MW00534920

Also by Paolo Bacigalupi

Pump Six and Other Stories

The Windup Girl

The Water Knife

The Tangled Lands (with Tobias S. Buckell)

YOUNG ADULT

The Ship Breaker Series

Ship Breaker

The Drowned Cities

Tool of War

The Doubt Factory

MIDDLE GRADE

Zombie Baseball Beatdown

NAVOLA

NAVOLA

A NOVEL

Paolo Bacigalupi

Alfred A. Knopf
New York, 2024

THIS IS A BORZOI BOOK
PUBLISHED BY ALFRED A. KNOPF

www.aaknopf.com

Knopf, Borzoi Books, and the colophon are registered trademarks of Penguin Random House LLC.

Library of Congress Cataloging-in-Publication Data
Names: Bacigalupi, Paolo, author.
Title: Navola : a novel / Paolo Bacigalupi.
Description: First edition. | New York : Alfred A. Knopf, 2024.
Identifiers: LCCN 2023037024 |
ISBN 9780593535059 (hardcover) | ISBN 9780593535066 (e-book)
Subjects: LCGFT: Fantasy fiction. | Novels.
Classification: LCC PS3602.A3447 N38 2024 |
DDC 813/.6—dc23/eng/20231127
LC record available at https://lccn.loc.gov/2023037024

Jacket illustration by Sasha Vinogradova
Jacket design by John Gall

Map illustration by David Lindroth, David Lindroth Inc.

Manufactured in the United States of America
1st Printing

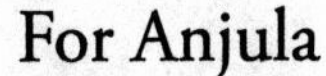

For Anjula

Cielofrigo
WUSTHOLT
Avillion
CHEROUX
CHAT
MERAI
Merai
VESUN
Oceana Sangue
Pardi
GEVAZZOA
NAVOLA
Romiglia
Paeninsula Ceruleana
SCHIPIA
Losiccia
TORRE AMO
KHUS

Tizakand
IMPERIX KHUR
Hekkat
Pagnanopol
La Cerulea
ZUROM

Part 1

Chapter 1

My father kept a dragon eye upon his desk. An orb larger than a man's skull, gone milky and crystalline but still burning with inner fire as if it retained life. He kept it on his desk next to the quills where he signed parchment debts and took trading signatories on linen and raw iron and neru resin and cardamom and silk and horses. He kept it on the desk where he made loans for shipbuilding and war. The dragon eye sat beside a Sag dagger and the Callarino's golden sigil of high office.

Trading codexes lined my father's library, the records of all the promises that he kept in far-off lands. He liked to say that he traded in goods, but more in promises, and he never failed to collect. This was how he came to own the dagger of the Sag man and the Callarino's sigil—the collecting of promises.

But the dragon eye he had purchased from far-off Zurom.

Of the dragon eye's authenticity there could be no doubt. It was not round, as one might think; it retained tendrils of draconic nerves crystallized—fine shards, sharp as daggers—that trailed from hind the eye so that it was less an orb than a teardrop.

The sharp trailing nerves made it appear as if it were the burning comet immortalized in Arragnalo's sketches upon the ceiling of the Callendra's rotunda, seen in skies from Losiccia to Pagnanopol, and now fallen to our human earth. The eye seemed to glow with the very fury of the heavens—a vitality that could not be extinguished, even by death.

When I was a small child, I would play in my father's library with my hound, and sometimes I would see it out of the corner of my eye: a fossil that was not bone, a jewel that was not stone.

I called my hound Lazy, for she only roused herself to play with me, and never for any other. When I was close, her tail would wag and she would seek me out, and then we would run through the galleries of my family's palazzo, up and down the wide halls, through the courtyards and porticoes and gardens, up and down the wide staircases of the living quarters, and round and round the tight spiral defenses of our tower. Our shouts and barks echoed across cobbles and parquet, bounced amongst the faces of my ancestors depicted in their portraits, and filled the frescoed rooms with their high painted ceilings where the Bull of the Regulai always paced.

We two had the run of the palazzo—and took it for granted as only the young and the innocent can—but when we were in my father's library, for reasons neither of us understood but somehow felt necessary, we were as silent as thieves stealing in the Quartiere Sangro.

The dragon demanded reverence, even from ignorant children and lanky-legged puppies.

While the authenticity of the eye was impossible to assail, its pedigree was less so. The trader my father bought it from claimed it came from a wyrm that had terrorized the sands and red cliffs of Zurom for more than a century before finally being slain by a great warrior with a blade cast of diamond.

The eye thence was offered to a rapacious sultan to forestall a terrible war and to rescue a princess. There was more to the story: the luminous beauty of the maiden imprisoned by the sultan, the lasciviousness and debauch of that cruel ruler, the nefarious sorceries the sultan cast to trick the warrior, the triumphant breaking of the maiden's chains, and the final tragic betrayal of the warrior. The fall of empires. The drifting of time and sand. The collapse of ancient cities into legend . . .

What could be verified was that the eye had been excavated from the crypt of a powerful ruler—with a touch of slip-speak as to whether this constituted scholarly discovery or outright looting—but in any case a turn of events that led to the eye falling into the merchant's caravan and traveling the trade routes over the icy Khim and Kharat passes, and thence traversing the whitecapped waves of Oceana Cerulea to our own fine city of Navola, the beating heart of banca mercanta for all the lands that spoke Amo's dialects, and finally to my father, Devonaci di Regulai, famous for his wealth and influence throughout the lands that touched La Cerulea's azure waters.

Whatever the merchant's claims about the eye's origins, my father maintained that the dragon's death had not come from a hero's sword but most likely old age. If a sword had ever pierced the great beast's scales, it had occurred in postmortem butchery, not heroic battle. Dragons did not submit to the likes of human blades—not even diamond ones.

But he bought the eye anyway, paying without bargaining (and assuring the merchant's name for a hundred years with the price), and he set the artifact upon his desk. When men came to sign contracts and make promises, he would make them swear upon the eye of a dragon. In this way, business partners were adequately warned that they dealt not with some mere notary-silver in Quadrazzo Maggi but with Devonaci di Regulai da Navola and nothing would protect them when he sought a return on his promises.

My father had a dragon eye.

That long-dead sultan of Zurom did not have one.

The king of far-off Cheroux did not have one.

Our own Callarino of Navola did not have one.

In fact, no one could say they had one. Perhaps a scale of a dragon. Or sometimes, maybe, a fossil thing a man might claim was a tooth. But this terrifying crystallized memory of power, this was something different indeed. The cat's-eye iris still held its orange color, even though the surface had gone milky. It glowed with an inner light that even death had not extinguished.

Whenever I was in my father's library, the dragon eye always seemed to watch me. It seemed to track me each time I entered there, hungry. It frightened me, but, if I'm honest before Amo, it drew me as well.

When my father wasn't present, away on one of his journeys to meet with the promissories of our far-flung empire of trade, I would sometimes sneak into his library and stare at it: the milky sheen of the surface, the trapped flaming rage within its winking cat-slit eye. An eye as large as my whole head. Staring with fury at our quotidian human endeavors. Our buying and selling of bales of champa wool and sacks of wheat.

It frightened me.

And it drew me.

And one day, I touched it.

Chapter 2

But perhaps I should explain to you my father and my father's sphere. Who were we, indeed, who carried archinomo Regulai? Who were we that my father could purchase such an artifact?

The Regulai name was old, stretching back to the time before Amo, and over time it had become proud. My ancestors witnessed the great wave that swept away thousands when Oceana Cerulea lashed us with her wrath in the time of old empire. We survived Scuro's plagues when they ravaged our land, leaving black-pustuled corpses piled as high as rooftops. Like so many Navolese, we fled to the mountains when the great capital of Torre Amo fell to the Khur, and the empire of the Amonese shattered to pieces, and petty dukes, priests, and brigands all declared themselves lords, and wars were fought for glory and territory all up and down the Cerulean Peninsula.

And like so many, when the wars were ended, we returned to our beloved Navola by the sea.

In our earliest days, the Regulai were simple wool merchants, trading with the villagers and herdsmen of the mountainous Romiglia and then hauling that wool out of the wilds to sell to Navola's loom guild. Later generations learned the arts of abacus and letters. Gradually our people became less of the country and more of the city. We settled in Via Lana, surrounded by the clack of looms and the reek of linen dye and the eternal chatter of mercantae bargaining with the loom guild. We sent proxies into the wilds to gather the wool while we instead learned to write and stamp contracts, using our name as guarantee. We made small loans to other merchants, insured traders against bandits and beasts, and slowly the power of our promises came to be known.

But it was my great-grandfather who made us one of the archinomo of the city.

7

"Deiamo di Regulai," my father's numerari Merio said, "would be much offended at your complaints of boredom at doing the work of a scriveri."

I was quite young at the time, no more than eight or nine years under Amo's light, and I chafed at my writing lesson. I desperately wished to be outside in the sunshine with Lazy, my newly given puppy with her silly fat paws and her whiplike wagging tail. Instead I was trapped inside the dimness of our bank's scrittorium, sitting beside Merio, surrounded by scriveri, numerari, and abacassi, all of them scratching away with their quills and clicking away with their abacuses. Merio clucked his tongue at my handwriting. "Your great-grandfather knew every part of his business, and scorned none of it."

I stifled a yawn.

Merio flicked my ear.

"Pay attention, Davico. The sooner you are finished, the sooner you run and play."

I bent once more to my labor. Around me, adults worked steadily, adding numbers in their columns, marking down deposits and withdrawals for acconti seguratti, reading and responding to the letters that came and went throughout the day. The walls of the scrittorium were filled with the evidence of their work: account books, correspondence, contracts, guidance for numerari on the rules of exchange and the Laws of Leggus. All of this was bound in books, written on vellum scrolls, stacked in paper piles—scribbled on linen rags in a few odd cases—and arranged by region, commodity, and merchant. All of it was locked in iron-latticed cabinets to protect our secrets from would-be spies.

In this shadowed and stinking vellum world I toiled, kneeling upon a chair to gain the height I needed to work at Merio's desk, all the while acutely aware of the day passing, sunlight stealing across the floor as Amo drove his chariot across the sky.

Beyond the window, a cascade of shouts and calls, bleats and barks announced that the streets were full of life. Carts clattered, livestock groaned, roosters crowed, peacocks cried, and the conversation and laughter of merchants, peasants, archinomi, and vianomae filtered up to me, all of them beckoning, all of it accompanied by intriguing smells—ripe fruit, new manure, bright perfumed flowers—and none of it was I permitted to go and see.

My task that day was to copy a contract whose meaning I barely grasped. The words were large, the numbers larger, and the terms of art abstract and cursed with hidden meanings. Words like *promissorio* and *fallimante.* Phrases like *usanza da Banca Regulai, controllar da Navola, cambio del giorno,* and *definis da Vaz.* Mostly, I remember the script as a tricksy serpent thing that led nowhere pleasant, and went on and on.

"Your great-grandfather understood that to practice every aspect of his business was not a duty but an honor." Merio peered down through the slit windows to the street below, each window designed very tall to let in light, but also very thin so a thief could not squeeze through. "From the most drudgerous to the most elevated, it was all his honor." He sucked his teeth thoughtfully. "*Tuotto lavoro degli scriveri,*" he said. "*Tuotto lavoro degli numerari.*"

He came to look over my shoulder and examine my progress. "Deiamo wrote this very promissorio that you now copy and turn to new purpose. Your hand follows his. Imagine that, Davico. A contract written by a man who has long ago ascended to Amo, and yet his words remain. His hand remains, reaching out to you from three generations past. His hand touches yours . . ."

I was not so moved to rapture as Merio at the thought of my dead great-grandfather's hand touching mine. The thought made me shiver and think of the catacombs below Navola where the bones of the ancient Amonese were stacked to the ceilings in dripping tunnels and crypts, but I knew better than to protest.

"Follow his hand, follow the grace," Merio said, his hand moving unconsciously as he paced back and forth behind me. "Follow and worship the smallest details of Deiamo's art. Give thanks to Amo that at this very moment your great-grandfather assists you."

At this very moment, I knew that my friends Piero and Cierco were in Quadrazzo Amo with wooden swords, playing at battle. At this very moment, Giovanni would be with them, sitting on the shaded steps of the Callendra, reading one of his many tomes. At this very moment, my friend Tono would be down on the docks fishing for Cerulean eyes. At this very moment, in our kitchens, Siana Brazzarossa was baking sweet biscuits with ginger and kha spice just the way my father's consort Ashia liked them. And closer to home, at this very moment, Lazy was sniffing around our palazzo's stables, hurt that I had abandoned her—

"Pay attention, Davico!" Merio flicked my ear again. "The details matter! Deiamo traveled far and wide to expand his mind. He was as knowledgeable of the rats that infested the grain ships of Vesuna as he was about the wood used to repair the looms that weave the linen here in Navola."

Merio gestured at the papers and tomes that lined the walls. "You can still read his letters and see his mind at work. The knowledge he built. He sniffed the necks of women in Merai to know the fashions of their perfume, and he drank camel milk in the tents of Bedoz to learn the lives of caravanners. We continue his traditions: the letters we read, the knowledge we glean . . ."

He motioned toward his own desk, piled high with water-stained and torn correspondence from our far-flung partners. "This is the foundation of everything your family does, and so you learn, just as your father learned, and your grandfather before him, each of you in turn learning from the genius of Deiamo—Go on, Davico. Keep copying. Don't stop your work just because I talk. Three perfect copies, and then you go and play. One for us. One for the merchant Sio Tosco. And one for him to carry to our branch in Vaz, where Sio Tosco will receive our loan of Vazziani silver fingers to buy his horses. You know that they count their silver in fingers, yes?"

I nodded.

"And what do the people of Vaz call their gold?"

"Thumbs."

"How many fingers to a thumb?"

"Twelve."

"Good. Keep copying. You should be able to listen to me and keep up your work, Davico. If I were doing this, it would be already done—" He broke off. "Nai, Davico. Two *t*'s in *lettera di credo.*" His finger stabbed my work, smearing ink, ruining my copying. "See there? Two *t*'s. The details matter. The day of repayment, the weight of the silver, and the two *t*'s. Throw that paper away. Start again."

"My hand hurts," I said.

Now, looking back, older and wiser, I suspect I had copied very little, but I was young and naïve and felt as if I had been at my labors for days. Such are the feelings of children. A minute of boredom is an hour, an hour is a day, and a day is a lifetime, and we share our feelings openly, for we have not yet learned the art of faccioscuro.

Merio's voice took on an edge. "Your hand hurts?"

Merio was typically a cheerful man, soft and easygoing as men of

Pardi tended to be, with the plump flushed cheeks and rounded belly of someone who knows good wine and better cheese. But I had apparently found some limit to his patience, for his eyebrows went up and his eyes no longer twinkled. "If your hand hurts, think of all the men who labor around you. The ones who labor *for* you." He turned to the scriveri at the desks around us. "Are any of you tired?" He jabbed a finger at the nearest man. "You, Sio Ferro, are you tired? Does your hand hurt?"

And of course Sio Ferro said, "No, Maestro," and all the other scriveri smiled indulgently at me, and bent once more to their tasks.

"These men write all day. They read all day," Merio said. "Sio Ferro began learning his trade at your age, and he wrote all day even then. So. You will do no less. Do not tell me your hand hurts."

I knew better than to answer, but I was not happy. I started again on a new sheet of paper, stifling my despair at the copying that had been lost to my single mistake.

"Ai," Merio relented, seeing my misery. *"Finis. Finis."*

He laid his hand over mine. "Put down your quill, Davico. Come with me." He motioned for me to follow. "Ci. This is no punishment. Come with me. I want to show you something. Come come." He waved me off my chair. "Come."

Merio guided me down the wide wooden stairs of the scrittorium to the ground floor, where the abacassi flicked and clicked their way through our profits and expenses. We threaded between their desks and out into the racket of the street.

Just to our left, the gate to my family's palazzo was thrown wide. Merio led me through the cool stone passage to emerge in the palazzo's peaceful sun-drenched quadra premia, cooled by the splashing of its central fountain.

Lazy sniffed our arrival immediately and came scampering over from the stables, her tail wagging. I gathered her up in my arms, as happy to see her as she was to discover me. She wriggled and shivered, snuffling her nose over my face and licking my cheeks.

I expected Merio to take me farther into the palazzo, but he did not, instead stopping right there in the quadra, looking at me expectantly. I juggled Lazy as she squirmed in my arms and looked about myself, trying to understand why he was gazing at me so.

Here were the three arched gates that led through to the quadra that held our stables, here were the quarters of our household guard along the street wall, with their upper and lower galleries. Here was the burbling marble fountain depicting Urula with her mermaids and her fishes, all their breasts bared and spouting water. The water was very nice and cool, especially on a hot day such as this. More arched passages pierced the farthest wall of the quadra, inviting access to the more private environs of our home, but Merio did not lead me farther. Instead, he pointed to the fresco that covered the last wall of the quadra. The solid wall that we shared with our bank next door.

"Have you ever looked at this?"

"Y-yes?"

I answered hesitantly, for of course I had looked at it. The painting was too large to miss, more than twenty-five paces wide, and tall enough that the only way to see the whole was to stand far back and crane my neck. It depicted Navola's battle against the invaders of Cheroux and Merai, and it was as unmissable as the fountain of Urula with her fishes and mermaids. But the fountain was at least good to cool my feet in, and even better for teasing Lazy with the splashes. And it was far less interesting than our stables full of horses, with colts and mothers and stallions, along with the pleasant smells of leather and the sweetness of hay and manure. I had seen this painting every day of my life, but I was wary, for I sensed a trap in Merio's question. Even at that young age, I knew when one of my teachers was about to sharpen a point, and knew to be wary of how it might prick.

"What do you see?" Merio asked.

"Navola and Pardi and Savicchi are fighting against Cheroux and Merai."

"What else?"

I struggled, my eyes moving over the clashing troops. Off to the right, Cheroux's objective, our own city of Navola, shone in the sunlight, perched at the juncture of Cascada Livia's river mouth and the vast Oceana Cerulea. The towers of our many rival archinomi rose high above Navola's walls, glittering in the sun.

Every child of Navola knew that this had been a desperate and important battle, but the painting was not something I liked particularly. My friend Piero, who came from nomo nobilii anciens and loved the lore of war, said that he would one day be a great general and fight glorious battles such as this Defense of Navola, but I did not like the way the blood ran on the battlefield, nor the corpses that floated in the Livia. It was a triumphant painting, but also unpleasant.

"See here," Merio said, assuming the attitude of a teacher. "Not only are we fighting against the invasion of Cheroux. Look here, up high in the sky? Do you see how Amo brings his divine favor and support? How he rides in his chariot to our defense? We are blessed by Amo, and protected by him, for we are righteous, and Cheroux is a kingdom of dogs. See also how green is the field of battle and how blue are the waters of the River Livia, where Cheroux has been pinned. This tells us that Navola is blessed with the sea, with the trade of the river, and with fertile fields, all of which make a worthy prize for Cheroux. And look, the invading dogs from Cheroux are now panicking, diving into the river, trying to swim, drowning in their mail. And here . . ." He tried to reach up, but of course could not touch, being far too short and more than a little too heavy to reach his target. "Here is your family's sigil, the Bull of the Regulai, flying amongst the banners of the Navolese army."

He looked at me expectantly.

I stared back blankly.

"*Ci!* History! We must teach you more history, Davico!" He wiped the sweat from his bald scalp. His head was already pinkening in the sun's heat, but he seemed determined to instruct. I hugged Lazy to me and tried to be attentive as he began pointing at the various banners and sigils, some of which I recognized from other Navolese families.

"Archinomo di Regulai was not always so proud as it is now," Merio said. "Before your great-grandfather, the Regulai name was the name of a merchant trader, and merchants are not often held in high esteem, and certainly not in those days. In those days, archinomo nobilii anciens dominated Navola, claiming blood descent from the old Amonese. They were the ones who held rank and honor and influence."

"Like Piero and Cierco."

"Yes. Just like your friends. They are of the old names. Di Regulai was a street name, vianoma. But here, in this moment, your grandfather has raised his banner alongside the banners of nobles who trace their names all the way back to the Amonese—"

"Did he?" I interrupted.

Merio paused. "Did he what?"

I looked up at the vast painting, at the men, the horses, our own banner, somewhat larger than all the rest, my grandfather upon his black charger Nero, his sword high . . .

"Was it really like this? Did it happen like this?"

"Why would you ask such a question?"

I wasn't sure. "Well . . . we painted the fresco. Maybe . . ."

"Yes?" Merio prompted.

"Maybe we make ourselves look powerful in the painting? The way Archinomo Furia hang their enemies from their palazzo walls until they rot and fall apart. To scare people."

"Go on."

"When people visit us here, they see this. It's the first thing they see. I've seen them look. And I've seen them whisper to one another. It means something to them. Maybe it is a message to them. Maybe it is more a message than real history."

"Ai." Merio beamed and pinched my cheek. "Just when I think that you are all wool between the ears, the glint of your father's mind pierces through."

"So, did we lead?" I asked, encouraged. "Were we part of the charge?"

"Does it matter?"

I hesitated.

"I don't know."

"Think on it then. Think hard. You like to read stories of legends. The journals of Marcel of Bis. Avvicco's *Travels*. I know you like the legends of the old gods. Are they true? Does it matter if they are true? Or does it only matter that they inspire a true feeling in you?"

I didn't know the answer. I felt happy that I had asked a question Merio respected, but now I had the feeling of swimming in deeper waters.

Merio smiled indulgently. "Think on it, Davico. It is a worthy question. One thing I can tell you, of a certainty, is that your grandfather was no coward. There is a reason Destino was called the Bull. He rode to battle, and he was party to the treaties after. As to the rest? Was his banner so bright and tall?" He shrugged. "Perhaps a wise man would say that we know that your family's banner rises high now, and the banners of the ancient names grow smaller with every passing year. But that is not what I want to show you. Come. Over here, at the bottom of the painting."

He walked the length of wall, pulling me along, all the way to the left, far from Amo, down at my own eye level, bringing us at last to a foregrounded forest upon a hill, with men and horses hidden, many of them cleverly blended into the trees, shadow shapes, subtle and brooding. "What are these men doing?"

"Nothing."

At Merio's frown, I tried again.

"Hiding?"

"Better. Do you see the sigil, upon their shields?"

"It's a wolf."

"Indeed. A wolf. Do you recognize it?"

I shook my head.

"Compagni Militi Lupari. A powerful army of mercenaries. They are Cheroux's reserve, meant to smash us from behind as we attack Cheroux by the river. Cheroux sought to bait the battle to this place upon the river plain, and put their back to the water, drawing us to attack. The Lupari were supposed to sweep down from the trees and strike us from behind. Smashing us between the anvil of Cheroux and the hammer of the Lupari. But the Lupari do not charge. Instead, they only watch. Because of this man."

He tapped a shadowy figure in a black robe, his features hidden under a cowl, sneaking through the forest. One hand held a knife, the other a sack of gold with coins spilling out. The figure radiated malevolence. "This is Vessio. He was your grandfather's stilettotore."

I sucked in my breath. "Like Cazzetta?"

"Very much like."

This was all I needed to know. "I don't like him."

Merio laughed, a surprised bark of laughter. He ruffled my hair. "Nor I, Davico! Nor I!" He continued to chuckle, then grew serious. "But you should also know Cazzetta is absolutely loyal to your father, and a loyal dagger man is worth more than his weight in gold, no matter the unpleasantness he brings."

I nodded doubtfully, unconvinced.

Cazzetta came and went on mysterious errands, a malevolent figure who appeared at any hour of day or night, galloping into our palazzo upon a lathered black beast called Avinciius, seventeen hands high and a brute of fury. Cazzetta would dismount, throw the reins to a guard, and stalk off to find my father. I had seen him burst into my father's bath, scattering bathing girls and attendants. I had seen him stride into the middle of a fete for the Callarino, sweating and stinking from his ride, interrupting music and conversation with his dark presence. And whenever Cazzetta appeared, my father would immediately sequester himself with the man. And then Cazzetta would disappear again, often that same night, like smoke, borne away upon the same ill wind that had summoned him.

But it was worse when the man lingered.

Cazzetta liked to play cruel games, and I was his favorite target. He would force me to test my speed in a hand-slapping game that he liked, numbing my hands with his blows. He would emerge by surprise from the shadows, threatening me with a stiletto that was hidden up his sleeve, or else the one in his boot, or else with the little punch daggers that he kept tucked into his stiff high collar. He would appear like a vicious fata, stepping from behind a column or looming out of a shadowy archway, and each time he would seize me and press his steel against my jugular, and then he would warn me that I was di Regulai and needed to be on my guard.

But for me, the worst was when Cazzetta brought me a white dove in a cage, as a gift. He gave me the caged dove, then he showed me a small golden thumb ring with a red gem. He flicked it open, to reveal a tiny needle. He reached into the cage and pricked the dove and the dove immediately collapsed, thrashing and dying of poison.

He then gave me the ring and told me to be careful with it. The ring was the gift. Not the dove.

Cazzetta was not a kind man, nor a good one, and I avoided him because of it.

Now I stared up at this other dagger man, Vessio, lurking in the forest with his stiletto and his bag of gold.

Merio said, "This battle was won not upon the open plain, but in the forest shadows. Not with the clanging of swords, but with the scratch of a quill. It was won because your family's promises were famous for their strength. As cold and unchanging as the ice of the Cielofrigo."

We both regarded the painting. I, the small boy, trying to understand. Merio, the numerari, perhaps considering how quickly he might have counted the gold necessary to buy the loyalty of the Lupari.

"But where is Great-Grandfather?" I asked finally. "You said you would tell me about Deiamo. But this painting is about my grandfather, the Bull."

"Why, all of this is your great-grandfather's work!"

Merio stepped back, gesturing at the whole of the painting. "His agile mind, his iron promises, and his contracts just like the one you are copying. Look up. Look, all the way at the sky. You see how our god Amo rides his fiery chariot through the clouds to battle on behalf of Navola? Now look who stands beside him in his chariot, the winged vincii there. The proud shape of the nose, the deeply set eyes—"

"Deiamo?"

Now that Merio had pointed it out, I recognized him from other portraits. Even the hunch of his body from long labor at the desk was captured, though in this painting he was winged and powerful and hurled a bolt of light.

"Deiamo," Merio breathed. "Indeed. The Bull raises a sword and charges into battle, but it is *his* father who hurls bolts of fire, and stands at the right hand of Amo. Imagine that. The Bull commissioned this painting, and yet he sets his father equal to the greatest of gods."

Merio's expression grew mischievous. "And I can tell you that Garagazzo considers this painting to be near-blasphemy because of it."

"He does?"

Merio winked. "Of course he does! Watch the next time you see him visit. See how the face of our canon priest purples. And yet still Deiamo stands, because your family wills it."

He crouched down before me. "Never forget this, Davico. Your family's true power comes from the unbreakable might of your promises, and the oh-so-tedious labors of your great-grandfather's quill. It is the foundation of everything." He clapped me on the shoulder, smiling.

"Now go and play. Tomorrow, you will copy that contract perfectly, just as Deiamo once did."

Born into a shadowy two-room apartment in Quartiere Lana, surrounded by clicking looms and the bustle and shout of traders, notarysilvers, and cartalitigi, Deiamo ended his days in a grand palazzo, draped in silk and attended to by the greatest names of the city. But even though he died surrounded by wealth, he remained vianoma in his heart, and always cared for the people of the street.

It was Deiamo who endowed the first colonnaded porticoes throughout the city of Navola, providing vianomae with shade from summer heat and shelter from wet-season downpours, and it was he who first paid laborers to dig down and repair the ancient sewers of the Amonese that were hidden beneath the city so that filth could be washed away from the Linen Quarter, and all people from highest to lowest could walk streets free of ordure.

When a hunger for glory swept over the archinomi of Navola and every great name demanded war against Vesuna, it was Deiamo who raised his voice in protest. He stood in the center of the Callendra and warned that it was foolish, and he lost deposits and accounts because of it. And when we went to war anyway, and our vianomae died by the thousands in the marshes of Vesuna, stuck by arrows and drowned in the mud, it was Deiamo who built a convent orphanage for the children who lost their fathers. The Convent Contessa Amovinci stands to this day, and in our palazzo's gallery of ancestors, Deiamo was depicted seated upon the steps of that convent, surrounded by all the children he cared for.

Deiamo was followed by Destino, called the Bull, who played such a role in Navola's defense against Cheroux. Destino's portrait showed him astride his charger, Nero, his black beard shot with gray, his dark eyes blazing, his blade drawn and ready.

Destino traded in coin and iron, flax and wool and linen, armor and arms, wheat and barley and rice. He created permanent branches in cities as far away as Villion and Bis, Hergard, Neft, and Sottodun, and he carefully chose partners to run those enterprises in our name. It was Destino who moved Banca Regulai out of the old Linen Quarter and into a grand new palazzo, and he who first took seat in the Callendra as archinomo.

Destino was not only a warrior, nor only a merchant trader. He was also a lover of art and nature. It was Destino who hired the genius Arragnalo to design and construct the wondrous Catredanto Maggiore at Quadrazzo Amo, where the named Navolese all prayed, and it was he who endowed the statuary gardens that ringed the city for all the people to enjoy.

Finally, there was my father, Devonaci di Regulai.

My father was not as kind as Deiamo, nor as valorous as Destino, though both those aspects were contained within him. He was something else entirely, almost otherworldly in his intelligence. It was said that he began to work the abacus before he was two, and that he wrote in Amonese Anciens by the time he was three.

Brilliant, sharp, observant, tireless, unbending, unafraid. I heard all those descriptions attached to him, and more. I heard them from the vianomae of the street, and from the men who served him in our palazzo, and all of them spoke with reverence.

My father expanded our Regulai Bank to the far corners of the lands where Amo's dialects were spoken, and even beyond. Kings and princes begged for invitations to dine at our table. It was my father who convinced Madrasalvo to come down from his hermitage to complete the catredanto commission when Arragnalo passed of poison from his apprentice lover. Madrasalvo painted the cloisters and domes of the catredanto with his own hand and no one else's—a commission that took ten years to complete, and was his finest work.

My father fed the vianomae when Scuro's pox killed our farmers in their fields and all our crops failed, arranging at our expense to bring great ships full of wheat from the Khur Empire to Navola, browbeating ship captains to land at our sickened docks and to feed our people on threat of losing all future trade. My father stayed with our sickened city when other archinomi fled, though the blue blossoms cost him his wife, my mother. He raised a shrine to her in Catredanto Amo, and you can find her there to this very day.

Our name was intertwined into the very bones of Navola; my forefathers had influenced its architecture, its twisted streets and shade gardens, many of them named for cousins, sisters, brothers, sons, and daughters of our ancestry. Via Gianna. Via Andretta. Giardina Stefana. For generations, we had been building our name and influence.

By the time of my youth, banca mercanta and the Regulai name were nearly synonymous. Archinomo Regulai rang clear across the sea, up and down the fishhook of the Cerulean Peninsula, across the deserts and the steppes, into Zurom and Chat and Xim. It crossed the frozen heights of the Cielofrigo to the barbarian hair men of the north. Our assigns and proxies made loans, purchased and traded, insured ships and goods, spied on rulers, bought mines, sold cities, and my father presided over all of it.

But who was my father truly?

I think it is hard for us to know a person in their heart. What I saw of him was different than what a notary-silver in Quartiere Lana saw in him, than what his consort Ashia saw in him, than what our Callarino of Navola saw.

I cannot speak for those others. I can only say that in my sight, he was a hard man, implacable in his business and unbreakable in his promises, but he was kind to me, and I loved him greatly.

Too, I would say that though he was powerful, he did not beat people about the head and shoulders with the stick of his strength. He was much concerned with preserving the pride of others, and so preferred polite agreement to outright demonstrations of power. He owned many a man's promise, but he did not seek to mud their cheeks upon his boot, not even when he collected their oaths. *Sfaccio,* it was called in the slang of Navola—to dirty the face—and my father did not take pleasure in such baseness. He was not one to force *sfaccire* without cause, not even when provoked by pettiness.

So, for example, in those days of my childhood, the Callarino was often at the palazzo on the business of the city. Unlike other cities, Navola had no prince or king to dominate us. Instead, we had a Callarino, elected by the archinomi, along with the guild representatives of our trades and crafts: the stoneworkers, the brickmakers, the wool collectives, the loom guild, the ironworkers' guild, the monastic leaders, and of course the district elected who represented the various quartiere of the city and the vianomae who resided there. One hundred men and sometimes women tasked with guiding the business of the city, a republic rather than a monarchy, with our Callarino at its head.

Navola in those days was civilized. We were utterly unlike the brutal principate of Gevazzoa, dominated by the Borraghese people with their blood feuds and revenge intrigues. We were wiser than the rash kingdom of Cheroux with its reckless wars and covetous king Andreton. And we were more content and civilized than the land of Merai, with its Parl who sat uneasily in his Red City and forever struggled to control his rebellious relatives. In Navola, the One Hundred elected the Callarino to high office, and with their guidance, that man ruled wisely and well. Borsini Amoforze Corso, the great Callarino of Navola, was elected by the many, obedient to the city, and guided by the interests of all.

So it was proclaimed by scholars, priests, and diplomats.

Now, often, the only warning of the Callarino's arrival would be when my father's numerari Merio cleared his throat in warning, for the Callarino enjoyed arriving unannounced. The Callarino was not one to wait patiently, nor to defer his valuable time to others. Merio would clear his throat and a moment later the Callarino would come sweeping into the library as if he owned it, strutting in his red-and-gold robes of office and preening as if his name were written upon Amo's crown.

And in response?

My father would simply look up from his writing, invite the Callarino to sit as if he were an expected and favored guest, and motion Merio to summon sweet tea and bitter cheese.

Such was my father. He was mild, for he had power.

And such was the Callarino, for he had none.

And then, in a dance of exquisite politeness, the Callarino—without asking—would beg permission to use his own sigil, which sat upon my father's desk; and my father—without acquiescing—would permit its use.

The Callarino might say, "General Sivizza says that the weapons of the Lupari Guards are dulled."

And my father would say, "This is not something that the pride of Navolese arms can tolerate. Our loyal protectors must be protected as well. They should receive meat for their strength, the sharpest and strongest of arms for their art, and those that are married . . . they should receive a golden navisoli in appreciation. The general and his Wolves should never feel as if the city is not grateful for their protection."

And so, then and there, the Callarino would write a proposal to the archinomi of the Callendra—many of whose promises my father had also collected, and whose cheeks my father had also marked—and the Callarino would stamp it with his sigil, dripping red ink, smearing the chop with authority that he did not have, proposing precisely the amount my father suggested, and the Callendra's Hundred Names would then vote and agree, and my father and other archinomi of the city would pay the taxes necessary to keep our troops at readiness.

Or else, the Callarino might say, "The Borraghese have sent an ambassador offering trade to Navola." And my father would frown and say, "But do we trust Archinomo Borragha, truly? Gevazzoa is such an ugly city. Populo Borragha, a base people. They would touch a cheek to your boot and then slip a stiletto between your ribs when they rose to kiss your hand." And then he would make a face, as if he had drunk from a bottle of poor wine, perhaps one of those famously cloudy wines of Gevazzoa, all murk and sediment.

In this case, the Callarino would drop the topic and move on to others, knowing that he had no authority to treat further with Archinomo Borragha.

Or else the Callarino might say, "The king of Cheroux wishes to send twenty scholars to copy the archives of the university and its knowledge of banca mercanta, litigi, and numismatica and would like to trade their texts of architectura and Amonese Anciens."

And my father would say, "Scholarship brightens all kingdoms who receive it, but even more those who provide it. Let the scholars of Cheroux come with the Lupari's guarantee of safe passage, but first let Andreton's son come to us and swear upon my dragon eye that they will never again make a blood claim upon our good neighbors in Pardi."

All of this, I would watch, and later Merio would quietly explain that ever since my grandfather had caused their defection in the war with Cheroux, the Lupari had become Navola's mailed fist—our soldiers exclusively, and paid well to defend our interests. But they were mercenaries at heart. They had come to us because we paid them better. What if another offer were to come? What if they were encouraged to change sides once more? What then?

Navola's archinomi paid well, and attracted the best from across Amo's lands. But these sell-swords were trebly valuable if they took wives in Navola and pupped new Wolves for the city—then they became bound to Navola not just by the suns and moons of our coinage but by blood. This was why my father gave the suns of Navola, navisoli, our gold, to those who made families. He sought to bind Compagni Militi Lupari to the city, to tie their survival to Navola. In this way, he encouraged the Wolves to fight not just for coin, but also for the survival of their own names and lineages, to become Navolese themselves.

Such was my father's wisdom.

"But why must the prince of Cheroux come and swear upon the dragon eye?" I asked.

Merio waggled his eyebrows. "Why, because if you swear an oath on the eye of a dracchus, you are bound to it, and it will burn you to ash if you play it false. A dragon sees into your very soul."

"Truly?"

I was much in awe then, and very frightened. Almost as frightened as I was when Cazzetta was about.

Merio ruffled my hair and laughed. "Ai, Davico, you're too credulous by half. How will we teach you, young princeling, to mask that open face of yours?" He sighed. "No, it will not burn you to ash, and no, it does not see into your soul. But still, it is a great fright to touch that which was greater than any man, and when you make an oath on such an artifact, you feel it in your bones . . ." He shivered. "You feel it deep. Symbol and ritual are as much a part of a man's promise as his coin and his stock of wool collateral and whether his cheek is clean of others' boot marks. When a man touches the dragon eye, your father watches him, to see how he shakes, to see if he hesitates. To see a little way into his soul."

Merio touched the corner of his own eye, seriously. "It is not the dragon who sees, Davico. It is your father."

This impressed me very much.

The Navolese are as twisted as the plaits of their women's hair.

—COMMON SAYING, RECORDED BY MARCEL VILLOU OF BIS

Chapter 3

"I want his head! I want that bedpisser torn apart, and I want his head on a spike in front of the Callendra!"

The Callarino's voice resounded as he stormed through the doors of my father's library.

I had grown, if not tall, at least tall enough to sit at a desk without sitting upon my feet, and over that course of time, I had passed from Merio's instructional hand to my father's. I was now often expected to sit alongside him when he worked in his library—sitting parlobanco, as we say.

It was an old phrase, *parlobanco,* from the times when all negotiations were made sitting across from one another over a rough-hewn plank filled with cheeses, cups of hot sweet tea, and slivers of good cured meats. In a pinch, any plank would do, or even a bit of fallen log, or even a three-legged stool if it came to that; so long as there was a bit of wood and food between the negotiating parties, all was right under Leggus.

In any case, when the Callarino came storming in, I was studying correspondence that my father had given me so that I could discuss with him and see how his mind worked, and learn better how he shaped our trade. I had been enjoying the strange missives, enjoying the generous crackling fire in the fireplace, enjoying the quiet snoring of Lazy at my feet, and the warmth of my father's company as a chill winter rain drummed against the windows. The letters were water-stained and ink-smudged, for they had had a hard journey, but all had been warmly cozy until the library doors crashed open, carrying cold damp wind and the Callarino's boiling rage.

"I want dogs to eat his guts and I want the rest of his pissioletto friends to see it!"

I stifled an urge to dive under my father's desk where Lazy—suddenly more than energetic enough—had already disappeared. Her attempt at escape was all the more comical as she had grown considerably over the years and now her long legs and lean body sprawled out in all directions from beneath the desk. She was no longer the bundle of puppy that she had been.

The Callarino threw his wet winter cloak to Merio as he passed and strode straight for the fireplace. Merio raised exasperated eyebrows to my father at the unceremonious use of his body as a coatrack, but my father made a placating gesture and waved that Merio should leave and take the Callarino's dripping cloak with him. I took this as a signal that I should leave as well, but when I made to stand, my father placed his hand over mine, stilling me, and from his look I understood that I was meant to stay, and listen.

"Borsini," my father said. "Come now. I take it someone obstructs your office?"

The Callarino stretched his hands to the fire, unaware of all that had passed behind him, and chafed his fingers in the heat. "La Cerulea's breath is full of ice today. She's put a chill in my bones."

My father winked at me. "Your blood isn't hot enough to warm you?"

The Callarino put his backside to the fire and made a face at my father. "You like to joke. But you don't have to keep a smile on your face when Tomas di Balcosi offers you a plate of shit."

"Balcosi? Really?"

"You doubt me?"

"You have so many enemies, I have a hard time keeping track."

"I'm glad you're amused." The Callarino turned to face the fire again. "That man is an asp in my bed." He stared into the flames and his face was orange like one of Scuro's demons. "I'm having him torn apart in Quadrazzo Amo for all his nomo nobilii anciens friends to see and learn from."

"Have you considered anything less gaudy?"

"I can't burn him alive. The wood's too wet this time of year. Nai. It will have to be a beheading. With blood all across the quadrazzo's stones, and his wife sobbing and his daughters begging for mercy."

Warmed by this imaginary vengeance, the Callarino came and flopped into a chair across from my father. He glanced around the library. "Where's that numerari of yours? The one with the cheeses."

"You gave him your cloak."

"Did I? Is he bringing tea?"

"I'm sure he's let the kitchen know of your arrival," my father said drily.

"You could loan me the services of Cazzetta," the Callarino said.

"To bring you tea?"

"Don't jest with me. You said you wanted something less gaudy. Cazzetta could deal with Balcosi most quietly. A stiletto. In an alley. A drop of serpiixis in his drink . . ."

My father gave the Callarino a sharp look. "A bad way to die, that. Vomiting blood is hardly quiet." He held up a hand to forestall the Callarino. "In any case, Cazzetta is not with me at the moment. He has distant errands."

The Callarino's lips pursed, disappointed that he could not unleash the ungentle attentions of Cazzetta upon Balcosi. He looked around the library again. "Will that numerari of yours bring the cheese as well as the tea?"

"Merio is well aware of your preferences. He has a mind for detail."

"That one should be a cook, not a numerari. Who ever heard of a Pardinese numerari? A numerari should be Navolese. Men of Pardi can barely count their sheep."

"Merio is very good at what he does."

"I would never hire a Pardinese. It would be like hiring a Borraghese to guard your back." The Callarino's eyes fell upon me, sitting beside my father. "Ai! Davico! I didn't recognize you. I took you for scriveri sitting there at the desk. You're all grown up!"

"Amo bless you, Patro Corso." I used the formal greeting that my father's consort Ashia said I should use with important men, but the Callarino waved off my words.

"Patro? You call me patro like a stranger? Ci. You don't have to use such formal language with me. Call me Uncle. Call me Sio. Call me Old Borsini and be done with it. We're nearly family. No need for formalities."

Stymied, I looked to my father, but he gave no guidance, so I ducked my head respectfully and stuck to Ashia's instructions. "Yes, Patro. Thank you, Patro."

The Callarino's smile widened. "Ai! You're a good boy." He reached over and tousled my hair. "A good respectful boy. And grown like grass since I last saw you." He studied me more closely. "And more like your father every day." He winked at my father. "It's always good to see confirmation that a pup is yours, veri e vero?" He settled back in his chair. "I have my servants watching my new wife day and night. Until she's pregnant, I'm not letting her out of my sight."

"I'm sure your wife feels blessed by your attention."

"Blessed or not, I won't be cuckolded like that clown Pazziano." The Callarino scowled. "At least not again."

"I'm sure you know best."

I did not fully understand the meaning of their words, but I sensed some unpleasantness. I could not name it, but still, like the dog who does not understand the words of human speech, I nonetheless sniffed a tension in the air.

Despite my ignorance of those matters of men and women, I had indeed grown, though not nearly as much as the Callarino implied. With almost twelve years under Amo's light, I stood somewhere between the sunset of childhood and the dawning of a man's resposibilities.

"What does your father have you at?" the Callarino asked.

"Letters from Hekkat," my father answered for me. "There is a new warlord."

"There's always a new warlord there. They kill them the way the Borraghese kill their friends. A new warlord, a new god to worship, a new flood of slaves for the misery trade and the Furia family fortunes." He quirked an eyebrow to me. "Well? What have you learned from Hekkat, young Davico?"

At my father's encouraging nod, I answered, "The warlord doesn't like cats. He doesn't take baths and he doesn't like cats."

"Cats and baths!" The Callarino laughed. "I always knew your empire was built on strange wisdom, Devonaci. But cats and baths is a new one. It would make a good song for a play. 'Cats and Baths.' 'Gatti e Bagni.' Something to go along with 'Terzi Abacassi, Senzi Gattimensi.' You could commission Maestro Zuzzo to write it."

My father did not return the smile. "Tell him the rest, Davico. What have you learned?"

"There is plague there," I said. "The warlord killed all the cats and now there is a great plague."

"Ahhh." The Callarino's eyes widened. "Now, that *is* a song."

Encouraged, I continued. "Silk will become expensive. And horses.

And Khazn hides. Sea captains refuse to land at Hekkat now. All the trade will have to cross Chat and there are brigands there. And the warlord has done the same to Tizakand and Samaa, so that route, too, is closed. We will now buy cargo from the merchants who are afraid to make the journey, and hire more guards for caravans through the oasis lands, and wait for the plague to pass."

This last I had not actually known, but had been explained by my father as he showed me a map of the few routes available to trade with distant Xim. He had also explained that we would have to rethink how we made our promises to protect merchants and their costs, and indeed, our partners in Hekkat had likely already fled the plague with the bank's silver. So now we would see if they came to us, or disappeared, or if the warlord had slain or robbed them, or if our branch still stood despite disease. All of this was now in flux because of a warlord who feared cats.

"That is truly useful knowledge," the Callarino said. "It's good that your father teaches you the wisdom of your name."

"He has a long way to go," my father said.

"Ci." The Callarino waved off my father's words. "Already your boy reads and writes and uses the abacus, and now he learns your talent for discerning the smallest details from the remotest places." The Callarino wagged an instructive finger at me. "Do not let your father's high standards demoralize you, Davico. If you were mine, you would already be a triumph. My own eldest is useless. He drinks wine, and fights duels over silly vendettae, and avoids his lectures at the university. I was too easy on him when he was young, and now he is a child in a grown man's body. I would trade for you in an instant."

"Children are always complicated," my father said.

"You should have another. I intend to have twenty if I'm able. I need someone with a better head on his shoulders than Rafiello."

"I think I am content," my father said.

"Ci. You are di Regulai. You deserve a harem of beautiful wives and an army of children as good as Davico. Ashia is a fine companion, but she's no reason not to take a new wife. Keep her as a concubine. A few more sons would do you good."

"Unless they're like Rafiello."

The Callarino made a sour face. "I blame myself for that. I was too easy on him."

"Yes, well, I think I will not play dice with the fatas." My father patted my shoulder affectionately. "I am content with the son I have. Now, tell me, what is this feud you have with di Balcosi?"

"That eel sucker. He came to the Callendra today and proposed that the nomo anciens be given a new 'advising counsel' of ten within the Callendra. A council made up only of nomo anciens, and none from others in the Callendra."

My father frowned. "To what purpose?"

"They would choose the candidates from whom I may pick my secretaries."

"Veridimmi?" My father's eyebrows went up. "Di Balcosi asks for this? When has he ever involved himself in politics?"

"I was as surprised as you. You should have seen him. Speaking with such humility and purity. Swearing under Amo's light that he seeks only what is best for the city." The Callarino scowled. "He was most believable. Half the Callendra were nodding along by the time he finished. He could have been Garagazzo at sermon, speaking on Amo's mercy."

"Who has put this in his head?"

"He claims it is his own idea."

My father snorted. "And how will these noblemen be selected for this council?"

"He has a list."

"How good of him."

"Avizzi, of course, D'Allassandro, Speignissi, Malacosta. All old names with history deeply rooted in Navola. Men who 'know her needs best.' And because they have land and title, they cannot be bought and twisted, unlike others . . ." And here he looked significantly at my father. "Who were born without lands, and who depend on trade in navisoli and promises."

My father sat back. "That is not subtle."

"Not subtle at all."

We were interrupted by Merio's return with servants and trays and glasses of hot tea for all of us, along with baked fennel biscuits and bitter cheeses. As the glasses and food were laid out, my father went silent, waiting until the servants had departed. The Callarino fell upon the food. Merio closed the doors and took up a post beside them, listening and guarding our council.

"Speignissi," my father said, finally. "You say that Speignissi was on Balcosi's list?"

The Callarino made three fingers off his cheek. "That one likes anything that makes trouble."

"Indeed. It is something I would expect of him. Speignissi slithers and sneaks."

"I sometimes imagine he is a serpent, hissing and dripping poison in other's ears. But it's not just Speignissi this time. All the nomo anciens like this idea. Even ones not on the list. They resent sharing votes with vianomae in the Callendra."

"A few guild names? A few men from the street? And now suddenly Balcosi puts his fingers into politics?"

"I'm going to send the Lupari for him tomorrow. We'll see how much he likes his fingers after he's lost a few."

"On what grounds?"

"Taxes, probably." The Callarino blew on his tea. "They all play games with their taxes." He sucked the tea through his teeth, thoughtful. "It doesn't matter. I'll catch him in the city, so he can't flee to his castello in the country. He thinks because he's old noble blood that he is safe from me, but every rat has to come out of his hole eventually."

"But still, he is an old name. And better liked than many. Well liked, in fact. He's not Speignissi."

"If he continues this talk, it will grow. Some of the guilds support the idea, too. You want some pissioletto like Pescamano to be the first secretary of war? To choose his friends when he decides where to buy our swords and armor? To choose the builders who will repair the gate towers? You want the first secretary of trade to decide who will dredge the harbor? Or where we buy the marble for the Convent of Sorrows? What about Amolucio with control over coinage? Next thing you know, he'll be stamping Amo's fire on the front of our navisoli and giving it to Garagazzo to favor. He who controls the purse, controls the city, and we both know it. Nai. I will stamp upon his neck, and I will not have you interfere. This is my sphere. We agreed upon it. And I am not wrong in this."

"Nai. Of course not. You are absolutely correct. If the man toasts you with blood, then drain the glass, by all means."

"Sei fescato. You have some thought. You always have some thought. Go on. Out with it."

My father inclined his head. "I think that one head on a spike almost always leads to more. We're both old enough to remember the wars between the names. All of us locked inside our towers, pitched battles in the streets. One archinomo's household guard against the next, against the next. Chaos."

"I have the Lupari—"

"And yet the dogs will still get fat."

"You want me to appease him!"

I flinched at the Callarino's outburst, but my father was not intimidated. "Absolutely not. Never weaken yourself. But this patro is well liked. He's not like Furia or Speignissi. And his cheeks appear unmarked. And yet . . ." My father broke off, considering.

"And yet . . . ?"

"And yet now our friend has stepped into the light. You see him. I see him. Others see him, too. So. What if you do not attack him, but instead make sure that he is seen even more. Give this good and honest nomo nobili anciens a chance to show us how a city-minded archinomo can serve the greater good. Give him responsibility for something important, and visible. The construction of the Convent of Sorrows, for example."

"He knows nothing of such work," the Callarino protested.

My father raised his eyebrows.

The Callarino's eyes widened. "Ai. That is clever."

The two began to scheme, leaning close to each other, sipping their tea and plotting, each pointing out ideas, working through the path and plan.

"Maybe he will learn—" my father began.

"—and maybe he will not—" the Callarino said.

"—but no matter how he performs, it pushes back the discussion."

"It certainly reasonably delays a decision on his proposal."

"And by the time the topic comes up again . . ."

"He will have made choices and agreements and contracts."

"Some names will profit—"

"And others will be slighted!" The Callarino was nodding vigorously now.

"Our clean friend will become muddy," my father said. "And a man with muddy cheeks is hard to love."

"He will certainly make others angry with his choices. He will become muddy . . ." The Callarino trailed off, frowning. "I think it should be the dredging of the harbor, not the convent."

"The harbor is not as symbolic," my father objected.

"Less symbolic," the Callarino pointed out, "but many of the nobilii depend on smooth trade at the docks. And it affects the guilds as well. There are more interests to balance. More enemies to be made."

My father's brow knitted, considering. "Ai. It would also affect the great merchants."

The Callarino leaned forward eagerly. "And the stevedores. And foreign ships. And the island fishers. And the vianomae of the docks. It goes on and on."

My father stroked his beard. "Ai. You're right. The harbor entangles di Balcosi in a wider web." He slapped the table. "You're absolutely right!"

And so it went. The two of them sipped their tea and ate their cheeses and schemed some more and eventually the Callarino left with a warmed cloak and a warmer expression.

When the Callarino was gone, Merio said to my father, "That was a good idea you had, to put Balcosi in charge of the harbor."

"Indeed," my father said. "The convent would have been disastrous. Garagazzo would have been irritated."

I looked between them, confused. "But it was the Callarino who suggested the harbor," I protested. "It was you who suggested the convent."

"Oh?"

"I heard you."

My father exchanged a knowing look with Merio. "Did you?"

I looked back and forth between my father and Merio, confused, trying to understand why the two men were smiling.

"You suggested the convent," I said again. "Not the harbor. I heard you."

"Davico," Merio said, laying a hand upon my shoulder, "you must not only listen to a man's words, but also think on why he speaks them. Does your father seem a fool?"

My father quirked an eyebrow at Merio, amused.

"No," I said. "Of course not."

"Indeed. He is not a fool. And yet the convent was never a good suggestion. If its construction were ruined, it would alienate an important ally of your father's, Garagazzo, our high canon priest. So, why would your father suggest such a terrible idea?"

I looked at Merio, stymied.

"Does the Callarino seem like a man who takes orders easily?" Merio prodded.

"Nai." I shook my head. "He likes to give orders."

"And therefore . . . ?"

Slowly it dawned on me. "You offered the Callarino a bad idea, so that he would have the chance to think of a better idea. Then he would think the idea was his, and would be happy to do it. You made him think it was his own idea."

My father leaned back, smiling proudly. "You see, Merio? He's learning."

"He is di Regulai," Merio said. "It's in his blood."

The two of them looked pleased, and I pretended to be pleased as well.

But in truth, I was troubled by the incident. I had been cowed by the Callarino's anger. The man had stormed into my father's library, dangerous and terrible, and I had only wanted to hide with Lazy under the desk. And yet my father had not been bothered in the least. Indeed, manipulating the Callarino had been a simple game to him, demanding no more effort than when a child rolls a ball in one direction or another, according to his preference. I had taken one look at the Callarino and wanted to flee his fury; my father had seen an opportunity to shape the politics of our city to his will.

"Merio," my father said, as he gathered his letters and made ready to retire, "I think I would like to sit across the plank from our friend di Balcosi. Perhaps share a bottle of wine with him."

"On what excuse?"

"Find out what his lands produce. Perhaps he would like help in trade. Perhaps he would benefit from a discretionary account with us, an opportunity to increase his family's fortunes. He will have some need or desire. Since he has decided to step into the light, let us take a closer look."

A week later, my father met the man upon a sunny hill, and took his measure. If Balcosi had been at all wise, he would have fled as soon as he received my father's invitation.

Chapter 4

I woke in the night to a feeling of wrongness.

I had been dreaming, bizarre and tormenting dreams full of swarming insects that boiled up out of the earth and crawled over me. I had lain rigid and still as they swarmed over me, knowing that they would consume me if I moved at all. Beetles of Scuro, ants, cockroaches, some as large as my hand . . . So of course when I woke—thrashing to get them off me—the night felt threatening. But even as my heartbeat slowed, a sensation of danger remained.

Feeling both foolish and apprehensive, I roused Lazy and climbed out of bed. I drew on a heavy robe and we two padded across the cold planks to my door and cracked it open.

Outside, there was nothing but the empty open gallery, the quiet columns and sleeping dark doors of the other apartments that encircled our garden quadra. Nothing seemed amiss. It was a cold spring night, clear and chilly and moonless. High above, stars twinkled, spangled across the arc of Amo's dome.

Lazy's ears pricked up. I froze, listening with her.

Men. Low muttering voices. A jingle and clank of activity. Following the noise, Lazy and I stealthed toward our quadra premia. We slipped through an arched passageway and emerged on the far side with a view over the rail into the courtyard. I sucked in my breath. Soldiers. Fighting men wearing the Bull of the Regulai upon their chests. More men than I would have guessed from the small amount of noise they made as they saddled their horses.

Staying low, Lazy and I slipped down the stairs and tucked ourselves behind an ancient urn. The soldiers were blackening their faces with charcoal and swathing their mail in wool to mute the clink and hide the shine. Others were wrapping their horses' hooves in leather, to muffle their tread. I recognized a few, men who were our personal guards. Rivetus. Relus. Polonos. The horses snorted impatiently, puffs of mist from cold muzzles. The men checked their swords, holding the gleaming edges up to the torchlight, scraping their fingers across the blades. The courtyard shimmered with an anticipation of violence.

A man emerged from amongst the press of soldiers, no taller than the rest but somehow taller anyway, taller simply in his presence. He spoke with a warrior here, gripped a shoulder there, joked quietly with a third. Aghan Khan, my father's guard captain.

Aghan Khan was a great swordsman, and, my father said, a great general. In my younger years I had only known him as an imposing man with a bushy black beard and deep-set eyes, who laughed easily and who always trailed behind me when Lazy and I went exploring in the city. We stole apples and oranges and small melons from merchants on the streets, and Aghan Khan came along behind and paid them to pretend that they had not seen us do so. This was the Aghan Khan I had known as a small child: a man who was kind and who indulged. Later, I faced a different version when he began to teach me swordskill. Then he delivered more than a few bruises: always fast, always hard, and always with a mild admonishment that stood in sharp contrast to the speed he struck.

Raise your guard, Davico.

Mind your left foot, Davico.

If you step like that, you will always hurt, Davico.

And hurt I did. Every time. But even then, his words were never harsh and his eyes had been kind, even if his strikes were not.

Now, though, Aghan Khan's gaze was implacably dark. For the first time in my life, the sight of him frightened me. He radiated violence. This was the great general my father had described. The Fist of Kharat, a man who had smashed kingdoms. And yet despite the violence that seemed to emanate from his very soul, the men seemed drawn to him. Indeed, each one seemed to grow a little, becoming more imposing, powerful, and dangerous as he passed—more like Aghan Khan himself.

Another figure emerged from amongst the crowd.

My father, not in armor but in silver-trimmed black velvet, finery such that it looked as if he were preparing to receive the prince of Cheroux. Where the men had crowded close to Aghan Khan, seeking his attention, his blessing, his power, they parted before my father, ducking their heads and touching their hearts. A different kind of power, a different kind of love.

The two men came together, gripping each other's shoulders. Their heads bent low, almost touching. They spoke for a little while, each one nodding in turn, their words too quiet for me to hear, then all at once they embraced tightly. A final shared look of grimness passed between them and then Aghan Khan was mounting his steed. He looked to the sky and raised an arm in silent order. In moments, all his men were mounted with him. With nary a shout or order they rode forth, two by two through the tunnel of our palazzo gates, and then out into the sleeping and unsuspecting streets of Navola.

Only my father remained, a silent lonely figure, gazing after the men and the gate through which they had disappeared.

"Father?" I emerged cautiously from behind the urn.

"Davico." My father turned, and his eyes were as dark and hard as Aghan Khan's. "I didn't know you were awake."

I shrugged, not having an explanation, not sure I needed one. "Where did Aghan Khan go?"

My father's eyes remained hard for a long moment. "He goes to fix my mistake."

I was surprised. "Merio says you do not make mistakes."

My father laughed and softened a little. "Anyone can make a mistake, Davico. Everyone does, eventually." He squatted down in front of me. "Do you remember our day with Tomas di Balcosi?"

It had been several weeks since I had seen the man, but I remembered. "In the vineyard on the hill."

"Very good. What else do you remember?"

The things I remembered were, I knew, not the things my father asked about. It had been a fine day, sunny, crystalline, with rags of muddy melting snow between the grapevines and a few faint kisses of overly eager grass upon the brown and dormant hills. One of the first warm days to attempt to pry open the cold fingers of winter.

The vineyard itself had been draped off three sides of an uneven hill, all of them proceeding downward from an ancient Amonese villa at the crest, much tumbledown. Unrestrained grapevines climbed the villa's walls and tore at its bricks but it remained inviting, and it was there that Tomas di Balcosi had come to meet us: my father, Merio, Aghan Khan, Polonos, Relus, all of us amongst the vines, pruning the ancient plants.

It had been a strange day, for my father never labored in fields. He was not so interested in the ways of growing things, nor did he particularly obsess upon wines as a typical Navolese was wont to do. In fact, he often said he had no expertise for wine himself, saying that his palate was not refined. He relied upon his concubine Ashia for her taste, and Merio's eye for a good price as to whether one vintage or another was destined for our cellars.

And yet there we all were, pruning the dwarfish vines that the vintner called bassalice, short chalices, for the way they grew from the ground like stubby trees, or alternatively calimixi—Caliba's friends—and that he claimed were a thousand years old. Perhaps they were not so old, but of a certainty, they were well established, thicker than Aghan Khan's thigh at their base, black-barked and stumpy, with widely spreading hands that touched our chests and that we now trimmed back, leaving only a few points for new buds to emerge. Trimming their fingernails, the vintner called it. And he and Merio were deep in discussion about the merits of different grapes and different ways of training vines when Tomas di Balcosi arrived.

"What else do you remember?" my father asked.

"He was not happy to meet with you, but he came anyway." More than that, was the contrast between my father and Balcosi. My father had been friendly, effusive even, where Balcosi had been standoffish. Balcosi had been well dressed and plump, in rich velvets with heavy golden jeweled chains about his neck, and a fat ruby-and-diamond clasp for his cloak. He rode upon a black horse and had three men to guard him, and his lips had pressed together as if he had tasted something unpleasant when he gazed upon us.

"He looked down upon us."

My father smiled slightly. "You're right. He did. But then, many archinomi do. The old nobilii are proud and often wary of us. What else do you remember?"

Despite di Balcosi's mien, my father had greeted the noble with pleasure, kissing the fleshy man on each cheek, then drawing him with some excitement down the chalice rows of vines to introduce him to the vintner. He then began asking Balcosi for his opinion of the vinobracchia grapes that we labored over. "My grandfather taught me that we should know the things we trade in," my father said, "the men we give our promises to, the businesses that they conduct, the details of their lives. So here I am, with a vine knife in my hand and a poor grasp of the art of winemaking."

"It is a fine grape," Balcosi said, his puzzlement softening his features. "But surely you knew that."

"But what about these particular vines?" my father asked. "Should they be trained so in chalices? Standing alone like this, and not upon a trellis or married to good fruit trees? Every man I talk to has his own opinions on such things, and they are all conflicting! I read both Petonos's *Land and Fruits* and Aeschonos's *Della Terra,* and they disagree. What do you think?"

Balcosi softened even more. "Ai. Well, for vinobracchia, on south slopes, the chalice is best. It has been so for more than five hundred years. Aeschonos's *Della Terra* is wrong in this. I read the same passage, and I knew in an instant that he was confused."

"And the wine?" my father pressed. "The wine these grapes produce. What do you think of it? Is it better than all others? The Comezzi claim it is."

"Well." Balcosi smiled. "My own lands are just there." He pointed to a nearby hill and a pretty castello, surrounded by many vines and trees. "I cannot speak against my own."

My father laughed. "Ai. Of course. *A true Navolese has his favorite vineyard, his favorite grape . . .* "

" *. . . and his favorite bottle.*" Balcosi finished the quote. "Quite so. But I think that if you are looking to buy wines, well, these are perhaps not as nuanced as those from my own vineyard, but no man—indeed no king—would be insulted should you pour it at table."

"So the land is good?" my father asked. "Merio tells me these grapes are good because the vines are wise and the land cradles them as a mother cradles her first child, but"—he shrugged—"he is from Pardi."

"Scuro's eyes!" Balcosi laughed and made a warding sign. "Trust a Pardinese with a sheep, not with a vine!" He sobered. "But in this case, your man is right. This land is very good. There is no finer near Navola, perhaps no finer in all the hook. I have often gazed upon these hills, these old vines, and thought how greatly they would prosper if cared for well." He shrugged. "The Comezzi will not sell them, though."

"They are an old name," my father said. "And very high above the concerns of trade."

"And stubborn," Balcosi agreed. "But you cannot have invited me here to discuss grapes."

"Well, not only grapes." My father took up his hooked vine knife once more and cut away a long trailing vine. "I have been thinking about what you said in the Callendra, not so long ago, about the importance of men without agenda to guide the business of the city, about the importance of nomo nobilii anciens."

"Ah." Balcosi eyed him. "It's said that Devonaci di Regulai never attends the Callendra but his eyes and ears attend to all."

"Ci. Vianomae say all kinds of things. I do not like politics, it is a messy business and unpleasant. But it's true that sometimes word comes to me." My father continued to trim at the vines, cutting away the previous year's growth, cutting back to the chalice of the grape's main arms. "I hear talk of this and that, and I am heartened that the ancient names worry for Navola as well." He cut another vine. "Am I doing this right?" he asked the vintner.

"Very correct, lord."

"Nai, nai. Don't call me lord." He jerked his head toward di Balcosi. "Our guest is noble. I am not. Did you know that the name di Balcosi stretches back even to the origins of Torre Amo?"

"I did not, lord."

"Ci. Don't be so formal. I am of the street, not the tower. True nobility is not bought with navisoli, it comes from good blood, and good marriages, and it takes generations to take its final form. Much like the best wines. Nobility is not something that appears overnight."

"Our name is old," di Balcosi acknowledged.

"And rightfully proud."

My father put down his hooked vine knife and shook out his hands. "Ai. This is hard work. My arms are already sore. Honest work for honest men, as they say, but not easy." He looked at Balcosi as he took up the hooked knife once more. "The truth is that I wanted to meet you, to know your character. To see if you were honest as well. I'm glad that you care so much for Navola, for we have need of more men like you. Respected men, who think not of power for themselves, but of the good of the city."

"They are rare," di Balcosi agreed.

"Too rare," my father said. "The great names all have their towers and like to preen and show themselves above Navola, but how many of them care for the life of the people in the streets? How many understand that the beating hearts of the vianomae are the true heart of the city? That when they prosper, we all prosper?" He sighed. "If the Callendra had more noble hearts such as yours, Navola would prosper for a thousand years."

"You flatter me."

"I never flatter." My father waved, indicating the sleeping vineyard around us. "These lands and vines are ours now."

Di Balcosi frowned. "I do not understand."

"I have purchased them."

"You jest. The Comezzi are proud."

"The Comezzi had many debts. Now they do not. This land is mine now, but as you can see"—my father laughed ruefully—"I am no expert. I asked you here to beg a favor, for you neighbor this land, and know it better than any. I would like to ask you to take these lands on my behalf, to manage freely, as you manage your own."

"Surely you jest."

"I hope not, and I hope you will consider it. I would be indebted to you. It is not a small thing, I know, to take on so much new land, but I would see these lands prosper, to be tended well, and our city as well. And when I look to your lands, just there, I think, aha, there is a man who is wise. My grandfather always taught me to seek wise men and their council. If you will do this boon for me, I would only seek a tenth of the profit, the rest to go to you. My only other request would be that you keep on this fine vintner who has labored long here and knows these hills well."

Di Balcosi had been surprised then, and warmed considerably, and he thanked my father effusively. We all drank toasts amongst the vines and then we went into the tumbledown villa and sat before a roaring fire and drank more wine, and it had been a happy day.

And now, in the cold darkness of our palazzo's quadra, my father asked again. "Do you remember?"

I thought back over all that had happened, how the wine had made my face warm, how we had eaten pigeon around the fire, how I had fed bits to Lazy, and how there had been many toasts.

"Di Balcosi toasted us and said that our names would rival the

Amonetti for their wines, and we would be known throughout the hook. And he said that forgers would stamp casks with our crest because no other wine would be so sought after."

"Indeed he did," my father said. "And when he made that toast, he met my eye, but his shoulders turned away."

I thought back, trying to recall the moment. It was as my father described.

"It seems a small thing," I said.

"It was not."

A few hours later, our palazzo's silence was shattered by our soldiers' return. They clattered through the gates, pikes gleaming and torches flaring, and herded before them, running and stumbling and crying for mercy, came Tomas di Balcosi, his wife, and his three daughters.

Not so proud as he had been on his horse, not so confident as he had been amongst the vines. A terrified man, stumbling and cowering as he was herded by our pikes. Five nomo nobilii anciens dragged from their palazzo, driven through the streets like cattle, and now crouched against our palazzo wall, beneath the looming fresco of our family's victory over Cheroux.

In the blazing torchlight, the painted banners of the fresco seemed alive, waving victorious, and the Bull of the Regulai even larger, looming above them all, seeming to trample not just Cheroux but our new captives as well.

How small those nobilii seemed, huddled before such an image.

How vulnerable.

How foolish.

Our gates crashed closed. The matra collapsed. Our men seized the patro and dragged him away, babbling and sobbing, to face my father.

Silence fell upon the courtyard. Torches crackled. The three daughters looked around themselves, stunned at their change in station. Gowns torn, hair tangled, faces streaked with soot, expressions so confused that they seemed as simpletons. The youngest sobbed. The tallest hugged her close, whispering fiercely in her ear, stroking her tangled braids.

Though torn, their silks were very fine. Gold brocade and embroidery shimmered in the torchlight. Diamonds glinted in their hair. Their throats and wrists and ears all dripped gemstones. I found myself fascinated by the opulence. They were as much peacocks as their father had been in the vineyard that day. It was not our family's habit to show our prosperity so casually. My father most often wore black, with only a simple embroidery of bulls or coins, except for the grandest of occasions. But then, we were banca mercanta and the Balcosi were ancient nobles. In every respect, we were different creatures.

The eldest girl knelt beside her fainted mother, trying to revive her. Our soldiers looked on, impassive.

"Only now do they begin to understand what it is to challenge us."

I flinched at the voice behind me. Cazzetta lurked in the shadows. I braced myself for abuse, for missing his arrival, but for once the stilettotore did not punish me. Instead, he joined me at the rail. A reek of smoke washed over me, choking and thick. Cazzetta's face was black with soot.

"You're burned!"

"Nai." Cazzetta's eyes gleamed beneath his mask of char. "Our enemies are burned. Every one. All burned alive in their tower. Not even Amo will be able to sift out their souls now." He looked as if he had clawed his way out of Scuro's pits.

He leaned upon the rail, and ash spilled from his coat. "How fare the Balcosi? Have they learned yet what it is to touch politics?"

I cleared my throat. "I thought they were supposed to supervise the harbor. Because they were popular. I thought Father didn't want to touch them. I thought we were in partnership with them. We were supposed to make wines together. We were going to make wines that everyone would clamor for."

"Indeed." Cazzetta brushed at his cloak and more ash rained off. "The Balcosi thought their name so high that they were invulnerable, and yours so low that you were nothing. Only now do they comprehend their mistake."

"But . . ." I screwed up my courage. "What changed?"

Cazzetta shrugged. "Two men shared a bottle of wine, and one saw the other clear."

"Father said that Balcosi turned his shoulders when they toasted."

Cazzetta smirked. "Is that what he said?"

"You think he lied to me?"

Cazzetta laughed. "Nai. Never. If your father says it was a turned shoulder, then I am sure it was, but I suspect it was more. Your father's mind is a restless beast, Davico. Like a tiger pacing. Always alert, always hungry. Always seeking to pounce. The things he notices and seizes upon—well, I do not think even your father can fully catalog. He may say it was the shoulder's turn, but I am certain it was more. Perhaps Balcosi drank too quickly after the toast. Perhaps he smiled too widely when your father proffered partnership. Perhaps he showed too many of his little yellow teeth. Or perhaps his brow wrinkled when he heard that your father was to be his neighbor. Perhaps all of those things. And then, at the end, he turned his shoulders one way instead of another. So your father sent me to follow the patro."

Cazzetta flicked three fingers off his cheek, throwing insult upon the captives below.

"I watched who Balcosi visited, and who visited him. I watched him when he knelt at catredanto, and when he lay beneath his mistress. I followed him to the Speignissi, a name that has never been friendly to our own. I gifted gold to servants and listened at doors and windows with ears that were sometimes mine and sometimes not. I listened to angry archinomo nobilii anciens. Small men with great names who remembered past glories and plotted murder." He spat in the direction of our captives. "Those creatures down there sought to destroy your family."

I stared down at the daughters, hemmed in by our soldiers' steel. Three frightened young girls, an insensate mother, all of them pinned below the grand fresco of our family's triumph over Cheroux.

"They do not look dangerous."

Cazzetta snorted. "Even a fool can be dangerous."

The tall girl was helping her mother to sit up, tending to the blood in her hair where she had struck her head when she fainted. My father's concubine, Ashia, had more steel in her than this noblewoman who had fainted, I thought. The matra was soft. Even the daughter was stronger.

"Let Balcosi be a lesson for you, Davico. Fools are dangerous. They are dangerous to you and they are dangerous to their allies. They are especially dangerous to themselves. Tomas di Balcosi was a fool to think he could throw in with the Speignissi. And he was fool to think that his popularity would protect him. But more than that, he was a fool for not understanding the limits of his own face. Whatever Aghan Khan may teach you with the sword, or Merio with his abacus, know that Tomas di Balcosi destroyed his family not with steel or gold, but with that face of his. He sought to play in politics, where the art of faccioscuro is both sword and shield, and he held neither. He imagined he could sit parlobanco with your father. That fool destroyed himself the moment he agreed to meet your father in a vineyard and talk of wine."

He gave the captives another flick of the three. "So now the Speignissi are burned to ash in their tower and Balcosi kneels before your father and begs for mercy. Take note of this night, princeling. Soon you will sit parlobanco as your father does, and you must read a man's face as well as he, and be as circumspect as di Balcosi should have been. Take note of this night, boy, for down there, that is the cost of failure."

Cazzetta's words filled me with foreboding. I wanted to ask how I was supposed to know. How I was supposed to read a face, but already Cazzetta was departing, disappearing amongst the shadowy columns of the gallery.

"Will we burn the Balcosi as well?" I called after him. "Will they all burn?"

Cazzetta's shadow paused, but he did not look back.

"Nai. Your father is too wise for that."

And so it was.

An hour later, my father and the Patro di Balcosi emerged from my father's library. The matra was reunited with her foolish husband, and I was summoned down to the quadra.

Guards parted before me as I approached where my father waited beside the Balcosi family. Men I had known all my life, whom I had only ever seen as companions or minders, now loomed great and terrible. Their steel lay bared. Blood splashed and stained their weapons and their armor. Aghan Khan's own face was slashed and his beard was matted with blood, blacker even than the hairs it tangled.

The patro, once so proud, stood beside my father, his head bowed in shame. The matra sobbed into her sleeves. Their three daughters huddled together, looking to one another for support and not to their shattered matra or patro.

My father took the hand of the tallest girl and placed it in mine.

"Show this sia the palazzo," he said. "Make her welcome. Sia Celia is your sister now."

Chapter 5

Such a strange night, such a strange turning of the Fates. I know I made for a strange host, and Celia di Balcosi a stranger guest. That tall willowy girl with skirts torn, hair tangled, skin sooty, and eyes wide, dark, and watchful. I still remember the chill of her fingers as my father placed her hand in mine. The mist of her breath in the quadra's cold night air.

Celia was much taller than myself. Seeing the way she had cared for her mother, and the way her sisters turned to her for support, I thought her much older than I. Later I discovered that she had but a year on me, and was simply sprouted as girls her age were wont to grow, but at the time, I believed her much older, and much much wiser.

Show this sia the palazzo.

Make her welcome.

Sia Celia is your sister now.

If I had been a grown and civilized man, hosting a young sia under such distressing circumstances, the appropriate thing to do would have been to take her immediately to audience with my father's consort, Ashia.

There, the young girl would have been indulged with hot sweet tea and soothing biscuits made with ground kha spice, just the way Ashia liked and just as she had eaten in her own homeland. Ashia, in her refinement and wisdom, would have arranged a hot bath for the unsettled girl along with servant maids to assist, gentle helpers who would wash away the soot of battle from Celia's skin and untangle the black knots of terror from her hair. Then Celia would have been swaddled in new warm clothes (that Ashia's sharp eye would have already sized correctly) and indulged with more hot milky tea before a warm crackling fire, and Ashia would have talked and talked and talked and talked of nothings until at last Celia's eyes began to droop with exhaustion and the frightened captured girl could be certain of a deep rest.

And then she would have been bundled off to bed to sleep, and to heal.

"Fieno secco, vino fresco, pane caldo," as we like to say. Dry hay to sleep, cool wine to drink, warm bread to eat. A promise of succor. An oath of hospitality and protection that all Navolese take seriously. Do not listen to those people who say that we Navolese are cruel and twisted. We know how to treat a guest.

But I was young and untutored in such niceties.

Instead, I dragged Celia around the palazzo, showing her the three quadrae that were the heart of our home, each with two and sometimes three tiers of columned galleries around them and with gardens at their centers, pointing to where my father kept his apartments, where Ashia kept hers, where our guards and servants slept, where the kitchens were, pointing out the baths, taking her to my own room and showing her my onyx-and-marble chess set from Cheroux. I showed her the paintings of my family that would now be hers, telling her of Deiamo, who was kind and took care of orphans, and of the Bull, who had defended Navola. I showed her the portrait of my mother, who had passed away long ago, and showed her my father's library with its tomes and letters from countless lands. I showed her the frescoes of the old gods and goddesses that told our family history and more.

Celia took in each detail gravely, but did not become alive.

I took her then up to the roof, to the place where our night gardens were, where shimmering lusca flowers grew, and where fireflies and luminescent butterflies would alight during the warm summer months, but nothing moved in that cold early spring, and indeed, when we looked across the city—past the domes of the Callendra and the spiking tower of the Torre Justicia where criminals were kept, past the great dome of the catredanto—something else was visible: two towers blazing like signal torches above the city—the defensive towers of the Speignissi and of her own family. The handiwork of my own.

"I'm sorry," I said, flushing with embarrassment. "I didn't think."

Celia shrugged as if I had caused no harm, but her wooden gaze did not waver from the burning towers. I tugged her arm, trying to pull her away from the awful view, but she resisted. I tugged again. "Please. Come away. I know a better place than this. It will make you feel better. I'm sorry."

Her gaze remained fixed upon the burning towers.

"Please."

She seemed to shiver, and then relented. I hurried her then, chivvying her down the stairs and through the gardens, away from that awful view until we at last arrived at the place I should have taken her first.

In the warm darkness of the stables, I lit a lantern. The soft feathery scents of hay and sweet manure surrounded us. Lazy came out from the shadows, head low, cautious, alert to the dark tenor of the night and the actions in the quadra beyond. Her tail wagged uncertainly as she approached. She did not leap up on Celia but instead sniffed her hand and rubbed about her legs and then sat and gazed up at Celia, her brown eyes querying.

"Who are you?" Celia asked.

"This is Lazy," I introduced. "Lazy, this is Celia. She is my sister now."

Celia smiled a little. "Lazy, is it?" She crouched and ran her hands over Lazy's head and neck, scratching behind her ears. "He doesn't think much of you, does he?"

Lazy wagged her tail and licked Celia's cheeks. Celia's guarded expression softened.

Stub peered out from his stall. "And this is Stub," I said.

I showed Celia the bin of wrinkled apples and carrots that could be fed to him. At Stub's rubbery lips upon her palm, Celia's drawn features softened more. Her shoulders relaxed. Her tightly held body eased.

I felt most successful.

Celia fed Stub another carrot, smiling softly as he lipped it from her palm. "And who is Stub?"

"Stub is my pony. He is from Deravashi stock."

"The Deravashi are very small," she said.

"They are stout," I disagreed. "My father breeds them with others, racers, for their stamina."

"But Stub is small," Celia said. She fed him another carrot, then walked down the length of the stables. Another horse poked her head out. "Who is this?"

"Wind. She is a Deravashi mix."

"Ai." Celia's eyes shone. "She is regal." She fed her a carrot. "I think you, Wind, you are who I would like to ride."

"But Wind is mine," I protested.

Celia glanced over. "But I thought you rode Stub?"

I looked away, embarrassed, and mumbled, "I'm not to ride Wind until my swordskill improves. Wind will not respect me until I can swing a sword, Aghan Khan says, and so far he is not impressed."

"Ah." I thought Celia would laugh at me then, but she did not, and instead only nodded gravely. "I think your man is wise. It's good to earn your place in the saddle, and not be given it."

I had the uncomfortable feeling then that she was speaking not of me, but of her father, and felt embarrassed at her family's stupidity.

"Will your father kill me?" she asked suddenly.

"Will he—"

"Will he kill me?"

Looking back on that moment, I think with some fondness on the directness of children. Shocking as the topic might have been, the guileless question stood in sharp contrast to the subtle ways of faccioscuro that made up my father's world—the twist of a shoulder, a pursing of lips, a sip of wine—that portended all manner of bloody events.

Here was a clear question, directly asked, to be directly answered.

Would murder be served upon the guest?

It was an important question, perhaps the most important. One worth asking (from Celia's perspective, certainly) but also one worth answering honestly (from my perspective, if we were to be good siblings).

I started to answer quickly, almost hotly with denial, but then paused to consider. Such a question deserved careful consideration.

Ai. To be so honest again. To be so unafraid as Celia, to ask the hardest questions and to expect the hard and honest answers. And in my own turn, to have the sturdiness to answer truly. What a gift that seems to me now, after all that I have seen and done, all I have suffered and inflicted. After all the deceits of politics that I have seen. I think now on Celia's question, and wish that all questions could be asked so directly, and answered so clearly as I answered on that night, without a trace of faccioscuro.

"Nai," I said, with all the solemnity that youth brings to the topics of adults. "My father will not harm you. You are safe."

"How do you know?"

I struggled to put words to my thinking. "I just . . . I know him."

Celia nodded solemnly but was obviously not assured. I sought some reasoning that might convince her. My father was not the sort who went to Quadrazzo Amo to see a thief's hands chopped off on the steps of the Callendra. Our family did not gather with crowds to see the adulteresses stripped and whipped, or to watch a murderer torn apart by horses. My father did not rant like the Callarino about how he would like to see someone's head on a pike, or bled before his family members.

"My father takes no pleasure in others' pain," I said at last. "He is not as a cat who plays with mice. He is di Regulai. He keeps his word. We keep our promises. It is our name."

"Men's lips speak honor, but their hands speak truth," Celia replied.

"Who says that?"

"My mother."

"My father speaks truth. Always."

"So your lips say."

I hunted for an authority Celia would trust. "Ashia says so as well, and she is a woman."

"And who is Ashia? Your mother?"

"My mother is dead. Ashia is Father's concubine."

"The sfaccita? I have heard of her."

I sucked in my breath, shocked. "Do not call her that."

"Is she not a slave? Does she not wear the three-and-three?"

It was true that Ashia was slave-scarred, but it did not sound right to say so. None of us said so, ever. Ashia ran the palazzo. She was my father's lover. She was always present. "She is powerful."

Celia shrugged, as if this was another person she did not believe. Men she did not believe. Slaves she did not believe.

"If my father wanted to kill you," I said heatedly, "he would have sent Cazzetta. He would have done to you just as he did to the Speignissi. If you were meant to die, you would be already dead. That is my father. When he strikes, he does not hesitate. But Cazzetta says my father is too wise to kill you or your family, so you are safe. I am sure of it."

"Who is Cazzetta?"

"My father's dagger man."

"Ai." She flinched. "That one I know. He is a scorpion."

"He's worse than that," I said, and liked her better, if only for our shared dislike of Cazzetta. "But if you were meant to die, you would have seen his blade by now. He is quick with it. You are safe here. I am sure of it."

"What will happen to me then?"

"Well . . . You are to be my sister."

"But I already have a family."

I was stymied. "Maybe your family will live with us, too?"

But of course, as soon as I said it, I knew this could not be true, and Celia's wise dark eyes told me she knew it as well. And indeed, by the time we returned to the quadra premia, all her family were gone as if they had never existed.

Tomas di Balcosi was not burned to ash. He and the remainder of his family were banished to Scarpa Calda to manage a tin mine on my father's behalf, and Merio took control of the management of the various Balcosi villas and estates. We sent sufficient navisoli to the patro for him to maintain a reasonable lifestyle—as long as he remained far from Navola. The patro was warned that if he ever returned he would be locked in the Torre Justicia and the Callarino would decide his fate according to our laws, for we had ample evidence that he had plotted to overthrow the Callendra and place the Speignissi and their cronies in control of the city. He was made to understand that the only thing that now sheltered him from the Callarino's wrath was my father's mercy.

"But why did you spare the Balcosi?" I asked my father the next day. "Why spare them, but not the Speignissi? Why is Sia Celia my sister now? The patro plotted against us, just like Speignissi, but you only sent him away and did not slay him."

My father smiled. "Think on it."

"Was it because they were popular? Would the Callendra not allow it? Was the Callarino angry that we sent him one way and then we went another? Do they have friends who spoke for them?"

"Think on it. Now go and see that your sister is well settled."

And I did think on it, but I came to no clear conclusion. We had had the Balcosi at our mercy, and Cazzetta always said that a serpent without a head was the best sort of serpent. The most I could conclude was that my father had a complex mind, and that he shaped the world to it.

The Speignissi family died, because my father willed it.

Celia's family was banished, because he willed it.

Celia di Balcosi was my sister now, because he chose it.

And when my father smiled and said that I should think upon the reasons, it demonstrated how little I still understood, and it troubled me.

"How can I match him?" I asked Merio later, when I was studying with him in the scrittorium. "He thinks and plans all the time. He plans in his sleep, even. He plays cartalegge blind, and always beats me. Always he has another plan or plot. He is never trapped or wrong."

"Did he not say that he had made a mistake with Balcosi? I know that he said so to me."

"He said so. But I do not believe it."

Merio laughed. "Ai, Davico. Your father is a man, as are we all. The events with the Speignissi were not ideal. Your father prefers to let the Callarino work the sphere of politics, and the Callendra to wield its power without the name di Regulai ever being spoken. It makes archinomi uneasy when towers burn and nobilii anciens beg for mercy. If there had been another path, your father would have taken it."

"But he saw the plot in time. We are alive and the Speignissi are dead and the Balcosi serve us now. You yourself say that the measure of a sailor is not how well he sails the blue ocean, but how well he sails the black."

"I do indeed. And your father sails both with skill, that is true."

"Cazzetta says I must be like him," I said glumly, "but I am not the same."

Merio laughed. "But that is why we make you study, Davico!" He ruffled my hair. "Do not think that you attain mastery overnight. It is a long and arduous process. Your father practiced long to become the man he is. In time, you will match him."

"Nai." I shook my head. "I'm not the same. He is something else entirely. As if Leggus and Scuro had a child. All business and twisty thinking. The Balcosi now make a profit for us, even though they once sought to destroy us. They make our mines productive, as if they are our friends. But they are not, and still I do not understand."

Merio laughed again. "Sfai! You are Navolese. It is your birthright to understand the twisted path." He added more seriously, "There's no escaping the work, though. If you wish your mind to be flexible and agile, you must practice with it. So, on with the study. Why is the gold of Cheroux something we reject?"

"What about you? Should your mind not also be flexible and agile?"

"Me?" Merio laughed. "I am from Pardi." He patted his soft belly. "The men of Pardi eat well, but we do not plot or plan. It is enough to see our pigs fatten, and see our white-horn cows fill their udders with good milk, and see our cheeses age. We are farmers. Our great trait is that we trust." He considered a moment. "Also, we are optimistic. A farmer must be, after all. We trust the sun to shine and the rains to fall. We trust our wives to come back to our beds at night, even when we drink wine all day. That is what a man from Pardi is good for. We are good for trust, we are good for drink, we are very good at table. Not so good in bed, but excellent at table."

"You're not a farmer, though. And you don't have a wife."

He waggled his thick eyebrows. "But I do set a very good table."

"You know what I mean."

"Well, Pardi men are also good for keeping numbers in their columns. We are trustworthy for that."

"Now you're just making things up."

"Not at all! My father was a farmer. But I was the sixth son. So"—he shrugged—"a numerari was willing to take me to apprentice and was my father's neighbor, so numerari is what my father made me." He ruffled my hair and pinched my ear. "But a numerari, too, is not a job for you twisty-minded Navolese. Too clever by half, the Navolese!" He pinched my ears again. "Twisty twisty twisty! Not to be trusted with numbers in their columns. Next thing you know the Navolese has stolen your business, your wife, your daughters, probably your pantaloni as well!"

I pushed his hand away before he could pinch again. "I think I should have been from Pardi," I said. "I am not twisty at all."

"Sfai," he said, turning serious. "You are di Regulai and you are da Navola. The twisted paths are your home and your safest thicket. Your mind is as sharp as Cazzetta's hidden daggers. It is your birthright, make no mistake. Your mind must be as sharp as a blade, as subtle as a fish beneath the waves, and as agile as the fox. For that is what a

Navolese is. It is your nature. You were nursed by Scuro himself, and no mistake. This is your birthright."

But I did not think so.

My father knew the price of wheat in Tlibi and the value of jade in Crechia. He knew how many blocks of pardago were aging in the great cooling houses of Pardi. He knew the percentages of gold in coinages from Torre Amo, Cheroux, Merai, and Vaz. He knew how many bolts of silk and how many Steppe horses were in the caravan bound for Capova, left six months previous and not due to arrive for a further three. He knew of planned coups in Merai, and also that he would extend credit to the Parl there to defend against them.

My father had sipped a single glass of ruby vinobracchia with Tomas di Balcosi and had taken the man's measure so perfectly that the Speignissi family was ash and Celia di Balcosi now lived in our palazzo and took her lessons beside me. Celia was not of our family, and yet she lived as one of us, because my father found it useful.

My father always planned, always anticipated, always triumphed, and I was expected to follow him.

Though I was of his blood, I was not well suited for the task.

Chapter 6

Nai. There. You see? Already I lie to you.

Already I seek to pretend that I was always the innocent—that I had no wiles, no sly ways. But that is not true. Of course I lacked the uncanny brilliance of my father, but to say that I had no guile was not true. All children have secrets. We keep them from our parents, our friends, the maestri of our lessons . . . Sometimes, we hide them even from ourselves.

I was not as wise as my father, nor as darkly scheming as Cazzetta. I was not even as clever as Merio with his books and his well-aged cheese crumbled with good crusted bread beside his abacuses. But still, I had my own secrets. And my deepest secrets were those of a young boy growing up, a boy who was fast upon the cusp of manhood. A boy growing hair upon his legs, and upon his eggs, who feels the first confusing rushes of a man's passion.

I was leaving that age of innocence and reaching a new age, one that suddenly discovers delight in the feminine form.

Was I duedezzi years under Amo? I think I must have been older. Thirteen? Perhaps. Our memories of the past become jumbled, sometimes mercifully so, and yet individual moments and events stand out as bright as gold in a strongbox. I know that this occurred after Celia's arrival, and after she became a part of my daily life, but to place a year or season is difficult. Perhaps Celia's arrival was even the cause, the arrival and presence of a girl more mature than I, waking something within me.

Perhaps you have never experienced this overwhelming rush, or perhaps you know exactly of what I speak, but for me, as I approached those early days of manhood, the sight of the feminine form suddenly became enough to make me nearly faint. I became out of mind.

Exomentissimo, as Merio used to say, though he used it to describe his relationship with cheese.

All of a sudden, I could scarce see a maid in the halls without seeing also how her skirts rustled about her hips. The open lacing in a servant's bodice was enough to make me swoon. The presence of Celia, always so close because of shared meals and shared lessons, was even more overwhelming. That tall (much taller than I) and maturing (much more mature than I) girl was suddenly always nearby. The scent of her, the breath of her, the sight of her, and most overwhelming of all, the thought that her bare shoulder was a mere hair's breadth away from my own pining skin (if we simply discounted that I wore shirt and vest and jacket, and she wore blouse and dress and cloak, and also of course that this thought was crashing down upon me like a lightning bolt in the scrittorium under Merio's watchful eye, where Celia and I were sitting at his desk and studying water-stained correspondence from the Khur Empire) . . .

But still, we were practically naked together!

Well, you understand. Such is the mind of an addled young boy.

But still, Celia's long dark hair whispering silky upon the page, and then tucked behind her ear so casually, the soft down of her cheek . . . Well, the words upon the page became as the sigils of Xim for all the meaning they had to me, so intoxicated was I.

My childish infatuation with that girl was mostly harmless in such cases, earning only a rebuke from Merio for my failure to note some line in a contract. But it was more consequential when we practiced at swords, when we exercised hard, and wore less so that we could fight well.

As Celia and I lunged and parried and panted and gasped . . . well, sweat glistened upon Celia's neck and soaked her blouse, and it all became so overwhelming that she stabbed me easily.

"Davico!" Aghan Khan shouted. "You've forgotten your guard again! Have I taught you nothing?"

I lay upon the ground where Celia had driven me. She pressed the tip of her wooden sword to my throat. "You'll never ride Wind if you don't attend your guard," she said with a slight smirk.

"Indeed he won't." Aghan Khan scowled. "Today, Celia, you ride Wind. And you, Davico, you walk to the hills beside us."

"But—"

But what was I to say? That I had not been watching Celia's sword or stance at all?

I walked to the hills that day, and stayed silent.

It only took a few more bruised ribs and cracks to the skull for me to set aside my illicit thoughts of Celia. It was too much a confusion and too painful a lesson. Celia was my sister, and that was that. She might be beautiful, but she was not for gazing upon with desire. Celia was for parrying, and teasing, and laughing, and knocking about with a wooden sword. That was Celia.

But if Celia was too dangerous (and too painful) to pine after, our maids and servant girls were everywhere. In the kitchens, in the gardens, bringing forth delicious dishes at dinner, and on their hands and knees scrubbing marble floors in the halls. My eyes could not stop drinking of them. And because I always thirsted, I discovered that if I was silent and clever, and if I climbed over a balcony and then stretched around a corner, I could then climb up and pad my way across the red-tiled roofs of our palazzo to rooftop windows that let in sunlight to the women's bathing chamber below.

I know that you will judge this. I am not overly proud of it myself, but if you are to understand me, you must know all of me. I will not lie to you, no matter how embarrassing it may be, for unvarnished truth is precious. I suppose I could tell you that I could not help myself, that lust's influence over me was too great, but that, too, would not be true. It is truer to say that I did not desire to help myself. I desired greatly to spy upon the servant girls, to see naked breasts and naked buttocks and naked figs, and so I did, and though I often felt ashamed, always, always, I went back to spy again.

Ai, such a confused and wonderful passion I felt as I watched them bathing. Anna and Gianna, Sissia, and many more. I feasted upon the sight of their forms, slick with water, foaming with soap. They fairly glowed in the natural light that flooded their bathing chamber. They were goddesses. They were wood nymphs and sylphs. They were the attendant fatas of the ancient god Caliba who drank wine and had the penis of a horse.

I had seen feminine beauty celebrated in the marble statuary of Navola; indeed, it was all about in our own palazzo, depicted in the splashing fountains of Urula and the tiled mosaics of Caliba's fatas in the bathing chambers where he chased them perpetually. It was everywhere. But never breathing, never alive. Never with the flush that comes from hot water on cool skin. Pale skin like milk, blushing. Dark skin like the teas of Zurom. Black thatches of pubic hair as tangled and mysterious as the deepest forests of the Romiglia . . .

Ai, the wonders of the flesh. Ai, the wonders of women.

Even now, remembering, I am overwhelmed by those first stolen sights. At that time, I was still too young to know exactly what I wished to happen with the beauty of those women, to know the pleasure that comes from lying skin to skin. But oh, I dearly loved to look, and the sight was a great gift to me. And even though I stole those glimpses, and it was not right, they sustained me much later, in painful wretched times, when there was nothing to see but darkness and nothing to hope for but death.

But that comes later.

In this moment, I was young, and in a fever of youthful fascination, and I could never satiate my cravings. One moment, I would be busy at lessons, or I would be riding Stub, or I would be fishing with my friends Piero and Cierco and Giovanni, and suddenly I would be struck again by desire, and stupidly, I would let it guide me.

And so it was on a day that the servant girls were not bathing that I hatched a plan to sneak into my father's library.

I was exomentissimo.

I knew that my father and Merio would not be present that day, for they were supervising the departure on the evening tide of a ship bearing Khurian pepper and saffron for the cliffs of Gavazzonero. If I was quick and stealthy, I could easily open the heavy oaken doors, open them just a crack, and slip into my father's vaulted sanctum.

In the library, I remembered that my father kept volumes of lustful drawings. When I was younger and cared less, I had seen them and thought little of them, but now, all in a rush, I remembered their contents and I burned for them.

Sketches in ink and charcoal and pencil. Women in their varied forms, their breasts and hips and rumps, women parting thighs, women with graceful throats, beckoning gazes turned toward the artist, their tresses trailing down over the ripe curves of their breasts, inviting the eye and stirring my hungers.

It was these volumes that drew me.

As the orange blaze of sunset pierced the library shutters, I slipped into my father's study and drew the volumes down. My hands shook at the delights I viewed. One volume had been done by Adivo himself, commissioned particularly by my father. Another was sketches of maidens done by Milas, and one other volume, of Vallese origin, bizarre and extraordinary—women coupling with bulls and tigers and demons, women entwined with one another, fingers and tongues busy with lust, women penetrated by the thrusting phalluses of men who matched the women in their splendor, men of rippling muscle and towering form, with their great roots rampant and red, all of them rendered in details altogether salacious, crazed, and exaggerated. Overwhelming to my young mind.

The women, the men, the beasts, the fantasies of coupling, of unrestrained lust. My root ached and my mind was dizzy as I turned the pages, each image further inflaming my youthful fevers.

And yet, even as I devoured those images of lust, I became aware of something else—

The dragon eye upon my father's desk.

I'm not sure why it drew my attention, but once I noticed it, it was impossible to look away. Somehow, the eye on that day seemed particularly alive. Blazing, even. The light of the setting sun glittered across it, refracted from the sharp trailing nerves, cast light in spangled glory around the library. I found myself turning from my books of lust and watching it instead.

Such was its power that it could even distract a youth from Caliba's favorite games.

Such was its influence.

There seemed movement within the eye. Life. Life, despite death. Almost unconsciously, I left my salacious reading and went instead to stare into the milky orb, and now, much as I had found myself hypnotized by the flesh of women, I found myself drawn to the eye. Storms whirled beneath its milky surface, the storms of its life, still raging. Bright and jagged sparks, like lightning spikes during a summer storm, all howling winds and monsoon rain and the raging spear strikes of Urulo's lightning as he whipped the winds, and as Urula sent her waves up to meet her brother and his frenzy, before the fish would come.

All this was contained in the eye. I felt as if I was peering into human history. The peoples that the dracchus had both studied and feasted upon. We tiny soft fleshy creatures, with our silly lusts, our small successes, our pedantic victories, our meaningless defeats. We were so small. Banca Regulai. The palazzo my grandfather had built with its flowering quadrae and shaded porticoes. The frescoes my father had decorated the ceiling of the library with.

Did my father's likeness push back the winds of Urulo and quell the waves of Urula? On the library's high vaulted ceiling, surely he did. And yet the dragon mocked him. The dragon seemed to say that all of his endeavors would pass, that di Regulai would pass, that Navola and the Navolese, the archinomi of the palazzos and the vianomae of the meanest alleys, all would pass. We would all become dust—but the dragon would endure.

Even now in death, the dracchus endured.

I stroked the trailing spines of the dragon's nerves, perfectly preserved. They glittered in the light of the setting sun, brighter than silver or gold. Beams of light seemed to strike it, seemed indeed to seek it, seemed to slip through the glazes and shutters of the windows to find it, as if the sun itself begged to worship its wisdom. And as I stroked those spines, I began to sense that the beast had not been some mere hundred-year phenomenon, but one of many hundred years. Not a centenato, more a millenato. Nai . . .

More.

It was ancient.

This beast had perched atop cliffs and watched not just human lives and the reigns of kings pass before its eyes, but whole empires, whole dynasties. It had watched as great cities were erected, and then in turn were swallowed by sands. It had seen mountains rise, explode, crumble to dust under the steady wearing of winds and rains . . . All the vistas of human life were contained in the eye, and if I looked closely, I could see their lusts, their hungers, their—

With a cry, I lurched back, bleeding.

My hand was gashed, cut by the sharp shards of the nerves where I had rested my hand upon them, no, in fact, where I had been leaning against them without being aware, so mesmerized was I by the great watching eye.

"You should be careful."

I whirled. Cazzetta stood in the doorway.

"Cazzetta," I stuttered. "I did not know you had returned."

I held my hand behind me, trying to hide the blood.

"A good thing I did." Cazzetta's gaze took in the library, lingered on the strewn books of nude women and their beasts, then turned to the dragon eye upon the desk. His lips pursed. I blushed deeply, wishing that I could melt into the carpets and disappear. I felt as if I were being turned inside out by his evaluating gaze, all my hungers, all my secrets, all my shame exposed to his pitiless gaze.

Cazzetta took my arm and forced me to bring it from behind my back. To show him what I hid. He frowned at the blood, gave me a hooded look.

"A deep wound, princeling. If I hadn't come, you might have been bled deeper."

His creased, scarred hand traced the veins of my wrist. The cut in my palm seemed to trend up toward the pulse of my wrist, a long malevolent line, almost as if the cut had been moving up my hand, digging and cutting . . .

"Do you see, princeling?" His finger traced the line.

I stared at the wound. Had I truly been dragging my hand along the vicious spine of the eye-nerve, that crystal cutting dagger of a tendril? Had I truly been driving it deeper? Bleeding myself at the dragon's urging?

Beside us, the dragon's eye swirled malevolently. My blood sheened the fossilized nerves. The eye seemed to whirl with unsated hunger as primal as the desire that had drawn me to images of women unclothed.

Had it forced my hand to the cut? Or had I simply been clumsy and unaware?

Cazzetta watched my slow cogitations. "You should be careful around the great artifacts, princeling. They have minds of their own. Even in death. And you are a child."

"A child?" I straightened at the insult, but he ground on, undaunted by my attempt at interruption.

"Children are easy marks for the wisdom of ages," he said. "Believe not that innocence is an advantage in the face of the cutting sword of wisdom."

He crouched before me, turned my cheek so that our gazes locked. He took my hand, his expression serious. "Do not look into the eye. Do you understand me? *Never* look into it."

His own eyes seemed to swirl with a madness that I had never seen before, as if he himself had come from the same crypt as the dragon eye. I nodded, but he seemed not to believe, for he drove his thumb into the open wound of my hand, pushing deep. I cried out but he did not relent. He pressed deeper.

"What are you doing?" I writhed, trying to shake free. Cazzetta's grip was iron. He drove his thumb deeper, forced me to meet his eyes.

"No more looking," he said calmly as I fought uselessly against him. "You are no match for it."

He let me free then, and I stumbled back from him, my hand smarting, my body shaking from the pain he had inflicted.

"Is . . . is it alive?" I asked when I finally recovered.

Now he was solicitous. "Come, best we speak elsewhere, away from its hungers. Best we take care of that wound." He led me out of the room and carefully pulled the heavy doors of my father's library closed behind us.

"Is it alive?" I asked again as he locked the door and pocketed a key that I had never known he had.

"Patience, princeling." He led me down many steps and through the vaulted corridors of the palazzo to the warm bakeries and open fires of the kitchens. Siana Brazzarossa took one look at my blood and waved us to the clean linen strips and grape distillates she kept for knife accidents there.

"Is it alive?" I asked again as Cazzetta bandaged my hand.

"Not in the sense that you or I understand." He shook his head. "It is a great power, though. The souls of dragons are contained in their eyes, and so they whirl and stalk. It should have been destroyed at death, pierced immediately, to let the soul out. It should not have been left intact. It is a dangerous thing."

"Why not break it now, then?"

"A dragon is hard enough to kill in life. Far harder to slay in death. That eye is harder than diamond now. I doubt you could find steel that would scratch it, a weight that would shatter it . . . It will last forever now . . . its soul as well, and that of course makes it angry."

"My father says it wasn't slain, but was found in old age. Does a dragon not naturally ascend to Amo when it dies? Must someone release it?"

"Who knows the ways of dracchi? I know that the eye is not a trifle, and should not be left out for children to find."

"I am not a child," I said.

Cazzetta finished bandaging my hand. "Before a dracchus, we are all children. Best to avoid it in the future, princeling."

After that fateful day, I promised myself to avoid the dracchus, and was exquisitely careful not to touch it again. But still, when I sat at my father's desk, I could not ignore its presence. Against my will, I would steal glances at it, peeking up from the correspondence and numbers that my father was explaining to me.

Some days it seemed to stare back. Other days, it seemed to forget me, and a part of me was relieved to see it lying quiescent, as if truly dead, and another part was disappointed.

I desired its attention, and feared it. I was drawn to it. I was wary of it.

Was it my youth that made me vulnerable to the influence of that ancient artifact? Was it simply that I stood near it on a day when my own animal nature was inflamed? Certainly, the dracchus was a creature of hungers, and in that moment I had been deeply consumed by my own lusts. If I had been a more disciplined mind, would it never have drawn my blood at all?

My father caught me staring. "Our enemies think I keep it to remind them that we are great, but it is not so. I keep it to remind myself that we are small."

I felt a sudden kinship to my father. "Is it truly alive?"

"Alive?" My father laughed, surprised. "You have been talking too much with Cazzetta. Of course it is not alive. That is a myth. But it is a true relic, and just as when we look upon the statues of Roccapoli, we cannot help but feel something." He gazed upon the eye, ruminating. "If you ever journey to see the ruins of Torre Amo, you will feel something similar. All those fallen columns, the vine-covered marble, those vast shattered domes, cracked like eggs. Ai. It is to feel the power of the ancient world." He focused on me once more. "But don't let Cazzetta frighten you. He likes to spread dark rumors. He does it to make outsiders respect and fear us, but it's his nature to play upon a person's fears. You should know better than to let him trick you."

"But what about its memories?"

My father's eyebrows shot up. "Its memories?"

"Its . . ." I tried again. "Its . . ." I fumbled for a word, stymied.

Memory was not the word. Memories inhabit the minds of men. They are the myths we use to explain ourselves to ourselves: who we are, where we come from, where we go—just as I tell this story to you. We embroider our stories to explain, to excuse, to justify. I have lost interest in hiding who I was or what I have become. I am tired of the lies and excuses, and wish only to lay myself bare before you, so that you at least will understand, even if you do not forgive.

And yet even now, I seek to pick the prettier memories, and struggle to admit the worst.

The dracchus was no such creature. Even to call what I had seen memory was inadequate. The dragon existed. It did not apologize. I did not care to explain. Past, present, future, memory and moment, all were contained and jumbled. The dragon had hunted, fed, and slaughtered. When I touched it, I had felt bones crunch between my jaws, blood spurting, as if it were happening in that moment. And at the same time, air currents had lifted me high as I watched terrified caravans fleeing below. Cities had risen up, minarets gleaming in the sun, and simultaneously they had burned in moonlight. Armies had conquered, leaving bodies strewn across fighting fields, offering green grass and red blood and easy feeding, and sandy deserts had boiled with heat even as mountain passes rimed my scales with ice. It went on and on. But all of it was present at once. Not as words, not as dry description, not even as emotions. Infinite time passed. No time passed at all.

I was a child; I could not find the words to explain to my father.

"It is old," I said at last.

"It is indeed." My father laughed. "You have been reading too much of Avvicco's *Travels*. He fills your minds with myths." He patted the artifact affectionately. "But it is indeed old."

I flinched, expecting an explosion of trapped reptilian rage. A flare of life. Something. Anything. But the dragon eye remained inert and my father's certainty remained unshaken.

It was the first time I doubted my father's wisdom. The first time I suspected that my father, for all his gifts, was not infallible.

And so I went elsewhere seeking answers, far from my father's sphere.

Virga's weave is all about us. Her winds rustle our hair and her warm earth hums beneath our toes. The fish in the stream luxuriates in the cool waters, the fox the green fern, the cricket mouse the shadow of night. Virga blankets us with her love. And yet we stumble blind through her weave. We cry out for her sustenance, when it is in fact all around us.

Such is man, fallen from the weave. Such is man, always.

—SOPPROS, *CONVERSATIONS II*

Chapter 7

"When dragons die, are they truly dead?"

It had taken several weeks to engineer an opportunity to ask this question. Several weeks of waiting impatiently not only for a person I trusted not to dismiss or chastise me out of hand, but also for a place and time that afforded sufficient privacy to express my questions without other listeners intruding, teasing, or reporting upon me.

This was impossible within the walls of our palazzo, and indeed felt impossible even within the walls of our city, and so I had waited, the question burning within me, until at last I had an opportunity to leave Navola in the company of the one person I felt closest to: our family physician, Maestro Dellacavallo.

I had met the maestro on a day when Celia and I had been playing a game of Frog and Fox. I had been the frog, hiding in the gardens, but had become distracted, entranced by the dance of honeybees as they scrambled about upon the tufts of purple clover that ringed my hiding place. I had been so dazzled by the activity of the bees that I gave up on hiding to instead watch closely as those clever fuzzy creatures scrambled and plucked at the clover, filling saddlebags of pollen upon their legs. I was so entranced that I missed the man's approach.

"They have their own language. Did you know that?"

I turned to find a bent old man, standing very close, watching the bees with me. He wore black robes with the green and yellow trim of a physician. His face was deeply lined and darkly tanned, and he had a formidable white bushy mustache and even bushier white eyebrows.

"Can you hear them gossiping?" the man asked. His eyes were kind. They reminded me of Lazy's.

"The bees?"

"Of course the bees!" he exclaimed. "How else do you think they find the flowers? One minute they are not at all about, and the next, when the flowers bloom, well here they are, *tuotti felici, tuotti integi.* All happy, all together." He waggled his furry eyebrows. "They tell each other where to find the flowers." He gently scooped a bee from a clover up onto his finger, eyeing it. "They're not like people at all, you know. They have no instinct for hoarding. Not these little ones. They only know to share."

I wasn't sure if the old man was saying that bankers hoarded or not, as I was of an age that I had now encountered quite a few people who were very much concerned with how gold grew in our vaults, and called it unnatural, so I was wary, but the old man was entirely absorbed in his examination of the bee.

"Lovely," he said. "*Reinius Insettus Dolxis.*"

He set the bee gently back upon the purple clover. "If you open their hives in the summer, you can listen to them singing to one another and telling stories."

"You understand bees?" I asked, wonderingly.

"Well, you have to listen very closely."

"Don't you get stung?" I asked.

"Stung? Sfai!" Those bushy eyebrows shot up with great offense. "What sort of Borraghese do you take them for? Who would sting a friend?"

A friend.

That was Maestro Dellacavallo.

From that chance meeting, a friendship formed that continued over the course of my childhood. In contrast with the musty darkness of the scrittorium or the fraught complexities of reading a man's face, Dellacavallo's world was drenched in sunshine, fresh breezes, and odd adventures, and it always beckoned. Dellacavallo indulged my questions and he introduced me to a myriad of mysteries, whether it was the singing of bees or the many uses for the plants and mosses and fungi that yielded up his salves and potions, unguents and perfumes.

The maestro delighted in taking me around our gardens, teaching me the *nomocanto anciens* for our plantings—the relic names—and each time he pointed at a plant and spoke its name, his words seemed to fairly burn with the power of banished gods. Every tree and flower and blade of grass had a special word, each one resonating with history and memory, each one laden with stories out of myth.

Of Caliba the trickster, there was the pink-petaled calxibia, known to invoke both great lust and great kindness. Of Scuro, that dark and twisted one, there were the purple nighthoods mortxibia and moraphossos that would drown someone in sleep and keep them there for all time. Of Virga, who had woven all the world, there was La Salvixa, with skeinlike root flowers that slowed infection. Of the capricious fatas, there was the mushroom caxiacn, also called toothrobe, with its red shards down its stalk that would kill, but whose innocent top would relieve pain. And of course there was the wound healer, fuzzy-leafed guxctosalvnia, also called conebalm, her green-and-yellow petals like the gown that La Cerulea wore when she walked across the waters for the sake of the fallen drift sailors of Hittopolis.

Old Dellacavallo would guide me around our gardens, his black physician's robes swishing about him, his green-and-yellow-trimmed sleeves gathering dandelion seeds and gattise pods, pointing his mottled finger at this plant or that, testing me as to what they were. He would try to trick me with foxglove, sapflower, and daisy vine. He tested me on the green serpent tongue and the white; the split, saw, and knot leaf. He tested my knowledge of mushrooms, of portola, bellabracchia, and carnecapo.

"Smell this," he would say. And I, with my eyes closed, would sniff and say, "Lavender. That is easy."

"What about this?" Another flower tickled my nose, luxuriously sweet, heady. Syrupy.

"Khus olive."

Chuckling, he guided me through the tall waving flowers, buzzing with the bees that he loved so much, with one hand over my eyes so that I could not peek. "What about . . . this?"

I inhaled. A sharp musty scent. "Chasa." Before he could ask, "It stops spider venom if it is made into a paste."

"But . . . ?"

"But it is no use against roachspider. For that, only neroscxo will work. The black lace. And only fresh, and that is only found in caves where bats live."

It went on like that. Venoss. Orange blossom. Thyme. Orega. Queen nettle. Basil. Silkwood. On and on.

I am not bragging when I say that I could touch any leaf in our gardens and know its kind and remember its uses, or sniff the cap of a mushroom and know if it was good to eat, or good only to bring a swift death, and Dellacavallo was much impressed.

"I need to gather fresh herbs. They are always weak when I buy them at market," Dellacavallo said to me one day. "You should come with me."

And so it was that when my duties of abacus and letters were fulfilled, my father gave permission. With the unlucky Polonos delegated to accompany and guard us, we sallied forth, Dellacavallo, Lazy, Stub, and I, exploring for the herbs and roots and barks and mushrooms of Dellacavallo's profession.

We quartered the hills around Navola upon steed and upon foot, up and down hills, through vineyards and estates, tumbling over rock walls and into farmyards, thrashing through tangled forests and crawling muddy along the banks of the Livia. There was always another place to explore, and Dellacavallo always required some new herb or flower. It was in those places where green grasses rustled with Urulo's breath and whitebark and pine swayed in rhythm that I discovered a comfort rare for me amongst the people of my city.

Raucous cauri birds flocked in the trees, squawking and staring down upon me with black sharp contemptuous eyes. Bluetip woodpeckers hammered for their dinners. Red foxes peered from beneath ferns with wide pricked-up ears and curious expressions. Dappled rabbits darted through raspberry bramble. Black boars dug for truffles like dogs hunting old bones. All of this and more surrounded us.

Sometimes Dellacavallo and I would sit and rest, our backs against the whitebark, listening to the sundry sounds of the forest. Lazy would rest her head upon my lap, her ears pricking up as Urulo's breath rustled the leaves and Polonos's sighs of boredom punctuated our rest. The soldier would shift from foot to foot, leaning against his spear, sighing, until Dellacavallo held up a hand to still him and he would fall silent.

And finally, just as I, too, was becoming bored, Dellacavallo would point into the ferns, indicating a tiny deer, no larger than a cat, staring back at us.

Other times, Dellacavallo would become excited when he found a fern-choked bog. "Look, Davico! Pig mud! And brush ferns!" And then he would lift up the leaves of the ferns and show me a new sort of mushroom that I had never seen growing, and around its base, a nest of fat black ants and their eggs, and he would tell me how the acid of their bodies could be used to clean a wound.

"Always look for the brush ferns. Horse ears like brush ferns, and the ants, they like the horse ears." He paused, ruminating. "The ants are also good on a salad of dandelion greens. The acid of the bodies is much like a young wine vinegar."

Much as a book opens for a reader, eager to share secrets, the wilds—to me—stood in stark contrast to the tangled streets of Navola and the plots of my people. In the wilds, there was no place for creatures like Cazzetta. Nor for the intrigues of faccioscuro. The wilds were a place of honesty, and Dellacavallo a man of honor. And so it was there, in those forests, that I broached the question that had been troubling me:

When dragons die, are they truly dead?

All morning we had been hunting along the southern edges of various copses of whitebark, dipping in and out of shadow and sunshine, alert for blackberry bramble and fallen whitebark, on the hunt for an herb called venxia, also known as Amo's crown for its golden tufts, that often grew in close proximity to the two. It had rained two nights previously, and Dellacavallo had high hopes that we would find the herb poking up.

We had been searching under a fallen tree, our knees damp in green grass, and it was into that darkness beneath the log—that damp and private confessional space—that I finally mustered my nerve to ask the question.

And it was from the far side of that log that Dellacavallo's bushy white eyebrows rose up, his kind eyes following, puzzled, to regard me.

"What have dragons to do with the pain of the joints?" he asked.

"Nothing. It's . . . It's just something I've been wondering."

I trusted the maestro, but now that the question had left my lips, I felt embarrassed. Indeed, speaking the words out loud after several weeks of keeping silent made me feel even more foolish, as if what I had felt in my father's library was nothing but my own fabulation, too absurd and strange to be credited as true when spoken aloud in the sunshine-dappled forest around us.

Maestro Dellacavallo rested his chin upon the fallen log, regarding me over the moss that had grown upon it. "You've just been wondering."

A comfortable distance away, Polonos leaned against his spear, observing our rooting and digging under the various logs, affably bored. He could not hear us, and yet still I found myself shy.

"Well . . ."

All this time I had waited for Dellacavallo. This was my moment. I screwed up my courage and pressed forward. "Cazzetta says that dragons do not die. That their souls remain in their eyes, unless they are let out."

"Cazzetta." Dellacavallo made a face. "That man." He stood and brushed the grasses and wood chips from his knees. "This is about your father's relic, then?"

"Do you know?" I pressed.

Dellacavallo favored me with a speculative glance and started for another fallen tree. "I saw a book, once, in an abbey in the north, in Kuln. But it was a book of myths." He knelt and began seeking under the tree and I crawled across to the far side and joined him beneath it, both of us pushing apart the wet grasses, leaves, and dirt to see if the venxia might be prodding forth, working our way down the length of the fallen tree.

I thought Dellacavallo had nothing else to say on the topic of dragons but then he said, "It was a madness book. That's what the monks called it. A *crookklibr* in their tongue, though they kept it anyway. It had no author, only tales, collected. 'The Girl Who Married the Dragon,' that sort of thing. Stories of people who had been chased by them, or seen them burn an army, or seen villages mesmerized by them to offer up virgins and treasure. Not the sort of question you are asking."

"So you don't know."

Dellacavallo laughed. "Do you take me for the Oracle Plythias? Such things are hardly my specialty. Come, let's try another tree."

We went scrambling over more fallen timber, eyes on the ground, poking through the grasses under each. "I'm sure that there's something here," he muttered. "I've found them here before."

"Maybe the fatas are hiding them from you."

"Maybe." He laughed. "Let's try that stand of trees over there. Maybe we'll have more luck."

We started across the open meadow, wading through the high grasses, Polonos trailing a distance behind.

"Why do you care what Cazzetta says about a fossil?" Dellacavallo asked. "He says many things and I doubt even half of them are true."

"I . . ." I hesitated, embarrassed by the circumstances, but the topic was well broached, and so I told him of my encounter with the eye, carefully embroidering around the shameful piece of how I had come to be in its company in the first place.

"I felt as if I was within it," I said. "As if I were . . . I don't know, swimming? . . . Inside its memories?" I shook my head, frustrated. "Nai. It wasn't memory. It wasn't swimming . . . but I felt inside it. Inside its life. But all of it . . . as if it were stacked like cartalegge cards and I was the stack. As if . . . I was old and young at once and in Navola and in Zurom at once." It sounded absurd when I said it out loud. To my relief, Dellacavallo did not laugh.

"A troubling experience, I'm sure. And you say it wounded you?"

I pulled back my sleeve and showed him the scar. "I didn't know who else to ask about it."

"I, too, have never heard of such a thing." He turned my wrist this way and that. "At least Cazzetta knows how to dress a wound." He bade me roll back my sleeve. "Where else would you like to search?"

Caught off guard, I scanned for signs of blackberries, or even raspberries, but spied none. "What about those?" I pointed to pair of fallen whitebark.

"Let's try," he said.

We began searching around them, parting the thick grasses. I found greenfringe, and knew immediately that we were wasting our time, but Dellacavallo spent another minute looking, and came up, pleased, not with venxia, but a flower with many stacked trumpet-like flowers. "Erostheia's tears. Do not eat the flowers, but the dew that gathers in them. It's good for joints."

"Like venxia."

"Much like, but harder to carry to a patient." He sipped the dew happily. "Ai, that's good."

We moved on around the edge of the trees, tracing the margin between meadow and forest, but found no other brambles. Still, I liked the look of a fallen tree and went to investigate. Instead of venxia, I found eggs, three of them, green-speckled, almost gemlike. Cauri bird eggs, carefully tucked under the fallen log, hidden behind a wadding of twigs and gathered grasses.

"Hidden treasure," Dellacavallo said. We both crouched down, inspecting them. "If you were not fated to inherit Banca Regulai, you would make a fine physician." He pulled the green-speckled eggs from beneath the log, one by one. "You have the feel for it, I think."

If I were Lazy, I would have wagged my tail and rolled onto my back for belly rubs. Dellacavallo's praise was always a joy, and a sharp contrast to the critical eyes of Merio, Aghan Khan, and my father.

"What does being a physician have to do with finding eggs?"

"The first and most important quality for a physician is knowing how to look and listen. To observe completely. The ones who are closest to Firmos always make the best physicians, for they know how to pay attention. You have the knack, of a surety. I would apprentice you in an instant if your father would permit it." He paused, thoughtful. "I'm not at all surprised you felt something from that dragon eye. Dragons are very great creatures, and you"—he held up the eggs—"are a sensitive soul. You felt the echoes of its greatness, even after all these millennia."

"But it felt alive."

"Ai. What do I know? For a sensitive one such as you, perhaps it was a little." He looked at me pointedly. "I think it would not be good for you to get too close. Firmos is clearly your friend but it has its tangles, and its thorns." He nodded toward my scarred arm.

"Firmos?"

"You don't know Firmos?" Dellacavallo's eyes twinkled. "Does our most excellent high canon priest Garagazzo not sing of Virga's weave when he makes his sermons?"

"I know Virga," I replied, not liking that he made fun of me. "And I know the weave. Virga wove the world at the behest of Amo, for the benefit of all."

The song was well known. The monks sang it upon the Apexia solstice, when Amo was high overhead and his power was at its zenith. And the nuns sang it in the winter, when we begged Amo's return. The first verses concerned Virga and her creations, given unto Amo for the benefit of all humanity. "Virga wove the world, after Amo brought order to the old gods and stopped their quarreling."

"Is that what Garagazzo says?" Dellacavallo's amusement redoubled, and it irritated me. I knew he was making fun of me, but I didn't know why.

"Of course that's what he says. It's what everyone says."

"Everyone up and down the hook, perhaps. Everyone, these days, perhaps. But you, Davico, you have all those ancient books and translations in your father's library and this is all you know?" He began to intone as if he were Garagazzo:

"Amo is the greatest of all gods.
Without Amo, the old gods would have destroyed the world.
Everything good is thanks to Amo.
Everything evil is thanks to Scuro."

He made a face and turned to Polonos, who was standing a short distance away, leaning against a tree, a mountain of muscle and weaponry, waiting for us to complete our herb hunt with his soldier's jaundiced eye.

"Ai. Polonos, come over here a moment. You're of the Romiglia, are you not?"

Polonos grunted affirmatively. "Those are my people."

"I thought I recognized the jut of that brow. What do the Romigliani say of Virga?"

Polonos gave Dellacavallo a speculative look. "We say we should not anger her, for her weave is all about us."

"Ah!" Dellacavallo pointed to Polonos. "That is closer to wisdom, I think."

"Is Garagazzo not right?" I asked, looking from Polonos to Dellacavallo.

Dellacavallo exchanged a knowing look with Polonos. "Right enough, for a high priest, in a grand catredanto, who sings the glory of Amo."

"Is he wrong, then?"

"Oh no, Davico. You cannot trick me that way. I'm far too wise to argue with priests. What I will say is that you should read more. Read more, Davico. Read widely and without favor. Read from many places and many languages, Davico. Your father does. He does not take the word of Garagazzo as the only word, nor the Solstice Recitation as the only story of the gods. There are other stories. If you go looking, you will find many references to Firmos. You have the knack of it already, you should learn it."

Chapter 8

Firmos.

The philosopher Soppros thought that the world was made up of two aspects: Cambios and Firmos. Cambios was that which man touched and influenced. Cambios: changeable, untrustworthy, the realm of human striving, of waterwheels and castelli, of axles, wagons, of lingua, steel, and cities. And, of course, in my family's case: trade and loans and the unbreakable promises of Banca Regulai.

Firmos, though, Firmos was that which lay beyond human power. Firmos was not just the dirt of the earth, as its name might imply. In Soppros's thinking, Firmos was a woven web exquisitely stretched: twinging and shifting, pulling and tugging in response to every creature, every plant, every season, every wind, every raindrop, each strand connected to every other, but instead of being woven by spiders this net was woven by the many gods.

Soppros wrote in the old lingua Amonese Anciens from before Amo banished the other gods and with the beliefs of one surrounded by the old religion, so in Soppros's concept the many gods were all present in Firmos, and all of them were powerful. Alongside Amo of the Light, there was Scuro of the Unseen Realms with his insects and bats, and Caliba the trickster with his many harems of fatas. There were Urulo and Urula, the twins of the sky and ocean: Urulo with his lightning and eagles, and Urula with her seahorse mount and her hair twined with shells, and of course their daughters Cerulea and Meridia, whom they fought over. There was Argo who wrought man with his forge, and there was Leggus who wrote the laws of the universe. And then there were the lesser gods and goddesses, the spirits and fatas, who took forms as varied as trees and dolphins and cats and birds. Cerulea was a dolphin when she wished and often saved sailors. Salvia was a fata made of tree shadows who liked to tease hunters to chase her nakedness through the woods until they fell off cliffs. Erostheia was beauty. Goriix was speed. Nubisia kept the stars warm upon the folds of her black sky cloak. It was all these gods and many others who contributed to the dance of the universe, and it was they in turn who gave their finest creations and most-loved treasures to Virga, who wove Firmos with their offerings, and created the world entire, the fishes in the sea, the animals of the land, the mountains and deserts and rivers and on and on, all woven by her skill and love.

But according to Soppros, there was one difficulty with the weaving: Man.

Man fought against the weave of the gods, and so out he fell, tumbling and falling until he hit upon the dirt.

When he fell, Virga looked down upon the man, scuffed and crying and alone, and took pity on him. She told Scuro to give him language so that he could at least talk to others of his kind, for he could no longer feel the singing of the web she wove, and after that she let him wander off.

This was the beginning of Cambios.

But still, man would be dependent upon the weave of Firmos. Still he would feel the changing of seasons, the rise of the sun, he would eat the seeds of grasses, he would beg the love of dogs, he would find sustenance from the milk of cows and goats, but he would never be truly one with Firmos ever again, and he would never be truly happy. He would never feel the thrill of the wind as the redtip hawk soared and he would never smell the passing of animals in the forest with that sensitive nose of the hare, and he would not feel the drumming of his ant brothers in their mounds, nor hear the singing of the leaves of the whitebark as they turned to shades of gold and their white gnarled trunks turned red.

Soppros believed that Firmos was too much missing from human life, and because of that our hubris was too great. Only by living in connection with Firmos could a person become wise. *Enruxos* was his term for this. To be rooted. To sink one's toes into the dirt and to become one with Firmos.

Soppros was almost always pictured barefoot because of this, enruxos. Rooted.

When I read Soppros's writings out loud to my father in his library, enamored of this new rationale for my increasing love for those things green and wild and of my time spent with Dellacavallo, he exchanged a wry glance with Cazzetta, who was lingering there like a waiting plague, browsing the volumes on the shelves.

My father said Soppros was at least partly right, for all men rise from dirt and all men fall back to it.

"And," he said, "the water in our veins is as salty as Urula's realm. So certainly we are part of the gods' great net and that is good to remember."

"And yet," Cazzetta said, closing his book and placing it back upon the shelf. "A man who gathers nuts and berries for sustenance and walks barefoot will not last long when the man with forged steel and wearing the skin of animals comes knocking. So perhaps the net of the gods is not so important as Soppros thinks."

"Any idea seems wise to at least some degree," my father said. "Altus ideux, yes?"

Cazzetta sucked his teeth in agreement. "Everyone who wishes to appear wise will say they have found some altus ideux. Garagazzo will tell you that Amo's Glory is the path of enlightenment, where Aghan Khan will tell you that no power comes without the strength of arms. Merio will say that the mind with all its quickness is the path to greatness. And your enruxos friend Soppros will say that you must go to the wilds and listen to the birds and trees and dig your toes in the dirt."

"And what do you think?" I asked him.

"I think the wisdom of one moment is the foolishness of the next. If you are very lucky, you will find one scrap of wisdom as the cauri bird found the emerald, and if you are truly wise, you will know when to throw that jewel away as nothing but glass."

"But how would I know?"

"If wisdom were easy, we would all be wise. Now come." Cazzetta motioned me to join him. "Leave your father to his work. I will show you how to make a poison that will turn the tongue black and kill a man within an hour."

"So this is your wisdom? Poison?"

He smiled thinly. "Nai. Silence is my wisdom. Poison is only a tool. Now come."

But still, I thought there was something very wise in Soppros's ideas. Firmos beckoned me. Firmos was as welcoming as the politics of

Navola were not. A tree rustling in the wind did not lie, the clouds did not lie, the deer in the forest did not lie, the flowers as they opened their petals to the sun did not lie. Even in trickery—as the fox was sly—there was something that remained true about them, a veritas deeper than the deepest roots of the tallest trees. Firmos spoke a language unlike any of Amo's dialects. It did not dissemble as human tongues did.

In Soppros's Firmos, I felt comfortable; its language was clear to me. And with a name attached to that which I loved, I found myself more able to see its influence in my life.

In contrast with the swinging of a sword, or the divining of lies in a letter from the Khur, when I hunted game with Aghan Khan, I did well. I excelled at tracking. I could follow the slyest of creatures. I knew the rustle of pheasant and the slow breathing of deer as they watched us from the undergrowth.

Still, despite my skills, Aghan Khan despaired of my ability to bring back game.

"You're too soft, boy," he complained when I failed to bring down a stag with a majestic crown of antlers. We had stalked the beast for a day, the two of us moving silently through the forest, having spied him drinking at a stream and then moving downwind, circling silent—a long process for the stag was alert and wise, having survived many hunters' ruses.

And yet, in the final moment, when I beheld the stag's eye down the long shaft of my crossbow, I did not pull the trigger, and then the moment was lost and he was gone, bounding away through the dappled trees, not to be found again.

"All that effort!" Aghan Khan groused as we slogged home. "And now we return without meat or trophy, not even a worthy tale. You must not hesitate, Davico! When the kill is before you, you must strike! You must not be weak."

But I was not apologetic. The stag had been too magnificent. It was enough in my own mind to know that had I been hungry, he would have made my dinner. It was enough that I drank of him with my eyes instead of drinking the blood of his heart in my cup, fresh from the kill. The knowing of the skill was enough for me, even if it was not enough for Aghan Khan. Aghan Khan wanted to dine upon the meat and the tale of the hunt; I fed upon the knowledge that the stag and I had lived—if only briefly—in the same wildness; bound together for a moment, enruxos in Firmos.

But my embrace of Firmos did not end there.

On occasion, my family would travel to the low Romiglia to escape the worst heat of Navolese summer. Our family had dealings with the archinomi who lived there, those small dukes and gauntlet lords who occupied that half-tamed land. The low Romiglia engulfed the south and west of Navola, and its lands yielded game and wool and hardened soldiers such as our own Polonos and Relus who sallied forth from their hardscrabble villages to earn money to send back to their families in the hills.

Deeper into the Romiglia, the land rose steeply, tangled and thick with forests and undergrowth, cut by deep ravines with crashing wild rivers, and ruled over by snowy craggy peaks. There were secret grottoes there, and high soft meadows, and, it was said, mysterious valleys full of shadow panthers, night wolves, stone bears, and other strange things. That was the true Romiglia. The deep Romiglia.

Or, as Aghan Khan called it with distaste, the black Romiglia.

But the low Romiglia was different, a place wild enough to test the mettle of a young man, but not so wild that my father fretted overly, and so it was that when we went to visit the Sfona (a family who held much land that yielded wool for the loom guild, and that my father financed to be sent to the cold wastes beyond the Cielofrigo), I was given wide rein to wander. Of course, I was only allowed to ride Stub for I still was not the swordsman that Aghan Khan wished, much as I was not the killer.

But the truth was I loved Stub dearly and did not take this as a punishment. Stub and I were friends. He was the finest companion I could have asked for in the wilds: more restrained than my friend Piero, who was always loud and wanted to swing his sword at the undergrowth, more willing than Giovanni, who preferred only to sit and read and did not care if he was indoors or out.

As our party journeyed along the trails, I dallied and lingered, entranced by the dappling sun as it filtered through the green bright leaves of the whitebark, climbing down to scout for frogs that hid near the rocks of the braided streams, and plucking the mint that I found there instead.

"It's nightmint," I said as I returned to our waiting party and offered up my discovery.

"Are you saying my breath is poisonous?" Celia asked.

Celia's personality had brightened considerably over the years. Contrary to the dark solemnity of her arrival, Celia's true personality was not a quiet one. She sparkled, occasionally even exploded, either with happiness or anger. A vintofrizza personality, of a surety, and a disruptive one. We had studied side by side for years, poring over litigi, numismatica, and philos under the stern eyes of our tutors, and she had not been quiet for any of it. But still, despite her loud protests and penchant for mischief, she had mastered her lessons, much as she had mastered the skills of the piercing sword, the honor knife, and the crossbow, enough so that Aghan Khan often turned to me with a raised eyebrow, letting me know that he measured me against her.

Now Celia twirled my offering between her fingers, her eyes amused. "Do I stink so badly?"

"Like Scuro's baths!" I said cheerfully. "Actually worse!" Then I added more seriously, "It is also good to drink in a tea when you are sleepy. It will wake you up."

"By Amo's crown, please, no," Merio said. "No one needs her more awake."

"Doesn't this grow in our gardens?" Celia asked.

"Well, this is nightmint. It's different than . . ." I trailed off as I saw that the rest of our party—my father, Ashia, Merio, Cazzetta, Aghan Khan, Polonos, and Relus—were all watching me with some exasperation. "I found it near the water snakes," I finished lamely.

Celia laughed. "Well, I'm glad you didn't bring me one of those."

With an indulgent sigh, my father said, "Why don't you linger, Davico? The rest of us will see you at dinner tonight. Aghan Khan, keep an eye on him, so he doesn't become too lost?"

And with that, the rest of them spurred onward.

I eagerly continued my explorations, poking through the undergrowth, pricking my fingers on a raspberry bush, tracking the rustle of squirrels, and sniffing the leaf of a plant I didn't recognize, all with Aghan Khan grunting and sighing as he kept watch over me with a jaundiced eye.

"You don't have to mind me," I said to the bearded warrior as I knelt at a stream bank and ran my fingers through the water, watching minnows dart and flee. "I know the path to the Sfona."

"Your father would have my head if I left you alone in these cursed lands."

"Why do you dislike the Romiglia so much? Look around. All is trees and water." I took a deep breath, taking in the pine and greenery, the damp humus of the soil, the flowers beside the stream, all of it so different from the stinks of the city. "We're in Virga's weave, here. We are safe."

"Safe in Virga's weave, are you? Well, so are bandits. If I were planning an ambush, I would hide behind those trees right there, and catch you as you crossed the water, while your footing was slippery and clumsy."

"Not everything is war and ambush."

"But when it is, it's better to be the ambusher. Come, you're only finally learning to swing that sword of yours. I won't have you eat a crossbow quarrel from the bushes. It's time we moved on."

I straightened with a sigh, brushing at the leaves and mud on my riding breeches. The whitebark that stood next to the stream was beginning to turn red. The coolness of the stream and the cooler nights were causing this bark to change earlier than most. When autumn came, the leaves would all be gold and the trunks would turn a deep rich red. This path would be bathed in colors more vibrant than even Arragnalo's paintings. Ai. It was beautiful. My eyes traveled down the blushing bark. It was scarred in numerous places where bucks had sharpened their antlers. It would be a good place to hunt . . . "Oh look! *Capaisix!*" I knelt beside the tree. The mushroom was a thick-headed thing, its red blunt cap only a little wider than its fat stalk.

"What is it?" Aghan Khan asked.

"*Fungi capirosso.* Cazzetta likes it for its poisonousness—"

"Of course he does. He only cares for murder."

I was not deterred. "And Dellacavallo likes it for it removes pain." I recited the old physician's lesson: "Capirosso shares the influences of Caliba and of Scuro, who are sometimes friends, and must be treated with deference. It must be soaked, and then dried, and then soaked and then dried. This must be done three times, over three days. This will take away Scuro's poison, but retain Caliba's medicine, and will not be so powerful that a person will fall into Caliba's realm of pleasure and not return." I did not touch the mushroom, for I had no gloves. But near it . . .

I began pushing aside the damp grasses, slowly widening my search in a circle around the capirosso.

"What are you doing now?"

"I'm looking . . . Here!"

Just as Dellacavallo taught, not far from the capaisix, I drew aside the grasses to reveal a stand of little pale mushrooms, small pale stalks, thin with tiny heads. "I found Virga's children!" I plucked one and ate it. "Look!"

Aghan Khan dismounted. I offered him one. He peered suspiciously at it. He took it, held it up to his eye, twirled it this way and that.

"Ai." He grunted. "It seems you have."

"Of course I have." I ate another, then offered one to Stub. "They grow with whitebark, but only in the shadows of north hills after rain, near capaisix. There will be more." I scanned the grasses. "There will be more. All in a line." I went to follow them, leading Stub with me. "If we had a sack I could bring back a feast."

"I'm sure the Sfona have their own mushroom hunters," Aghan Khan said gruffly, glancing at the sky. "We should be on. The sun will soon drop behind the hills."

"I just want to look a little longer."

Stub and I followed the lines of mushrooms, picking and eating them as they led us deeper into the forest. The grass was damp. We wound through, finding our way into fallen timber where pine needles had fallen. Whitebark and gnarled rock pine were intermixed here, and that meant there would be no more of Virga's children. They didn't like rock pine.

I crouched down, studying the ground beneath a fallen tree, the soil sweet with wood rot, and here I found fata fans, bigger than both my hands spread, bluish on top, with gray gills beneath. Not good for eating, nor for poisoning, nor for medicine. *A waste of a good mushroom,* Dellacavallo always complained, even though he also said that Virga never made mistakes and every creature had its place, but still he complained about fata fans. *Only good for fatas to cool themselves.* But I liked finding these, too; reminders that some things were not meant for men, but meant only for the gods and their handmaidens.

I led Stub around the fallen pine and through a clearing. The settling sun peeped through dappled leaves. We pushed on, our eyes roaming across patterns of shadows and greenery. There is a trick to mushroom hunting that requires not so much looking as perceiving, letting the gaze wander along the ground without effort, until suddenly your eyes begin to catch and hook upon that which was not previously visible, even though it was right before you all along.

Here was Caliba's nose, the one that made you drunk and silly. I had seen it fed to Garagazzo, and Garagazzo had been much inebriated by it, and cursed later that the degenerate creations of Caliba had no place on the palate of a priest, even though he liked Caliba's influence over wine and never complained when he drank heavily.

Now here was sweet grass. And here were the blue petals of monkface, all fallen. But the dry heads were still attached. I plucked one and sucked on it. Tartness there. I picked a few and offered them to Stub. He liked them better than the mushrooms. His warm lips tickled my palm. He ate happily, and then quested over me for more, turning his face, snuffling at me—

"Davico!"

Aghan Khan's shout shattered the solitude.

"Davico! By the fatas! Where are you hiding?"

With my attention on the ground and the flora of the forest, I had not realized that we had become separated from the warrior. Now trees and shadows separated us. We weren't hiding at all, but now, delighted by the idea, I touched Stub, urging him to silence.

Aghan Khan shouted again. "Davico!"

By the fatas, he was loud.

With increasing pleasure, I guided Stub through the forest, using Aghan Khan's crashing movements to avoid him. Stub instinctively intuited my desire for mischief, and his own steps grew as furtive as my own. Step by careful step we eased through the forest, keeping to the shadows of the late afternoon, moving only when the cauri birds called or the wind rustled the whitebark leaves, navigating always to avoid the brute noise of Aghan Khan—

Aghan Khan stopped moving; he was listening for us.

I touched Stub's muzzle in warning, but he already knew the game. We both became absolutely silent. As still as the marble statues of Roccapoli. We breathed in rhythm with the forest, our ears alert for Aghan Khan even as he listened for us. Aghan Khan took a step in our direction. The leaves and twigs rustled. Another step. We held our breaths. Now that he was moving quietly, it was impossible for us to move.

We held our ground.

Closer and closer he came. If we had not been downwind, he would have scented us easily. Instead, I smelled him. His sweat. The leather of his riding clothes. The oil of his sword. The clove scent he used in his beard. His rustling movement stopped. We were separated only by a few bushes. I could hear his breathing, mere feet away.

I stifled a sudden urge to laugh.

Was he playing me? Was he pretending not to see us, the way our street merchants had once pretended not to see me stealing their fruit when I was younger?

He had to be tricking me. Why, I could reach through the bushes and tug his beard if I wanted. I stifled the urge.

Who fooled whom?

Aghan Khan didn't move. He was absolutely silent listening for signs of us, but Stub and I were equal to the challenge. We held ourselves stony still. We became as one with the rocks of the cliffside. Our feet as rooted to the earth as the great whitebark that swayed and rustled overhead. I imagined us as part of Virga's weave: breathing with the breezes, our feet sunk deep in the earth. As restful as the stones. As belonging as the trees.

Aghan Khan was but a man, alone. He had fallen from Virga's weave and now walked alone. I felt a sudden wave of pity for him. He walked alone when life was all around.

I would have reached out to him then—not to trick or startle but to make connection, to bring him close to Firmos. But just as I was about to break our silence, Aghan Khan cursed and turned away.

"Davico!"

A flight of cauri birds took wing down near the trail and Aghan Khan went crashing back the way he had come, chasing after the sounds that he surmised were myself and Stub, making our escape. "Davico! This is not a game!"

I tugged Stub to follow. Not too close, not too far. Who was hunter now, and who was prey? It was difficult to say, such is the tangle of Virga's weave.

"Davico! Where are you?"

We crouched in the undergrowth and watched as Aghan Khan

mounted his great black steed, turned in a circle, scanning one last time for evidence of us, and then spurred up the trail for the castello of the Sfona, where he believed we had already gone. His hoofbeats faded.

"Aren't we clever?" I sought in my pockets for a carrot and fed Stub, patting and ruffling his neck. "Aren't we the clever ones?"

Stub snorted agreeably.

We started to follow where Aghan Khan had disappeared down the trail, but I had a sudden prickle of suspicion that the master soldier might be teaching me a lesson about warcraft and ambush.

Perhaps he really had seen me, and now was playing with me as a cat plays with a mouse.

I reined Stub to a halt. "I think our friend might be planning an ambush. What do you think?"

Stub's ears twitched.

"Yes, that's what I think, too. He thinks he's going to teach us a lesson about being alert in forests."

Determined not to be caught, we turned away from the trail and instead wound between the trees, forging into the untracked forest. When we came to a steep slope broken by cliffs, I dismounted and led Stub up through ferns and undergrowth. The way was stony and there were water seeps everywhere, making for muddy uncertain ground. We scrambled and slogged. At last we reached a high rim of cliffs. The forest was somewhat thinner here, but still our travel was impeded by fallen trees and more small streams.

The sun was beginning to sink. I began to think now that I was not so clever. I guessed we had perhaps an hour, two at most, before darkness would swallow us. Through the canopy of the trees, the sun was already sinking to touch the highest hills. The shadows would soon become thick and close, and more so in the valleys.

Annoyed at myself, I began guiding Stub down the cliffs again and back toward the trail. If we hurried, we might still make our way to the castello before dark.

We made it down the steep hill, but to my surprise we did not meet with the trail but instead came upon a rushing stream, nearly a small river, deep and fast. I turned about, confused. I did not recognize the stream, nor the shape of the land around us. The stream was wider, rockier, faster, and more swollen than it should have been, and on the far side, a new hill rose steeply. None of this matched the familiar shape of the valley, nor the trail that led to the Sfona.

I led Stub across the stream, thrashing through icy knee-deep water, and climbed the opposite bank, my breeches squishing and dripping, thinking that the hill would be small, and I would find our trail on the other side, but the hill kept rising and the timber thickened. I stopped, panting, and turned around, confused.

Stub snorted impatiently.

"You have some idea of where we are?" I asked, testily, feeling the chill of the water. "If you have an idea, tell me then."

He looked at me as if I were a fool, and I believed a little that I was, for we were well and truly lost.

Chapter 9

It is a dizzying sensation to realize that you have lost your sense of direction. Up becomes down. Left becomes right. South, north. It all seems to spin. The woodcraft I had learned from Aghan Khan and Dellacavallo told me that this was the precise moment when a man could lose his head. Disorientation made people panic and dash about, scrambling this way and that and getting nowhere until they starved. Even an experienced hunter could become lost. Could run in circles until exhausted or injured. Could die, far from anyone.

I pushed down my panic, and regretted getting myself wet.

"We'll follow the stream," I told Stub, trying to make my voice authoritative. "We will follow the stream until the sun is no more, and then we will camp."

The stream might not lead me to the trail, nor the lands of the Sfona, but it would inevitably run down through hills where it would meet other streams, and these would all eventually find their way out of the Romiglia to the wide-open plains, where they would join the great Cascada Livia and she, eventually, would take me home to Navola.

"We're not lost," I said firmly to Stub. "We're just a little farther from home."

We started along the bank of the stream. The going was muddy and tangled. My boots and breeches remained soaked and the waters were cold. Seeps and tributary streams added to the waters, deepening and speeding the flow, and turning it into a lively river. The rush of water blotted out other sounds. I thrashed through ferns and brush, leading Stub, using the noise of the river to guide me. Despite my plan, I still held a secret hope that I might still find the trail back to the Sfona. This fortified me as wild roses and raspberry pricked and ripped my skin and clothes. That hope lasted until we fought through a wall of bracken and emerged to find the river spilling out into open air.

A cliff.

The river's water poured down its granite face, all foam and mist, falling and tumbling and finally plunging into a roiling pool of black shattered timber, far below, before collecting itself and disappearing once more into the darkening forest. The cliff was too steep to descend and I had no confidence that I would find a different path now that darkness was fast upon us.

Stub looked at me accusingly.

"Yes, I know. This is my fault."

I led Stub away from the water, hunting for ground less chill and soggy, depressed that a warm bed and a warm meal were both impossible now. Even under the pines it was cold and damp. I carried no blanket, nor any items for making camp, and so it was with some misery that I unsaddled Stub and brushed him as well as I could, and then curled up against a tree root that was less damp than anything else, including my boots and breeches.

My belly growled. I tucked my cloak more tightly around myself. "There's a lesson in this," I said to Stub's shadow. "One moment you're clever, and the next you're a fool."

Stub snorted agreement.

It was an uncomfortable night, restless, shivery, half awake, half dreaming. I tossed and turned, huddled tighter in my cloak, and shivered. My dreams were strange and troubled, my mind working at the problem of how to find my way out of the Romiglia and how I had become lost in the first place.

In my half-dreaming, half-awake, entirely chilled and shivery state, I retraced my steps, considering each turn, each fold of the hills, each valley that we had crossed both before and after I had snuck away from Aghan Khan. I stalked down the river again, puzzling at the winding and tumbling way of the waters, trying to understand how I had come across it, and where it went.

And what about the cliff? Where had that come from?

In my dreaming state, I was better at avoiding the mud, and more skillful at avoiding the thorns and spines of the raspberry and wild roses, but still I arrived at the cliff's edge, and gazed out over the dark Romiglia. In my dream, the trees were silvered with moonlight, somnolent and mysterious, and the dark shadows about their trunks rustled with wild fowl, the whispers of rabbits, and the clever sneaking of foxes. A deer bent her head to drink from the waters far below.

Dreaming still, I turned away from the cliff and followed the path that Stub and I had taken as night had fallen, tracking Stub's hoofprints and my boot prints out of the mud and onto drier ground until I came at last to the clearing where we had made our rest, and where Stub slumbered, my saddle laid upon a log beside him, and where I lay curled upon the ground, the two of us, unaware and uncautious, smelling of sleep, of meat and warm blood—

I woke with a start, and scrambled back against the tree.

I expected to find a bandit standing over me, but I saw nothing in our little clearing. Only moonlight and silence and Stub's gentle breathing. No scent of man. Only pine. But something was wrong. My fingers felt for my dagger, carefully drawing it forth as I peered into the black shadows of the surrounding forest. My skin crawled with the unpleasant sensation of being watched. My knife felt small and silly in my hand. Every frightening story I had ever heard of the Romiglia raced through my head. Bandits who fell upon unwary travelers. Wolves who tore apart livestock. Fatas who lured men off cliffs. Golgozza who wandered undead and ate the hearts of the living . . .

I couldn't take my eyes from the shadows. Something was out there.

I crabbed sideways toward my saddle, still holding my dagger out to defend against attack, and fumbled blindly for my sword, trying to watch the darkness and also to get a grip on the weapon, trying to be as silent as possible, and also frantic to arm myself. My hand found the pommel and slowly drew the gleaming steel. I held sword and dagger as Aghan Khan had taught me, but I didn't know where to turn, only that danger lurked in the darkness. My breath steamed in the cold. I wanted to shout and challenge whoever it was, to get the fight over with—and at the same time, I was terrified that if I did, I would cause the battle and I would die.

Was I the Bull, meant to charge?

Or the mouse, meant to hide?

"Who goes there?" My voice cracked and I immediately regretted speaking. It was the sound of prey, not the sound of a man. "Who goes there?" I tried again, but the sound of my voice in that wildness made me feel worse, not better.

I knew suddenly, deep in my bones, that I did not belong in the Romiglia. Virga's weave was not for me. Like all men, I had thought myself greater than I was. Such hubris. The weave was vast and full of shadows and watchful eyes, and I was small, and I was alone. No wonder Aghan Khan hated this place. The Romiglia was no place for a man—

A shadow sharpened at the edge of the clearing. My breath caught. A black shape, almost as large as Stub, with green eyes glittering, watching me.

A shadow panther.

Its head was low, its hips were bunched, and its tail swished like a whip. I could lie and tell you that I brandished my sword, that I shouted, that I felt no fear, but it would all be lies. In truth, I was so terrified at the sight of that great cat, prepared to pounce, that I could not even act like a rabbit and flee. I pressed my back more tightly against the tree, holding my sword before me, and shivered with fear. I prayed to Amo, to Dellacavallo, to Virga, to my father, to any god that might hear to simply make that great creature not attack.

We faced each other for a long time that way. Me, frozen in fear, my sword shaking in my fist. The panther, crouched and ready, measuring me. Each of us tangled in Virga's weave, each of us playing our part, our beings tied, our fates entangled, hunter and prey.

I felt suddenly too much a part of Firmos.

As proud as I had been of my skill at eluding and stalking Aghan Khan, I now comprehended how small I was within the greater weave. It was almost enough to make me laugh. I had thought myself great, as a child who has learned to toddle thinks himself a king. And so here I was, part of the weave as I had imagined I desired, me and the shadow panther each with our part to play.

A strange sense of peace swept over me. We were neither important. We were simply two brothers, entangled in the weave, tiny sparks in the pulse of Firmos. Brothers, both breathing the same cold air, both smelling the same rot of mud, feeling the same chill mud beneath our paws, hearing the scuttle of hop-mice in the undergrowth. We were enemies. We were friends. We were prey. We were hunters. We all had our parts to play. I braced myself for the attack.

With a contemptuous flick of its tail, the cat turned and disappeared into the darkness.

I blinked, surprised. Peered into the shadows, unbelieving.

The forest shadows shifted and shivered, but the cat did not reappear.

Was it playing with me? I strained my eyes at the darkness. I listened. Tree leaves rustled, high above me. Small creatures scuttled through the underbrush. In the distance, the river continued to rush over the falls. My breath steamed in the chill moonlight. No great creature leapt forth to attack.

Stub slumbered on, unaware of our visitation.

I did not sleep again.

With the rise of the sun, the Romiglia changed her character once again.

Her robes became once more green and curious, warm and welcoming, so much so that a shadow panther seemed an impossibility, a fragment of my troubled chilly sleep. Such creatures were almost impossibly rare, and more so this far from the deep Romiglia. I had never heard of one so close to where men lived and hunted and farmed.

With the sun up, my courage returned. I quartered the clearing, seeking evidence of our visitor, but to my frustration and confusion, I found none. No paw print, no trace of fallen black fur. I began to saddle Stub, but then, unable to let it go, I went back to the edge of the clearing and went over it again in more detail, pushing aside ferns, crouching, crawling nearly, while Stub watched in placid perplexity.

When I found it, I almost missed it. The print was so large that I had not taken it for a paw print at all at first. When I pressed my palm to it and spread my fingers wide, the print was larger still. And once I found one, I could now find others, could follow them back toward the waterfall . . . I found a deep print, in wetter mud, could see the shape and pad of the foot in exquisite detail.

Around me, the birds were waking, chirping and calling and squawking at the rise of the sun. Stub snorted impatiently that it was well past time for us to go. I stared at the print for a long time, then with a shiver realized that I was deep in the bushes, and if the creature was still about, I would never see it before it pounced.

With more than a little urgency I returned to Stub and finished saddling him.

In the golden light of day, we soon discovered a path down the cliff and past the falls, and then, to my surprise, we pushed through a bramble of raspberries all heavy with fruit and came upon the exact trail we had been seeking—and in an instant I felt my sense of direction return, and understood how I had been misoriented.

It was a dizzying sensation, as odd and uncomfortable as when we had become lost initially, for now the land was familiar and friendly once again, and I knew my place in it, and I was so relieved that I laughed out loud.

I mounted Stub and spurred him up the trail, and a few hours later we arrived chilled and muddied at Archinomo Sfona's castello, where the household was in an uproar, preparing a concerted search.

The Sfona troops were already mounted with Aghan Khan at their head, my father and another group were also readying themselves, and the entire quadra premia was full of activity as troops mounted and prepared to ride out.

"Davico!" Celia cried. "Where have you been?"

All eyes turned as Celia dashed across the courtyard to me. My father. Aghan Khan. Cazzetta. Merio. Patrinomo Sfona. The guards.

"Look at you! You're a mess!" she cried as she tugged me down off Stub. "What have you done to yourself? Are you hurt?"

Everyone stared, shocked, and then a babble of cries filled the grounds as everyone joined in the rush for me: *Davico! Sfai! Dove saiai segretinato? Davico qui!* and on and on, everyone pulling me to them, everyone fussing over me, everyone inspecting me from head to toe as if they thought I was the shade of ancient Ciranaius risen from the dead, and with questions tumbling down so fast that I could answer none of them until my father at last put a stop to it, and gave me a chance to speak.

When I explained what had happened, Aghan Khan was angry that Stub and I had so well fooled him.

"This is no game, Davico! Look at all the people you roused! All the people made to worry!" He stripped off his riding gloves and turned to stalk away, then turned back to wave his gloves at me. "You are nearly a man and yet you persist in a boy's games!"

My father, however, had a slight smile on his face. "Do not trouble yourself, Aghan Khan. This is no fault of yours. You cannot protect a boy who does not wish to be protected. As you say, he is becoming a man now. Men choose their own paths."

"Young men choose foolish paths," Aghan Khan said sourly. "If he had encountered brigantae we would all be singing a different tune."

"Ci," Patro Sfona said. "He lost himself and found himself as well. What more can any man hope for in all his life? *Veri e vero, nai?*"

Aghan Khan grunted sourly and stalked off.

My father jerked his head toward the castello. "Go and wash yourself, Davico, and next time, perhaps, be a little less sly. It is best not to raise alarms unnecessarily." But even with the admonishment, I could tell that he was proud of me, and I was warmed by it.

Later that night, at table, emboldened by my successful return, I told them of my midnight encounter with the shadow panther. "It was no farther from me than that doorway over there."

"Ci. You don't need to embroider your deed," Celia said. "You already fooled the great Aghan Khan. You don't need to pretend to more greatness."

"I'm not embroidering," I said. "I saw one."

"He didn't fool me," Aghan Khan said.

"Nai?" Celia's expression turned mischievous. "So you lost him? The inheritor of the Regulai? You *lost* him?"

"I did not lose him." Aghan Khan shot her a hard look. "He lost himself. And you, Davico, if a shadow panther had seen you, it would have eaten you."

"I saw it," I said. "I don't know why it didn't eat me."

"You probably saw your own shadow," Celia said. "You turned around, and there it was, chasing you! Ai! A shadow!"

"My shadow is not half the size of a horse."

"It's half the size of Stub, that's about your size—"

"Enough," my father said.

"I don't mean to insult Stub, he's a lovely pony—"

"Celia."

My father's words carried enough warning that Celia at least closed her mouth, but her eyes continued to sparkle with amusement. Every year she was more this way: more confident, more vivacious, and more difficult, and I might have felt relief that my father had at least quelled her, but his defense of me did not extend to believing my story. Indeed, from his expression I knew that I was only saved from rebuke because he was too kind to call me out at table. It made me regret speaking of it at all.

The Patro Sfona was more indulgent. "We often say that the Romiglia sees us more clearly than we see her, and that she only reveals herself to the innocent. Perhaps he did see one."

"You're lucky you didn't see a fata," Merio said. "That close to water, she might have drowned you in the falls."

"Fatas," Cazzetta scoffed, "do not exist."

"Here in the Romiglia?" Merio made his eyes wide. "Sfai. What do you know of such things? You play with daggers and poison. You do not have dealings in the veils and whispers of the old gods."

"The old gods are no more," my father said, plainly happy to shift the topic. "Amo ran them off, and Scuro ate their bones."

"Caliba and his playmates, even?" Patro Sfona asked, smiling.

"Well," my father said. "Caliba was always Scuro's friend."

"There you go," Merio said. "Caliba was always Scuro's friend, and where Caliba goes, fatas follow. And especially in wilds like these."

The patro laughed. "It's true what you say, numerari. If any land still breathes with the old gods, it's here. But not all fatas are treacherous. Caliba's maidens are many and varied. Some are tall and beautiful, like the finest porcelain of Xim, the ones Caliba collects and makes his concubines. They are kind and generous. Others are tricksy and clever, the sort he plays his pranks with—the ones who teach young boys to look through keyholes." He winked at me, making me blush, seeming to see right to my most guilty thoughts of spying on our servants, but to my relief, he did not linger on my embarrassment. "And of course, there are the ones who may like the taste of blood, Caliba's war maidens, who lead a man to his death. I myself know a man who says he met one of Caliba's sweet companions bathing in a stream, and she only smiled at him and dove and disappeared. And I know another whose niece shared a bottle of wine with one of Caliba's maids upon a sunny stone in one of the old groves, and the wine did her no more harm than wine always does when we have too much."

"But have you ever seen a fata?" Cazzetta challenged. "You yourself?"

"I have not." The patrinomo paused. "But then, I have never seen an elephant, and yet I know that they exist."

I could not help but think of the dragon eye sitting upon my father's desk, with the power that lay within it.

"What about dragons?" I asked.

"What about them?" Cazzetta asked sharply.

"They, too, are legends," I said, "but we know they existed. And we know they have great and unexplained powers."

"Even in death," Cazzetta acknowledged. "But still, they are not gods, nor the playmates or consorts of gods. We find their eyes." He looked at me significantly. "They are not evidence of myths and legends, who are most evidenced by their very lack of evidence."

Aghan Khan shook his head. "In Zurom there are efrit and djinn. I do not know why they would not be here as well. Though maybe water chases them away. Efrit and djinn like dry lands, not wet ones."

"Have you seen one of these efrit or djinn then?" Cazzetta asked.

Aghan Khan frowned. "I have not been so unlucky, but—"

"Yes, yes," Cazzetta interrupted impatiently. "We all hear stories. We all hear legends. We all hear of a man who met a woman who had an uncle who saw this or that. I'll believe in Caliba's fatas or Zurom's djinn when someone brings back an eye of one that can sit on Devonaci's desk beside the Callarino's sigil. Then I'll believe."

Everyone laughed at this.

"And yet, I believe even so," Patro Sfona said. "Just because I have not been privileged to meet one, I cannot dismiss them. The Romiglia is not as those lands around Navola where every inch of dirt is farmed or fished or cobbled by man. When Amo rose and stood above all the other gods, the deep Romiglia was where the rest of the gods fled, to escape Amo's rageful fires. There were dark caverns and cold pools to save them, far and isolated places; it takes weeks to find paths into their valleys." He nodded at me. "In such places they could throw off the scent of Amo's blaze hounds, much as you threw off your protector Aghan Khan, and so here, more than anywhere, the old gods still hold sway and we respect them. In the deep Romiglia—the true Romiglia—well, we live at its periphery, and even here sometimes see strange things, but I know men who dare to hunt the deep for the skins of stone bears, for the pelts of mist wolves, and the claws of shadow panthers, and they say there are strange things there, still. I have not seen them myself, but those men are not the sort to live by peasant magic and superstition. They may be unlettered, but they are . . ." He paused, seeming to consider his words. "They are *awake,* yes? Awake to their surroundings. Awake to the Romiglia in ways that perhaps our young bull might understand a little of, given his woodcraft. In any case, I do not doubt them."

"Ci." Cazzetta still shook his head. "I have seen many things that men thought were magic, and that men thought were the gods, but when I looked closer, I saw nothing but trickery and priest-talk and superstitions. I will never be convinced. It's all kissing Amo's amulets as far as I'm concerned."

"Really?" Merio asked, pouring wine around the table. "Even in Pardi we know that if we want a cheese to age well, it's good to give a little to Caliba, for he likes goats and will take care to make sure the milk comes out well."

"Cheese? You use cheese as your evidence of Caliba?"

"What have you against cheese?"

And so the conversation continued, and so I subsided in frustration, wishing that Dellacavallo had been present, for he at least would have believed me. Dellacavallo would have asked me about the size of the paw print, or if I had felt Firmos in that moment. And then I wondered if that was true or only wishful thinking, and wished again that I had said nothing at all.

Around me, the wine continued to flow, but though I was present at the table, I felt very far away, and not a part of the people or the evening. I saw my father avoiding looking at me, so as not to show his disappointment. I saw Merio taking apricot jam and pardago, saying that he couldn't possibly fit any more in his belly, but then taking more anyway. I saw Aghan Khan growing less and less gruff as his cup was refilled, showing us how the soldiers of the Khur hung their swords about their hips with only a bit of rope; and I saw Cazzetta observing every move of every servant, guard, and person at the table, every plate cleared, every glass lifted, every knife dropped . . .

I saw them all, and watched them all, and felt very far away from them all—a creature of Firmos, accidentally in the company of the creatures of Cambios. But then I looked upon Celia, and was surprised to find her watching me as well, and that her expression was tender.

When our eyes met, she mouthed words of apology and I knew, instantly, that they were genuine. Celia loved to tease, but she did not like to wound, and I was grateful for her concern, and felt better and less distant because of it—perhaps not so far from Cambios as I had thought, and perhaps happier there than I often liked to imagine.

Thinking back on that moment, I suspect perhaps it was not an accident that it was Celia who drew me back from my lonely musings of Firmos, a girl who did not fear the tangled paths of Cambios, and who walked them with aplomb.

I wonder how different my life might have been, had she not been my sister.

Part 2

Chapter 10

"Come and ride with me, Davico."

Celia slapped her riding gloves upon my desk. She was dressed in a gray riding skirt and breeches and had a flush on her cheeks. Her dark eyes sparkled mischievously.

"I'm bored, and the sun is shining."

I'd known of her arrival in the bank by the stir she caused below, that familiar ripple of excitement and awe that came from the abacassi and numerari as they greeted and fawned over her. Her voice had filtered up the stairs, sparkling and breezy, teasing and joking with the scribes, all of them ensnared in their labors of gold counting and ledger marking or else they would have surely followed her up like dogs starved for treats.

As soon as I heard her entrance, I knew that I would find myself in difficulty.

As Celia reached womanhood, she had only grown more assured, leaping reckless into whatever took her fancy, and dragging me along—sometimes willing, sometimes not—but dragging me along, regardless. When we had been young, her schemes had been those of a child, sneaking through dim servant passages, pretending to be fatas to frighten the servants Sissia and Timia and Giorgio in the darkness. Now that we were older, it was galloping across the hills at reckless pace, or spying upon ambassadors who came to my father for favors and loans, or dressing as manservants to listen to gossip in the Dye Quarter, where vianomae spoke without respect for archinomi and where the gutters ran thick with color.

Celia was quick of action, and quicker of wit, and as the years passed she had become more than simply my sister. She was my friend—if a disruptive one.

"I know you heard me," Celia said, slapping her gloves again. "Come and ride."

Around us, my father's numerari clicked their abacus beads, checking numbers and reports, but I knew they were no longer focused on their work. Celia was as much a distraction to them as to me, if for different reasons.

"I'm busy," I said, trying to remember the next words I had been about to write. In truth, I desperately wished to escape with her and the idea of a ride appealed. To escape not only the scrittorium, but also the walls of Navola . . . but my duties beckoned, and I was determined not to disappoint either Merio or my father, no matter how soul withering the tasks before me.

"It's a lovely spring day. Why waste it indoors?"

"He is sharpening his brains," Merio called out from his own desk, where he sat upon a dais above the rest of us, his face smudged with ink. "As you should be doing also, young sia."

Celia made a face at him. "My brains are as sharp as the knife that split Urula's hair, thank you very much." She leaned over me, examining my ledgers. "What are these lists of yours?"

I scanned the column. "Silk, horses, gold from Cheroux—"

"That's weak gold."

"And rain is wet, thank you for your insight. So, I must convert the value into navisoli, and Andreton in Cheroux keeps making his coins less pure, so it's impossible to make a good conversion."

"Best you wait until tomorrow then, because the value will change again. Your fingers will blister from the abacus and still you will not have an answer. So"—she jerked her head—"come and ride."

Her dark hair was bound up in coils with blue silk braided through it, the knot rising above her head, as if she were one of the Sianae Justiciae of the ancients. Her maturing features showed a sharp patrician face and flashing dark eyes. She was no longer taller than me, for even though she had continued to grow, I had finally outstripped her, but still, she could have been Arragnalo's muse when he first began the Callarino's rotunda and was painting the Just Ones.

"I can't," I sighed. "Soon it's my name day. I must finish this."

"And so the boy will become a man."

Celia's tone was so freighted with seriousness that I turned to catch if she was mocking, but she was already pacing around the desks of Tullio and Antono, teasing them.

"Well," she said as she circumnavigated Tullio, making him fight to keep his eyes from her pretty swaying form. "I am going to ride. And Aghan Khan is coming as well." She nodded at Lazy, who lay at my feet. "And Lazy wants to run, doesn't she? Doesn't she, my sweetheart?"

Lazy's ears pricked with understanding and her tail banged against the marble. I half expected her to leap up at Celia's beckoning, but in the critical moment she held her ground. Still, she looked up at me with despair, brown eyes pleading, her opinion of her choices clear.

"Do you know why we do not lend to the Schipians?" I asked, ignoring Lazy's pleading.

"Because you don't like how they cut their mustaches?" Celia hazarded as she toyed with Antono's inkwell. His cheeks flushed a bright and uncomfortable pink. "Because they're too short? Because they're like lice in a whorehouse, once they get in they never want to leave?"

Antono blushed more furiously.

"Because they never pay back," I said. "They take your loan, and then they flee back to Schipia, and the next time they come to Navola, they send another of their family and act as if they do not know one another. The Borraghese lost a fortune that way, trusting Schipians. Well, that and their Xmo simply refused to pay Borragha—"

"Their Xmo." Celia winked at Antono. "They have a leader called a Xmo, Antono. Would you lend to a Xmo?"

Antono stuttered something, his skin nearly purple he was having so much trouble breathing. Celia gave up tormenting him and returned to me and Lazy, crouching down to scratch Lazy's ears. "And why do you care about Xmos and Schipians?"

"Because Merio has asked me to come up with a way to insure against non-payment from Schipians. Imagine that! A way to secure against someone who will always rob you!"

"Don't lend to them?" Celia suggested.

"Not acceptable," Merio interjected from his own desk. "We want them to support us, if Cheroux should come calling again. Cheroux fears them at their back, after the battle on the peninsula. Also, they have relationships in Merai. Banca Regulai can always use more eyes there. The Parl rests uneasy upon his throne, and his brother Ciceque covets endlessly. Even our best spies are sometimes pressed to see what happens within his Red Palace and to gauge the risks of loaning him more money."

"And you've loaned him quite a lot?"

I glanced at Merio, unsure of how much of our business I was supposed to reveal. "We . . . keep him entertained."

The truth was that we had made enormous loans to the Parl, supporting him as he built a glorious palace in Merai, paying for mistresses—all sorts of favors—and in return, we had first refusal over his wheat, and a letter of permission for untaxed trade through his territories, which made the expenses of maintaining the Parl's extravagance worthwhile, in comparison with the trade we sent through, and the letters of protection we sold to other merchants who traveled that way.

On a political level, my father considered Merai an essential buffer state against Cheroux, and wished it well tied to our influence, instead of loyal to King Andreton as they had been in the past when they let Cheroux's armies march over their passes into our own lands. The Red City, as Merai was sometimes called, was at a crossroads, its wet fertile river lands surrounded on three sides by mountains. Us to the south. Cheroux to their west. Wustholt to the north. And Vesuna to the east along its seaboard. Its passes were difficult to cross, if they chose to defend them, and their taxes ruinous if they considered someone an enemy. It was cheaper to invest in friendship.

"And so Davico sits, tangled inside his father's clever nets with yellowing ledgers and three abacuses, living in the moldery shadows, while poor Lady Lazy languishes." Celia scratched more vigorously behind Lazy's ears and under her chin. "Poor Lady Lazy."

"I have a place here beside me for the young sia if she's not careful," Merio warned.

Celia laughed, unfazed. "*Terzi abacassi, senzi gattimensi.*" Three abacuses, but no brains. Or, more specifically, missing the minds of the cats. *Senzi gattimensi.* A story from our childhood.

Merio gave her a baleful look, but she only winked at me and said it again. "*Terzi abacassi, senzi gattimensi.*"

"I heard you the first time," I said.

She began to hum the tune, and then to sing:

"Once there was a man
who thought
he would make himself rich.
He was a master of numbers,
A master of ink and things that do not exist,
With his abacuses he could make money appear
In ledger books,
And people believed, oh they believed . . .
But!
His three cats played the abacus as well,
And they played as cats
With mice
So mice appeared
And squeaked and ran and ate and danced—"

"I am not the three abacuses, nor the three cats," I interrupted. "I have serious work to do."

"Ai, Maestro Not-Three-Cats! So . . ." She went and took a chair from Tullio and pulled it up beside my desk. Plopped into it. Laced her hands upon the wood and rested her chin upon her hands, playing at solemnity. "What other task makes our young bull believe he must ruin this spring day?"

"Well, I also have to write a letter to our capo di banco in Torre Amo, and invite him to make the journey north for my name day. I'm supposed to flatter him and make him feel as if I am a man he can respect when my father steps down one day."

"But his cheek is already marked by your father. Why flatter?"

"Because Merio says—"

"Friendship is as powerful as pay and pledges." Merio wagged a finger. "And sometimes more, sia. The words a man speaks when he marks his cheek are but the dry desert winds of Zurom, if they are not wet with the blood of the heart."

"Sia Navetta says that any word a man speaks is nothing but dry wind, regardless," Celia said. "Dry wind at best, the wind of his buttocks more likely."

"Sfai, sialina! You are too young to see the world so darkly."

"This man Filippo," I went on, "apparently appreciates jokes about whores and priests. He collects and trades them."

"And goats," Merio added. "Don't forget that he especially loves the goats."

"And goats."

"A charming man, then." Celia considered. "So tell him a story about our canon priest, Garagazzo. Something about a fat man of religion who makes his nuns scour the folds of his belly with their tongues."

"A good blasphemy, then."

"Not at all. All the nuns speak of it. His folds stink like Scuro's baths, they say. I'm sure you could add something about goats as well and it would not be untrue." Celia returned her attention to fawning over Lazy. "It's a crime that Davico named you Lazy," she said, scratching vigorously and cooing. "Such a terrible slander of such a good girl. Such a good girl who just wants to run outside and play instead of being stuck here in the shadows with the ledgers and the ink."

Lazy's tail thumped all the harder. She gazed even more desperately up at me.

"She doesn't do that for anyone else, you know. Not even that tail wag."

"If you didn't hold her in your thrall, she'd be mine in an instant," Celia said, still scratching. "She's a good girl and she senses my pure heart."

"She senses that you feed her twelve-month-aged Mantollo ham under the table."

"More slander," Celia cooed, scratching Lazy's ears more vigorously. "I will defend your honor, dearest Lazy."

And with that, she leapt up and seized the quill from my hand before I could stop her. She danced back, quick and laughing. I lunged after her.

"Come out with me, Davico! Come out with Lady Lazy! Gold will lose its value! Cities will fall! Schipians will steal from you in the morning! We will all be dust draped over your father's dragon eye! And tomorrow Cheroux will mint more of her fescatolo coins, and you'll have to do the numbers all again, while your capo in Torre Amo dreams sweet dreams of goats!"

Lazy panted up at me, her gaze pitiful and begging, her tail wagging so hard that her hindquarters shook to and fro.

I made another try for my quill, but Celia tucked it behind her back. I turned to Merio for help but he waved his hands in mock surrender.

"The young sia is too much for me, Davico. Go out and enjoy life. Soon you will become a man, and your responsibilities will grow. I think today the abacus can wait."

"You don't fight fair," I groused to Celia.

"I was trained by the Regulai," Celia replied cheerfully, saluting me with the quill. "Come! Ride! The light is bright, the air is soft, and the apricots are blooming!"

Chapter 11

Soon we had horses saddled and were clattering through the narrow maze of Navola's cobbled streets, accompanied by Aghan Khan and a small guard, jostling through a mélange of vegetable carts, guards, servants, palanquins, ladies, and laborers. All around us, the stone walls of grand palazzos rose up.

Navola had always been a proud city, of proud noble families, and so the palazzos were imposing and their walls high, hiding the lives of their occupants from view. But because it was Navola the proudest families were like ours: those who involved themselves in banca mercanta. According to the writings of the Amonese historian Niccos, Navola had long been a place of trade, well placed beside the Livia's wide river mouth and protected by off-coast islands that made for gentle tides, facilitating travel up and down the river.

According to Niccos, merchant houses had always flourished at this nexus of raw materials, skilled labor, and transport, where marble and wheat and barley and iron ore and wool and flax came down to the city, and weaver guilds and blacksmith guilds and artist workshops all plied their trades. And so now, as we made our way from Palazzo Regulai toward the city's southern gate, we passed all manner of merchants crowded under the shade of the city's columned porticoes, calling out goods newly arrived and busily crating items for far-off shores.

We passed the gold alley and the silver, along with the emerald and jade markets, all of them grouped close together and with Lupari standing guard at the Callarino's order, alert to the call of a merchant in distress, and with eyes out for the known pickpockets and purseslits who might relieve a man of his gold or a woman of her necklace in the narrow confines of the alleys. We passed the Cloth Quarter with silks and wools and linens woven fine, long sample strips shimmering, advertising color and quality, flapping in the breeze.

We passed alleys reeking of river eels, silverscale, spine fish, and Cerulean eyes. Poisonous blue squid were laid out glistening, fresh for beauty ointments and dried for inks, alongside tiny fish that would be fermented into pastes, and great ones that would be baked with delicate baby pigeons within. The morning catch was still fresh, and yet in a few hours it would all be sold to the marsh guild when the evening catch arrived, the older fish to be dried and preserved or turned into seasoning using the sea salts that the marsh guild controlled.

We passed stalls where strawberries and young pea shoots and bitter greens were newly arrived with spring, easing our horses through the press of servants and cheek-scarred slaves buying for the most noble of archinomi alongside the most common of vianomae wives. We passed spice sellers with red chili bags open, and golden turmeric sacks, and cardamom and cloves and pepper, their voices lifted in steady thrumming cantos offering samples to sniff and taste for freshness.

We passed open gates that showed the hidden interior courtyards of Navola's archinomi, fountains bubbling merrily, with inlaid mosaic tiles tinier than my finger in the Accran style. We passed the closed temple gates of the Sag who lived in Navola as refugees from Xim, where they had been driven out, bringing with them old Amonese books that had been previously lost to our light. The Sag carried daggers on their arms at all times, both the men and the women, and were said to worship blood. They were prized as assassins when the disposal of a wayward husband or a useless son-in-law or henpecking wife was necessary, for they cared not for Navolese intrigues and so were tight-lipped when the job was done.

We passed down a narrow alley between the palazzos of the Gibberti and the Varrasoza, with only a few guards standing at their open gates. It had been several years since the honor wars between the two close families and their shouted accusations of fathers sleeping with daughters and cuckolding sons rang out across the Via Luce. The blood had all been shed, and whatever scandals still remained within their walls were now confined to whispers in markets when the son escorted his mother to pray at the catredanto.

It was good to ride through the city, and I was grateful that Celia had dragged me out, away from the shadows of the scrittorium. To see the sights and sniff the smells. Stub and Lazy, too, were happy to be out. I felt especially guilty that I had not given Stub more time free of the stables. His tail swished eagerly and I had to rein him back constantly as he anticipated the open hills and green grasslands that awaited us. Alongside us, Lazy explored this way and that, winding between Stub's legs, circling and snuffling, sometimes ranging farther, each time returning, tongue lolling, pleased with the stinks of the city.

Despite the pleasure of the day, Aghan Khan remained alert. He rode ahead and then trotted back to see who watched and who observed our passage. Two other guards assisted him: Polonos, who often accompanied me into the fields with Dellacavallo, and also his brother Relus. They were raw men, used to the brutality of the wild Romiglia where petty lords and made-up dukes bowed only to the laws of sword and fire, rather than those of book and quill and guild litigi. They were astonishingly quick with their blades, but also—surprisingly for their barbaric origins—kind as well.

I had seen battle-scarred Polonos buy apples for the beggar children at Quadrazzo Amo, cut the fruit, and share it along with crusted brown bread and bitter pardiluna cheese, sitting on the steps of the catredanto, he and Relus eating with the children who braved to approach their nose-broken faces. Their big callused hands had nearly engulfed the apples. When I asked Polonos about it, he had huffed, somewhat offended, "Well, I'm not Borraghese!" And then, with more seriousness, he added that when he and Relus had been young, they had often begged for bread and gotten kicks instead.

As we traveled through the city, Polonos would drop back as Relus scouted ahead. They and Aghan Khan chose our route at random, never following the same path through the tight echoing streets.

When I was younger, I had not understood their wariness, and had complained to my father once about all the twisting and turning. He, in turn, had taken me down to the river to watch a body dragged from it.

Madrico di Gibberti, the second son of that family.

"The Varrasoza did this," my father explained as Relus and Polonos stood tight around us. "You see how many times he has been stabbed?"

I did see. Madrico had been stabbed in head and body and arms and legs, as if he were a stuffed dummy used by Aghan Khan at blade practice and not simply murdered. The slashes gaped like mouths. Fishes and eels squirmed within the red ragged wounds.

"He sent his guards away to rendezvous with a woman and did not want tongues wagging," my father said. "And the Varrasoza took advantage because they were angry about losing their hold over the silk trade.

"It is not enough that you have no enemies. You must understand that I have many. You must understand that what we cannot see and do not anticipate is our greatest threat. Madrico was well loved by everyone he knew. And now he is dead. Because he had not the sense to be alert to the unseen." My father touched his eye. "What we fail to see is that which destroys us. So. Do you see Madrico?"

I nodded, mute. I had known Madrico. He had been full of life. Laughing, enjoying. He had smiling eyes, Celia said, and that was as good a description as I could have fashioned. He emanated joy, and I always thrilled when I saw that he was at a festival or dance or dinner. He had once given me chocolate from the famous cioccolatisto Etroualle. The chocolate had been stamped with the Gibberti crest of the fisherhawk, and was filled with layers of hazelnut and raspberry jam. Madrico told me that it took Etroualle a whole day to fashion only a few treats and so I should carefully savor every bite.

"Just like life!" he'd said. "Savor it!"

And then he'd laughed and given me another.

And now he was nothing but a pale wet corpse with gaping wounds. He had been rendered lifeless. No, even that wasn't enough to describe it. Madrico was my first corpse. Not the first person I had seen die, you understand, for of course I had seen thieves hung, and men dragged through the streets, or beheaded for traitors, and nerisae religiae burned alive. But he was the first whom I had known, and so the missing life was jarring. He was . . . empty. I stared a long time at Madrico, at that emptiness.

I never suggested again that I should travel without Aghan Khan or others, or that we should not follow an unexpected path.

"I wanted a companion," Celia said, interrupting my thoughts. "Not a meditator on Amo's lumen."

Polonos, who had just returned from scouting, smiled and said, "But our Davico is such a thoughtful one. Sfai on you for interrupting his mystical thoughts."

Celia stuck her tongue out at him.

I tried to make myself smile, but the memory of Madrico hung with me. "If you must always be alert for a danger that you cannot see, how is it possible to live at all?"

Polonos considered. "But that is simply life. Danger abounds." He half drew his sword. "When it comes, you stick it. Until then, why worry?"

"How can you not think on it, though?"

Celia regarded me with an expression almost pitying. "My, Davico, you think dark thoughts for a sunny day. Should I have left you home?"

"I think, is all. It's my mind. It is not quiet."

"As noisy as a tavern," Polonos agreed. "All wine and song and wenches."

"Not quite like that," Celia said, frowning. "But still, noisy. And worse lately." She continued to regard me. "The things you think, Davico, they keep you from living. If you live in fear, you are not living. You are dead already. Dead long before any danger comes for you."

"Now who thinks dark thoughts?"

"You see? It's too easy to become dark. Better to be light." She grinned abruptly. "You, Davico, are not living right now." She leaned over and smacked me with the loop of her reins. "You are not living! Enjoy the spring! Enjoy this moment, now! Not those twisty turns inside your brains."

I fended her off. "I wish I did have twisty turns inside my brains," I said. "Then I'd know what to watch out for."

"Nai! No more complaining, Davico. I won't have it." She swatted me again with her reins. "Enjoy! Your sister commands it." She flipped her reins at me again and again, relentless.

"Ai!" I flinched from the sting, laughing despite myself as she continued her assault. "My sister is a tyrant! Defend me, Polonos!"

Polonos grinned. "I would not dare, young prince."

Celia paused, reins raised for another attack. "There, you see? If Polonos yields so must you."

I held up my hands laughing. "I yield."

"Then say you are happy. Say you will enjoy this day and not ruin it with dark thoughts."

"I am happy. I promise."

And I was. The day was a gift I would not have given myself. My determination to prove to Merio and my father that I had their stamina of mind would have kept me at my labors until the sun had set. If Celia had not come along, I would have been there still.

We rode under an arched causeway that connected the twin palazzos of the Amonetti family. Flowers hung from the arches of the walkway, marigolds and lupines, the purples and oranges of their family colors, and the street beneath the walk was nearly paved with all the fallen petals, as if we were riding through Amo's blessings, simply by riding beneath the arch.

"Why does your family not have a palazzo as pretty as the Amonetti?" Celia asked as she plucked a marigold. She twirled and sniffed it, and then playfully tossed it at me. "You're rich enough."

"I don't know. It's the way my grandfather wanted it."

Aghan Khan said, "The Amonetti have little to fear. They trade in the wines of their own vineyards, and the distillates of their name. They touch politics little. They have few enemies, and the ones they do have, they keep too drunk to bother them. A split palazzo would be foolish for us."

"I just got Davico to cheer up. You're going to make him unhappy again."

"He won't make me unhappy. I just . . ." It was impossible to describe the jumbled lessons and admonitions, the warnings and risks that filled my mind. "It seems impossible to know and see every danger."

"Nai." Aghan Khan shook his head. "That is not your task. And to think that way is a poison. Think instead about reasonable precaution. If your father sends a ship to the far side of the Cerulea, she may indeed encounter a storm, and she may indeed sink. If he sends her in the month of Argo, she most certainly will. Do not worry about safety, think instead about stupidity. I have found that a man who is not stupid is also a man who is generally safe. So, we do not have a split palazzo."

We turned into a short way that wound tight into another alley, and from there we turned into Via Uva where the finest vintners in the city offered up bottles from near and far, and where the Amonetti crest, not coincidentally, was prominently displayed. I began eyeing the vintages, wondering if there was something that would suit my father's table. He might say that he did not have a strong opinion about wines, but I had seen him fairly glow with pleasure when he tasted the right grape—

A feeling of darkness swept into the street.

A bottle shattered on the cobbles.

Suddenly merchants were scrambling back, making way for a quattore of riders. Matched black stallions in red and black colors forged into the bustling lane like the dark prow of a murderous ship. Their riders wore black armor and carried bared steel, despite Callendra laws against such displays.

"Back!" Aghan Khan called as more black riders flooded into the alley. "Back!" His hand was already at his sword, half drawn. Polonos and Relus closed about us. I reined Stub short and gripped the hilt of my own sword. Celia mirrored me.

Following the four soldiers, a woman rode a black war stallion. My heart climbed into my throat. She wore fine maroon leather embroidered with silver, and her skirts were of silk and black. She observed the scattering shopkeepers with a pleased contempt.

La Siana Nicisia Furia. The Lady Furia. A name to strike fear in the hearts of all decent Navolese. A name used by mothers to frighten their children. *Be good my child, or La Siana Furia will come for you, and you will never be seen again. La Siana Furia will cut out your heart and eat it while you watch, if you are lucky. And if you are not, the siana will sell you as a slave to the filthy Borraghese. Be good my child, or La Siana Furia will come for you.*

Lady Furia was flanked by a pair of giants, black-skinned and rippling, their mailed armor shining. Lances shipped in their scabbards, trailing pennants with the Furia raven crest. Javelins in quivers upon their backs. Hook knife and stabbing sword at the ready. Men of Khus. Their helms gleamed, marked in the strange lettering of their people, said to be poetry dedicated to families and gods. Around the face guards were the four tusks of the Khusian lion, a beast I had only seen in illustrations from the travels of Demesthos and Marcel of Bis.

The Khusian lion was a creature with rough leathery skin like that of the crocodile but with the lithe form and movement of a cat. Six-legged, the Khusian lion was said to be viciously fast, and also poisonous both in its fangs and in the quills it flicked from the tip of its tail. Tezzi of Athos claimed it was something Demesthos had made up, but the four tusks around each helmet made me think Demesthos had the right of it. According to Demesthos, the tusks and armor these men wore would have been from lions they had killed themselves, alone, with nothing but their traditional hook knife and a quiver of javelins, a test of manhood that Demesthos said left half their number dead at the end of each coming-of-age season.

Regardless of the truth of lions, the truth of the men of Khus was that they were warriors forged. Empires fell when they rode. Khus had never been conquered in all its history, not by the ancient Amonese, nor by Zurom, nor by the Empire of the Khur. All had tried, and all had shattered like glass on granite.

Behind Lady Furia came another quattore of warriors, much like her lead riders, but less impressive in the shadow of Khus. All of them rode with blades bared. The men on the right held their blades right-handed, the men on the left, left-handed. None of them slowed to give shopkeepers time to make way. They simply forged through. More glass bottles fell. Crates shattered to splinters under iron-shod hooves, and still they came.

"Steady," Aghan Khan ordered.

In the confines of the street there was no room to maneuver. The merchants continued to scatter, scrambling to rescue their wares as the horsemen forced through, and then, suddenly, the street was clear, and our two parties faced each other.

Furia and her riders did not slow and did not pause, they simply came on, forcing us back, pressing us as if we did not exist, backing our horses, backing and backing. They didn't speak, but simply pushed. Polonos and Relus made a barrier between the pressing soldiers and Celia and myself. Aghan Khan's sword came fully out of its sheath as we were maneuvered back down the alley. Polonos and Relus, too, bared steel. Celia and I mirrored them, drawing our own thin blades though we had nothing of our soldiers' skill.

At the sight of our steel fully bared, Lady Furia finally acknowledged our existence. She reined her steed to a halt. Her guard halted with her without a word of command.

Furia's gaze swept over me, over Celia, over our guard. "Ai," she said. "The Regulai. Out of their palazzo. What a surprise."

She radiated menace as naturally as the sun seemed to shine. Her dark hair was drawn up in plaits and coiled above her head. Her dusky skin was smooth and flawless, her eyes were a startling green. "So," she said. "This is Devonaci's young bull." A small smile curled as she evaluated me. "How such a small guard for such a vulnerable charge?" Her hand went to a silver-and-malachite brooch at the hollow of her throat, and for a moment I felt as if she were drawing me to her, drawing me to touch her brooch, drawing me to kiss her skin, her throat, the slope of her breasts—

By the fatas! I tore my gaze away. Lady Furia was perhaps the most beautiful woman I had ever seen, and yet at the same time, all I wanted to do was flee.

"We are a sufficient guard," Aghan Khan said. "For a time of peace between the names."

"Peace." Furia's tone was pleasant and yet there was monstrous hunger behind her eyes. "It sounds enticing, but it's something I've never really understood. One moment here, the next moment . . ." She shrugged. "Sadly gone."

She did not look sad at the prospect. More than anything, she seemed to crave the breaking of peace. At any moment, I expected her to wave a careless hand and cause her men to suddenly spur forward and hew us down like wheat. Blood would splash the stone walls, would drench the cobbles beside the broken bottles of wine, would mingle there . . .

"Perhaps if you did not ride with bared steel against all the laws of the Callendra, you would enjoy more peace," Aghan Khan suggested.

"Sfai." Furia made a face. "I ride as I wish, where I wish, and no Regulai canisfincto sfaccito will instruct me otherwise. The Callendra is stuffed full of Regulai sfacciti." She touched her cheek. "So many sfacciti there. All of them secretly marked, all of them panting like dogs to please Devonaci." She made a lazy motion of dismissal, brushing away the Callendra, my father, everyone, none of them deserving her attention or respect. "It's a pity you decided to become one of them, Aghan Khan." She glanced at the two men of Khus beside her. "I think even my finest might learn from you. And"—she paused, her eyes glinting—"I would never make you sheath that fine blade of yours."

"When I draw steel, Siana Furia, it is for a purpose, not to frighten children and wine merchants."

Furia laughed. "Aghan Khan, what a man you are! A giant!" She became serious, evaluating him. "A giant indeed. I would have rewarded you with suns and moons and all the love slaves of the Furia pleasure baths if you had come to me. You were a fool to choose the Regulai."

"And yet I am satisfied."

"Satisfied to coddle children? Really? Then you're not the soldier I remember."

Aghan Khan was too disciplined to rise to the bait, and yet I could see that she had somehow stung him. For a moment I thought that he would retort in anger, but instead he mastered himself. He sketched a bow from his saddle.

"And yet I choose who I serve. And while one name offers gold, another, greater name, offers honor that outshines all the suns of Navola."

"Honor?" Furia made a face. "Not from the Regulai."

"I would not expect you to measure a man whose gold is not filthy with the misery trade. Perhaps you could study from Archinomo Regulai, instead of lashing out like a child ashamed of the filth you have smeared upon yourself."

Lady Furia's eyes narrowed. I sensed her warriors readying themselves. Their muscles quivered, as tight as wound crossbows, begging to be triggered free. I wondered if these few stray words would see the streets of Navola once again drenched with blood. The palazzos and towers of the city had been built in a time of anarchic honor wars between the city's families. In my grandfather's time, Furia and Regulai troops had met in pitched battle in the streets. I held my breath, waiting.

Furia laughed.

"Ai! Old soldier, you are a wit! Ai!" She slapped a hand upon her thigh. "Ai. Yes. You are sharp with wit. The Zurom tongue stings like a bee. But I do not hold grudges. If you ever lose that upright master of yours, your fine sword will always find a welcoming sheath in Palazzo Furia. A warm and welcoming sheath."

Aghan Khan began to blush furiously, a man mastered not by swordplay but by entendre. Before I could consider how her words had struck so well, Furia was turning her attention to me, and to Celia.

"Well, they're a beautiful pair, at least." She weighed us each in turn. "I could sell them for a chest of suns. Brother and sister. Innocent." She smiled. "Delicious."

Polonos and Relus bristled. Aghan Khan motioned them still. "Beware, Siana Furia. You speak of the Regulai."

"Of course I speak of the Regulai. Regulai children, in chains."

Her lips curled. "Regulai children in pens. Regulai children, on their knees—"

"You go too far!"

It was Polonos. He and Relus raised their blades.

"Hold!" Aghan Khan commanded. "Hold, you dogs!"

Horses jostled and steel flashed on high.

"Hold!"

Polonos and Relus drew back at the last moment, barely restrained. Our horses jostled in the narrow alley. Furia's men, superbly trained, held back, but they quivered like wolves, eager to tear upon a fawn. Horses and men huffed and called out at one another, taunting, Celia and I were buffeted as Aghan Khan and his men sought to protect us, and all the while Furia sat atop her steed, a calm island in the swirling storm of steel that seethed around her. "Ai. What a treat," she said as she held her reins. "Delicious. To see Archinomo di Regulai trembling to kneel and pleasure a buyer—"

"Sfacirritai!" Celia made three fingers off her cheek. "May you wear your own chains, sfaccita fescata! May you wear chains and may you choke on cock!"

Lady Furia's gaze fell upon Celia like an icy blanket smothering fire. Celia fell silent. "Perilis, my child." Furia was smiling slightly. "Perilississimo." She touched her cheek with three fingers. "I could mark your face so easily. You and your brother. By the time I was finished with you, you would both be begging to feel the fire of sfaccire upon your skin."

Celia quivered with rage but Furia's gaze had already passed to me. "Ci." She made the sound of dismissal. "The young bull." She made a small laugh. "Not even a shadow of the great man." She twitched her reins and set her charger in motion. As she passed, she said, "Felicitations on your approaching name day, young bull. May Sia Fortuna preserve you."

And then she laughed and was moving past, with all her guard.

None of us moved.

The sound of Furia hooves receded, leaving in its wake a silence as deep as a forest thicket, where the rabbit huddles in fear and prays that the wolf has truly passed.

Slowly, finally, the street began to breathe. Merchants began to emerge from their shops. Apprentices ran to collect shattered glass. I realized that I had been nearly frozen. We all looked at one another, blinking. It felt as if we had all been swept up in a menacing dream, and only now were waking.

"By Amo, she frightens me," Celia said, breaking the silence.

"Slaves and horses." Aghan Khan spat. "I have seen her pens on the Issolae Tristezzae and they are not pretty things." But it seemed to me that it was not only her business that made him irritable.

"I didn't like how she looked at us," Celia said. "Like a serpent thinking about swallowing mice."

"It is how she looks upon all people," Aghan Khan said. "Her family is not a kind one, nor a good one, and she did not rise to rule it by being kind or good herself." He spurred his horse forward. "Devonaci would have my head if I allowed you two to fall into her hands. We should move on."

"You don't really think she'll break the peace?" I asked.

"I think that she is a cat. And cats eat mice. I do not tempt her, and so I never need find out what the Siana Furia will or will not do. Your father should have had Cazzetta put a dagger in her ribs and been done with her long ago."

We all spurred onward toward the city gates, eager to put some distance between us and Lady Furia. But while the others soon were laughing and enjoying the day once again, it took quite some time for me to dispel the unease that Lady Furia had engendered. She seemed to encapsulate everything that I feared and more, a threat that appeared from nowhere, and that always lurked, ready to pounce if I were ever unwary.

Chapter 12

"You see?" Celia said as she reined up beside me atop the hill, breathing hard. "It is good to be out in the sun." She took in a deep breath. "I can smell the sea," she said. "Flowers and the sea. What a glorious time of year."

As soon as we cleared the city gates, we had urged our horses into a gallop and ridden hard, shaking off the city and memories of Furia, thundering through bright-green open meadows and half-wild orchards, before at last slowing to an easier pace that allowed Lazy to catch up—at least until she started chasing rabbits and pheasants, joyfully terrorizing them. She returned each time at my whistle, her tongue lolling with a pleased and gaping grin, but as soon as I looked away, she was off again, delighted with her game.

Now, atop the hill, all of us breathing hard, all the world seemed to spread below us: the Cascada Livia blue, serpentine, and lazy in the fertile plain; Navola and her many towers gleaming in the sun; the wide Cerulea stretching to the horizon . . .

"What ships do you think those are?"

I followed her gaze to the many ships tied at Navola's docks. The waters around the docks were clogged with skiffs. More merchant vessels anchored in the deeps, waiting for berths. One large vessel was unfurling her square sails and setting out for open ocean.

"I think that one is *Fortuna del Delfino.* She's out of Torre Amo. Cloves and saffron from Khus to us, then linen and wine from us to Pagnanopol, then Suvian olives and pottery back to Khus."

I was pleased that I knew. Years of Merio's relentless tutelage, paying off. I knew the trade routes, the captains, the ships, the cargoes, the costs . . . I followed the *Delfino*'s departing shape, white happy sails, the blue ocean beckoning, only a few barrier islands standing in her way before she was free and clear . . .

For many days, the only ships and people the merchant vessel would see would be the red-striped triangular sails of pescatorae triremes, the fisher people who chased the schools of white gill and red, the great bass, the bone shark, and the vicious serratine. Those people passed all their lives upon the ocean and seldom touched their feet upon dry land.

The world was wide, and I was struck by how little I knew of it, except from the entries in our ledgers that told of places and ports through numbers and columns and contracts. I watched the departing ship hungrily, wondering what it would be like to live a life entirely upon Urula's waves, under Amo's sun. I knew its cargo, but not its life.

"Davico! Celia!"

At the shout, we turned. A figure was clambering clumsily up the hill, his arms wrapped around an enormous book. "Thank Amo!"

"Giovanni!" Celia exclaimed. "What are you doing out here?"

It was indeed our friend Giovanni. Face flushed and sweating, knees muddy and grassy, and, of course, his book entirely undamaged, thanks to his protective embrace. The hills often attracted clusters of students from the university, out with bread and wine to enjoy the day, the poor afoot, the wealthy on their own steeds, but Giovanni appeared entirely alone and ill-equipped.

"Shouldn't you be at the university?" Celia asked. "Hiding in some shadowy library? And what are you doing with that book?"

Giovanni wiped ineffectually at the sweat that sheened his face. "I was in the Librixium Lucia—which has lovely light and is not at all shadowy—and then Piero and Cierco came round, and convinced me to come out here. They were meeting some friends with wine, and wanted to talk philos."

"*Piero* wanted to talk philos? I don't believe it."

"Well, he wanted to drink wine," Giovanni said. "And he said I could sit under a tree as well as I could sit in a library."

Celia scanned the dandelion-spangled meadows. "And where are Piero and Cierco now?"

Giovanni sighed. "I think, perhaps . . ."

"Yes?"

"I think perhaps I forgot to tie our horses properly."

"*All* of them?"

"Well . . . yes."

Celia laughed. "That sounds like a mistake."

"Well, it wouldn't have been so bad, but Piero scared them when he started singing, and they ran away, and now . . ." He shrugged. "Well, they're looking for the horses in the woods." He gestured vaguely toward where the hills became more forested, in the direction of the Romiglia.

"And so you're walking home."

"I don't really think they're going to come back for me today. Even if they do find the horses."

Celia quirked a mischievous eyebrow at me. "What do you think, Davico?"

Giovanni looked so miserable, I couldn't help but play along. "Well, according to the philos of La Salvixa, we should help him. That is, if we're talking philos."

"That book does look heavy," Celia said.

Giovanni looked hopeful.

"But . . ." I let the word trail off.

"But?" Celia asked.

Giovanni gave me a sour look. "Don't you start as well."

"He did lose his friends' horses, as well as his own," I said.

"Ai. That's true." Celia stroked her chin as if it were a beard, thoughtful. "Doesn't your father often say that a hard lesson makes for a permanent reminder?"

"That's right!" I snapped my fingers. "And Aghan Khan says something similar as well!" I deepened my voice to match the soldier's. "*You remember the right, when you've eaten the fruit of your wrong,* he says."

"He does say that!" Celia exclaimed.

"If I thought you'd be as bad as Piero and Cierco—"

"I've also heard him say"—and here Celia deepened her own fair voice to a basso mimicry of the warrior—"*A child doesn't eat rotten fruit twice.*"

"Ai!" I slapped my thigh. "That's right, sister! I had forgotten that one. *A child doesn't eat rotten fruit twice.* It's a good lesson, don't you think?"

"I do indeed."

"You are always so wise, sister."

"Nai, it is you who are wise, brother."

"We should study philos more."

"I feel my mind expanding already!"

Giovanni gazed sourly up at us. "I should have kept walking."

Aghan Khan, Polonos, and Relus rode up. "What's going on here?" Aghan Khan asked.

"Our friend has lost his horse," Celia said.

"Has he?"

"He didn't tie it up."

"Oh my." Aghan Khan stroked his beard. "That is a mistake."

"It's quite a long walk home," I said.

"That book looks heavy," Polonos said.

"Those shoes look soft," Relus observed.

"We were considering helping him," Celia said.

Aghan Khan rested his hands upon the pommel of his saddle and frowned down at Giovanni. "I've always found that a soldier learns his best lessons upon his blistered feet."

Celia beamed. "Oh, that's a very good saying. We should remember that one, brother."

Giovanni looked so forlorn that I couldn't continue the farce any longer and broke into laughter. "Don't look so sad, friend. Of course I will give you a ride back. We won't leave you here alone. Stub can carry us both."

"Stub is barely large enough to carry you," Celia said. "Giovanni will ride with me." She slapped her thighs. "I'll let him sit right up front. Right here."

Giovanni blushed, which was undoubtedly Celia's intention, and Aghan Khan and Polonos and Relus all laughed at his discomfort.

"Don't worry, Gio, we'll find some solution for you." Celia dismounted. "In the meantime, let's have lunch."

Giovanni flopped down on the grass, exhausted and relieved, and we all dismounted after Celia.

As we made our lunch ready, I saw Giovanni's fingers almost unconsciously reaching for his book where it sat beside him on the grass. The very book that had undoubtedly caused his distraction from tying the horses was calling to him once more. It was his way. The sun was shining, the bees were buzzing happily in the dandelions around him, and he only had thoughts for his book. He had always been thus, and

I had always liked him. He was greatly respected by the maestri at the university. He was much unlike Piero and Cierco, who were nobilii anciens more interested in battles and soldiering and the ancient days when their ancestors had raised swords and bloodshed up and down the peninsula. Giovanni was a calmer sort, though it was also true that he was more pale than any of us because he seldom came outside. Even now his nose and cheeks were reddened by the sun. He needed a hat.

"So, what is this book that has brought you to such difficulties?" Celia asked.

"Avinixiius. His *Observations*. In the original Amonese."

"I hate reading Amonese. It's such a struggle."

"I learned it early, so it's easier."

"You learned it when you were three. You're not natural."

"So what has Avinixiius observed?" I asked.

"I don't know yet," Giovanni sighed. "I sat down to read, then Piero started singing, and then he and Cierco started to wrestle as they always do, and then the horses ran, and . . ." He shrugged.

We set out bread and thinly sliced Montallo and cheeses and Aghan Khan produced a bottle of wine, and we all settled to eat underneath a blossoming apricot tree, its flowers pink and perfumed with sweetness such that it seemed the warm air around us was kissed with syrup. We passed the bottle amongst us as was right between friends, and for a time the only conversation was of happy attack upon the feast.

And after that, as a challenge, Aghan Khan set out apples atop the pikes of Polonos and Relus to use as targets, and Celia and I took turns with Aghan Khan's crossbow, trying to knock the wavering apples from atop their perches. Giovanni settled back against the apricot and immersed himself in Avinixiius, occasionally announcing things like, "Did you know that he wasn't supposed to be emperor at all? It was only because all his cousins died of bad shellfish."

"All of them." Celia snorted. "All at once. At a single banquet. A terrible tragedy."

"He didn't poison them," Giovanni said with a scowl.

"No, I'm sure he didn't." She took aim at her target, loosed her bolt, and scowled at the result. "Veri e vero, I'm sure that Aghan Khan gave me a smaller apple than you."

Aghan Khan snorted. "They are the same size, sia. You are impatient."

The apples wavered in the wind, mocking us. I took aim and also missed but Lazy ran to retrieve my quarrel, managing to pull it from the ground far distant where it had buried itself and bringing it back to me proudly.

"It's not fair that she does that for you," Celia grumped. "It's part of the game that you should retrieve your own quarrels."

"You're just jealous that Lazy likes me better."

Celia made a moue of annoyance. "No, I just think it's not natural."

"Reading Amonese is not natural. Having a loving friend is not natural. Naturally, you're jealous."

"No one should be loved so much that they don't have to do the simple work of retrieving their own quarrels."

"How did you train her to do that?" Polonos asked.

"She decided to do it on her own." I grinned at Celia. "Because she loves me, naturally."

"Fescato!" Celia made the three off her cheek at me. "It's all shit you speak. All shit."

"Jealousy makes you ugly, sister." I tossed a bit of apple to Lazy as reward for her work. She leapt to catch it, twisting gracefully, jaws snapping, and came to earth.

"And she eats apples!" Celia exclaimed. "I do not think she is even a real dog."

"She likes apples."

"She should eat meat."

"But she likes apples," I said, crouching and rubbing her behind her ears. Lazy rolled over and let me rub her belly. "Don't you, girl? You love the apples, don't you?" Lazy lolled her tongue and grinned up at me, shivering happily, paws in the air.

Celia flopped down beside us in the grass. "Do you have clothes picked out for your great event?"

I looked at her blankly.

"Your name day? You come of age? You become a man? Become designated as your father's heir?"

"Oh. That."

Celia rolled her eyes. "You will soon bear the standard of the greatest nomo banca mercanta under Amo's light, and you say *oh, that,* as if it's a curse from a fata." She shook her head. "Only, you, Davico. Only you."

In truth, I was not happy at the reminder. I had been so enjoying the day, enjoying the sunshine and the company of Lazy and Celia and

Giovanni, that my coming change of station had fled my mind. Now it all came rushing back, a dark storm looming on the horizon, filling me with an amorphous dread.

"What's the matter, Davico?" Polonos and Relus came and joined, sitting comfortably cross-legged in the grasses with us. Relus plucked a bright dandelion and chewed it placidly.

I shook my head. "Nothing. You wouldn't understand."

"Try us."

"He doesn't have clothes for his name day," Celia said. "Poor baby."

"It's not that," I protested, but Polonos and Relus were already laughing, which caused Giovanni to look up and come over. "What's this?"

"Davico's name day. He has no clothes chosen yet."

"Avinixiius wore armor on his name day."

"To protect against his remaining cousins, no doubt."

"You should don a suit of armor," Polonos said. "You will need it to protect yourself from all the sialinae who will come calling."

"You should run," Relus advised. "Once Siana Ashia has hold of you, you'll never escape her clutches. She'll have you swaddled in silk and jewels so you look like a child's doll."

Celia gave them an exasperated look. "You aren't helping."

"Helping?" Relus turned to Polonos, aghast. "Was that our purpose? To help?"

"'Twas not mine," Polonos said. "I hoped to make it worse."

"And I as well!" The two men grinned at each other. "We must be brothers!" they exclaimed and then fell back laughing.

Celia gave them two fingers off her eye. "Sfai, the two of you. If a man were drowning, you would dance pedi a pedi upon his head."

"Only if the water was deep," Relus said.

"I do like to see a man sputter," Polonos agreed.

Aghan Khan joined our party and sat cross-legged in the grass. "What is this merriment?"

"Davico is about to become a man," Polonos said as he plucked another dandelion. "He's terrified. All the pretty girls of all the Hundred Names will flock to him, and he'll have his pick of beauties. Sialinae stretched as far as the Cerulea stretches, all the way to the horizon and even beyond. He'll make kings and princes quake in fear that he'll withdraw their credit. All will bow before him. And here he sits, miserable." He winked at Celia. "Poor baby."

To my surprise, Aghan Khan did not join the jocularity. Instead, he frowned. His brow knitted. "It is a burden," he said.

Polonos and Relus guffawed but Aghan Khan silenced them with a look. "The duties are real. The burden of responsibility is not light. You are perceptive to see it, Davico. You are not like the children of the old nobilii who strut like peacocks and think their wealth something that they simply deserve, much as they imagine the obedience of their slaves and servants is theirs. We have all seen them, those ones who spend their days recalling the ancient glories of their name, chasing the concubines that Sia Allezzia trains, whoring in the glass window quarter, drinking all day in Quadrazzo Amo, and calling out and challenging anyone who looks at them to a duel." He made a face. "They think that because their name is ancient, they are noble, but it is not true."

I glanced uncomfortably at Giovanni, wondering if he might take offense, for he was as much nobilii as Piero and Cierco, but Giovanni was listening closely and nodding as Aghan Khan continued.

"To inherit a great name, a great family, a great history, this is not trivial. When I was in the guards in Zurom, I saw this. I saw how children of the sultan behaved and I swore that I would not serve such creatures. So it does you credit that you think seriously upon the duties that you take up. But, too, it is not the hell you imagine, Davico. You have friends and family who love you." He gestured at Celia and Giovanni. "You have men who have known you since you were a child." He gestured at Polonos and Relus. "I am not ashamed to serve your family. I am honored. Polonos and Relus are honored. We may tease you, we may push you, but most of all, we are honored to serve you, because you do not sully our honor. That is your strength, Davico. So enjoy that you live amongst good company, and loyal friends, and pity those creatures like the fallen nobilii who live only to count revenges, and who make children who are as poisoned as they." He slapped my knee. "In any case, you were born to this life. This was your fate. So, with its burdens, you should remember to enjoy its fruits as well. You are a serious soul, it's true. You always have been so, but that is not all of life. If you practice joy as well as you practice misery, you may find yourself a happier inheritor."

"I'm sure Ashia has something picked out for you," Celia consoled. "She has impeccable taste."

"She's already measured me twice," I said glumly, thinking of my father's consort and how she had studied me, head cocked, like a prize side of beef that she planned to carve up and serve to all and sundry on my name day.

"You'll look dashing and all the girls will swoon over you," Celia teased.

"She'll dress me up like a mannequin and her tailor will stick me with pins."

"Ci. I will help, Davico. I'll stay close and defend you. Just as Polonos and Relus defend your body from swords, I will defend it from tailor's pins."

I laughed. "You promise?"

"I promise that I won't let the tailor prick you, and that when Ashia has done her work, you will look so resplendent that every sialina will swoon before your handsome figure."

"He still won't have any idea what to do with them," Polonos said. "He'll be like one of those cakes that Etroualle puts in his window, that look so beautiful but are made of paper and covered in colored sugar."

"I'm not a fool." I scowled. "I know what to do with girls."

"Ha!" Polonos guffawed. "No boy your age knows more than to twitch like a rabbit for a few seconds."

"You give his stamina too much credit," Relus said. "Look how he blushes!"

Celia, too, was laughing at my discomfort. "Did you know that your father keeps books full of the most salacious drawings in his library?"

"Does he?" Giovanni asked. "Are they old?"

"That's the question you ask, *Are they old?* You're as bad as Davico. You should be asking, *Are they scandalous?*"

I blushed at the memories of those books, the figs and phalluses, the breasts, the maidens on hands and knees before bestial men. All of it rose up so strongly that I felt an uncontrollable trembling in my loins. Of course, Celia took my blushing discomfort not for memory but for innocence.

"It's true!" she teased. "Just beneath the bust of your grandfather. Right there in plain view! You have only to look for them! Men and women all intertwined. Women and squids. Women and minotaurs. Men and she-devils . . . Ai! So much sex! So much scandal!"

"Enough, Celia, you're breaking him," Aghan Khan intervened, but Celia only laughed.

"Oh, Davico, all the pretty sialinae will have a time with you, and with that blush of yours. You have so much to learn now that you're to become a man! You should read those books, or else you'll go to battle entirely unequipped!"

And with that she leapt to her feet and ran off, laughing.

And to my dismay, Lazy followed her.

VESUNESE SONG

The Navolese love their gold,
Hoard it like dragons old,
Navisoli fill their minds and their banking vaults
But if you cut a purse you'll find an asp,
Ai! The Navolese love their gold.

Now Torre Amonese love their women,
Dress them in silk so sheer their nipples pop
Wind their braids with diamonds
But leave their skin all bare to stroke,
Ai, Ai, the women of Torre Amo!

The Borraghese love their blood,
Drink goblets drained from enemy throats.
The cats of Borragha never starve
For blood fills begging bowls like milk.
Red runs life, and red runs wine and red run the streets of Gevazzoa
Ai! Ai! Ai! The Borraghese love their blood.

Oh, the Men of Pardi love their cheese
And the Ladies of Merai love their jade
The Sons of Treppo love their shoes
And the Daughters of Corregi love their pride
The Men of the deep Romiglia love their hunting bows

Ai Ai, those men are beasts in forests high and far
But of all the lands and all the peoples
There are none so fine as the children of Vesuna
Who love the fair blue Cerulea,
Who sail upon the breast of Urula,
Who worship her bounty,
None so fine, as they.
None so fine. Ai! Ai! Ai!

Ai Ai Ai! The Navolese guards his gold with jealousy
And the Borraghese spills his blood most zealously
But none are so fine as Vesunese,
With wind and sail,
And a land far away to hail.

Ai! Ai! Ai!
A land far away to hail.

Chapter 13

As Celia predicted, my father's consort Ashia had very specific ideas of image for me. I was to appear regal, but not ostentatious. Wealthy, but not crass. Well appointed, but not foppish. But above all (much to Celia's amusement, and my anxiety), I was to appear eligible. When I took my name, I would become my father's heir officially. Heir to fortune. Heir to power. And Ashia was determined to ensure that I would stand first in every archinomo patro's mind as a man of substance, and every matra's mind as a figure of romance.

And so, as the day of my celebration approached, I found myself more and more circled by Ashia, her flashing dark eyes always seeking fault as she brought in tailors and chose outfits for the various celebrations that were to occur. When I complained that the embroidery at my collar chafed she slapped my hand away, her tongue tut-tutting admonishment as was her culture's wont.

"It is right," she said. "You will bear it. The clothes you wear are not for comfort. They are for status."

On that day, the windows were all thrown wide for it had grown warm, spring falling before summer. Sea and river breezes kissed us but only in the most teasing and seductive ways, causing us to yearn for relief, but never giving satisfaction as they touched our skin. Soon we would be in the blazing heart of summer, that time that Celia dreaded, when heat hung heavy and still upon the city, but it was not yet full upon us.

"Where is Celia?" I asked as Ashia plucked frowning at the high-collared embroidery of my jacket, making me turn to left and right.

"She has her own lessons to attend." Ashia pointed to the cut of my sleeves. "This is much too long," she said to the tailor. She clicked her tongue disapprovingly. "He is not some Velanese actor. Take them in."

"Yes, mistress," the tailor said.

Ashia's cheeks were slave-scarred, three slashes on each cheek as was the custom in Navola. She had come to our household at the age of fourteen, purchased by my father as a concubine to warm his bed after my mother died. Though she had been marked young, the scars remained, distinct, even after many years. She would die with those scars upon her cheeks, no matter how long she lived.

Despite this, she commanded our household with the authority of true nobility, which she had once been in her faraway land.

"And I want his slippers to match," Ashia said.

"Of course. I can also embroider diamonds . . ."

"Ci." Her tongue clicked again. "Not for the shoes. The Regulai are rich, not stupid, maestro."

"Of course, Siana. My apologies."

"What studies does Celia have?" I asked. "She promised that she would be here."

"She has her own duties," Ashia said as she continued to fuss with the fall of my coat. "It is not your affair."

I had the distinct impression that while I was being poked and prodded and pricked by tailor pins, Celia was out having some sort of fun. "But she said she would be here and give her opinion."

"That girl is not the one you must impress. There are archinomi you will be encountering now."

"Archinomi with daughters," I said sourly.

"Beautiful daughters," Ashia said as she and the tailor hemmed my sleeves. "Now hold still or you'll be pricked."

I subsided, but still, I was frustrated. Celia made such events bearable. She at least lightened the moment with wry comments. Even now she would have been teasing me about how the daughters of the archinomi would swoon at my long sleeves, or else telling me that my neck resembled a chicken's, stretched long by the high scratchy collar, something—anything—to relieve the tedium. Instead, she'd run off, leaving me to Ashia's depredations.

Ashia circled. Plucked at the hang of the long jacket. "Yes. This is better." She fingered the fabric. "I'm not sure about the color, though. The cream . . ."

"This is finest Xim silk," the maestro protested. "Better even than what our own workshops produce. It was meant for Xim royalty, and only smuggled out at great risk. We cannot make its like, even here in Navola."

"Yes, you and I both know it is better silk, but the Navolese . . ." She frowned. "They like their bright colors."

"If Celia were here she could tell you," I said, testily. "She thinks like a true Navolese."

Ashia's eyes narrowed, taking the thrust of my barb. "And yet," she said, "you yourself are true Navolese, and are of no help at all."

She pursed her lips, standing back with the tailor as she considered. "Merio will be sufficient, I think. Go and show him the color, Davico. Quickly now." She clapped her hands at me like I was a servant. "Quickly, young bull. We don't have all day. The maestro must sew and embroider and he cannot do so with you wearing this coat."

I sullenly left the room and descended the stairs from Ashia's apartments. I passed through a long reception hall that we used for family celebrations, full of images of the various gods of old, and then emerged from under shading columns into our garden quadra.

Here, on one wall, my father had ordered a fresco dedicated to my mother. She was depicted as Erostheia, sleeping beside a stone bear in the high mountains, all the other animals peeking out to look upon her beauty, all of them guarding over her. The image was stronger than my own memories of her, a woman whom I associated most now with the scents of cardamom and honey, the softness of her touch upon my cheek. Looking upon the image, I felt a creeping stain of mind that I had called Ashia not of Navola. I had known the words would cut, and they had. I would have to apologize later. Ashia wished me well, and she loved my father. In her own fashion she wished the best for me. But still, she was a foreigner and I had not liked her acting as if I she were my true mother. And yet, in veritas I had no other.

I made my way through the garden, mulling the unpleasantness of apology.

I should have proceeded out through the ranked archways to our quadra premia—but instead of continuing on to the banking offices with their clicking abacuses, I paused. A staircase led to the upper galleries, beckoning, and my own chambers lay beyond.

Celia was playing Frogs and Foxes.

Why not I?

Almost before the thought was formed, Lazy appeared, tail wagging, looking up at me mischievously.

Freedom beckoned.

Should I follow Ashia's orders?

Or steal my freedom?

We were up the stairs in a flash, hurrying along the gallery that overlooked the courtyard, and then I was in my rooms, throwing off the fine silks and pulling on breeches and linen shirt.

"We must hurry," I said to Lazy as she wagged her tail with pleasure. "We don't want Ashia catching us, do we?"

I tucked my dagger into my arm sheath as Cazzetta had taught me, and then we were down the stairs again, both of us silent as thieves in Quartiere Sangro, our noses up for any hint of Ashia's perfume, our ears pricked for the whisper of her soft slippers on stone.

Polonos was sitting near the gate, flipping a dagger. As soon as he saw us stealing around Urula's fountain with my wary eye cast over my shoulder, he guessed our intentions. He was up in a moment, the dagger disappearing, matching our step.

"No more tailors and silks today?"

"We're getting out of this tomb of a palazzo and as far from Ashia as possible," I said. "Wouldn't you like a cool cup of wine?"

"La Siana will be angry."

"She rules my father, not me."

Polonos snorted, but he didn't stop us from slipping out of the palazzo.

In truth, despite my bravado, I felt guilty at my escape. Now I would have even more to apologize for. Ashia had come to our palazzo in chains; it was not her fault that she was foreign, and sometimes strange. And in truth, despite her foreignness, she was masterfully adept in the politics and customs of the ambassadors and archinomi with whom my father sat at the plank. She infused our house with intelligence, culture, and grace. Few in Navola could match her, and this despite the fact that she was marked three-and-three. But today, for whatever reason, her ministrations were simply too much to bear. Too, it was infuriating that Celia ran free while I was sentenced to scratchy collars and Ashia's tutting tongue.

"Did you see where Celia went?" I asked Polonos.

His eyebrow went up. "She said shopping. Those chocolates of Etroualle. The maid Serafina was with her."

"When did she leave?"

"Half a candle, half a turn of the sand, perhaps."

"Excellent." I turned our steps toward the streets where fancies were sold and where Etroualle plied his trade.

Soon we were surrounded by sweets and chocolates and flowers and lovers' trinkets, and were greeted by the sight of Celia emerging from Etroualle's shop with Serafina in tow.

I was about to call out to her when Celia handed off all her packages to Serafina, piling all her boxes and paper-wrapped fancies—all stamped with Etroualle's gold crest—precariously into the arms of the servant girl, and then strode away down the street alone.

What was this?

Celia's stride was quick and purposeful, squeezing down the narrow street, slipping between ladies and couples, merchants and maids. She glanced behind her once, but by the barest luck, I anticipated the turn of her head and pulled Polonos behind a great spray of daisy reds.

Celia's gaze lingered for a moment, searching the street, and I had a strange feeling of almost being seen by her, but then she was turning down another narrow street, her green dress swishing. I held back a little, then followed. This alley was nearly empty, and so we were forced to hang back more than I wished, allowing Celia to reach each bend in the alley, and then dashing after her, hoping to catch sight before she made the next crossing of ways.

We made an absurd sight, I'm sure, myself and Lazy and Polonos all in a rush: Lazy delighted by the game, running ahead of us, hungry for the chase as if tracking a rabbit; Polonos indolently laggard, making comments about it being too hot for children's games; and me, between the two, attempting a semblance of leadership that neither Polonos nor Lazy respected.

Lazy dashed ahead, tongue lolling, and then looped back, then dashed ahead again so that I was sure she would burst upon Celia and give the game away. Polonos longingly studied cool taverns, with trays of Pardi cheese and barrels of wine and crusted breads and summer pickles of asparagus and onions and long beans.

Lazy lunged ahead once more. It was all I could do not to shout after her and give up the game, but at the last moment, as if understanding my desire, she held back at the corner. She waited impatiently for us to catch up.

"Velociti!" I urged Polonos. "Velociti! We'll lose her."

"Velocimi, velocimi," Polonos muttered. "I thought we were going drinking."

"Soon, but first I want to know where Celia is going."

"Have you considered that it might be best to leave the sialina to her secrets?" Polonos asked, wiping sweat from his brow as we peered around another corner.

"What do you know about it?"

"I know that a woman who doesn't want to be followed, doesn't want to be followed." He scratched at his beard stubble. "Too, I know that when a man follows a woman, sometimes he does not like what he finds."

"I am not a man, I'm her brother!"

Polonos smirked.

I gave him a sour look. "You know what I mean."

We reached the belly of the alley's curve just in time to catch a glimpse of Celia making a new turn. It was puzzling, for her steps took her not toward a quartiere known for flowers or trifles, nor for workshops known for art, nor where tailors and dressmakers made their trades. This was Quartiere Lana, known for merchants and trading. Here, long ago, linen merchants had kept their looms. As the trade grew, the looms had moved to larger shops, with warehouses closer to the river, and now merchants of linen, silk, and finished wool filled the empty places. Here, my great-grandfather had been born, amongst the click of looms, and here he had built our trade.

Today, the street was filled with the bustle and shout of commerce. Long tables and benches clogged the street, stuffed with merchants bargaining. Scriveri wrote contracts. Notari took pledges and stamped their sigils. Merchants stole one another's business, shouted competing offers, and then acted as witnesses to trades that they had feverishly opposed just moments before. Barmen and wine girls shuttled frantically amongst the tables, serving the teas and cheeses that were traditional to bargaining and the plank, and bringing wine when agreements were sealed.

I knew this place well. Merio had brought me here many times so that I would understand our family's roots. This was where we had started, where our family had lived in cramped quarters for generations, before Deiamo effected our precipitous rise.

"Never forget," Merio said, as we sat sipping sweet tea and eating bitter cheese and meeting with one merchant after the next. "The leaves of the great oak of Banca Regulai are gilded with the gold of kings and princes, but this is where we sink our roots so that we are not blown down when great winds shake kingdoms."

Here we offered letters of credit, here our numerari made agreements to extend cash in cities as far as Wustholt and Bis, and across the Cerulea in the glittering city of Vaz and even as far as Xim. Here, a merchant could send a bale of wool or a ship's hold stuffed with tea across the world, and at the far side, when he made his sale, he could record it there, in a distant branch of Banca Regulai, and return home, carrying only a slip of parchment and the seal of our bank branch to be made whole here in Navola, without need to transport the gold himself. Here, he could buy insurance for the journey, protecting himself against sea storms and brigands, and sometimes even a change in price on his precious cargo.

We squeezed between the crowded tables, trying to keep Celia in view. All around us, trade continued and deals were made. Litigi feverishly drew up papers, working by the contract. Women of pleasure sat and sipped their own teas, their eyes bright and alert, eager to help a merchant celebrate a successful deal, all of them as savvy at contracts as the men they pleasured. Deep cellar–cold wines were brought out and uncorked. Friends and enemies mingled. This, as much as anything, was the beating heart of Navola's banca mercanta, but Celia had no business here. She could not be visiting any friend here.

Too, she seemed furtive.

Abruptly, Celia turned into a tavern, ducking through the low doorway. We dashed after and peered in through the unshuttered windows, trying to see into the dimness without giving ourselves away. Nothing.

"I'm going in."

Polonos shrugged, as if to say, *You know what happened to the boy at the keyhole,* but he didn't prevent me and I stepped into the gloom. The tavern was small, the tables all occupied by lawyers and scribes, all making notes on contracts, their stamps and ink boxes beside their sharpened quills. But Celia was not with them, not making some bargain, not collecting some contract. I ducked under a low door to a second room, but she was nowhere in sight.

The princi di taverna came up behind me. "You wish to eat, or sit at the plank?"

"Did you see a girl come in here?"

He made a face. Jerked his head toward the kitchen.

"She cooks?" I asked, puzzled.

"She goes out."

I started for the kitchen, but he held up a hand. "If you wish to go out, you must pay."

"Does she pay?"

He tipped his head. "All pay."

More puzzled, I reached for my cash string and unknotted it, offered him a quattopezzo. He jerked his head toward the kitchen. "Go on, then."

I pushed through. The kitchen fire roared, the cooks shouted, a wave of scents and sauces and steam enveloped me. Pigs turned on spits. Cleavers hammered at meat and vegetables. Boiling teas, muslin-wrapped cheeses coming up from the cold room below, but no Celia. I went out the back and found myself in a stinking narrow alley where two men plucked chickens over a bloody drain.

There was no sign of Celia.

"Looking for the sialina?" One of them smirked.

"Did you see her?"

"She was a piece. Enough to make the root poke right up."

Polonos and Lazy came through. "Well?" Polonos asked.

"She went that way," the man said, grinning and winking and pointing down the lane. We hurried in the direction he pointed, but almost immediately encountered a split, three claustrophobic alleys leading off at odd angles. I looked to Lazy. "Where is Celia?"

Lazy cocked her head.

"She won't track without a scent," Polonos said.

"You don't know Lazy." I crouched beside her, held her face in my hands, rubbed her ears. "Celia? Can you find her? Celia?"

Lazy blinked, quirked an eyebrow, quizzical.

"Celia," I said. "Hunt."

Lazy looked down the alley, then back to me, then roused herself.

She started to circle, sniffing. A moment later she was off, trotting down one of the streets.

Polonos grunted. "That is not natural."

"She's a very smart dog."

To my disappointment, Lazy lost the scent as we came to a new larger street, Via Amoluce, with shading porticoes and much bustling activity, fine dust and trampled manure puffing up in the hot air. It was one of the great avenues, with many people coming and going, bound either for Quadrazzo Amo at the center of the city, or else for the city gates. Lazy wound between carts and horses and people, circling, sniffing, confused. She looked up at me apologetically.

"It's not your fault," I consoled as she rejoined us. I scratched Lazy's ears and studied the activity of the street. Celia had meant to elude followers, and it had worked. "It's not your fault. She tricked us all . . ." I trailed off, struck by a new suspicion.

The street whose verge we stood upon did not only lead to shops, but also led to residences. With a growing certainty, I waved Polonos to follow and, unseemly as it was, I began to run, hurrying across the street and toward Quartiere di Marco. Not the grandest of quarters, but pretty, full of blooming trees in the streets and climbing vines on the walls. Celia wasn't shopping, and she wasn't eating. She had passed too many such establishments. She could only be going to visit someone who lived in this quarter of Navola. I made my way between two walled palazzo gardens, and emerged on another street. The houses here were larger, the walls higher, and there, at a gate with a guard, was Celia, just slipping inside.

The guard swung the gate closed. Celia was lost.

But I did not need to follow. I knew the house.

Everyone in Navola knew the house.

Chapter 14

Everyone in Navola said that Sia Allezzia di Violettanotte was a beautiful woman, but that was like saying La Cerulea was vast, or that the Navolese were twisty-minded. I had seen her twice, and both times I had been struck dumb. One time I had been with my friends Piero and Cierco. They had pointed her out to me.

She had been sitting at a table outside a tavern known for its small bitter spirits. An establishment not of benches and long tables, but of small round ones, meant for intimacy. She had worn a gown of green with white lace, her breasts much exposed, her eyes darkened, her lips reddened, and her silky black hair in plaits and coils so complicated that it would have taken servants many hours to sculpt her so. She was as a portrait by Arragnalo, unearthly and mesmerizing as a fata, except that she was alive, within reach. A creature out of legend, and yet there she sat before us, sipping red bitters while the man across from her—archinomo nobili anciens, by his hose and jacket and embroidery—preened for her attention, desperate to keep the treasure of her gaze upon him.

Allezzia di Violettanotte.

A courtesan, Piero and Cierco had whispered. A courtesan who kept four different men, who in turn kept four different palazzos for her comfort, for whenever she chose to visit them. A woman so seductive that they were content to share her charms and attention, for to go without would kill them. Sia Allezzia was said to have ruined Archinomo Taglia, causing the patro to spend all his money attempting to win her back after she had discarded him for his jealousy.

Allezzia di Violettanotte.

Ai! Even seeing her door was enough to stir my ardor. Polonos was studying the door as well, and from his expression, he too recognized it.

What was Celia doing in the palazzo of such a woman? What could such a woman want with Celia?

Piero had told me that Sia Allezzia sometimes arranged parties for men she favored, pairing them with young vianomae women, girls who enjoyed games of seduction, the daughters of mattress makers, of weavers, of candle dippers, delivered to Sia Allezzia by mothers and fathers who wished to use the treasures between the thighs of their daughters to please, to seduce, and ultimately to ascend in Navola.

Piero and Cierco told stories of those girls. Piero claimed he had bought one for a night of dalliance, and instead of singing her praises had sung the praises of Allezzia, who had trained her so well.

"Ai, Davico." He had waxed poetic. "The things she did with her fingers. Her tongue. She was a fata of the bedchamber. Ancient Caliba could not have asked more from his own attendants. Ai." He sighed dreamily. "Every man should spend a night in the arms of a girl trained by Sia Allezzia."

I peered through the iron gate to the fountains and trees beyond, but caught no sight of Celia. The guard in turn watched me and Polonos. "If you have no business here . . ." He jerked his head. "Move on."

Polonos tugged my elbow. "Best we go."

"What business could Celia have?"

"You know the business that is conducted," Polonos said, pulling me away.

"But how could she . . . ?"

Was she, even now, draped seductively in Allezzia's gardens, one of her nymphs? Piero had described the experience of being invited within. The sparkling company of the girls, Allezzia's pleasure fatas. Was Celia one of them? Was Celia even now crouching between the thighs of some archinomo rake?

I turned away, fighting to suppress the images that invaded my mind: confusing, arousing, disgusting, appalling, intriguing. My imagination was full of images. Celia as one of Caliba's fatas, clad in diaphanous silks. Celia shrugging off her gown, letting it fall to her feet. Sia Allezzia in all her beauty with Celia. The two of them entwined, as I had seen women drawn in the pages of the books in my father's library . . . For a long time I wandered, Polonos and Lazy in tow, my mind roiled by visions that I fought to smother, questions that could not be denied.

"You want me to watch her?" Polonos interrupted my thoughts. "Next time she leaves? I can watch. See if she meets . . ." He trailed off.

Men.

That was the word he wanted to say. See if she meets men. See if she goes to tavernae and if she sits in the laps of rakes and archinomi with lust in their hearts. Young wastrel nobilii or old, wizened, fat mercantae. See if she follows the profession of Allezzia. If she soils the Regulai with licentious antics. This was what Polonos wanted to ask, but did not.

"No." I shook my head. "I don't know."

I doubted that she did . . . well, whatever she did, in public. She had been too secretive about her visit to Sia Allezzia. But I had a feeling of foreboding. Celia's visit to the house of a woman so notorious—and with such furtiveness—boded ill.

"Perhaps she is only meeting . . ." He trailed off, for of course, there was no meeting at Sia Allezzia's that could not involve fleshly entanglement.

Unless . . .

Allezzia's influence touched many spheres. Numerous archinomi sought pleasure with her and her nymphs. Many men had reason to visit. Friends and enemies. Celia kept her visit here secret, tried to keep it hidden. And if she kept secrets . . .

Cazzetta rose up in my mind, whispering and unpleasant, suspicious of anyone who kept secrets, asking the one question that poisoned his mind at all times, and now poisoned my own:

Is she treacherous?

I thought of Celia laughing, teasing me, urging me to join her in the sun for a ride. Could my sister be treacherous? I wondered if I should tell my father, or go directly to Cazzetta. Cazzetta would certainly waste no time rooting out the meaning of Celia's deceptions. He would stick to her like her own shadow. He would watch, he would listen, and eventually . . . I shivered.

I was loath to unleash Cazzetta's darkness. Cazzetta stripped secrets from people the way a fishmonger ripped bones from a Romiglian trout. To set Cazzetta upon Celia . . . well, he might find her purpose at Palazzo Violettanotte, but there was no guarantee that Celia would not end up as a bloody offering to my father.

Deep in troubled thought, I wandered the city with Lazy and Polonos in tow, not paying much attention to where my feet carried me, thinking only of Celia and the questions that her secret provoked.

I was only brought back to myself by a sudden cascade of bells ringing terzi, a crush of black-robed bodies all around me, and shouts calling out in recognition.

"Davico! Ai! Davico!"

I looked up, confused, taking in my surroundings. I was in the Quartiere Universita.

"Davico! Get the wool off your eyes!"

A river of students was pouring out of Studio Litigi, all of them pushing and shoving out through the grand tulla wood doors. The doors had been carved with images of famous masters, depicting students listening rapt and attentive (though if you looked closely, you could also find slyly carved images of students napping), and now they were thrown open, and within the seething mass of ejected students, I spied a cluster of familiar faces.

"Davico!" Cierco called. He was half tangled in his robes, trying to strip them off mid-escape from lecture. "Where have you been? We thought you lost to us!" He pointed at me. "Look, brothers! Our long-lost Regulai!"

I think I instinctively must have been seeking company and succor, to place myself at that precise place at that precise time, that place where I often met my friends, for along with Cierco Altosevicci was his brother Piero, as well as my studious friend Giovanni, and also Antono Veradicca, whom we called Tono. All of them were juggling disarrayed papers and quills as they stripped off their black student robes in the heat, free at last from university custom.

"I told you I saw him just the other day," Giovanni said as his robes came over his head, leaving him flushed and disheveled. "After you and Piero left me in the hills."

"You mean after you lost our horses," Cierco said, but before that argument could be started he rushed forward to embrace me, his robes still half on and flapping. "Our long-lost friend!" he cried. He wrapped his arms around me, entangling me in his garments, and hopped up and down like a child who has found a favorite toy. "As lost as the sailors of *La Demeta* when Cerulea took her down! He was lost, and now he is found!"

I fended him off, laughing. "Not so lost as that, Cierco. Though I may not swim long if Ashia has anything to say about it."

I fended off a second attempt at capture, then set about helping free Cierco of his self-inflicted tangle of robes and books.

"Ai. That foreigner," Cierco said. His head popped free, revealing a sweaty black tangle of hair and a pair of deep-set eyes sheltered by bushy eyebrows, mobile and expressive. "She controls your father too well. And now you, too."

"Even worse," his brother said, "she makes him pretty." Piero managed to get his own robes over his head, revealing similar eyes, but with a sharp nose like his mother's, as sharp as the naked swords he often trained with. His hair, in contrast with his brother's, was straight and the color of straw. Piero was light where Cierco was dark, but the two were clearly brothers, for their brows were heavy, their eyes were sharp and blue, and their grins and energy were exactly matched.

"Look how nicely his hair is trimmed and curled!" Piero reached out to tousle my hair. "Such a handsome boy now!" He pinched my cheeks. "Such a handsome boy, approaching his name day! My, how big you've grown." Now he had both his hands on my cheeks, pinching. "Such a big boy!"

"Fescato." I pushed him away and flicked three fingers off my cheek.

"Do you flick your three at me?" Piero demanded, mock-enraged.

"I not only flick," I said. "I flick again! Three-and-three upon you!"

"Dare thee flick me the three, Regulai dog?"

"I do not dare, I double-dare!"

"We must duel!"

With a battle cry, Piero charged, seizing me and driving me back against a column.

"Peace!" I begged as we slammed laughing against the stone and Piero tried to wrestle me to the ground. "Peace, Piero! It is too hot to duel!"

But still we tangled, Piero entirely outmatching me with his quickness and strength. He dragged me to the ground. Lazy leapt to my defense, barking and scrambling atop us, wagging her tail and nipping at us both until at last Piero rolled off me and sat up, face flushed and panting, and holding Lazy at arm's length as she tried to lick his face.

"Ai!" he gasped. "You're right. It is too hot. You yield, then?"

"I yield." I collected myself with as much dignity as one can muster after being dragged to the ground by a half-dressed litigi student. "I yield and salute." I ignored Polonos's smirk as I straightened my linen shirt. "But only if you promise me that you are drinking."

"When are we not drinking?" Piero wrestled Lazy off him and wiped her slobber and his sweat from his face with a sleeve, then paused. "*Is* there a time when we are not drinking?"

"There's never a time when you are not," Giovanni said.

"Well," Piero said as he climbed to his feet and shot an acid gaze at the Studio Litigi doors. "It's only because I must wash away the bad memory of our Maestro di Culolingue."

"Sfai. That's not called for—" Giovanni started.

Cierco cut him off. "Maestro Cultalangue is standing right behind you."

Panicked, Piero whirled and fell to his knees, on the verge of marking his cheek to apologize.

Of course, the maestro was not to be found, only more fellow students, chattering and stripping off their own black robes.

"Fescato!" Piero sprang up and punched Cierco's arm. "You scared me!"

"Don't call our maestro an ass-tongue then."

"Fuck that fescatolo pigfuck—"

"As wise Plaesius advised his young apprentice," Giovanni interrupted, wagging a finger of instruction. "*Use not words in the privy that you would not also use in the quadrazzo.*"

"Ci. Plaesius," Piero spat. "I have too much of Plaesius."

"You could learn something from Plaesius."

"You could learn to swing a sword."

"Wisdom is sharper."

"Well, then you can use it to manage my country villa and give me sharp fat profits."

"What country villa?" Giovanni snorted. "Your family sold it."

Piero laughed good-naturedly. "That's what the sword is for. To win a new estate. I will march with the Lupari and win great riches."

"You could always just excel in your studies."

"Indeed. But that would require—"

"Studying Plaesius?"

"Exactly!" Piero gazed about. "Weren't we going drinking? I for one could use a drink. Even Plaesius liked wine."

"He wrote a poem about it," Giovanni said.

"Wisdom at last! At least we can all agree on drink."

With this, we collected their various belongings and set off down the length of Via Raiana.

Here, it was said, the young Sia Raiana Bellapensi had inspired her suitor, the aged and ugly Pagamello, to construct an intricate and beautiful shading portico along the entire length of the long street, to shelter her from freezing rain and scalding sun as his beloved beauty went to and from the university. It had undoubtedly been a lovely passageway in the past; however, despite the romance of Sio Pagamello's intentions, the supporting columns were now liberally charcoal-scrawled by students, with images of enormous horse cocks crowding up against clever phrases of philos and litigi, which were in turn overlaid with curses against the shriveled buttocks of this or that instructor who had offended the students.

"You see!" Piero pointed to a sketch of a university maestro with a supernaturally long tongue buried in the ass of a student on hands and knees. Below the picture, a rhyme about touching and tonguing asses was scrawled: CULOTOCCHI, CULOLINGUE, CULTALANGUE, MOLTO . . . "Everyone calls him Culolingue!"

I recognized the hand that had written the poem. "You drew that!"

"But now everyone names him so," Piero said. "So, my words are true and correct; everyone calls that ass-tongue what he is, and I can take the oath under Leggus with a clean conscience: Everyone calls him Culolingue." He beamed with pride. "It is fact, in fact. Even noble Plaesius would agree."

"It seems," said Giovanni, drily, "that our wayward friend has at last become a student of litigi. And here we thought all he did was sleep at lecture."

"A worm turns into a butterfly when it sleeps," I pointed out.

"An excellent point."

"Fescato!" Piero said. "I am a master of the thickets of the law—" His words were drowned out by a cascade of ribald commentary from the rest of us.

"More a master of tongues—"

"A master of bums!"

"For Piero, that counts as coming up in the world."

"I squeeze a tear of pride—"

"I squeeze a spruto of spremi!"

"A scholar at last!"

"Piero Altosevicci, maestro di fescatolo."

"I'm a maestro di litigi!" Piero protested.

"Well, you are full of shit," Cierco said, thoughtfully. "So you've got that going for you."

This earned him a punch in the arm from Piero. "Fescato," he said, "For that, you pay Siana Grassa for the wine."

We turned from under the great columned shelter of Via Raiana and from there, into the cramped and jagged way of Vialetta Dell'Occhi, wherein lived Taverna L'Orso Banco, with its image of a stone bear sitting at the plank of negotiation, alongside a great pot of honey.

Chapter 15

The Bear was a popular place for numerari, scriveri, and litigi students, always welcoming. In winter, it was all tightly packed tables steaming with warm broths, and in the summer it was stocked with cold pastas that could be had at any time, from a great groaning kitchen that was kept working from late in the morning until far later in the night. The mistress of the place was a fat woman—Siana Grassa behind her back, Siana Grazzurula to her face—the original Bear at the Plank, Piero joked, and a well-fed bear at that, and even though Siana Grassa kept the wine heavily watered and never let the serving girls sit in student laps, she and the Bear were well loved.

Taverna Orso was a place that smelled like home, but without the home pressures of name and family, a place where students could find succor for their bruises from fights in rougher taverns or from arguments with other students, or else shelter from their failures before the maestri of the university, or—for me—from the expectations of my family.

For me, Taverna Orso made it possible to briefly become someone other than di Regulai. I liked the warmth. I liked the long, knife-scarred and tankard-dimpled tables. I liked the crowding of the students and the occasional university maestro, slumming with the youth. I liked that girls and boys flirted here, and sometimes kissed in front of others to our great amusement, all of us drumming our spoons upon the dark wood of the tables when it happened. Sometimes a few students would appear with instruments and then there would be songs, and we would lean against one another, rocking to and fro, singing of spring, of the boy at the keyhole, of the fatas, of Navola.

When I was in the place, I always found my spirits lifted, as if the warmth and pleasure of the others were raising me up. I could almost feel them within me, making me smile. The Orso was a good place, our friend Tono opined. Built on good dirt, filled with good fatas, and so filled with goodwill.

Today, the shutters of the tavern, made of heavy wood and closed during the winter months, were thrown open to let fresh breezes flow. And at one of the wide windows, our friends Benetto Cucchiaio and Dumont D'Enrit, a foreigner from Cheroux, had already claimed places at a long table ideally suited for fresh air and light, and were playing cartalegge.

Benetto caught sight of us and leaned out the window. "*Culotocchimi!* Do Caliba's fatas deceive me? Could this be Davico di Regulai whom my eyes perceive?"

I sketched a bow.

"Ai, Davico!" Dumont smiled. "We wondered about you!"

"Wondered? Ci!" Benetto said. "We thought you lost to Urula's tempest, sunk perhaps to the bottom the Cerulea and drowned. Or else eaten by a stone bear in the deep Romiglia. Or perhaps kidnapped for ransom by those dirt-drinking Borraghese. For how else could he become so scarce to us, his closest friends? I myself told Dumont you would never abandon us, and so you must have been lost to some great calamity far beyond your control."

"If a calamity is called Siana Ashia, then you have the right of it," Piero said as he climbed in through the window, pushing Benetto aside to make a seat. "Our boy barely escaped with his life."

Dumont made room for Giovanni to climb in through the window and join Piero on the opposite bench. "Everyone says that you will no longer study with us," Benetto said. "I did not credit them."

"It's true," Cierco said, clapping an arm around my shoulders. "Give him another month and our young Davico will have his name, and then his marriage, and then Banca Regulai, and then he will have no moment for we vermin vianomae."

"That's not true," I protested.

"You, my friend, are smoking hazesap," Cierco said. "If it's this bad now, imagine how it will go once you sit beside your father at the plank." He forced himself in through the window to much grumbling and jostling. "Ai! Make some room, you fescatolo pigfuckers. More are on the way."

"Why should I make room? It was I who seized the table," Benetto groused, but still he shifted himself and Cierco squeezed in despite dark looks from students farther down the bench.

I would have followed my friends in through the window, but with Lazy and Polonos along, it was impossible. Too, Siana Grassa was watching me from the door of the taverna, frowning. She didn't like dogs, not even good dogs like Lazy, so there was no chance of smuggling her in.

I told Lazy to sit outside the window and wait for me, and then, under Siana Grassa's formidable gaze, I retrieved a bowl of good pickled pork paquapezzo for Lazy to eat, and a bowl of water. Though Siana Grassa was clearly annoyed that I fed Lazy with food meant for students, I like to think that there was at least a glimmer of approval for my loyalty.

Lazy taken care of, Polonos and I joined the rest of my friends via the more traditional entrance. Today, thanks to the early arrival of Benetto and Dumont, we had control of the critical end of our table, against wall and window, with a good breeze, and so now we set up a defense against other students intruding upon our territory, taking full advantage of the scarred visage of Polonos, who sat with his back to the table and his legs kicked out as he casually cleaned his nails with the tip of a dagger.

Over time, more and more students crowded in as lectures were released and more and more of our friends arrived and slowly our merry band took territory like the Schipians had once taken the Peninsula of Becchame, slowly taking it piece by piece, crowding and crowding until others gave way and we were all well-wedged at the table, with heavy pottery carafes of Siana Grassa's watered wine and good crusty bread and bowls of paquapezzo pickled and cool. As more people joined we started more games of cartalegge, with others observing and encouraging various tactics, and sometimes outright cheating.

A while later, Celia appeared at the window, along with her friend Niccoletta. "I saw Lazy outside, and knew you would be here. Ashia won't be happy. She's looking for you."

"How would you know?" I retorted. "You've been gone all day."

"I had errands."

She said it breezily, and I would have believed her if I had not seen her sneaking through the streets of Navola. "Errands? Is that what you call it?" I tried to keep my voice light, but she gave me a strange look, and I knew that I had failed to hide my irritation.

"Why so offended, Davico? I have tasks, just as you. Shopping for chocolates and carrying messages for weavers, and instructions for cooks—Ashia nearly makes me work as her maidservant these days. So many tasks, this way and that, and all for the sake of you and your celebrations."

"So that was where you went?"

I searched her face, seeking some hint of dissembling, and was discomfited to find none. No guilt or shame at her lies. No embarrassment that she kept secrets. By the fatas, Celia had the skill of faccioscuro. It bothered me greatly to see how clever she was with her face. I changed tacks.

"You were supposed to be with me," I said. "To fend off Ashia."

"Ci." She clicked her tongue the way Ashia did and pretended to pity me. "Poor Davico, his father's concubine has been hard on him." She pinched my cheek. "Poor little boy. Pricked by tailors' needles and made to stand still. Poor sad boy. Poverito siolito."

"I was pricked, in truth." I pushed her hand away, irritated. "Several times. And all with Ashia clicking her tongue that way, and looking me over like a cut of beef."

Niccoletta, Celia's friend, laughed at that. "You should be grateful, Davico. The sfacciana has a good eye. Half of Navola follows her tastes, and"—she looked me over—"it's not as if you couldn't use the help."

"Davico gets dressed in the dark, picking blind," Giovanni said, not looking up from his cards. "He can't be blamed for making choices without his eyes."

"That does explain much," Niccoletta agreed.

"My clothes are fine." I elbowed Giovanni but my attention was on Celia. "So where were you?" I pressed.

"Ai, Davico, you are tiresome." She waved a hand airily. "I was here and there, thither and yon, and none of it is your business. Now move over." She gathered her skirts and clambered in through the window, wedging in beside me, followed by Niccoletta. "Deal us in."

And so the girls took hands of cards and the game became more chaotic, just as it was meant to be, with many gambits and shifting alliances as we all vied to make our hands and rob others of theirs, and if

I allowed myself, I could forget for a time that Celia kept secrets from me, and that she had a hidden life that none of the others at the table knew of, either.

The version of cartalegge we played had a great deal of cross-talk and double-talk, and Dumont, who was from far north Cheroux and whose father was one of that king's ambassadors, complained about the game.

"It doesn't make sense!" he groused.

"It makes sense to us."

"That's because you're Navolese. 'Twisty twisty twisty,' my father says."

"Twisty twisty twisty," Celia agreed amiably. She played Urula the ocean and wiped the cards Dumont held in his hand. "Ci ci ci. Bad fortune, there. Malafortuna all the way around."

"She's building the twin castles," Tono said. "She picked up the bridge."

"I did not. That was last round." Celia gestured with two fingers from her eye, sending him Scuro's luck. Tono stuck out his tongue.

I picked up the castello. "Well, then you won't mind if I take this."

Celia pouted. "And you call yourself my brother."

And so it went, round after round. Dumont gave up in despair and, in an act of singular self-immolation, went to sit with Celia.

"You play ciessa, in Cheroux," Celia said as she picked up a blind card.

"Chess," Dumont corrected.

"That's what I said."

"All right then. Yes, we play ciessa. It is a game of true skill and knowledge. Not like this madness of cards."

"We play ciessa here as well," Piero said.

"Really? I've never seen it here."

"Well, it's a child's game."

Dumont gave us a look of horror. "It is an honored game of deep skill and subtlety! Not a child's game!"

"I suppose it's interesting, if all you care about is the board," Celia said. "But it's all on the table. Sul tavolo."

Niccoletta was nodding. She picked up three crossed swords and threw down a red castello that Tono snatched up.

"He wants all the castelli," Niccoletta said. "But where is that black castello that he wants?" She held up her hand, taunting, her eyes bright with pleasure. "Where could the black castle be?"

"Why would you tell him?" Dumont asked.

"Why would I not?"

"She could be lying," I said.

"Is she?"

"That's the fun," Niccoletta said. "Is she, isn't she, will she, won't she? Where did the black castle go?"

"For us," Celia said, "we like a game where the challenge is not what's on the board. The board is not interesting. It's too obvious. Too simple. It's not a game for Navolese."

"But I do actually like chess," I said. "I've always liked it."

"That's because you are as simple as a child, Davico."

"And you are as kind as a cauri bird upon a dead rat."

"I'm the one with the black castello," Celia said. "Niccoletta is a liar."

"No. You're the liar," Niccoletta said.

"Actually, it's mine," Piero said, flicking one of his cards.

"That's your sword knight," Celia said. "I saw you pick it up."

"I shuffled my hand."

"You did not."

He gave her two fingers, sending Scuro back at her. "Just because you missed it does not mean it didn't happen."

Dumont interceded. "But if the game is not a challenge of skill, what is there? If not two minds vying for triumph through careful thought and subtle action, what fair and true contest is there? If it's all luck and lies, what contest is that?"

"When two men draw blades, is it a fair contest?" asked Piero, who brought almost everything back to swordplay.

"It is a fair test of each one's skill, yes."

"Ci. You are daft. It is the skill, plus the trickery, plus the strength of one, and the friends of the other, and whether the one was drunk the night before, and whether the other got him drunk and so his skill is already broken. It is not simply a measure of each one's skill."

"Those could apply to chess as well."

"What he's saying is that every move in chess is a known move. Everything that must be interpreted and prepared for is on the board," Celia said. "As I said before. Sul tavolo. Life is not like this. Life is not all laid out before you, with all the legal moves agreed upon, and not a single other move allowed."

"Sul tavolo," everyone else agreed. "Not interesting. *Troppo semplice. Basico. Per gli bambini.* For little babies."

"In your game of chess," Piero went on, "you cannot blind a man with the flash of sun on your blade, nor can you trick him with a false stumble, nor throw sand in his eyes—"

"Those are all part of the skill of combat," Dumont interrupted.

"Nor can you be stuck in the back by one who you thought a friend," Celia said as she played the red assassin card and I lost the king of my cups.

"I thought we were working together," I protested.

"You did," Celia agreed amiably. She winked at Dumont. "You see, every play in your ciessa is known. There are no mysteries. But in Navola, as in life, there are many mysteries. There are things that will affect your life that you will never see. There are alliances you may never know of, there are cards you may not have expected existed, for the seventy-seven of the deck can be altered with the shrouded cards. There are plots and plans, and, above all, there is the player, sitting before you, and he or she will tell you many things, if you read them. If you watch them closely." She gestured around, pointing at each of us in turn. "If you see the players clearly, you may know their cards without ever seeing the suit or count, for the face of the player reflects all."

Dumont made a curse of disgust in his own language. "You and your Navolese obsession with facciochiaro and faccioscuro. Clear-faced this, hidden-face that. It's a sickness with you, everyone hiding your feelings and thoughts, and calling that a virtue. Twisty twisty twisty."

"Sfai, Dumont! It is not an obsession, it is life! How do you read the people around your own table? How does your father read the merchants and princes and kings he treats with? What are the plots? What are the plans? There is much to read. But in your game there is nothing to read. In your *chessss* . . . you play the pieces and the board." Celia smiled and her teeth flashed mischievous. "In *chessss,* you play the table. In cartalegge, you play the people *around* the table."

And with that she lay down the black castello, along with king, queen, assassin, and horse.

We all threw down our own cards in disgust.

Chapter 16

"You really are terrible at cartalegge," Celia said as we walked home late that night, trailed a short distance behind by Polonos and Lazy.

Our footsteps echoed on the marble of the long portico gallery where we walked. Overhead, the arches that covered our colonnaded walk glimmered, mirrors and polished copper and glass reflecting oil lamps, making the walking path bright and light and the cobbled street that we paralleled, low and dark. Merchants in the gallery were gathering the last of their wares into their shop fronts, or else loading them into carts to take back to their more distant homes.

"Thank you, sister. You are a veritable fountain of kindness."

"For a Regulai," she amended. "You'd be passable otherwise. If you were mere vianoma, say, you'd be fine."

"Maybe it's that I don't like to lie," I said, trying to prick her conscience.

"It's not a lie. It's a game. A game of faces. You should practice it. Your role demands it."

I glanced over at her, wondering if she was trying to hint at something, to admit that she had lied to me this very day, but I saw nothing in her demeanor except admonishment. I could not read her face. I wondered if I had ever been able to do so. I wanted to confront her, then and there, but I worried that if I pressed her, it would lead to accusations, and then to harsh words and then . . . Well, sometimes words can cut as deep as swords. I had seen it happen between friends. At one time, Piero and Cierco had been very close, and then one day they had had a quarrel and after that they were still brothers but they were no longer quite so close. I could not be certain that our words would not become sharp. "I don't like these games of faces," I said.

"And you say you're Navolese."

"Maybe I'm not. If it were up to me, I would not take up this duty."

Celia laughed. "Ci. What would you be then?"

"I don't know. Maybe I'd drink wine and sing songs with my friends."

"Of course. And play cards all day. How would you pay for such a habit?"

"Well, if I had simple needs, I think could work the abacus as a numerari. Or maybe work in the Callendra for some third secretary of the treasury."

"Sfai, Davico. Do not set your eye so low," Celia teased. "You should aspire at least to serving a second secretary."

"Really, if I had a choice, I would apprentice with Dellacavallo."

"The physician?" Celia's brows knitted. "You would be a physician?"

"Why not?" As I said it, I liked the idea more. "Dellacavallo said that I have the knack. I have a skill for herbs and balms, and finding necessary remedies, and I have a sense for sicknesses."

"You know what ails Stub, or Lazy, and think this makes you a healer."

"There is no play of faccioscuro in the faces of the sick," I said.

"You only say these things because you doubt you can match your father. That is what this is about."

I barked a bitter laugh. Her works had struck cleanly. "You know me too well." Despair welled up. I swallowed, fighting to keep my emotions bottled, my voice steady. "You read too well, sister."

Her expression turned gentle. "Well, I read *you,* at least."

"I think you see into the very center of my soul."

As I said the words, I knew that they were true, and I wondered how it could be that Celia could see me so clearly, when she herself was so full of secrets. How could she know me inside and out, and I know next to nothing of her?

"I think . . ." I swallowed, trying to keep my emotions in check. "I think I am not well suited to this life."

"What is the cause of this worry, Davico? All this sadness because you struggle at a game of cards?"

"If a man cannot play cartalegge, is he Navolese at all? Isn't that the saying?"

She laughed. "They also say that if you don't have a favorite vine and a favorite wine you are not Navolese. It's a small thing. Nai, it is smaller than small. Picomito. Picotissimo. Pico—"

"Enough. *Basti.*"

"It's a failure of your teachers, is all." She waved her hand, dismissing. "If I were your teacher you would already be a master at cartalegge. *Un maestro di faccioscuro.*"

"Cazzetta has given up. You think yourself better than him?"

"Cazzetta? Ci. I am twice the deceiver that Cazzetta is," she said loftily.

I could not help but be troubled by her words, her pride at secrets. "You think yourself skilled in this?"

"Better than Cazzetta. He is but a man. Faccioscuro is the weapon of the woman. The sharpest weapon a woman can wield. *A man will never know her heart, for her face will always reflect himself, like a pleasing mirror.*"

I recognized the line. "That's Lisana di Monetti. From one of her poems."

"'The Pool of Forest,'" Celia acknowledged, and then recited:

"A woman's face must be a mirror,
must never show her soul,
for her man would fear her,
should he ever know her truth.
He would call her
Demona, Fata,
though she only desired love,
he would cut her heart from her breast,
for the crime of being true."

"You don't believe that," I said.

She shrugged. "I know that men like to see themselves more than they like to see their women's truths."

"I'm not like that," I said.

"No. Of course you aren't."

I stopped short. "Ai! You're doing it to me now. You're saying what I want to hear."

"I'm not—"

"You are! I see you. Don't think I don't see you. You say one thing but you mean another! You are Sia Lisana's acolyte! Today you snuck off, and left me to Ashia and her tailor, and without any explanation—"

"Leave some secrets for your sister. I must have my womanly secrets." She made it sound girlish, teasing and coquettish, but after seeing her disappear into the pleasure gardens of Sia Allezzia, I saw it more darkly. I did not know her at all, I realized. Where did she learn such a teasing tone? Such a playful batting of the eyes? Such a manipulation of my feelings, such that if I had not been on guard, I would have been distracted, her teasing would have tricked me away and led me astray, much as the fatas of the wood led the angry husband when he sought out Caliba for revenge. She sought to trick and inveigle, even now.

"I saw you," I said abruptly.

That brought her up short. "What did you see, Davico?"

The words were out now, I would not take them back. "I saw you sneaking through the streets. I saw you go to Sia Allezzia di Violettanotte's gates. I saw you enter there."

Celia laughed. "You saw me enter. Ci." She waved a hand, dismissing me. "You saw nothing, then." She turned to start walking again, but I caught her wrist.

"I saw you enter the door of a courtesan. And when I asked you where you went, you lied. And when I asked again, you tricked. If I had not seen the truth of it, I would not have known your words for falsehoods, or your face for a mask."

"It is nothing. I lied because it was not a thing for you to know." She tried to pull away again, but I dragged her back to face me.

"You put the Regulai name in the dirt."

"Your sister can no more put your name in the dirt than you can."

"You are not my sister in this. You make yourself a toy for men."

"Ai? Mi veri dichi?" Her dark eyes flashed with anger. "We are not brother and sister now that I embarrass you? One minute I am di Regulai, but now I am nothing but di Balcosi? Sfai, Davico. So quick to adopt, so quick to discard. All because you are embarrassed."

"Embarrassed?" I stared at her, shocked. "That is too small a word. What will people say of my father that you became a concubine while he guarded your name's honor beneath his roof?"

"They will say nothing, because they know nothing."

"Then how will you explain to my father? To Ashia? How will you explain to them that you have become a whore?"

"A whore?" Celia's lips twisted and she gave me a pitying look. "Ai, Davico. I will tell them nothing, for they already know."

I stared at her. To say that I was stunned is to say that the cow slaughtered by the butcher's hammer is stunned. I had a sudden feeling of the city tilting beneath my feet. Nothing was solid anymore. "They . . . know?"

A tight smile played across Celia's lips. "Sometimes Ashia herself takes me. Oh. Does that bother you, Davico?"

"*Ashia* takes you there?"

"Often." Celia flipped her hair. "She prefers to accompany me."

I couldn't find words. I simply stared, mouth open like a gapefish, dying on the muddy banks of the river. Celia watched me, amused, smirking, and in her dark eyes I saw knowledge swirling, eyes that seemed to tell me that I was a child, and she was a woman, and that I knew nothing of the world.

"Well? What do you think of that, Davico? Can you imagine it?" She ran her tongue along her lip, teasing. "You've seen Adivo's sketches in your father's library, so you must be able to imagine. Think of it. Me. Ashia. Sia Allezzia. Three women, drunk with wine, our limbs entangled, men watching. Think of it. Bodices unlaced, breasts heaving, skirts raised, fingers questing beneath . . ." She moaned. "Oh . . . oh . . . oh . . . Sia Allezzia is so skilled, her tongue, her kisses on my thighs—"

She broke off, laughing at my shock.

"Ai! Davico!" She pinched my cheek. "You linger over Adivo's sketches with your tongue hanging out like a dog's, and yet you have so many judgments when it comes to real women."

"That is truly . . . what you—?"

"Isn't that what you imagine?" Celia's eyes sparkled, but then she relented. "*Matra di Amo,* Davico. Your face . . . I can't bear to torture you more. Why do you think such things? Why is your mind so full of such thoughts?"

"Because I saw you!"

"Ci. You saw me. You saw me enter the lusty demesne of Lady Allezzia, and when I entered, I stepped into the realm of your fevered boy dreams where you yank your root every night until it falls off."

I could see that she was playing with me now, but I couldn't stop myself from blushing. "Please, Celia. I don't understand."

"What if I said it's not your right to know? That it's not your right to ask? If you have so many judgments, ask Ashia. Or ask your father. He's the one who sent me."

"My father?" I was dumbfounded. "He trains you as a courtesan?"

"Sfai, Davico!" She smacked the side of my head, but kindly. "That mind of yours! If I say it is not your affair what I do with my time, then why would you press?"

I didn't know what to say. I was confused and ashamed, for I could not see Celia as a courtesan, nor could I see my father sending her to such a profession. Celia was my sister, my friend . . . she was more than I could put simple words to.

Celia's expression softened. "Ai, Davico," she sighed. "You are such a boy still. Everything for you is good or bad, right or wrong, simple and clear. You are Navolese and yet you wish the world were clear as glass when in fact it is all mud and confusion. And so here you stand, wanting everything simple, as clear as Amo's light. For you, there is only a sparkling mountain stream, or a sewer drain. You think now that I have no virtue, that I am a whore, and that your father prepares me as such."

"Nai—"

"Nai, Davico." She held up her hand to silence me. "You have judgment of me. I will tell you that Sia Allezzia is a good woman, regardless of her profession, or perhaps because of it. She is who she is, and I respect her greatly. As does Ashia. As does your father. Whatever she is in your or your friends' fevered imaginations, she is more than that, more than you imagine. And not despite her life, but because of it."

"I don't understand."

"Allezzia understands the world of men," Celia said. "She understands the minds of men. She bends seven men to her will, and they follow happily."

"I thought it was four."

"It is seven. One for each day of the week." She laughed at my shock. "Listen to me carefully, Davico. Ashia takes me to Sia Allezzia because Allezzia is wise in the realms where men and women intersect. She is wise to the ways of men and power and she shares her knowledge graciously. You and I, we live in the same world, Davico, but we walk very different paths through it."

"Do you . . ."

"Ai! Davico! Always with the sex!"

I hung my head.

"Nai, Davico. The arts of love are not what Sia Allezzia teaches. It is the art of companionship. It is a different thing, though much related. I was not playing when I said that faccioscuro is a woman's weapon, far more than a man's, for often it is the only weapon a woman is allowed. So, I learn to read banked emotion and repressed feeling and hidden hurt and black intention. I learn the things a woman must know in order to survive in a world of men, and Allezzia knows much. It is not for sex that your father sends me to her, but for protection and defense, for he would have me know the depths and darknesses of men, and would not have me go forth into this world defenseless against them.

"I go to speak with many women now, and all of them teach me that which I must know, because it is not enough for me to know how to poison as Cazzetta does, or wield a blade like Aghan Khan. I must know the paths that my sex have walked, and know the traps that they have avoided. We are both of Navola, Davico, but men and women walk different streets, even when we walk together, holding hands. Your father knows that. Ashia knows that. Allezzia knows that. So put away your suspicions and your fears and be assured that your father and Ashia care for me, perhaps as much as they care for you. And so they ensure that I am prepared for the paths that I must walk."

I felt ashamed again for doubting her. "I'm sorry. I should not have imagined . . . should not have thought—" I broke off in a turmoil, and Celia laughed at that, too.

"Ai, Davico. Do not make me some pure maid, either. Let me be myself, only. Nothing more, nothing less. From you, I would have you know me as I am, and hope that I will always know you, as well. We are as we are to each other."

She took me by the arm, pulled me close, and laid her head upon my shoulder.

"Let us simply be ourselves," she said, and I felt at last that our friendship was renewed.

The Myth of Erostheia

—AS TOLD BY A MINSTREL IN PARDI, AND OVERHEARD BY MANY

This is a story from the days before the great empires, before Sienelleus was king of Baz. Before the wide blue Cerulea touched Zurom and Chat. Before the great city of Aenezzium fell. This was a time when gods often walked the land, and man and animal were equal. This is a tale from before Amo came to power.

In that time, Erostheia was a name well known. It was sung atop the tallest mountains, and murmured in the deepest valleys. It was whispered upon the farthest shores, for Erostheia was known for her beauty, and she was known in all the lands where people know the music of language.

But though Erostheia's name was known, she lived far away from man, deep in the hidden forests of that place we now call the deep Romiglia, for beauty is both a blessing and a curse, and any who saw Erostheia were filled with a terrible longing and desire. Men hungered to lay their hands upon her body and sought to force apart her thighs. Women longed to lie beside her, to kiss her lips, and then to jealously steal her skin as their own. And so Erostheia fled her home and lived far from people, amongst solemn towering trees, clear cool streams, with only the company of birds and beasts. There, in that wild land, the language of man was not spoken, and so she was not coveted.

And yet still she was remembered. People who had seen her spoke of her beauty with awe. Poets composed epics. Sailors sang songs. Women compared themselves to the very idea of her. Even as her presence dwindled, her memory grew, for that is the way of people.

They make up stories about that which they have not seen.

As for Erostheia, she lived free in the mountain valleys. She sheltered from sun beneath the green dappled canopy of swaying whitebark. She ate of the fruits and nuts of the forest, and bathed in the streams that tumbled pure and laughing from the high snows of the mountains. She was sung to by the birds, and warned of danger by those tiny deer, famous in the Romiglia, who pricked their ears and sniffed the air on her behalf. When men ventured near, shadow cats and mist wolves pursued them until they fled, and each night, Erostheia slept safe, cradled in the warm company of stone bears.

But one day, as Erostheia bathed in a splashing stream pool, Scuro, who was much about the world in those days, caught sight of her. He was returning to his Realm of the Unseen, and the pool she had chosen was close to a sulfurous cave that gave entrance to his realm.

When he saw her bathing, he hid himself in the cave and spied upon her from the shadows, and when she climbed from the waters and the sun kissed her skin, he found himself in awe—Erostheia, beauteous and at ease, was more lovely than any woman in the world for she was free of men's gazes, and thought her nakedness for herself alone.

As Scuro gazed upon Erostheia's unselfconscious beauty, Scuro became ashamed, for he saw that he stole beauty that was not given, and so he went away, reproaching himself.

But Scuro could not keep the memory of Erostheia from his mind, and so he returned, first once, then again and again, to watch her bathe. To let his eyes taste a beauty that could never be his, for he was ugly, and all men quailed when they looked upon him. This was why his realm was darkness.

But at last, besotted, he called to her. She was much frightened at his voice from the cave shadows, and sought to cover herself and flee, and he was sad to see her fear, and hurried to assure her that he meant no harm, and was not as men, but was something else, something that lived all around, like a fata in a lake, or the fish in their streams or the deer in the forest. Just so, he was a creature of caves.

Which was true, but was also less than true.

But Erostheia was comforted, and curious, and perhaps even lonely for the music of language, and so she came to the edge of the cave where Scuro hid in shadow, and there they spoke with one another, and enjoyed each other's company.

Thereafter, Scuro would often climb up from his Unseen Realm and converse with Erostheia in that cave where light and shadow met. They talked for many days and many nights. He gave her opals from the darkness of his underworld, and he gave her the finger bones of kings. When the sun fell behind the mountains, and the stars were kind enough to hide their faces behind cloud, he would even come out and sit near her, and marvel at how close their hands might lie upon the grass, without ever touching.

But never did he reveal himself to her, for he was ugly.

In shadow though, his appearance did not matter. He could tell her jokes that made her laugh. He could spin epic tales of lands far away. He could tell her the hidden secret stories of the gods. He told her that he was a prince of his realm, which was true, but he did not speak of the creatures that he lorded over.

But at last, driven foolish with longing, Scuro desired to let Erostheia see himself, in his true form. But he did not know how to do so, and was shy and frightened, so he called upon his brother Amo for aid, for Amo walked always in light, and knew the ways of the people who had fallen from Virga's weave. If anyone could help, it would be Amo, with his great knowledge of humankind, whose affairs he often meddled in.

Amo teased Scuro for his shyness, but agreed to help him press his suit for he was pleased to be of aid, and flattered that Scuro bowed to his knowledge. But when Amo laid eyes upon Erostheia he became desirous of her, and decided that he would have her for himself. And so he led Scuro from his cave and into the bright light, telling him that the only path to a woman's heart was unadorned truth, and so he brought Scuro before Erostheia and, as Amo had known, she was much appalled and frightened and disgusted at the sight of Scuro, and she was much enamored of Amo, who was made of light and radiance, and whose form was ever-pleasing.

She rejected Scuro.

Amo, in turn, made his own desire known, and so Erostheia lay with Amo. They had the children Elo and Ela, who walked amongst men and gods alike.

But Scuro, being Scuro, was not finished.

Scuro never lost his affection for Erostheia. He still brought her gifts from the darkness. When she asked for stars, he came with a net full of them. When she asked to see a flower she had never seen, he quested for the raven orchid, which only blooms under the shine of the moon in the desert of Zurom, and then only if the rain has fallen, which only happens once in a hundred years.

All of this Erostheia smiled upon, but never would she lie with

Scuro, for Scuro stank of smoke and charnel, and his voice, even when he crooned, was the sound of skulls crushing. His breath was of carrion and his cries were those of vultures, and his teeth were all taken from graves. Where Amo stood tall and clean and powerful, with matching limbs and rippling muscle, Scuro stood with the leg of a goat, and one of a crow, and his body was covered with matted hair, like the tangled pelts of the bears that had fallen asleep in his caves and never woken, and from which Scuro had himself been fashioned.

Scuro was a horror. But still he loved Erostheia.

Now, Amo was much amused by his brother's attempts at seduction. Amo enjoyed that where he strode straight, upright, and proud, Scuro hopped and scuttled sideways, hunched. Amo liked this comparison, and many more, and so he kept Scuro close. He laughed at Scuro's clumsy desire for Erostheia. He enjoyed watching Scuro lay his gifts at Erostheia's feet, and enjoyed how she spurned him anyway. But eventually he tired of Scuro's obsessions and so one night he called to his brother to watch him as he lay with Erostheia, as she ministered to his lusts.

"See her wondrous flesh?" Amo teased. "See how she clutches me, hungry for mine own body? See how I touch her? See how she sighs? See how she arches and spreads her thighs? She gives herself to me. See her pleasure and her desire?" he taunted.

"Why did you think you were meant for her? No woman could love such a creature as Scuro. No woman desires the slash of fangs upon her lips, nor the scratch of claws upon her breasts. No woman hungers for the roughness of scales when a man thrusts, and no woman desires the stink of dead bears and carrion breath when she lies down for love. Go back to your caves, brother. Be content with the Unseen Realm. The light is not for you."

And so Scuro went away, much saddened, for Amo spoke truth.

But too, Scuro being Scuro, he was not finished. He did not return to his caves. Instead, he traveled. He sailed distant seas, he lived for a time in Atalat and in Hephaestos, he crossed deserts larger even than those of Zurom. He scaled mountains higher than the peaks of the Cielofrigo, he rode upon cloud chariots alongside the wizards of Xim. Across the many lands he traveled he met many kinds of men, but wherever he went under the light of Amo, woman or man alike, none looked upon him with desire.

But Scuro being Scuro, he was not defeated. Scuro made a disguise and went to see the blind oracle Plythias, and begged him for help, but Plythias recognized him in an instant, and said that Scuro would never see himself reflected beautiful in the eyes of others until all were blind, and even then they would know him as Scuro, and so they would not love him.

"Go back to your caves." This was what Plythias advised. "Be content with the Unseen Realm."

But Scuro being Scuro, he was not content. Still, he was tired of the fear and disgust he conjured in the eyes of Amo's creatures, and so he fled the lands of men.

I will live in the forests, Scuro thought. *The beasts do not recoil from my smell. The trees do not stare down upon me with disgust. The streams do not recoil to touch my flesh. I will go to the wilds.*

And so he did, and lived alone. (It is said that while he was in the wilds, he showed Soppros how to walk without stumbling in darkness, and advised the warrior Ishebe on how to defeat the Hydra of Tyros, but that is another story.) But no matter how long he sought to distract himself, he never could forget Erostheia. She lingered with him always, a fata of memory. Again and again, he turned and reached for her, and caught nothing but air. She visited him in dreams. She kissed his fangs and embraced his scales and in passion, she pulled aside his rough garments and straddled upon his serpent cock. In his dreams, she did not recoil from his hideousness. She loved him as she had loved Amo.

But always he woke, and always he was alone.

At last, in a torment, Scuro determined to die. He would throw himself from a high cliff, and be shattered on the stones below, and thereby rid himself of fancies and dreams, and finally escape Erostheia's memory.

Now, if Scuro had simply gone and drowned himself in one of his dark cave pools, none would have known except the cave crickets and gray spiders and bats and rats and spores and mushrooms of his realm, and they would have all fed happily upon his body.

But instead he stood atop the highest cliff, over the deepest chasm, preparing himself to plunge and die, and it was thus that Caliba came upon him.

"What's this?" called Caliba. "What are you doing up there, Scuro?"

"Do not look upon me!" Scuro shouted down. "I am hideous and now I will die!"

He made to leap—and would have leapt—except that Caliba began to laugh at him.

Caliba laughed, and clutched his belly, and he pointed at Scuro, and gasped to speak but could not, and so he laughed some more. He guffawed and gasped, and wiped tears from his eyes, and still he laughed.

Scuro was much annoyed.

"My heart is broken, and you laugh?"

Caliba rolled his eyes. "Ci. You have a heart of stone, then, that it shatters so easily."

"I have a heart with blood and life," Scuro said, "and it curdles with shame at my hideousness."

"A curdled heart does sound unpleasant," Caliba admitted. "But tell me, brother, why do you think yourself hideous?"

"I am scaled."

"Dragons are scaled, and all bow before them."

"I am horned."

"The mountain ram is horned, and he is grand."

"I have fur."

"Rabbits have fur and they are soft and loved."

Finally Scuro said, "I look nothing like Amo."

"Amo!" Caliba exclaimed. "Is this about that bedpisser? Amo is a prick! He is the spremi I wipe on the grass! He is the shit that clings to the cat's anus!" (I am paraphrasing, here, but you must give a poet some license. And in any case, Caliba had even more to say, but it is too rude even for me to relate, at least near the catredanto.) "Why," Caliba said, "Amo would steal a fig and tell you that you had eaten it. He walks in light, but his heart is small and withered like a prune. Now come down from there, brother. Quit this foolishness."

"But I am sad."

"Then I will entertain you. Come down and let us enjoy ourselves. This is not a problem of your appearance, this is a problem of the ugly company you keep."

"It won't work."

"Up the ass, then! What do you care, anyway? If I'm wrong, you can dash yourself on the rocks tomorrow, and you will have lost nothing.

Today or tomorrow, the rocks do not care when your thick skull cracks upon them. It's not as if this is some special appointment as far as the rocks are concerned. The cliff, too, will be here tomorrow. So come with me tonight, and let me entertain you. You can always smash your brains tomorrow."

Eventually Caliba coaxed Scuro down from the cliff, and he set a feast for him beside a stream where the water slowed and became deep turquoise pools and was warmed by the sun. And then Caliba's fatas came. There were wood fatas and stone fatas and water fatas. They emerged from the boles of trees and the cracks of boulders and from the deep slow pools of the stream. There were crop fatas from fields, and wine fatas from the vineyard, and they all set a grand table. They drank wine and laughed and sang, and the fatas stroked Scuro's tangled beard and curled happily into the shelter of his arms. They did not fear his serpent cock, but kissed it and teased it, and they ran their hands all across his furred body, and praised his great strength, and soon the wine was spilled and the table overturned, and there was much running through the forest and splashing in the pools, and many sighs and murmurs after.

"Why would you want a mortal woman?" Caliba asked when they were sated, and all lay in a stupor of spilled spremi and splashed wine. "We are gods, not men. Why trifle with those fools who have fallen from Virga's net?"

"You have not seen her," Scuro said.

"But do you not love Chira?"

Chira looked up at Scuro with her wide eyes, and pressed her naked green flesh against him. "Do you not like me, Scuro?" she asked, and arched, offering her green breasts with nipples as hard and bright as early grapes, but sweeter.

"If you saw her, you would understand," Scuro said. But he did not reject Chira's offering, either.

"Nothing good comes when gods mix with men," Caliba grumbled.

But Caliba had never liked Amo very much, for Amo was always after him to obey Amo's rules and to bow to Amo's edicts, and all of this amounted to tonguing Amo's asshole as far as Caliba was concerned, so Caliba decided to go and see if he could see what Scuro saw.

He disguised himself as a dog and went to see Erostheia for himself.

Now, Caliba very much enjoyed that Erostheia cooed over him and stroked his ears, and scratched under his chin, and he was especially pleased that when he rolled to his back, panting, tongue lolling, and belly offered, she rubbed and patted him most vigorously, at least until his canine prick poked out, redly impertinent, impolite, and uninvited. And Caliba being Caliba, he especially liked how Erostheia blushed when she saw his vile offering, and then quickly looked away.

But still, she was only human.

"Well," he announced when he returned. "I would not throw myself from a cliff for Erostheia."

But still, Amo was besotted, and Scuro was a friend, so Caliba came up with a plan to draw away Erostheia.

He returned to her as a dog and he spoke to her. He told her that while he might be a rude dog with an impertinent prick, still, he was a dog, and dogs knew something of the meaning of loyalty, and Amo was not loyal to her.

She did not believe him, so Caliba lit a fire and showed to her in the fire and shadow light how Amo had exposed her to Scuro when they had made love. He showed how Amo had told Scuro to look upon the lushness of her nakedness, and showed her how Amo had encouraged Scuro to watch closely as she arched and cried with lust. And then Caliba showed how Amo had exposed every detail of how she pleasured Amo, how she had stroked him, kissed him, worshipped his loins, and in this Caliba went into every detail, sharing intimacy after intimacy, pressing the thorn deep, until Erostheia was red with anger, for her love was a precious thing, privately given to Amo alone.

Angry, she left Amo and his palace of light, and Caliba followed. And Amo chased them. Amo ordered Urulo to make storms with terrifying lighting, to kick dust and sand in Erostheia's face to slow her, to raise seas so that she could not sail, and to make trees fall to block her path, for he was angry at her departure.

But Caliba came to her aid and called upon the fatas of the desert to shield her face from the sand, and the fatas of the water to bargain with Urula to defy her brother's winds and quell the waves, and the fatas of the woodlands to guide her safe through the cracking raging forests, and so she reached the wild Romiglia once more and was safe, and Amo was forced to come begging, beseeching her to return, and there, Scuro barred his path, and there they quarreled until she came upon them.

"I gave love where I thought I was loved in turn," she said to Amo. "But I was not loved. I was as a prize, and I was used. I will look upon your light no more, for you are ugly within."

And then she turned to Scuro. "Though you love me, I am not for you," she said. "But at least you have never insulted me."

To both of them she said, "I will not be part of your brotherly fight."

And then she turned herself into the moon.

So now it is that Amo, of the light, can never see her beauty truly. He pursues her all across the sky, and always she is ahead of him, for Caliba aids her still, and even when Amo does catch sight of her, and sun and moon both cross the sky together, it is only the palest memory of her beauty that Amo sees. But Scuro, Scuro sometimes sees her still. When shadows stretch and darkness falls, he sometimes scuttles from his Unseen Realm to gaze upon the sky. And on occasion, when she chooses, and only then, Erostheia rises high and bright above him and shares her beauty for a while.

And here my story ends.

Except.

Except, perhaps, a coda.

It is sometimes whispered—and I believe these rumors, for I have known the players in this sorrowful comedy, and this has the ring of truth. It is sometimes whispered that what neither Amo nor Scuro know is that Caliba (that sly but loyal dog) sometimes visits Erostheia in the sky.

And there he makes her laugh.

They talk often through the night, and she looks forward to these visits, for they love each other's company and at these times she is as free with her beauty as if she were alone beside a forest stream, and she feels as safe and happy as if she were protected once more by stone bears, but with a difference, for now she has true companionship, for Caliba desires only fatas.

Erostheia likes this very much.

Chapter 17

"And so," the merchant Melonos Pakas concluded, "the trade in porcelain from Pagnanopol is much increased. I would like to import Navolese wine—"

"On credit," Merio murmured.

"—and return with porcelain that can be sold at double the rate."

The occasion of my Assumption was one of celebration, but it was also—in Navolese style—an excuse for business. In the weeks that preceded my event, a steady stream of partners and debtors and trade delegations had made pilgrimages to our palazzo, loudly and publicly offering gifts of goodwill, then privately and quietly begging favors of money and trade.

Pakas was looking expectantly at my father, but my father only dipped his head toward me, indicating that whatever favors we might bestow would come from my hand. We two now sat together, side by side, father and son, as men came to sit parlobanco before us. The sweet tea and bitter cheeses of our trade littered the desk, and the crumbs littered Pakas's shirt. He was a short man with a thin mustache that quivered like a mouse's whiskers, and he leaned forward eagerly, as if he were already enjoying the profits of his venture.

At my father's indication he focused all his attention upon me. "What say you, young Davico?"

"Eight hundred navisoli," I said, "is not a small sum."

"Two thousand in your hand when I am finished, far more than double the profit."

I stifled the urge to look to my father for guidance; it would make me look weak, and I was determined not to look weak. Not before this merchant. Not before Merio. And especially not before my father. I schooled my expression to indifference, even as my stomach twisted.

"What surety do you offer?"

"The same I offer myself. Profit. With your funds and my labor, we all benefit. This is a unique moment." When I did not reply, he reluctantly added, "My home, on Vialetta Manara. Six rooms. In the heart of the Quartiere Lana."

I didn't like him, I decided.

I didn't like that he came asking for great sums when smaller sums would do. I didn't like that he sought to cloud my mind with greed for easy profit. I didn't like that he offered his house, which was not worth eight hundred navisoli in any circumstance—but especially I did not like him, for I knew rumors of his son.

"Is your son still attending the university?" I asked.

His eyes darted sideways. "Not at the moment. I sent him on an errand."

"An errand to . . ."

"Vesuna, carrying a purse of payment."

"Would not"—I hunted in my mind for the name of a patro who had roots in Pagnanopol—"would not Archinomo Pulikas be better suited for this trade?" I asked. "They have family there. Many contacts. Many alliances. They would be useful for negotiation. You would almost certainly get a better price on your porcelain."

Pakas's eyes narrowed.

It was subtle, but it was all I needed.

I stood and bowed to the merchant.

Startled, my father hurried to stand with me. Merio, too, straightened in surprise that our meeting was ending. "Seek out the Patro Pulikas," I said. "I'm sure he will be eager to make such a profitable agreement with you. Tell him I"—I glanced at my father—"*we* recommended you."

And that was that. I bowed again. Pakas bowed. My father bowed. We all bowed. Merio led him away.

I flopped back in my chair, relieved.

"The offer could have been improved," Merio said as he returned from closing the doors behind Pakas, "but that was rude. You should not have dismissed him so. You were too abrupt in your decision."

"Nai." I shook my head. "Pakas offered an oily hand. He will flee to Pagnanopol and will not return."

"Impossible," Merio said. "He has a good reputation."

"And yet Pakas will not return."

I could not help but enjoy how flummoxed Merio was that the meeting had not gone as he had expected. I leaned back, enjoying the numerari's irritation.

"You cannot pretend to see the future, Davico," Merio remonstrated. "You must behave with reason, not act like a child, smashing plates because no one will stop you now that you are to be a man. Your family's business is not a game. This is not a game."

"I do not *pretend* to see the future," I said. "In fact, I see it perfectly. And I never play games with our business, because I am already a man—no matter the date of my Assumption." I wanted to make my voice firm, to tweak Merio for challenging my decision, but I could not help smiling.

Merio's eyes narrowed. "What do you know?"

"You have to ask?" I pretended surprise, enjoying our interplay even more because my father watched. "You didn't see it, too? Why, it was written squarely on his face. You always tell me I should master the art of faccioscuro. That I should learn and listen, watch and observe, dissemble and obscure, *Watch, Davico, watch closely. Watch this, notice that* . . . And here I thought you were paying attention when you were teaching me!"

"No one likes arrogance," Merio said sourly. "Have I taught you that, yet?"

I had pushed Merio far enough. "You didn't miss anything on the merchant's face. The truth is, there is gossip in the university. That is what I know, and how I know. Pakas's son was bedding the unmarried daughter of Maestro Boccia."

"Boccia . . ."

"Boccia's wife comes from Archinomo Tazzia," I supplied.

"Ai!" My father's eyebrows shot up. "They are proud."

"They are bloodthirsty and their honor is wounded," I said. "And I know it, because her cousins came to the university with swords drawn, looking for him." I couldn't hide my pleasure at knowing something Merio and my father did not. "Pakas's son has already fled the city. I think Pakas is seeking a letter of credit because he cannot close all his business dealings fast enough without meeting a stilettotore in an alley. I would not be surprised if he intends to flee as far as the Khur."

"If his son has gone to Vesuna . . ." Merio's eyes widened. "Why, the son could be setting sail as we speak!"

My father's hand gripped my shoulder. "Well done, Davico. Very well done."

Merio's expression also became one of open approval, and it felt glorious to me that I had impressed them both. "Ai, Devonaci, if we had any doubts about the boy's mind, we can set them to rest."

"Indeed," my father said. "I would not have trusted Pakas, either. But I did not know that tidbit about the son. We need more ears in the university. Children's tongues wag—" He broke off as a great commotion rose outside the library doors.

Someone was singing, loudly, and from the sound of it, drunkenly.

Merio raised his eyes heavenward. "No. By Amo, please tell me that it isn't so. He's here already?"

My father favored Merio with an amused smile. "When has that man ever delayed riding to wine or dinner?"

Merio grimaced. "I'm sure he set sail as soon as he opened the envelope."

"Who?" I asked.

"You cannot guess? Use that sharp mind of yours, Davico. You sent the invitation yourself."

My father ushered me out of the library and down the stairs of the gallery to the gardens, and then through the archways to our quadra premia, where the cacophony reached new and greater heights. In the center of the quadra, cantering atop a great white horse and circling Urula's fountain, a man was singing at the top of his lungs. Around and around he went, singing:

"Behold the hero has returned.
Behold the hero upon his steed.
Behold the light of Amo upon his crown.
Behold, Behold, Behold!"

He was being chased by several of our guards. They had their swords out, but they seemed unsure if they should attack or indulge the drunkard, for the stranger wore fine clothing and a shining and thickly woven gold chain about his neck, and he seemed entirely unbothered by their bared steel.

He waved a floppy velvet hat at them as if it were a shield, flipping it this way and that as if he were a bullfighter, teasing them to charge. One guard made a lunge for the drunkard's reins, but the man turned his steed neatly, reversing direction, and smacked the guard upon his head with his floppy hat, even as he twisted the words of Amo's Celebration.

"Behold, the blessings of his might,
Behold, he wields the light,
But it is not Amo whose gifts he praises,
For our hero is blessed by Caliba,
And his cock is the size of a—"

He broke off as he spied us. "Devonaci!" he cried. "You have terrible guardsmen!"

He leapt off his horse and threw his reins to the nearest guard, who had been on the verge of capturing him, and the guard was so surprised that he took them, even as the stranger crossed the flagstones to embrace my father.

"Filippo!" my father said. "By the fatas it's good to see you, you ribald bastard."

And now I knew. It was the capo di banco who liked his jokes about nuns and goats. Filippo di Basca. Our man in Torre Amo.

From his foul writings and his position in our bank, I had always assumed him an ancient slavering drooling man, some crusty and frustrated imp of lusts, obsessed with the scatological and sexual. Instead, Filippo was tall, not at all old, with well-formed features and wild sparkling dark eyes.

"My ass is as raw as a linen boy's after a day behind the tavern!" Filippo said. He slapped his buttocks and waggled them suggestively. I half expected my father to remonstrate with him, for he was always decorous, but he only laughed.

"Ai, Filippo. You are uncouth as always."

"And yet still welcome?"

"Always." My father kissed him on both cheeks, and then clapped an arm around Filippo's shoulders. "Always welcome. Now come. We will have a bath prepared, and then food."

"What about wine?"

"I assumed you would drink in your bath."

"What about a few nice girls to scrub beneath my eggs?"

I was appalled, but my father only laughed as he guided Filippo out of the quadra. "If any of my girls scrub anything, it will be your mouth."

"Not even that lovely girl . . . what was her name? Sissia?"

"Sissia is married, her husband would take more than your eggs."

"Say it isn't so! Is she very plump now? I wager she's plump. I like plump women. Perhaps I can pay her husband." Their voices receded as they disappeared down the passage toward the baths. Filippo's voice echoed back to us. "I've eaten soap, you know? A man once made me eat three fists of the stuff."

"Ai. Filippo." My father's rueful laugh echoed. "Why am I not at all surprised?"

"So," Celia said. "That is your man in Torre Amo." I had not noticed her come up behind me. Now she was staring after where they had disappeared. Their voices becoming muddled, twined back and forth: Filippo's bright blasphemies erupting and echoing, followed by my father's deeper tones, placating and chivvying him on. "Filippo di Basca da Torre Amo."

"As uncouth in person as he is on paper," I said. "Though I thought he would be shorter."

"Oh?"

"And uglier. Like a troll."

"And here he is, taller than your father, and pleasing to the eye."

"You think he's handsome?" I snorted. "Even knowing what he puts in his letters?"

"Better to see him clearly than have to guess. Many a woman would count herself lucky to know exactly where her husband's eyes wandered and where his thoughts followed. There are worse surprises for a woman."

"You can't be thinking of him as a match for you."

"Why not?"

"He's old!"

"Girls marry men their father's age all the time, and he is far from that." She saw my horrified expression and laughed. "Ai, Davico. It would be absurd for me to marry such a man. What advantage would it give our family? Your father has already marked his cheek." She looked after Filippo speculatively. "But they do say he is very very very rich."

"Enough, sister. Enough."

Filippo was a puzzle: always with a bottle, always lascivious, always rude as an imp conjured by Caliba—and yet my father and Merio tolerated him, and even deferred to him.

Despite Filippo's many failings of character, he was not lazy. As soon as he had bathed and drunk and pinched the bottoms of all our servants (and not a few guards as well), he set to work in the scrittorium, cursing and joking with our abacassi, a steady stream of filth spilling from his lips—all cocks and cunts and assholes, priests and goats and more—even as he urged them to greater effort.

Reflecting lanterns were hung in the scrittorium and frantic moths swarmed around their light deep into the night. Cups of sharp black tea shuttled back and forth to the bank—arriving full, departing empty, returning full once again—keeping abacassi minds sharp and litigi eyes like pinpricks as my father and I met with delegations, merchants, diplomats, mine owners, guild leaders, and craftsmen. The list went on, and our business was as the River Livia in spring, swollen and fast, and seemingly unending.

I tried to avoid Filippo as much as possible, for he was never polite, but he seemed to greatly enjoy being underfoot, whether in the scrittorium or the palazzo. He especially seemed to enjoy annoying Ashia. As gifts arrived for me from various supplicants, and as we prepared and packaged gifts to be sent out to our many allies, he would look over her shoulder and comment upon every item.

"You think the Callarino's mistress needs rouges from Merai? Give her a muzzle for those horse teeth, and the Callarino will thank you more."

Or . . .

"Tea from Xim? Everyone knows that tea from Kethia is finer. The Xim never send out their best teas."

Or . . .

"You're giving the district elected the Grantinero vintage? Emeralds before cockroaches! Why waste such good wine on such untutored palates?"

And so on.

Regardless, as many gifts as arrived for my name day, a greater number issued forth. Gold and gems and carved elephant tusks and serratine horns for those archinomi who supported the Callarino. Pottery and chocolates for district elected in the Callendra. Teas and Cerulean eyes for guild representatives. Peacock feathers, perfumes from Cheroux, and rouges from Merai for various mistresses. Ox bone medallions commemorating our name in the old Navolese style for vianomae who had done us good turns upon the docks and in the warehouses and in the taverns. A grand racing horse for the Callarino. All day long, Ashia busied herself directing our servants Sofia, Sissia, and Teresa in wrapping these gifts of regard and giving them to our well-wishers as they departed. Such was our largesse that at this time, Polonos and Relus were ordered to dole out sweets and apricots and honey for any child who came to our gates, no matter their station.

But all was not work in the final weeks before my celebration. There were dinner parties. There were expeditions into the hills to view the profusion of summer blooms and to escape the heat. There were cool wines and games in the quadra when the evening fell and the heat had faded.

My father paid the young and talented artist Arvino Casarocca to paint Celia's likeness.

This was how Celia ended up one day, reclined upon a hillside richly vibrant with yellow Caliba's crowns and purple neft blossoms, her arms akimbo, her white gown stark against the color as she stared up at a blue sky.

And this was how a group of us ended up sitting nearby: myself, Giovanni, Piero, Cierco, Niccoletta—joking and teasing—as the young maestro d'arte remonstrated with her for moving.

"Please, sia Celia. A little more still," Casarocca begged.

"Yes, hold still," Niccoletta said, and threw a neft blossom so that it landed on Celia's face.

"Sei fescata!" Celia said, brushing off the flower and sitting up. She threw the three in our direction. "Niccoletta, you come over here and lie down. We have the same shape."

"Nai, Sia!" Casarocca protested. "Please! It is important that I paint only you. This will hang in Palazzo Regulai."

"Ci." Celia fixed him with a sour look. "If you were half as good an artist as you claim, you should be able to look at me once, and know all my looks, and yet here I lie for hours."

Giovanni, who was currently taking his turn holding a parasol over Celia so that she would not scald under the sun, said, "Not everyone is painted by such a maestro, Celia. You should be honored and pleased. He does you as much honor as you do him."

"Then you lie down here."

"Indeed, Giovanni!" Piero piped up. "You have the ass to stand in for her."

"Don't you start, Piero. If anything is a perfect double for my ass, it's that face of yours," Celia said.

We all howled.

"Ci! We two are nobilii anciens," Piero protested. "You should treat your people better." He crawled over and tried to capture Celia's hand to kiss it, but she slapped his arm back.

"You and your nobilii anciens. Your face is certainly an ass, for your lips spill nothing but shit." Celia flopped back into the flowers. "Paint, me, Maestro. Paint me."

Piero scowled. The rest of us teased him for her rejection. "She is a fata of chaos," he said bitterly, but even Giovanni, who was kinder than most, both the veritas and the amicus of us, laughed.

And so the days went on, sunny and bright and increasingly busy and warm, and soon, the painting was done.

When it was finished, my father ordered it hung in the columned gallery that led to where his library lay on the second floor.

"Ci. That is not subtle," Celia said when she saw it.

"I think you look pretty," I said, staring up at it. "And I like the flowers. Casarocca is very skilled."

"I do look pretty," she said, with irritation.

"Isn't that rather the point?"

"To lie pretty amidst new blooms?" She gave me a pointed look.

I frowned, trying to see the problem. "You do not think he made the flowers very nice? I like it very much. See how it becomes a field when you step back a little?"

"And here I dangle," she said, "beside your father's library door, where his most important business partners pass."

"But isn't it good and right that you be displayed so? You're practically family. Look at you there, right beside the old Bull. Who could ask for more?"

She gave me an exasperated look and stalked away. I studied the painting, trying to see what had elicited her pique. It was well painted. She looked teasing, knowing. It was her, by Amo, captured in oils. Playful and alive and beautiful. Casarocca had outdone himself. He was as much a master as Arragnalo.

I stepped back, trying to take all of her in, when behind me I felt my father's presence. He had come quietly, but still I must have felt his breathing or else heard the tread of his velvet slippers, for I was not surprised to turn and find him there. He joined me in study of the painting.

"Celia doesn't like it," I said.

"No. She wouldn't." He smiled slightly. "She sees the waves of Cerulea, but she feels the deeps of Urula. A clever girl, Celia."

I wanted to argue this, for I sensed a criticism of my own perspicacity, but my father changed the subject.

"The ambassador of Merai is throwing a party tonight," he said. "In celebration of the Apexia. It will be important for you to attend. Ashia has chosen clothes for you."

I sighed. "I'm sure they'll itch."

My father laughed. "Very likely. But you represent us now and Ashia knows best how to ensure you cut a good figure."

"Will Celia be there, too?"

"Of course. And Filippo as well."

"You can't be serious."

My father shrugged. "Filippo likes parties."

Scratchy collars and Filippo. I resolved to avoid at least one of them.

Chapter 18

My collar itched and Filippo's eyes glowed with excitement as we approached the ambassador's residence.

"It's always nice to see the Navolese celebrating," he said. "So much more pleasant than when they're sticking knives in one another's backs."

"You yourself are Navolese," my father said. "You shouldn't speak so harshly of your own people."

"I was Navolese. Now . . ." He shrugged. "I do not know. Something in between. A bit of Torre Amo, a bit of Navola, I am a foreigner here, though. I recognize this city, but I do not think it is mine anymore."

"Are the people of Torre Amo so decent and kind, then?" I asked, tugging at my collar for the hundredth time.

Filippo laughed. "Oh no! They're much much worse. Always drawing blood for no reason. Always feuding between the princes. Always robbers in the streets. Cutpurses and whores and goats all about in the quadrazzi and the ruins of the old palazzi. When they throw a party, you never know if you'll walk out. Perhaps someone will slay you, perhaps someone will wine and drug and love you to death." He sighed. "They are a lovely, terrible, lovely people. But very alive, you know? When you're in Torre Amo, you always remember that you are alive. You should see the way they celebrate the Apexia there."

The ambassador's residence glittered, even from the street. Urchins had gathered outside, wearing Masques of Amo as was traditional for Apexia, and waving sparkers in greeting. They had been given sweets—with more promised after—so that they would welcome the archinomi and not disturb the great names as they arrived, and the children now cheered and waved their masques and sparkers at the guests in a merry swelter of excitement and sugar dreams.

The envoy from Merai rented the palazzo from the Archinomo

Taglia. The family had fallen on unlucky times, the patro struck down by the strangling disease, with four children still young, and then it became apparent that the patro had debts from gambling at cartalegge and at dice and spending on illicit loves, so the matra's choices were limited. She had given over the vast majority of the palazzo to Merai, and now lived near the village of Montevino in a small farmhouse and on land they had once rented to others and that it was said she now learned to till herself, while the vast amount of the money she earned from the letting of her palazzo went to the men who owned her husband's debts.

In any case, the palazzo was lovely, in the old style of the Imperial Amonese, with many walled gardens, and tiled pools dusted with rose petals for bathing. It had been occupied for many generations.

"I think I like Palazzo Taglia better than Palazzo Regulai," Celia pronounced as we were escorted through the gates. "It has a true grace and elegance to it."

"It has lovely low walls," Cazzetta said. "Easy for assassins."

She gave him two fingers in response. "Not everyone is out to kill you, stilettotore."

Cazzetta only raised his eyebrows in response, as if she were a child and he knew more than her, and then Celia swept indoors and I followed her, leaving Cazzetta to fade into the shadows outside, to watch the arrivals and departures and count the number of people and do whatever dark things he did with such information.

Inside the palazzo walls there were exquisite mosaics and secret gardens, places where lovers were rumored to often slip away. The great rooms and balconies were lit with lanterns, and the halls were filled with people. Courtesans glittered, their rouged lips and dark eyes promising skillful companionship, the professional women intermixing easily with women of lesser names who plied a similar trade but in quest of connection rather than navisoli.

In one quadra, actresses in scandalous dress and actors with codpieces stuffed to the size of cantaloupes performed a play of desire written specifically for Apexia by Zuzzo, who stood to one side, his lips mimicking the lines of the actors, his hands alternately tugging at his great gray beard and conducting the musical accompaniment.

Goblets of Meravese d'Affrizzo wine were offered in crystal cut by the glassmakers in Ferreine with great effort and expense, and transported with even greater care.

In addition to the envoy from Merai, the envoys and ambassadors of numerous other city-states and kingdoms, dukedoms and principalities were all there, all of them watching one another like suspicious dogs, trying to discover who spoke with whom, who made alliances and who made nemeses. Did the Duke of Savicchi smile at the guild master of the linen weavers? Did the envoy from Cheroux speak too long with the wife of the envoy of Chat?

And so it went, on and on: the glitter and the laughter, the song and music and drink and spetaccolo, and of course, because the Meravese liked to think themselves patrons of the arts, there were included many painters and sculptors of renown. Casarocca, who had painted Celia, was present, looking young and out of place, despite the respect everyone paid him. Madrasalvo was there, with a new lover in tow, dressed as one of Caliba's fatas, his face prettily rouged. The boy blew kisses at the ambassadors and irritated Madrasalvo greatly.

"He's always jealous," Celia observed. "I don't know why Madrasalvo brings them if he'll only be jealous."

And of course the archinomi of Navola were present, not the complete One Hundred, but still, many of the guild names and the banca mercanta. Lady Furia was there, seeming irritated that the ambassador had forced her Khusian bodyguard to remain outside, much as Cazzetta had been forced to loiter outside with our own guards and Aghan Khan—though Filippo pointed out a girl who attended Furia, a dancing slave from Zurom whom Filippo said had been taught to kill with the pins that held up her hair.

"Would that not be a magnificent way to go to Scuro?" Filippo exclaimed. "With that minx atop you, twisting those lovely dancer's hips, riding you like a horse, frothing you right to Caliba's apex, and then . . . Pop! Your eyes! Your eyes! Ai! Your eyes are popped! And then off to Scuro with you!" He laughed, delighted, and toasted the girl with his crystal goblet. "Ai, she can have my eyes. If she were my last sight, I would be most content."

But I had no eyes for the slave girl, for beside her, Furia stood, and Furia was looking at me, toasting me, her smile wry. I looked away, blushing, uncertain of how to interpret the jumbled fear and desire she engendered. The sight of her inspired lust, of a surety: her tightly laced bodice and the rise of her breasts with the gleaming golden medallion of her name nestled between those globes, and then, higher, green eyes so malign that I might as well have been drinking arsenic.

How could someone be so beautiful and also so terrifying?

I fled the quadra and Filippo's suicidal contemplations of lust, making my way toward rooms where guests played the games of cartalegge and finger dice that had brought Archinomo Taglia low, and where eager players gambled for omens of luck and wealth, as was traditional when Amo's light was highest in the sky. I spied Piero dicing—shouting, flushed, drunk already and laughing.

"Amo lights my path to Fortuna!" he shouted as he won a throw of the finger dice and everyone cheered. He looked as if he might call for me to join him, but then there was another great shout as the dice turned in his favor again, and he turned away, calling out that the year was his, foretold.

Feeling a little lonely, I continued to wander the sights and distractions, seeking someplace where I might moor myself with a friend or two. I edged past a swirl of revelers dancing in the quadra, moving in their intricate patterns of joy to Amo, as strings and reed pipes and drums kept the time. In an alcove, I spied a fortune teller, with a line of people hoping to know their fate now that Amo's light was at its highest, and all truths could be seen. The fortune teller wore the gold mask of truth, as was traditional, with only a slit for the mouth, and the painted-on eyes of that tragic emperor Catxaiin, so that she could not examine the features of those who came before her, or guess who they were in any way, ensuring that her fortunes would be honest. I didn't go to her. I knew my destiny too well already.

Eventually I stood off to one side and simply waited, wishing that it were proper for me to depart, but unable to do so—and so it was that the ambassador of Wustholt found me.

"Not enjoying the Apexia, young Davico?"

He was a man with a very luxurious mustache, blond hair that hid his gray, and blue eyes that were much like the ice of his homeland beyond the high Cielofrigo. There, his kingdom fought against barbarian hair men and lived in winter snows. He was wearing civilized clothes not of fur, as was his people's wont, but velvets of Navolese design, his only declaration of Woltish loyalty the sigil of the bear embroidered upon his collar, and the fringe of that very beast's fur that spread across his shoulders, coarse and brutish.

"I am not . . ." I shrugged. "The society of many strangers is too chiachichiacalda for me."

"Chia . . ." He puzzled at the word. "Chiach . . ." he tried again.

"Chiachichiacalda." I said it slowly. "Chiachichiacalda. Too much noise and heat, too much pressure, too many voices. It becomes as a great crowd of untuned instruments to me. Chiachichiacalda."

"Ai!" He nodded. "I understand! We have a term in Wustholt for this. *Horgus.* 'The heat and the noise.' It's a positive connotation for us, though. Our winters are cold, so we appreciate a warm cozy house, full of family. Or a loud and boisterous inn. Something that is *horgus* is very good indeed. Full of life, full of women with great warm breasts and men with big red noses, and much beer flowing. Good songs. Good life. Much happy life. Or a good group of friends, packed close in a warm home, beside a bright fire, telling tales. And drinking."

"It sounds like there is a lot of drinking."

"We like our beer." He smiled. "It is better than what you Navolese make. Your kind are not much for beers."

"It sounds as if you enjoy this *horgus*."

"How could I not? It's one of the finest things. It's the feeling of having a good harvest. Plenty of meat strung up to smoke. Great deep pits full of cabbages and carrots and beets well buried for the winter. A full larder and a full house. That, too, is part of the feeling of *horgus*. Plentiful food. Plentiful drink. Laughter and good company." He considered. "Also, we like people better than the Navolese do. So *horgus* is probably not something you would like, no matter what."

"We like people," I protested.

His brow wrinkled in the way of Wustholt, signifying polite disagreement. "You Navolese . . ."

"Yes?"

"You see people with suspicion. You watch your backs. I think . . ." He paused, considering. "I think in my land that we must trust more, cooperate more. We must, you see, if we wish to make it through long hard winters. In Navola you have your warm weather, you have your fat fisheries . . ." He shrugged. "It is different."

"So you have no rivalries?" I challenged. "No feuds between brothers? No wars between kings? No jealous sharp tongues? No men who steal? No women who lie? No angers? No moment when cold steel draws and hot blood flows? No—"

"Ai, ai, ai! Mercy, young Davico! Mercy, di Regulai!" He was laughing, holding up his hands in apology. "I did not mean to offend! I mean only to say that there is a difference. Perhaps I was clumsy with my words. I simply mean to say that when we war, we war; and when we make peace, we make peace. When we drink, we drink from one another's tankards and fear no poison, and when we do not drink, we fight, and there is no doubt as to whether there will be drinking or bloodletting.

"Navola, though, with its whispers and knives and rumors and poison and promises made and broken . . ." He shook his head. "That is not our way." He waved at the assembled people. "How many of the people who smile and dance here also sharpen daggers for one another? How many plot some rivalry or betrayal? It is a luxury we in Wustholt simply cannot afford. You here in your great glittering city have too much wealth. Too much food. So you do not love one another, or support one another. And your cities are so big! All the cities on the hook! There are so many people that one person more or less is no matter. I think this makes it difficult for you to find the warmth of other people. Maybe it's simply that it is too hot in these lands. In the north, we are cold, so we seek the warmth of one another, for love, for survival, for pleasure, for life . . ." He shrugged. "You southerners . . ." He shrugged again. "I do not know."

We were abruptly interrupted in our discussion by Filippo, drunk and cheerful, carrying glasses of d'Affrizzu, that wine from Merai, light and cold, that frizzed on the tongue. He offered a glass to the ambassador. "Here, try this, it's very cooling, Ambassador."

"No, thank you."

"I insist! It's a party! Caliba and his fatas ride tonight!" He leaned close, conspiratorial. "These Meravese people, they are useless with money, but they at least make good cold wines."

The ambassador accepted ungraciously, but Filippo was unconcerned; he pressed a glass upon me as well, spilling a little on his sleeve. "Ai! I should learn to juggle!" He took a sip of his wine. "Ai. That is good." Now he regarded us. "Please tell me that you aren't filling Davico with the mistaken impression that the cold men of Wustholt are the handmaids of Amo."

The ambassador smirked and quoted from Zirfan, the legendary general of Zurom. "If a man does not like the thunder of the charging army's boots, covering his ears will not improve his condition." He toasted Filippo.

"He talks about Navola the way we talk about the Borraghese," I said. "You would like him."

"Sfai! Say it isn't true!" Filippo laughed, then looked mischievously over the rim of his glass. "But then I'm sure he has worse to say about Torre Amo."

"That . . . *cesspool*?" The ambassador made a face. "I barely escaped that wretched city with my soul. A place of terrible temptation."

"Sfai! Temptation is not terrible!" Filippo made eyes at me. "Our cold friend speaks of the famous silk girls of Torre Amo." He waxed rapturous. "Ai, Davico, you have not seen such creatures. Navola has her beauties, but Torre Amo? And silk girls?" He kissed his fingers. "Magnifica. A healthy mix of Zurom from a long-ago invasion and the southern Romiglia from when the Amonese used to raid there. Good blood there, very lusty. They know something of what it is to suck life from the pomegranate, as they say. And if you like boys, well, you have never seen such vitality. When they play their games of war, your loins will throb. Just watching will make your root explode, long before they get their hungry mouths upon it!"

I could not help but feel embarrassed at Filippo's raw words.

The ambassador was shaking his head. "It is a dark place, with dark desires," he said.

"We were talking about the Borragha," I said, trying to steer the conversation to safer shores.

"Ech." Filippo made a face. "A nasty place and nasty people, the Borraghese. As bad as their wine. Those ones leave a bad taste in your mouth. In love and trade, both."

The ambassador laughed, and the atmosphere between us all improved slightly. "Well, there you are. Always one people will find a reason to think another is strange and terrible."

"Or fuckable!" Filippo said. "Detestable or fuckable. One or the other." He paused to consider. "Or sometimes both, now that I think of it." He shrugged. "But at least everyone can agree the Borraghese cannot be helped."

"Certainly not their wines," the ambassador said. "I could never accustom myself to them. The grit of sediment on the tongue." He made a face of revulsion.

I remembered something Merio had said about them. "They call the sediment *la vita uva.* The life of the grape."

"I can spit in your wine and call it Amo's tears, but it doesn't make it taste any better," Filippo said. "Speaking of spitting, I have a joke for you. It's an old one. When a man grasps his root, what time is it?"

I didn't want to know, and from the ambassador's expression, neither did he. Filippo was not deterred and I was ashamed when he blurted, "It's time for the priest's dinner!"

"That is not a joke," the ambassador said.

"Sfai, you men of Wustholt respect your priests too much. They are still men, after all."

But the ambassador was already turning away, offended.

"They still have roots!" Filippo called after, sloshing his wine, but the ambassador was gone.

Unfortunately, this meant that Filippo now turned on me, and so I was now subjected to a stream of increasingly infantile and bawdy jokes about whores and fishmongers, demons and nuns, wives, horses and priests, and, of course, goats.

". . . and the nun said that she had simply done as she was told—she milked the billy goat!" Filippo guffawed. "Milked! The billy goat!"

To my vast relief, in that moment, my father arrived. "I'm sorry, Filippo," he interrupted. "We have business."

Anyone else would have taken the hint immediately, but Filippo waggled his eyebrows at my father. "Veridimmi? Business for the young bull? An Apexia assignation, perhaps?" He now waggled his eyebrows at me. "Is there a lovely courtesan waiting for our newly made man, a sweet and knowledgeable woman who will guide his plow into her furrow? Or mayhap a rippling young soldier who can show this young boy how to wield his weapon?"

My father smiled slightly, and I was again surprised at how unbothered he was by Filippo's impertinence. "Alas, it is the business of the plank, not the root. I think you would not find it so interesting."

Filippo made a shuddering face. "Indeed. I have had enough of the plank for the day. I am here to celebrate! Now where shall I sink my root?" And with that he staggered off, calling after a servant who had a carafe of the d'Affrizzu wine that he was drinking so liberally. The last

I glimpsed of him, he was ruffling a young man's hair and whispering something undoubtedly bawdy in his ear, for the youth was blushing.

"Why do you tolerate him?" I asked as my father guided me away.

"Who? Filippo?" My father shrugged. "He is absolutely loyal. And he makes more money than any ten of our other branches."

"But he's a fool. He's . . ."

"Uncouth. Foppish. Rude." My father recited. "Lecherous. Wild. And always an embarrassment."

"Well . . . yes."

"Filippo is also brilliant. He is profitable at the plank, and his face hides no secret from me. If tolerance of goat jokes and lechery are the worst that he demands for his skill and loyalty, well, that makes him a truer friend than most, and a fair bargain for our family."

"But—"

"*Never discard a friend when your table is full . . .*" my father began to quote.

" *. . . for you will find no friends when your table is empty,*" I finished for him. "Grandfather. I know."

"Then you also understand."

I was about to press again, but my father waved me quiet. Our host, the ambassador of Merai, awaited us at the foot of a staircase that led to the upper floors. He exchanged kisses with my father, touched his cheek to mine, and led us up the stairs, flight after flight carrying us higher above the crowd.

"The Taglia knew something of architectura," the ambassador said as he guided us around a turn, indicating the carvings of fatas that peered out from niches lining the wide staircases. "They were clever."

At the fourth turning of the stairs, there was another staircase that split away from the central one, this one guarded by soldiers wearing the blue-and-yellow livery of Merai. Up we went again, and thence through a sequence of richly tapestried and decorated private chambers—the ambassador's own, it seemed.

We came to a lushly carpeted library, arches all along one side, with a door in each arch, all of them thrown open to a great balcony half covered and half exposed to the sky.

"Here," the ambassador said. "You see for yourself. Patro Taglia was brilliant with design. A fool for love and dice but a great mind for pleasing proportion." He guided us out onto the open balcony, into the warm night air. "A generous balcony, open to cooling breezes. Many choices of where to sit, depending upon weather, heat, and preference. Good light in the library so that reading is always easy—and of course, this pleasing vista of all of Navola."

"It's impressive," my father said.

"I can see ships on the river from here. I count them sometimes. This one from Vesuna. That one from Torre Amo. The galleys of the Khur. I wonder sometimes if it is Scuro's influence that makes me so very pleased at Archinomo Taglia's poverty, which has gifted me with this glory of a residence."

The red-tiled roofs of Navola were shadowed now, but I could make out the black shapes of domes and towers. Here, the three domes of the Callendra, there the somewhat greater dome of Catredanto Luminere Amo. The night sky was spiked with the defensive towers of our various archinomi, dark shadows against stars. I could name many, easily. Serpieri, Furia, Vianotte, and dozens more, the legacy of our honor wars. I could see our own tower from here.

Torches and lanterns flickered wherever I looked. From on high, in this darkness, the city looked much like what I imagined Scuro's great City of the Unseen was described as, a place of both deep shadows and warm light, a place mysterious and dangerous, and, depending on the teller—priest or minstrel—sometimes horrifying, but sometimes enticing as well. Beyond it all, the dark river and ocean beckoned, and the stars blazed above.

How had I never looked upon my own city in this way? Our own rooftop gardens did not afford such a vista. But still, we had our tall defensive tower. And yet I had never looked upon the flickering of the city so. Patro Taglia had designed these rooms specifically for this grand view, and because of it, I felt suddenly that I could see and understand my own city better. I could almost feel its breathing. Up here, on high, I felt at one with—

I must have heard the footfalls, for I turned to face the man before he even cleared his throat. Indeed, I was already looking at him when my father and the ambassador finally noticed his arrival. I should have been afraid at the arrival of a stranger from behind, but the man who stood in the lantern light was not an assassin (though Cazzetta would have been irritated at my so easily dismissing the possibility). He wore fine linen and silk, and stood with a very straight back. His dark eyes were sharp with intelligence, as sharp as his goatee. His mustache and beard were shot with streaks of gray, but his skin was not heavily lined and he had a vitality and a presence that were extraordinary. As soon as I saw him, I understood that it was he whom we were meant to meet.

Indeed, he was the sole reason for our attendance at this party.

Chapter 19

"Patro Dellamont," my father said, and moved to embrace him. "Amo's light be upon you."

I knew the name. I had heard it discussed between my father and Cazzetta. The newly appointed first secretary of Merai, Count Dellamont.

"He's slippery and sharp," Cazzetta reported when he returned from one of his mysterious journeys. "Almost Navolese."

"And he's thrown his support behind our young Parl," my father said.

Cazzetta made a lemon face. "At least until the lion sees fit to eat the peacock."

His sourness was not unmerited. The Red City had been in turmoil. The old Parl had unexpectedly fallen from his horse, likely because of trickery, and had taken such a blow to his head that he never revived. He had lingered feverish a few days, then died, leaving his son, Roulait Dominoux, in possession of the Parl's ring. But the young Roulait was not much older than I, and so the transition had not been smooth. Only when Dellamont had thrown his troops and influence behind the young Parl had disruption been quelled.

Standing before us, Dellamont was a formidable man. Lean and tanned and fit, clearly a man of horses, swords, and war. His nose had been broken and badly set. A scar split his lip, and it, too, had been badly sewn, as if it had been done in the field rather than by a skilled physician, but even so, he was not ugly. His eyes, though. They were blue, and unpleasant. Unsmiling, even when his expression seemed so. The blue reminded me of the eyes of the Wustholti, and I wondered if some of that blood coursed through his veins. The Cielofrigo laid jagged teeth across Merai's northern border and in times past, Wustholti men had raided across those summer mountain passes, stealing livestock, scavenging gold, and leaving their seed in the bellies of Meravese women.

Dellamont leaned casually against the balcony rail. "Patro Regulai." He nodded to me. "And the son as well. Congratulations on your coming name day, Davico. It is a great thing for a young man to make his Assumption."

I tilted my head to him, careful to give no more respect than my father gave. Dellamont smirked, as if amused that I aped my father. He wasn't slighted; more, he simply saw me as too small to insult or concern him—like a minnow posturing before a razorgill—but then he was speaking to my father.

"I am grateful for your accommodating secrecy," he said. "I know it is not convenient to meet thus, but as you can imagine it is imperative that my presence be kept from prying eyes. If word of my presence spills into the mouths of the streets, it would not be beneficial for my Parl."

My father waved a hand as if his favor were nothing. "Well, we sit at the plank, in any case. All that occurs here is not for the street to know or speak." Even as my father spoke, I realized that the ambassador had faded out the door. We were entirely alone.

"So," my father said. "Roulait's uncle, Ciceque. He harasses you."

"The ambassador warned me that Banca Regulai casts a fine net."

"He exaggerates."

"Not at all. *The Regulai have ears in audience halls and noses in taverns. Fingers in cookeries, and tongues in the ears of courtesans. All across the hook and even beyond.* That is what he said."

My father laughed. "Well. A bank without knowledge is soon a bank without gold."

"Is that a paraphrasing of Vittius?"

"My grandfather, actually."

"It sounds like Vittius."

My father inclined his head, neither agreeing nor disagreeing.

"Vittius liked spies," Dellamont said. "He thought it necessary to know not only what was said to his face but also what was said in bedchambers and tavernae. If I had a man like your Cazzetta, I think my Parl would never be surprised. With a man like Cazzetta, we would have no fear."

"I suspect you are not so unequipped as that."

"I have some skill, but your man Cazzetta . . . Spymaster. Stilettotore. My ambassador tells us that rumors abound in Navola's streets that he is actually a golgozza yoked to Scuro, clawed up out of the Unseen Realm to wreak bloodshed upon the living."

"Cazzetta is many things, but not a golgozza. Of course we listen for gossip, and sometimes it is helpful. But this is far from spying. We are not like the Borraghese, who pay men to play the double-face game. That is not our custom."

"I don't mean to offend."

"You cannot offend."

"I simply wish to pay respect."

My father shrugged in that way that only a Navolese can. The shrug of a man who does not care, who is listening, who might walk away, who might (as Merio liked to say) steal your wife, who might give you the finest wine in his cellar, who might be your greatest friend, or your most dangerous enemy, all depending upon what you said next.

There was a sparring occurring between my father and this man, a subtle vying for advantage. Each of them outwardly calm and yet engaged in the thrust and parry of faccioscuro. I felt goosebumps upon my skin as they both leaned their elbows upon the balcony rail and studied the view.

The silence stretched. I could hear hooves clattering far below. The call of a wine bag man, offering pours. Children laughing and playing, teasing one another and stealing one another's sweets. The bell of a priest trying to call them back to Amo's contemplation.

At last, the first secretary broke the silence. "I only say that you know what I have come to request."

My father leaned his back to the rail, elbows resting upon it, outwardly relaxed. "Tell my son, then. He is my inheritor, and already sits at the plank beside me. Do him the honor."

Dellamont could barely restrain his irritation. It was a wonder to watch my father play him. With ill grace, Dellamont addressed me as my father asked, and as he did, it became apparent how desperate the man was. To allow my father to push him about like this. To accept dealing with the son who was not even yet of age. It was astonishing how much the man revealed. He was not Navolese.

"As your father surmises," Dellamont began, "Merai finds herself harassed by the troops of Ciceque."

"Roulait's uncle," I said. "He wants the ring. Roulait has the inherited claim. But Ciceque has the experience. And he is loved in Merai's north."

"You are as informed as your father. Indeed, he wants the ring, and while he does not have the troops to lay siege to and take the Red City, he has more than enough to spread fire in the fields, rape the women, rob and murder caravans, and impoverish everyone. Eventually, Merai will starve." He made a face. "It is an ugly business. Ciceque will create enough havoc that people will lose faith in Roulait, and beg to be yoked in slavery to Ciceque, the man who has manifested all their suffering." He spat over the rail. "It is against Amo. It is against reason. And I fear that brigand will be welcomed as liberator by next spring."

"He has pretext," my father pointed out. "He is elder. He is of the family."

"*Fecca fesculo!* He has a black heart. He has always schemed for the ring. Now, with his brother out of the way, he will take it from his nephew."

I nodded sympathetically but did not rush to speak, aware of the faith my father placed in me. I held silent, waiting, as I had been trained. My role now was to wait, to listen, and not to speak until the other person had truly finished speaking.

Love not the music of your own voice, Merio had once instructed. *Love the music of your opponent's. Wait. Listen.*

And then, Cazzetta had added, *wait a little longer. Draw the silence as you would a hunting bow. Draw it until it sings with tension and desperation to break, let it tremble there, desperate for release. Love that silence, for it is your friend. If you are patient, if you wait, a false man will often reveal himself into that silence.*

Merio agreed. *He will rush to fill that silence, for he cannot bear listening to the falsity that echoes within his mind.*

He will lunge to justify himself, Cazzetta said. *He will babble. He will explain. He will reveal his true face. Facciovero, facciochiaro.*

All you must do is wait, Merio said.

But now, to my frustration, Dellamont waited as well.

I waited.

He waited.

I gazed up at the stars. Beside me, my father gave no hint of his preferences. I could just make out his shadowed figure from the corner of my eye. He was watching us. Watching me. The silence between us stretched.

This was a test, I realized. Likely a consequence of my success when I had bested the pottery merchant from Pagnanopol, weeks before. With Pakas, I had been gifted with knowledge that had given me advantage, and because of it, I had succeeded. So now, of course, my father in his infinitely clever way had set a new test for me, one where I knew nothing and had no advantage at all.

I felt a wave of resentment that my father had tangled me in his net, throwing me into the teeth of this Dellamont, who, for all his urbanity, seemed as dangerous in his own way as Aghan Khan with a sword. Even more irritating was the knowledge that my father would not apologize. This was his way, as much a part of his nature as it was for a wolf to test the doors of a sheep shed. Devonaci di Regulai never trusted. Instead, he tested. Again and again and again.

And still, Dellamont waited me out. I had gone to a party, and arrived at the plank.

I was tired of being tested. Of being tangled in others' nets. I was not a card to be played at my father's will. I had my own will.

I turned to Dellamont. "And you wish what?"

My father stiffened as I spoke, as near a shout from him as I had ever felt at the plank, and this increased my irritation, for I had not asked to be tested. I had not asked to be thrown into negotiation without warning. I didn't want to be standing here, playing his games of faccioscuro. Damn my father and his games. I could barely restrain my anger at his manipulation of me, his judgment of me, his disappointment that I did not play the game that he himself had manipulated me into.

Dellamont at least was speaking. "We need to hire compagni militi to root out Ciceque. At least one thousand soldiers."

"One thousand?" I was on more familiar footing, now. "And you wish Banca Regulai to loan you the necessary monies."

"Do I not stand here asking?"

I could feel my father judging, but I no longer cared. "Let us speak plainly. How much do you require?"

"Thirty thousand navisoli."

It was an enormous sum. I could sense from my father a deep desire to take this conversation from me, to take back control of that thing that he had tossed upon me. To me, he was as a coiled asp, writhing with restrained emotion, with desire to strike. But at what? And how? And did I care? I could almost enjoy his discomfort.

"What guarantee is offered?" I asked.

"The word of a Parl."

"The Parl." I let the word hang, hoping to draw Dellamont out, but he simply nodded. "The Parl," I said, "has only worn his ring for three months. And already he faces troubles on all sides. Too, Merai already has loans with Banca Regulai under Avetton's old promises. Will Roulait honor the promises of his father?"

"With your support, Parl Roulait will wear the ring for decades, and he will honor all his family's promises."

I thought of all I knew of Merai. How to guarantee loans from a Parl under siege? It was as bad as trying to get Schipians to repay their loans. Roulait was truly in a precarious place, and he seemed ill-equipped to pay back his already existing loans. How to guarantee . . . ?

"I think we must . . ." I trailed off. I wasn't sure. I knew that it was best not to be forced to do something unless it was on my own time and terms. Perhaps that was the lesson here, not to be herded forward—not even by my father.

"I only come to Banca Regulai as a courtesy," Dellamont pressed. "Banca Serio has long desired a relationship. Banca Cortesa. Archinomo Furia—"

I didn't like the sound of that. Particularly Furia. "With a little time to consider and consult—"

My father cleared his throat. "There is copper in the Cielofrigo. Ciceque has mines there."

I felt like a puppy kicked aside. Dellamont paused. His attention went to my father, then back to me, and I thought I saw a satisfaction there, that he had drawn my father out.

"He does have copper," he acknowledged.

My father was brusque. "Just so. Once Ciceque is cleared, the mine's revenue will be sufficient as payment for our loan, and sufficient guarantee."

Now it was the first secretary who hedged. "It is a valuable mine."

"It is inaccessible with Ciceque in power. Already lost to you, in a very real sense."

"Di Regulai is only the first name I have approached," Dellamont said testily.

My father made a dismissive noise. "Furia? You wish to sit across the plank from a slaver? You know what sorts of payments she likes."

"There will be better offers," Dellamont insisted.

My father shook his head. "No matter how many planks you share tea over, you will not find such an offer."

"The Parl will not be pleased to lose his mines."

"Roulait does not have the mines. He is weak. Merai is weak. Avetton spent unwisely before his death. He bought tigers from the Khur and elephants from Khus. He kept expensive courtesans for his pleasure. He built an entire palazzo for Maria Ascolacasca, and another for Simon Tourneau. We both know how vulnerable your young Parl is; he has not inherited a healthy country. So, I will say with an open face that the risk of further loans to him is considerable. He is young. He is unproven. He has no heir. His power comes entirely from your loyalty. And what is that? Is your loyalty the unending ice of the high Cielofrigo, or is it the spring melt of the low?"

Dellamont scowled. "You seek to pick our corpse like dogs."

"I seek to speak plainly. It was not I who told old Avetton to spend his loans on women and piles of marble and elephants he did not know how to feed."

"And yet we all know what the vianomae say about banks. A bank will tear you naked, it will starve your family, it will strip your bones and then complain that your bones make a poor toothpick after the feast. Always banks say the loans they make are risky, and yet, always, the coffers of banks grow full while the mouths of children go empty."

"You sound like that mad priest Magare."

"Sfai. That fescatolo pigfucker?" Dellamont made a noise of disgust. "He has no love for nobility, either."

My father laughed at that, then grew serious. "I can only make an offer that protects Banca Regulai. But my offer, at least, does no harm to Merai. But go and sit at the plank with others, drink their tea, see what they offer. I will warn you, though. Whomsoever you approach, they may offer better terms on parchment, but they will require you to hire compagni militi who are their friends, for they will care not if you survive or die as long as they profit. They will suggest Caninero's Black Company, or Francino's Compagni Borragha, and those handpicked compagni will bleed you as surely as a butcher bleeds a pig. They will drag out battles, they will avoid decisive action, they will march hither and yon, up and down, around and around Merai. They will flash their spears, and shout their war cries, and fuck your women, and billet in your towns, and eat your bread, and then they will march some more, saying that they must maneuver. And the seasons will turn and they will demand more money. They will bleed you until you are nothing but a husk. Merai will be as blood-dry as the mummies they dig out of the sands of Zurom."

Dellamont shifted uncomfortably. I sensed that the moment of bargain and promise approached.

"Do as you will, First Secretary," my father said. "Slap away our hand of friendship and take up the oily hands of Archinomo Serio, or Cortesa, or Furia, instead. Then go back to your young Parl with whatever one you choose, and know that when Ciceque marches upon you, and you are besieged in Palazzo Rosso, cursing Amo and Scuro equally, you chose your fate."

Dellamont gave my father a look of near-hatred. "And you will not demand your own choice of general? I'm no wet babe mewling from my mother's cunt. You will have your own conditions."

My father's lips twitched. "Oh, of course I will."

Dellamont waited, like a cow waiting to be struck with a sledgehammer.

"General Sivizza," my father said, smiling.

Dellamont drew back, surprised. "You offer the Lupari? Navola's own?"

"Better than that, I offer Ciceque's head on a pike before winter."

Dellamont hedged. "The copper mine for ten years," he suggested. "It will recoup your investment—"

"I liked Avetton, even if he was a fool for spending," my father said. "For the sake of his son, I offer, but I do not sip tea to taste the sugar. This is my only offer." He motioned to me. "Come, Davico. We are undoubtedly missed downstairs."

"Wait!" Dellamont seized his sleeve. "Let me think, by Amo!"

My father paused, looking down at Dellamont's fingers upon his arm. Dellamont, seeing the direction of my father's gaze, quickly withdrew his hand. At that motion, I saw once again how skilled my father was. In the course of a few words, he had shifted the power of the conversation back into his favor. What I had tossed away in a fit of pique, he had seized and then taken more.

"Let it be done," the first secretary whispered. He touched his cheeks, both sides, and kissed his fingers. "Ink the paper."

My father softened. Suddenly he was smiling, as if he were the beams of Amo's light. "Then we are allied!" he exclaimed. He pulled Dellamont to him before Dellamont could crouch to formally mark his cheeks on my father's boots. "Nai. There is no need for that. We are allies," my father said, kissing both his cheeks. "Ciceque is no more!"

Dellamont called to the ambassador, who had been waiting outside, and sent for wine. We drank small glasses and sealed our bargain there, though there would still be stamps on paper to be arranged by Merio.

"You must attend Davico's Assumption," my father said.

"Nai. I must return to Merai with the news. My Parl waits anxiously."

"Another time, then. But know this, Count Dellamont, you will always be a welcome guest at Palazzo Regulai."

We drank again, and then we were being ushered back to the party below.

"Why did you offer him such good terms?" I asked, as we descended. "The copper mine is not so valuable, is it?"

"Valuable enough. We have other interests in the lands of the Red City," my father said. "The fall of the old Parl complicated certain ideas of mine. It is very much to our advantage to bind the new Parl to us, and to protect the loans we already have with them."

"You're not worried about throwing good money after bad? Or that the Callarino will protest sending away the Lupari?"

"Why did you give Dellamont an advantage?"

I was surprised by the swerve in conversation. "I—I was angry."

"You were angry." My father paused abruptly on the stairs, forcing me to stop a step below and turn back to look up at him. "I put you in the very position of power that you will one day inherit, and you were angry?"

"You tricked me into it."

"And so you wounded yourself, because you were angry at me. Does that seem wise?"

"I didn't ask to sit at the plank tonight!"

The words came out more loudly than I intended and my father's eyes widened with surprise. I expected him to be angry at me, to chastise me for my disrespect, but he only frowned.

"We are di Regulai, Davico. We always sit at the plank. We sit at the plank when we bargain over tea, and when we drink wine with ambassadors. We sit at the plank when we play cartalegge with our friends. We sit at the plank when we attend wedding celebrations, and when we go to catredanto. We are di Regulai. Our every action matters. You are soon to be a man, it's time you acted as one. We always sit at the plank. Always. And we never, *never,* give advantage to others."

And with that he favored me with a look so disappointed that I thought that I should melt immediately into the floor.

Chapter 20

I wandered the party, feeling numb and stupid, lonely and adrift.

We always sit at the plank.

My father's words followed me and changed the party's tenor. Everything was bargaining. Everything was negotiation. I had given up an advantage. I felt the fool.

I caught sight of Garagazzo the priest, wearing a mask and trying to push grapes down the bodice of a servant girl. He apparently wasn't worried about how he was seen or what advantage he gave up. I turned away and spied Lady Furia watching me speculatively from across the room, looking at me as if she were a raven observing carrion. She toasted me. I tried to keep my expression still, to not show her how much she unnerved me, but she only smirked.

This was Navola, I thought sourly. Crass priests and vicious slavers and enough wealth to buy and sell armies and kingdoms, and meanwhile, the men from the loom guild cornered the Callarino for some new monopoly and the wine merchants plied the names of the Callendra with their wares and asked them for lower taxes and on and on it went, with everyone smiling and everyone watching and everyone scheming.

Celia always smirked at these maneuverings, at the little lusts and little plots of small men, everyone strutting in their plumage, pretending to greatness in the eyes of others. "They'll all go home to wives and mistresses and lover boys. They'll fuck and pretend that they have effected greatness. That they are special, that their lives matter."

Cazzetta was more succinct. "They will all be dust."

All this plotting and striving, and for what?

I spied Filippo in the act of pinching another wine server's bottom, and at that very moment Filippo looked up and saw me, seeing him. He grinned, utterly unabashed, smacked the servant onward, and started for me.

I immediately turned and squeezed through the crowd, seeking escape. I had no more appetite for Filippo, no appetite for this party at all. I felt hot and trapped, surrounded and drowned by mouths laughing and drinking, voices shouting, all the embroidered gowns and jackets. The tight hose and breeches. The coiled braids, the complicated plaits with ribbons, the faces behind masks. The drunkenness and revelry.

"The great heaving mass," the Amonese emperor Vittius had once called them. Vittius had always been disgusted with people. It had made his art depictions revolting and twisted, even as he had risen to glory as a statesman. He had hated vianomae most assiduously, but really, all it took was a pair of eyes to see that archinomi, too, were monstrous. It mattered not whether we drank from Ferreine crystal in grand palazzi or slept as beggars in the alleys.

I spied Celia, chatting with a handsome man, a painter and sculptor, I thought. Art at least was pure. I forged through the crowd to her. She must have seen my desperation for she said something to her companion, and he bowed to her and left.

"Where did you go?" Celia asked, pulling me close and kissing my cheeks. "I saw you with Filippo and then pfft!" She made a motion with her hand. "Gone like a fata."

I leaned gratefully against her shoulder, feeling a relief as total as the drowning fishermen of Ossos must have felt when Urula sent her mermaids to kiss them full of air. "I just escaped him again," I said. "Him and his fescatolo goats."

"He told me a joke about a goat with a tongue as long as a baby's arm—"

"Please, sister."

She laughed. "I've decided he's harmless. But yes, tiresome."

"Who was that?" I asked of the departed man, who was gazing longingly back at her.

"An artist," Celia said, smiling and nodding at him. "He wants to paint me as Casarocca did."

"Another painting?"

"Well, he thinks my naked skin would look very fine if it were wet with water. He would see me *jeweled with the laughing waters of the Cerulea,* he said."

"He said that?" I couldn't help but feel disappointed.

Her smile did not slip. "He is a pig. But he is favored by Garagazzo and makes sculptures for him. Better to appear open to him than be immortalized as a slave of Scuro."

"I liked the ambassador of Wustholt." I sought across the crowd. "He would not act so."

"Well, that would be refreshing." But she said it in a way that told me she doubted I knew what I was talking about. I decided I didn't care. Of all the people who filled the palazzo with their revelry, the foreigner from the north had been the most pleasant.

"I would have liked to talk to him more, but Filippo insulted him."

"What would you talk about?"

"Anything at all. Talking to him feels like you are bathing in a clear mountain stream instead of the muddy mouth of the Livia. I could talk about . . . Well, I've heard they have snows there for more than half the year, and they make tunnels through the snow to one another's houses. I would ask him about that."

"And I have heard that they make rooms and heat them so hot that they take off all their clothes and mingle there, men and women all together, naked," Celia said.

"Of course that's what you've heard."

"Ai, Davico. Always so proper. What shall we do with that proper mind of yours?" She cast her gaze across the revelers. "Ah. There. The sisters di Pardi would be happy to give you less proper thoughts."

Of course, like the child I was, I turned and looked. And of a certainty, the two sisters were looking at me with undisguised interest. I blushed and looked away and Celia laughed at my discomfiture. "Do you prefer the elder or the younger?"

"Neither." The truth was that I found them both appealing and also terrifying. Easily available sialinae like the di Pardi sisters were to me like doors begging to be opened, and though I desperately hungered to experience the mysteries that lay beyond, I also feared them, and felt more than a little overwhelmed by their possibility. The sisters kept looking at me. I found myself looking in every other direction, avoiding their gaze, embarrassed. I searched the crowd again. The Wustholti was no longer attending. Inwardly, I cursed Filippo for running him off. "In truth, I like the idea of a quiet place to hide from all of this."

"But we're having so much fun."

"Fun for you. Torture to me."

"I suppose this means you do not wish to go to the fortune teller and have her read your tea leaves? She's quite skilled, they're saying. I'm sure we could ask her about how rich you will be and how kings will quiver at your name. She doesn't have anyone waiting at the moment."

I looked at the fortune teller, sitting cross-legged with her golden mask with its dark slit for a mouth. "I think I've already seen my future, and it is full of bitterness."

I meant to say it lightly, as a joke, but as I spoke, I felt a sudden grief rising, as if I had cut open my chest by accident, and now the blood was coursing out. I was shocked at the feeling, how strong it was. An encapsulation of the evening, for me. The ugliness of our peers, the complexities of my family's dealings, the muddiness of negotiations, and more than anything, the sense of not belonging. This was my father's world, not mine, and yet this existence was my destiny.

Celia prattled on, unaware. "I went to a fortune teller near Quartiere Sangro. She said that I would one day marry a king. I laughed in her face—" She broke off, turned to examine me. "*Caromio.* What is the matter?"

I shook my head, trying to master my emotions.

"Ai, Davico." Celia took my hand. "Come. Let's go outside." She pulled me with her. "We'll find some air. Some privacy. Best that no one sees your face so clear."

I let her draw me outside, out into the Taglia gardens and down the marble steps to a maze of sculpted hedges. There was a large fountain at the maze entrance. Celia drew me to sit upon its edge.

"There," she said, dipping her fingers in the water. "That's better, isn't it?" She dipped her fingers in again and touched them to my brow, leaving cool relief. I leaned against her.

"*Caromio.* What is it?" she asked.

I tried to answer, but all I could see was Count Dellamont and my father. Their battle of wits, the balancing of bravado and risk, two masters of a game that I wanted no part of.

Celia's cool hands touched my cheeks and turned me to face her. "Are you sick? You seem flushed."

Celia, the girl who played cartalegge and always won, gazed into my eyes. The girl who hid all that she wished to hide, and showed only that which she wished to show. A maestra of faccioscuro. I took her hands from my cheeks. I stared at her face, trying to read her, trying to know who she actually was.

"Davico, what is it?" She tried to tug her hands away, but I held her tighter, still trying to see. "Really, Davico." She laughed uncomfortably.

I could not read her. I did not know her. "Promise me something, Celia."

"Promise you? Really, Davico, what happened with Filippo—?"

I gripped her hands tighter. "Promise me you will never lie to me."

"Promise—" She paused, on the verge of making a jest, but she saw my expression and grew abruptly solemn. "*Caro significo,* Davico." Emotions flitted across her face, uncertainty, almost an anguish. "*Caro-mio,* Davico. Ai. This is silliness."

"Promise me," I pressed.

"Why are you suddenly so worried about such things?"

"Everyone around me is a master of hiding truth. My whole life is faccioscuro. Who is my father? What does he think? How does he plan? Ashia? My tutors? They speak of things behind my back, they discuss me, they measure me, they test me. They shape me, train me like a horse—"

"They love you, Davico—"

"They hide things from me. Just as you have hidden things from me."

"Everyone has secrets. It is natural. Think of Sia Lisana, she wrote many poems of secrets, of the three faces of a man—"

"Please, Celia, I would like to think that with one person, at least, there are no lies. Please, Celia, promise me this."

There was a long pause as she searched my face. Her expression was one of pity. "But Davico, how would you know? If I made this promise, it, too, could be a lie. I could promise you the moon in the sky, and you would believe me if I did. I am too good at this game. Why ask for a promise that you cannot know is true?"

"Please, Celia. Do not play your clever word games. Promise me. Promise you will never lie to me."

Her hands twisted in mine, her expression anguished. "Do not ask this of me, Davico."

"Please."

"I can promise, Davico. I can say I will never lie to you. But I warn you, some lies are a kindness." She freed herself from my grip and took my hands in hers. "Are you sure of this thing? Are you sure you want this thing?"

"Never lie to me," I begged. "And I promise I will never lie to you."

Still she hesitated.

"Please."

Her eyes held mine, dark and sorrowful, so deep with knowledge that for a moment I wondered if I understood what I asked for. If perhaps I was stupid for voicing my honest desire, for speaking of my hunger for one safe haven of honest concourse. I wondered if I was a fool. I wondered if I asked too much, and yet stubbornness and—if I'm honest before Amo—also desperation and loneliness made me steel myself.

"Please," I said again.

At last, she gave a solemn nod of acquiescence. "And so it is sworn," she said. "I promise you."

I moved to embrace her. "Thank you," I whispered. "Thank you." I buried my face in her hair and she held me close, stroking my hair, holding me.

"Caro, Davico," she whispered. "My poor Davico."

We held there for a long time, and when we drew away, her eyes shone as if with tears, but then she blinked and they were gone, and I was not sure I had seen correctly. She smiled, then, and the old Celia was back. The one of play and mischief.

"Well," she said. "That was very serious."

"Thank you," I said earnestly. "I mean it."

"We are one, Davico." She squeezed my hand. "We are forever in trust to one another. So." She cast about us. "What shall we do with this party we find ourselves at?"

Light was spilling from within the palazzo, lanterns and candelabra flickering and reflecting from beaten copper, making the room bright and alive, full of life, full of laughter. We exchanged glances, and it was obvious that neither of us had the appetite to return. In the gardens behind us, I heard the giggle of a woman, followed by the low laugh of a man.

Celia heard it, too.

She smirked. "Aha . . ."

"Celia . . ." I warned, but she was already up and tugging my hand. "Come," she whispered. "Let us spy, as Cazzetta spies from shadows."

"I don't think we should."

"Of course we shouldn't! That's the pleasure." She tugged me on. "There are many lovers' nooks in these gardens. Palazzo Taglia is famous for them."

"Did you hear that from Sia Allezzia?"

Celia winked back at me. "That and more." She pulled me onward. "Patro Taglia ruined himself for her, he made all these gardens for her. She told me that only after he was ruined did she learn to control her powers over men. So come, we will hide, and we will listen, and we will see what noises Navola's archinomi make under cover of drink and darkness."

And of course, as with all things Celia, I followed.

Never insult a Torre Amonese's taste in women.
Never insult a Pardinese's taste in cheese.
Never insult a Vesunese's taste in ships.
Never insult a Navolese's taste in wine.
Never insult a Borraghese, for he is brutish and he will kill you.

—MARCEL VILLOU OF BIS, FROM HIS *TRAVELS*

Chapter 21

The garden maze of the palazzo was indeed something of a legend, for it had been made under the influence of obsession, with all the money that Archinomo Taglia had borrowed and all his need for hidden places for his hidden life. It was rife with dead ends, maze passages, circular ways, and secret pass-throughs.

"It's impressive," Celia whispered as we explored.

And it was. Pinkfall hedges and marble statuary of Caliba and his nymphs. Fatas and goatmen. Fountains depicting Urula and Urulo, water gouting from her breasts, surrounded by spitting fishes, and him atop storm clouds that hissed with water, and mouths of drowned sailors and their drowned visages ringing. They were strange images, obsessions. It had driven him into debt, and then into sickness.

Celia studied the green bronze features of a fountain of Caliba chasing his nymphs. "Ashia says that Archinomo Taglia is a good lesson for women. That we should never depend upon a man, for it will destroy us in the end."

"Ashia says."

"Indeed she does."

"Not Sia Allezzia?"

"They both say it, if you must know." She took my hand and dragged me deeper into the gardens and maze. The pinkfall was blooming, and so the heady perfume of the hedges was almost overwhelming. Somewhere amongst the greenery, I heard someone sneeze, the scent having overwhelmed them as well. My own nose itched. "What exactly does Sia Allezzia teach you?"

"You still think we must engage in some debauchery."

"I do not."

"I thought we agreed not to lie to each other."

"Well . . ."

Celia laughed. "Ai, Davico. You and your obsession with what women do and what lies beneath their skirts. And then the di Pardi sisters set their eyes upon you, and you blush and run away. You remind me of Lazy, afraid and delighted and afraid that she might actually catch a rabbit." We turned a corner in the maze, then made another turn. "If you stopped pining and simply just took the plunge, you'd be better off. Then you might actually have enough of your mind free to practice at faccioscuro. Instead, you're still being dragged about by that root of yours."

"I'm not dragged about by my root."

"All men are dragged about by their root. And yes, Sia Allezzia says so."

I started to retort, but Celia hushed me with a wave of her hand. "Listen!" she whispered.

I listened. All around us, there were scufflings and sighs. We were surrounded by couples engaged in the parry and riposte of courtship. This, too, was Apexia, the moment of heat, the time when futures were gambled, when fortunes were told, and when lovers unbound themselves.

"Patro Taglia built these gardens well," Celia whispered. "He's inspired them."

Murmured protests and sweet surrenders. Small gasps of pleasure. Low laughter. The rustle of silks and skirts, the popping of toggles. The gardens hummed with sexual desire and promise, it permeated the air, as heavy as the flower perfumes. I felt a tingling in my root. I shifted, suddenly uncomfortable. Celia covered her mouth with laughter.

"Ai. And there it is. The serpent stirs."

I adjusted myself, embarrassed. "We shouldn't be out here."

"Sfai, Davico. Stop running away from the things that make you curious. You love this as much as I."

"I do not."

"Nai? I know you looked at those pictures in your father's library. I heard Sissia say you spent hours poring over them."

I sputtered. "She what?"

"Oh, don't act so caught out. You look like you expect Urulo to strike you down with lightning. So the princeling Regulai likes to feast his eyes. So what?" Her own eyes sparkled at my discomfiture. "I liked looking, too. It is natural. Permit yourself to be yourself, and stop pretending you wish to be some monk for Amo." She took my hand. "Now come. We will spy. We will play Cazzetta and see what we may learn."

We moved as if we were night fatas. We spied, using the moans of the great names of Navola to guide us. We peered in on the bulk of Garagazzo as he grunted over some poor courtesan that he had bought, and we listened to Madrasalvo begging for the attentions of his lover, while the young man made him a fool and made him beg all the more. We saw men and women entwined, face-to-face and tender, and we saw them rooting like dogs, women with their skirts raised, panting as their men frantically humped behind them. We saw the shadows of men worshipping the roots of their young attendants . . . it was as if I were seeing the lust books of my father's library brought to life in all their carnality.

But it was a different sort of couple that ultimately caught and held our attention: my father with Ashia, speaking in quiet tones.

And speaking not of love, but of me.

"It is time, Devonaci," Ashia said. "He is old enough."

"He still needs time."

"Time you do not have."

"There is Celia," he said.

Celia and I exchanged puzzled glances. We could only make out their shadows, but somehow I knew Ashia was shaking her head. "Look at how the di Pardi sisters look upon him."

Celia pinched my arm at their mention. I pushed her hand away, trying to listen. Ashia went on. "If you do not arrange something, he will arrange something himself. He is of the age. More than."

"He is not like that," my father said.

"All parents think their children do not feel the rush of desire, and then they are surprised at how quickly it happens. You Navolese especially. You spend all your time obsessed with sex, and then you are surprised when the young follow your example."

"Davico may have the sword but he still does not wield it," my father said. "He does not have interest in that way."

I could feel Celia's body shaking with laughter beside me. She bit the heel of her hand, bottling up her mirth. I gave her a dirty look.

"Ci. So you say. What if he finds himself a lover?"

"I had lovers. What of it?"

"You had lovers, and you have a bastard to show for it."

Celia and I both startled.

"Bastard?" Celia mouthed at me. I shook my head, as confused as she. I had never heard tell of a sibling. "What bastard?" Celia whispered.

"Who is that?" Ashia asked.

I hushed Celia with a sharp wave of my hand. Just beyond the hedges, my father and Ashia fell silent. They were listening, listening to the night sounds of the garden much as a deer pauses and listens at the rustling of leaves in the Romiglia, suspecting a panther may be stalking.

I was sure they sensed us, simply from the way Celia fairly buzzed beside me, unable to contain her excitement at this strange secret. For my part, I willed myself utterly still, and willed Celia still as well, thinking of myself when I hunted with Aghan Khan, imagining myself part of the garden, one with the pinkfall and the happy gurgle of the distant fountains and the rustling of the hot night breezes. Imagined myself as shadows, and my breath as the breeze, and let myself become still. But beside me, Celia was as loud as an elephant. Her breathing might as well have been that of a bull preparing to charge, and she did not even notice. I glared at her to be silent. The listening stillness stretched between my father and Ashia, between Celia and me, all our shadows frozen.

My father stirred. "Many men have children," he resumed. "A few bastards is a sign of virility."

"What family will let us bind their daughter's hand in flowers if they see a pack of bastards following Davico the way Lazy follows him?"

"A pack?" My father snorted. "You make it sound as if he's plunging his root into every fig in Navola. No. Davico is coming to manhood, but he is not like I was. He cares more for plants and flowers than a willing fig. And even if he were determined to plow every open field in Navola, still I would not take the pleasures of Caliba from him."

"Sfai, Devonaci, you treat me like a wife!"

"A wife!" My father barked surprised laughter. "A wife!" He reached out to Ashia. "Ai, miti, you have a sharp tongue."

"Yes, a wife." Ashia batted away his hands. "A Navolese wife. One of those pretty flowers who you men say you worship." She mimicked a man's voice: "*A Navolese worships his woman as he worships Urula, for he knows to anger the ocean is to court disaster.* Ci." She made a noise of disgust.

My father shook with laughter. "Ashia, miti . . . Are Navolese all so terrible?" He sought to capture her to him, but she batted away his hands again.

"Sweet miti," he coaxed. "I would never presume to treat you as a wife."

"You think I make a joke!"

"I do not."

"Keep your hands to yourself and listen, then."

"Do I not always listen? Do I not truly worship you as sailors worship Urula?"

"And now comes that famous Navolese sugar tongue." This was followed by a stream of words in her own language, all staccatos and sibilants, strange in comparison with Amo's favored tongue, and yet the irritation was clear. If I had been subject to that tone, I would have wilted, but my father only laughed.

"Oh, how I love you, Ashia. How you warm my heart."

"Stop laughing."

"I'm trying."

"And take your hand away."

My father sighed, and at last turned serious. "I hear your words, and attend them. You are right, as always. But now is not the time to bind our name to another's. It is not . . ."

"Yes?"

"We are unsettled now."

"Merai?"

"We are vulnerable. It will take some doing to get agreements to send Sivizza's troops to secure Merai. I need the Callarino—"

"That dog."

"I need him."

"He is sfaccito. He must obey."

"You and I both know that obedience and loyalty have limits. Publicly stripping the Lupari from Navola to send to Merai is something that will test him. Archinomi will complain. Furia and her dogs will push—"

"Cazzetta should have put a knife in her neck years ago."

"And yet such is our situation. To wish otherwise is to close our eyes and dream instead of facing the tiger and his teeth."

"And Davico?" she prompted. "How did he negotiate?"

My father said nothing. In the darkness I could not see his expression, but I sensed he was scowling. I felt Celia's eyes upon me, curious. This was almost worse than having her hear the dissection of my sexual likelihood and prowess.

"He was foolish," my father said at last.

The words came as a blow. I knew that I had behaved rashly in the moment, but some secret part of me had still hoped that my father had at least seen that my spine was strong. That I was a man not easily controlled. Even if I had disappointed him, I had still imagined that he might find some aspect of my behavior laudable.

Such are children: We always hope to be loved in our parents' eyes, no matter how disobedient we may be. But my father's words were a judgment as final as the sultan's knife across the throat of Perfinas. I might as well have had my bleeding head held high.

Ashia shifted in the darkness, her silks rustling. "You treat him as a child, still."

"He is still learning."

"He is about to become a man."

There was another long silence between them. Celia's hand found mine, gripped it.

"He will learn," Ashia said, finally. "Children act as children, and then, all in an instant, they act as men, and make their fathers proud. This will pass. Anyway, I'm sure that you will find a solution. The great Devonaci di Regulai is too clever to be defeated by the simple difficulties of fatherhood."

"Don't patronize me."

Ashia laughed at that, a bright sound I had not heard from her before. She leaned close to my father. "Patronize? You? Devonaci di Regulai? Sfai! I would not dare. The great di Regulai would see through all my deceptions if I were to patronize him."

"Ashia . . ."

"After all, you are the wisest and most intelligent man in all of Navola," she said. "A master of politics and trade . . ."

"Ashia . . ."

"... with a perception unmatched. A mind as sharp as a bone knife, as quick as a silver fish beneath the waves ..."

"Stop it."

"Stop what? I say it not because you are my master but because it is true."

"Don't use that word."

"What word? *Master?* Am I not your slave? Do I not bear the scars upon my cheeks? Do I not obey and serve? I am a slave—"

"Ashia—"

"—and I am content, for the man who gave me the three-and-three is wiser than the ancients of Fusza in their hermitages. My master sees more of the world of men than the sun and moon combined. He bargains better than the Schipians. He is stronger than the bull—" There was a sudden movement from my father. Ashia gasped. Their shadows joined.

"You make it very difficult to think, miti." My father's words were thick and dark.

"I ... *Ai* ..." Ashia's breath hitched. "I have forgotten my place."

"When have you ever forgotten anything?"

There was a rustling of silks, and Ashia's breath came more quickly. "Mercy, patro."

"Oh? Now you beg for mercy?"

Ashia gasped again at something that my father did. "I was ... impertinent."

"And now you wish to atone."

"Yes." Her breathing became ragged and desperate. "Ai. Yes. Let me please you, patro."

"Ai, miti. You are too good for me." I could hear the smile in my father's voice. Ashia gasped again. "You are too good," he said. And then was a rustling of silks and brocades. Their shadow breathing became as one.

Celia tried to linger, but I pulled her away, leaving them to their lovemaking.

"Well," Celia said, tugging a bit of pinkfall from her hair. "That was most enlightening."

"I don't think we should have done that."

"Sfai, Davico. Did you know you had a sibling?"

"No." To me it was the least interesting news amongst the flurry of judgments I had endured at their discussion of me. All I wanted now was to escape the festivities. To be away from all the people, their lusts, their plots, their secrets, and most especially their evaluations of me.

"A bastard . . ." Celia clicked her tongue thoughtfully.

"Are you still thinking about that?"

"How are you not?" She was entirely unbothered that we had listened to my father and Ashia in their privacy. "Cazzetta would know who it is," she said. "He would know your father's son."

"It might be a daughter."

"Nai." She shook her head. "A bastard is a son. A girl . . . we are not bastards. We are nothing."

"That's not true."

She glanced sharply at me. "Ci, Davico. You are an idealist. The bastard is most certainly a boy."

"Go back and ask my father, then, if it interests you so much."

"You should ask him," she said seriously. "It is something you should know. This bastard may one day challenge your inheritance. If he reveals himself, he could take your place. With your Assumption approaching, it would be best for you to know."

I shook my head emphatically. "And how would I explain my question? My father would see through my face in a moment. He would know that we had been spying upon him."

"Aren't you at all curious?" she prodded.

"Maybe he is dead," I suggested. "My older brother died of Schipian fever," I said. "My younger sister of the blue blossoms with my mother. Perhaps he died as well."

"Ci," Celia scolded. "Don't be daft. Of course he is alive, or Ashia would not speak of him so. She would not care about your father's early loves and the seeds he scattered if they were all dead and gone. His root was busy rooting—"

"Please. Enough."

She threw up her hands. "Fine! Enough. Enough of bastards. Enough of thinking. Enough of looking into shadows. Enough of knowledge." She pinched my arm.

"Ouch!"

"You should listen to me, Davico. I am wise."

I rubbed my arm where she had pinched. "Well, you are certainly twisty-minded."

"You should ask him." She made to pinch me again but I dodged.

"Nai. It would be foolish. It would only prove to him that we have eavesdropped." I fended off her hands again. "If he wanted me to know about a brother or sister—Ai! Stop it!—he would have told me already." I captured her wrists and held them together, fighting to keep a grip as she struggled. "*Sentimi.* No matter what his answer, he will deflect and I will not be able to read his truth or falsity. He is too skilled."

"So you'll just give up?"

"I didn't say that."

"Nai?" Celia stopped struggling. A knowing smile spread across her features. "Ai. You have an idea. Tell me what it is."

"Maybe. I don't know." The grain of a possibility was in my mind, but I didn't want to say anything to Celia, for fear that she would place even more pressure upon me.

"Leave it for a few days. I'll see."

Chapter 22

If anyone knew of secret loves and secret children it would be Aghan Khan, a man who had guarded my father for years, in all his travels, in all his meetings, and all his assignations. Aghan Khan would know, just as Polonos knew more than he wished about whitebark and mushrooms thanks to trailing me over the years. And unlike Cazzetta, Aghan Khan was far less likely to take my questions as threads to be pulled and follow them back to my father.

I found Aghan Khan in the dimness of our guards' common room, where the stink of oiled leather and the tang of sharpened steel twined with the sweat of men well-worked from sword practice. Swords and crossbows gleamed dully in their racks along the walls.

When I arrived, Aghan Khan was instructing Polonos and Relus as to how the household guard would be arranged during my Assumption and how they would prevent thefts—urns of wine and sides of pork were already disappearing thanks to the extra servants—but this quickly turned to a discussion of how our guards were to greet and search guests. Listening at the doorway, I gathered there had been an incident with an envoy from Hekkat, where a new warlord once again held sway, and the man had been insulted.

"That fescatolo flea?" Polonos exclaimed. "What of him?"

"You searched his kivis," Aghan Khan said.

"His *whatsis*?"

"The wooden thing he wears around his neck," Relus supplied.

"I didn't search his kivis. You searched his kivis. I searched his eggs."

"And you think that's better?" Aghan Khan asked.

"We didn't know he was an envoy," Polonos said. "He smelled like a horse stall."

"He had just arrived after twenty days overland," Aghan Khan said, tiredly pinching the bridge of his nose.

"Ah. That makes sense then. Twenty days overland does make a man stink."

"Him and his kivis," Relus agreed.

"The envoy," Aghan Khan said, "was doing us an honor by coming immediately to the palazzo. The people of Hekkat do not delay when they arrive. To them, it demonstrates respect."

"Well, he wasn't polite to me," Polonos said.

"Well, you were searching his eggs," Relus said.

"I found a knife inside his thigh, didn't I?"

"And so you then searched his kivis?" Aghan Khan asked.

"Nai," Relus said. "First, he put a curse on us. Then we searched his kivis."

"He put a curse on you?"

"And we found another knife," Polonos said.

"You still have it?"

Polonos drew the knife from his belt and handed it over. "What envoy hides two knives when he comes to sit at the plank?"

Aghan Khan sighed. "It is a Hekkat custom to carry knives." He turned the blade in the light, inspecting it. It was a gaudy thing, covered with jewels that were either rubies or glass. "When they're being polite, they tuck them away. That is how you know they will do no harm. It is a point of honor for them."

"No one told us."

"I'm telling you now. That man's lord represents our best trade passage to Xim. Devonaci has only just reestablished a bank there after many years, and now you've created an incident that Ashia will have to smooth over. Also . . ." He paused. "You missed the knife on his forearm."

"We *what*?" They both goggled at Aghan Khan.

"It's customary for them to wear three." Aghan Khan flipped the knife up in the air, caught it, and handed it back to Polonos, hilt-first. "He's coming back today. You two are expected to apologize."

Polonos scowled as he shoved the knife back into his belt. "I don't like all these people coming and going in the palazzo. There's too many of them."

"Gird your loins then, because it only gets worse from here. Hekkat, Pagnanopol, Cheroux, Bis, Deravash, Wustholt, Zurom, Khyza, Kharat. Them and many more. Ashia has made a list of people for you to look out for." He wagged his finger. "*And also their customs.* Try not to make Devonaci's labor more difficult—" He broke off when he saw me. "Davico? What brings you here?"

I hesitated on the doorway's verge. "I don't want to disturb." Even though these rooms were part of our palazzo, I never felt as if they were my place. This was the realm of men who relished violence and sought it out, and I was an interloper.

"It's not a disturbance. Come in. Come in. These two were just leaving to practice their diplomacy."

"I was wondering if I could practice a little with my sword," I said.

"I'll do it," Polonos volunteered.

"You will not," Aghan Khan said. "You will apologize to the envoy. Ashia will instruct you as to how to kneel and mark your cheek so that he takes the apology seriously. Now go. Both of you."

The pair left obediently enough, but as soon as they were outside, a bickering rose up.

"How did you miss the third knife?"

"I searched his bottom. His top was yours."

"Three fescatolo knives . . ."

Their words faded as they passed out of the courtyard. Aghan Khan listened to the last of them, shook his head with indulgent exasperation, then turned to me. "I'm very busy now, Davico. Perhaps Celia has the time to practice. Your name day has us all in an uproar—are you all right?"

At the mention of my name day, my stomach had twisted, making me wince. It had been happening more and more of late. The frenetic meetings with merchants, the deliveries of wines and sweets, the gifts from dignitaries along with the increasing arrival of guests all served to remind me that my Assumption was fast upon me, and now my stomach pained me daily.

My friend Piero had approached his name day with relish, taking his family's name and sigil, and draping himself in its glory—however tattered and ancient—with delight. Giovanni had passed through his Assumption with aplomb, barely looking up from his books as the celebrations occurred around him. To me, it continued to represent a nameless dread. Another kind of door, as threatening in its own way as the di Pardi sisters, that once I passed through, I could never reopen or escape back from. I dreaded the responsibilities. My stomach twisted again at the thought.

"Are you all right?"

"Nai. It's nothing. My stomach pains a little is all."

"You're nervous."

"In truth, I am. And actually, I was hoping . . ." I had a speech prepared, about my approaching name day, about wanting to sharpen my swordskill, to deserve the mantle of manhood, but in the moment, the words wouldn't come out. I didn't want to trick Aghan Khan. Our world was made up of too much trickery, and he was too honorable. It would dirty him, and it would dirty me to play games of faccioscuro. Instead, I chose to be direct.

"Did my father have other children?"

"Children?" Aghan Khan's eyebrows shot up. "He had two. Your older brother, and your younger sister. You know this."

"I was wondering about . . . others."

"Others?" Aghan Khan regarded me.

"Children that weren't recognized."

"Bastards."

"Well, yes."

Aghan Khan pulled out a chair and sat down. He motioned me to join him, then glanced around the empty guard room and lowered his voice. "That's an interesting question, coming from a young man on the verge of his Assumption. But not one I would have expected from you."

I puzzled at the tone of his voice, then realized with horror what he was implying.

"I don't want to kill them! Why would you think that?"

Aghan Khan held up his hands in apology. "Forgive me, Davico. It seemed a strange question, is all. And coming at such a portentous time . . ." He shrugged. "Well, one might wonder at your motivation, asking here. Asking alone." He looked at me significantly. "Asking a commander of swords and not your father."

By the fatas, the man was sharp. I didn't want to admit to spying upon my father, so I deflected. "In truth, it was Celia who wanted to know."

"Ai." He laughed ruefully. "That makes more sense. She's a sharp one."

I didn't like the admiration underlying his tone, and my expression must have said so.

"Don't take it as an insult, Davico."

"No. Why would I?" I couldn't hide the sudden bitterness I felt, though: not on my face, and not in my voice.

"That was not my meaning," Aghan Khan said.

"Nai? We both know it's true, though. She is true Navolese."

"And you're not?"

"I'm not like her."

I expected him to deny it, to puff me up in some way or another, but instead he was quiet. He regarded me, frowning. "Be wary of the stories you tell yourself, Davico. You may begin to believe them." He held up a hand to forestall me. "The Navolese like their intrigues, that is true, but if that was all there was to Navola or her people I should have left here long ago. Celia has her way of thinking, and you have yours. Don't take it further than that."

I shook my head. "I'm sorry. It's just . . ." I didn't know how to explain the burst of irritation I had felt at his admiration of her. "I sometimes think Celia should be making this Assumption, not me."

"She is not di Regulai," Aghan Khan said sharply.

"Is she not my sister?"

"Don't be clever. Celia is reckless and she enjoys chaos. We are all very lucky that she cannot inherit."

"What about others? Are there others who could?"

"Bastards, you mean." Aghan Khan shook his head. "In truth, I do not know. Nai. That's not true. I know for certain that no one other than you is di Regulai. Your father has never wavered in this. There is no secret offspring waiting to take your place, no dispossessed brother like Ciceque waiting in the wings to foment revolution upon you—"

"That's not what I mean," I said, frustrated at Aghan Khan's assumption of my concerns. "That's Celia's thinking. Not mine. I only mean to know if I have a sibling."

"Why haven't you asked your father?"

"It seems . . ." *Like I've been spying on him.* "It seems delicate."

"Delicate. Hm. Indeed. Well, you've wasted your time, for I do not know. I know that your father was wild when he was younger, and most accomplished at wooing women. But that was well before my time. Young men of your age and your position attract women like flowers attract honeybees. It is something that I'm sure you've already experienced"—the di Pardi sisters once again flooded my mind—"so I assume there must have been some pups along the way. But if some man's wife bore an extra child, she would have claimed it was her husband's for the sake of everyone's good name. And if some family's daughter became heavy in the belly, they likely would have benefited from your family's goodwill, and would not have complained—even if they had to send her for a time to a convent to birth and see the baby off for adoption. Men love to plow a willing field and there are many willing fields here in Navola, and far more willing fields for a name as revered as di Regulai. I've often suspected that half the archinomi here are fathered by someone other than their own, the way you Navolese behave—"

A shout at the gates interrupted us: Polonos, arguing. Aghan Khan looked up at the noise and shook his head. "Ai. It seems Polonos took the wrong lesson." He stood. "With your permission, Davico?"

Of course he didn't need to ask, but of course he did. I stood as well. "We don't want to lose another trade route."

"Indeed."

We both started out, but as Aghan Khan reached the doorway, he paused. "I know that we are hard on you, Davico. That we push you more than others, more than your friends, more than"—he shrugged—"well, anyone, but you should not think that this is because we are disappointed in you. The role you take upon your name day is twice the one your father inherited, which was twice that which the Bull inherited. The task has grown larger, and we are all but men."

I was surprised at his speech. "Why are you telling me this?"

"I hear . . ." He sought for words. "I hear how you speak about yourself." He looked at me significantly. "And about Celia. Do not think that you are somehow not Navolese enough. You are Navolese down to your bones, and you are di Regulai, deeper still. All people tell stories of themselves, and if they say them enough, they begin to believe them: The Borraghese are bloodthirsty, the Torre Amonese are debauched, the Meravese are lovers of luxury, the Navolese are twisted, and on and on. But they are only stories. The next time you hear that the Navolese are twisted, remember that is not what I see of Navola, and it is not why I serve your family. When a Navolese's heart is true, it flies swift and straight, and it is more pure and brilliant than the snow of the Cielofrigo. I watch you, Davico. I see you. Your heart is good and it is true, and that, too, is Navolese. Never doubt that this is a great and awesome strength."

I stood for a long time after he left, thinking about that. Thinking about how I measured myself, about how others measured me, and I continued to think about it as the last days before my Assumption ticked away.

But as I met and greeted delegates and sat at the plank beside my father, my belly twisted and burned. We were always watching for advantage and for risk, always practicing the art of faccioscuro. And always my father's eyes were on me. There did not seem much room in his library for a heart that was open, straight, or true. And though I was warmed to know that the tasks expected of me were larger and more complex than those he had faced when he took our name, it was a small comfort, for the mistakes were present, real, and costly. If we loaned money to a prince that would not pay, or did not know that the wool of a merchant was moldy, or if a gold ship sank under the wrath of the Cerulea, the costs were there, all the same.

My stomach worsened.

On the day before my great event, I woke to terrible pain. I barely managed to find my chamber pot before vomiting. Blood and bile spilled out. I heaved and gagged. I clutched my stomach. It felt afire, as if a rat was gnawing its way out of me. I retched some more, spit streamers of blood, and stared into the chamber pot. The red and black of my guts stared back.

I fell back into bed and resolved to tell no one.

I know that you think that I should have raised some alarm, but all I could think of was the disappointment of my father. How he had spoken to me on the night when I had blundered with the first secretary of Merai. How bitterly he had spoken to Ashia of me afterward. We were always observed. I could not give up advantage or show weakness. And so I pretended health.

But it was a struggle.

It was a struggle even to try on my celebration jacket one last time with Ashia and the tailor examining everything for perfect details. Ashia tugged at the fall of my vest, fingered the height of my collar, spoke under her breath in her own tongue.

I stood, swayed, endured. I closed my eyes as they poked and prodded. I willed the pain away. But when I opened my eyes, Ashia's gaze was hard upon me, as dark as Scuro's coals, probing.

"Are you well, Davico?"

"My stomach pains," I said.

"Badly?"

I wanted to tell her that my stomach was knives and that my chamber pot was red with vomit, but instead, I only shrugged. "It's been bothering me, is all." Remembering how she and my father had discussed me in the gardens. Any new weakness I revealed would be dissected by them. I would not reveal it to her. "It was the peppers last night, I think."

"Well." Ashia frowned. "Eat lightly today, princeling. Tonight you dine with Archipatro Garagazzo and the Callarino. Best to be your best."

"My father has some scheme, doesn't he?"

"It is to honor your family's closest friends before your great day. Tomorrow, the Hundred Names will fill palazzo, quadra, hall, and balcony, and in that bustle, the most important might be lost." Her eyes flicked to the tailor, warning me to ask no more questions, and telling me, too, that my father did indeed scheme.

"My stomach will be fine." I exhaled slowly, hiding the pain I felt. "I'll be fine."

"Good," she said. "It is necessary." As if the matter were settled.

But still, the way she said it made me imagine she might have more to say. After overhearing her thoughts of me in the Taglia gardens with my father, it was dawning on me that she attended me much more closely than I had ever suspected. She might be obsessed with the quality, color, and cut of my silk, but that was not where Ashia started or ended when it came to me.

Ashia plucked at the embroidery of my jacket.

"There is a thread here," she said to the tailor.

"Ai. You have a good eye." He took scissors and cut the thread.

"Good." She clicked her tongue. "Better."

Her eyes were as sharp as a falcon's as she circled me. The tailor followed, nervous that she would find more fault.

Who was Ashia? I wondered. What did she truly see when she looked at me? She wore her beauty and slave scars like a mask, so what lay behind? I imagined her thoughts, lurking there, thoughts and judgments as secret and cold and deep as the eels that swam the undercurrents of the Cerulea. Ashia was as skilled at the art of faccioscuro as any Navolese—so skilled in fact that I had never noticed her playing our game. She was my father's concubine. She was the property of Archinomo di Regulai. But now I wondered at what else she was.

What was it Celia had quoted?

A woman must never let a man see her truth, for he will find her horrifying. Something of the sort.

How much more so for a woman who was a slave?

On the heels of this thought, I wondered if Ashia hid things also from my father, in the same clever way that she had hidden her judgments of me. The truth was, I had not seen Ashia clearly. If Celia had not led me to spy that night, I would not have guessed how closely Ashia observed me, or how she advised my father. I was not surprised that she had thoughts and feelings, but rather that she kept so many of them perfectly hidden. *Mensa obscura. Occulta. Obscolta. Nascolta. Segreta.*

There were oceans of Ashia that I did not know, and I did not like knowing that she measured me so closely with those dark secret eyes.

The tailor finished. "Ai! It is perfect!" He stood back, admiring his work. "Archinomi will seek to copy us, siana, but they will never match."

When Ashia did not respond, he turned to her for affirmation. "Is it not perfect, siana?"

Ashia's eyes never left mine. "It will have to do."

My pains increased as the day progressed. I could find no comfort, not in our gardens, nor in the library, not even when the heat of the day came on and we retired to our rooms for afternoon sussirre.

Sun blazed beyond my shutters, beating upon the palazzo stones. If I looked outside, the red-tiled roofs seemed to nearly boil with the heat. In my room, the air felt hot, close, stifling. I lay naked, the humid air heavy upon me. All through the palazzo we lay napping, servants, guards . . . family. I imagined that I could almost feel the palazzo itself breathing, a lazy heavy rhythm in time with the breaths of its inhabitants, all of us drowsy and insensate under the high sun. All at rest.

My stomach twisted. I stifled a groan. Lazy pricked up her ears. She climbed up on the bed and licked my face worriedly. She was not supposed to climb upon my bed—had not since she was a bare puppy—but now she licked my face anxiously. I pushed her away.

"Stop it. I'm fine."

But she wasn't deterred. She licked me again, licked my face, licked my hands when I tried to push her muzzle away, and then pulled at my hand with her teeth as if trying to drag me out of bed.

Her expression was so full of concern that I found myself holding back a sob of gratitude. This was love. Lazy was true. Lazy, more than any person I had known, cared for me. I felt a terrible loneliness at that thought. Lazy wanted nothing but comfort and happiness for me. Could that be said of anyone else in the palazzo? Celia, perhaps, but even Celia pursued her own agendas. Lazy's love for me was entirely selfless. It was both warming and humbling to feel such care from another.

This is not the life for me.

The thought came to me as if handed down from Amo.

This was not the life for me.

Almost before I knew it, I was out of my bed and drawing on clothes. This life was not for me. I was not suited for it. This was a place for Celia. This was a place for my father. This was a place for Ashia. It was not for me.

Lazy wagged her tail uncertainly at my sudden movement but when I pulled my riding boots from their chest, she rushed to the door, tail wagging and eager.

To my surprise, as soon as I started moving, the pain in my stomach receded. Even as I dressed it was disappearing, as if it had never been. I felt a lightness suffusing my being. With every decisive motion, my taking up a cloak, my sliding a dagger into my sleeve, my taking down my broad-brimmed riding hat, I felt lighter. I could scarce believe what I was about, and yet, with each step, I felt better, and my determination grew.

Lazy and I slipped outside and gently closed my door. We stole along the columned balcony that circled our palazzo's garden quadra, moving from column to column, more silent even than when I had fooled Aghan Khan in the forests of the Romiglia. We eased down the stairs, looped around the quadra premia, keeping to the walls, feeling the blazing, baking heat of the sun, then made our way through to the horse yard and the shadow heat of the stables.

Stub whickered greeting. His head was over the door of his stall, anticipating my arrival.

"Hello, old friend," I whispered as I ran my hands along his neck. "True friend." I laid my head against his neck and felt him breathing. There was a steadiness to animals that stood in sharp and painful contrast with the whirl of men, and it firmed my conviction that I was doing the right thing.

This was what Soppros had been trying to explain in his philos. Man had fallen from the woven net of life, and had been alone ever since. But Virga's weave was still present. It was all around us, if only we sought it. It was here, in the steady rise and fall of Stub's breath beneath my hand. It was here in the warm scents of hay and manure. It was here, if you pressed your ear to listen, in the placid heartbeat of a creature still connected to Virga's weave. One had only to listen.

I became aware of my own heart beating eagerly, full of anticipation that I had not felt for a long time. With every step away from my rooms, I felt as if I were parting a veil of confusions and dark dreams, and now, at last, the world was clear. As clear as the air after a heavy storm, when the sky glitters blue and sharp in the sun, and the far hills of the Romiglia are visible from every rooftop in Navola.

Lazy licked my palm. Stub butted his head against me. I felt as if the shards and fragments of my soul were finally being assembled, a shattered pot made whole.

I was not alone. And I was no longer in pain.

There was only one path for me.

I seized Stub's saddle and laid it across his back. I wasn't even sure what I planned. It was as if my hands controlled my mind. In moments the straps were tight around Stub's belly and the bit was fitted between his teeth. Lazy went to the stable doors and peered out, as if scouting on our behalf.

I tightened the belly strap one last time. Stub immediately sucked in his stomach to help make the strap more secure. He did not try to trick me. Did not try to keep the saddle loose. Stub was a friend, just as Lazy was a friend. My friends and I slipped out of the stable.

The palazzo courtyard shimmered in the heat. We eased our way across. Three sly friends, passing under the closed shutters of the palazzo, those shutters closed like sleeping eyes, the palazzo sleeping, just like all who dwelled within.

The guard at the gate was Vissius, who had been in my father's service for only a year, come to Navola from the Romiglia, like Polonos and Relus.

"Riding in this heat?" he asked as he began pulling aside the bars.

"I cannot rest," I said, which was truthful enough.

"I imagine so," he said, grinning. "You have a grand night waiting for you. Just a moment, sio, and I'll be back with a horse."

"Do not trouble yourself," I said. "I'll be fine."

He hesitated, caught between orders from Aghan Khan and my instruction.

"If I cannot ride alone for even a moment," I said, "I hardly deserve to assume the Regulai name. Don't you think?"

He laughed at that, shook his head in agreement, and stepped aside.

I ducked through the gate and emerged on the cobbled way that ran before our palazzo. I laid my reins across Stub's neck. We turned west, aiming for Via Andretta, which would lead out through the city gates, and then into the countryside, and then onward, south and west. The wilds beckoned. The Romiglia beckoned. I could smell the flowers already, feel the dampness of fallen whitebark, could hear the calls of redthroat and bluetip.

A shadow emerged from a door alcove.

Cazzetta, blocking our path.

"Whither away, princeling?"

For a moment, I imagined spurring Stub forward, riding over him, but Cazzetta was already beside me, his hands reaching up for the bridle, tugging down Stub's head, patting him in a friendly manner.

By the fatas, the man moved like Urulo's breath. Even in bright sunshine he was hard to follow. One moment he stood ahead of you, the next he was at your side and had control of your horse.

"Whither away?" he asked again.

I could not answer.

Cazzetta waited.

"I thought I would ride," I said finally.

"I thought you might, as well."

I swallowed, my mouth dry.

There are moments when we make decisions that define our life entire. Looking back, knowing what I know now, this was my moment, as full of fate as Caliba's decision to steal Erostheia from Amo. From this one decision, everything proceeded.

All would have been different if I had ridden on. Cazzetta would not have stopped me, I think. He did not truly bar me. But he forced me to see myself, and what I saw reflected in his eyes, I did not like. I did not like to see myself fleeing in secret, fleeing name and duty. It reeked of childishness. Of caprice and cowardice. Another sort of recklessness, much like my reckless bargaining with the first secretary of Merai, that would harm my family. I did not like that mirror that Cazzetta held up to me.

And so, though my deepest soul yearned to flee to the wilds of the Romiglia—to seek the woven net of life, to follow the wisdom of Soppros—instead I chose the path of name and family. I chose the path of the Regulai.

I turned Stub and Lazy back to the palazzo, and in that moment I ensured all that followed, both the horrifying and the sublime.

Chapter 23

My father's carefully selected group of honored allies arrived in the deep evening, as the stones of the palazzo were finally cooling, and as the night winds of the Cerulea began to whisper over the roofs of Navola.

These were the people that Ashia had said should not be lost in the noise and revelry of the general celebration.

Garagazzo, Amo's voice, archipatro and iron fist of our faith. The Callarino, our master of politics and the Hundred Names of the Callendra. General Sivizza, the first name of the Lupari. With these men, my father had forged prosperity in Navola. He had bent their purposes and promises to him, and because of it, peace had held in Navola for nearly two decades.

Of my own family, there was my father and there was me, and there was Celia. Ashia was present but did not sit, refusing to eat with us as it was not her place, though still she acted as hostess for the evening. Aghan Khan also joined us, a military man for Sivizza's entertainment.

But there was one discomfiting addition, whom I did not understand at all.

Lady Furia.

She came with an attendant girl, slave-scarred, whose pale watchful eyes reminded me much of Cazzetta and who tasted every dish before Furia let it pass her own lips. It started when we began with our ritual toasts of past, present, and future, and continued on throughout the meal.

"Really, siana?" my father asked as Furia made her servant taste a small piece of potato crusted with parsley and Pardi tomato. "You think I would poison you in my own house? Am I the pig who spits?"

"Not at all," Furia said. She cut a head from a dish of eels and offered it to her servant girl. "Here, Silxa. This will be divine, I'm sure."

The girl, instead of taking the food with hand or tongs, bent to Furia's hand and delicately plucked the oily flesh from between Furia's fingers using only her teeth.

We all watched, revoltafame, that strange mix of fascination and disgust that one feels when one catches one's uncle having sex with a servant. Revulsion, fascination, embarrassment, the sensation that you should not look but stare anyway. The girl nibbled at the treat. It was uncomfortably intimate. It was like watching two women, entwined as if they were one of Arragnalo's sketches, but not in private, instead performing their lust upon the public steps of Catredanto Amo.

The girl swallowed, her pale bare throat showing the passage of the eel.

"It's good, isn't it?" Furia said. "Siana Ashia is famous for her table."

The girl did not reply, but opened her mouth for the next morsel. I was reminded of a falconer feeding her pet.

Aghan Khan had told me that Polonos and Relus had nearly come to blows with Furia's own Khus warriors when she arrived at our palazzo and wanted them to accompany her within. Eventually they had compromised on this single handmaid, whom Aghan Khan warned me to avoid, for her fingernails were sharpened like knives and poisoned with distilled serpiixis, such that if she scratched anyone—even herself—that person would die within minutes.

I had been much discomfited to find Furia and her strange handmaid at dinner, but now, watching the woman feeding her pet, I felt oddly grateful for the table's distraction from me and my own condition, for my stomach once again was paining me greatly.

"You are behind my walls," my father said, "beneath my roof, at my table. *Fieno secco, vino fresco, pane caldo.* And still you do not trust?"

It was an ancient promise, and a powerful one: Dry hay to sleep, cool wine to drink, warm bread to eat. The Navolese oath of hospitality and succor. An assurance of safety and protection, and one that no honorable Navolese would ever breach. It was this point my father now pressed.

"You cannot say you do not trust the honor of the Regulai," my father said. "So what is the meaning of your fear?"

"Fear?" Furia laughed. "I have no fear." She selected a small shrimp poached in lime and offered it to her girl. "I trust no one," she said, "so I fear nothing. It's as simple as that." She watched closely as the girl chewed and swallowed. "I have not the smallest speck of fear in my eye."

"Do you really think he would poison you, here?" Garagazzo asked.

Furia smiled slightly. "I think only that I could poison myself here. Little Silxa does not protect me; she protects my dearest Devonaci. Come girl." She offered a spoonful of cold soup. The girl bent to taste. Again Furia watched closely, with an almost anticipatory fascination.

"Really, Nicisia," my father said, testily. "It's as if you expect that poor girl to turn purple and die before you."

"You make an excellent point. It could be a slow poison," Furia said. "I shall wait a moment." She sipped her wine and continued to study her slave with close interest, seeking signs of death.

"She seems to breathe yet."

"You sound almost disappointed," General Sivizza said.

"Nicisia . . ." my father began again.

"Look at it this way, Devonaci: If I were to fall poisoned in your own palazzo, the names of many would rise against you. I'm doing you a favor."

"Don't feed me fish guts and call it caviar."

"Call it what you will. I really don't care."

When Furia's slave did not collapse purple in a heap, Furia took a morsel of eel for herself. "Ai! Siana Ashia!" Her face suffused with bliss. "This is almost good enough to die for." She made an act of swooning at the flavor, smirking at my father as she swallowed. "The Regulai always did fill a fine table."

"It's a lonely way to live," Aghan Khan said.

"What is?"

"Trusting no one. Living in fear. Never letting your guard down. Never able to relax, even amongst friends."

"Are we friends?" Furia asked. "I hadn't heard."

"Allied in interest, no?" the Callarino suggested.

General Sivizza said, "I myself cannot imagine what a misery my life would have been, if not for the trust and loyalty of the Lupari." The old warrior swirled his wine thoughtfully. "Trust, the love of good companions, they are as vital as food and wine. Perhaps more so, for a soldier. We could not win through the terror of battle without a brotherhood of trust."

"Nor could I survive without the love and support of my priests," Garagazzo agreed as he scooped garlic and Amotito mussels onto his plate and cracked into them with relish. "As it says in the Libri Luminari, *If we do not feel the love of Amo, we gasp as the fish gasps on the beach.*"

"Thank the fatas I am not a fish, then." Furia offered her slave a spoonful of mussel broth, then took some herself before returning her attention to the priest. "Perhaps our difference is that of sex. You are men, I am a woman. We sail different seas. Trust is a vice a women can ill afford."

At Furia's words, I noticed Celia perk in interest. I was reminded of our own conversations on this topic, and how closely she and Furia compared. Celia was on the verge of speaking, but the Callarino challenged Furia.

"Do you think our seas are so different, siana?"

"Is the sky blue? Is Scuro not hungry for Erostheia? Let us speak plainly. When I sit at this table, every man here thinks first of what lies beneath my bodice," Furia said. "Not how many great names have marked their cheeks upon my boot. Not the troops I order. Not the slaves I own. Not the navisoli I command. Only my thighs and what lies between—"

"I don't know about that—" the Callarino started.

"Nai, you are not true. You see me almost as naked as you see Silxa here, and she can kill men dead in an instant. It is thus, and it has always been thus."

"Men worship a women's form," Aghan Khan said. "How is this an evil?"

"Ci. Worship our form. Men make poems about our pretty lips, and then rage when we move our lips to speak."

"Sia Lisana," Celia said, her eyes glowing.

"Very good, Balcosi girl." Furia's eyes turned to me. "And what does the princeling think of all of this?"

"I—" I was caught out.

"Oh, Davico likes the forms of women very much," Celia said airily. "All the servant girls speak of how he spies on them when they bathe."

Conversation stopped dead at the table. I stared at Celia, feeling my blush and embarrassment rise but she simply winked at me, wickedly pleased. I was reminded of Aghan Khan's description of her: a lover of chaos. Piero had said similar, but I had not taken it seriously, because I was not the target. I felt angry, betrayed, and embarrassed.

The silence stretched, and then, suddenly was broken by a guffaw from Garagazzo. "Spies a lot, does he?"

"All the time," Celia said.

Furia's eyes were glittering. My father was hiding a smile. Garagazzo was laughing, and the Callarino with him. I could feel myself blushing, my face explosively red and hot, more facciochiaro than chiaro can be. I wished the ground would swallow me up, but the Callarino seized on my example.

"Ai! And well he should!" he said, pounding the table. "It's hardly something to be embarrassed of. It is natural to desire to see beauty, and there is no shame in it. If a man appreciates the form of a woman, it is a compliment."

"Even in her private bath?" Furia asked.

"Who amongst us has not played the boy at the keyhole?"

"Not I," General Sivizza said. "Girls are the same as any to me."

"Only because you prefer to root the boys," my father said.

"But of course!" Sivizza said. "A young man, blooming with strength . . . Ai. Now, that is a fine and wondrous creature! They are like lions. Lean muscles, coiled with power. Manes of thick hair. Long lashes. Ai. It is wondrous that Argo has wrought us so." He glanced at Furia. "But does this not also show that whether you are a pretty girl or a pretty boy, everyone endures a hungry eye or two?"

"Nai!" Celia protested. "It is different!"

"It is simply life," General Sivizza disagreed. "A man's eye seeks to drink of beauty, and a woman's eye is no different. We all have desires. Our bodies were formed by Argo at his potter's wheel, and fired by the light of Amo's sun, and kissed to life by Tressia, and woven into the net of all living things by Virga. All living things desire beauty. It is gift and a delight, not something to scorn."

"Agreed," Garagazzo said. "The Libri Luminari says that we should not scorn any part of the body, but must love all."

"With balance," Aghan Khan amended.

"Of course with balance," Garagazzo said, testily. "A madness is a madness after all, but the life sensations that Amo fired into Argo's clay are not to be scorned. Amo desired, and so does man. It is no sin to love beauty."

"And if the beauty does not like it?" Celia asked brightly.

"Ai. Clever girl. You pin the wind with that, though you do not realize it," Garagazzo said. "This is not a problem of women, but the problem of beauty. The lesson of Erostheia is that beauty has always been both blessing and curse. It matters not whether root or fig lies between the legs. If you are beautiful, you will be pursued and hungered for, man or woman."

"And yet the tale of Erostheia is that of a woman pursued, not a man," Celia pointed out.

Garagazzo scowled. "By the fatas, you are a stubborn girl."

"She is that," my father said, smiling faintly. "But what of her point? Erostheia was a woman, pursued by Scuro and Amo, not a man."

"In the text, the lesson is clearly about beauty," Garagazzo insisted. "Not about sex."

"I seldom hear of armies raping boys and men," Lady Furia said. "But I often hear of armies raping girls and women."

"Both happen," Sivizza rumbled. "Both happen." But he seemed discomfited.

"It happens, yes, but Plaesius's logic demands we gather many stories, not a single one. Only if we gather many stories do we discern a pattern, and then perhaps a truth."

Celia was nodding along with Furia's words, her eyes shining.

Furia went on: "Too, how many women stand as archinomi? How often do we speak of matranomo and not patro? It is the patronomi who speak and cast cartadecisi in the Callendra, not the matra."

"Men are naturally born to seek power," the Callarino replied. "Women naturally desire to nurture. The sphere of men is politics and war. The sphere of woman is finance and household."

Furia raised her eyebrows. "So I am unnatural?"

"You"—the Callarino wiped his mouth carefully—"are unique."

Furia smirked. "So diplomatic. I see how you made your rise in the Callendra."

"I made my rise because I speak with reason."

"Reason." Furia's eyes narrowed. "I give you a Plaesius Pattern and you ignore it. This is your reason. So, let us ask another." She turned, and at first I thought she would speak to Celia, but instead, she spoke to Ashia, standing behind, observing the table and its service. "Let us ask Devonaci's slave. No one can deny that she sails the treacherous seas of men. Perhaps she can convince you, where I do not."

We all stiffened at her words. My father's expression went dangerously dark. "My slave?"

"Is she not sfaccita?"

Aghan Khan's hand fell to his knife. Garagazzo and the Callarino exchanged concerned glances. Sivizza's glass had paused, halfway to his lips. Celia's eyes darted between Furia and my father. Furia's handmaid curled her poisonous fingers into claws. Furia, unconcerned by the blow she had dealt, took another eel and popped it into her mouth. She caught us all staring and paused.

"Oh come now. What is this fastidiousness?" She gestured with her eating tongs. "Does Ashia not wear the three-and-three upon her cheeks?"

"Siana . . ." the Callarino started, delicately.

Furia interrupted him with a look of contempt. "Oh, stop it, you piggy eel. I deal in the misery trade. I am not afraid to speak plainly. Ashia is marked. She is bought, and bought for a purpose. Men are bought to fight and labor." She tossed the eel into her mouth. "And women are bought to fuck."

"Scuro burn your eyes—" my father started.

"Sfai, Devonaci!" Furia taunted. "Why so angry? Break the mirror if you like, but the truth remains. Ask your slave what she thinks. Here she stands behind us while we eat. Ask the sfaccita what seas she has sailed. You, Devonaci, may have fallen in love with a sfaccita, but that does not change—"

Aghan Khan rose, tugging forth his blade. "Furia, by the fatas, you go too far—" He broke off as Ashia, standing behind him, touched his shoulder, restraining him.

On Ashia's face, where one might have expected rage or hurt, there was only serenity. "It's quite all right," she said as she gently pressed him down into his chair. "Please. Do not rise with steel, old friend."

She waved for our servant Sissia to bring a chair for herself and motioned for it to be placed beside my father at the table. She took the seat, and turned her attention to Furia.

"My cheeks are indeed marked," she said. "And I am indeed a slave. And"—she took my father's hand in her own, twining her fingers between his—"the world of men is indeed a dangerous sea for a woman to sail. You are most correct."

Furia smiled slightly. "So, sfaccita. You do know your place. I had wondered."

My father's face purpled, but Ashia's hand restrained him. She remained unruffled.

"My place, Siana Furia, is where my master desires. Tonight, he desires for me to host you, and so I obey. His pleasure is my pleasure." She stroked my father's hand. "It is lucky, I think, that he sees value in you, for if it were my choice, you would lie gutted like a fish upon our marble, and your own intestines would be your final meal. And that poisonous fata behind you would make no difference."

Her speech was so serene that if you listened only to the tone, you could be fooled into thinking that Ashia offered sweets instead of murder.

"So, in this case," Ashia continued, quirking a smile, "perhaps you are more grateful for the politics of men than you had imagined, for if these politics were my politics, you would not see the sun rise."

A shocked silence stretched between us. I watched Furia's handmaid hungrily flex her poisonous fingers. I could almost hear them cracking, and then silence was cracked by laughter.

Delighted, pleased, enchanted.

Furia's.

"Ai!" Furia exclaimed. "Ashia, ti amio. You are too good! Too excellent by far!" Her laughter was as bright and merry as a forest brook. Her expression was almost rapturous with girlish delight. It was utterly unlike any face I had ever seen from the feared Lady Furia.

"Ai. She is too brilliant for you, Devonaci." Furia wiped her eyes, still chuckling. "You do not deserve her. You may set a dragon eye upon your desk, but Ashia. She is your true treasure." She fanned herself with a hand, recovering her breath. "He does not deserve you, Ashia. Run away with me. We would be so fine together. We would rule all of Navola and all these weak men here. Their great names and their steel swords would fall prostrate before us, worshipful. Ai, miti," she said, using the term of endearment, "we would make a fine pair. Navola would tremble before us."

"A good thing for Navola that I am content, then," Ashia said.

And then she toasted Furia with my father's wine, and just like that the conversation turned and the dinner's brooding menace dissolved. Furia ate her dishes without first feeding her girl. There were jokes about archinomi in the Callendra, and discussion of the play by Boltiricchio where the men become asses and the women whipped them, and the girl Cilizia was forced to decide whether to save them, with Caliba arguing that men are asses in any case, and so there is no difference, except that they are better endowed as animals, and worked harder. There were more jokes and more wine flowed, and it was almost, almost, as if there was no conflict between us.

More food arrived. More laughter filled our hall. Ducks were brought out on golden platters and there was much admiration expressed for their tender meat and crackling skin.

Garagazzo sang praises as if he were singing Amo Valoris in the catredanto, and people's hands became oily with duck flesh, all of us eating in the traditional way, digging our fingers into the birds, then dipping our prizes in the berry and sage sauce, sweet date sauce, and others, all of them made according to Ashia's knowledge, and everyone was so busy with their own meals that no one noticed that I picked at mine and piled the food in different ways so that the carcass appeared eaten and yet I consumed little.

Furia's baiting of my father and Ashia had not made my stomach any more comfortable, and though everyone smiled now, I knew that a smiling conversation under the moon sometimes results in murder under the sun, and so I remained wary while the others enjoyed.

"Well, now we're all oily-handed," Sivizza joked, leaning back at last, dipping his fingers in a water bowl, and then wiping them upon the tablecloth.

"I don't know why anyone would speak ill of an oily hand," Garagazzo said. His fat hands were plunged deep into a second carcass that Ashia had prepared specially for him. He turned to eye my own plate, hungrily. "You should eat, Davico. The siana's bird is not to be scorned." His chin dripped with grease.

"I've eaten," I protested, not liking that others were now looking at me.

"More is better," Garagazzo said as he dipped another bite. "Ai, siana, this is a fine bird. Why will you not give my cook the trick of it?"

"But then you would not visit!" Ashia said.

"Not true!"

"Archipatro, I know you have sent servants to spy and discover the recipe."

"I would never."

"Annetta, Amosina, Patruccho, I have caught them all."

Garagazzo laughed. "Mercy, siana. No matter how many times my cook girds himself for the assault, always the result is . . ." He shook his head. "I do not know. The bird always has an emptiness to it."

"Love," Ashia said. "It's missing my love."

Furia snorted.

"Amo's love for you," Ashia continued, unruffled. "That is the secret ingredient. Your cook does not love you as the Regulai love you."

My father's eyes twinkled. "It's how I guarantee that the church will pray for our prosperity, and guide the vianomae to love us all the more."

"I believe that better," Furia said.

"You could make it a gift to Amo," Garagazzo suggested. "Something that all the religious orders could enjoy. Every monastery could make it. Every nunnery. And then every voice would rise in praise of the Regulai. And Navola would be famous for our ducks. More famous than our wine!"

"I've known wars won with the bellies of soldiers," General Sivizza said. "But this would be new."

"I could declare a feast day!" Garagazzo declared. "And I would lick the grease from every finger!" He was waving a drumstick like a baton. People laughed.

Celia smiled mischievously. "You could have a painting made, Archipatro. A worship of the divine and most oily and luscious duck. It could decorate the ceiling of the central rotunda in the catredanto. Priests and nuns and ducks, and you at the center."

"Nai. Not me at the center. Saint Ashia of the Duck."

"Oh no," Celia said. "It should be a religious painting. It should be you." As she spoke, she winked across the table at me, and I knew—knew absolutely—what she was thinking: the rumors of Garagazzo.

She was imagining Garagazzo, painted fat and naked upon the catredanto's ceiling, his body oily with duck, his nuns' faces buried in the folds of his belly, worshipful tongues busy. I don't know how I knew the exact image she was thinking of, but I knew that I was right, and now Celia winked at me, knowing that I knew. And now I couldn't get more images out of my mind, the whole mural and all its details.

There would be lines of priests with duck-oiled roots, and Garagazzo would be at the center of these monks and nuns, the nuns sucking his belly, and him sucking the roots of priests as sensuously as he just now was sucking at his own oily fingers.

Celia's eyes twinkled, knowing that she had poisoned my mind.

She was truly awful.

"I can arrange a feast for your priests if you so desire," Ashia was saying. "A duck for every devotee."

"Don't forget the nuns," Celia interjected with another wicked glance at me. "The nuns shouldn't miss out!"

"The nuns as well," Ashia agreed, unaware of our interplay.

I glared at Celia.

Garagazzo continued sucking the grease from his fingers. "Sfai, Siana Ashia," he said. "If I let you feed my priests and nuns, the next thing I know, you will be leading prayers at the catredanto, and all the people of Navola will be marking their cheeks upon your feet."

"There's an image," Furia said.

Celia crossed her eyes at me. I choked on my wine.

"Are you well, princeling?" Lady Furia asked.

I coughed, trying to get my breath back. "I'm fine."

"But you eat nothing."

"He's nervous!" Garagazzo defended me, clapping me on the back. "What boy would not be nervous, faced with his destiny? I remember my own Assumption, and it filled me with terror, if I'm honest before Amo."

"It's true," the Callarino said, looking up from a separate conversation with Aghan Khan. "Passing through the veil of manhood is no small thing. A boy becomes a man, a man has a name, shares it with a wife, becomes a father, passes on his name . . . It is no small thing."

The other men around the table were nodding, all of them clearly remembering their own name days, their own Assumptions.

"It is a great day for the patronomo," General Sivizza said. "A great thing for di Regulai to have a named heir. And a great day for Navola. A clear path through the thickets of Navolese politics is a great gift for the city." Though he was speaking of me, his eyes were on my father, who lifted his wineglass in acknowledgment.

"Better than the Borraghese," my father said. "All of them with their knives, fighting for the recognition of their favored archinomo."

"Thank Amo, Scuro, and all the fatas that Navola is not Gevazzoa, and we are not the filthy Borraghese," Garagazzo said.

"Well said," agreed the Callarino. Furia made a face of agreement as well, and we all drank to our luck that we had not been subjected to the horror of being born filthy Borraghese.

When we had finished our toast, my father said, "It is not solely by my hand that Navola has come to prosperity," he said. "It is thanks to all of you seated here that we enjoy peace."

I was surprised that he said so in front of Lady Furia, for I had never seen her craving peace of any sort, but she did not argue, and in fact raised her wine again in toast.

"To a long peace," she said. "May it outlast all our mortal lives."

We drank to that toast as well, and then my father leaned in, and I knew instantly this moment was the true reason for the dinner. Everything before it had been but prologue. My stomach tightened.

"There is something we must discuss," my father said.

"Merai," Sivizza said.

"Just so. They are unsettled."

"Bad business to have them in chaos, with Cheroux on the other side, chafing for opportunity. Andreton would be more than happy to find an excuse to 'rescue' the Red City. And then he will be on our borders."

"Indeed," my father said. He paused. "Which is why I have forged an agreement to send the Lupari to aid them."

People around the table startled, exchanging troubled glances.

"But who will defend Navola?" the Callarino asked. "What if Pardi were to attempt to break from us? Or if Vesuna were to sail upon us? Duke Umbrusco would love to see our ships in flames."

"And what if that mad priest Magare were to rouse the countryside?" Garagazzo asked.

My father waved aside the chorus of protest. "Worry not, I have a plan."

Furia smirked. "When do you not?"

"Indeed. I would like to train and arm a new militia, to defend Navola."

General Sivizza frowned. "You would replace the Lupari?"

"Not replace, supplement."

Furia's eyebrows were up. "You would give weapons to . . . what?

Farmers? Guild laborers? Stonemasons and weavers? Painters and woodcarvers? The shopkeepers?" She laughed. "Well, you always were prone to fantasies."

My father shot her an irritated look. "Don't act as if it hasn't been done before. Navola has defended herself before. This is not unprecedented."

"In your father's time," Aghan Khan said, "it was done. When Cheroux came, we armed the vianomae and held the invaders at bay."

"Yes, yes, we know. The Bull raised the peasants and gave them arms, Navola Valoris," Furia said. "It's splattered all over the walls of your quadra premia. But it was the Lupari who gave us victory, not that rabble."

"I believe that if a man has his toes rooted in Navola's dirt, he is worth a hundred," my father said. "He will fight for family and friends and survival, and that is sufficient for defense."

"*A man defending his door is as a lion,*" Garagazzo quoted, agreeing.

"But what of the Lupari?" Sivizza asked. "Have we not served well? Now you will . . . exile us to Merai?"

"Exile? Sfai!" my father exclaimed. "My general, my old friend, no! That is not my meaning. My meaning is that we must increase our strength. To arm our people will give us a different weapon in our armament."

"And one less expensive," Furia said drily.

My father shot her an irritated look. "We know that an army of both sword and bow is more dangerous than an army with only one or the other. An army with both foot and horse. Navola is stronger when she can fight the distant war and defend her own walls simultaneously." He looked around the table, serious. "We know that Cheroux covets us still, even after all these years."

"And their path leads through Merai," Sivizza said, waving a hand in agreement.

"Indeed. Merai aided Cheroux in my father's time," my father said, "and Merai has kinship ties there still."

"I still do not see why you wish the Lupari to leave Navola."

"Or to give weapons to farmers and craftsmen and villagers," the Callarino said. "It is a terrible risk to arm vianomae."

"With the church and Callendra working together, it can be done. We can offer both assurances of Amo's love for those who serve loyally, and offers of lower taxes for those who join."

"This is not temporary, is it?" Furia pressed. "You wish to tie Merai to us. Once the Lupari defeat Ciceque you intend to billet them there."

"You do?" Sivizza asked. "For how long?"

"Until Merai agrees that her interests are those of Navola. If we can defend our own walls with our own people, our professional swords can march as they please. If Merai were not always ready to open her skirts to Cheroux, we would be more secure. Binding Merai assures us of real peace, and the Lupari are the key."

"And also . . ." Furia trailed off, considering. "If Merai is tamed and you have militia swords to guard our walls . . . would our professional soldiers stop their march in Merai? A militia here would mean that the Lupari could march at will." Furia's eyes narrowed. "Empire. You dream of empire."

Everyone turned to her. My father was smiling slightly and I felt a pang of jealousy. I had not seen what she saw clearly. I had been on that balcony when we negotiated with Merai, when my father gave the first secretary the impression that sending the Lupari to aid them was a gift. A gift that he himself had thought of. And now Furia saw not just this single maneuver of my father's but a wholly more complicated game. It was as if he had plucked all the cards from the deck of cartalegge, and let all the others play their short games of points, small slights, betrayals, and gambits.

And meanwhile he played an entirely different game.

Empire.

The word hung in the air.

In Navolese minds—indeed in any mind that occupied any dukedom, city-state, or petty kingdom on every barb of the Cerulean Peninsula's hook—it conjured images of greatness. Imperix Civix Amonese. It conjured tales of armies on the march, spears glittering in sunlight. Burnished cuirasses of bronze. The Imperial Chrysanthemum. The broken and shattered monuments of Torre Amo and Prisephetheom. The legendary burned and drowned Pirividium. Fallen statues. Great tombs. Towering domes that still we could not rebuild. Silks that could no longer be made, except in Xim. Paper and books in plenty, and with them the poetry and thought of Soppros, Tician, Plaesius, Avinixiius, Aeschius, Vittius, and so many others.

It was a heady vision, a dark deep wine for those of us who had grown up on the legends of our past, of Imperix Civix Amonese, for those of us who walked past its ruins. Any who lived on the peninsular hook could tell tales of empire. The word tasted of memory and nostalgia, regret and desire.

Empire.

"The Amonese marched their citizens upon the world," the Callarino said thoughtfully.

"The Amonese made all the world their citizens," my father corrected.

"The priests of Cheroux are so very tiresome," Garagazzo mused. "They insist their translations of Libri Luminaria are more correct than ours."

"So we should fight a war with them?" Sivizza asked, doubtfully.

"Cheroux has never denied that she coveted us," Garagazzo said. "Were it not for you and the Lupari. For the alliances of the small princes. For the arms of Navola, we would all be affecting the lisp of King Andreton even now."

"Well, you are bold," Furia said, smiling faintly. "Devonaci di Regulai da Navola is bold. I give him that."

"So it's true?" the Callarino prompted. "Merai is just the beginning?"

"If our peace and prosperity can be forged to continue, and be defended." My father inclined his head. "We here, at this table, represent the great powers not just of a city, but of an ideal. We here are the merchants of gold, the shepherds of Amo, the masters of steel, the whisperers of politics. And here we are allied. We, here, are unique. The world could be united. The world could be at peace. The world could be Navola's, if we chose to make it so."

Silence again descended upon the table. Celia's eyes were as wide as mine must have been.

"Well, I like it," Furia said.

"You only want more slaves," Sivizza said. "An empire's worth of captures and misery, paid with the blood of my soldiers."

"I nurture my business," she replied, unruffled. "Don't act as if this does not benefit us all. More taxes, more laborers, more glorious monuments to Amo, more palazzi, more territory for sons' inheritance and daughters' dowries. And as for your men, did they become soldiers to get fat and skin their eggplants alone, or seize glory and land of their own, and gold and women? If the Lupari fear a fight—"

"We fear nothing!" Sivizza exclaimed.

Furia laughed. "I only goad to see your cheeks flush, General. I do not doubt your bravery, in truth. And I do not doubt you will make short work of any who stand in your path."

I looked around the table at all the faces. Speculation, greed, fear, calculation. The room seemed to pulse with the fundamental humors of man, the lust and rage and hunger and ambition and opportunism, and it filled me with an awful dread. Even Celia's own cheeks were flushed. Her eyes blazed with an excitement that I did not share.

For myself, all I could feel was fear, rising.

"It's not coincidence that we speak of this tonight," I realized, my stomach twisting. "Is it, Father?"

"No, Davico." My father smiled slightly. "It is not a coincidence."

"Nothing is a coincidence in Palazzo Regulai," Aghan Khan said.

"Every piece has its place in Amo's glory," Garagazzo said. His gaze had fallen upon me with renewed interest. In fact, all of them were looking at me speculatively.

"Tomorrow the boy becomes a man," the Callarino said. He cocked his head, examining me as if he were studying a horse for sale.

"A man must have a wife," Garagazzo said, his expression hungry.

"And a wife . . ." General Sivizza tugged his goatee. "A wife should bring gold and armies."

"Vesuna and her fleets? The Princely States?" Furia studied my father, frowning. "Nai. Farther afield." Her eyes glittered, "Ai, Devonaci. Cheroux? You would seek to defeat them through marriage, not the sword?"

"A battle won without steel is still a battle won," my father quoted.

"Cheroux would see us as the weaker party," the Callarino objected.

"Ci. What an opponent sees, and what is truth?" My father replied. "Well, that is a vast chasm, and a vast opportunity."

"Avinixiius," Sivizza said, nodding sagely. "The greatest strategist of empire. The greatest manipulator of enemy minds."

"Just so." My father inclined his head. "Tonight, we sit at a unique nexus of opportunity, friends. Tonight, all the world lies prostrate before us. And it does not know it."

Everyone was looking at me. My father, Ashia, the Callarino, Sivizza, Aghan Khan, Garagazzo, Furia. Celia.

Profit.

Power.

Empire.

I vomited blood, all over the table.

Chapter 24

The next hours were a crash of sensations and blurred visions. Cries of poison, accusations of betrayal, refutations of horror, rejoinders of suspicion, all jumbled with my own struggle to explain my stomach, my sickness, to admit the pains that had been plaguing me, to calm the suspicions of a plot, and all this even as Ashia was shouting for servants, and as my father and Aghan Khan were carrying me to my rooms.

There, Maestro Dellacavallo fed me strange potions, and I fell into unquiet sleep.

In the morning, I woke to find the old maestro sitting on the edge of my bed.

"How are you feeling?"

"Tired." I sat up slowly. "My stomach . . ."

"It's been paining you for some time."

I startled. "Yes."

"Getting worse?"

I nodded, surprised that he knew. He grunted. "It took quite some effort to convince your father that it was not poison. Of course I knew as soon as I saw the contents of your stomach upon the table, but I was not the one who needed proof. Not mortxibia because you were not sleepy. Not Erostheia's tears, for you were not numb. Not necrxi, because the blood did not form lace when I touched it with vinegar. Not toothrobe because you had no blackness on your tongue, nor capirosso, because the blood was from your belly and not your ass—"

"It was none of those," I said.

"Indeed it was not, but everyone else had to be sure. Why did you not tell anyone you were ill, Davico?"

I looked down at my blankets. I felt tired. Tired and stupid. "I didn't want to seem weak." It sounded foolish when I said it out loud. I hadn't wanted to seem weak, and so I had gotten sicker and sicker, until at last I had showed everyone that I was weak. In hindsight, it seemed obvious. And yet here I was, in bed, having ruined my father's dinner with his closest allies. And Furia. My stomach twisted at the thought of Furia. The cat who liked to eat mice. I dragged my thoughts away from her.

"Is it bad? My stomach?"

"Better than you have any right to expect." Dellacavallo gave me a piercing look. "But worse than it had to be."

"But . . . will I heal?"

"I don't know. If you were me, what would you do for yourself?"

His reply surprised me, and then relieved me, for I saw a glint of his old humor as he regarded me. He wouldn't be asking me if he was overly worried. It was the old game. The familiar and friendly game of herbs and unguents, potions and mushrooms, all of Virga's weave there to be visited and explored and understood.

"Calcixs, to ease the burning of the stomach?"

"Good. And?"

I ran through various plants in my mind, their associations with myths, gods, sprites, and fatas. Green and yellow fuzzy-leafed petals. The physician's colors. "Guxctosalvnia. The wound healer."

"As useful on the inside as on the out," Dellacavallo said approvingly. "What would you take it with?"

I tried to think of what he would choose. Something to make it stick. Something to help on the inside of the stomach. "Khusian parsley?"

"Why?"

"To thicken the blood. Or parchment parsley, if Khusian is hard to find."

"Very good! And one other herb as well. Foxbite."

I made a face at the thought of the bitter stems. "It's for infection, though."

"It is. And it works." He stood. "You will heal, Davico. If you had stopped to think at all, you might have even healed yourself, and saved us all a lot of worry." He squeezed my shoulder. "And don't worry about your Assumption. With a few more hours' rest, I'm sure you will be fine for the festivities."

My stomach clenched. I tried to mask my expression as pain seized my guts, but Dellacavallo was not fooled. His eyebrows shot up.

"Ahhh . . ." He sat back down beside me. I breathed gingerly, waiting for the spell to pass. "This makes more sense now," he said.

"I don't want to appear weak," I said, willing the pain to ease.

"Sfai." Dellacavallo sighed. "You are not weak. Dispense with the foxbite, though. Your pain is not an infection, it is a wound. I should have guessed sooner, but it is an affliction of older men, whose natures are not at ease. It does not normally eat the young."

"When has my mind ever been at ease?"

I meant to say it lightly, as a jest, but it came out too seriously, and too truly. A wave of bitter grief surged up within me, and I looked away, blinking water from my eyes. When had my mind ever been at ease? Always it was full of fear. Always I struggled in the waters of my life.

Dellacavallo was watching me, his expression pitying. "It's an important question, Davico. And one that only you can answer. Your soul is at war with itself. And so you suffer."

"I don't suppose there's a medicine for that?"

"I can give you herbs to ease the pain," Dellacavallo sighed, "but no cure for this affliction can be found in Virga's weave. Yours is a disease of men. An affliction of Cambios. No other creature in Virga's weave suffers so. The cure will not be found in potions or herbs. It will be found in that unquiet mind of yours." He stood. "I will tell your father."

I reached out. "Please. Don't."

"I think we are past hiding this, Davico. Your father must be told." And he was gone before I could stop him.

I slumped back, exhausted. Lazy climbed up on the bed and nuzzled my face. In the room's dimness, I pulled her to me. A new wave of sadness engulfed me. Ai. Such a lonely feeling. I was surrounded by duties and expectations, and all of them filled me with fear and doubt. No one had tried to poison me. I was poisoning myself.

By the fatas, if only I had ridden for the hills and not looked back.

There was a knock at my door. My father leaned in. "How are you feeling?"

I wasn't sure how to answer. "I am sick," I said, finally. "Something is wrong in my stomach. It was not the poison—"

"It's all right." My father held up a hand to forestall me. "Maestro Dellacavallo explained. I understand now. Cazzetta wanted to question the servants—"

"He didn't!" I lurched upright. "None of them—"

"Nai! Do not trouble yourself. It's fine. Dellacavallo convinced him. No harm was done."

I lay back with relief, shivering at the thought of Cazzetta unleashed upon the servants. It filled me with a different kind of nausea, to think what he might have done in the heat of his paranoia. "I've been sick for some time," I said. "I knew it, but I didn't know it was serious."

"He says it comes from an unquiet mind."

I looked away. "I don't want to disappoint you again."

My father laughed, a sharp bitter sound. "You do not disappoint me."

I shook my head sadly. I didn't know what to say.

We both knew that I should get up, get dressed, and prepare for the Assumption, but I felt as if a weight sat upon me, pressing me down in my bed, and I had no urge or will to fight against it. It sat upon me as an elephant. All I wished was to sleep, to simply rest. To stop pretending that this was my place, or my world.

My father settled beside me on the bed, studying me. I was surprised that his expression was not stern, but wistful. "It is not easy, what we ask of you, Davico. Don't think I don't know the toll of it. It is not a thing that any of us are born to, and yet we are born into it. Like children tossed into the Cerulea and expected to swim. It is no man's true nature. It has terrible costs."

I knew that he was trying to soften the blow of my failure, but all I felt was exhaustion. "I thought it was the birthright of all Navolese. To walk the twisted path, to play at politics, to master business . . ."

He laughed wryly and shook his head. "Nai. It is difficult no matter what. It was difficult for me. I ran wild because of it. I fought duels. I drank wine. I seduced . . ." He shook his head. "You are a more sincere and decent soul than I was. Than I think I am, in truth. Instead of chasing maids and drinking wine and dallying with courtesans, you instead strive to be more and more dutiful. And you wound yourself more and more."

"I just . . . I don't want to fail. I feel as if I'm always failing."

"You put too much pressure on yourself. Far too much." He stood abruptly. "Nai. I put too much pressure on you. I see that now. I should have seen it sooner. Rest now. You are sick. You must rest."

"What about the Assumption?"

"We cannot celebrate your Assumption with you ill. It would be a bad omen for the family. To have what happened last night, happen today . . ." He trailed off. "Well." He touched his eye, with his two fingers, the mark of Scuro. "Malasignifica, nai?"

I tried to sit up. "But if I do not take our name today, people will say Amo does not favor us. It will be as a curse. Garagazzo would say—"

"Ci, Davico." My father pressed me down. "Do not listen to the priests. Let the priest worry of priestly things. We are family. We will arrange a solution. But now, you must rest. I will send for Maestro Dellacavallo again. Perhaps he will have a potion to ease your discomfort. In the meantime, the Assumption will be changed. I will not have you attempt the day while you are ill."

"I'm sorry, Father."

"There is nothing to apologize for, Davico." He shook his head, smiling down at me, an expression of pity and kindness on his face that I had never seen before. "Ai, Davico." He reached down and tousled my hair as if I were still a young boy. "This is a small thing. Your health is most important. Now rest."

And so I lay in the dimness, with Lazy abed beside me. I dozed in fitful dreams, both guilty and relieved that the Assumption would not occur. My pains eased.

But a few hours later, Ashia came to my room.

I did not know it was her at first, thinking that it was Dellacavallo come to give me more advice and medicine, or perhaps Celia to entertain me, or perhaps even my father again, to look kindly upon me once more. But then I smelled her perfume and I shut my eyes tight, hoping that she would go away. Instead I felt her weight settle beside me on my bed. I curled in on myself, hiding my face from her, but Lazy watched her with pricked ears and curious expression, for Ashia had never entered my bedchamber before.

"Davico," she said at last. "You must rise. This day is yours."

"I'm sick," I said, not turning to face her. "Dellacavallo says I must rest."

"Nai, Davico. You are a child. It is time to become a man."

Her voice was so stern that I rolled over. She was regarding me with a steely gaze that made me forget my sickness. I had never seen such an expression upon her features. Not even Furia had evoked such an expression. Ashia was beautiful and elegant and warm, not cold steel. She was the creature who lit our dinner parties, who smiled upon my father, who made his eyes soften when she was near. The queen of our palazzo, sometimes wry, sometimes sharp with her opinions . . . but now her dark eyes were so icy and unsentimental that she could have been my father when he destroyed a man at the plank.

Abruptly, she stood. I thought she would leave me, but instead she went to my windows. She yanked open the shutters. Hot sunlight blazed in. I flinched and squinted against the stabbing glare and heat. She went to my door and spoke to her servant Sofia, waiting outside.

"Go to his father," she said briskly. "Tell him that Davico is now well."

"I'm not well—" I started to protest, but she turned on me with a glare so fierce that my words froze in my throat. She shut the door again and strode over to me, sweeping toward me with such imperiousness that I had a momentary urge to bolt the bed and flee.

"Nai, Davico, you are well." She settled once again by my side and regarded me. "You are well, but you are acting the child."

I felt pierced by that gaze. I stared up at my ceiling, avoiding it, hoping that my father would hear of her invasion and make her leave. I let my eyes follow the images painted there. The mythical lands of Nebbistrano. Depictions of unicorns and pegasi and other, stranger creatures. I wished that I could disappear into that world. When I had been younger I had pretended that I could go to the mythical lands of Nebbistrano, that I was not here at all—

"Davico," Ashia said. "Please look at me when I speak. Give me this respect, as I have given you respect these many years."

By the fatas, she was hard to deny. I wanted to continue to pretend she was not sitting beside me, but it was too shameful to treat her so. She deserved respect. It lowered me in my own eyes to withhold it. And so I met her solemn gaze.

"Davico," she said. "You know how I came to your house."

I nodded slowly. Though we did not speak of it, indeed avoided the topic, I knew well that she had been purchased, bought to please my father soon after my mother died, just as Lady Furia had said. Ashia had once mentioned that when she first came to us, she had been silent for nearly a year, for she had not spoken our language, coming from a land where not even the lesser dialects of Amo were known.

"Today, you are a man, Davico," she said. "You have been protected from much of your father's burdens because of your youth, but now you must learn. And you must learn quickly. Tonight, your father announces you as his heir, and you announce yourself as a man. And Navola and the wider world will attend you in ways that you will not like."

I looked away. "And that is why I should not go."

"Sfai!" Ashia seized my chin and turned my face to her. "Listen to me, Davico. You are fortunate to have lived swaddled as you have. Your father loves you very much, and so he protects you from the sharp thorns of life, but he does you no favors for it. He is soft with you when he should be hard. He is too kind, and he is blind to the fact."

I regarded Ashia with surprise. "You think him soft?" I asked incredulously. I was shocked not only by her opinion, which did not match my experience, but because I had never seen her in anything but accordance with my father.

"You are your father's heir, Davico. You are di Regulai, and you are da Navola, and no amount of hiding in your bed or pretending to be sick will protect you from this fate. And yet he allows it, because he is kind. Too kind."

"I'm not pretending!"

"You think it matters? No matter how innocent you wish to remain, or how you wish to deny your inheritance, your enemies are not innocent. And they. Are. *Everywhere.* Your father protects you, but he cannot do it forever. You must be prepared."

"Why are you telling me this?"

She gave me a bitter smile. "Can a slave not love her master's child?" Her words stung and she saw it. "Nai, Davico. I do not wish to make you think I resent your father. I love him dearly. He is kind, and we . . ." She shook her head, smiling slightly. "Well, I love him dearly."

She turned serious. "But because I love him, and because I love you, his son, I will tell you that which I do not tell others. I was once of a great family. We lived in wealth. I lived with my mother and sisters and my aunts and we all were loved and coddled and protected. We, too, had our gardens and our fine horses, and our city was one of the most beautiful . . ." She trailed off, for a moment lost in memory.

"Ai, Davico, Navola is pretty, but my homeland was . . . the city of Jhara, was beautiful. I wish you could have seen it. Could have seen our fortress where it overlooked the lands. And Jhara with its high roof terraces, its gardens . . . its fertile fields and the River Nish, blue and dotted with the sails of traders . . ." She trailed off again. "I lived in a heaven. I knew enough of the world to know that I lived in softness, and that others did not, but I was never told of the plots and poison that also twined through my world like serpents." She turned her gaze to me, and her expression hardened.

"My family was destroyed, Davico. Almost all of them were killed. I was sent into slavery, but only because an uncle of mine took pity on me, and kept me from the swords of his men. It was luck, Davico. That was all. He liked me because I once shared a sweet with him, and he took it as an honor, and so when he slew the rest of my family, he took pity upon me, and sold me instead. So. Here I live. Far from my homeland. All my family dead. My world changed in an instant."

I wanted to look away. I wanted to cover my ears. To hide from this story that I had never heard, but Ashia's words ground on, relentless.

"My family was a glass goblet, Davico, and when we fell from the table, we shattered. I was kept like a princess, and so I was ignorant of our fragility. When parents coddle children, it is to make them feel safe, but the coddling does not make them truly safe, it makes them ignorant, and it puts them in danger. Your father has enemies. Your family has enemies." Suddenly she reached out and seized my arm, her fingers digging in like claws. "And those enemies see that you are weak!"

I shook her away. "I'm sick!"

"If you wish to be weak, be so! But know that it will cost all your family and all those who depend upon you. Navolese politics does not tolerate weakness, any more than the politics of my own homeland did."

"You don't know—" I started to protest, but Ashia overrode me.

"Look to Celia if you wish to see the costs of failure in this game we play. Ask her if she would prefer to be at home, with her family still, or living here with strangers."

"We aren't strangers—"

She quelled me with a look. "Ask Celia. She knows the stakes. She keeps her eyes wide and her ears alert. She is alive to the world that surrounds her. Now you must become alive as well, Davico. It is time. It is past time. Time to wake from your slumber and see clearly what surrounds you. Listen to me, Davico. I will tell you what your father cannot bear to say. He needs you to be his heir, not only in name, but in competence. There is no room for failure."

She stood. "Now get up, Davico. Be a man. Be the man your father needs you to be. And if you are not strong, then pretend. People are watching you. People will be watching to see if you stand strong or fail when you are presented as his heir. You must be a bull, Davico."

She leaned down and pinched my cheek, hard. "You. Must. Be. *Strong.*"

And with that she left.

A few minutes later I heard a gentle rap at my door. Celia, standing at the doorway, looking apologetic.

"I'm sorry," she said.

"You sent her?" I asked. "You listened to what she said?"

Celia gave me a sad look, and I saw now what I had not seen before. Without Ashia to say it, I would not have seen it. It was true; Celia was alert all the time. She was always listening. Celia had been the one who had suggested we spy on my father and Ashia, as if it were a game. Had suggested we should find my bastard brother, as if it were an interesting puzzle. But now I saw that none of it was games or puzzles to her.

I sighed and threw my legs out of bed. *"Mouse listens for the tread of Cat, and must listen all the time,"* I said, quoting Aeschius.

"And Cat listens for the tread of Mouse, only when he is hungry," she replied, favoring me with a small smile.

"You told me that you would not lie to me."

"Ask me a question, then."

When I was silent, she sighed. "It's not that I don't love your family, Davico, for I do. And it's not that I do not appreciate the honor your family does me. I would not have been educated so by my own family, had they a choice. I would not . . ." She trailed off. "But they are still my family, and I have not seen them for a very long time."

"What do you remember of them?"

"My mother. I remember my mother. She was a serious woman, but kind, and she always had time for us, whenever we had need. I remember my sisters, Ellia and Tissia. We used to play cartalegge together and I would let them win. I miss them."

"And your father?"

She gave me a sharp look. "I prefer yours. My father was a fool, and not kind. He liked the stick and he liked a person's fear. Your father is hard, but he is fair. My father . . . he was only ever hard." She quirked a smile. "So, not all rotten fruit, not all fresh, as they say. You should prepare. It's your day."

She started for the door.

"Celia?"

She paused. "Yes, Davico?"

"I'm glad you are in our family."

"So am I, Davico." She seemed wistful. "Sometimes, I am very glad indeed." She turned serious. "So do not fail. We all depend upon you."

And so, borne up by Celia's faith in me, and pressed forward by Ashia's iron will, I began preparing myself for my Assumption, girding myself as if for battle. It was my Assumption; it was time for me to become a man. More than time. I would not shrink or hide from my duties anymore. The pain in my stomach was still there, but with my clear decision it also seemed to fade—forced to obey me, and not the other way around.

I dressed and straightened myself and stood before the mirror, gazing upon myself. I made my face still and strong.

I would not falter.

Chapter 25

Musicians played and acrobats spun from high wires and fire spitters illuminated the darkness. Lanterns glimmered like fireflies throughout the quadrae. They dangled from all the high balconies, so that when you looked up from the center of the garden quadra it felt as if you stood amongst the hanging gardens of the ancient Amonese.

As it turned out, my greatest difficulty as my Assumption began was that as the sun sank over the palazzo and festivities approached, as armies of servants and suppliers, cooks and entertainers flooded into our home, Lazy became miserable and cowered in the stables with Stub, only venturing out in short spurts. I glimpsed her dashing several times across the courtyards and through the gardens, an arrow of canine distress, and then she would dart back to the stables and hide once more.

It had started even as I was dressing for the event, when she slunk to hide under my bed, and no matter how much I tried to convince her, she would not come out. I empathized, but after Ashia's lecture I was determined to do my duty, and so I was much irritated that I could not convince Lazy to follow my example.

"Be Lazy, then," I said spitefully as I gave up on dragging her out from under the shadows.

Her expressive golden eyes roved past me much distressed, but she did not emerge.

"Ci. I named you right, after all."

It was unfair of me, but I was jealous of her.

When the revel began, I was seated on a red velvet cushion embroidered in gold upon a raised dais in our great hall, with its high ceilings and frescoes of the creation of Navola, and with the faces of our family and allies depicted within. Amo drove Scuro and his darkness down into his caves with flaming dogs and a chariot of light. He yoked Urula and Urulo to his will, and made the seas safe for ships. He bid Virga make the plains fertile, and on and on, and it was there, under his light, that I accepted formal gifts from our guests.

Merio stood behind me, whispering names in case I forgot some archinomo's position or family constellation, for it was difficult to remember that a silk merchant we insured in his trades along the dangerous roads to Xim was twice married but had returned to his first wife after the second was poisoned; or that the archinomi of the salt monopoly and the marsh guild despised the vianoma elected by the spice merchants to represent their interests.

And so the great names of Navola lined before me with their gifts, drinking iced wines—ice that had been hauled from the Cielofrigo, packed in hay, and then buried in the earth so that it could be excavated for this sweltering occasion—and fanning themselves in the hot night as jugglers juggled, and as the Teatro Pericolo spat fire.

Gifts of honey, of incense, of jewels, of embroidered slippers, of sigil rings. Necklaces of gold, squares of rare chocolate, bolts of Xim silk, a procession of gifts many of which I would never see again, for they could not be tasted for poison without showing insult, nor worn in public without showing favor to one faction or another, but still the gifts and the procession continued.

The Callarino came before me with a sandalwood box. He opened it and offered it with a bow.

It was an ivory dagger. Extremely long and vicious-looking.

Nai, not just a dagger.

"A claw?"

I took it up, examining its wicked curve. Intricate engravings of a princely land covered its length. There were women dipping water from a river, there were strange tufted trees, there were men with curved swords riding to battle, there was a great fortress and a queen riding upon a palanquin with her people bowing down to her. The handle was textured with interlocking tiles reminiscent of Zurom's mosaics. A dagger, made from a single claw.

"It is of a dragon," the Callarino said. "Something to match the eye that your father wields."

I studied it carefully, reverently. It was valuable beyond my comprehension.

"My agent discovered it in the city of Zir," the Callarino said. "That place where ruins and dreams intertwine. Perhaps it is from the self-same dragon. Perhaps from a mate. In any case, it is ancient, and when he sent it to me, I thought of your name day."

I turned it in my hands. "This is too valuable."

"Nai. It is too little. It is already yours, in any case. I will not accept it back." And with that he stepped away, his hands raised, leaving it in my possession. "Guard it well, Davico. Now that you are a man, you will have need of a sharp claw. When you do, never doubt that I will be at your side." He bowed one last time and turned away, leaving the next guest before me.

Garagazzo the high priest gave me a special prayer rug and a golden image of Amo for my own rooms for my meditations upon Amo.

Avinci the poet had written a poem in my honor.

Aghan Khan gave me a hawk.

"He is a battle hawk. If you learn his language, he will spy in the sky for you and tell you what he sees. His name is Blood of the Skies."

There were more people, and more names, and more forms to be observed, and then, to my surprise, the crowd parted and Lady Furia stood before me, her deadly handmaid Silxa behind.

Cazzetta, who was nearby, stiffened at the sight of the pair. I could almost see his hands itching to draw a weapon. Furia made a formal sweep of her skirts, a perfect suttoflectere, her head dipping to a calculated angle of respect. "*Amo ti dava buonizza fortuna* on your name day." She unwound her curtsy and smiled. "And so good to see that our young bull lives after all. I worried greatly for you." Despite her smile, I could not escape the feeling that she played with me. "How does it feel to be a man? Do you feel taller? Stronger? More capable?"

There it was. I suddenly felt as if I were a dog seated upon my red-and-gold cushion, a dog pretending to be a man, dressed in foppery and absurdity.

"Ready to take the field?" Furia asked. She tilted her head, as if by changing her perspective she might see me in a different light. "Ready to charge and thrust? To drive home the sword? Or maybe you think yourself less a warrior but more a farmer, ready to plow and seed. Perhaps you will be the sort of man who instead of fighting for the field, seeks to fill its furrows? All those wet furrows, wide and open, begging for your plow?"

My cheeks flushed. Furia flicked her fan, amused that she had unsettled me. She opened her hand. A golden chain rested in her palm, punctuated by polished white stones. She pressed the chain into my hand. I stared at the stones, they were very light, not stone at all.

"Finger bones," she said. "Slaves who disappointed me."

I stared at the awful prize and tried to control my face. She was testing me. Testing me publicly, seeking to strip my name from me before I could even take it. Testing to see if I would recoil, if I would hurl her gift away. The passage of time seemed to slow. I felt my father's eyes upon me and Ashia's as well, both of them holding their breaths. Cazzetta's fingers were plucking for the stilettos he kept hidden up his sleeves. The Callarino was watching with a glint of fascination. Garagazzo had covered his mouth to keep his surprise hidden. It felt as though the whole hall was watching. As if the acrobats had paused mid-tumble and the jugglers' balls had frozen midair so that even the entertainers could turn and watch.

Before me, Furia's presence seemed to grow. In that moment, she seemed something other than human, something terrifying, lovely, and awful, a goddess otherworldly who traded in human lives and human bones. Around her, all the others seemed to fade, like flowers withering under the ice of first freeze. Furia, though, Furia seemed to blaze like fire. I saw now how she had defeated her brothers and come to rule Palazzo Furia—

She stepped close. She lifted my chin. She stared into my eyes. She turned my head, this way and that, studying me. "A lamb amongst leopards," she murmured. For the briefest instant I thought I saw an expression of sorrow upon her face. She closed my hand around the awful gift.

"Take these bones and remember that if you are not feared, you will always be tested."

The tumult of the hall returned. Juggling balls fell into jugglers' hands. Acrobats threw one another high into the air. Music swelled, conversation poured over us like a wave held back, and to my surprise, I found Furia standing where she had been, far below where I sat upon my dais, as if she had not moved at all.

She made suttoflectere once more, but this time her obeisance was so low as to make a mockery of bowing, an excess of respect, the respect one pays to emperors and priest-kings, not to boys.

The procession continued.

Filippo came before me.

He gave me a book. "In all honesty, I very much enjoyed the jokes you sent me when we corresponded," he said. And then he lowered his voice conspiratorially. "Someone told me that you have a taste for such things as this."

It was a book of the illustrated sort, and as soon as I opened it, I was shocked. I slammed it closed as if it were full of vipers, for what I saw were drawings even more lewd than the ones in my father's study.

Filippo laughed at my embarrassment. "You're a man now, Davico!" He wagged a finger. "No need to be shy of your desires! But you must learn to control that face of yours. You performed . . . well, *adequately,* with the Lady Furia, but we both know how badly you do when you are faced with a true challenge." He wagged a finger again and winked. "The pretty maidens are quite the weakness for you."

Hurriedly, I set the book aside.

Of course, Celia seized it and opened it immediately.

"Why, it is all bulls!" she exclaimed.

"How could they not be?" Filippo laughed delightedly. "Is this not a day for the Bull?" He turned and raised his wine and shouted out to the crowded hall. "To the Bull!" he cried, and everyone cheered. He repeated his toast, to another cheer, and then seized the waist of a serving girl and whirled away with her.

At Celia's cry of shock, Cierco and Piero and Niccoletta and Giovanni came running, and clustered around the tome with her. Judging from their whispered exclamations, Filippo had outdone himself. He had apparently commissioned the drawings especially, and they were either flattering to our name or else deeply insulting, depending on one's perspective, for the well-endowed Bull cavorted wildly with maidens and fatas, priests and nuns, Caliba in his pleasure gardens, and more. My father and Ashia were both smiling indulgently, so I pretended I was not embarrassed as my friends all gathered around the disastrous thing, turning the pages and exclaiming at the salacious acts contained within.

I could hear Celia exclaiming, "But I don't see how that is meant to fit!"

The envoy from Hekkat gave me a musical instrument with eight strings and two necks, inlaid with diamonds at its frets, and his kivis was about his neck, apparently unmolested by Polonos this time. The envoy from Zurom gave us a living cliff tiger. The ambassador of Cheroux gave me wines from King Andreton's own vineyards. But there was one whom I was disappointed not to see.

"What of Wustholt?" I asked. I searched for the bearded ambassador whose company I had enjoyed only a few weeks before, but could not spy him in the crowds.

Filippo, who had returned to enjoy the reactions of my friends to his licentious offering, laughed. "Have you not heard? Wustholt is gone in the night, fled in darkness, his wife and daughter both killed at table, and him only alive because he came late to dine, and found them fallen in their soups, their tongues black from toothrobe."

"Poisoned?" I was shocked.

Filippo shrugged. "It is said that he was whispering the departures of ships to ears in Vesuna. And making a profit when their pirates struck."

"Ours?" I was aghast.

"Oh no! He wasn't that foolish. But someone seems to have found him out at last."

"But . . . he seemed such a good man."

"Indeed. One of the finest practitioners of faccioscuro I have ever met." He paused, meditating on the ambassador's skill. "For a foreigner," he amended. "Not a Navolese."

After the procession there was dancing and feasting and because I was now of name and age, there were entertainers of the commedia lasciva brought to tease me into manhood. Women dressed in diaphanous silks who draped themselves over me while the adults laughed at my distress and embarrassment. There were short and bawdy plays celebrating the confused lunge into adulthood, and the adults laughed harder than those of us who were younger, for they recognized their own incompetent fumblings in the clowns and jesters and ladies of the night who pantomimed youthful lusts and loves and foibles.

I did my best not to appear embarrassed, but my face was red as an apple. As Filippo noted, it is easier to hide some emotions than others. This night afforded me little respite. My emotions blazed upon my face, entirely facciochiaro, and even Cazzetta, who had taught me so much of faccioscuro, seemed not disappointed but amused.

And so when a beautiful courtesan trailed her silks around my neck and brought me up to clumsily dance with her, and though it was a dance entirely (well, almost entirely) chaste, it set my mind whirling in ways that previously my mind had not, and to my horror I stiffened in my pants and this, too, set the crowd laughing and applauding, both for the courtesan and for me.

It was not a night for subtlety.

All of this and more whirled by. I talked with my friends. Cierco and Giovanni and Piero, as well as others, Tullio, Antono, Dumas . . . too many to remember. We admired my new hawk, Blood of the Skies, as he sat upon his perch, hooded.

The Callarino came to me and murmured in my ear. "I saw that which the Lady Furia did. It will not be forgotten. Do not concern yourself with her." Garagazzo patted me on the back and gave me a glass of wine and reminded me that it was best not to drink too much on the Night of Assumption, and then winked and laughed and assured me that even though Amo taught moderation, even he had his excesses. Shuro of the Schipians pressed me for information about trade with the Khur, and if we would take his loans again. Garagazzo's priest friends asked what sort of interest they might anticipate from our bank in the coming year, for all their deposits were with us. Later, General Sivizza came to me, that creased and tanned man who never stopped drilling his soldiers, and who had been loyal to Navola for more than two decades.

"I am relieved you are better, after your sickness at table." He gave me a gift of a gold dagger, bejeweled. "It comes from the south, where men wear blades for honor, and where killing is common, but they love their weapons, and the man I took it from fought hard to keep it. Cazzetta knows much of such men and their steel."

I held the dagger cautiously in my hand. "It is good steel," the general said. "Do not be fooled by the gold. It is a blue water steel, you can see it is folded many times."

"Thank you," I stuttered. "But I am not the warrior for this blade."

The general shrugged. "Then someone will take it from you, as I took it from someone else. But I see steel in you, Davico. You stand here, where you were sick before. You stand tall against that which would bring another low. That is more important sometimes than skill." He gave me the dagger's sheath and showed me how to strap it to my arm, replacing the simpler one I had had before. "There," he said with satisfaction. "Now you are always ready to defend your honor, as they defend it in the south."

"Thank you."

"You are a man now, Davico." He clapped me on the back. "Now let us drink as men!"

And I did drink. I drank the wine of many countries and I laughed and danced with the courtesans again while my father and Ashia looked on and Filippo leered, and there was a great deal of laughter. My friends came around again and they had that disastrous book of Filippo's still, and Celia and Niccoletta were with them, and Celia said, "Look at these, Davico. I think that he must have spent many navisoli on this gift. He must make a great deal of money in his work in Torre Amo if he commissions such a thing, for simple pleasure."

"Or he curries favor with you," Giovanni said.

"This is not how he will curry favor with me," I said.

Cierco piped up. "Well, he has all my cartadecisi!"

"Your family doesn't have any votes in the Callendra anymore," Celia said.

"He is a foul man," Niccoletta said. "He never stops with his jokes or his crudities."

And then we were dancing again, men's dances and women's dances, and whirling men and women together, our feet thundering and people clapping, and all of us flushed with the excitement.

I remember particularly the clapping and the joy, and all the people's faces red with wine. Bodices loosened as well as reserves, the breasts of courtesans exposed to Filippo's kisses . . .

I saw many things, but I did not see the blade.

Piero was laughing and offering me wine, and as I took it a strangeness crossed his expression, a blazing intensity I had never seen before, and then I felt a burning across my stomach and Cazzetta threw me aside.

I crashed to the floor, confused. What had I done to anger Cazzetta? All around me, people were shouting. Piero tumbled to the marble beside me, blood gouting from his mouth. I stared at him, stared deep into his eyes, and in the instant that his life fled, I saw a hatred so deep that it was like staring into Scuro's madness.

"The princeling! The princeling! To me! To me!"

It was Cazzetta. He stood over me, paired daggers drawn from their hidden sheaths. His blades were a blur. I tried to crawl away. Another man fell atop Piero, clutching his throat, spurting blood. Cazzetta moved like a shadow, here and gone. Liquid lunge and thrust. Men collapsed like sacks of flour. Blades skittered across the marble. People screamed and ran.

Piero held a dagger. It was still tight in his fist, glazed with blood.

It was only then that I comprehended that Piero had cut me. I had been attacked by him. My friend had stabbed me. I fumbled at my clothes, expecting to find my guts spilling out, but the slice was shallow. There was much blood, but my belly was intact. Somehow Cazzetta had seen Piero's intention and saved me from a deeper cut.

Someone dragged me upright. Aghan Khan. I glimpsed Merio, caught in a crush of men and women, falling, blood on his face, his eyes wide with terror, and then the crowd swallowed him. Aghan Khan's sword flicked forward and caught a man in the throat. Steel clashed all around, our guards against men dressed as servants, against others, some of whom I recognized—

"Assassino! Assassino!"

"Betrayal!"

"Wake up, Davico!" Cazzetta was dragging me back. "Fight!"

I fumbled for the gold dagger that Sivizza had just given me. Men and women screamed. People trampled and ran. Blood made the marble slippery as steel clashed and men died. I tried to glimpse Merio again, but he was lost to view. The fight was in earnest now. Assassins seemed to be all around us, swords drawn, and our guards were dying.

Polonos took a sword in the neck, and fell, gouting blood, his hands trying to stanch the wound. Cazzetta and Aghan Khan, two unlike men, stood side by side, defending me, but we were becoming increasingly isolated. Relus fell, surrounded by attackers as he fought to reach us. We were an island in the fight, the three of us facing half a dozen.

"Come and die!" Aghan Khan shouted.

He lunged and spitted a man. Blood sprayed, the man collapsed, but more arrived to replace him. We were cornered. There were near a dozen enemies now, but after Aghan Khan's strike they were wary.

"We just want the princeling," a man said as they circled. "You two can walk away."

I crouched and pried the sword from Polonos's dead hand, nauseated that I robbed him, horrified that he had died for me.

"We just want the boy," someone else said. "Walk away."

Cazzetta sagged, seeming to give up. "I just want your life," he said, and a dagger flicked through the air and sank into the man's eye. Another dagger appeared in Cazzetta's hand. The assassins rushed us.

I parried a man's attack, parried again, our steel scraping and crashing. He was fast and strong, but Aghan Khan's lessons held. The assassin made a third pass at me. I slid inside his guard and buried Sivizza's golden dagger in his belly. It felt just like the pigs that Aghan Khan had made me practice with, and it sickened me, but I kicked my opponent back as Aghan Khan had taught me. Someone thudded against me and I slipped on the marble. I fell, scrambling on the slick bloody stone, expecting a sword to fall upon my neck but suddenly Celia was there.

"Get up!" She dragged me back to my feet. A sudden gap opened before us as Cazzetta murdered a man and shoved another aside.

"Go!" Cazzetta shouted. We plunged through the gap and kept running, with Cazzetta close behind. I could hear shouts all around as we plunged out into the garden quadra. I caught glimpses of more fighting in other halls, and heard men coming from many sides, and was horrified to realize I had no idea where our allies were. Enemies seemed to be everywhere.

"Where are we going?" Celia panted.

"Up the stairs!" Cazzetta said. "The library!" He threw me the key as we ran.

"What about my father?" I hadn't seen either him or Ashia in the melee. "Where is my father?"

"He'll rally the guard with Aghan Khan, do not pause!"

Until that moment I hadn't realized that Aghan Khan was not with us. In my own desperate flight I had abandoned him. I felt an ugly shame, and tried to stop but Cazzetta yanked me onward.

"Do not pause! Your father would not want it! Run!"

Cazzetta's face, always coolly impassive, blazed with emotion. His skin was flushed and his eyes darted everywhere, and that, more than anything frightened me. Cazzetta was worried.

We reached the library. I fumbled with the key, the door swung open, and then we were through, slamming the heavy wood behind us.

Silence enveloped us. On the other side of the door, people were fighting and dying, but here, there was nothing but stillness. Rows of books, the wisdom of the ancients, sitting peaceful on shelves. The ledgers of my father's business. Thick carpets. Finely woven tapestries and painted ceilings. The quills and inks on my father's desk sat patiently, awaiting his return, the dragon eye beside them.

Something thudded against the door. We all jumped. Our pursuers struck another blow. The door shook in its hinges. Dimly I heard men shouting for axes.

"Did you recognize the men?" Cazzetta asked.

Piero.

"One was Piero." I swallowed. "The first one."

"One was a servant," Celia said. "I saw him with wine, earlier."

"We'll have to inspect all the stores for poison then."

The door thudded again. I cast about for a path of escape. If we squeezed out the windows, we might be able to make the rooftops if our foes weren't waiting below with crossbows.

Something heavy scraped at the door's edge. "They'll try to pry the door off," Celia said.

I went and threw open a window. It was too far down and the roof overhung us. A good way to break our legs, but not to escape.

Celia peered down beside me. "Headfirst, it might steal the satisfaction of them killing us themselves."

"We're trapped."

"Not trapped," Cazzetta said. To my surprise, he was standing before a portion of a bookshelf, running his fingers along the edges, pressing here and there, seeking something. He pressed again, and suddenly the shelf slid aside, revealing a gaping darkness. "Come," he said. "Our time is short."

Celia hurried into the dark chamber he had revealed. Her voice echoed out. "It's stairs!"

Cazzetta waved for me to follow, but I hesitated. An axe thudded against the door. Cazzetta glared at me to hurry, but something held me.

The dragon eye.

It sat upon my father's desk, and it seemed to be glowing.

There was a cracking from the library doors as they levered against the hinges. The axe blows became rhythmic, sinking hard each time. The wood shuddered, splintered, groaned.

"Davico!"

More axes slammed against the door. A blade cracked through, splitting the wood grain with its gleaming edge.

"Come, Davico! Now! Before they see!"

The dragon eye seemed to be calling me. I could not leave the library without it. In fact, I realized, it would not let me. With sudden determination, I strode to it and wrapped my arms around the ancient thing. It was heavy. I had never hefted it before. It took both hands to lift and cradle it to my body. I was careful with the nerve spines, which made it awkward, but I lifted it, and as I did I felt that thing I had felt all those years ago: The dragon was still with us. Alive within.

I could feel its life. Its rage. Its contempt for humanity. As I held the orb close to me, I could feel the dragon soul stirring. Uncoiling. Coming awake. Its scales scraped across my chest—

The door shuddered with another axe blow and the edge splintered through again, widening the crack.

"Davico! Come now!"

An eye replaced the axe, peering in. Cazzetta went and jammed his dagger through the slit. Someone screamed. I stared around myself, confused. Surprised that I hadn't moved yet. It felt as if I had been dreaming, as if the dragon had mesmerized me.

More axe blades thudded. Cazzetta wiped his dagger on his sleeve.

"Now, Davico!"

Carrying the weight of the dragon eye, I hurried to the hidden passage. Cazzetta's hand pressed me forward. I smelled dampness. Stone. Old dust and carrion. Celia waited anxiously at the top of a stone staircase that wound downward into blackness. Her eyes were wide with fear. Cazzetta pulled closed the secret door.

Darkness swallowed us.

Chapter 26

"Go carefully," Cazzetta whispered.

Heavy wood scraped as he barred the hidden door against our pursuers. "The stairs are uneven, and they circle tightly. Count them, one hundred and twelve steps."

One questing step after another we went down through a darkness deeper than that of Scuro's blind hells. It was a darkness that smothered, a darkness so thick, it felt as if we pushed through curtains with every step. I quested forward with my foot, found the smooth worn edge of the stair, stretched my toe downward, not knowing how far—

There.

The steps were uneven, as Cazzetta had said. Some wide, some narrow, some deep, each wedge of the circling stair like a pie cut by a baker who cared not for the fairness of the portions he sold. Celia's breathing. I could smell her perfume, I realized. I could smell her sweat.

I smelled her fear.

We circled clumsily down. With my arms around the dragon eye, I could not use my hands to balance and was slowed. I could feel Cazzetta behind me, impatient.

"Conti permissio," Cazzetta murmured. It was not a question. He squeezed past me, and I heard the rustle of Celia's skirts as he pushed past her as well.

"A torch would be nice," Celia said.

"A torch is smoke," Cazzetta said. "Smoke is a trail."

His voice was already falling distant below us. Celia's skirts rustled as she resumed her own descent. I followed. It was exhausting, feeling for every step, never knowing how far down it might lie, never knowing what my foot would rest upon.

Once, I stepped on something that crackled and slid from beneath my foot and I smelled carrion. I leaned against the wall, breathing heavily. The sounds of Cazzetta and Celia seemed to be far below me. The darkness smothered me. It weighed upon me. I had lost count of the steps. They seemed to go on forever.

A heavy crash resounded above us. I instinctively looked back, though all I could see was more darkness. Our pursuers had breached the library. I heard their dim shouts, their bloodlust cries of triumph and then dismay as they found the library empty.

"The hounds still bay," Cazzetta said. "Do not tarry!"

The thumps and shouts of search filtered down to us. They were not so far above us as I had hoped or imagined. We had barely started our journey down, it seemed.

"Hurry, Davico!"

Celia was getting farther ahead of me, moving quickly, her skirts rustling and spiraling down, growing fainter with every step. I began again to feel my own way down, step by clumsy felt step, leaning against the curving wall for balance as I carried the awkward weight of the dragon eye.

Deeper and deeper we went, spiraling down into the cool earth, while our pursuers hacked apart library shelves, ripped down tapestries, tore aside carpets, and shouted for our blood.

Down and down, spiraling down. The darkness grew heavier upon us, a physical thing.

I heard water dripping. Smelled damp earth. Rot. We were below the ground now, I was sure. Down amongst the worms and roots of the city, so deep in darkness that it became an embrace, a living presence all its own, as alive as the dragon eye in my arms, a thing that stirred and circled and enveloped us, sucking us deeper in, a creature wholly alive, swirling with malevolence, scales scraping against the prison of its orb, scales rasping across my chest, body coiling, stretching, flexing. Testing confines. Leathery wings unfurled and poisonous spines rose like hackles. Its tail lashed, coiling around my heart.

It was inside me, I realized. I could feel it within me now, a slithering horror, coming more and more alive with each step of our descent into darkness, an eager hungry presence, exploring now not within the prisoning orb but within the casing of my mind.

I wanted to drop the eye, then, but I could not. I tried to alert

Cazzetta but my lips instead pressed closed. I wanted to reach for Celia's aid, but my arms remained wrapped around the living orb. Alone in the darkness, I fought against the presence of the dragon in my mind. I fought it silent and alone as step by step we spiraled down.

"What is this place?" Celia whispered. Her voice in the darkness was a relief to me, and to my surprise, the presence of the dragon seemed to withdraw, as if cautious of others near.

"Old catacombs," Cazzetta replied. "Ruins of the city that stood before Navola. From the time before Amo. Not as old as the ones in Torre Amo but still, old." His footsteps slowed. "This is the bottom," he said. "Have care now. Wait."

Celia and I stood silent. Her hand touched me, questing, found my arm and gripped. Her fingers were cold against my skin. She was trembling. I could feel both her fear and her relief at my presence, and I was comforted as well by her. The two of us, at least, were together. And with Cazzetta, we had hope of survival. I still remembered how he had fought against the assassins, how his knives appeared as if conjured, how he had buried them in the throats of our attackers. By Amo, he was fast. Without him I would already be dead, lying on the marble instead of Piero.

Celia and I waited close, our bodies nearly one as we waited. Water dripped. A streamlet gurgled nearby, but I could not ascertain its source. The echoes of the catacombs made everything difficult to fix upon.

I heard Cazzetta muttering, something in his own dialect. Stone scraped. Something tumbled heavily, thumped and rolled. He was moving stones. More stones scraped and clattered after the first. Celia and I waited, dependent upon him, listening to his mysterious work.

I had the feeling of time passing quickly, of events crashing down upon us while we were stuck here, immobile. I imagined our hunters above us, searching to and fro, throwing aside books, tearing at tapestries, raging at our disappearance, circling like hounds hungering for scent, eager for our blood. They were close. Time was passing.

Cazzetta's stony excavation continued.

At last there was a heavy scraping and a grunt of satisfaction.

The smell of camphor filled the darkness. Sparks flew, bright showers like fireworks, and suddenly there was fire, bright and red and alive, making us squint.

A torch, spitting sparks and smoking damply.

"Hold it high," Cazzetta said as he offered the crackling brand to Celia.

Aided by torchlight, he continued digging. In the flickering light, it became clear that we stood amongst the bones of the dead. All around us were shadowy niches, sepulchers, and sacramortae chambers filled with skulls and bones and whole skeletons, all neatly stacked. Water glistened in the wavering torchlight, dripping from the walls. Mold and mosses grew upon some of the bones, filling in the sockets of skulls and softening the crests of ilia. Finger bones lay scattered on the floor like tavern dice abandoned. A rivulet of water ran down the center of the chamber, following the uneven path of sunken flagstones.

Cazzetta was digging into a particular sacramorta, shoving aside bones, letting them clatter all around, uncaring of respect or ceremony. Abruptly he straightened, dragging out a prize, a sword that he handed to Celia to complement her dagger. More prizes followed: daggers that he hid about his body; a lantern of wrought iron with strange sigils embossed upon it; a leather pack that he opened and examined closely.

"The rats haven't been at it," he said with satisfaction. "We have food for a week."

"Are we running away?" I asked, as he yanked the straps tight and slung the pack over his shoulder.

"We are preparing for whatever we discover. I do not know how deep this plot has sunk its roots."

His words filled me with foreboding. In the halls of our palazzo, perhaps my father was already dead, his blood staining marble. Perhaps everyone was dead.

Perhaps we were alone.

Cazzetta turned his attention to the lantern. He popped open a small hinged door and withdrew a candle. He lit the wick upon Celia's torch and replaced the candle in its niche. He slid open a trap on the opposite face of the lantern and suddenly light cast forth as a bright beam. It disappeared instantly when he closed the trap.

"Good," he said, with satisfaction. "Douse the torch."

Celia did as she was told, rolling the torch in the rivulet that ran beside us. The flame hissed out, smoky. Darkness rushed in.

As soon as the light disappeared, my other senses came alive. I could hear rats squeaking. The water dripping from the walls. The rivulet at our feet. Could smell the lingering torch smoke—

Cazzetta's lantern scraped open. A beam of light blazed forth, tight and focused as if it were the sun poking through a tiny hole.

"It is mirrored within, to better throw the light," Cazzetta said. "A tool of thieves and fugitives." He turned the light toward the tunnel arch and led us through to a passage that stretched far into blackness, despite the strength of the lantern light.

"Quietly," Cazzetta said, as we started forward. "As if you were Caliba, stealing Erostheia."

We began our journey, slinking past bone chambers, easing along water-slick walls, stepping carefully around great fungal fans that spread like the beds of Caliba's fatas, with gills that seemed to breathe and that recoiled abruptly when light touched them.

We went silent and we went stealthy, and yet it felt as if we revealed ourselves with every step. A thousand eyes studied us. Spiders and skin mice and sewer rats. Roaches and centipedes. We waded through knee-deep sewer-stinking streams, trying not to splash, and on the far side brushed off pale maggoty trucco worms that attached themselves to us, worms that liked to burrow into warm skin to lay their eggs.

The dragon eye, wrapped in my arms, felt almost warm, a strange contrast with the chill of the catacombs. There was an unholy vigor to it, a malevolence unhuman. It seemed to crave to catch and eat the pale cave crickets that chirruped on the ceilings; to pounce upon the blind hairless mice that skittered ahead of us and clung to the ledges of the catacomb vaults.

And then I realized with some creeping horror that it hungered for us as well. We three people were as rats and crickets to it, but warmer. And fatter. I longed to drop the eye, but my arms were unable. I could still feel the dragon within my mind, slithering. Seeking. Exploring. Furling and unfurling its wings almost incessantly now, scraping its scaly coils against the confines of my skull, tunneling and burrowing into the softness of my mind. My head ached. And still I could not let the eye fall. I lacked the will. It refused to be abandoned.

Cazzetta led us onward and I followed, tangled in silent war with the artifact. He turned left and then turned right. We clambered through half-collapsed passages, stepped over crushed bones, waded through more sewer streams. He did not stop or look for landmarks, though all the tunnels and sewers and ossuary niches looked identical.

The oppression of the darkness increased. The sewer deepened and the stink made my eyes water. I breathed shallowly, and sensed Celia doing the same. Our watchers increased. I could feel them all around, could feel the opportunistic interest of the spiders and the rats. With a start, I realized that there were black eels swimming undulous in the sewer deeps that ran beside our feet, unwelcome creatures blind and toothy, full of ravenous malevolence. And with that realization came another: It was not I who sensed the watching and seething hungers of Scuro's creatures; it was the dragon. As much as it shared my senses, I shared from it as well.

"We're under Quadrazzo Amo now," Cazzetta whispered. "It is not much farther."

Suddenly I felt a new set of eyes. Not small ones like rats or crickets, but large ones. I felt the dragon's soul flare in my chest, a sudden heat of eager anticipation. I found myself hungering, my mouth salivating, my lips parted, pleasure . . .

Bloodshed.

"Stop!" I whispered. "Stop here!"

Cazzetta and Celia froze. "What is it?"

I had difficulty putting what I sensed into words. The language of the dracchus was not the same as the language of Amo, and it was a struggle to shape the surging feelings into human meaning . . .

"There are men," I managed, finally. "There are men waiting for us. They—they know . . ." I swallowed. "They know we are coming."

"You are mistaken," Cazzetta said. "We are at our terminus. Conquer your fears, Davico."

"Nai." I shook my head. The soul of the dragon was fairly thrumming with pleasure, anticipating the murder ahead. "They are waiting." I could feel their crouching malice. "I smell their steel. It . . . it is an ambush." Even as I shaped these sensed truths and forced them into the configuration of words, I could feel the dragon hungering.

Cazzetta dimmed the lantern. He was looking at me with concern. I realized I was sweating, nearly overwhelmed by dragon hunger—our blood, their blood—it cared not.

"There are . . . f-four."

Celia looked uncertainly from me to Cazzetta. "How can you know?"

I began to fear that the dragon's hunger for death was a siren song, calling our ambushers to us. Its bloodlust suffused my body. I felt as if I were lit within by a signal fire. It wanted me to call out. To call attention to us. To provoke the battle. To begin the feeding.

"They are close," I said through gritted teeth. "Ahead in the passage. They know we must pass this way, and they mean us violence." It took all my effort to form the words.

Cazzetta's eyes narrowed. "The dragon eye tells you so?"

"I feel it. As if its senses are my own." The orb fairly throbbed with eagerness for violence. An unbridled desire to feed, uncaring which of us warm-blooded animals fell to its teeth and claws. Its presence was growing in my mind, a purring power that threatened to crack me open. "They have swords," I gasped.

"Four?" Cazzetta queried. "You're sure?"

All I could manage now was a nod.

"Bows? Crossbows?"

I could not feel teeth with wings, only long steel claws—"N-nai. Swords."

"How far?"

I knew with a precision that was uncanny, but converting the distance into human measures was impossible. "Ahead . . . within the . . . third arch. I can see them there." I startled at a new sensation. "They know we come."

"Hold the lantern," Cazzetta said to Celia, suddenly decisive. "Count to sixty, then slowly make your way forward." To my surprise, he began stripping off his clothes, unlacing the ties of his trousers, unlooping the buttons of his jacket, dragging off his shirt. Celia's eyes widened at his increasing nudity but Cazzetta was unmindful. "After the count of sixty, make noise," he said. "Make all the foolish noise of a foolish and fearful archinomo child. Do not be cautious as you approach. I will need your distraction."

Cazzetta's naked flesh was shockingly scarred, a tapestry of whippings and stabbings, slashes and burns. I had never seen him thus exposed, and I could not help my eyes traveling his body, studying the cage of his ribs, the thin hips, his stringy thighs, the limp pud of his penis, and everywhere—across all his body—scars. A lattice weave of torture and misery. We did not have long to look, for now Cazzetta slid into the filthy waters of the sewer.

"Count to sixty," he reminded us. He bit his dagger between his teeth and disappeared below the fetid waters, leaving nothing but ripples in the black and stinking murk.

Celia shuddered, staring at where he had disappeared, but she began to count, just as Cazzetta had ordered.

"*Uniz, duiz, terz, quattra, cinqua, sezza, setta . . .*" Her count was steady, perfect as a heartbeat, a procession of numbers almost holy in their rhythm, each number falling from her lips as if it were a prayer to Amo.

We stood close together, looking into each other's eyes as she counted. Her dark eyes were soft with fear and hard with determination. She drew the sword that Cazzetta had given her, silently sliding it from its sheath. Her count went on. "*Terzia, terzuniz, terzaduiz . . .*" On and on, and ending too soon.

When Celia reached sixty, I found myself doubting that we had given Cazzetta enough time, but Celia turned authoritatively and started down the passageway, the lantern held high, her sword held ready.

"How much farther, Davico?" Her voice echoed, girlish and fearful in the passage. "How much longer in this awful place?"

I realized she was playing for the benefit of our ambushers. "Keep going," I said, and was surprised that the words came out. The dragon did not interfere, now that we were once more proceeding toward conflict. I went on, pretending a confidence I did not feel. "This is my father's most secret escape. Soon we'll be safe."

"I don't know what I would do without you, brave Davico," she said breathily.

I shot her an irritated look for her overacting, but her expression was tight with anxiety, and she was entirely focused on the passage ahead. We passed the first arch. I sensed the menace of the men ahead. I hated not being able to hold a sword. I hated how the dragon hungered.

"I'm sure we'll be fine," I heard myself saying. "Once we're out of these sewers, we will regroup. And then we will revenge ourselves."

"If anyone's alive. Oh, Davico, do you think anyone else is even alive?"

"Then we will flee. We will run to Cheroux. Or Torre Amo, or . . ."

"Oh, Davico—" She broke off, for there was the sound of a scuffling ahead.

"Who's there?" she shouted. "Who is that?"

From the darkness ahead there was gasp, and to my surprise, I gasped as well, for I felt a blade sliding into my guts. A terrible cold steel, probing, violating. It was slick and cold and deep inside me, quickly there and quickly gone. And then it was in me again, thrusting, pushing. I groaned at the violation, and then there was nothing but emptiness, a void darker than the catacombs.

I had felt a man die. I had felt his life leak from him. I wanted to retch, to cleanse, to scrub away the violation that felt like blasphemy—but all that was overwhelmed by a surging, rising scream of triumph.

The dragon eye blazed alive.

A light brighter than the sun flooded the tunnel, revealing Cazzetta in its glare. His body was black with sewage filth and his knife flicked like the sting of a scorpion. He moved like liquid night, a blood demon risen from Scuro's darkness.

And the men he battled did not move at all.

They were mesmerized. They stared at us, at me, pinned under the glare of the blazing dragon eye. They stared at the brightness without squinting, struck dumb. Cazzetta's blade pierced them, slashed them, bled them, one after the next, and they fell like string-cut marionettes—one, two, three, falling—their blood gushing ruby-bright.

And I felt each one die.

I felt the violation of Cazzetta's blade again and again. Steel slit my throat, making my neck gape wide like a fish's mouth. I fell and I died, I died and then fell, and each time I felt my soul leaking from my body like air from a pig bladder. I recoiled, trying to flee the awful sensations, but the dragon surged, ravenous. It lunged and snapped after those souls. It bit and shook them like a dog shakes a rat as they came hissing from the dead men's wounds. The dragon whirled and flapped and snapped, and fed.

Together, we gorged on souls.

Triumph, pleasure, shame, horror, lust, revulsion—all raged through me. Sensations without end, wanton and orgiastic in their matings. I lost all awareness of Cazzetta, of Celia, of the sewers, of Navola. There was nothing except rampant bestial desire, unfettered, exultant, and ultimately, too much for my fragile vessel.

I collapsed to my knees, overwhelmed. My arms fell open. The dragon eye crashed to the stones and rolled unevenly, coming to rest against a wall. I fell forward, gasping. Celia rushed to me. I tried to curl up, but could not take my eyes from the artifact that ravaged me. Its reptilian eye stared back at me, flaring red and hungry. The mists of ages that had clouded it were gone; its colors were brighter than jewels. I stared into the eye with awe and horror. The dragon's soul seemed to loom within the tunnels, its dark wings stretched wide. With all my might, I fought to look away, battling the sensation of the dragon gorging, trying to hold on to my own soul before it was lost. I wanted to look down, to look at the stones there, but sensed instinctively that to do so would be to bow to the dragon's might.

And so, with a last desperate effort, I hauled myself upright, to my knees, and fought my eyes upward, up, up, up to the ceiling. Up. Up—the tether snapped. My soul seemed to slam back into my body, once more mine and mine alone, even as the dragon crashed back to its own prison. I fell backward and hit the stones hard.

With the last of my strength I crawled away from it, retching, and curled up.

Cazzetta padded over to me. His knife was slicked red with blood. Shit and sewer slime coated his body. More than ever he seemed to me a demon. A bloody creature born of Scuro, otherworldly in his skill. Watching him in combat had been like watching a dancer almost, a graceful whirling amongst the men who wished him ill. The elegant cutting of the tethers of each man's life in turn, each death seeming as beautiful as falling autumn leaves and as ugly as maggots on a butcher's offal pile.

Now Cazzetta crouched beside me. "I owe you a debt." His eyes blazed with passion. "I owe you a great debt indeed, princeling."

In that moment, I saw great beauty in Cazzetta. This man, with his savaged flesh and his blackly shit-covered body, seemed to me to shine brighter than a bonfire. Bloody, filthy, terrifying. But beneath it all, a banked and hidden love. It was all there, blazing behind his eyes. He was beautiful.

"It is we who are indebted," I gasped, and reached out to embrace him, uncaring of anything except that I clasped a good man to me, vital and alive and unique.

With his and Celia's help, I climbed to my feet, but when Celia moved to pick up the dragon eye, I yanked her back.

"Nai. Do not touch it."

I limped over to the artifact, studying it warily. It no longer glowed. It seemed sated. Its surface had gone milky and crystalline once more. If I listened closely, I thought that I could hear the barest scrape of scales and claws within, but perhaps it was only my imagination. I crouched and studied it more closely. At last, I extended a cautious hand and brushed it with the least of my fingers, ready to draw back in an instant if it attacked. It did not react. It lay quiescent. I was not sure if I was relieved or disappointed. I took a breath and gingerly, carefully, gathered it into my arms. I turned to find Celia watching, her expression considering.

Cazzetta finished his dress, buckling on his blades. "We have little time now," he said. "We must move before others know of us." He went to rifle the corpses. "They wear no colors." He examined an assassin's sword, then tossed it aside with disgust. "And no sigil upon their weapons. I do not know these men."

I watched silently. I had seen thieves and murderers hung, but something about these men, who had meant us ill and now were dead—it was a different feeling, new, uncomfortable, angry and sad simultaneously.

Cazzetta rolled the next man over and repeated his search, examining the man's face, frozen in a final gasp of horror from when Cazzetta's blade had opened his throat.

"This man's mustache is trimmed as mercenaries out of Cheroux sometimes favor, but . . ." Cazzetta shook his head. "It is impossible."

One of the bodies groaned and stirred. We all startled. One of them still lived. In the dragon's frenzy, I had not sensed any survivors, and so now it seemed to me as if the man rose from the dead—but no. He was grievously wounded, clinging stubbornly to the last flickering candle flame of his life. I half expected the dragon to leap upon this new prey, but the eye seemed to have lost interest in our mortal lives.

Not so Cazzetta, who fell upon him like a wolf.

He crouched beside the dying assassin and took his face in hand, pinching it, turning it to and fro, studying. The man was deathly pale, but breathed shallowly. Cazzetta rolled the man roughly over, yanked up his shirt, and inspected the wound he had inflicted. "His spine is severed, but he is stubborn." He motioned me and Celia close. "Stay here. Keep him alive."

"You want us to stay? Here?"

"I will bring others. A physician, if I can." He scowled down at the man. "We will keep him alive, we will revive him, and then we will see what tale he tells." He became brisk. "Quickly now. Use the others' shirts for bandages. Do not let him bleed out." He clapped me on the shoulder. "I will return soon."

"What if you don't?" Celia asked.

"Then you must run."

"We have no idea where we are!"

"Sfai." Cazzetta cut off her protest. "If I do not come back, follow these waters. They will flow to a grate. It is locked, but there will be a key, high above the arch. You will not see it. You must feel for it. But only if I do not return."

"How long?"

"An hour. No more. If I do not return by then, I will be dead. Go then to the Sfona. They are true friends and can smuggle you out of the city to their castello in the Romiglia. Then you must go south. Go to Torre Amo."

"Filippo?" I asked, surprised.

"If he yet lives. If not, to the second manager there. Torre Amo controls much of your family's wealth. It is the richest branch." He gripped my shoulders. "Do you understand?"

I nodded, feeling numb.

"Good. Now keep that man alive!"

Cazzetta disappeared down the tunnel. Celia held her sword tightly, staring after him. After a moment, she went to one of the dead men and cut rags from his clothes. She pressed the soiled linen to the man's leaking wound.

Her face was pale and ghostlike, tight with strain. I wondered if mine looked the same. Water dripped and gurgled. I wondered what had happened at our palazzo. Was my father dead? Was all my family? Were we the last? Was I now the last Regulai?

I felt a crushing weight at the thought.

I tried to slow my breathing, loud in my ears. I imagined I could feel eyes upon at me. All the eyes of all the creatures of the catacombs. All the eyes of Navola. All eyes, watching and waiting to see what would happen to Archinomo di Regulai. All of them, watching me, and then something else: that crawling sense of power emanating from the dragon eye. Cradled against my chest, it was stirring once more.

"Davico!" Celia said. "Help me!"

I realized that I was staring deep into the eye. I didn't know how much time had passed. I roused myself from my stupor and with uneasy reluctance set the eye aside. Celia was crouching over the assassin, trying to stanch the flow of blood. All the rags were soaking. I had been lost in the dragon eye for quite some time. The man's eyes were open. He was awake, staring at me. He tried to say something. Blood stained his lips.

I leaned close. "Who sent you?" I asked him. "Who sent you?"

Of a sudden thought, I went and seized the dragon eye. I placed the artifact beneath his hand and asked again. "Who sent you?"

But the eye now seemed dead.

The man licked his lips. Whispered something. I knelt close, trying to hear his last words, wondering if I should feel pity or revulsion or hatred for him.

He tried to speak again but only bubbling exhalation came. He died. His body fell limp in that way that bodies do when the soul escapes. I flinched, expecting the dragon to feed once more, but it lay quiescent.

"Well," Celia sighed. "Now we'll never know."

I stared at our would-be assassin. He was young, I realized. Not much older than us, if at all. He could have been a student at universita. Might very well have been, given Piero's involvement.

I sat back on my heels. It felt strange to think about. Someone a bare few years older than me had lain in ambush, waiting to murder us.

Footsteps echoed in the darkness.

"Hide," I whispered. We stole away from the bodies.

Torches and footsteps. The echo of men's voices. Cazzetta appeared, trailed by soldiers bearing the wolf and sun sigil of elite Lupari. "Come!" he said. "The plotters are dead." He looked to our dead patient. "He no longer breathes?"

"No."

Cazzetta made a face as if he had bitten rot. "No matter." He motioned to the Lupari. "Take these corpses into the light and hang them with the rest. Hang them from the balconies of the palazzo, hang them at the city gates. Hang them before the Callendra and at the catredanto. Let them hang and let the vianomae see." He frowned down at the dead young man.

"The street will see the faces, and the street will give us names."

Part 3

The Dogs Get Fat—Navolese Children's Rhyme

CANI INGRASSANO

Cani ingrassano!
Cani ingrassano!
Patri, matri, tuotto stilettano.
Nera la notte, rossa la strada,
Fratri, figli, sono garrotano.
Amici, cugini, perche no?
Vino d'insetti, sangue viscoso.
Cani ingrassano!
Cani ingrassano!

THE DOGS GET FAT (LOOSELY TRANSLATED)

The dogs get fat!
The dogs get fat!
Father, mother, stabbed with knives
Black the night, red the street,
Siblings and offspring, strangled with wire,
Friends and cousins, too, why not?
Wine of insects, sticky blood.
The dogs get fat!
The dogs get fat!

Chapter 27

"Veritano di Amolucia. Carlo Cavallini."

The names came as whispers. Names of the dead, the names of our attackers.

"Domiono Assignelli."

My father ordered the corpses of our would-be assassins laid before our palazzo gates, arranged like merchant's wares, body beside body, neat and orderly, tall to short, oldest to youngest, some with slashed throats, some with punctured bellies, this one missing an eye, that one with an opened thigh.

"Marco Pardi."

Blood made rivulets between the cobbles and flies buzzed in the street and dogs slunk about, hoping to seize prizes, and the gossips of Navola came as well, stealing to us from alleys and shops, guild offices and servants' quarters, eager to see the dead, seeking opportunity, knowing that in the aftermath of murder, always there is trade.

"Rodrico di Cartabrisi."

Names for gold. A practice as sacred to the Navolese as light is to Amo.

"Vinci Occhia. Serio Bellanova."

Cloaked figures stole through hot mist darkness to the gates of Palazzo Regulai, appearing as apparitions in the night and disappearing just as quickly, lest they be seen profiting from blood feud.

"Giorgio Broggia, Giovanni Vesuna."

They whispered the names of former friends and faithless lovers. They shared the names of neighbors. Sometimes, they even offered names of blood relations, for hatreds run deep in Navola, and grievances, though buried, live long.

"Amodeo e Amolumio Picobracchio."

The names came as sacred offerings, for gold, for favor, for revenge, some even for loyalty to Archinomo di Regulai, and as each name arrived, it was given into Cazzetta's care, so that he could make an offering in turn.

"Deiamo Pescirusso, Bruno di Lana, Antono Lupobravia."

Wives woke at dawn to find husbands dead beside them, stilettos through their eyes, their heads pinned to the pillows. Sons clutched their throats and vomited black bile, mid-song in tavernae, surrounded by their closest friends. Daughters disappeared from catredanto education, gone like smoke, as if seduced by Caliba. Corpses appeared in black alleys, necks gaping with red second smiles. Dogs carried severed hands through the streets like prizes, chased by children desirous of golden rings left gleaming upon the fingers.

Cazzetta became a name to frighten by.

Be good, my child, or Cazzetta will come and steal you while you sleep at night.

Be obedient, my child, or Cazzetta will come and take your tongue and cook it.

Be silent, my child, and never share the secrets of our family. Whisper nothing of our associations, our dinner companions, our palazzo visitors.

Be discreet, my child, or we may join Archinomo di Lana—all found hanged from the windows of their palazzo: patro, matra, figli, too. Necks stretched long, tongues gone purple, eyes bulged like fish, and the vianomae all pointing up and laughing at how they pissed down their legs while they kicked to breathe.

So please, be silent, my child. Be more silent than a thief in Quartiere Sangro. For if Cazzetta hears a whisper of us and ours, we will join the di Lana, the Broggia, the Cartabrisi, too. Our tongues will be nailed to the catredanto door and our bodies will float in the Livia, and you, my child, innocent though you may be, will be sold to the misery trade . . .

Are you surprised? You shouldn't be. Such is Navola. Such is politics. When families clash, the dogs get fat, as the children's rhyme goes. But perhaps I am too hardened. My sufferings, I know, have hardened me.

At the time, I was at least unnerved. I had grown to majority in a time of relative peace. I had not seen Navolese politics at its most fevered, and so the ferocity of our retribution was unaccustomed. I had known Cazzetta to be dangerous, but I was not prepared for the scope of his campaign.

I was not prepared for the mothers who came to beg mercy at our palazzo gates, how they waited, hollow-eyed and hopeless, but still driven by their mothers' hearts. When we rode out to the hills or to the catredanto to pray, they laid themselves flat upon the cobbles and marked their cheeks, pressing their faces again and again to the grime of the street, prostrate in dust and manure, praying and penitent, praying for reprieve, desperate to save their still-living sons, or else begging permission to take their dead, that they might be buried well—bodies sent to Scuro, souls to Amo—their flesh protected, at the very least, from the bellies of dogs and pigs.

I was similarly unprepared when my friend Giovanni came to me, begging mercy for a cousin. Giovanni, my friend who memorized the Laws of Leggus and read Avinixiius under blooming apricot trees, and lost his friends' horses and ensured his thoughts were rigorous though the principles of Plaesius. The student, the scholar, the veritas and amicus of our circle, petitioning me, not as friend or peer, but as archinomo. Me. Simple Davico. Not my father. Not Merio, Aghan Khan, or Cazzetta.

Me.

"Of course he comes to you," Celia said. "You're the only one soft-hearted enough to listen."

And I did listen. Giovanni and I sat in our summer garden, beside blue-green pools of lilies that cooled the air where we sat beneath the columns of the quadra periphery. We sipped sweet tea and shared bitter Pardi cheeses, and pretended that we were friends at leisure, instead of negozziere at the plank.

The late-afternoon sun blazed down. Lavender and spikebush rustled and bent as bees lit upon their flowers. Water spilled from the fountain, Caliba lifting a ladle of water to shower his pleasure fatas in their postures of bathing.

The gardens were tranquil, and yet Giovanni's eyes darted. They darted whenever Anna approached on soft footfalls to pour more tea, and whenever a laugh from Celia echoed from the balconies above the quadra. But most of all, they darted to Argonos and Ferros, the Romigliani soldiers Aghan Khan had set to guard me, meant to replace

Polonos and Relus, and a heavy reminder of loss—more heavy than if no one had stood in their place at all.

But to Giovanni, they symbolized something else, for his eyes darted like a rabbit's whenever the men shifted or scratched. This was what my family had wrought. Even here, sitting as friends, under my name, in my house, with my food and wine, he feared the hand of violence.

Fieno secco. Vino fresco. Pane caldo.

And yet he feared.

It said a great deal about Giovanni's loyalty to his family that he braved our palazzo on his cousin's behalf.

"He was always swayed by altus ideux," Giovanni said, after we had made small talk for a time. "It was always his weakness."

"Altus ideux?" I looked at him askance. "Is that what we call murder plots now?"

"I don't defend Vettino," Giovanni said. "He is a fool, no doubt. A bitter and stupid fool. But he is a fool as Berecchio was a fool when Caliba made promises to help him sleep with Siennia. Our Vettino, he reads the pamphlets of that fescatolo priest Magare and thinks banks breed vipers and that priests should walk barefoot. He sat with Piero, and Piero talked of a Callendra that would return to glory once it was ruled by nomo nobilii anciens." He waved a hand, tiredly. "It filled his brain with shit. Someone tells him that he is righteous, and he believes them. Someone tells him that he is downtrodden because of his name, and he believes it. But he has no malice."

"So he is blameless, even though his circle tried to kill me?"

"I don't say he is blameless! I was there, too! I saw Piero raise his sword. I saw good men die. And I fled, just as you did." He reached out to me, entreating. "But Vettino was not there. He did not raise a sword. He did not participate in their plot. These were his friends, yes. His acquaintances, of a surety. Men he drank with, and a circle he philosophized with. But he did not lift a blade."

"Did he know of the plot?"

Giovanni looked away.

"Did he know they planned murder?" I pressed. "Did he say nothing? Nothing to you? Nothing to us?"

"I—" He shook his head. "He says he did not know."

"But you won't swear your name upon it."

"It is not something I can know."

I smiled bitterly. "You sound like a true maestro di litigi, saying only what you know before Leggus. No more, no less."

"I swear he does not have evil in his heart."

"That sounds like another oath for Leggus. If he's innocent, why should he worry?"

Giovanni gave me a dark look. "Your family's stilettotore is not famous for restraint. Half my cousin's circle lie dead already, despite the fact that they were not the ones who came at you with steel. Now Vettino cowers in the countryside, expecting any day that some villager will sell his name for Regulai gold. He does not sleep for fear that the demon Cazzetta will come calling." Giovanni reached out to clasp my hands. "He just wants to come home," he pleaded. "He promises to forswear such circles. He will never again speak your family ill. Please, Davico. As a favor to me. Help Vettino. Give him mercy. I told him that your oath is good. I told him that you are kind."

Giovanni pleaded his cousin's case with sincerity, and this—more than the terror of being attacked, or our frantic flight for survival, or the bloody aftermath of vengeance—this was the moment I understood everything was changed for me.

Nai. Not changed. Broken.

Here I sat, beside a friend whom I held in great esteem, as he pleaded for his cousin's life. It was as if Virga's weave of connection between us had come all unraveled, leaving only a few ragged fibers and the two of us far separated. But more than that, I found myself unable to answer Giovanni's plea for mercy. The distance was too far between us, though we sat side by side, and this was the worst unraveling.

We all seek the trust and companionship of other human beings. This is natural. It is necessary. Few of Amo's creatures can live entirely without love and company. And yet, in that moment, as Giovanni waited anxiously for my reply, I found my lips unwilling to form the assurances that my heart wished to give. I found myself unwilling to repair the unraveling bindings of our affection.

Perhaps you will think badly of me. We idealize the trust and friendship of Sevius and Rivus, those soldiers who were like brothers, and never, ever—not even under the most awful duress—betrayed each other or failed to come to each other's aid. We all want to believe ourselves to be so loyal. But myths make poor instruction when words are shrouds and faccioscuro is a razor-sharp skill.

So, this is what I faced: caution against faith—the Conundrum of Arachea. The bargain with the spider. The question of true natures.

Was cousin Vettino a danger or a fool? Could he be trusted to stand by his oaths? Would he join once again with plotters? Was he sincere, or was he only frightened now that his friends had been run to ground? Did I dare show mercy? Was I brave enough to grant absolution to one who had traveled roads with men who had plotted to put a blade between my ribs? And then, even more darkly, how to know Giovanni? He was my friend. I thought him good. But then, I had called Piero my friend, too. What did I know? What could I trust? What was real? It was all unknowns. As scuro as Scuro can be.

And yet I am still ashamed of what I said to Giovanni on that day.

"It is not mine to decide."

Such a coward's words.

"But . . . you're Archinomo di Regulai," Giovanni protested. "You are recognized. You have made your Assumption—" He colored, recognizing the mistake of invoking my name day, the very reason we now sat negotiating without admitting we were doing so. "You have power," he finished lamely.

I wish I had said something then, even if it was to damn his cousin and his plots. I wish that I had embraced my good friend and risked the gift of mercy, or else that I had stood and promised vengeance. I wish, looking back, that I had chosen.

"Tell your cousin to petition Cazzetta. If Vettino is innocent, Cazzetta will know, and no harm will come to him."

Giovanni's face fell. Giovanni, who had always been good and decent and wise, and had always been steadfast. But I was afraid, and so I no longer trusted even those who were trustworthy. I saw the hurt I inflicted on him and desperately wanted to take back my words. But I was afraid, so I let them stand.

To this day, I remember Giovanni's despair, and to this day, I feel ashamed. Friends are to be treasured. They deserve at least forthrightness.

Looking back, I regret so many of my failures and weaknesses, but my failure with Giovanni still binds my heart with thorns. I was not the person I imagined myself. I did not pretend to be the finest swordsman, nor the most skilled in faccioscuro, nor the most astute when I sat at the plank.

But I had thought myself at least a true friend.

This is what I lost when assassins came at me with swords.

They did not take my life.

They took my trust and decency.

Nai. If I am honest before Leggus, I discarded trust and decency myself, for fear that they would kill me.

Chapter 28

Cazzetta's hunt did not end. But despite the opinions of some archinomi, his was no murderous frenzy.

Each public act of vengeance was calculated and precisely chosen, for with each name we sent to Amo, we gained more names, and with those names, we began to discern a tapestry of treachery that had long lain hidden.

Each name was a thread, and the more threads we pulled, the more we discerned the greater weave, slowly revealing an awesome piece of artistry, rich with color and figures. One could marvel at the image revealed, despite its malice . . . so delicate and subtle and exquisite in detail.

As the image took shape, it was not surprising that Giovanni's easily influenced cousin was associated, for it was a motley collection of names and brotherhoods, driven by differing passions, but bound together by hatred for our name.

Some hatreds were political in nature. Archinomi that resented our influence in the Callendra. Others were resentments of trade. Merchant names, who sought to profit from the breaking of our monopoly on marble shipped on the River Livia, or spices from Torre Amo, or who hated our influence with stevedores on the docks, or the loom guild, or the prices shipowners set for the shipping of finished wool and linen and dyed cloth. There were acolytes of the mad priest Magare with his hatred of banks and gold that multiplied unnaturally within our vaults. And there were those like Vettino and Piero, passionate students of the universita, seduced to recklessness by ancient tomes, hungry for glory and full of desire to see nomo nobilii anciens inscribed once more upon the face of history.

Some names were too well-defended for us to reach directly, and so we turned to our allies to force the reckonings we sought.

The Callarino was more than happy to call for votes in the Callendra, for his own blood had been drawn that night as he defended my father. He had taken a slash to the cheek, an inconvenient mark that smarted his pride more than it had endangered him, for now people whispered that he was Regulai sfaccito, marked and owned for all to see.

Between his influence, alongside the exhortations of Garagazzo from his high altar, and with the help of our own loyal backers, the Hundred Names of the Callendra were brought forward to cast cartadecisi. The governing names of the city, the old nobility, the guilds, the artisans, the banks, and the streets, all agreed to inflict decisi exodis against the plotters, stripping them of wealth, properties, and rights of protest in Navola and her territories. And to enforce the decision, they sent General Sivizza and the Lupari.

Battles raged in the streets but family guards were no match for Navola's fearsome Wolves. Soon the Lupari were looting the traitors' palazzi and dragging men from their homes. They slew them on their doorsteps and left the discarded bodies as warnings. Not all died, of course, but all felt the lash of vengeance. Sons and daughters were whipped through the streets, naked and pelted with shit. Cousins and siblings and associates of lesser plotters were dismissed from their offices in their guilds and banned from trade. Others were barred from positions in the Callendra. First secretaries fell. Petty bureaucrats in the ministries of war, trade, tax, and diplomacy were evicted to the streets, left begging to support their families. Students were barred from universita, shunned by maestri and pupils alike. Artisans lost their commissions, and apprentices lost their maestri. The lesson was clear: Those who broke Navola's peace would be held accountable, nomo in tuotto.

Every day families fled Navola, some banished by the Callarino, others simply unable to bear the weight of scrutiny, others fearing that the axe of vengeance would soon fall upon them as it had upon others. I was saddened to hear that the foreigner Dumont D'Enrit, son of Cheroux's ambassador, fled with his family in disguise—whether from guilt of association, or some hidden participation of Cheroux, or simply an abundance of caution, I never knew.

But though Cazzetta and our allies searched high and low, we could not locate the hand that had guided the plot. It was more scuro than Scuro. A puff of smoke, ungraspable but acrid in the nose, making you turn again and again, like a dog trying to catch its tail, seeking the thing that was just beyond the glimpse of your eye, knowing it was there, but unable to catch it.

We discussed the question constantly.

None of those who had plotted or participated, or had associated themselves with the plotters, seemed endowed with the necessary intellect. We had lost the majority of the assassins to the various melees. Some, to Cazzetta's irritation, had been dismembered by the Callarino when he and my father retook the palazzo, a fit of vengeful butchery that ended with bodies stabbed like pincushions.

"He is an idiot prick!" Cazzetta fumed.

My father raised an eyebrow. "He did take an unfortunate mark to the cheek."

"And so he thirsts for blood, and we now starve for intelligence."

"He has his own ways of finding truths. And in the Callendra he is of use. The Hundred Names do as we desire. The Lupari roam as we prefer."

Cazzetta sucked his teeth. "He is still a shortsighted fool."

"As I recall, you yourself felt little restraint in the sewers. Four opponents taken. And yet none with tongues to wag. I thought you more skilled than that."

Cazzetta scowled, and still called the Callarino an idiot prick, but not to his sword-slashed face. Still, Cazzetta was frustrated. He had learned how the men had infiltrated our gathering, how they had replaced servants, how they had brought in their weapons, but he could not pierce the veil hiding the hand that had pulled the strings of the plot.

In the end, it was not Cazzetta's net that dragged up our fish. The cleverness of the plotters was too great and their loyalties were too tight. But still, mistakes were made.

As it happened, there was a servant girl who had been ill used by the son of a certain patro, a man with an oily hand and an oilier tongue, and that son had made allusion to expectations of power. The girl eventually, quietly, made overtures through her communities of women. The scars on her back were shown, her tale was attended to, and at last a name was whispered, not into Cazzetta's ear, but Ashia's.

Celia later told me that the name had come from the concubine Allezzia di Violettanotte, whispered first to her, then confirmed, and finally offered to Ashia, as a gift of esteem.

Archinomo Avizzi.

They were an old noble name, from Amonese times, and they thought their blood very pure. They had lost a monopoly on salt many years ago when my father took the side of the vianomae and made the salt monopoly into a guild monopoly. They had lost money in trades afterward, and they had burned with resentment ever since. And, as it happened, they were old friends of the Speignissi, whom we had burned in their tower all those years before.

"I thought all the Speignissi gone," I said.

Cazzetta shrugged. "Even if you burn a cockroach nest, a few always manage to scuttle away. One of the brothers hides in Gevazzoa. They married a daughter to the Borragha." We both made faces of distaste. "The girl is nothing, but the brother has been corresponding with the Avizzi. So." He shrugged, as if all that was needed had been said.

"So," my father said, in much the same way.

So.

We made an example of them.

A few days later, in the predawn light, we rode with our guard to the fortified palazzo of Archinomo Avizzi. That day, I rode a warhorse called Lightning instead of loyal Stub, and sat tall in my saddle, and when we arrived, we lined our horses in the street to watch as Aghan Khan sent our guard to the gates. Merio trailed him, along with two of our numerari.

The Avizzi guard captain stepped forth as if to fight, but then surrendered, trading his Avizzi sword for di Regulai navisoli. All his soldiers followed. Merio paid each soldier in turn from sacks that our numerari held, sacks heavy with gold.

That silent humid morning, with the mist of the river not yet burned from the city, we paid each guard more than five years' wages, and then the gates of the palazzo swung open and our troops stormed through.

I heard shouts from the palazzo and watched as the Avizzi were all dragged out in their nightclothes, fettered and bruised. I saw my father raise his hand and let it fall. I watched as our guards put each person to the sword, one after the next, grandfathers and grandmothers, wives and concubines, sons and daughters, all of them crying and begging mercy, and all of them dying just the same. I watched swords plunge through soft bodies and I watched blood gush upon the street. I watched the Avizzi die, one by one, and did not avert my gaze until the totality of Archinomo Avizzi lay dead, that ancient name expunged from Navola.

I remember that the blood pooled thickly that morning, viscous and sticky in the heat, and that the flies and dogs found it quickly.

You may ask what I thought of such murder, so vicious and unrelenting, and again I will say that such is Navola, and such is politics.

You may ask what I thought at seeing a whole family put to the sword, the innocent alongside the guilty, the young beside the old, the men, the women, the boy and girl children, all without regard for anything but a shared name.

What did I think of this? What did I feel?

I felt *nothing.*

—Nai. That is a lie. I will not lie to you, I will not pretend before you, I will not dissemble, though it has become my habit because of all I have seen. I will tell you the truth, though it is not a wise thing, for I would have you know all of me.

In truth, I felt many things. I felt horror. I felt pity. I felt anger and relief. I felt the urge to vomit on the street. I felt all those things and more. But I showed nothing on that day.

I gave no reaction as the Avizzi were slain, one by one, marionettes falling with their strings to Amo cut.

I felt much. But I showed nothing.

And when we rode home, still I gave no sign of my whirling thoughts.

I locked myself in my bedchamber. And only once I was there, alone, with no one to know, did I vomit in my chamber pot, and at last let myself feel that which I had kept hidden.

Later, I secretly rinsed that chamber pot with my own hands, doing it in the darkest night, so that not even the servants would have a chance to suspect my weakness. I scrubbed away my fear and horror at what my family was, and what we had done, and in the morning, I showed nothing of what lurked inside my mind.

Ashia would later say approvingly that I became a man that day.

Chapter 29

Of course, even with the extermination of the Avizzi and the unmasking of Speignissi influence, the politics of Navola continued.

The vianomae, who loved us very much, followed our example and so there were petty abuses and petty murders that aped our archinomi bloodshed. There were maneuvers in the Callendra to make a new force of soldiers, composed of citizens, though it was much slowed by bickering over which families and which guilds could be trusted to contribute men for training.

There was argument about whether it was wise to use farmers from the villages that surrounded Navola, or if the levee should come only from within, and there were doubts about if it was wise to give steel and training to any vianomae who might have resentments of some archinomo that might shatter the newly fragile peace of Navola.

There were arguments about how soldiers should be nominated and there were arguments because the highest merchants and guild representatives who controlled the wealth of the city did not want to contribute their own blood or effort to the defense, but also did not trust the vianomae, the craftsmen, the builders, or the laborers, nor the farmers who could have filled the ranks.

Such is Navola. Such is politics. It is a messy process.

But slowly, my father's influence bore fruit, and man by man, sword by sword, the Lupari slowly began to train a few men in defense of the city, with the promise of more once they demonstrated their loyalty and utility.

I tell you all of this, but in truth, I was not much in attendance, for I had found a different distraction.

After the attack on my name day, when we had fled through the catacombs and I had felt the power of the dracchus, I had imagined myself somehow special. I had felt a dragon's soul stirring, after all. I had felt it feed. Indeed, I had seemed almost to feed with it. And for a time after—if I were to use a word, I suppose I would say that I felt more . . .

Alive.

More alert and more aware. More like Lazy, who could prick her ears and twitch her nose and know that Siana Brazzarossa was carving a side of beef in the kitchen. Indeed, I felt as if I could almost track game with my nose, just like Lazy. I fairly quivered with a feeling that the world was alive around me, full of tastes, smells, movement, and color.

Of course, we are all more attentive to our lives when we have nearly died, but to me, it seemed more than that, indicative somehow that the dragon had worked some power upon me, and so I became fascinated with the thing.

It is true what they say about the great artifacts. They are indifferent to us, but they are hungry. And it is easy for us to mistake the siren call of its hunger for a hunger of our own. I was drawn, nigh obsessed, with the artifact, but after that strange moment in the catacombs, the dragon eye no longer swirled, and I could not rouse it.

I could touch it. I could run my fingers along its ocular spines, I could peer into its depths, but it did nothing. Indeed, by the time we had retaken the palazzo, the eye had become milky and still, more like dead quartz than a living fossil of a great and ancient creature.

Cazzetta reported to my father what had happened in the catacombs, and my father summoned me to lay my hand upon the eye and show him the dragon's power, and it did nothing at all.

It was quiescent, much as it had always been.

My father was disappointed.

"It lived?" he asked, trying not to sound skeptical.

"I don't know that it lived, but . . ." I explained what I had felt in the catacombs, what I had seen, how it had felt to sense every creature that lurked in every corner of the sewers, to feel my way through the darkness, to simultaneously crawl with rats and to hang from the ceiling with spiders, to slither in the sewers with the eels, to see as the dragon saw, and then sense the men waiting, and know they meant us harm.

"It wasn't so much that it lived," I said. "But it was . . ." Still I could not adequately describe. "I felt as if I were the dragon. I was the living one, but the dragon became a part of me, or used me—" I could find no other words. "It was as if we were one, and bound. And together we could see every living thing. I felt as if I were part of . . ." I sought words. "Well, everything."

My father gently stroked the surface of the eye, studying it closely. "But you feel nothing now?"

I shook my head. "I think maybe it is dead now. Maybe those souls it consumed, maybe it went with them?"

Cazzetta suggested that perhaps it was a dangerous thing to keep so near. "We should lock it in the vaults with the coins and jewels. Better that it disappears and is forgotten."

My father quirked a smile. "I thought nothing frightened you, old friend."

"It is an ancient thing. It lay forgotten beneath the sands of Zurom. Who can say why it was buried there? Perhaps it was cursed and the people who buried it meant for it to never be found."

"I thought that you didn't believe in such things as fatas and djinn and curses," my father needled.

Cazzetta was unruffled by the chiding. "I do not understand it. And I do not toy with things I do not understand. It should be buried."

"Nai." My father brushed off the suggestion. "It is a reminder of our power. It will remain." Again he studied the dragon eye. "It does nothing now?" he pressed me. "Nothing at all?"

I shook my head. "It is . . . quiet."

He studied me a moment longer. "Well, then we will watch it. You will watch it. And you will tell me if it stirs once more."

Cazzetta made a disapproving hiss, but now my father was all briskness, his decision made. We agreed we would keep these events close, and that Celia, too, would be reminded by Cazzetta not to speak of anything she had seen. We would watch the eye. We would see if it moved again.

And so the dragon eye returned to my father's desk, and our attention turned from the artifacts of the past to the conspiracies of our present.

But I had lied.

While the soul of the dracchus had not stirred visibly when I touched its fossil, I had very much felt its life. The creature's essence had seemed to fill the confines of the eye, quiescent surely, but entirely present and thrumming with contentment. Not at all dead. Sated. Beneath the milky surface of the eye, there now burned a furnace full of life, a heat that I could feel as soon as my hand rested upon it.

It slept, of a surety, but it was the sleep of a snake when it has gorged and now must lie still, weighed down by the prey in his belly. The sort of slumber where it grows and grows until it sheds its skin, and slithers forth to hunt greater prey.

I do not know why I did not tell them this. I do not know if it would have changed anything that happened later. Certainly, in that moment, I would have gained more respect, if I had explained my sense of the creature within, the strange connection I had made to that ancient monster. I could have made wild claims, even. I could have said that the dragon and I were bound by fate. That I read its mind. That I touched its power. I am sure that my father and Cazzetta would have been impressed.

But instead I held the secret to myself.

Perhaps I had lived too long amongst people who practiced faccioscuro. Perhaps I wanted to hold something private in a life where I was much examined, pushed, and prodded, and where everyone seemed to believe they knew me, inside and out. Perhaps I still remembered that long-ago time when I told my family of seeing a shadow panther, and they had not believed. Or perhaps the dracchus itself influenced me, making me as greedy for secrets as dragons are said to be for gold.

Even now I do not know my motivation, but I told my father and Cazzetta nothing. This was my own secret, and I was determined to keep it.

Over the following weeks, I found myself often returning to my father's library. Sometimes I sat within, furtively studying the eye from beneath my brow as I worked at ledgers or listened to the negotiations of the plank. Sometimes I stood frustrated without, stymied when the library was locked. And sometimes, deep in the night, I stole to the library when all others were asleep and I pressed my hand against the doors, and felt for the creature that dwelled beyond.

It was there. Like an itch. It was alive. We were connected somehow. And yet . . . I pressed my hand to the door, feeling within, feeling for that presence, that eldritch creature, hunting for the sense of its slow breathing, of its great furled wings, of its coiling tail—

"Ai, Davico. What is this you're about?"

I jerked my hand away, feeling a flush of embarrassment, as if I'd been caught doing something private, ashamed of being discovered.

Celia stood in the corridor in her nightdress, a cloak around her shoulders to protect her from the chill of deepening autumn. She was frowning, studying me quizzically. I did not know how she had snuck up upon me, except that my attention had been too focused on the dragon. "I'm not doing anything," I said, then tried to turn the conversation. "And you? Why do you wander the halls at night?"

Celia shrugged. "I go where I like, when I like, and I like the quiet of the night." She studied me curiously. "But you, Davico, you sleep in the night. You're always so reliably in bed, and so reliably awake in the morning, and yet here you are, missing your rest." She came to join me beside the doors and examined the carvings upon it: many fatas, drinking and pouring wine. "Were you feeling the fatas?" She smirked.

"No!"

In the aftermath of the attack, the doors had been replaced with heavier wood, and decorated with great artistic effort to obscure this new strength. Intricate carvings of mythical women cavorted across the surfaces, sensual and almost shockingly alive. They played across the panels and hid amongst the doors' twining grapevine motifs—leaves and fruit clusters placed ostensibly to preserve modesty, but in fact inflaming the observer's curiosity and imagination.

Some of the fatas played hide and seek amongst the twining vines; others swam in river pools and bathed under waterfalls. There were fatas sitting cross-legged in meadows, singing to huge bulls who laid their heads in the fatas' laps, content and at peace. Other images showed the fatas tempting men into their forests, or plucking flowers, or pouring wine.

"I wasn't feeling fatas," I said.

"No. You're just touching them." She sighed. "You're di Regulai, Davico, and yet here you are, cold in the dark, pining after naughty nymphs when a thousand hot-blooded girls would willingly warm your bed. You should visit Sia Allezzia and be done with it."

"I wasn't pining after nymphs."

"Nai. Of course not. You were merely admiring artistry." She ran her hand down a door, feeling the forms. "Well, at least you have good taste."

The doors indeed were impressive, commissioned from the di Bicci workshop for the sum of thirty navisoli. Enough to feed an artisan and his family, indeed his entire workshop, for more than a year. Guardio di Bicci claimed credit for the intricate work, but it was an apprentice named Orvik, a foreigner from the north who had done the carving. Orvik was said to be able to feel human forms buried within marble and to hear wood singing as he carved, guiding his hand to find the forms buried within oak and cedar and whitebark, guiding his hand to release them. This apprentice was the reason Ashia had commissioned di Bicci, and though it was not publicly known, di Bicci had been given the commission on the condition that only the apprentice would touch the wood.

"The foreigner is skilled," Celia said. "But still, you need warmer bed friends than these."

"Why is it always sex with you?"

"Why are you always so easily embarrassed?"

I had no answer. Piero—and it pained me to remember him as he had been, drinking and bragging—Piero had always loved to speak of his conquests: bragging about the baker he had cuckolded, the widow he had warmed, the farmer's daughter he had taken in the haystack. Antono spoke of how his father visited a young woman in a house just down the street, paying her husband a monthly sum for daily lunchtime visits. Dumas, before he had fled, had spoken of courtesans and their secrets, their tricks of tongues and fingers, how many times he had plowed their fields . . . and I had been of course interested, but still, it seemed a thing private to me, not something to be bragged about.

"You miss your father's secret books, is that it? But why, you have your own now."

The term she used was a double entendre. *Libri segreti,* which could refer to our bank's ledgers of trade and promise, the master accounting books that he kept in the library. Or, if you were not a banker, the same term could be used to describe the erotics my father kept.

"It's not the books," I said.

"I don't believe you."

"You're exhausting," I said. "I pity your husband. You'll suck him dry like one of Caliba's fatas."

"I pity your wife. She'll dry up like a corpse waiting for you to fill her." She lifted her hand theatrically, pressing it to her brow. "Ai!

Where is my Davico? He should be stroking my thighs but he leaves me alone at night, all alone while he strokes cold wood. Ai. Pity poor me, all alone."

"You always think you're so clever."

"In a word."

"I'm not stroking wood," I said, immediately regretting it.

"Yanking the root, skinning the rabbit, strangling the priest—"

"Why won't you just leave?"

"Why won't you tell me your secret?"

She was like a dog with a rat. Now that she'd set her teeth upon me, it would be difficult to shake her off. I turned and went to the balcony rail, seeking to distance myself from the doors. I stared down into the quadra below, trying to think of some way to distract her.

She came to lean upon the rail beside me. Her breath steamed in the chill of the night air. She pulled her shawl around her shoulders. "We agreed once that we would not keep secrets from one another. That we would tell each other the truth."

"I'm not lying."

"But you're hiding. It is the same."

I looked away.

"Do our oaths mean so little?" she asked. "I tell you all my secrets. But you keep yours." She sounded wounded. "I am your sister, but still you think me untrustworthy."

"It's not that."

"Then what? Do you think me unkind? Do you think I would pass judgment upon you for your desires? For your predilections and obsessions? I do not care, Davico. I would simply know you, as you know me."

When I did not respond, she sighed. "Keep your secrets then."

She gathered her shawl and turned to leave.

"It's the dragon eye."

The words were out of my mouth almost before I realized that I had made the decision to tell. If she had been angry at me, I think I would have kept my secret. If she had raged at my hypocrisy, or harassed me for my secrecy, I would have built walls against her. But all I felt from her was grief at loss of intimacy.

Or perhaps it was my own loneliness. The desire to be known truly, by at least one other person. As the pressures upon me had increased, as my circle of friends shrank, as the watching eyes of others seemed everywhere, my sense of isolation had increased. As I discovered that people I had thought my friends were instead enemies, and as I discovered that those friends remaining saw me as an instrument to influence my father.

I remembered Giovanni begging for my intervention on behalf of his cousin. It had felt as if we were upon different boats, proceeding down different rivers. I was di Regulai. He was someone who wanted something from di Regulai. We were bargainers, not friends. I was not on the same boat with anyone. I was not connected at all.

I think all of this weakened me. I desperately craved someone to confide in. Someone to alleviate the loneliness of faccioscuro, of suspicion, of caution.

"The dragon eye?" Celia asked, quizzical.

"I'm . . . listening to it." I did not meet her gaze. Down in the quadra, the fountain of Caliba gleamed pale in the moonlight, drained of water now that the cold had come. "I'm listening to the dragon."

"But"—she frowned—"you said it was dead to you."

"Nai. It's still there. If I listen, it's there."

"You . . . lied to your father?" Celia laughed, surprised. "You fooled Cazzetta?"

"I'm not proud of it."

"Well, I'm proud for you, Davico. You're a man at last." She glanced at the door. "Well, except that you're still groping wooden nymphs in the dark."

"I wasn't groping. I was listening."

"With your hand."

"I don't know why I told you."

I turned to leave but she caught my arm and pulled me back. "Sfai, Davico. I was only joking. Tell me. Tell me, and I will listen. Tell me, and I will hear you. I will not tease anymore."

"Put your hand on the door, then."

She looked at me, bemused. "All right." With a shrug, she went to the library doors. She pressed her palm to the wood beside a huge brass pull fashioned in the image of the di Regulai Bull. The Bull dwarfed her hand, making her seem even more soft and delicate in comparison.

"Like this? This is how you were listening?"

"It's not . . ." I sought for an explanation. "It's not listening, exactly. It's . . . it's *feeling.*"

"Well, I feel oak."

"It's not oak, its catredanto wood."

"Now who's being clever?"

"You're not supposed to be feeling the door. You're listening *past* the door."

"With my hand."

"Just try."

In truth, I didn't even have to try. It had been tickling my mind for months. That great beast, initially satiated and quiescent, of late had been stirring. And I had been watching it.

As the months passed from summer into fall, as we rooted out the plots of the Avizzi, it had slowly stirred, and I had watched it.

As we sent the Lupari to Merai, I had watched it.

As we heard our first reports that Ciceque had been trapped in open fields and lost many men, I watched it.

As my father's plan for a Navolese militia slowly formed, I watched it.

As we received reports that Ciceque the wily fox had escaped across marshlands, tricking many Lupari into drowning, I had watched it.

And as Ciceque successfully escaped to his stronghold in the Cielofrigo, wounded, yes, but safe now to lick his wounds and cause more trouble, I watched it.

And all this time, it had slumbered. Sometimes it stretched, like a great cat, and I would sit up, surprised at how powerfully it moved, but then it would settle back and the sensation would fade.

But now it seemed to be rousing itself.

"What does it say to you?" she asked.

"It—" I shook my head. "It's not like that. It has dreams. If you listen, you can swim in them."

"You swim in a dragon's dreams. And do that with your hand."

"No. But it helps to . . ." *To reach.*

It helped to reach for the thing, to stretch toward it. But in truth, I had some sense of the dragon often now. It disappeared when I was far from the palazzo, but it became loud when I lay abed, deep in the night. It was much like my heartbeat. Always present, but seldom attended to during the tumult of the day. When I was focused on a task, riding Stub, say, or balancing a ledger, my heartbeat was of course present, for were it not I would be dead, but it didn't announce itself particularly. But when day became night, and all the palazzo slumbered, then my heartbeat became loud in my ears.

"I don't feel anything."

"It's because you won't be still. You have to be still."

"I am being still."

"No, you're not. You're always moving. Like a butterfly. Be still for once."

"How—"

"Think of how you sometimes lie abed and only when you're very still and quiet do you feel your heart. If you are very very still, if you listen, you can hear it. You feel it beat within your chest. You hear it thudding in your ears. You feel your own blood throbbing through your body. You feel it pulsing in the very tips of your fingers. You feel it touch your face. You feel it pulse under your skin, it rushes through your body, again and again and again. It is always there . . ." I trailed off. "Listen as you would listen to the throb of life within you."

I pressed my own hand to the wood beside hers, trying to regain the moment that she had interrupted me from. It was like trying to gather up strings of knitting, everything unraveled. I forced myself to slow my desire. To breathe. To feel the chill night on the skin of my face. The cold air in my nostrils as I breathed. To listen.

Where was it?

I heard torches crackling. The wood was smooth beneath my palm. My pulse raced from my heart to my fingertips and back. It was there. Slumbering like the Colossus of Hippatos. It had always been there. Just like my heartbeat. I reached . . .

Beneath my hand, the door seemed to come alive. I felt the grain of the wood, the life it had once been, a towering catredanto pine. And then it was as if the wood parted before my hand, and suddenly the dragon was there, its presence flooding my mind, filling my head until it seemed there was no room to hold it, and yet still growing larger.

It was vast.

I felt again how small we were to it. How simple. How meaningless. I felt the weight of its years. Desert winds hissed across sand dunes. Strange trees grew tall, taller than catredanto pines, became forests, grew taller than our actual catredanto, and then crashed to earth. Cities grew and spread, and then fell back, swallowed by sand, or war, or famine. Ice crept down from mountains and slowly covered the land, and then slowly, slowly it melted back, leaving new green lands growing. It was as if I watched all the ages, all the way to antiquity. What must it have been like to have accumulated so many years? The knowledge of the dragon seemed wider and deeper than the Cerulea. My father was a learned man. He had read the wisdom of the ancient empire and he listened to everyone from craftsmen to farmers to kings for wisdom that he might apply, and yet his experience encompassed mere decades—

"I don't feel anything," Celia said, dragging me back to the chill of the palazzo. "And I certainly don't hear anything."

"I told you. You have to be still."

"I was still."

I took her hand and forced it back against the wood. "Be still for once. Just once, be still."

It was right there, to be sensed, if only she would try. It was almost impossible to ignore now, for me. It was hard to credit that she could feel nothing. I closed my eyes, and reached out to where the dragon reached for me.

Green fields. Sheep. Forests. Snow. Forests so rich and dense that it was impossible to catch game in their shadowy hearts. And then the forests were cut. Sun beat down and fields covered the land, and the hunting became rich. Mountains cracked apart, became tumbled stones and gray ash. The fields withered and dried, the mountains became hidden bones, covered beneath drifting sand . . . But still there was hunting, caravans crossing to the few emerald pools of oases in the desert. Gazelles in grass seas . . .

"I don't feel—" Celia started again.

"Hush." I stood behind her and I laid my hand over hers, gently pressing it to the grain of the door. "Feel." I kept my hand over hers, pinning her. Keeping her still. I sent my mind questing once more, not just through the wood, but also through her hand . . . "Listen," I whispered.

Questing through, her hand and mine, reaching into the library beyond.

There.

Celia gasped. *"Oh . . ."*

The power of the dragon flowed through us. I could feel it, and I could feel Celia react as well. She knew what I felt now. She could not refute the feelings. We could both sense it. All that wisdom, all that history, all the world, all those hunts . . . I could feel its hunger for us, its desire for our flesh, our warmth, our blood, its jealous desire for the life surging beneath the softness of our flesh. Our warm supple skin. Our hot breath. Our bright blood. Our speeding heartbeats, Celia's soft skin, her hand beneath mine, wildly alive . . .

Our fingers were intertwined, mine over hers, clasping. Her head was turned, staring back at me, her dark eyes wide and startled, her breathing quick. My hand pinned hers. My body pinned hers, pressing her to the door, the two of us breathing as one, our cheeks touching, our lips close. I pressed myself hard against the curves of her body, and she pressed back, leaning back into my arms, one hand coming up, pulling me closer, pulling my lips closer to hers as she let herself be embraced by me. I wanted her. I wanted Celia. I wanted her as a man wants a woman. And suddenly, I could scarcely breathe. Our bodies were pressed close, the two of us nearly joined. I was shaking. I was aware of everything about her, her gaze, her breath, her skin, her breasts, her ass . . .

"Oh . . ." Celia said, sounding even more surprised than when she had felt the dragon's power. Her eyes were wide with some expression I had never seen before.

She was trembling—

No, I was the one trembling. "I don't presum—"

"No. Of course—"

"I didn't mean—"

"No," she said. "Of course not. You would not—"

"No."

I realized that I hadn't actually moved away from her.

When my friends spoke of love, they spoke of how they acted with vigor, pursuing their desire without restraint. They boasted that they plunged into battle without fear or hesitation. But I was not as such. In fact, I was almost entirely overwhelmed, shocked by the intensity of my desire and the confusion of my body. I could not draw away from her—did not want to—but I did not take her as men say they do in the tales of their love conquests.

I was frozen. As frozen as she.

Her breasts rose and fell rapidly. Her breath came in short gasps. I could feel all the length of her body touching mine, not withdrawing, not fleeing. Her parted lips were close. So close.

"You're holding me."

My hand had fallen to her hip. My fingers were digging into her flesh, pulling her to me, pulling her hard so our bodies pressed close. She gazed up into my eyes. I had the feeling of standing before a door, not one locked like the library, but one half open, inviting a push. Daring me to explore what lay beyond.

I felt myself blushing. I wanted to run. I wanted to force her lips to mine. And yet I remained frozen, intensely aware of the touch of her body. The door was open, all I needed was the bravery to push it wide. Instead, like a fool, I hesitated upon the cusp of decision.

I saw a flicker of disappointment in Celia's eyes.

Behind us, a man coughed.

We sprang apart as if scalded. Celia's shawl tumbled from her shoulders, revealing her sleeping shift. She scrambled for it as I turned to face the interloper.

A shadow separated from the deeper shadows of a balcony column and resolved itself into the shape of a man. Silent as was his wont, observant as was his habit. He eased out into the orange light of the torches, his expression hooded.

"Cazzetta," Celia said as she dragged her shawl around her shoulders. "You startled us. Davico was just—"

A contemptuous look from Cazzetta froze her tongue. His eyes flicked from her to me, taking in our flushed faces, her disheveled shawl, her thin sleeping shift. He cleared his throat.

"I had business in the library."

He continued to evaluate us. I could feel Celia trembling next to me, but before Cazzetta's frown, I dared not look at her. Still, I was acutely aware of her presence, the frantic beating of her heart, fast and terrified, much as I had felt the dragon's living pulse beyond the door. We were still connected, and a part of me reveled in it, even as I quailed under Cazzetta's gaze.

I sought an excuse. "We were—"

"It's late," Celia overrode. "I should go to bed." Summoning admirable poise considering her disheveled state, she nodded to us. "Good night to you both." She turned to make her escape.

"Sia Celia," Cazzetta called softly, and though his tone was honeyed, she froze, mid-step. "I believe your rooms are in the opposite direction."

"Ai. Yes." She spun, flustered. "Of course. This way. How silly of me." She pushed past us, murmuring apologies, a deep blush staining her cheeks, apparent even on her dark skin and under the flicker of torchlight, and then she was gone, her slippered footfalls padding hurriedly away. Her perfume lingered.

Cazzetta's attention fell upon me.

"A beautiful girl," he said.

"Is she?" I tried to make light. "I hadn't noticed."

Cazzetta did not smile. "Do not play the fool, Davico. You are not a fool. Do not pretend it, ever." I hung my head. He nodded, satisfied. "Good. Better." He took out his keys and unlocked the library. "There was a ledger I required. Perhaps you would like something to read as well, before you sleep."

"I—" I hesitated, trying to read Cazzetta's expression, to see how he judged me, but of course he was faccioscuro as always. "Yes," I said at last. "Thank you."

I followed him through the doors and into the night stillness of the library. I half expected the dragon eye to come alive at my presence and reveal another of my guilty secrets, but though I felt its presence thrumming, it did not stir.

In the moonlight streaming through the windows, Cazzetta went to take out the ledgers. He lit a candle and set it beside him, then lit one for me as well. I took the offered candle and pretended to peruse the shelves, pausing on Caphii's translated *Histories of the Emperor Reixiin,* which would surely put me to sleep if I opened one of the volumes.

The library was silent except for the dry turn of pages as Cazzetta studied the numbered columns. I made my way down the shelves, pausing on poems of Soppros in their original Amonese. I wondered if Cazzetta had forgotten the encounter with Celia. Already, it felt like a dream to me. It seemed impossible that we had pressed so close, our bodies, our skin, our breaths blended. That I had drawn her to me, tight against my body, that her eyes had gazed up at mine, dark, questioning, open—

"She is not yours to touch," Cazzetta said.

I turned but Cazzetta did not look up from his ledger. "Sia Celia is a promise to your father." He turned a page, ran his finger down the numbers. "If he gives her to you, that is one thing, but if you take her, it will be another. Not even for his son will Devonaci allow his promises to be broken."

I might have protested that I had no such intentions, but one sharp look from Cazzetta warned me. I took another tack. I turned back to the volumes on the shelves, pretending the same nonchalance that Cazzetta displayed.

"How did Celia come to be here?"

"Sia Celia," Cazzetta corrected.

I turned back to Cazzetta, surprised. "We never use that honorific."

"Perhaps that is why you have forgotten to respect her position."

"Sia Celia, then. Why did Father keep Sia Celia? Why not kill her and her family the way we killed the Avizzi? The way you burned the Speignissi? Or why not exile her with her father?"

"That is your father's business."

"It affects me."

Cazzetta shrugged. "She is part of a contract. The Patro di Balcosi failed in his promises once. It will not happen again. She ensures obedience."

"She cannot only be a hostage. Not for the great Devonaci di Regulai. There has to be some other purpose than to keep a knife at her neck."

"If there is, it is not your affair."

"Is she an investment?" I pressed. "Will he sell her like wool when her price rises? I know he sends her to Sia Allezzia for instruction. Will he make her a concubine? Why keep her alive at all? Why let di Balcosi work a tin mine, instead of feeding dogs in the street? What does my father gain from keeping any of them alive?"

Cazzetta snorted amusement. "Don't be simple, Davico. Not every conflict ends in bloodshed. There are advantages to mercy, where it is warranted. Sia Celia ensures a peace between two families. Eventually, she will make a good match and a good wife, and she will do both di Balcosi and di Regulai proud. That is all. She is your father's ward, and you will respect her."

"What if I want to marry her?"

Cazzetta's eyebrows went up. "Do you?"

I looked away. The words had flown from my mouth too quickly. They felt true, but also frightening, a commitment from the heart rather than the head, and all the more foolish because of it. I felt as if I had leapt valiantly into battle, only to land upon quicksand.

Cazzetta considered me. "It's time you had a companion, I think. A girl to keep you company."

"That's not what this is about."

"Your father thought it would be soon. Ashia will arrange someone."

"I don't want some girl 'arranged' for me."

But Cazzetta had already returned his attention to the ledgers. "You are not in love, Davico. You are intrigued by the undeniable attractions of the sia. And in any case you would not marry so low as Sia Celia. We both know your father has greater plans for you."

"Cheroux?"

He looked up again, his dark eyes glittering. "Whosoever is of value. Sia Celia, of a certainty, is not."

"She is nobility. Archinomo and nobilii anciens. She has lands. Di Balcosi has lands. It's not as if she's some dog found on the street."

"Their holdings are like an ant's in comparison to di Regulai. Nai. You will marry a bright jewel from Banca Metano or Belanche, or yes, maybe a princess from faraway Cheroux. But of a surety, you will not marry a girl from a family that has already been swallowed by your own, no matter how old or noble the blood."

"So my own desires do not matter?"

"Sfai. Davico. Look about yourself. Use your eyes. Use your head. There are wheels turning around you. Great wheels that your father turns on your behalf, like the gears of a mill, turning and crushing wheat into fine flour, flour that will one day be baked into bread. Perhaps even royal cake."

"And if I desire something else?"

"Then your mind is clouded." He closed the ledgers with a thump. "Come. It is late. I will speak with Ashia in the morning. First, we will relieve that ache in your loins that the fine young sia has inspired. Once your head is clear and your lust is cooled, we will talk. No man thinks well when his blood is all in his root, a young man least of all. What little wisdom he has is all leached away."

"You know my father's plans," I accused.

Cazzetta shrugged, that Navolese shrug that seemed to say, *Maybe yes and maybe no and maybe I don't care to tell you.* "I know you cannot be a fool. Not a fool for yourself, and not a fool for a woman's swaying hips, nor the blush of her breasts. We will make sure your root is milked dry, then, perhaps, we will talk of the future your father works to his will, and of all the lives he grinds into useful flour."

"I am not flour," I said.

Cazzetta gave me an appraising look. "Mark my words, princeling, before your father, we are all either kernel wheat, well-ground flour, or useless chaff. And if you are chaff, you will be burned."

Chapter 30

I should have taken Cazzetta's warning, but, much like the dragon eye, Celia drew me.

I could not help but look at her differently. Previously, I had seen her as my sister—beautiful, yes, pleasing to the eye, of course, but also familiar. Now I saw her anew. How her skirts clung to her hips and how the exposed skin of her breasts swelled above her bodice. How she gathered her lustrous dark hair back from the seductive curve of her neck. The endlessly twisting plaits of her hair when it was bound up. My fingers yearned to trace the enticing hollow of her throat where an amber necklace rested. When I heard the rustle of her skirts and the soft pad of her slippers upon the marble, I tingled with anticipation at her arrival.

But most of all I felt her eyes. Her dark eyes, burning upon me.

We were closely observed. Ashia said nothing, but watched us with hawklike intensity. My father said nothing, but had me sit in his library with him often. Aghan Khan said nothing, but took me riding and hawking. Cazzetta said nothing, but took me to the dark cellars where he made poisons. Merio said nothing, but entangled me in correspondence with our far-off bank branches. And too, Anna and Gianna and Ferrio and Sissia and many more servants suddenly all seemed to be about, always underfoot, always in the same room as me, in the garden with me, on the streets with me.

Cazzetta and Ashia conspired to create another distraction for me as well. They sent me one day to Sia Allezzia's palazzo, hoping to entice me with the charms of more appropriate women. There I was given into the hands of a very skilled and pretty girl for several hours. I could tell you that I did not thrill to the sight of her naked body, offered up to me in her rooms, before the flickering light of a grand fireplace, but that would be a lie. I felt a hunger as deep as the dragon eye, and I went into her arms willingly. But in the moment of our union, when we were twined and close, I looked into her eyes. And there I saw a coldness more howling and remote than the winds of the Cielofrigo, and I drew back. I think it is the first time that I saw with certainty past the mask of a person's faccioscuro, and it would have been a triumph were I sitting at the plank. Instead, it left me feeling as if I were not a man, but a lumpen block of wood, unimportant and discardable, and the contrast was so stark in comparison with the way Celia had looked at me that my lust died.

I returned to the palazzo with only an increased desire for Celia.

Under constant observation and unable to find time alone with her, I attempted to communicate with Celia through more subtle methods. With the offer of biscuits from Etroualle's, or the pouring of tea, or an invitation to come and walk with me and Lazy. Innocent, unreproachable acts that once would have elicited no notice at all, but now seemed weighted with intrigue.

And yet she dismissed my invitations.

Though she did not rudely refuse my offers of biscuits or tea, neither did she indulge. She thanked me without affection, as if I were a servant. I wanted to ask her if Cazzetta had had words with her (or more likely, Ashia), for in every action, every glance, every word, she was rigorously correct.

For myself, I could not help but watch her all the time, whenever she was in the room. But she now seemed uninterested in me. She ministered attention upon stitching and reading and spent time at the bank, harassing the clerks and numerari. She lavished attention upon Lazy, cooing over her.

All this I watched, and all this time, she ignored me.

We attended catredanto services under guard, and listened as fat Garagazzo preached to us about the importance of moderation. The body was the temple of Amo, and so should be treated with respect, much as the mind was also Amo's temple, and neither should be polluted. He admonished that we should spend our time amongst those who uplifted our minds, and did not drag them down, much as we should seek nourishment but not gorge ourselves.

I tried to catch Celia's eye, hoping to at least share the quirk of an eyebrow that would indicate her dark amusement that someone as polluted as Garagazzo spoke on the temple of the body, but she never turned her head and never took her gaze from Garagazzo as he burned the incense and made the prayers of absolution.

It began to feel as if I did not exist.

Had I offended her? Had I imagined the moment between us? Had I actually forced myself upon her, and she, chameleon-like, gone along, faccioscuro, until she could escape me? And yet, when she had gazed into my eyes, she had seemed desirous. And her body, I did not think it could have lied. I had desired her. I had felt her respond, felt her breath quicken, her lips part . . .

Every night these questions crowded my thoughts, intruding enough that I forgot even the dragon eye and its siren songs. When I slept, I dreamed of her. I dreamed that she came to my chambers and pulled aside my bedclothes. I dreamed that she lifted her nightdress to expose her fig to me, and then laughed at me lying there, saying, *Why, Davico, you're still in your nightshirt!* And I would wake, groaning, my nightshirt sticky with Caliba's honey.

I dreamed of her so much that I began to fear to sleep. I lay in the darkness, imagining her lying abed on the far side of the palazzo. I imagined myself stealing through the dark corridors to her chambers.

I even went so far as to step out in the middle of the night, and would have gone to her then, to demand an explanation for her coldness, but in the darkened halls, I sensed a presence, lurking. Cazzetta in the shadows. Guarding the path to Celia's chambers. I could feel him there. Could hear his breathing.

I pretended instead to go to the kitchens in search of snacks—even though I wore too little for the cold, and even though my ruse must have been transparent to one such as he—and when I returned to bed, still Celia haunted me.

My days became as gray as the winter clouds and fogs that now stole into Navola's streets.

I missed her presence. With Celia withdrawn, I felt a loneliness that I could not shake away, as if a fata of sadness had come to press her hands down upon my shoulders, and whisper despair in my ear.

To escape the feelings, I rode Stub into the cold hills with the gray clouds and all the fields cut and brown and chill mists drifting across the sleeping lands, and they all matched my mood.

I tried to play cartalegge with those friends who remained, loyal

Antono, along with Niccoletta and Benetto, but the game felt empty without more to play, no matter how we tried to pretend that it was satisfying. The missing Giovanni, the dead Piero, the fled Dumont and Cierco, the absent Celia . . . It was as if we played with ghosts.

Celia was more a part of me than I had ever known. And now she had cut me away, as if I were the rigging and sails of her swamped ship, cutting me away, leaving me to drown, while she floated away on the tide.

It was in the depths of this despondency that I was summoned to dine one night with the rest of the family. Hot soups and heavy spices for the winter. Spiced hot wines, of low quality but warming and soothing.

I no longer looked at Celia across from me. I no longer bothered trying to read her face, to catch her eye or make her laugh, or pour her tea.

And that was when I felt it: a toe beneath the table.

A toe, stroking up my leg, touching me. I was so startled I almost jumped, and instead coughed so that Ashia and my father and Aghan Khan and Cazzetta all looked at me, surprised.

Celia's toe disappeared.

I pounded my chest and apologized.

I resettled myself. The conversation resumed.

Celia's toe returned.

Her touch spread tingles up my legs, made me flush. I took a sip of hot soup and fanned myself, pretending that it was the cause. Meanwhile, Celia spoke of how she had been reading *The Philosophies of Queen Epeia of Khus,* which had been translated and sent to her as a gift from Filippo di Basca da Torre Amo, of all people.

"She suggests that we are only as high or low as the people we surround ourselves with. A thief is not a thief if he is not surrounded by thieves. A noble is not a noble unless surrounded by nobles."

Aghan Khan laughed. "That describes the Callendra, certainly."

Celia's toe slid up my shin, spreading fire.

"I wonder if that is why the Siana Furia is the way she is," Celia went on.

My father paused. "And what do you think Siana Furia is?"

"A monster," I said, trying mightily to both revel in Celia's touch and lock it away from my face. "Furia is a monster."

Cazzetta snorted. "I've known worse."

"I think she is surrounded by evils, but she is not so," Celia said.

"If you saw her slave pens you would think differently," Aghan Khan said.

"Why do you dislike her so?" Celia asked. Her toe was stroking slowly up and down my leg, rising higher. I scooted my chair closer, slipped my own toe from my shoe, and reached for her as well.

"As Davico says, she is a monster."

"You haven't seen enough to know," Cazzetta said.

"I have seen enough of her to know," Aghan Khan said firmly.

I slipped my own foot up Celia's leg but was met with a swift kick. Her touch withdrew from me. I drew back my own foot, confused.

"She killed her brothers," I said, trying to keep the conversation going.

"Maybe they were monsters, too." Celia's expression was entirely bland as she gazed across at me. "Monsters abound in Navola." I wondered if she was talking about me.

"If Furia is a monster, she is entirely of her own making," I said. "Twisty."

Cazzetta laughed. "Ci, Davico. Still you think you see the world, and still you miss the light and shadow of it."

"What is there to know about Siana Furia? She is entirely chiaro. She revels in her monstrosity."

Cazzetta regarded me. "What if I told you that she cried when her brothers' remains were returned to her?"

"I would say you're lying."

He shrugged and went back to his dinner.

"You're lying, aren't you?"

Cazzetta glanced at my father. My father shrugged. "Nai. It is true."

"She cried because she couldn't torture them," Aghan Khan opined.

"But she did kill them," Celia said. "That's true, isn't it?" Her toe was at mine again. Caressing, playfully touching and withdrawing, making me draw sharp breath, so sharp that her eyes flicked to me briefly, warning, and then slipping higher, caressing up my leg, touching my knee, pressing between my thighs. And all the while, she kept up her conversation.

She was truly a maestra of faccioscuro. She carried on the conversation. She inflamed me. She ate her meal. She passed the salt bowl and sipped her soup, and all the time, she played her dangerous seduction of me. She was an artist.

I would have been in awe, had I not been so preoccupied.

"I still wouldn't believe that she cried," I said. "She is what she is. Entirely chiaro. Not a trace of scuro."

Celia gave me a disappointed look. "Ci, Davico. Do you not see it? She plays at monstrosity, to hide her vulnerability. The face she shows is not her face at all."

My father snorted. "Well, I wouldn't go that far."

Cazzetta was nodding though. "Still, there is more to what you say than you know, Sia Celia. She cried when the remains of her brothers were returned to her. And it was with true feeling."

"I heard she threw a ball," I said, "and gave sweets to the poor, and tossed the bodies in the river, unblessed, unburnt, doomed to walk the earth forever."

"What you have heard and what is true can be different things."

"Not with her," I said firmly.

"And the fact that she cried?"

"I do not believe it."

"And yet I tell you true that the night her brothers' bodies were returned to her, she sobbed in her bedchambers. Sobbed all the night through. What she showed the world was different from what she showed herself."

"You could not know that," I said, but in my own mind was suddenly the memory of the night we slew the Avizzi family, and how carefully I had masked my face as their bodies fell, and how I had thrown up in my chamber pot after.

"Not unless someone whispered it in my ear," Cazzetta was saying. "A chambermaid perhaps, with a lover who used to ask her questions, who used to ply her with gifts and so she told stories. Siana Furia cried as if her heart had been sawn from her body. And then, in the morning, her face was clean of tears, and she threw her party, and tossed her brothers into the Livia to feed the razormouths, and celebrated her own sort of Assumption."

"Is that why you treat with her?" Celia asked. "Because she's not all bad?"

My father shrugged. "She is dangerous, but she is . . . reasonable." I thought of what I had seen of Furia, and my face must have said more than my mouth for my father added, "Reasonable in her own way. She will not hesitate to protect herself, but she has a strong sense of what is right and what is not. She pretends to more mischief than she believes."

"That act with her slave," Celia said. "At our dinner. Before Davico's Assumption. The girl with the poison fingernails that she fed from her own hand."

"Indeed. Her insults. Her testing of propriety." My father shrugged. "It is all of a piece. When you see her clearly, you see how carefully she grooms her image. Fear is a weapon, and she wields it well, but it is not the whole of her."

"But how can you be sure?" I asked. "If someone pretends to something all the time, isn't that precisely who they are?"

Aghan Khan nodded. "I agree with you, Davico. If you pretend to something long enough, the difference between a true self and a pretended self becomes meaningless. They become the same."

"Furia is more than that," my father said. "She plays her game, just as we all do. But she is more than that."

Celia's toe slipped between my thighs, questing, pressing farther, making me swallow. And then she was feeling my root. Massaging me to hardness. I stifled a gasp. My father's eyes narrowed.

"How can you be sure of Furia?" I asked again. "I don't see any of that."

Celia's dark eyes flashed.

"Ai, Davico. You have simply to look. Everything is revealed if you look closely."

Chapter 31

It is a special thing to know that someone burns for you as you for them. This fire of knowledge warmed my winter much as my sense of loss had previously made it cold.

It is a strange thing that something as absolute as winter's chill can be either so cold that it seems to break the soul, or else a trifle barely remarked upon. The winter chill does not change, and yet it is changed. Aeschius spoke on this phenomenon of perception. He imagined that the world was perhaps not even the world at all. He surmised that it was a construction entirely of his mind. Was winter cold? Was hunger hunger? Was a journey debilitating or thrilling? I had never put much stock in this idea. To me, it seemed that the world was the world. A disappointment was a disappointment, a triumph a triumph, but now as the sun rose over Navola's chill mist winter, I saw beauty where I had seen dolor, and I wondered if I was so correct.

With the warmth of Celia's attention I was suddenly warm where I had been cold. I was delighted where I had despaired, and it was in this mood of pleasure that my father called me to our bank offices, to show me recent reports that had arrived.

Reports from Sivizza and the Lupari in Merai, bogged down by the wily Ciceque and now wintering there. He offered me more reports, these from the branch in Bis, in far northern Cheroux, where ships had been observed and loans for canvas had been secured. Great amounts of canvas. And after this a report from our branch in the Red City that spoke of seeing an envoy from Cheroux wearing King Andreton's colors in a tavern, along with whispers from palace servants that fine apartments—empty since the young Parl had taken his father's—were now being scrubbed and hung with new tapestries and the furniture beaten of dust, and wood laid in for fireplaces.

The pattern was plain. "The Parl has grown impatient," I said. "He's negotiating with Cheroux."

"And Cheroux is preparing for war." My father nodded. "It would be in our interest to bind Merai more tightly to us."

"If not with money and the Lupari, then how? It is a bad business," I said. "We will only lose more if we keep making loans." I looked at the books. "We should write off the loans. We cannot continue to extend ourselves."

My father and Merio exchanged glances.

"What?"

My father motioned me to follow him. We went out through the small triple-locked door in the upper floor of the bank that led directly to our palazzo along a catwalk, and thence along a hall to his library. He went to his shelves and pulled down his master account books. Pushed them across to me, without a word.

I turned the pages, frowning, for the numbers that we kept in the bank were different from these numbers. These numbers were enormous.

"Where did these totals come from?" I asked. "I've never seen these."

"These you can trust."

"Why are they different?"

He gave me a sour look.

"We have spies in the bank?" I was shocked and disturbed. "Why have we not gotten rid of them?"

"It's sometimes more useful to know who spies, so that we can control what they know."

"Who spies on us?"

My father laughed. "Tomas and Primo. One for the Callarino, one for Banca Cortesa. We rid ourselves of Federico, who spied for Furia, to make the other two spies feel more confident that they are undetected and well trusted, and to make the information we feed them seem more legitimate."

"The Callarino spies on us?"

"Of course." My father looked surprised. "We are allies. Not friends." Merio snorted at this.

"But . . . these debts are greater than . . . we have borrowed money from other banks. Our last loans to Merai . . . we did not have the money."

"We used the Borragha in Gevazzoa."

"We used the Borraghese?" I could not hide my shock. "Why would we let them know our business?"

"We used proxies," Merio said. "They think they make loans to a shipbuilding company in Vesuna and a spice merchant in Torre Amo that they do not know we control."

"These numbers are huge, though!"

"They think it is for a bribe to dominate spice imports across the Kharat and Khim." My father waved his hand impatiently. "That is not important. You see that we are extended. That we are vulnerable. If we lose Merai, we are nearly bankrupt. It would take much of the capital of the other branches to cover the amounts we owe."

"Is it even possible?"

"Once we control Merai," my father said. "Once Ciceque is vanquished. Once the Parl sits comfortable on his throne. Once he is convinced that he cannot renege on his promises to us."

I was still astounded, trying to understand how we had become so at risk. It defied everything that I understood. "How . . ."

"The old Parl was trustworthy," my father said. "His promises were good. We saw each other clearly. We had agreements that were never written, but were iron, as long as he lived. This young one . . ." He scowled. "His promises are like the ice in the harbor. One moment firm, the next so thin that when you step on it, you drown. He's a boy, tempted to rashness."

I was still trying to comprehend the terrible risk we were in, but my father was already speaking. "You will go to Merai," he said. "I will send you with Cazzetta. You must make a new agreement with the Parl to bind him more closely to us."

"But we have no more money to offer. We have no more troops to offer. He has the Lupari, already! We are vulnerable."

"We have one thing to offer, still."

It took me a moment to realize what he was implying.

"Celia." I could scarce believe it. "You will offer Celia." I felt sick at the realization.

"Just so."

"She's not . . . She's not the highest nobility. Why would the Parl accept her?"

"She is as a daughter to us, and that is a powerful guarantee. With her dowry, with our bound loyalty, he could be assured of support that no other bank could offer. She is one with our family. He will accept."

"But we are bankrupt! It is all pantomime!"

"Not once we win. Sivizza will root out Ciceque, and the money will flow from Merai. We can hold off the Borraghese bank until then. It will work, Davico."

Suddenly, I saw what he was doing, saw through the entire scheme. "You're trying to separate us."

My father looked at me, steady. "Cazzetta mentioned that you had grown close."

"Are these books even real? Are these the true numbers?"

Merio sucked in his breath, shocked at the insult, but my father shot him a quelling glance.

"She is your sister," he said. "She is not for you."

"She is di Balcosi!"

"She is as a daughter to me. You can never marry her."

"What if I love her?"

"Love?" My father laughed. "Love does not fight off ships from Venzi, nor does it pay back loans to Borraghese bankers. I thought I had taught you to see more clearly—" He broke off at my expression. "Ai. I see. You care for her greatly." He took a deep breath. "I speak with too much heat." He took a moment, breathing deeply, calming himself, then looked up at me. "What I wish to ask is, do you care so much for her that you would ruin your family for her sake?"

I stood stubbornly.

My father made a motion of dismissal to Merio. Merio backed awkwardly out of the room. The doors closed behind him, heavy and final, like the closing of a tomb. My father sighed. "You are a man, Davico. I cannot control you. But hear me and think well, for as you are a man, you must think as a man. If you would marry Celia, you would forgo alliance for yourself with another family, a royal one, perhaps, a wealthy one certainly, with lands and power and influence. If you forgo that, you set us alone, like a boat upon the Cerulea without a sail, to be blown by fate, rather than steered by strategy."

"I could be a physician, like Maestro Dellacavallo. I could steer a different course."

My father barked surprised laughter, but waved a hand before I could argue. "Nai. I'm sure you are sincere. And I am sure you would make a fine physician if it were your destiny to do so. But think on this, what of Celia if she marries you? What prospects do you offer her then?"

"A physician's life is not so bad."

"But you will not be a physician. You will be di Regulai, and as our bank crumbles and fails, as it surely will, do you think it will fall quietly? Do you think our enemies will be content to leave you alone, just because you have gone to mix herbs and count the heartbeats of patients? Nai. They will see you as a shrouded card in cartalegge—a threat—and they will seek to ensure that you never are played again." He sucked his teeth. "I love you, Davico. I love you so much that my heart seems sometimes to be outside my body, but if you marry Celia, you will set events in motion that will not come to stillness until all of us are dead or fled to exile."

"I could take her as a lover, then. As you have taken Ashia."

His eyebrows went up. "Ashia is a slave. Do you see Celia so?"

"You know that's not what I mean," I said.

"Would you ruin Celia's hope of good marriage, by making her yours?"

I didn't like this turn. The conversation seemed to have strayed into uncertain ground, much like the grass seas to the south of the city, where river and salt sea met and made marshes, and where fishermen made traps for fish. There were solid grounds and muddy grounds and no one could know the difference except the fisherfolk who made it their lives to know those places. People drowned in those marshlands, and now, returning my father's gaze, I saw that I was upon similar marshes.

"She loves me," I said stubbornly.

My father sighed. "Use your head, Davico. Even if Celia were so willing, I have both the power and influence to protect Ashia. I can keep my promises."

"You think I do not know my promises?" I shot back. "You think my hand oily?"

My father laughed. "Is this sigil of Navola yours?" He lifted the stamp of city office. "It is not." He gestured at our surroundings. "Is this palazzo yours?" His lips formed a thin line. "It is not." His expression hardened. "The promises of our allies?" I did not reply but we both knew the answer. "What you offer Sia Celia," my father said, "comes from my hand, for I am the one who supports you. Now, whatever you may think of your own promises, I have promised Celia's father that she will be well placed, in return for his loyalty and obedience. Will you now break my promise to her father? Will you have me say to him, Ah yes, Sia Celia, your daughter, is now my son's marked slave—"

"I didn't say that!"

"—she will ever be held at a distance, never to marry with honor, perhaps to later be discarded if he grows tired of her, her children by him bastards sent to our farthest branches of banking. Would you go to the Patro di Balcosi, who stood by his promises and gave up his daughter for his honor—and who now depends on my promises and on my honor—and say you wish to make his daughter into a bauble in your bed?"

I hated how he made my love for Celia tawdry. "That's not what I want from her!"

"Well perhaps not only that, at least." He laughed a little. "My son, Davico, you have a good heart, if not a wise one. If you think yourself Celia's friend, then you will speed her on to a good marriage and good fortune, and not interfere. But regardless, she will be married and you will find your own match. There is no more to discuss."

"I will have her for a wife and damn you!"

My father paused. I was on my feet with a hand upon my dagger. Rage had moved me before I knew it was there. I longed to draw my dagger, to plunge it into his heart, to teach him to respect me at last, to hear me, to no longer show contempt.

My father's lips compressed as he looked upon my quivering rage. "Forgive me, blood of mine," he said. "I had thought you not a fool."

I would have stabbed him then. I would have ended him and spat on his body and sent him to Scuro, but I became aware of the dragon eye beside us, resting upon the desk. And I was struck by a sudden feeling that the thing was watching us. It was watching, and it wanted to see blood spilled. It wanted my father's blood spilled upon the desk. A reptilian coiled hunger for blood, a twisting, writhing, snakelike desire to see the violence. And something more . . .

It wanted not just to see blood, but to see us fight as fathers and sons must always fight. It wanted to see the young supplant the old as must always happen, whether through age or violence. The dragon knew that the old always lingered too long, and that the young rose always against them. The young would stand tall and place the boot of youth upon the weak neck of age—until they, too, were crushed by their own children. And on and on.

On and on, through all the ages.

And suddenly I was aware of time, of the dragon's sense of time. It desired to see the workings of human trifles once again played out. No matter what I did, it would confirm the dragon's judgment of humanity. I could strive against my father, I could spill his blood, or I could bend my knee and obey, but no matter, I would not break the pattern of humanity, the long chain of fathers and sons, mothers and daughters, stretching through the ages, always the same, always in pattern. The dragon had watched the rise and fall of generations, had watched the rise and fall of empires, of dynasties, indeed of the land itself, watching as Zurom turned from a lush land to one of sands and devastation . . .

I took my hand from my dagger.

My father watched without reaction, faccioscurissimo. The man who designed and pulled the strings of all the actors in his play. Such a maestro. A player of cartalegge who tossed out card after card, knowing as each one was played how the others around the table would respond. He was a maestro without peer. I was just another card.

"You will leave for the Red City tomorrow," my father said. "Cazzetta will accompany you."

I didn't reply. I turned on my heel and left, striding from the library and slamming the doors behind me. Let him think that he had won. He had not. I would not surrender so easily. And though I was unsure of how I would defeat him, I was sure of one thing:

Whatever I did before the eye of the dragon, I would not do as expected.

Chapter 32

I woke in the deep night. Cazzetta stood over me, a shadow shard, eyes gleaming in moonlight as he poked me awake.

"By the fatas, you scared me!" I exclaimed, scrambling back and drawing my bedclothes around me.

A small grunt of laughter escaped him, but before I could remonstrate with him, he tossed breeches and shirt upon my face. "Get dressed," he said.

I clawed away the clothes so I could see him. "Why?"

"We leave the city before dawn. Hurry."

"I will not."

I had gone to bed intending to resist my father's plans, and if Cazzetta thought himself intimidating enough to chivvy me forth, he would be sadly surprised. "I'm not leaving."

"You don't think so?" Cazzetta's shadow sounded amused as he rifled through an armoire that held warm clothes. A riding coat landed upon my bed with an unceremonious thump.

"I'm certainly not leaving until I say goodbye to Celia," I said.

Cazzetta's shadow, now busy finding my boots in a chest, snorted. "What would you say to her?"

"It's not your affair."

"Ha. You have no words. You're a pup." He went back to his noisy digging in my chest. "She is not here in any case. Ashia took her to Calda di Livia, for the baths there. She won't be back for several weeks."

"She's gone? Why didn't she tell me?"

My boots landed atop my bed, as unceremoniously as my clothes. "Because she was told to go. And she obeyed."

"I don't believe you." I climbed out of bed, taking my bundled clothes and boots. "I'm going to speak with her."

"I tell you, she is gone." Cazzetta laid a pair of daggers atop the pile of clothes in my arms. "Now get dressed."

"She's not. And I won't."

"So you intend to go hunting for her like that?" Cazzetta laughed. "Get dressed, princeling. Then go look if you don't believe me. Hurry and look, so that we can go."

Scowling at him, I pulled on my breeches and shirt. In the chill, my skin was gooseflesh. I hurried. "There," I said, tugging on my boots, tucking my daggers in their sheaths. I strode for the door. "Wait here. I will not leave until I have spoken to her."

Cazzetta bowed himself out of my way. "Of course, my lord. Woo as you will."

But as I pushed past him, his hand came up to tap my neck. I felt a pinprick. Almost instantly, numbness began spreading through my limbs. I managed two more strides before my legs gave out.

Cazzetta caught me as I stumbled against the door. "You really should be careful of who you let close to your person," he grunted.

The poison was thickening in my body. My eyes were becoming heavy. I could feel the numbness spreading with each beat of my heart. I fought to stay awake but the poison was powerful, just as Cazzetta had taught me it was.

"Why didn't you just prick me while I was asleep?" I slurred as I slipped down to the floor. "Why bother with all of this?"

Cazzetta laughed shortly. "Have you ever tried to dress a limp body, Davico? Ai. It is a clumsy and difficult task. Much better to let you do the work for me. For which, young princeling, I thank you."

I stared hate at Cazzetta, but that was all I was capable of as I sank into his realm of shadow.

The Story of King Nemaius

This is a story from the time before Amo, in the city of Roccapoli, that place where statues still are dug from the earth, finer than any that can be carved in workshops, finer than any that have ever been known.

King Nemaius was the ruler there, and he was in love with the human form. He commissioned artists from Roccapoli but also from every distant land to come and carve their finest for him to gaze upon. He wished to see man and woman in their truth, their nature captured in art. He craved for them to be chipped from marble, cast in bronze, fired in clay, and given him to admire.

But each time he saw a form, he was dissatisfied. The hands of the men were carved too small, their cocks were carved too large. The breasts of the women did not hang as breasts should. A woman's waist was wrongly twisted as she reclined upon her bed. A man's posture was not balanced as he hurled the discus. Always he found a flaw and always he was not satisfied, for he craved a perfection that did not exist.

Nevertheless, he became obsessed. He demanded more and more statues be made. He refused to let the artists leave him, ordering that they try and try again. He enslaved his own people to go to quarries to cut more marble, and go to forests and cut more trees, and to dig in the rivers so they would have more clay, and to mine the mountains for more copper for more bronze.

All this so that his imprisoned artisans would make more statues.

King Nemaius did all this, for he was mad for the human form.

And because of this, he was blind to all other creatures.

Foxes and deer and birds were chased from the great forests, where wood was cut. Fish were driven from their crystal streams where clay was dug and mud made the waters filthy. Bears and wolves and shadow cats were driven away from the mountains by the cacophony of King

Nemaius's mines. All the creatures of Virga's weave suffered, and they all cried out for aid.

And Virga answered.

She disguised herself as an artist, and she went to King Nemaius.

"I will carve you a perfect human statue," she said, "if you will stop this madness."

King Nemaius, greedy for more to look upon, agreed, and Virga set to work. She was no carver, but she loved her creatures and wished to help them, and so she asked for help from Argo, who had first fashioned man from clay. Argo had always liked Virga, and he agreed to once again take up his tools alongside her. They worked together for a year, and at last, they were finished and she presented to Nemaius a marble statue of a woman so beautiful that when the people of Roccapoli laid eyes upon it, they fell to their knees and worshipped it.

But Nemaius was not satisfied.

"It is too perfect," he complained. "This is not what I wanted. Make another. This does not capture the true human form."

Virga was angry then. "You care only for yourself. You care nothing for my weave and nothing for Argo's craft. But still, I will give you the statue you demand."

And then she cursed him, and turned him into stone.

All the people of Roccapoli saw this and were afraid and fled, and the city fell silent.

Then Virga called to all the creatures of her weave, and invited them into the silent city, and invited them to make it their home. And so birds perched upon King Nemaius's head and wolves pissed upon his feet. Deer grazed in the quadrazzi of his city, and shadow cats perched upon the roofs, and stone bears slept upon the bed of the great King Nemaius. Grass sprouted up between the stones and vines climbed the columns of his palace, and all the many glorious statues that he had made slowly tipped and fell, became broken and pitted, and at last the human form lived in harmony once more with Virga's weave.

—Soppros, *Meditations IV*

Chapter 33

I woke to bright sun, hot on my face, and myself tied across the back of a horse like a sack of grain. The horse was ambling along a dirt road, its hooves raising small puffs of dust in the heat. Clop. Clop. Clop. The horse walked. I bounced. The sun burned down upon me.

I struggled to lift my head, but it was too much effort. I closed my eyes. My head weighed as much as a boulder. With effort, I lolled my head to one side and forced my bleary eyes open again. The amiable haunches of another horse filled my view, long black tail swishing, with Cazzetta in the saddle. A lead connected my horse to his. Squinting against the sun, I lolled my head in the other direction, looking back the way we had come.

We were far from Navola.

I recognized the hills. We had crossed the Cascada Livia. Piled stone walls marked where fields had been cleared for tilling. It was lesser farmland than that on Navola's side of the river. All the fields were brown, but with early spring, there were hints of green along the track that we rode. I stretched my neck and strained to orient myself with the sun. I couldn't even see the river anymore. Not even Navola's highest towers or the Callendra dome peeked above the horizon. Judging from the height of the sun, I suspected we were at least twenty miles from the city, perhaps more, if Cazzetta had been efficient.

The horse whose back I was strapped across was not Stub, but some great gray dappled beast, a warhorse, judging from the height at which my head dangled above the dirt. I had never ridden him before, and did not recognize him. I tried to move, to pull myself up into the saddle, to sit, but I was well tied.

"Good. You're awake."

Cazzetta was looking back at me.

I scowled. "Did my father tell you to do this?"

He reined himself over and dismounted. My own horse drew even and halted docilely before him.

"Did he?" I pressed.

Cazzetta shrugged, a Navolese yes-no-maybe that I found infuriating as he unlooped a series of ropes binding me to the saddle. "There. You can get up now."

"What about my hands?" I asked.

Another shrug. My problems were not his problems.

With difficulty, I hauled myself to a sitting position. I swayed, dizzy, as the blood left my head. I felt vaguely nauseous. Cazzetta handed me a wineskin. I drank the watered wine awkwardly, clasping the skin between my tied hands. We were near a farmhouse, and there was a farmer in the field, walking behind an ox, one of the great and powerful humped cattle that our region was famous for. His wife and children were out as well, busily preparing the fields for planting. One field already showed early bitter greens sending up their tops. A line of vines for wine also grew. The house was made of stone, and there was a barn separate, also of stone, all of it gathered from the fields. There were chickens and ducks. A prosperous farm. A trio of children had paused in their work of hauling water from a well and were staring now at us. The presence of the well made me think we were not so far from the Livia after all.

I turned and scanned the horizon to the south, but I could not make out river or city. I sniffed the air. There was moisture and a faint scent of fish. We were far from Navola but not so far from the river. I turned and looked north. Far ahead of us, the high Ruia jumbled rocky and purple across the horizon, streaked with white. Not so high and sharp as the Cielofrigo, nor so ragged and fierce as the peaks of the Romiglia, but still, high enough to retain snow.

"This is not the road to Merai."

"Nai. That road is too well traveled." Cazzetta looped the ropes that bound my wrists around my saddle pommel. "We will cross into the Pardi Valley. Then we will take one of the high passes into Merai." He yanked the ropes tight, tested them with a sharp tug, and returned to his own horse. As he remounted, he said, "We should reach the Luz valleys in four days. Merai herself in another two." He clicked his tongue and his horse started forward, tugging mine along by its lead, all of us moving together at a lazy amble.

"You were afraid I would make a fuss on the main road," I accused. "You were afraid I would escape you."

"It crossed my mind."

I scowled.

Cazzetta turned himself in his saddle. "Ci, Davico. Do not look so sad. Look." He gestured at the surrounding hills. "It is spring. The land comes to life once more. There. Look. Dandelions already! And once we cross the Ruia, it will be warmer. In Merai it is full spring, for the Blood Ocean sends warm winds to her. I know you enjoy the wide web that Virga has woven. And here we are, smack in her net. Out of Navola. Away from the twisty streets and twisty minds that you complain about. It's not all bad."

I scowled at him. "I can still ride off in the night."

Cazzetta shrugged again. *Yes-no-maybe.* "You can do many things, but most of them are stupid."

"I could hide from you."

"I am well aware of your woodskill. Aghan Khan still smarts from it."

"Untie me, at least."

He laughed and turned his attention forward. "You start with the threats and only then take a try at negotiation. Have your father and Merio taught you nothing? Did they not tell you that starting with sugar often yields more than steel?"

"Ah, yes," I said. "Because you started with such great respect for me."

"Respect." He laughed. "Of a certainty, Davico. You deserve respect." He glanced back at me. "Give me your word and I will release you this instant. Promise not to run back to Navola and not to make further trouble, and you are as free as the cauri birds released by Caliba."

"I promise."

"Do you?"

I started to reply, then shut my mouth and scowled. Cazzetta waggled his eyebrows, irritatingly pleased with himself. "Ai, Davico. I sympathize. It's a difficult thing to be honorable, but it does speak well of you. That goodness will serve you well, someday."

"But not today."

"No. Right now it is inconvenient," he said. He paused, considering. "But it is entertaining."

"Scuro damn you!" I burst out. I yanked at the ropes, struggling to free myself. "Damn you, Cazzetta! Damn your mother, *matracazzo, pissioletto, canifescato* . . . !" I yanked harder at the ropes, but the knots held fast. "Let me free, Cazzetta!"

Cazzetta burst into laughter. "Ai! Davico, you're a man after all!"

I glared at him.

"Give your word, Davico. It is all I ask."

When I did not reply, Cazzetta nodded, knowing me too well. I would not break an oath with him, no matter how enraged I was. I settled back on my saddle, stewing, considering how I would escape. It would have to be while Cazzetta slept. I would have to work the ropes free. Perhaps chew them off in the night. Then steal the horse—

"You should know," Cazzetta said, "that the horse you ride is most loyal to me. He will not abandon me, any more than Lazy would abandon you." A pause. "In case you were considering taking him."

I refused to give him the satisfaction of responding. Perhaps I would bash him on the back of the head. Give him a good egg on his skull. I could tie him up and bring him and his loyal horses back together.

It was an enjoyable fantasy, and it kept me occupied as our horses made their easy way up and down hills. The sun moved across the sky, warm and pleasant and all the more irritating because of it. If I was honest before Amo, I was happy to be away from Navola, happy to be amongst greening hills instead of trapped inside the claustrophobia of the city, and that, too, I found irritating. Cazzetta was right. Scuro damn his eyes.

"Why is it," Cazzetta asked, after a time. "Why is it, Davico, that you are so determined to defy your father?"

"Because I love Celia."

"Ci. Love."

"You don't believe in love?"

"I've heard of it. It comes." He shrugged. "It goes."

"You won't understand then."

Cazzetta snorted, amused. "I think that you are like the Cat Who Watched Mice. Hypnotized by the mice all dancing about on the floor, all of them dancing and making him pounce again and again—and him always forgetting the ones he had already caught right beneath his paws. And so he chased and chased until he starved to death."

"And Celia is a running mouse?"

Cazzetta shrugged.

"Put Celia under my paw, and we can test your theory."

"Nai." Cazzetta laughed. "She is going to marry a Parl."

"She won't. She loves me."

"Has she said so?"

She had said no such thing, but I didn't feel it was a stretch. "Of course she has."

Cazzetta wagged a finger. "Do not tell me that my pants are upon my head, and I will not tell you that your shirt is upon your ass."

I wondered how he always seemed to read me. Was I so very chiaro?

"If you are so sure of your love and hers," Cazzetta said, "why fight this journey? In a few weeks we will be back in Palazzo Regulai, and the Parl will not be marrying Celia, and you and she can continue this teasing dance you have begun. If you think your love as strong as granite, as pure as marble, as passionate as rubies, then what harm to humor your father's whim?" He looked back at me. "Unless you think your connection to Celia too weak to withstand even a few weeks apart."

"It is not weak."

"That's good. For if a few weeks apart is enough to break you, then it is weak love indeed."

"Our love is not weak."

"Then maybe just confused. Celia is a difficult girl to read. Perhaps you have mistaken her intentions toward you."

"Shut up."

By the fatas, I was tired of his taunting. More, I did not like that he had found my softest vulnerability. A point to press, like sliding a dagger around the breastplate and into the heart, from beneath the arm. Cazzetta knew how to press. Scuro eat his eyes, the man knew how to probe.

I thought myself sure of Celia, but he had cleverly prevented me from saying goodbye. What would she think of this? Would she imagine me changeable? I wished we'd had time to exchange promises. She had to know that I was unwavering in my desire for her. But what of her desire for me? In that moment in the hall, our hands entwined, our pulses entwined, our lips so close—it was as if we breathed each other's breath. I had felt I knew her then, had seen into her soul as clearly as I had seen into the dragon's. She had wanted me. The door to her heart had been open. We had been one.

And then she had turned cold and ignored me. Until I gave up hope.

And then she again inflamed me. Was I a toy to her? By Scuro, perhaps she was the cat, and I the mouse. As soon as I was caught under her paw, she lost interest, as soon as I turned away, she pounced again—

Nai. That was uncharitable. She was true. We were true to one another. But of a surety, Cazzetta had pressed a soft spot, and I did not like it. I resolved to knock his head well when I finally had my opportunity.

For three days we rode that way: Me, refusing to give my word, and plotting various escapes, and Cazzetta supernaturally alert to all my ruses. At last, exhausted by being treated as a prisoner, I made a bargain.

"I won't help you marry off Celia. But I won't try to escape anymore."

"Is this your new offer?" Cazzetta asked. "My knees tremble at your wooing of me."

I scowled at him. "I won't try to escape."

"But you will obstruct."

I shrugged. "I am a fly caught in my father's web, so of course I will tear it if I can."

"You are more a fine silk strand of the web, rather than a fly within it. The Parl, I think, is the fly."

I gave him a sour look. "And that should please me? My father weaves and plots, and I am forced to his design."

"And so you seek to ruin the pattern he weaves. Perhaps disrupt an alliance marriage. Or maybe . . ." He considered me. "Maybe run away with the girl you love."

"Why wouldn't I?"

Cazzetta shrugged. "Where would you go that your father does not reach?"

"Pagarat. Citadel by the Sea. Cheroux. Bis." I recited the names easily. "Wustholt. Zurom, even. There are many places outside his reach. He is not Amo. He does not see the world entire."

"And yet if you fled so far, you would place yourself within the reach of others—men and women who wish your family ill."

"So I'm a pawn, whatever I do."

"No." Cazzetta's voice sharpened. "To outsiders, you are a pawn. To your father, you are the only piece that matters."

"And yet still, he moves me as he wills."

"Then move yourself, princeling! Amo's balls! This whining, this victimhood. It does not become Archinomo di Regulai. If you are of the Bull, you must charge as the Bull! You must stamp the ground and make it tremble as the Bull! You must conquer as the Bull of Navola. Be not some mewling kitten begging scraps in the offal alleys." Cazzetta made a face. "You complain that one thing—one girl—has been barred to you. One girl. Fagh. *Una fescata nubila. Una verginale nubila!* It sickens me."

"I love Celia."

"This is how I know for certain that you are still a child. You speak of love as if it is some clear apparent thing. As if there is only one, as in Boltiricchio's play. A single Alessiana for a single Rodrigo. Boltiricchio's play. Fagh."

"What do you know?" I shot back. "You are alone. No one loves you at all. You probably poisoned your own mother."

For a moment, I thought I had gone too far. Cazzetta's expression darkened. "If I poisoned my own mother," he said coldly, "you can be assured that she never saw it coming."

We regarded each other with venom. At last, Cazzetta shook his head. "How can you be so very stupid when it comes to reading people, Davico? So closely observant with herbs, so wise to the movements of a stag in the Romiglia, so inspiring of loyalty from your hound, and yet when you attempt to read people, such a simple ass."

"So you agree," I said, sensing victory.

"I agree you are an ass."

"If I am an ass for not helping you sell Celia like a sack of forged relics from Torre Amo, just to fix my family's finances, then yes, I am that ass."

He flicked his hand in agreement. "Fine. Promise me you will not go riding off and getting yourself killed, and I will free you. Perhaps eventually you will see how shortsighted you are."

"Nothing will change my mind."

Cazzetta dismounted. "Everything changes," he said as he untied my hands. "It is the one thing that is certain."

I rubbed my wrists, restoring blood to them. "I do not."

"Another sign that you are an ass," Cazzetta said as he remounted, but I didn't mind. I was free, and I knew my heart, and whatever my father's plans, I would make my own.

Chapter 34

We made our crossing into Merai over a nameless pass, scrambling up muddy rock and slushy slick snow, Cazzetta and I leading the horses, for their footing was as uncertain as ours. The final climb took us up a steep face of snow softened by spring melt, with all of us, horses and men alike, scrambling and scrabbling, crawling at times.

As we fought our way up that final slope, alternately plunging our legs into deep holes and skidding across the snow's crusted icy surface, I wished mightily for Stub—not so long of stride, not so daunting in battle, but tough and wise on his feet in ways that these warhorses were not.

At last, we reached the top of the pass, and came to a remarkable divide.

Here, we looked down upon the land where the winds of the Blood Ocean swept up, always warm, often damp, raining heavily during the monsoon, mitigating the winters. Flowers known only across the Cerulea in wet southern forests were found on the Blood Ocean's shores and thrived in farmers' fields deep into Merai. Soppros had journeyed to the city of Gevazzoa and the western borders of Merai and written in amazement at the sight of strange fruits and great melons and lush extravagant flowers wider than his hand.

It was not so warm as that this high in the Ruia, but still, the difference between the west side of the peninsular hook and the east almost defied the mind's belief. Below us, the slopes that descended toward Merai's territory were already green, the grasses covering the shoulders of the mountains, like gently draped thick verdant robes.

"You see?" Cazzetta said with satisfaction. "Merai sends warm greetings. Just as I told you."

I breathed deep of Merai's perfume. Everywhere there was new growth. The vibrant grasses were embroidered by dandelion fields, bright and inviting. My heart felt as if it would burst with pleasure at the sight. I had a sudden childish urge to hurl myself down the steep grassy slope before us, rolling and bouncing and laughing down through the green and yellow. To play. To revel in unalloyed delight and joy.

Already warmth was seeping into my bones, more healing than the finest of Dellacavallo's potions. Behind us, on the Pardi side, the Ruia was all dirty muddy patchwork snow, the high land still very much gripped in the last cold claws of winter. It would be more than a month before our side of the mountains enjoyed a similar awakening. But here, all was joy.

I tugged my mount forward, for the first time leading, eager to be embraced by Firmos.

Fat bees hummed amongst the dandelions, greedy for nectar. The grasses danced under a gentle breeze. It was wildly different from the plains and hills near Navola, or the forests and crags of the low Romiglia. I found myself captivated. Even the bees were different when I looked closely, fatter and heavier than our own, their colors tending to oranges rather than yellows.

"Virga weaves a different net here, does she not?" Cazzetta was smiling.

The descending trail zigzagged back and forth across the grassy headwall of the valley, thin but not dangerous if we led the horses, and once we were halfway down the face, we reached a wide verdant shelf where we could remount and ride at ease.

The shelf rimmed the valley, a wide U of rolling hummocks and blue-green kettle lakes. Below it, ragged cliffs tumbled steep into the deep crease of the valley's heart, where marshy streams glimmered and then were swallowed into whitebark forest. We did not attempt the cliffs but paced ourselves along their edge, keeping the steep fall to our left, the mountain peaks rising to our right. Along the shelf we rode, easy and soft as a farmer's pasture. We paused to let the horses drink from a small crystalline lake. White marsh lilies clustered at its edges, stamens yellow with pollen. The trail had disappeared.

"No one rides here," I said.

"There are easier passes," Cazzetta agreed. "The descent from here is not ideal for horses. Deer and mountain goats, small hoofed animals more commonly." He nodded down the length of the valley, along the shelf we were perched upon. "We ride to the mouth of the valley. There is a path to descend there, but it is not easy. Horses are not well-suited."

Overhead, a hawk gave a cry. I looked up, shading my eyes. It circled high above us, lazy against the blue of the sky. Its wingtips were red, as was often true of hunting hawks. A breed apart, traded and coveted from Zurom to Cheroux.

"Do redtips nest wild on this side of the mountains?" I asked.

"Nai." Cazzetta spat. "Merai knows we have arrived."

I scanned the valley, but I could spy no master of the hawk. "There are people here?" I asked, surprised.

"Rangers," Cazzetta said. "Perhaps near, perhaps far."

We watched the hawk circling. It did indeed seem to be studying us, looking down from on high. If it had been wild, it would have circled on, looking for prey more its size, but instead, it circled us, and then, instead of simply widening its circle, it bent wing and beat its way downvalley in a manner unnatural for a wild hawk.

"Merai patrols all her borders," Cazzetta said. "She is accustomed to invasion, what with Cheroux, Wustholt, Gevazzoa, and Navola all at her borders. It is not surprising. But still, I would have preferred it different. I thought it might be different."

He untied a cloth bundle from his saddle. Steel spilled from the folds, gleaming in the sunlight. He tossed me a sword. "Arm yourself."

I studied it, surprised, recognizing it. It was Polonos's. The one I had taken from his hand on my name day. I had killed a man with this sword.

I suddenly missed Polonos desperately, and then I wondered if that was why Cazzetta had brought this blade, instead of my own. To remind me of my duty, to remind me of the dangers our family faced. I caught him watching and tried to hide my expression, hating that he sought to manipulate me without saying a word. And then I wondered if it was my father's doing.

For a moment here in the Ruia I had felt free of all of Navola's intrigues. Free and alive and happy, and now, with a single act, Cazzetta had ensnared me once again in all the tangled grubby machinations of our world, making me think not only of Polonos and his sacrifice for me, but the many schemes of my father.

"Are we in danger?"

Cazzetta shrugged as he buckled on his own sword and tucked daggers into his sleeves. He tossed me a stiletto and an arm sheath as well. "Take this, too."

"Do rangers not owe their loyalty to Merai?" I asked again as I caught the knife and began securing my own blades.

"We are very far from the city," Cazzetta said. He tugged his horse from grazing the marsh lilies and remounted. "The Ruia is still wild, there are wolves and bears and bandits. Two men can easily disappear, no matter the oaths of rangers." He spurred his horse. "Come! We should hurry. There is only one path of descent from here. It is a choke point and it puts us at a disadvantage. I want to be deep in the forest before anyone comes."

We rode quickly then, trotting over the tufted grasses and splashing through trickling marshy streamlets of snowmelt. Eventually, we reached the end of the valley, and there picked our way down a series of steep cliff shelves, step by step, coaxing our horses down. Cazzetta and I proceeded ahead, clearing the rough natural stair of loose stone and fallen rocks so that the horses would have better purchase. The horses followed, unwilling and unsteady. Though the descent was but a few tree heights, it took more than an hour, and my heart was in my throat throughout.

At last, we found ourselves standing on soft forest pine needles, stable ground, and safety, and I could breathe again. "Ai, that was unpleasant," I said.

"It is not a common route," Cazzetta agreed. He scanned the sky again.

"The hawk is gone," I said. "I looked already."

Cazzetta grunted sourly and we started to mount.

Suddenly I felt eyes upon us, an almost physical presence. I spun, searching the forest shadows.

"What is it?" Cazzetta asked.

I held up a hand, listening, peering into the forest thickets that surrounded us. Shadow-dappled forests, low pine boughs, bushes, raspberry and emperor berry. Soft brown forest floor, needles, scents of pine and whitebark. Someone, or some creature, was out there. I strained my eyes, listened for the crackle of feet upon breaking pine needles. I tried to make myself still, to ignore my pounding heart, to breathe the forest, to follow the movements of the breezes, the chirp of birds—

Behind me, Cazzetta's sword hissed free. I found myself irritated that he made so much noise. But my hand strayed to my own sword as well, too uneasy not to draw.

"Who goes there?" Cazzetta demanded.

I was about to admonish him when undergrowth crackled and a shadow separated from the thickets. A man emerged from amongst the trees, his clothes all dull browns and greens with little metal gleaming so that he blended well with the forest. As he approached, he threw back his hood.

I gasped. His face was a horror. Sword-split lips revealed cracked teeth and a ragged hungry grin. His nose had been split by the same blade, chopped and resewn ragged. Gouges raked his cheeks like slave scars. We faced a monster.

"Fescato!" Cazzetta exclaimed. "You should announce yourself!" He sheathed his sword and strode to embrace the man. "I might have stuck you!"

"Scuro will shit upon Amo's throne before that happens."

The man's accent had the lisp of Merai. He turned from his embrace of Cazzetta, and his expression turned solemn. "So, this is our young bull." His eyes seemed to burn, and for a moment I thought I saw rage, but then he swept into a bow of obeisance and fell to his knees. "I am your man," he said, and marked his cheeks upon my boot. He straightened and threw a dead hawk at my feet.

"We should go. The rangers of Merai are difficult to escape if they catch our scent."

This was how I came to meet Lugo.

Chapter 35

Lugo Terrademezzo. A man unlike any other I had known. Lugo seemed a creature of rage, always banked. You could see it whenever his guard was down. Where some become still and happy when they rest or feel at ease, Lugo, when his guard was down, when his face was not controlled, was entirely bottled rage, seeming to burn like a bonfire. He was capable of donning a mask of humanity, as when he bowed to me, or embraced Cazzetta, but when no one looked or he was not distracted by activity, his rage would slowly emerge once more.

Lugo was Meravese by mother and Navolese by father, and spoke both the dialect of Merai as well as the slang of Navola, and he slipped between those languages in a way that made him difficult to understand. Added to his badly sewn lips and the ragged scars upon his face, and his protruding teeth, it took effort to attend his words and not to stare.

"Do not spurn Lugo," Cazzetta murmured as we followed him through the forest. "He is our finest man in Merai."

"I haven't seen his name in correspondence."

"He does not watch for our bank," Cazzetta said. "He watches the bank for us. He is our shadow man."

I knew that we kept observers upon our branches, both reporting on the state of the cities and kingdoms where we did business but also keeping an eye on the branch managers and clerks, a second set of reports, shadow reports designed to test if they agreed or conflicted with those of our branches.

But by the fatas, his face was truly a horror. If one didn't know better, one would think him a slave, well marked and brutally owned. It was difficult to decide if the scars were truly slave scars on his cheek, for there was a thick embroidery of other ruin there, but it made me wonder, and it made me think about what it would be like to go through life with such terrible marks . . .

I realized with irritation that Cazzetta had been testing me once again. He had not warned me of Lugo, or the surprise of Lugo's face, and he had smirked when Lugo marked his cheek upon my boots.

"You didn't tell me of him or his scars on purpose," I accused as we led our horses through the forest bracken, away from the cliffs. "You were testing me."

Lugo grunted. "You did better than most, princeling."

"Lugo had an unfortunate encounter with a stone bear," Cazzetta said.

Lugo grunted again. "He opened his jaws eventually."

"He did indeed."

I didn't know what to say. The two of them clearly shared a bond, two men scarred and experienced, and I sensed a deep history between them. I fell back on ceremony.

"Well, Patro Terrademezzo," I said. "I am honored to speak your name."

"Patro?" Lugo favored Cazzetta with an amused look. "The prince's words are as sweet as the shit clods of the honey weasel."

"Our good friend Lugo does not spend much time with sweet wine on his tongue."

"I am more a man of sour bucket wines," Lugo agreed as we wound between the trees. "Sour wine and sour cunt. Those are enough for Lugo."

He was a shadow man. A stilettotore, like Cazzetta. If you wanted a dagger in someone's ribs, he was your man. If you wished thievery and rooftop work, he was pleased to serve. If you wanted a man kidnapped from the streets and questioned until he cried and shit ran down his legs, he would not flinch.

"He's very good at what he does," Cazzetta said.

"Pisso." Lugo spat on the ground. "Not so much a shadow as this one," he said, jerking his head toward Cazzetta.

We came to a clearing where Lugo's horse was hobbled, and we all mounted. There were deer trails now, and he led us along them until we reached a stream and thence followed it to a farmhouse, where a man was waiting. The man lit a fire, and drew sausage and cheese and turnips, beets and carrots from a hatch beneath the floor. Soon a stew was bubbling. He did not speak, nor did he question us, and when the food was made he retired outside with a bottle of wine.

"What is this place?"

"One of our houses," Cazzetta said. "A place for our whispers and shadows to hide if necessary. To shelter for aid. And a place to keep gold and weapons. It does not cost much to secure the man's loyalty."

"You trust him?"

Cazzetta shrugged. Lugo snorted. "We trust his ignorance. He does not know who comes or who goes or who pays him. He does not know when we arrive. He does not know how long we stay. He does not know there are bags of gold and silver beneath the hearth, nor weapons buried beneath the privy. So, he takes our gold and forgets. We trust him that far."

Lugo stretched out his legs and drank from his wine bottle, staring into the fire. And there, I saw again the rage that seemed to boil within him. It was there like the flicker of the fire shadows upon his face, there and gone, there and gone. He caught me watching him. The rage disappeared like smoke, replaced by a twist of smile.

"Ai. You're an observant one, though."

"Oh, he has his skills," Cazzetta said. "Take him out into the forest, and you'll never find him again."

"Really?" Lugo looked interested.

"He tricked Aghan Khan," Cazzetta said. "When he was still a child."

"Ai! That is good! He was angry, I expect."

Cazzetta smirked. "He was most embarrassed."

"The wooded lands." Lugo shook his head. "Back alleys and taverns. Whorehouses. Warehouses. Docks. Those are more my pleasure. I should learn your woodscraft, princeling."

"He's stupid about people, though," Cazzetta said.

I glared at Cazzetta. Lugo snorted amusement. We were quiet for a while before the fire.

"It was a stone bear?" I asked, finally. I touched my cheek. "The scars?"

"Aivero. It was a bear." He made a face. "A large one."

"All of them. All of the scars?"

"He wants to know why you look like a slave," Cazzetta said. I blushed, mortified at the blunt translation of my question.

Lugo waved his wine dismissively. "You tell the story. It is boring to me."

Cazzetta took the bottle from Lugo and drank before passing it to me. "Lugo sold himself into slavery to infiltrate the household of an archinomo. He was a spy for your father."

Lugo smiled and his eyes lit up. "And then I burned them in their tower. Burned them all to ash."

"The Speignissi?" I looked to Cazzetta, confused. "In Navola? I thought that was you."

"Me?" Cazzetta laughed. "How could I do such a thing? I was outside their tower."

"But everyone says it was you."

"And so everyone watches him," Lugo said, plucking the bottle from my hands. "And everyone fears him, and no one looks for me."

"We owe you a debt then." I touched my cheek. "We owe you a great debt."

"Nai," Lugo said. "All the debts are settled."

"But you let yourself be scarred."

Lugo's split lips hitched into a nightmare smile. "Do you think me a slave because my cheeks are marked?" The words were almost dangerous.

I picked my words carefully. "Other people will. Other people will look low upon you."

"Aivero." Lugo drank again. "That is true. Sometimes I correct them."

"But then, what of the bear? You said there was a bear."

"Ai. That. Well. That Speignissi fescato thought to feed me to a pet. Speignissi liked to keep pets. Liked to make bets on battles between men and beasts. Between this animal and that. I made a bargain with the bear, though, and he let me go."

He said it so seriously that I didn't know how to respond.

"You doubt me?" Lugo asked. "I spoke its language. It's not that different from Navolese."

Now I was certain he was making fun. "You play with words."

"Not at all. The bear decided that we were better off as companions. My master made a poor negotiator in comparison with my own silver tongue."

"He does have a certain skill of negozii," Cazzetta said when I looked to him for refutation.

I had heard of people who could whisper to the beasts of the forests. There was a story in Navola of a maiden who whispered up wolves and lay with a white tiger and survived for years in the Cielofrigo. A maiden, pale and beautiful, who walked through snow without feeling its chill and called to hawks and wolves and that great tiger. Poiivi had claimed in the books of his travels that the people of Xim could take the forms of hawks and fly. There were numerous stories, and a part of me was willing to believe such things, but at the same time, it was also possible to disbelieve.

And yet here Lugo sat beside me, saying that he bargained with a bear.

"I wish that I could bargain with a bear."

Lugo looked up sharply at that, and I expected that he would rebuke me, but instead he said, "You bargain with princes. It is more dangerous. Bears speak truth. The tongue of a prince drips lies. Bargaining with bears is simplicity in comparison." He shook his head. "I do not envy you."

If you visit Torre Amo, do not accept a drink from a stranger, for they are a debauched people and will offer you elixirs that excite the senses. I watched a man rut with a donkey there.

—MARCEL VILLOU OF BIS, FROM HIS *TRAVELS*

Chapter 36

The next day we reached wide tilled fields, and that night, for the first time in days, we slept at an inn.

"We're not hiding now?"

Cazzetta shook his head. "This is the main road to Merai. We will make the Parl and his first secretary nervous that they somehow missed us on the way. It will trouble them that people move along their roads so easily. Too, the people who most concern us are back in Navola."

And so we found hot baths in the great tubs that they kept heated behind the inn and later, well scrubbed, we sat in its tavern room, no longer hiding our presence, playing scuro, and later, cartalegge.

I enjoyed playing the card game of scuro with its rising and falling princes, its thrice-paired lovers, and its changeable thieves. Coins and castles, swords and chalices. But to play cartalegge was to play not with cards but with players.

In Merai, they had changed the cards so that there were staves instead of swords, and instead of castles they had trees. I still do not know the reason for this; perhaps to make the game seem more peaceful, and because we were in Merai, we played a Meravese variation. Round after round, each of us taking our cards and points, depending on the ranks of princes. Tree princes falling to staff princes falling to coin princes falling to cup princes, and then back up through the ranks, until the trees once again ruled over all.

Cazzetta carried a somewhat damaged deck that Lugo looked upon with complete contempt before drawing forth his own.

"You don't trust me?" Cazzetta asked.

"Even Davico must see the marks of the cards," Lugo said. "We will use my good clean deck."

And so he dealt out the seventy-seven cards. And so we began selecting, trading, betting, and the time went by easily, though Cazzetta was infuriatingly blessed with luck.

Lugo shook his head as Cazzetta won again. "I do not understand how you do that."

"I cheat," Cazzetta said.

"You know, old friend, some people enjoy a game of cards without abusing the skill."

"Cheating is a skill," Cazzetta said.

"You know my meaning."

"Ci. Any game worth winning is a game worth cheating at," Cazzetta said as he gathered up the cards and began shuffling again.

"I do not agree," I said. "What is the purpose of a game if the players ignore the rules? What contest is that?"

Cazzetta laughed. "Ai, Davico. That is a deep question. As deep as the Cerulea."

"Can you not surrender to Sia Fortuna even once?" I asked. "Even for something so unimportant as a card game?"

"Sia Fortuna," Cazzetta said, as he dealt a new round of cards, "is a nasty little bitch. Best to beat her hard, or she will be tempted to bite."

"What about Amo's will?"

"Amo's will?" Cazzetta snorted, shuffling the cards. "Am I speaking to Davico di Regulai or that fat fuck Garagazzo?"

"Call it what you like," I said. "Gods, fatas, fortuna, there is such a thing as chance, as luck, and you know what I'm saying."

"I know what you are saying, and I tell you this, Davico. Sia Fortuna is too fickle a mistress for the likes of us." He wagged a finger of warning. "And we should never seek to woo her, for she will always reach to pull us up, and then reveal an oily hand." He began arranging his cards. Laid down the prince of fools. "To play at cartalegge is to play with fortune. But to win at cartalegge? That is to spank Sia Fortuna's ass until she obeys your will."

"No one controls Sia Fortuna," I said. "That is her nature. She is beyond the control of men. That's her essence. The thing outside of our control. A reminder that we must have humility, for we are not gods. We are people."

Cazzetta looked up. "You think so? Truly? You think you have no power over the lady?"

"She is either with you, or against you," I said firmly. "It is not within your control."

Cazzetta was thoughtful, touching his cards, his fingers running over the edges. His fingers lingered over one, then another, finally he selected one. Laid it upon the splintered wood of the table. It was Urula, the sea, her great wave cresting against the shore, rising high.

"Here," he said. "Let us play a game of understanding, here."

"Are we still playing the game?"

"We are always playing the game," he said sharply. "Let us say that the sea is Fortune. Powerful one day, and angry—sometimes taking a whole city, as Navola once was swallowed in the ancient times. But the next day, she is blue and pliant, inviting us to sail upon her soft breasts. Now," he said, "perhaps there are times when we are always at her mercy. Out in her blue deeps, much is beyond our control."

"But that is exactly my point."

Cazzetta shot me a quelling glance. "The bull charges at shadows. Listen to me, Davico. Now what about the sea near the coast of Navola, where the sandbars and the jewel cranes stalk the waters? Have you ever noticed how in that place the waters are not only of the ocean, but are sometimes salt, and sometimes clear?"

"Yes, because of the Cascada Livia," I said, impatiently. "The waters mix at the river mouth."

"Just so, fresh water, sweet water, from the deep Romiglia. Lugo, if you would play the river, if you please?"

Lugo favored Cazzetta with a suspicious look. "You're cheating again."

"I don't have to cheat to read your hand. The card. It's the only one that makes sense, in any case."

With another dark look at Cazzetta, Lugo played his river.

"Good. Excellent. Now, let us name this river Deciso. The acts of man. The sea is Sia Fortuna. The river is Il Deciso." He motioned to me. "And now Davico will place his city of staves."

"Do you know all the cards in our hands?" I asked. "Did you look as you dealt?"

"I don't have to look."

"That's not an answer."

Cazzetta was arranging the cards on the table. "Now, here in the city, in the realm of man, we find both the river flow, and the tides of the sea, and this is where they meet. Thus we have the dreams, activities, and lives of man." He touched the city. "Isn't it interesting that we often place our cities at the mouth of river and sea? Is this an accident? That the scope of our human endeavor often finds itself here?"

"I think you are tangling the knots in your braid," Lugo said drily.

"Sfai. Who is plaiting this braid?" Cazzetta laid down the seven of cups.

"Not I, Maestro." Lugo played his eight upon Cazzetta's seven. Cazzetta pushed the pile of cups up against the river. "Now," he said, "if we take our cups, and we go to the river mouth, will we dip sweet water, or will we dip salt?"

"It depends on the time of day," I said. "If the tide is high, then it will be salt. If it is low, then it will be sweet."

"So, this is how I think the Lady Fortune works. She is always present, yes, and sometimes has great influence—as at high tide. But the sweet water, that is the steady pressure of all human deciso; that is us, Davico. That is us, striving, pushing, and at times, the deciso, it is stronger, greater, and it pushes back against Fortuna, and all is sweet water at the river mouth."

I considered. "No. I think you're wrong. The sweet water is always swallowed by the ocean. It disappears into the sea, and all is eventually salt. Fortuna is always present."

Cazzetta eyed me. "Fat Garagazzo must truly love you. You've learned his lessons too well." He made his voice mocking and trembling. "Oh, oh, all striving is useless, for the sea is too large! She is too great for the likes of me! Ai ai ai! Sia Fortuna does her will. Amo is all the sky! Ai ai ai!" He shook his head. "Use your mind, Davico. Look again at that tidal place, where they meet and mix. There are places that belong solely to Sia Fortuna, it is true. And if you choose to float a castle upon the deepest sea, you will be at her mercy. Just as if you decide to blindfold yourself and run headlong through the streets, you will surely run into stone eventually."

"Who would do that?"

"Who indeed?" Cazzetta laid down another cup card to follow Lugo's. "You use your eyes, yes? And so you only occasionally bump into a wall. And then only you receive a bruise, instead of a broken nose."

Lugo laid down the knight of cups and took up a shrouded card. The cards had been falling steadily in my favor. I held the cup king, and Cazzetta and Lugo had been building cups for me. Too, I held the assassin. Barring Cazzetta or Lugo holding the concubine, I was on the verge of a powerful hand.

Cazzetta continued, "But why do you focus so much on the rough seas of fortune, Davico?" He tapped the river card. "Why not follow the river, instead? Upriver, from the sea. Up far enough, it is not Fortuna who triumphs, but deciso. How much does the sea influence if I place my tower here?" He picked up a shrouded card and dropped the white tower, which did nothing for me. "She cannot even reach. Here, all is within my power, and nothing is within hers."

"No place escapes some aspect for fortune," I said.

"Ci." Cazzetta filled his wine from the flagon and toasted me. "Sia Fortuna does not decide if I lift this cup. She does not dictate if I drink." He sipped. "This is the realm of deciso, not Fortuna. This is where I choose to live."

"I think your metaphor is too simple."

"And yet I drink again, and Sia Fortuna has no say."

The draw went around the table again. Lugo rearranged the cards in his hand. From his expression as he picked up the white tower and laid down the heart queen, he was looking to make a play of towers and cities. "Davico is right," he said "We have a foot in both realms. It is as the city. Sometimes the river runs strong, sometimes the sea rises high. We are touched by both."

Cazzetta made a face. "Sfai. We have great power. We have the power to set the table at which Sia Fortuna dines. And the more we exercise deciso, the more we influence her, and the more she favors us when she comes to table. Fortune favors work and planning and intention, and sometimes, sometimes, there is a flood of sweet water, and the whole harbor is full of your actions. That is what I see."

He laid down the concubine, to join the heart queen. The concubine was the only card that could have troubled my assassin. I tried not to show my pleasure. "It's impossible to do all the time," I said as I took up another card and stilled my face. The cup queen. Now I had king and queen, and the knight. And I still held the assassin.

"Is it?" Cazzetta asked.

"Nothing can go always according to plan," I said.

"Perhaps. But in the minds of many, because it is difficult, it is not to be done at all. In the words of Garagazzo, there is no point in striving." He lifted his hands and pretended to pray to the sky. "*Woe, Sia Fortuna does not love me! Woe, Lady Fortuna has turned her back upon me!*" His expression hardened. "Lady Fortuna cares nothing for us. She is here, or she is gone. I have killed fifty men, and many of them blamed fortune. I killed fifty men, and I think that Lady Fortuna helped my hand five times, truly, and I was happy for it."

"Now you're arguing the opposite—"

Cazzetta wagged a finger and overrode me. "But in the opposite cases—those instances when she turned hard, very hard against me—I was more than ready." He stabbed his finger on the table for emphasis. "More. Than. Ready. You understand, Davico? I cannot say I will kill a hundred men, or a thousand, but I think I have a good chance at killing sixty, and it will not be because of luck."

He laid down the heart king and fanned a royal family wide.

"Your preparation is one thing, but I still think you need some luck to win." I laid down the cup king, and his family, the higher suit for the round. "Like this. Sia Fortuna, and my planning. And I have won."

Lugo made a noise of annoyance and laid his cards facedown on the table, acknowledging defeat, but Cazzetta just sighed.

"No, Davico, you prepare, so that you have a better chance to win, certainly. But Sia Fortuna is far too fickle. One moment there, the next not. If you depend on her gift of chance, you are already lost. What I am saying is that victory is always stolen. It comes not from her favor, but from your action. You must pluck victory from her hand, you must take it, and leave her gasping and wondering in awe at your cleverness."

"And yet this time she has favored me," I said, indicating the cards on the table.

"She favored you. But I am a good thief."

And with that, Cazzetta laid down the assassin, upon my cup king.

"That was my card!" I exclaimed. "It was in my hand!"

"It was," Cazzetta agreed amiably.

Chapter 37

The famous Palazzou Rosso of Merai was constructed of red sandstone. Atop a cliff at a bend in the river, it stood formidable from a distance, and then became friendly when you came closer, full of long red colonnaded walks and garden courts that burst with flowers and life—the vibrancy of spring that would not come to Navola for another month.

If I had not known the state of the Parl's finances I would have been much impressed. My father said often that wealth should not be displayed ostentatiously, that it was better to give visible gifts to the city and the vianomae, for this would garner their love; your wealth would be seen to benefit them. But if you spent it all to draw attention to yourself, resentment would grow in their hearts. We might richly furnish our palazzo behind our walls, but this would never be seen from the street.

Merai followed a different standard.

"They seek to awe with wealth," Cazzetta said as we entered the city, no longer accompanied by Lugo, who had split off from us long before it came into view. "They like to make their visitors feel small when they enter the demesne of the Parl." And this seemed true wherever we went in the city. The archinomi aped their Parl, much as children ape parents.

Much of Merai surrounded the hill that the castello topped, all of it contained inside a bend in La Cascada Rossa, so called for the color of the clay that choked the river in flood season. This clay was in turn used to make the bricks that cobbled the streets and decorated the buildings, and so the Red Castle stood over the Red City in the bend of the Red River and all of it was quite pleasing to the eye, as long as you only looked where the Meravese wanted you to look, and squinted past the grimy parts.

Those streets and quadrazzi where noble names held sway were full of flowers and shaded porticoes and clear of filth, but if you turned toward meaner smaller alleys, nightsoil and rot lay in neglected piles and they had no sewers, only open canals that channeled water from the river through the city to then pour back into the Cascada Rossa, where women washed their linens and the catfish were pulled from the selfsame pools. Merai was not as Navola, where the districts and quartiere were managed by the Callendra, regardless of an archinomo's territory, and where a working sewer was thanks to the efforts of the city as a whole, and not to individual archinomi, currying power and influence and vying against others.

"The difference between republic and monarchy," Cazzetta said as we rode between tightly packed red-brick buildings, and the stinks in the heat became dizzying. "No politics avoids self-interest. If only archinomi rule, they rule only for themselves." He spat. "It's why we limit the number of nomo nobilii anciens who sit in the Callendra, and balance guilds and vianomae against them. With all interests represented, politics becomes a fairer sport, if only because everyone is equally corrupt."

I think that whenever we come upon a foreign land and a foreign people, they always seem strange and either all brilliant, or all backward at first. Habits and customs that are not yours leap out strongly, and it takes great effort to see their beauties and barbarities not as a single story, but as something more nuanced and complex. But though I was young at the time, and Merai was new to me, I do not think I was wrong in my judgment of her.

What I saw was that the Meravese had beautiful palazzi and filthy streets. They had the Palazzou Rosso that they took great pride in, and they closed their eyes to the orphans who lurked in alleys and dropped their trousers and offered their asses to us, calling out prices in quarter moons. There were no orphanages organized by district or guild or city that I could see. They had no nunnery bakeries to feed those who were ill or maimed. I saw more flower-strewn quadrazzi than ever in my life, and I also saw more urchins, diseased beggars, and open sewers.

Such a strange city, that patchwork quilt. We could pass down a street guarded by some archinomo's soldiery, and it would be entirely filled with flower sellers, with rose blooms for sale that were larger than my head, and merchants bargaining with women whose silks gleamed diaphanous and sheer and whose scent was that of honeysuckle, and in the very next alley, where the guards cared not at all, I could see a man being kicked like a dog by thieves, and all his silver taken. The city was not a city, it was many cities, quadrazzo by quadrazzo, street by street, open sores and powdered beauty all up against one another.

We turned down an unpromising and narrow stinking alley, where men leaned against the walls with bottles of sour wine, and spat and scowled at us as we rode past. I would have protested the choice but I didn't wish the observers to hear my discomfort, and so I put my hand upon my dagger and urged my horse up beside Cazzetta. Cazzetta jerked his head toward an unsavory tavern.

"If you ever must hunt for Lugo, you will find him there."

The name was the Shoe Dog, and the dog in question was pictured pissing upon a shoe. The place looked rough, dark, and reeking in the middle of the day, as bad as the untidy stitchwork of Lugo's face. A gap-toothed whore squatted drunk upon the stones before it. She lifted her skirts to us as we rode past.

And then, as was typical of Merai, we turned a corner and suddenly found ourselves in a tidy little quadrazzo, sunny, with well-swept bricks and small round iron tables set out before tavernae in the style of Cheroux. Fine ladies in silks and men with gleaming sharp swords and tightly buttoned jackets were languorously drinking red bitters together, and on the far side of the quadrazzo our own bank branch waited, with a long polished wooden table set out in the sun, and a pair of benches on either side, upon which sat a few numerari engaged in discussion over a contract.

As soon as we approached, one of the numerari straightened and ran inside, and a moment later, even as we were tying our horses, a plump man with a trimmed goatee came hurrying out—Maestro Paritzio Ferro, as it turned out, our capo di banca in Merai.

The capo was clearly unnerved by our arrival, wringing his hands and bowing and making as if he would mark his cheeks upon our boots, and stopping his ministrations only when we insisted. Indeed, he seemed so anxious that I studied him as my father would have, and yet I found nothing obvious to criticize. His clothes were black as was my father's preference, with only little silver coins embroidered upon his collar. His fingers were ink-stained, and the tips of his fingers were well-callused from the abacus. His numerari and abacassi returned to their work immediately, despite our interruption, and without him ordering them to do so. When our greetings were finished, he shooed his men away from the front benches so that we could sit and have privacy, and though his eyes were questioning, he did not ask, until Cazzetta spoke.

"We are not here to audit your good work," Cazzetta assured him. The maestro pretended not to be relieved, but his shoulders immediately slumped and his smile become warmer. "Ai. You worried me. If you ever wish, of course you should, but I am glad to know I am trusted."

He waved to a tavern man standing in the door of a nearby establishment, and soon red bitters arrived on a silver tray. "It is cooled with snow from the Ruia," he explained. "Later it will come from icehouses and be more expensive, but right now it is not excessive luxury." He repeated this as the glasses were set out. "It is not an excessive luxury."

He seemed to be saying it to himself more than us, and I liked him all the more for it, this tidy man with his thoughtful ways, and we drank our bitters as Cazzetta explained to the maestro that we were meant to meet with the Parl and so would need apartments and introductions to be arranged. This was done with some alacrity, and so within the time it took for us to take another round of bitters and share a roasted chicken, all was arranged, and soon we were stabling our horses and knocking upon the doors of a dwelling called Palazzou Navou.

We watched the Sio Navou—an unfortunately minor noble—vacate before our eyes, along with wife and children. His "palazzou" stood in a pretty private garden quadrazzo with climbing flowers on all the walls of the surrounding homes, and if you stood on the balcony overlooking the quadrazzo, you could see over the roofs of the palace, high atop its red sandstone cliff, with stairs carved into the face that led up to it—part of the defenses. From there, high walls rose, straight up from the cliff, punctuated by domed towers with blue and gold pennants flying.

Almost as soon as we were installed in our rooms, a messenger appeared on our doorstep with an invitation to dine with the Parl. Cazzetta read the invitation and handed it to me. "You will attend the Parl. I will not."

"You're not coming?"

"You think Roulait would invite a stilettotore to his table?"

"Why would you send me alone? I will not help you auction Celia."

"That will not be broached tonight in any case," Cazzetta said. "All that is required of you is to attend the Parl. You represent Banca Regulai and your family." He raised his eyebrows. "I assume that you are not so angry with your father that you will insult Merai's hospitality. Whatever your feelings about Celia's marriage, you do understand the necessity of good relations."

"How is it that Merai owes us so much money, and yet we attend to them? Should they not come begging for our attention, and we decide if we will grant them audience?"

Cazzetta shrugged. "It is always better not to force nobility to mark their cheeks too publicly. They do, after all, control armies. If we give them the feeling of control, so much the better."

"Is that what you're doing with me? Giving me the illusion of control?"

"So suspicious, Davico. You do your family proud."

"Celia is not for Merai."

"As you will. But regardless, tonight you dine. And when you return, you will tell me what you see and what is said, just as I have taught you."

So it was that I found myself walking across a wide quadrazzo, past a statue of Amo holding up the sphere of the sun while the lesser gods all crouched at his feet and marked their cheeks, and of course, in the heart of the quadrazzo, Marlonne di Vien was commemorated in statue upon a charger, his spear pointing with authority to the west and Cheroux. A reminder of a long-ago victory against that much larger kingdom.

The men of Merai wore their hair longer than we in Navola, and tied it in a knot that was their tradition. The women wore high shoes, and tight-waisted dresses, influenced by Cheroux, and their hair, instead of being bound in plaits, was drawn up high and loose so that it was upswept and then fell down in cascades, something that looked very strange and felt very intimate to me, to see hair so loose and wild that way.

Lugo had remarked that the Meravese might block the soldiers of Cheroux, but Cheroux had conquered Merai's women anyway, and now Cheroux caressed their flesh day and night, and ran its fingers through their hair and made them wild, while the men of Merai looked on.

I was bowed into the palace and then met by Count Dellamont, the first secretary, whom I had last seen in Navola.

"Archinomo di Regulai." He bowed. "It is an honor to have you in our city." He smiled but did not seem glad.

"How goes the fight with Ciceque?" I asked.

"That dog." He grimaced. "Now that it is spring, we will have him. He has nowhere to run. Wustholt lies at his back, and we have assurances from them that he has no place to escape in the north. This summer he dies." He favored me with a jaundiced eye. "Or so your Sivizza assures me."

"If Sivizza says it is true, I would believe him," I said.

"You know him well?"

I felt confident answering. "He is too experienced to make a reckless promise."

"Ai. That is good, for it drags on too long already." He led me through a maze of pretty courtyards, and from there, to my surprise, not into the palace residence but to the stables, where we found the Parl currying a horse.

"Davico di Regulai!" the Parl exclaimed, and came to embrace me.

I was taken aback at his enthusiasm. In Navola we are more careful with our open pleasure, but he was most chiaro, clasping me with a heartiness that reminded me of Wustholt and those open and chiaro people.

More than his unalloyed excitement, though, I was surprised at his youth. He truly was barely older than I.

"It is an honor to meet you, Your Majesty," I said.

"Majesty? Ci. Set aside such talk," the Parl said. "It is not necessary. I am Roulait! And you are Davico!"

Dellamont looked on indulgently as we made our acquaintance. We spoke of nothings as I studied the young ruler. His hair was blond shading dark, like straw in winter fields. His face was handsome and smooth and his skin was darker than many of the north, as if he spent much time in the sun. Looking more closely, I had difficulty deciding upon his exact age, for the life that animated him seemed young, and he moved as one driven by the excitement of childhood. But there was also grace and an assuredness of power. He was the sort of man that Aghan Khan would have described as comfortable in his body. His words were honeyed enough that he would have charmed even Ashia, but his eyes were quick and attentive and Cazzetta would have warned me against him, for even as I examined him, he examined me in turn.

I wondered what he made of me. Shorter than him. Darker. My black hair unruly, curly and thick. My clothes, though woven of fine cloth, were simple black, the only adornment a bit of gold embroidery at my cuffs and upon my high collar.

The Parl finished his assessment of me, and then, to my surprise, introduced me to his horse.

"This is Imperix," he said proudly. "The finest in my stables."

For a moment I wondered if he was mad, introducing his animal as if it were part of his family.

"He is very fine, Your Majesty," I said uncertainly.

And he was fine. A great black beast, seventeen hands high, perhaps more. Bred for war, thick and strong, and with a gleam of violence in his eye. As soon as I saw the animal I could see that he was formidable and dangerous. The Parl stood beside the stallion, grinning with seeming delight, but with a glint of violence in his own eye that matched that of his warhorse.

"Come and say hello!" he urged.

My estimation of the Parl changed. He was less the foolish boy than he first appeared. Not as friendly, nor as happily informal as I had thought. He liked to test, and he intended to intimidate, and that made him dangerous in ways somewhat worse than those of his steed.

The first secretary was watching closely.

This was a tableau well staged, I realized. The Parl had schemed to wait here, knowing I would be calling. I wished suddenly that I had arrived an hour late as was fashion in Cheroux. To have kept this dangerous pair waiting impatiently, like actors frozen upon the stage, unable to begin without an audience. For this was a play, of a surety. Staged for me alone, the fool in their pantomime.

Imperix snorted and tossed his head.

"He is beautiful, is he not?" The Parl fondly stroked the war beast's muscular neck.

In fact, the stallion fairly boiled with bottled violence. If he was well-trained, he had been conditioned to attack any who attempted to ride or approach except the Parl. His hooves would easily shatter a skull. His bite would tear a man's arm from his shoulder.

The Parl patted his beast with unalloyed pleasure, a creature viciously loyal and blood-hungry.

"Indeed," I said. "He is beautiful."

I stayed well clear of the animal. Its eyes followed me like a bloody fata, hungry to rip out my throat. "I had heard that Merai bred great warhorses," I said, "but I never suspected they were so noble."

"Ai. It's true. His great-grandfather was Victoriix, whom my grandfather rode in the Southern War."

So, a threat and a message and a test, all in a single horse. The Parl's grandfather had ridden with Cheroux against Navola. We still told tales of how that army had raped across the plains to lay siege upon us.

"Your grandfather is much respected," I said carefully. "We have a painting of the River Treaty in our palazzo. He brokered our peace with Cheroux."

All of us were smiling, but the danger was real. Victoriix and the Parl's grandfather had nearly destroyed us by allying with the Cheroux and aiding their attack upon us. If my own grandfather had not rallied the alliance of Navola, Pardi, and Sevicchi, and bought away the Lupari, our women might have been wearing their hair high and loose, just as those of Merai did, walking on their high shoes and speaking with the affected trills and lisps of the north.

Only when loss was imminent had the old Parl of Merai changed his alliances, recognizing that Merai would likely suffer and Cheroux would not, and so he had forced a peace, dragging Cheroux along with him to the plank to negotiate, and keeping them and their armies bottled below the passes of the Ruia so that Cheroux could not escape until restitution was paid—and Merai was safe by treaty, despite the ruin that they had caused us. The man had been wily. My father said that without him, Merai would have been Navola's, much as Pardi was.

"Come and see him," the Parl urged. "He is my favorite."

I wondered if he intended for me to die here. To say that his horse slew the heir of the Regulai. Slew the grandchild of the man who had once humiliated his family. Such a tragedy.

"You're not afraid, surely." The Parl patted his beast. "I had heard you enjoyed to ride and knew horses well."

It took all my discipline not to shy from the animal, not to simply turn and leave the stables. Violence emanated from the beast the way heat boiled from a blacksmith's forge. I held out a hand. Predictably, Imperix snapped at it.

"He seems unwilling," I said.

“Nai.” The Parl waved a hand of dismissal. “He merely teases. Dellamont, be a good man and give Davico a sweet to feed Imperix.”

Dellamont, with a hooded look, produced a clump of sugar from his sleeve, luxurious and expensive—especially to be given to a horse—and offered it to me.

It was all so obvious. Of course the first secretary had sugar up his sleeve. The play was well-staged. I could see the entirety of their planned entertainment. I could see the roles they two played, and I suspected my role was—well, to at least be injured. Nai. The horse would be well-trained to the Parl’s voice. So, they sought to terrify me. Imperix would put me in my place. He would leave me blooded, but alive. And frightened. And weak in comparison to the Parl.

They knew we had come to negotiate. And this time, we came to them, not they to us, and so now they set the table to their advantage.

All this I saw.

But more, I saw Imperix, that great and terrifying beast, chained by his master’s commands, conditioned with whips and shouts and cuffs, the spirit of the animal molded like wax into a form that was no more his nature than it is natural for a tree to grow sideways.

No animal is born with violence in its heart. They are always twisted to it. Even shadow cats and stone bears carry only hunger, not a desire for cruelty.

But still, Imperix was well twisted, and that was dangerous.

And yet, too, I could not dismiss that there was also a nobility in the creature. A nobility that was greater than that of the young man who stood beside him, this vicious boy who pretended to be ruler. This stage that the Parl had placed me upon was not dominated by the Parl, nor by Dellamont. In fact, there were only two actors who mattered.

This was a drama between Imperix and myself.

I took a step closer. And then another step. But I came closer not as a man seeking to rule, but simply as one of the many creatures woven into Virga’s net, all equal. All part of the weave. Imperix and I were one. We were not separate creatures, but one.

Man had fallen from Virga’s net, but still there was kinship, we creatures formed of Argo’s clay and fired by Amo’s light, and all of us part of Virga’s weave. I let go my held breath. Let my body loosen. We were not master and slave. We were companionable creatures, sharing this stable. Companions of the moment, neither of us ruling, neither of us serving. All of us were creatures of Virga, myself and Imperix, just as myself and Stub, or myself and Lazy, myself and a majestic stag in the deep Romiglia. Did we all not yearn for care? Were we not all as kittens? All of us seeking our mother's tongue, to be warm and purred upon and washed and loved?

I stepped into the circle of Imperix's violence.

For a moment, I thought he would rear and strike me down. He trembled and the Parl stepped back from Imperix's flank, anticipating the surge, the beast to rise up and drive his hooves down upon me, the horse to lunge and bite and tear at me—but Imperix did not move.

I stood close before him, caressing his noble face and staring into his great eyes.

We are all creatures of Virga's weave.

I produced the sugar, and there before the astounded Parl and first secretary, I fed Imperix. I ran my hands down his neck and patted his huge chest, murmuring admiration for him, offering not domination as men always do upon horses, but friendship.

Imperix lowered his head to my face, and lipped my cheek. I saw the Parl flinch, and I laughed.

"He is mighty!" I said.

The Parl and Dellamont exchanged uncertain looks. I might have taken pleasure in their disarray, but in truth, I did not care, for though the Red Palace of Merai might be full of human asps, I had found a friend.

"Imperix never has let another man touch him," the Parl murmured.

"Perhaps he senses my pure heart."

Dellamont snorted his disbelief. The Parl looked troubled.

Chapter 38

I was unable to divine if the test of Imperix had been designed by Dellamont or the Parl, but in any event, with their pantomime in shambles they became rather more pleasant company.

The Parl and I shared much interest in riding, hawks, and hunting. Too, the Parl set a good table. Various nobles dined with us in honor of my visit, those men and women who controlled the patchwork prosperity of the city, and we drank good vintages from Merai, though they did not match those of Navola. There were hams and cheeses and peculiar red fruits, pickled both tart and sweet, red as tomatoes, long as my pinkie.

"Cherupin," explained a young pretty woman who was seated beside me. She had peacock feathers woven into her hair, and wore a blue silk gown with green embroidery, tight at her waist and low across her breasts.

"I'm not familiar."

"Cherub cocks," the Parl said loudly. A titter went around the table as he held one of the red things up and bit it. "Try them with the wine."

I did, and was surprised that the vinegar and fruit matched the vintage well, and did not clash.

"This is a fine vintage," I complimented the Parl as I sipped.

The young woman with the peacock feathers smiled coquettishly. "It is the finest of the cellar," she said. "You are much honored."

"Ah. Of course." I sipped again. "I'm honored."

"Are you?" The Parl watched me. "Do you find it most excellent?"

I felt myself caught between honesty and diplomacy, and also wondering if this was another test, intended to put me on the wrong foot. Was it truly his finest? If it was, it was not so impressive. If it was not, and I were to lavishly compliment it, would I be made a fool? I sipped the wine again, pretending to think on it, and wished mightily that Merio were here, always complimenting good food. Or that Aghan Khan with his blunt honesty were at my side.

I settled for avoiding the direct answer. "It is extremely pleasing with the cherupin," I said. "Perhaps I could send a few bottles from Navola to add to your cellar."

There was a collected intake of breath from the table.

A man stood. "You insult Merai."

I looked up at the man. He was handsome and strong, with a powerful jaw and a thick nose that clearly had been broken at least once, and an attitude of aggrievedness that seemed to go beyond the wine. He reminded me somewhat of the lordlings of Navola, who enjoyed strutting in Quadrazzo Amo. They liked very much to be seen, and very little to be forced to do much of anything, but more, I was surprised that he had his hand upon a dagger.

"Are gifts an insult in Merai?" I feigned confusion. I looked to the Parl. "If so, Majesty, I meant no such thing." I turned back to the disgruntled man. "As for you, if you do not desire to taste Navolese wine, sun-sweetened in the fertile hills of Valle Livia, pressed under the feet of laughing maidens, aged in the oak of the wild Romiglia—well, then, you are fortunate, for I did not offer it to you."

Someone snorted laughter.

The man gripped his dagger and turned a deep shade of red. I let my hand stray to the stiletto in my sleeve, wondering if this was another test, or if this was a true challenge, and then wondered why the people of Merai liked their brute bloodshed so much. They were worse than the Borraghese.

"Ceinot is loyal," the Parl said, smiling, motioning him to sit. "We are a proud people."

I was glad to see my hand did not shake when I took up my wine. "Well, you are fortunate, both in the loyalty and pride of your people. While our wine is excellent, our people are not so straightforward."

"The minds of the Navolese are as twisted as the plaits of their women's hair," the Parl quoted.

I had heard the quote, and did not like it. "So many people say."

"A Navolese's heart is as black as his gold is bright," the girl with the peacock feathers quoted.

"I have heard that saying as well." I tried to keep my voice level.

"The Navolese are as dark and crooked as their alleys," Ceinot said.

"And just as narrow," the Parl added, smirking slightly.

"Outsiders often say so," I acknowledged through gritted teeth. "But it is not so bad."

"Sfai. You yourself were nearly murdered by your own friends," Roulait said. "Is this not crooked, twisted, and black?"

I remembered Piero lunging at me with his dagger, and pushed away the memory. "Merai has plots and intrigues, too, does she not?"

"Not like Navola," Roulait said with distaste. "Even a dog like my uncle Ciceque at least has the decency to declare his intentions. He does not come as an assassin in the night."

"Is Navola such a twisted place?" the girl beside me asked, laying a hand upon my arm.

"Not to us," I said, trying not to show my irritation.

"But there are so many stories of betrayal," she said. "I think I would be afraid to visit there." Her hand remained upon my arm. She was quite beautiful, with her dark hair drawn up, her eyes green, wide, innocent, and curious. Of them all, she struck me as without malice, only curiosity. She might be ignorant of Navola, but she held no malice.

To my surprise, I found myself paraphrasing Aghan Khan. "Navola's alleys are indeed crooked, and the hair of our women is indeed twisted, but our hearts are straighter than the straightest arrows, and we always fly true toward that which we love."

I held her gaze boldly, until she blushed and looked away.

I was actually shocked at my own presumption. I almost tried to apologize, for it was an illicit feeling to speak so boldly, to transgress upon a lady's honor in such a way, and yet also, I saw that my words had struck and that I had conquered, for she lowered her eyes, and was blushing, and was also, clearly, much enamored with me.

Somehow, with a few words, I had fooled her into believing I was more of a swaggering man than I truly was, more powerful, more bold, more knowledgeable of women—

The Parl laughed and slapped the table with approval, shattering the moment. Others around the table also were nodding and smiling and repeating the words, and the girl, whose name was Allessana, peeked up at me from under her lashes, not at all insulted but instead blushing and complimented.

A new course was brought out by the servants and suddenly the table felt easy to me, warm in a way it had not before.

The dinner and conversation flowed smoothly then, with many stories told by the Parl about hunting, and only the man with the dagger glowering at me, and I did not care for I had the attention of a girl with peacock feathers in her hair, and the wine of Merai was warm in my belly.

Chapter 39

Cazzetta was pleased when I returned to the apartments, but when I spoke my mind he was less pleased.

"You wish to see Celia bound to Merai?" I demanded as I threw off my cloak and unlooped the togs of my high collar. "To those dogs? How could you?"

Cazzetta seized my arm. "Not here!" he whispered fiercely. He dragged me outside, into the open quadrazzo where a small fountain splashed. Around us, the flowers and vines that covered the buildings were dark. In the distance, torches glittered atop the walls of the palace, a looming presence in the chill of the spring night. I wished I had not discarded my cloak so readily. It was warm in Merai, but the night still had its bite.

"You did well tonight," Cazzetta said, after he had ensured that no one was close. "But have a care of where and how you speak, my prince."

"How would you know about my night?" I asked. "And what is wrong with the apartments? There are no servants to spy."

"Just because we see no one listening, does not mean there are no ears," he said. "As to your night, I know that a horse did not bite you, a man did not stab you, a young woman is smitten with you, and the Parl respects you."

"I very much doubt that."

"And yet it is true."

"He says he wishes to hunt tomorrow."

"Will he take the man Ceinot? The one who sought your blood?"

I tried not to show surprise at Cazzetta's knowledge of the dinner's details. "I do not know. They are close, though. The Parl did not flinch when he put his hand to his dagger."

Cazzetta quirked an eyebrow approvingly. "Ai. You are wiser than Merio gives you credit for."

"How nice to know."

"Speak no business before that one. He wishes the Parl ill."

"He acts as if he is the Parl's closest friend."

"Indeed he does."

I thought back on the evening, trying to remember any hint of what Cazzetta accused. "He seems arrogant. And performatively loyal. But still, I thought him adoring of the Parl."

"He shares blood with Ciceque."

I startled. "The Parl does not know?"

"Did the Parl seem at all on guard?"

"Nai." I shook my head. "By the fatas, he seemed completely trusting. He's a fool," I realized.

"And it is to our advantage. He needs true friends."

I couldn't help but remember Piero again, the painful hurt of his betrayal. I almost pitied the Parl, and did not like it, for I did not want to care about him at all. But it made me think that I understood something of his desire to challenge and frighten. He was on guard, much as I was. I found it irritating to see a reflection of myself in him.

I changed the topic. "Do you truly think the walls listen to us in our apartments?"

Cazzetta gave me a jaundiced look. "The apartments were arranged almost immediately. As soon as our capo di banco made the request. The patro we evicted is a dependent of Dellamont. If the walls are not hollow then Dellamont is not doing his job. There will be both eyes and ears, peeking and peering and listening there."

I shook my head sourly. "I do not like this place. There is cruelty here."

Cazzetta shrugged. "There is cruelty everywhere."

"Nai." I shook my head. "It is different here. It feels . . ."

Something about the ways of Merai. The air seemed to fairly tremble with a viciousness that even here in the quadrazzo seemed still to exist. The way people had behaved at the Parl's dinner had not been subtle. The way the Parl behaved in his stables. They liked to bully. They liked to dominate. They liked to flaunt. Even Piero, who had tried to murder me, seemed somehow less brutish. He might have sought murder, but he had done it because he had been stupidly passionate and glory-starved. He had not done it to bully.

"For the Meravese, everything seems to be strutting and challenge," I said. "They flaunt their wealth. The control their streets and quadrazzi. And they press and test you. And then they press some more. They like to see people flinch before them. They are the sort who, if you knelt to mark a cheek, they would step on your neck, and press you harder to their boot."

That was the closest I could come to describing my sense of the day I had spent. It struck me that I suddenly believed—fervently believed—that some places were diseased. Torre Amo was said to be a place of decay and debauch. Gevazzoa a place of revenge and bloodshed. Pardi a place of warmth and hospitality. Navola a place of scheming.

But Merai . . . it was a place that felt its wounds, and yet did not seek to salve them, but only to cause wounds upon others. Whether it was a street controlled by some archinomo, or the Parl's testing of me, they seemed to want to strut and dominate. Every aspect of this day had been engineered to test and prod, to see if I could be broken. Except the girl.

"Who was the girl I sat beside?"

"The Sia Allessana D'Evangeline Du Tesse."

"She seemed somehow different to me."

"She is of a lesser house. A lady's companion to Contessa Ulain. She has been sent to the Parl's court in hope of a gaining an advantageous marriage."

"Why was she seated beside me?"

"She is of low house. So, a useful pawn." Cazzetta shrugged. "It is likely Dellamont seeks to twitch a line and see if you will bite upon her. She is pretty, is she not?"

"She is," I admitted.

"Then she is bait."

I wondered if it was true. And then I wondered if she knew herself to be such.

"She seemed guileless."

"Perhaps she is," Cazzetta said. "But her family lacks powerful allies, so she will be at Dellamont's mercy if he has a use for her."

"Not the Parl?"

Cazzetta favored me with another jaundiced look. "Did the Parl seem capable of leadership to you?"

"Nai," I admitted. "He seems too simple. Too blunt."

"Indeed."

"You cannot think that Celia deserves such a match."

"Most people do not deserve what occurs in their life. And yet still it occurs."

"Well, I would sooner see Celia fed to a wolf, for it would be kinder."

Cazzetta laughed and clapped a hand upon my knee. "You think too little of the sia."

He stood to return indoors, but I remained seated by the fountain.

"I do not like this place," I said. "It is full of cruelty and it has made the people cruel as well."

"Ci. Do not be fooled by a single day amongst a people," Cazzetta said. "If this girl Allessana intrigues you, whatever her true purpose, perhaps there is more to them than you discern."

"Nothing about the Parl would be good for Celia," I said.

"Is that the prince of the Regulai who speaks? Or the jealous boy?" He held up a hand to forestall my angry outburst. "Nai. Do not answer, Davico. Use that mind of yours. To be di Regulai is to think. To plan. To see the distant goal, and set sail for it, though it may be beyond the very horizon and out of sight.

"Regardless, Sia Celia is not yours to give, nor to keep. She is a promise your father made to di Balcosi, And your father will not see you disrupt his promises, to di Balcosi or to any man. And if that does not convince you, then think of Cheroux, sidling close to our young Parl, making alliance, and looking south to us. It is difficult, I know, but sometimes, we are small, and the demands of our roles are great. Now come, it grows cold and there is a warm fire waiting. Tomorrow you will hunt and perhaps you will see a different side of the young Parl."

We went inside then, but the fire did not warm me. I thought hard on Cazzetta's words, and on the tangle of duty and promises and the roles of families, and all of it felt like a black and tangled mass. I saw no good solutions, and no clean choices, and my heart was heavy. I wondered if this was what my father had protected me from in my early years. I had been taught to work the abacus, to sit at the plank, to swing a sword, but I had not been taught to ruin my loves and destroy my desires for the sake of politics and family. No one had told me that my inheritance was to be not power, but pain. I wondered what would be left of me if I continued down this inexorable path, and I wondered what was left of my father, and then I thought of Merai, with its petty cruelties and constant challenges, and I thought that we were all sick, for still we kept at the game, even though we all suffered.

Chapter 40

The morning was gray to fit my mood when I went hawking with the Parl, and soon it was raining.

"Don't worry," the Parl said. "Once the sun is high, these rains will fade. They are always thus. Wet in the mornings, but gone soon enough."

"As you say, Majesty."

"Roulait, I beg of you. Roulait."

"Roulait, then."

Ceinot rode beside us. I thought on Cazzetta's accusation of Ceinot. The man was strong and handsome. He laughed easily. He remained always close to his Parl. But when he stood close, Roulait seemed smaller. The Parl was vital, not at all unfit, but he was also awkward. I had seen it in the stables as he baited me to touch his horse. He was full of bravado that I had first interpreted as strength, but now, watching him beside Ceinot, who made easy jokes with guards and courtiers, I saw that Roulait was stiff.

When Ceinot rode close to the Parl, I watched him for signs of contempt or disgust. A narrowing of the eye, a twisting of the lips or nose . . . I had been taught by my father and Cazzetta to look for small signs in men, to look beyond faccioscuro, and yet Ceinot seemed to hold no ill will toward the Parl. He was even solicitous. And the Parl, in turn, seemed to crave some approval from him.

We rode on and the sky did indeed clear. We sent ahead the beaters and soon hawks were aloft and dogs were running ahead baying, and our bows were out. I brought down a pheasant with my bow, and my hawk caught it mid-fall but did not return it to me, instead bringing it to the Parl.

"A fine bird, Ma— Roulait. She is loyal."

The Parl smiled slightly. "If only men were so loyal."

He signaled our hunting party to halt, and to prepare lunch. The servants quickly went about preparing a tent and chairs, while Roulait and I sat atop our respective horses, watching. He motioned his men to dismount, surveying them all, but when I moved to dismount he tapped my thigh and shook his head.

A moment later, when all were down and were tying their horses, he abruptly wheeled Imperix, and kicked him into a gallop.

"Ride with me, Navolese!" he shouted. "Let us test your skill!"

And with that, he set off hard down the trail, with me in pursuit, leaving all the others behind and surprised. Ceinot, Dellamont, and all the rest.

We spurred hard, crashing through bracken, leaping small streams. It was a reckless gallop, ducking under branches, scraping between tight trees, hurtling over fallen logs. I hung on and rode hard, summoning all my skill to keep up with him, grateful to Aghan Khan for years of instruction. Too, I was grateful at least that Roulait had chosen to test me in the saddle rather than in the hunt. The Parl could ride, but so could I, and the horse he had loaned me was also very fine. He was called Nero and I could feel his eagerness to charge, to run, to gallop with wild abandon, and after feeling trapped and tied by duty, I was more than ready as well.

We burst through a thicket. Open grassland spread before us. The Parl was ahead, shouting Imperix to greater effort. We charged after him. Imperix widened his lead on us, but we kept him in sight, and Nero did not flag.

I rode out of my saddle, crouched low over Nero's neck, shouting encouragement in his ear. He was a good steed, fast and prideful and unwilling to defer even to the Parl and his own favorite, and so we all rode hard. It was marvelous, the speed and the risk and the wide lands, and now, a hill rose before us, and the Parl was charging up its flank, leaving the valley below us, charging for higher ground.

The spine of the hill was rocky, red sandstone and grass interspersed, and yet still the Parl spurred up. He looked wild, almost mad. He looked as if he desired to leap into the sky and challenge Urulo as Gienna had done when her husband was drowned in a storm. It was harrowing. We skirted a cliff, and then fought for higher ground, lunging upward, upward, the ground uncertain, becoming steep. I fought the urge to rein in Nero for fear, and instead let him have his head, trusting him to feel the ground, to avoid the plunge.

Abruptly, the Parl reined in Imperix. He swung out of his saddle below a sharp face of red stone. I hauled Nero to a halt as well. Roulait was breathing hard, sweating and grinning, his eyes wide and excited.

"Well ridden, di Regulai!" he exclaimed. "My spies said you were a man of the horse, and now I believe it!"

He did not pause, though. Now he began to climb, scrambling up the gritty face. "Come!" he called back, and I followed. We climbed, gasping, clawing upward, until at last we reached the crest of the hill. The Parl stood atop it like a god, gazing out upon his lands, pleased.

Fifty feet below us, our horses still heaved for breath, their sides lathered with the effort of the climb. And below them, the cliff faces tumbled far to the plain below. From here it was possible to see the Cascada Rossa, to see the tidy fields and vineyards of the Meravese, and in the far distance Merai's red walls and red-tiled roofs, with her fortress palace standing high above it all. Below the fortress, the catredanto's domes dwarfed the smaller buildings, but they in turn were dwarfed by the palace. Garagazzo would not have been pleased.

"Well done, Navolese," the Parl said when I reached him.

"I haven't ridden like that . . . ever."

"Even better then!" He was breathing hard, but still seemed to have energy.

Down on the plain, the Parl's guard and retinue had finally burst out of the forest.

"Your people are distressed." They were seeking this way and that, turning their horses, circling, all of them desperate to find their ruler. "See how worried they are for you."

The Parl made a sour face, and his expression was different from any time I had seen him before. "Some, perhaps. Some would be just as pleased to see my neck broken."

"Surely not."

"It has not been long since Ciceque rose against me. And when he did, it was a very near thing. Poison in my cup. If my cousin had been less greedy for my good wine, I would not be alive."

"I heard that there had been an attempt."

"The Regulai have a reputation for listening."

"The gift of fear," I said sourly.

"What is that?"

"Something a tutor said, many years ago. Something he taught me. He made me fear. He made me alert where I had been asleep."

"A useful lesson."

"He tells me I still haven't learned it."

"Then you are lucky he is loyal," the Parl said. "I could use a man who I could be sure of. Someone who feared for me as much as I should fear for myself. Count yourself lucky."

"He is my father's man, not mine."

"The one you travel with?"

"Cazzetta. Yes."

"I have heard that the parents of Navola warn their children not to be naughty or the stilettotore of the Regulai will steal them away and sell their souls."

"He does have a certain reputation."

"I could use a man like that. As it is, I have bluff fools. Ceinot and the like."

"As I said, Cazzetta is not mine, he is my father's man."

"Then you should seek to bind him to you as well. A man like that is worth a vault of Navolese gold."

He seemed strangely earnest. It was surprising to me that we discussed such intimate details. Was this his true face, or another ruse? Another test? I made a decision. "There is something you should know," I said.

"Oh?"

"We listen to the rumors of Merai, much as you listen to Navola. Your man, Ceinot, we think is not trustworthy. We think he has blood ties to Ciceque."

"Ceinot?" The Parl scoffed. "We have known each other all our lives."

"It could be that the whispers are wrong, or misdirections. I do not know. I watched him myself, and discerned no mud on his cheek. So I wonder if my contacts are incorrect in this. Still, I thought I should say something."

"Are your contacts often incorrect?"

I shook my head. "Not often. But all men make mistakes." The men of the retinue had at last spotted us, and were galloping across the open ground. "Do what you will with the information. Perhaps set another to watch him, someone you trust well."

The Parl made a face. "Again, the problem of trust."

"Dellamont?" I suggested.

He gave me a dark look.

"You do not trust him, either?"

He spat. "He is cruel, and he likes to brutalize. It was he who wished you brought to the stables, to meet Imperix." He glanced over at me. "He still smarts from the negotiations with your family."

"But you do not?"

The Parl shook his head. "I am not like these people. Sometimes I feel as if I am surrounded by asps. They all slither, they all like to be close to a warm fire, and they all will not hesitate to strike."

"But Dellamont supports you."

"For now. While Ciceque yet harasses us." He made another face. "I am sorry for the stables. It was not . . ." He paused. "It was low of me."

I sighed. "I know what it is to be pushed and prodded by those around us."

"Do you trust those around you, though? Are they good?"

I thought of Merio and Aghan Khan and Cazzetta, and then of the Callarino, and of Garagazzo. "I have never known them to fail my father, but some I trust more than others. Some are generous in spirit, and some are . . . *selfish* is not enough of a word. Avaricious." I shrugged. "But we are not rulers. The stakes are different for us."

"Ah yes. The Regulai. Humble bankers. Holding money, making trade, extending credit. And yet you keep the Callarino's sigil in your palazzo, and he must come begging to use it."

"Our family prefers not to touch politics, but it is sometimes wiser not to leave things to chance."

"Indeed. So. Quickly then, before my sycophants arrive. Why are you here, Navolese?"

I shook my head. "That is something for you to discuss with Cazzetta."

"Not with you?"

I shrugged. "He is empowered to speak with my father's voice."

"And yet, I wish to hear it from you."

I made a face and looked away. "My father seeks a durable alliance."

"To what end?"

"The defense of Navola, the protection of our interests across Merai. A more reliable defense and ally against Cheroux, should she seek again to invade the hook."

"And you offer?"

I looked away. "That is for Cazzetta to say."

"Nai nai nai! I know what you offer! You offer Celia di Balcosi. A minor noble. A ward of your father, a girl of little worth—"

"She is my sister!"

"Ci. I do not believe it. She does not share your name."

I looked away, not wanting to be further baited.

"I did not know the offer had been made," I said stiffly.

"Nai? The emissary arrived more than a month ago. I should have thought you would know such an important negotiation. The girl, a substantial dowry, a complete forgiveness of my father's debts, the Lupari, even." He was watching my face. "You truly did not know?"

I tried to master myself, but I felt a fury rising. My father had made the proposal almost as soon as Cazzetta had seen me with Celia, I realized. He had wasted not a moment. He had moved against me, quickly, efficiently, without sentimentality.

"What is so special about this girl?" the Parl asked.

I looked away. "Nothing. She is my sister. That is all."

"But she is not your sister. She is not your blood. She is a mere hostage. Why does your father seek to sell her to me? She is nothing. Offal from the slaughter of di Balcosi. Not even fresh—"

"She is not to be spoken of so!" I burst out. "She is of our family! She is ours!"

My hand went to my dagger and I would have drawn it for the insult, but the Parl was watching me, observing, and suddenly, I saw my father's scheme.

In my defense of Celia I had betrayed her. And in a great burst of clarity, I saw my father's entire plan. All his intentions laid out.

The Parl would of course resist the offer of a girl below his station. But if he were convinced of her value, he might be persuaded.

But how to convince someone like the Parl? Why, show him that Celia was greatly valued by our family. My own care for Celia would convince the Parl that she was a prize, and his own pleasure at winning prizes would drive him into matrimony.

Far below us, the Parl's men were climbing the hill, coming to his rescue. Trails of ants climbing, following their lord.

For a moment, I considered pushing the Parl from the cliff. It would destroy my father's plans, at least. I would die, but I would at least be free of my father's schemes—

"Ai. Do not resent me, Davico," the Parl said. "I had to be sure. The promises that your father sent—" He shrugged. "Well, words are beautiful, but if you cannot see beyond that man's face, it is impossible to know him. The Navolese are difficult to read."

He nodded down at all the men approaching, scrambling up the hill. "I am surrounded by asps. It is impossible to know who is true and who is false." He looked at me. "But you, I trust." He took me by the shoulders. "You have a reputation for decency that precedes you. Dellamont said that you were easily moved, and easily played." He held up a hand against my angry outburst. "So what, Davico? These intrigues are not for you. Do not sorrow for it. It does you credit. You are a decent man."

It felt as if the world were crushing down upon me. All my father's plans, landing atop me like an avalanche. He had played me too well. I closed my eyes, fighting down the anger and grief and feelings of betrayal. I would not mewl and cry in front of the Parl. I would at least hold that much dignity. I met the Parl's eyes.

"You must treat her well. You must swear to it."

"I so swear," he said. "You will have no cause to regret our union. Now let us go and see to the snakes, before they all fall faint."

Chapter 41

"This was why you wanted me to come to Merai!" I accused as I stormed into our apartments. "You knew that I would hook that pissioletto better than any other person. You used me against myself!"

Cazzetta didn't look up from where he sat upon a low couch. He was sharpening one of the many daggers that he kept secreted about his person, and now the noise of it was grating. The rasp of the whetstone on steel. This particular knife was a short thing, no longer than a finger, with a grip perpendicular to the blade. A sort of punching knife. He slipped it into a pocket of his cloak and brought out a long stiletto.

"That was the intention, all along, wasn't it?" I pressed. "To make me the authenticator of Celia."

Cazzetta examined the blade in the candlelight, then set stone to it. "The offer is indeed more trustworthy coming from one who admires her greatly."

"And I have a face that cannot dissemble."

Cazzetta inclined his head in agreement, continuing to sharpen the stiletto.

I wheeled, pacing. "Even when I am sure of my own direction, it seems I walk a road my father has long mapped out for me. Everything is to his plan." I couldn't hide my bitterness. I did not wish to. "Do you know, these Meravese, they make jokes about us? About our intrigues? And then I say that we are not so bad as that, and then I find that *I cannot keep even the tangled threads of my own family distinct.*"

"Be glad that we work so many threads on your behalf. We weave a tangled skein, but always to your benefit." Cazzetta began sharpening another knife. "You should go and write letters to your father and Sia Celia, so that they will know of the Parl's agreement."

"I will not."

"Ci. You're angry because the Parl played you," Cazzetta said. "Does that not make him worthy of Celia?"

I scowled.

"Does it not?" he pressed again.

"No one is worthy of Celia."

Cazzetta sighed. "Well. Write the letters, or do not. Celia will be informed, regardless."

I wrote the letters.

With regret and bitterness I wrote. I informed my father in the coldest language that the Parl was amenable to Celia, and I wrote to Celia and tried to explain my disappearance from the palazzo. And I tried to explain why it was that we could not be together, and how I still burned for her but that it could not be, and that I hoped that she understood, for she would be a queen, and if I was honest, this was a better match for her.

The Parl is handsome. He is intelligent and vital. He is assured enough of his own self that he will likely appreciate your counsel. With him, I think, you will be more than a pretty ornament—

I crumpled the paper and threw it away, grinding my teeth.

If she had been my true sister, in blood and parentage, I could not have found a better match of man or station. And yet, still I raged. I started again.

It took me three attempts, but eventually I had a letter. I read it over, my throat tightening on the honeyed words. No matter how I tried to reconcile myself, I could not. I was about to crumple this one as well, but Cazzetta plucked it from my hands, his cold eyes warning against my trying to fight him.

He read it over, expressionless.

"Well?" I asked acidly. "Does it meet your approval?"

"It is good enough." He took wax and sealed the letters, then, to my surprise, rang for a servant. "Have the maestro di palazzo send these to Navola."

"They will read my letters, though," I protested. "They are sure to steam the seals and lift the wax."

Cazzetta gave me an amused look, and I saw that I had been used once more. Cazzetta wanted the Parl to read my letters. To see my private communication with Celia. The Parl would now have new assurance of my esteem for Celia.

He would see me transparent, facciochiaro.

More than.

As wheat bends before winter winds, so must a people bend before politics.

—AVINIXIIUS, *OBSERVATIONS*

Chapter 42

Weddings in Navola are not drawn-out affairs. As soon as our letters arrived, the preparations began. By the time Cazzetta and I returned home, the household was awhirl with activity. Ladies coming to fit Celia with new gowns, cooks and vendors for the foods and gifts, actors who would perform plays for the city in honor of the wedding, pyromaestri for fireworks, and of course acrobats and sword swallowers and fire dancers and bawdies for the feasts and entertainments.

The Callarino ordered a scrubbing of the city streets, paying urchins and vianomae to scrub soot from the marble columns of the walks and galleries, to shovel and scrub dung from the cobbles, to wash and paint over the graffiti of the University Quarter so that Navola would gleam for the Parl's arrival. Quadrazzo Amo was filled with a new stage for a performance of *Erostheia,* as well as *The Mule and the Merchant, The Boy at the Keyhole,* and a new comedy by Maestro Zuzzo, called *Cinezzia,* about seven merchants besotted of a young maid.

And of course, as this was Navola, there were contracts and promises to be signed and stamped and filed with the guild litigi. My father was paying a great dowry to the Parl, and there were other terms as well, favorable to Merai and Navola, promises of untaxed trade through Navola's port, promises of new loans for the Red City's coffers, promises of free and untaxed roads and bridges for Navolese goods as they crossed Merai on their way to the passes of the Cielofrigo and the northern lands of Wustholt, and of course there was the land route to Cheroux. Free passage as well along the silk and horse routes that led to Chat and eventually to Xim.

Maestri litigi from the Universita da Merai were on hand to negotiate for the Parl against our own Navolese maestri, ensuring that the drafted agreements would be ironclad. And then there were notari and numerari there to make the final letterings of the agreements, and make all of the necessary copies for filing with the legal guilds.

Our quadrae were full of arriving guests. The Callarino was present, bowing, making proclamations as if he ruled Navola and not my father. Three days of feasting were declared. Barrels of wine were sprung on the streets, offered to anyone who could bring a cup. Goblets of gold were offered as prizes for the strongest men in the city, the most beautiful women, the finest poetry . . .

Celia, though she was not royalty in name, was more than royalty in stature.

But amid all this warmth of wedding preparation and the imminent arrival of the Parl, Celia was a rageful fata.

Cold as she had been before, it was now in earnest and I could sense the difference in her every word and movement. There was no hint of another version, no tease of her quick and mischievous mind peeking out from behind faccioscuro.

When I gazed upon her beauty, now there was nothing but contempt. Peel away a layer of her hidden mind and the next was just as rageful. Layer after layer, all of Celia, to her core, was nothing except disgust for me. Her gaze did not take me in, her ears did not hear my words. I was as a ghost.

The preparations became fevered. I had a sense of days draining away, like blood from a man cut. Days as blood. Days as life. The life of our once true and real connection. Our relationship was draining away, and there was nothing I could do for it.

Finally, in desperation, I caught her in the quadra, seizing her arm and forcing her to look at me.

"Celia—"

She looked down at my hand as if it were a crawling roach. "Let me go, Davico" was all she said, and the words were so cold that I thought that I might have died in the snows of the Cielofrigo. My protestations strangled in my throat. She did not look at me, so much as look through me. My hand fell from her arm. Helplessly, I watched her walk away.

When I turned, I found my father watching.

"This is your doing," I said.

He shrugged, unapologetic. "You rage as a boy who has lost a bauble. It is time you became a man."

"I have my name now. I am a man."

"Your emotions control your actions. That is childish." He held up a hand to forestall my outburst. "Nai, Davico. I sympathize. I know what it is to be young, to feel those hungers. We are animals first, and to deny this is to deny our true selves. So, go to the glass window street and buy a girl."

I remembered my one encounter with one of Sia Allezzia's trained companions, and it did not appeal. One coldness in place of another.

My father read my face. "Do as you will, then. Find your solace however pleases you. Later, we will speak, and I will explain."

But we did not speak. I did not want another woman. I wanted Celia. I missed her laugh. I missed her taunts. I missed her companionship. I missed the thrill of her close by, her hand touching mine.

News came from Merai that the Lupari had at last vanquished Ciceque. Our preparations redoubled as news came from the Parl that he would arrive within days, and it was this that precipitated the open speaking of Celia's dissatisfaction.

It was to a cold dinner that we sat down, cold not in temperature, and not of repast, but icy of temperament. The candlelight glittered in Celia's eyes as she gazed across the table at me. The rage at her perceived betrayal was more than apparent, but when she spoke, she did not speak to me, but to my father. She cut into her capon, picking out the small bones.

"The Parl, I understand, is a fool," she said.

The table stilled.

"What makes you say so?" my father asked.

"Davico told me as much."

I startled. "I did no such thing."

"Nai?" She gave me a cold look. "No. That's right. You didn't. You told me he was handsome. You told me he was vital. You told me he would honor me." She made a face. "You did not say that he is deeply in debt to your family. That he holds power thanks to Navola's Lupari. That he is not even able to put down a small rebellion without help. What have I forgotten? Oh yes, he is surrounded by sycophants, and leans upon his first secretary—who is a serpent—like a crutch."

My father wiped his face with a cloth napkin, and leaned back to regard her. "You seem exceptionally informed."

Celia scowled. "Do not condescend to me."

"I would not dare." My father seemed amused. "The wrath of Celia di Balcosi is famous."

"Indeed, my lord." Cazzetta smirked. "The princess flicks poisonous barbs from her tongue."

"I will not be married away like a piece of meat," Celia said.

"Does meat marry?" Merio asked. "I hadn't heard."

Celia scowled at them all.

Ashia interceded. "What do you expect of the Regulai?" Ashia asked. "That we marry you to Davico? Your own brother?"

"We are not tied by blood," Celia pointed out.

I was surprised at Celia's words, for I had thought her disgusted with me, but Ashia wagged a finger. "Nai, child. It would do you disservice and it would do the Regulai disservice as well. The most you could aspire to within this family is concubine."

"You are a concubine," Celia pointed out.

"I am sfaccita," Ashia said. "Is that what you wish for yourself? To become a slave? After all that the Regulai have given you, would you make yourself a slave to them? Do you aspire to so little?"

"What do you care, sfaccita?" Celia shot back.

My father laid a hand upon Ashia's arm, stilling her. "Ashia is saying that I made a promise to your father. An oath that I would care for you as I care for mine own and I would find a match worthy of us."

"A fool?" Celia protested. "That is my worthy match?"

Cazzetta made a hiss of disappointment. "Sfai, Celia. I thought you sharp as a dagger. Where are your wits?"

"Perhaps you did not school her as well as you thought," my father said.

"It is not I who failed," Cazzetta said. "I teach poison and facciolegge. Merio teaches politics."

Merio waved a hand of dismissal. "I did not fail, lord. She has knowledge. It is not my fault she refuses to use it."

Celia glared around at the table. "You will not shame me," she said. "You match me with a weak man, in a weak kingdom, beset by enemies. His only value is that Merai is so deeply in debt to you that if he falls, your bank falls with him."

My father laughed at that. "It is not so dire as that, sia."

My father seemed unconcerned by her knowledge of us, but I was astounded at how much she divined of us without being told, how closely she observed her surroundings. I had no time to linger on this thought for Celia turned on me.

"And you, Davico? Do you truly wish to see me sent to the bed of Merai?"

"I—" I stuttered. "He is not—not unpleasing to the eye."

She huffed.

"The kingdom is wealthy," I said. "They have good farmland. They have mines. They control trade. There is wealth there—"

"Yes yes. That is what you Regulai care about. Money. Navisoli here, navilunae there. Always the money. Always protecting your investments. I thought better of you, but you're di Regulai after all." She turned to my father. "And you. You say you honor your promise to my father, while sending me to the bed of a man even your sfaccita"—she said the word harshly so that Ashia's eyes narrowed—"even your slave would despise. The sfaccita honors you because you are a bull. And yet the Bulls of the Regulai send me, the girl they call *daughter,* to the bed of a calf."

"Sia Celia." My father wiped his mouth on a cloth napkin. "You misunderstand."

"I think not."

"I promised your father to place you well. You go to a man with lands and influence."

"And no sense in his pretty head at all! He needs di Regulai to save him from his money troubles and his rebellious nobles. We provide him with troops. With spies. With gold. And now you send me. What do we not do for this silly man?"

"Enough!" My father slammed the table with the palm of his hand, making glass and cutlery rattle and making us all jump. "Do you think, for even a moment, that I do not know the measure of the man we send you to? Your future husband's faults . . . do you think I do not know them? Do you think I do not understand them completely? Do you think I do not weigh and measure every aspect of him?" He glowered across at Celia, his dark eyes sharp as a hawk's. "Do you think for one moment that you see something I do not?"

Celia started to retort, but suddenly I saw it. I saw it all. I had understood only a portion of my father's intentions. I felt my world tilting, as if I were falling into a pit, falling and falling and struggling to orient as I finally saw the full shape of my father's plan.

"The Parl will be devoted to you," I said.

"I care not!" Celia slammed down her fork, rattling on the plate. "I care not for this so-called man!"

"Ai." Ashia smiled approvingly at me. "There. Davico sees. At last." The others were nodding as well. My father, Aghan Khan, Cazzetta, Merio. All of them looking at me with warm approval.

Merio raised his wine to me in toast. "Better late than never, as they say."

Celia glared around the table. "What does he see?"

Cazzetta lifted a glass of vinobracchia and toasted her. "Devonaci di Regulai da Navola means for you to rule, sia. He means for you to take the lands of Merai for yourself. Your patro wishes for you to rule as you will, with unrestrained hand and wide autonomy. He wishes not to give you to a prince. He wishes to give you all of Merai, and he expects that you will reign over the Parl with your skilled hand. The di Regulai have but one son, and he must remain in Navola. But we expect our daughter to use her wits and skill to take and rule the Parl. To take him and control him, and rule Merai completely."

Celia goggled at Cazzetta.

"As you yourself pointed out, the Parl is a fool," Ashia purred.

Celia stared around the table, her assurance lost. "But . . . but if I did such a thing . . ." Her expression hardened. "Nai. If I ruled truly, why would I not make my husband march against you? If he's besotted with me, then I would have true power. What would stop me from allying with Cheroux and marching our troops on Navola? From burning away all our debts? From crushing you entirely?"

"Do you truly hate us so?" my father asked.

Celia looked away.

My father took a sip of wine. "It's true, I suppose. You could attempt to smash the Regulai if you wished." He set the glass back upon the table, spun its stem between his fingers, throwing light from the cut crystal.

"That is always the difficulty of truly worthy allies. An ally who is truly valuable is also truly powerful. Powerful enough to withhold their power, or even to betray. Any ally worth having will have the ability to choose their own path, for an ally is not a slave. An ally—a true ally—chooses you. They choose you for friendship. For advantage. For reward. For shared purpose. Now." He took another sip of his wine. "If this were only about myself and your hatred for me—and I do see your hatred, Celia, do not mistake—I would not be at all surprised if you betrayed me." He glanced sideways at me. "But then, you have a brother. A brother whom you care for very much."

Celia closed her eyes. "You kept me close. You kept *us* close."

"I did."

"It was deliberate."

"Yes."

"You raised me as a daughter," she said. "You made me literate and numerate." Her gaze went to Ashia, Aghan Khan, Merio, and Cazzetta. "You taught me swordskill and accountancy and languages and poisons. You taught me the tricks of women, and the tricks of politics. You did not chain me as a prisoner in your tower as you could have; you chained me instead to Davico."

It was clear in retrospect. Not only had he honed Celia's mind and knowledge, but he had allowed our closeness to flourish. Nai, he had encouraged it. We had grown together, as the roots of plants grow entangled when they are planted in the same pot. Binds of friendship, of love, of care, of family, and at last of desire, and when that had finally flowered, he had acted. Even our shared resentment of a man who would one day, inevitably, pass—that too had likely been nurtured.

It was all finally clear.

Celia stormed out of the room, leaving us all at the table.

In the silence, Cazzetta took a sip of his wine. "Well played, Devonaci. Even by the standards of the Regulai, it is well-played."

After much searching, I found Celia alone in the gardens, pacing under the porticoes, the shadows of the columns casting lines across her pensive features. The evening had turned warm with oncoming spring, and soon it would be hot. Soon the only shelter from the heat would be these cool central gardens, with the fountains trickling and the ponds and the citrus trees blooming, and these dark shadow corners under the porticoes. She caught sight of me watching her, and waited, her expression cold.

"So this is what we are," she said bitterly. "Puppets in your father's play." She held up her arm and wiggled her fingers. "How did I not see the strings?"

"We both know my father is right."

Celia didn't seem to hear me. "To think that I believed myself blessed by his caring heart that he saw me educated as one of his household. That he was kind to me and not a despot. He taught me the same accounting methods as you, taught me the same politics, taught me the same . . . all to become one of his shrouded cards. Hidden until the last, and then used."

"We are all cards in his hand."

"He is a true Navolese. All twisty thinking and clever stratagems. And a heart as black as his gold is gleaming."

"Don't say that. He cares for you. He just does it in his own way." I did not know why I felt it necessary to defend him, and yet I found myself doing so. The son's loyalty to the father. "It isn't personal. It is his nature."

"The nature of the Navolese."

I laughed. "If that were true, I'd be better at the intrigues."

My laughter seemed to clear the storm of Celia's mood. She shook her head ruefully. "And I thought myself so clever before him." She touched my face, gently. "Ai, Davico, it's true you have little of the skill. It's why I like you so very much. You, at least, are trustworthy."

We gazed into each other's eyes and I felt a quickening of my heart as she looked up at me, her hand upon my cheek. I was taller than her, I realized. When we had first known each other, she had been the taller. I had not noticed how I had grown. How we had changed. Celia's hand fell, touched my chest, feeling my beating heart. I could not look away from her eyes, did not want to. Desire welled up within me, the lust and desire that had been suspended since that night when we had felt the dragon's power outside my father's study door. I could kiss her. I could take her. She was gazing up at me. We were bound together.

A clatter of horses arriving in the quadra made us turn, guilty, and step away. It was the Callarino and Garagazzo, arriving, dressed in finest raiment.

"The Parl arrives!" they called. "He is at the gates!"

Like an ant's nest kicked, their words threw the palazzo into a whirl. Servants running hither and thither. Guards calling out. My father and

Ashia, Merio and Aghan Khan all hurrying to their duties. Celia was pulling away from me, pulling away, leaving me . . .

I caught her arm. She turned back. Our eyes locked. In a flash she drew close. She pressed her lips to my cheek and whispered in my ear.

"Come to me tonight. After the torches die. Come to me."

Chapter 43

In deepest night, I slipped from my rooms. My family's portraits watched sternly as I stole past them like a shadow thief. Their eyes seemed to follow me: Deiamo, the Bull, my mother. Even the frescoes of the gods seemed to judge me, gazing down from the shadowed ceilings.

Below, in the courtyard, I could see a pair of our guards. They were awake, but their backs were turned to me, looking toward the quadra premia, and in any case I was as the shadows.

I moved with the chill breezes of the palazzo. I was as still as the marble of the columns, as quiet as the flagstones. I was a breath of night, nothing more. I slipped along the high gallery that ringed the garden quadra without raising notice or alarm.

There was no easy way to Celia's rooms. We were separated by an entire quadra and several guards who kept watch on the passageways that led through. I supposed that such had never been an accident, that we had been kept far apart, always. Deliberately.

Footsteps echoed. I faded behind a column. Our maid Sissia hurried across the quadra below. She came up the stairs, bearing linens for more soon-to-arrive guests. At the top of the stairs she met Demestino, one of the men who guarded my father's chambers. They exchanged low greetings. A joke, a laugh, and then she was passing by and the rustle of her footfalls covered my own as I eased along the gallery walk and Demestino's gaze followed Sissia's pretty disappearing form.

I found the door to a small receiving room and eased it open, feeling the catch of the hinges, wincing at their squeak, holding my breath, and then I was inside.

A minute later, I was out on the room's balcony and climbing. The cold stone gutter spouts made for easy purchase, familiar, just as they had been when I had been younger and driven by adolescent passion.

I was quickly up on the roofs and hurrying across them, but this time I ignored the cupolas and windows that gave light and view to the women's baths below, and continued stealthily to the far side of the palazzo to the quadra where Celia's rooms lay. Here, the drop was neither easy nor familiar. I dangled for a moment, reaching with my feet, stretching mightily, until I found purchase and dropped clumsily down upon a wide stone rail. I slipped and fell heavily from there, landing hard on the marble, wincing, fighting not to cry out, afraid that I would make noise and raise an alarm. Then, with horror, I realized that I had nearly fallen into the quadra below.

I was exomentissimo.

I lay still as shadow, waiting to see if I had made too much noise, but no alarm came. I hauled myself to my feet and peered down into the quadra. All of this garden's shapes were unfamiliar in the night. Stealthily, carefully, I moved along the shadowed colonnaded gallery, then froze. Ahead, the black shape of a guard.

He snored.

I couldn't decide if I was grateful for this laziness, or annoyed. Aghan Khan would have his head if he caught him. He snored again. Nai, I was glad. I waited, though, in case there were others, spying about the gallery and the quadra, letting the moonlight show the shadows, the air carry the scents and sounds of the inhabitants. The palazzo slept, just like the guard.

Still, I waited there for a long time, forcing myself not to rush the last distance. Nothing moved within the shadows of the colonnaded walks, nor in the gardens. And yet still I did not move. The implications of what I was doing loomed. I steeled myself. I had come too far. I would not turn back.

I made the final quiet dash to Celia's door.

My hand shook as I knocked, the barest tapping.

In an instant the door was open and Celia pulled me within.

"Were you seen?" she whispered. Her eyes were wide and bright. She wore a diaphanous sleeping gown, ethereal in the light of bedroom candles.

"Nai. No one."

Her hair was down. The promise of her body beckoned, barely hidden beneath the thin shift. Her breasts, the slope of her belly, the hint of darkness between her thighs—she pulled me to her. Soft curves pressed against me, thrilling. We held close, body to body, both of us trembling, staring into each other's eyes, each of us uncertain and yet both of us determined. By the fatas, I felt such a lust for her. It was as a hurricane, threatening to whirl through me and spirit away my mind.

Exomentissimo.

I know that you will think ill of me, but I do not care, for I have sworn to tell my truths that you may know me. I will not dissemble. This girl whom I had grown beside, whom I had seen blossom, who had been my sister in all but name—I felt such desire for her. Such explosive flame as when olive oil falls upon a bonfire and it bursts alive.

Her body pressed tighter to mine. I wanted to kiss her. To devour her. To—I did not know what I wanted to do. I wanted all of her. I wanted to steal her, I wanted to force her close to me, I wanted to drag her body up against mine. I wanted to rip her shift from her body.

But I hesitated.

The enormity of being alone with her. Alone in the silence of her sleeping chamber. Alone and without anyone to rein us back made me hesitate. It was wrong.

"We—" I broke off. "We should not."

She searched my face, anxious. "You do not want me?"

I touched my finger to her lips. "Do not say such a thing."

Though I was now suddenly determined not to go through with this act, still I wanted her. I wanted . . .

I pulled her close to me, savoring the press of her body against mine, the ache of my loins, the feel of her hips under my hands. My hands of their own accord slipping around to grip her ass and pull her close . . . By the fatas, I wanted her. I wanted her so very badly. But it could not be.

"We cannot," I said.

And yet still my hands lingered on her. "You are my sister. I—I am your brother. I have a duty to you." I forced myself to raise my hands from her hips to her waist, but I was loath to release her. Still I held her. I drew her to me, drew her head to my chest. This felt more brotherly. Her unbound hair was like silk beneath my hand. "I have a duty to you."

Celia let out a small sigh. She clutched me and then I felt her laugh, a small laugh of defeat, a surrender to the truth of our predicament.

She drew away. Then drew farther still, out of reach, leaving me with such an emptiness in my soul that I felt as if I were the Cerulea drained.

Celia went and sat upon the bed. Sighed again. She gave me a wry smile.

"Come." She patted the bed. "Sit with me."

I hesitated. She laughed with sad exasperation. "Am I so terrifying? I know . . . I know that it—*we*—cannot be. Just sit with me. Sit with your sister." She patted the bed again. I went and sat beside her, aware now not of our closeness but of the distance between us. The chasm that I had opened. Celia reached over and clasped my hand. Intertwined her fingers in mine.

"What am I doing, Davico?"

She looked so sad and despairing that it took all my effort not to embrace her once again in an attempt to comfort her.

"He is a decent enough man," I said at last. "It is a good match. You will rule him." I felt like my father or Ashia, pushing her to fulfill her duty, to play her role, to become a card in our family's hand, played to neutralize a threat and turn it to our advantage. "It's . . . I do not think you will be unhappy."

She gave a little laugh and looked away. Her shift rustled about her body. A silk so fine that royalty in Xim could not have desired better. I could see the dark points of her nipples under the fabric, pressing. I looked away, fighting my desire.

"I am . . ." She paused. "I do not want . . . *Fescata,*" she cursed softly. "It's all a tangle, isn't it?"

"It will not be so bad. Merai has its beauty. It is warmer there. There are flowers, so many flowers as you would not believe. The women wear tall shoes. Their food is strange, but it is not unpleasant. And we will write to each other. And I will visit often."

"Do not lie to me, Davico. We promised not to lie to each other."

"I will visit as often as I can."

She laughed and shook her head sadly. "That. Yes. I believe that."

For a while we sat in silence, holding hands, our fingers intertwined. A bell clanged, and other city bells as well, announcing the darkest hour of night. Time was advancing. Soon the servants would begin waking, stoking fires in the kitchens, summoning the sun and her marriage day.

"I must go."

I moved to stand but she gripped my hand and tugged me back. “No. Please. Don’t leave me. I don’t want to be alone. Don’t leave yet.” Her gaze was starved and lonely. But there was something else, something more. That hunger that I had sought to steel myself against.

“It’s dangerous. I should go, now, before the dawn.”

“It’s hours until then.”

“Still.”

“I want to show you something.” With sudden purpose, she took her candle and went to the chests that held her clothes.

“Close your eyes,” she said. “Turn away.”

I did as she asked, and soon heard silks rustling. The shift and rustle of garments.

“I’m ready,” she said. “You may look now.”

I turned. My heart tightened.

Celia glimmered with pearls and diamonds in a gown of elegant white. The dress she would wear on the morrow when she went to the catredanto to make her vows before Amo and was at last married to the Parl. The skirts fell in layers, accenting her hips and her tiny waist, the bodice accenting the rise of her breasts. Around her throat was a white silk lace, adorned with pearl and diamond. It stood stark against the dark luster of her skin.

“Do you like it?” she whispered.

I swallowed, unable to speak. Nodded. “You . . . are beautiful.”

She took a step toward me. “Do you truly wish for me to go to him?”

She had pulled back her hair. The plunge of the gown showed the hollow of her throat, the cleft of her breasts. It hugged her waist. Accented the flare of her hips. She looked like a queen. She took a step closer.

“Do you truly wish me to lie with him? To go to his bed?”

“Celia . . .”

Another step closer.

“He will be a good husband—”

She touched her fingers to my lips. “I do not want him.”

“Sister—”

“Brother,” she whispered. Her lips were close, upturned, questing. Inviting. The power of her gown was as a drug. It fired my senses more even than her sleeping shift. The softness of fabric, the sight of her, as a woman, prepared for another man.

I had tried to steel myself against her, but now I was more aware of her than ever. Aware of the silence in the room. Of our privacy.

"Davico?"

She reached up to stroke my cheek. I closed my eyes to avoid her gaze, but I could not help but lean into her touch, could not help but place my hand upon her waist, to draw her closer, to feel her breathing. To know her beneath the beadwork and gems and jewelry, to know her, to feel her breath quicken for me.

Celia.

Her lips found mine.

How to describe the first kiss of love? That trembling terror and joy of another desirous of you? One kiss became two. Two became many. Became frenzied, frantic with desire. Kissing lips and cheeks and brows and throats. We sought to devour one another. She was whispering in my ear and our embrace was no longer that of brother and sister.

"Please," she whispered in my ear. "Please don't make me go to him . . . Not without knowing you."

I could feel my heart pounding. Could hear the blood in my ears. My hands . . . I was trembling, shaking as if I were full of palsy, but it was desire, a desire so wild that it threatened to overwhelm me. I could not hold her enough. I could not draw her close enough.

Celia's eyes were wide and yearning, her breath fast and hot, and suddenly it was as if a dam had burst. We fell upon one another, full of hunger, full of bestial need. I fumbled with her dress, pulling at it, yanking at the embroidered loops of her bodice, her helping me, both of us panting and desperate. Our mouths found each other's again. Kissing. Her lips soft. Her breath sweet. Her tongue flicking to taste mine, something so intimate, the touch of tongues. Tasting, kissing, biting, suckling. I could not get enough of her. I was kissing her lips, her neck, kissing down her throat—

Her bodice opened. She clutched me to her, pushing my head lower, pressing my lips to her revealed breasts. I found her hardened nipples, sucked at them, heard her gasp. She pulled me tight to her breasts, urging me to suck and tease, to bite, to lick, to consume her . . . and then she was dragging me up to meet her eyes once again, and we gazed into one another's eyes anew and there was only desire, mirrored.

Our hands tore at each other's clothes. I found her laces, fumbling with them, pulling at them, drawing them out, dragging open her dress even as she was fumbling with the laces of my breeches, and then our clothes were falling to the floor and we were naked, gasping, our skin touching, our skin alive. Her hand gripped my root and I was hard, shaking with pleasure as her fingers played upon me, sending bolts of sensation. She knelt before me. She looked up once, wicked-eyed, and then she was upon me, licking, sucking, swallowing me, root and soul, just as Adivo had depicted the fatas pleasuring Caliba. I was transported.

Feeling her hands upon my shaft, her mouth soft and wet upon me, her tongue lashing my length. She was mewling, needy, almost desperate upon me as she sucked, moaning with lust, and then she was up again, her lips slick with her spit and my own essence, and we were kissing again.

We fell together upon the bed. I pushed apart her thighs and dove between them, hungry, starved, desperate to taste her as she had tasted me, to know her, to find her essence. I was as an animal, as a beast, and I thought then that I understood the drawings in my father's library better than I had ever known, for we were not man and woman anymore, but beasts—nai, demons—for pleasure. We were lust incarnate.

I licked, I tasted, I plunged my tongue deep into her. I loved her scent, her taste, the slick feel of her cunt on my tongue, I wished that I could devour her, I could not have enough. I feasted upon her. Her fingers tangled in my hair urging me on, and then she pulled my mouth hard against her sex, moaning. The folds of her sex opened as a flower, and I was as a bee, desperate for nectar. I found the nub of her, the hard knot of a woman's pleasure, and worked it with my tongue. Kissed it. Licked it. Worshipped over it as she moaned and pulled me tight to her. Her thighs closed around me. There was only her. There was only this moment. I slipped fingers into her, pressing into her wet slickness. Her thighs opened. She arched—

"Oh!" she cried. Her hips rose to take more, greedy and gasping, taking my fingers, riding against them, and then I was atop her, and she was guiding my cock between her thighs. Both of us panting, both of us desperate. My cock was harder than iron. It felt nearly a weapon and I could not think for my desperation to find her sheath.

The feel of her flesh was dizzying, as if I'd drunk a barrel of wine, I was drunk with her, with the feel of her, and her eyes were drunk as well upon me, wide and needy. She began to pull me into her, guiding me into her slick wet folds. Her hands clasped my buttocks. We stared into one another's eyes as I slid into her, inch by inch. I felt myself engulfed.

"Ai," she panted. "Ai. Yes. That. Yes." Pulling me deeper.

I felt a resistance. Her maidenhead, I knew, and in that moment, I hesitated. I had heard the stories that a woman's first time was different than a man's, I did not wish her to feel—

With a groan she pulled me hard into her, and there was suddenly no resistance, and I was deep inside her and we were both staring at each other wide-eyed. We were joined. Joined completely. My breath was gone. She was beautiful.

"Slowly," she whispered. "Slowly."

It was all I could do to restrain myself. Already I felt the power of my seed building within me, but I did not want it to end. I fought not to lose myself. I held myself still, our bodies slick and close. I gazed into her eyes, astounded at the depth of feeling there, the wonder and desire and love.

She drew me down to her and we kissed, tender.

When my friends had spoken of the act of love, this was not what they had spoken of. We kissed again and then she was kissing my cheeks, my eyelids, my forehead as I fought to hold still within her. And then her hands strayed down my flanks and took hold of my ass. She pulled me closer, deeper.

"I'm—"

"Shh. Slowly."

The crisis passed. We clutched together, moving as one, our bodies twined and urgent. Now it was too late, we had done the deed, we were one, joined with as much tenderness as Scuro and Erostheia, as much lust as Caliba and his fatas. We were love and lust, we were separate and yet we were one. We became a creature of pleasure, a single greedy desperate beast seeking pleasure. I began thrusting harder, I could not control myself, I was too full of need. I felt her fingers at our joining, playing, driving herself to greater pleasure as I thrust into her. The wave was cresting.

"Celia. Celia. I cannot—"

"Yes! Ai! Now, Davico! Now!"

I felt her womanhood clench around me. It was too much. I thrust into her with a cry and felt her pulling me even deeper. My body shook with release. My seed poured from me, the pleasure coming in waves. Her womanhood clenched and seemed to milk me, and then her own crest took her and she arched, crying, "Davico! Davico! Davico!"

The pleasure seemed to go on and on, slowly ebbing, finally releasing us, the high tide of Caliba's lust retreating, revealing the shining diamond sands of Erostheia's love, a love so generous, a gratitude and kindness so deep that I was left as Celia's slave, so in wonder was I.

We lay close, our bodies twined. At last, I moved to lift my weight from her, but she held me close still, pulling me down, kissing me gently, embracing, only letting me free of her jealously, my cock slipping from her body, used, slick, expended. Our skin gleamed with sweat in the candlelight. Celia looked at me bemusedly.

"Celia—"

"Hush." She kissed me gently. "I love you."

"I think I have always loved you."

"Ci. Such a boy, still." But she was smiling when she said it. She touched her womanhood carefully, probing with her fingers.

"Are you . . . ?" I could not help but be concerned. "Did it hurt?"

"Not so much." She showed me her fingers, glistening with my spend. "And look. The young bull is virile."

The enormity of what we had done finally intruded. The sight of my seed, clinging sticky upon her fingers. "Celia . . ." I started.

But she was smiling. "Nai, Davico. It was what I wanted. I would not go to the Parl's bed without knowing you." Her expression clouded, and then became determined. "Even when I go to him, I will think of you."

"You cannot go," I said. "Not now. You cannot."

She smiled sadly at me. "That is not something we choose. This." She placed her hand upon my chest. "This is what we choose. Tomorrow I will marry, but you—you I will always love."

I was about to reply when I heard a small noise outside the door. I froze, listening.

"Davico—"

"Shh."

It had been subtle, but I did not think I had imagined it. I strained my ears, listening to the night sounds of the palazzo. I sat up and turned my ears to the door, straining. Celia sat up as well, gathering the bedclothes around her nudity.

"What is it?" she whispered.

"I . . . I don't know." I had not imagined it. I had heard something. And the sound . . . I listened hard, straining. I heard nothing more, but I was gripped with foreboding.

Something felt wrong.

I was suddenly aware of the dragon eye in the far distant library. Alive, present as ever, and yet something about it seemed strange. Malevolent.

Hungry.

I scrambled from Celia's bed and began pulling on clothes.

"What is it?" she asked.

"I don't know. Something isn't right." But it was worse than that. Something was deeply wrong. I could feel it. Feel it as a foreboding warning, a storm of evil. Hurriedly, I pulled on my breeches. Celia watched me with wide eyes, her hair disheveled, beautiful. And suddenly also small and vulnerable.

"Davico—"

"Wait."

I eased open the door and peeked outside, slipped through, letting the door slowly close behind me, hating the sound of hinges rasping. I held still in Celia's doorway, straining my eyes against the shadows, my ears against the silence. Nothing. Darkness. My breath steamed in the chill. Behind me, there was a click and the door swung open. Celia, in her nightdress. I wanted to tell her to go back inside, to stay behind, but her expression was determined. I motioned her to wait.

Was someone spying upon us? Had I been seen sneaking to her room? By a servant? A guard? Was our secret already known?

"A rat?" Celia suggested in a whisper. I waved her silent, still straining my eyes—

There.

A man, tucked into the shadow niche of a doorway, so subtle as to be part of the palazzo itself.

Cazzetta.

Of course.

I knew without needing to see his face, and as soon as I saw him, I knew that all our secrets were lost. A part of me felt ashamed at how I had gone against my family, and wished I could sink into the flagstones. I wished I could run away. But still, another part of me was determined not to hide. If I was a man, then I would face the wrath of my choices, without apology. I had chosen.

And yet Cazzetta made no move to remonstrate with me for my transgressions with Celia. He did nothing.

"Cazzetta?"

I took an uncertain step toward him, peering into the doorway, wondering if perhaps my eyes deceived me, a trick of my mind, a phantom of my guilt. I took another step closer.

"Cazzetta?"

Still he did not move.

I took another step, straining to see. Gasped.

Metal glinted. Eyes gleamed, wide and surprised.

That is what I still remember: that first sight of Cazzetta, tucked into the shadows, but not by his choice. His eyes were white in the moonlight, but black blood ran from his mouth. He hung from the door like a suit of clothes. A dagger had been rammed through his mouth with such force that it had pinned his head to the door.

His sword was still in its sheath.

Behind me, Celia gasped. I unpinned the dagger from Cazzetta's mouth and slowly let him sink to the ground. I felt a sense of unreality. Cazzetta was dead. Cazzetta was murdered. In our own palazzo. In silence.

It seemed impossible. Yet his corpse lay before me.

"Who could have done this?" Celia whispered.

I shook my head. My hands were shaking. Something was terribly wrong. Cazzetta had been following me, I was sure. He had stalked me as a cat stalks a mouse when I went to Celia, and yet someone else had stalked him. And had caught him as he spied upon us.

I could picture it—Cazzetta, never one to be fooled easily, watching me steal toward Celia's bedchambers. But someone else had followed him. And he'd been distracted by spying on me, and so his murderer had ambushed him.

But still, it was hard to credit. When had Cazzetta ever been surprised? His sword was still sheathed. His daggers were still up his sleeves.

A cold realization washed over me. "He trusted them."

He had trusted his murderer. And that could only mean—

"We're betrayed," Celia said, with conviction. "It means we are betrayed."

Chapter 44

A shout echoed up from the courtyard below, followed by the clash of steel. We ran to the balcony. Aghan Khan and some of our household guard were pelting across the quadra, disappearing under the porticoes. More shouts rang out. Steel clashed where they had disappeared.

"To me!" Aghan Khan shouted. "To me!"

"Alarm! Alarm!" A bell began to ring. Clanging and harsh, tolling doom. *"Alarm! Alarm!"*

The call came from all corners of the palazzo as we woke to our danger.

I wanted to run for my rooms, for my sword, but they were far across the palazzo.

"Get dressed! Get your sword!" I shouted to Celia as I stripped Cazzetta's own sword from its sheath. I hefted the blade, trying to get the feel of it. Wishing I had something more than breeches and a bare chest. A chain shirt at least, a buckler, anything to protect.

Servants were stumbling sleepy-eyed out into the courtyard, emerging onto balconies. More steel clashed. The sounds of battle came from the quadra premia, along with bellowing shouts. A man started screaming like a wounded animal, then suddenly went silent. A second later, the bell stopped ringing.

Celia returned wearing her riding breeches and carrying her sword. "Who is attacking? Is it over?"

The silence was eerie. "I don't know."

I didn't like the new silence that was upon us. "Go back to your room. Lock your doors."

Celia spat in disagreement. "I will not hide like some mouse."

New clashing steel forestalled argument, along with hooves clattering across stone. "Stay close." We ran for the sound of Aghan Khan's shouted orders, through a passage toward the garden quadra. As we rounded a corner, we stumbled across our maid Sissia, lying like a rag doll upon the tiled floor. Blood everywhere. Gutted. I froze, staring down at her body.

The battle sounded as if it were farther from us, in the quadra premia, and yet there were bodies here. Cazzetta. Sissia.

"To me! To me!" I heard my father calling out. "Hold the gates!"

More and more of our people were pouring out of their rooms, coming downstairs and streaming across the gardens below. Servants. Guards. Guests. Many with swords or daggers, a few even with iron pokers. Celia and I ran down to join them. Our guards were gathering together, armor half-buckled. I suddenly missed Polonos and Relus.

Aghan Khan appeared through an arched passage, bloody but alive. "To me!" he shouted. A quattore of horsemen came crashing into the gardens, fully armored, their steel flashing. I gasped with relief at the sight of them. They bore the wolf upon their breastplates. The Lupari! We had allies!

Except they did not slow their steeds.

They rode down upon Aghan Khan.

He fell beneath their horses as they came charging for us. Everyone scattered. I grabbed Celia. We lunged over planter urns and a low wall, diving for safety under the shadows of a portico. The Lupari circled back upon Aghan Khan. Astoundingly, he was up again, staggering, still with his weapon—

A Lupari swung his sword. Aghan Khan's head spun from his body.

I dragged Celia deeper into the shadows of a side passage that led to the kitchens. More horsemen surged into the quadra, circling and hunting for our guards, chasing them as they scattered. Shouts and steel echoed. Throughout the palazzo, battles raged, knots and clots of Lupari battling our guard, appearing and disappearing from our view.

More Lupari came clanking through a passage, these ones on foot. Our servant Gianna exploded from hiding behind a decorative urn and ran from them, pelting toward us. A soldier leapt and seized her. He stripped her garments from her body, shouting with lust. Her honor knife flashed. The soldier cursed, and then Gianna was falling, her throat slit. She hit the marble not far from us, staring up at us where we hid in the shadows. Her mouth worked but no sounds came out. Her eyes stared at us. She died.

"The library," I whispered. "The secret passage."

Celia nodded. We waited until there was a break of opportunity and bolted across the garden quadra and up the stairs. At the top, we found Ashia. She was slumped against a wall, a sword in her guts, her gowns bunched around her, drenched with blood. Her honor knife lay beside her, alongside the man who had killed her. He had stabbed her, but she had paid him back before she died. Her eyes stared at nothingness, but then to my surprise she stirred. Her head turned. Her eyes focused upon me.

"Run," she rasped. "Run, Davico." Blood trickled from her lips.

"Who is it? Who attacks us?"

She slumped dead.

"Davico!" Celia cried, pointing. I turned and ran to where she stood. Down in the quadra premia, dozens and dozens of men were charging through the main gates. More and more. The fortified gates were flung wide and soldiers were pouring through, straight into the heart of the palazzo. I recognized the colors of the Lupari, and—

"Merai," Celia said grimly.

I stared, struck stupid. It was true. The blue and gold of Merai. It made no sense, and yet, even as I watched, a figure appeared at the gate. The Parl. Roulait. Strutting in his young and childish way. I felt such a rage then that I made to leap the balcony, but Celia dragged me back.

"Nai, Davico! We must run! It is lost!"

All around us, men and women were dying. My family. Our guards. Our servants, many of whom I had known all my life. They were being hacked down. I stared at the butchery, frozen. Struck dumb with horror and confusion. It made no sense—

Celia yanked my arm. "It is lost! Davico! It's lost!" She yanked again, harder, shaking me from my stupor. "We must run!"

We ran.

We ran, gasping, back to the garden quadra and up the stairs, up toward the library and the hidden passage there. Cazzetta, even if he was dead, had taught me the way of it. Too, I thought, there was the dragon eye. I could feel it calling to me. Could feel its soul flaring as people died. There was power there. There was vengeance.

An armored soldier emerged from a corridor, barring our way. "The princeling!" he shouted. He brought his sword to guard.

His cry echoed through the palazzo, and was repeated. *"The princeling! The princeling!"*

Another pair of soldiers appeared, dashing down the hall to join their friend. All wore heavy armor and the sigil of the Lupari. All held sword and dagger.

I stepped back, feigning confusion, lowering Cazzetta's sword. Stepped back again, keeping my own dagger concealed. "Ai! Lupari!" I cried. "Good! You must help—"

They did not even allow me to finish my ruse, they simply lunged at me. I was only saved because they thought me too simple to fight. I stepped past the first one's lunge and brought up my dagger, ramming it into the gap in the side of his plate. Celia was beside me, her blade flicking. I heard her man die, and then I was kicking my own opponent off my dagger. The last man stepped back, wary. We circled him. He watched us like a viper hoping for an opening, but he was too smart to try us by himself, and so he let us circle past him. Behind us, his shouts echoed. "The princeling! I've found him! The princeling! To me! To me!"

"They mean to kill you," Celia panted.

"They mean to kill us all."

But it made no sense. Why had Merai turned upon us? How had Merai bought the Lupari? It was all a jumble in my mind. Merai had been about to secure greater loans, a great dowry, the alliance of Navola. Had they come here with enough troops not simply to act as honor guard, but as invaders? It seemed impossible. They could not hope to—

"The Callarino," I realized, feeling sick. "He has made alliance with Merai."

I could hear the soldier still shouting and following us, but we made a new turn and he went wrong. We hurried up the last flight of marble stairs, headed for the library as I tried to understand what had occurred.

It was as a game of cartalegge. All the cards I had not seen, that we had not seen, all coming into play at once, all of them turned from allies' hands against us, all of them laid together, king, knight, castello, horse, and assassin. And all of them falling to the table without so much as a hint of warning.

We had been played. My father had been played. This, more than anything, terrified me.

Ahead, the library doors loomed. We slammed up against them.

Locked.

I wanted to scream frustration. Of course they were locked. Everything was falling apart. I tried not to let despair overwhelm me. My father had a key, but I did not know where he was. Cazzetta had a key, of a certainty, but his corpse now lay far across the palazzo and too many soldiers stood between. I pounded the door with frustration.

I could feel the dragon eye on the far side of the door. Could feel it pulsing. Could feel its pleasure at the bloodshed. I wanted it. I wanted it to do something. I had a feeling that if only I could touch it, it could somehow help. It had power.

Celia rattled the doors, trying to move the unmovable. "Why don't you have a key?" she cried.

We hacked at the doors with our swords, but they were far too strong, well-reinforced after the last attack. We wasted precious time there, wishing for that which could not be had. To have reality itself somehow bend to our prayers and make the doors not be locked. Celia pressed her back to the doors, casting about.

"What about the tower?" she said. "If we get to the tower, we can go out through the bank, above them all. You have that key."

"In my rooms."

We started in that direction, but a pair of men came clattering into the hall. "Ai! Our princeling!" one said, grinning.

I pushed myself away from the library doors and lifted my blades. Celia came to stand beside me. We were trapped—

The roofs! If we could simply defeat this pair before us, we could climb out a balcony, we could be atop the roofs and from there to the women's baths, through those windows, into the baths, then through the servants' passages . . . with luck, it could be done.

If we could kill these two.

"This must be the one who poked a hole in Mattreo's belly," one said.

"And cut Vinnetto's throat," the other said.

These ones would not be surprised by our swordskill. They moved cautiously. Experienced, careful, hardened men. I lunged at one, trying to drive him close to the other to tangle him, but he backed instead.

The other lunged for me and was only prevented from skewering me by Celia's own flashing blade.

"Well," the one said, as they circled, "the pups have teeth."

"And here I heard the Regulai pup had no skill with a sword."

They attacked again. Celia again defended my flank. A sword tore my shirt though.

"The girl won't save you, boy."

"She might delay us if you give her to us, though," the other leered. "Maybe we give her a little poke."

"I'll give her a little poke in a second," said the first.

"Well, there's pokes. And then there's *pokes.*"

Celia hissed at them and made her own lunge, but they were too quick. They were Lupari.

"I think I'll like poking you," the first Lupari said.

Throughout the palazzo the clash of steel and the cries of the dying continued to ring out, but here, before the doors of my father's library, we were alone.

I could feel the dragon behind me. Just beyond the doors. I could feel its power. I felt for it with my mind, trying to . . . draw it to me. To beg its help. To unlock whatever power lay within it. I didn't know why I did so, didn't know what I hoped to attain. I did it out of desperation. It was there, waiting, another sort of locked door. And there was a key. I knew there was a key. The dragon's power would come, would save us—

The soldiers made another play at us and we beat them back.

"Maybe we'll poke you both," the Lupari said. "The princeling would look good on my cock, I think. Maybe I'll make you both take a good poking."

"Maybe we'll poke you!" Celia lunged.

The Lupari parried easily. "Maybe I'll fuck your skull, girl."

It was obvious that they were not serious. They did not press the attack. They did nothing that gave us advantage. They were biding their time, knowing that eventually Celia and I would tire, and that more of their comrades would arrive. I tried again to reach the dragon eye as the Lupari continued to play at the edges of our defense.

"If you surrender, we'll go easier on you."

"Liars," Celia said.

They both grinned. "Worth a try."

They were like wolves truly. Content and patient, knowing that they had us. Like a pack knowing there was no escape for a deer they pursued. Relaxed, easy, confident. The hunt was theirs. Soon they would feed. And there was nothing Celia or I could do about it.

"Which do you want, Avo?" the one said. "The girl's ass? Her cunt? Or her mouth?"

"She has a pretty mouth."

Celia bared her teeth. "I'd bite your cock off."

The Lupari laughed. He made a swift pass with his sword. His dagger flicked for her and nearly caught her. If it had been me, I would have been dead, but she was quick and the Lupari backed off.

"I think the princeling might have a nicer mouth," the other said. "He seems more like a willing bitch."

"We can train them to share."

The Lupari made a lunge at me. I beat back his sword, but as I did, I backed against the library door and nearly failed to keep him from gutting me. I realized they'd been maneuvering us. They'd taunted and joked and threatened like thugs, but all that time they had actually been circling and pressing, giving us less and less room to fight. Unconsciously we'd been giving ground to the professionals, not even realizing it.

The wood of the door pressed hard against my back. The Lupari grinned, seeing that I had at last realized our predicament. Celia seemed to comprehend the ruse as well, for in a flurry of attacks she went for them, beating them back a little. I tried to join her, but all our attacks were for naught. They gave a little ground. They defended themselves carefully. They made no mistakes.

I wished that I could do something, anything. Suddenly, in my rage, I felt the dragon with me, seeming to whisper for blood, filling me with a sort of new strength, or at least resolve. I was not powerless. Even if I were to lose this battle, I could still make them pay dearly for their victory.

"I swear by Scuro that I will slay one of you," I said. "Though I may die doing so, I will take one of you with me to Scuro's darkness. This I swear. By Scuro, I will make an offering of you. I will not make the journey to darkness alone."

At this, their smiles faded slightly.

Even an unskilled peasant could kill when he cared nothing for his own survival. I could make good on my threat, and they saw it. A warrior who cares not for survival, but simply to take another to the grave is a dangerous man indeed. The suicidal are sometimes difficult to counter.

"So." I feinted again. "Who will join me in death?"

I could feel the power of the dragon, just on the other side of the door. I could feel it watching us. Could feel its approval at my words. The willingness to war until the last breath, to never surrender—

The Parl came striding up the stairs, flanked by soldiers in the blue and gold of Merai. His armor was splashed with blood and his sword dripped with it, but he was as composed as he had been after our wild ride to that rugged hilltop of Merai. Handsome, smiling, alive. Behind him, his first secretary, Dellamont, came, the man's own armor spattered with gore.

Roulait came to a stop. In his armor, he looked less a boy and more a commander, a leader of men. His eyes were almost pitying as he gazed upon me.

"Yield, di Regulai."

"Ti matra fescata," I said. "Why would I yield to you? So that you can kill me freely? I will not."

He gave me a pitying look. "It is lost. You are lost. But"—he paused, glancing from me to Celia—"you can still end this with honor."

"By giving myself to you like a goat to slaughter?"

"Nai. By saving this sister you love so very much. You can save yourself, even."

"Why should I believe a villain and liar like you?"

"Believe or not." He shrugged. "My archers will be here in a moment, and after that, all things will end the same, but with more blood."

"Why have you betrayed me? I trusted you."

"You have to ask?" He wiped the blood from his sword, eyed the edge, frowning at something he saw there as he held it to the light. "You, my trusting little princeling, thought you could take my kingdom with a cheap bed bauble." He sighted his sword down his arm, aiming the tip at Celia. "Pretty enough, but a bed bauble, nonetheless."

"I would have given up anything for her!"

"Which you now have, you poor trusting wretch. Did you truly think a pretty girl from fallen nobility would blind me to the true aims of the Regulai?"

"But I spoke true! We sought to make alliance!"

"Well, yes." He sighed. "You, poor Davico, speak true. Facciochiaro, you. Too chiaro. A lamb amongst wolves." He went back to examining the blade. "It's nicked," he complained to Dellamont. "You said it was blue steel, it should not nick."

"You fought Devonaci di Regulai," Dellamont said. "You think his sword would not be a match?"

"I want it."

Dellamont nodded affably. "It will hang above your throne."

The Parl turned his attention back to me and Celia. "Of course you spoke true, Davico. But di Regulai . . . Ai, your father is a different beast. Well," he amended, studying the nick in his sword again. "He was."

My stomach felt hollow. I thought I would collapse, my string to Amo cut. I think perhaps that I had known my father was dead. Of course he must have been. Aghan Khan had fallen. Ashia was murdered. Cazzetta was dead. And yet . . . somehow, my mind had played tricks with me, hiding this truth.

The Parl was still speaking. "Your father sought to dominate me, and dominate Merai, just as he dominates—dominated—Navola. I am not some cow to yoke at a plow, to be mounted by the Regulai Bull. Nor are the Navolese, it seems."

Another man was climbing the stairs, a man in rich velvet. Wearing the red robes of the Callarino.

"Ai," the Callarino said. "Here we are. Just one last door between myself and my sigil."

More men were following him. Men with iron bars, ready to pry the library doors off their hinges. I felt a glimmer of hope but tried not to show it. If they would but open the library, the dragon eye lay beyond. I did not know what it might do, but I could feel it waiting there, expectantly. I could feel its hunger.

If only they would open the doors for me.

"You made alliance with Merai," I said to the Callarino, stalling. Trying to see how to gain access to the eye. "You made alliance, against your own people."

"Against the Regulai, anyway."

I remembered my father smiling at the petty rages of the Callarino. How unbothered he had been. Years ago, I had wanted to hide under a desk when he arrived raging. To seek to assuage, to run, to hide, but my father had manipulated the man with ease. He had thought the dog well-leashed. Everyone had. My father. Merio. Cazzetta. No one had taken him seriously. But I had been right to be afraid.

"So this is how you entered the city in force," I said to the Parl. "The Callarino welcomed you."

"He even loaned the aid of the Lupari. Although"—the Parl considered—"General Sivizza was more than happy to support. He has little appetite for foreign adventures. He likes his Navolese boys and his Navolese wines. War is for the young, he likes to say."

"And you . . . you snuck your men amongst ours? You cut us down, and then held the doors for the rest?"

"Ci, Davico." The Callarino looked askance. "Think! I tried to infiltrate your palazzo once. It almost worked." He made a face. Touched his scarred cheek. "But not quite. You were a little too quick, and I had to take a mark to throw off suspicion. I knew your father was surely too wise to be tricked twice. So, I had to find another way to play the assassin's card."

"Who?"

He smirked. "You cannot guess?"

I stared at him, blank. A servant? Someone angry at us? Someone who had killed Cazzetta, someone deadly. Yet I could think of no one.

Dellamont sighed. "It's astounding that Devonaci thought this one could possibly succeed him. The boy is as simple as a touched beggar in the quadrazzo."

More men came clattering up the stairs. The archers that the Parl had promised. The Parl glanced from them to me. "So, Davico. Your time is finished. Save your sister. Surrender. Let us end this conflict. I swear that you will be treated honorably."

"I do not believe you."

"Ci. Your family is broken. There is no need for further bloodshed."

The Callarino scowled impatiently. "Take him. Finish this."

The Parl held up a hand, forestalling him. "Davico? Is this truly how we will end things?"

The Callarino motioned to the men with their axes and pry bars. They advanced on me and Celia. We retreated slowly, our surrounding circle moving with us. The Callarino's men started hacking at the door. We all watched. I fought not to show my one hope. My one slim hope. Beyond the door, the dragon eye pulsed with life. A great roaring power, seething to be unleashed. Baited alive by the bloodshed.

I had but to delay.

I wasn't sure exactly what I would do when the door opened, but suddenly, I knew, knew with certainty that if I could but place my hand upon it, I could triumph. With each blow of the axes, as they shattered through the carvings, I could feel the dragon's power flare. It was a wonder that no one else could sense it. The power of it. Our blood was joined. The dragon and me. If we could become one . . .

"What is your offer?" I asked as the men hacked at the door. "For our surrender?"

The Parl shrugged. "Lay down your weapons."

"With what guarantee?"

He glanced at the Callarino, at Dellamont. "I suppose . . ." He laughed. "None." And with that he waved to his archers. "Take them."

"No!"

I lunged forward, my sword flashing. It all happened so quickly. I saw the Parl's look of surprise as I came at him. He brought up his sword just in time to parry. He fell back and his men rushed forward. I was fast. I took a blow to the arm, but the Meravese had been so surprised that it was only the flat. I felt a pommel crash against my ribs, and yet still I came on. The Parl stumbled back before me, and now the Callarino was there as well—they were both there. The knot of men was too close for the archers and I was fast.

By the fatas, I was fast.

It was as if Aghan Khan himself guided my sword arm. As if his spirit worked through me. I knew how the men must attack. Knew their movements before they made them. My sword met theirs, parried blades, struck back. Quick as an asp, I struck. I drew blood. A man fell. Another, but they were all around me. I fell beneath their weight. I fell to my knees as a man slammed into me from behind and dragged me down. I could smell the man's breath, heavy with onions. I felt for my dagger. Hands seized my wrists. Cold steel fell across my throat. I froze.

The Parl, Dellamont, and the Callarino recovered their composure. From the corner of my eye, I saw Celia struggling in the grip of more soldiers. She had wounded one as well; his guts were strewn upon the marble, making her captors slip and stumble as they dragged her over.

"Drop your blade," the Lupari said quietly to me, his razor edge across my throat.

"Kill me," I rasped. "Kill me so that I may go to Scuro with word of your treachery." I glared at the Callarino. "You will live reviled. You have poisoned Navola. You will be cursed."

The Callarino looked bored. "Is that your final curse? I had hoped for better."

Celia was thrown to her knees beside me. A soldier held a knife to her throat as well. She was struggling to breathe, to move at all, but the man's grip was iron. She was looking desperately to me.

"Release your blade," my captor said again.

"Kill me," I said. "Be done with it."

I waited, expecting him to open the smile in my throat. To feel my blood gush out. But he did nothing.

"Be done with it," I said. "I curse you all."

"Be done with it?" The Callarino laughed. He and the Parl exchanged sly smiles.

"You see? Duller than the dullest knife," the Parl said.

"Sometimes, you wonder if he's di Regulai at all."

"Kill me!" I shouted. "Do it. I do not fear!" It was a lie, but I was in a rage, and I knew I was lost. "Do it!"

"Oh no, princeling. We still have uses for the Regulai." The Callarino glanced at Celia. "Perhaps we'll kill the girl though. She has no practical use."

"*No!*" I shouted as a guard raised his sword over Celia's head. "I will do anything you demand, but set Celia free."

With Celia free, I had hope. If only I could convince them. "She is nothing in your intrigues. She was a captive of my father. She is nothing to this. She is innocent."

"Ai. Our princeling cares greatly for her," the Parl said. "Perhaps she has a use."

The Callarino shot the Parl a look of disgust. "She sat with them at table," he said. "She is one of them. She must die. Rape her if you wish. Throw her to the Lupari. But she must die."

"No!" Celia protested. "Please," she entreated the Parl. "I beg of you. I was their toy for barter. That is all. Please. Spare me. I was but a card to be used at whim."

The Parl glanced at Dellamont. The adviser shrugged. "Either the girl is close to the princeling, in which case she is far too close to the Regulai, or she is a useless card who can be discarded. I don't see the difference." He shrugged again. "As our friend the Callarino prefers."

The Parl nodded, seemingly regretful. "Alas, Celia, you were raised as Davico's sister. He wrote with much affection to you. I think you are very close."

"Nai." Celia shook her head vigorously. "I was raised in his house. But I was never his sister. I was a captive, dependent upon them. What else could I do but pretend obedience? I was their captive. Of course I tried to survive amongst them as best I could. But I had no choice."

"You had no choice?" The Callarino's voice dripped disbelief. "No choice at all except to dine at table, and take lessons from their tutors, and sip their wine, and wear their finery? If she's not of the Bull then I'm a cock crowing dawn."

"I was their captive!" Celia insisted. "I did what I had to, to survive! You know nothing of what it is to be a woman. To be forced to survive under the hand of men. You know nothing of what we must bear. I was their hostage. Of course I smiled under them. How else could I survive the Regulai for years?"

"And you say you resented it?" the Parl asked.

"Of course I resented it!" She spat. "They destroyed my family!"

The Parl looked thoughtful. I felt a glimmer of hope. He shrugged to the Callarino. "Perhaps she speaks truth. She seems most truthful."

"She is Navolese," Dellamont snorted. "They always seem truthful, until they stick you."

"Well then"—the Parl drew his dagger—"why don't we have her show us?"

Chapter 45

"Show you?" Celia hesitated.

"Yes," the Parl said, impatiently. "Show us how much you resented your captivity. Show us how angry you are at the fall of your family, young sia."

A silence fell upon the crowd of soldiers, an odd anticipation. The Callarino was smirking. Dellamont was looking thoughtful. I struggled against the big guard holding me, but it was like struggling against a mountain.

"I don't understand," Celia said.

"I want to see your resentment." The Parl flipped his dagger and handed it to her hilt-first. "I want to believe it."

The guards stiffened as Celia hefted the blade. I watched closely, trying to understand her ploy. She could not possibly think to escape. Would she kill him? Take him to Scuro with her, screaming like a fata? She was fearless, and she was skilled. She had once even bested Aghan Khan. She could do it. She could take him. Bleed him like a pig, revenge us.

Celia's fingers were white upon the dagger's hilt. I prepared myself to fight when she made her move against him. I would try at least to break free of the man who held me.

"Go on," the Parl said. "Show me how you resented your captivity. Take something from your not-so-dear Davico. Take something from him that he will always hate you for taking."

"I . . . I thought you wanted him alive."

"Yes yes, alive. Of a surety." The Parl smirked. "But there are some things he will not need now. So . . . geld him. Show us how much you hate the Regulai. Geld your 'brother' for us, and I might believe you hated them all along."

Celia looked up at the man, tested the edge of the knife. "You want me to take his manhood?"

"What better way to show you hate the Regulai?"

"Celia . . ." There was something growing between Celia and the Parl that I didn't like. Some interplay of understanding. Within the library, the dragon felt it, too. It was coiling and twisting with awful anticipation.

"Celia . . ."

She didn't look at me. "What do I get in return?"

"Why should you care?" the Parl replied. "You hate the Regulai, you say. You should want to do it for free."

Celia laughed harshly. "I am still Navolese. I know when I sit at the plank."

"Celia," I said, "what are you doing?"

"Do be quiet, Davico. I am no longer your sfaccita."

She said it dismissively, as if I did not exist. She did not even look at me. Her eyes were only for the Parl.

"My . . . sfaccita?"

The world seemed to be tilting under me. Guards' hands tightened upon my shoulders. I swayed, trying to find my balance. My face felt numb. The palazzo's floor seemed to be melting beneath my knees. My ears were ringing. I stared at the people all around. Their voices tumbled over me, confused and muddy, distant, echoing. The guards. The Callarino. The Parl. I stared at Celia, dumb as a slaughtered calf, trying to comprehend.

"My sfaccita?"

"Ci, Davico." She finally deigned to turn her gaze upon me. "Ci. Don't look at me like that. Did you really think I loved you? That I loved your family?"

"But . . ." I tried to make sense of the resentment upon her face. "We made you one of us."

"Made me one of you?" Her lips twisted. "Is that what you did when you took me hostage?"

"You're my sister!"

"Do you fuck your sister?"

A gasp went up from the assembled men.

"We . . . I . . ." I stared at her, wounded. "But . . . I love you!"

I said it, and it was true, and for the briefest instant, I saw acknowledgment flicker in Celia's eyes. She knew my love was true. Of course she knew. We were too close, she and I. Closer than brother and sister. Closer than lovers. There was no secret of mine that she did not know. But in that moment, I saw her clear as well. I saw past all the masks and games of faccioscuro that she played so skillfully, to her true and constant self. And what I saw was sorrow, sorrow as deep as the Cerulea, for not only did I love her, but she loved me as well. Ai. Sia Fortuna had played an awful trick upon us, to give us love so profound that with a single glance we could know each other's hearts—and know also that it would change nothing.

"Do you remember the night your family took mine?" Her words were soft.

"I . . ."

"Your soldiers came to our palazzo in the night," she said. "We had guests that night, so our gates were open. It was late, and we were saying our goodbyes. And then your soldiers broke through with swords and pikes. A horde of those Romigliani you love to hire, screaming for our blood."

Her voice cracked. She paused, fighting to master herself. To the watchers, she was telling a story of never-forgiven wounds, proof that she played no ruse. Justification and assurance that she was my enemy. But between us, it was something else. It was a final parting. A last chance to look upon one another before we were lost to one another. One last moment of softness. Even as she spoke, the Celia I had known was disappearing. That blithe and clever and happy girl was saying goodbye, to be replaced by another girl. A stranger. Word by word, memory by memory, as Celia's voice cracked with raw emotion, the Celia who had loved me was being hidden away, swaddled and protected, muffled from this place of betrayal and hurt.

"Aghan Khan killed men I loved," Celia said, her voice hardening. "All your men did. Polonos. Relus. All those men you worshipped and laughed and shared wine with. They ran us down. They cut us down. Guards, servants, they did not care. Good people, every one of them. People who had sworn oaths to us, and we to them. People I loved died because they kept their oaths. Because they tried to protect us from you."

Her cheeks were becoming flushed and her eyes colder. Layer by layer she was swaddling herself in protective rage.

"Celia . . ." I wanted to reach out to her. To convince her not to do this to herself. To convince her there was some other way, some path through for both of us, but the Celia I had known was being smothered and a stranger was emerging—a girl capable of anathema.

"Did you think I would forget, Davico? Forget being dragged from under my bed by soldiers? Forget being dragged past the trampled bodies of my servants? My friends? Forget my palazzo burned? My sisters exiled?"

"Celia—"

"You drove us through the streets like dogs!"

I flinched. The rage was real. The hurt was real. She was no longer playing to an audience. This was Celia, in all her truth. She had been a child, and innocent, and we had shattered her world. We had wrought terror and bloodshed and pain upon her. And now she would take revenge. I tried to find words to convince her to find some other way, to create some clever plan, to turn from this awful path she was choosing, but Celia turned to the Parl.

"My family's freedom," she said. "They return to Navola. That is my price."

"Done," the Parl said.

"Done," the Callarino echoed.

"Good," Celia said. Her knuckles were white around the dagger as she turned to me. She stepped close. I tried to shy back, but the soldiers blocked my retreat.

"Hold him," she said grimly. "Hold him down."

They grabbed my shoulders and dragged me flat. "Celia! Please. No!" I tried to glimpse again the Celia I had loved, to beg her mercy, but she was entirely gone. There was no sorrow, and no hesitation, only the eyes of a bloody fata. I tried to kick but she sat upon my legs and yanked at my belt. I felt fresh horror and began to howl. All around, the guards began to hoot and urge her on.

"Ai!" the Parl laughed. "She plays for keeps, young princeling!"

I fought, bucking and trying to get free, but the guards' grip was iron. Against my will, I felt my bladder empty, terrified, as Celia yanked at the laces of my breeches.

"Look!" Celia laughed. "The princeling is pissing himself!"

All of them were laughing. Celia and the guards and the Parl and the Callarino. How had she become such a monster? More guards grabbed my legs. She was pushing me back, kneeling astride me as the men pinned me. I bucked and fought, terrified as she brought the blade between my thighs.

"Nai! Celia! Please!"

I don't know why I cried for mercy, for there was no longer mercy in her. She was possessed. There was only cruelty now. All the men were laughing and cheering. The Callarino was watching wide-eyed, his hand at his mouth, either shocked or delighted to discover someone willing to do more violence than even he could contemplate.

Cold steel touched my eggs. Played across my root. I felt it small, shriveled, wet with piss.

"One egg or two?" she asked, playing to the men. "Or should I take his whole little root?"

"Celia!"

She cocked her head. "Yes, dear Davico? You don't wish to lose the root?" The cold blade played across my sack. "You don't want to sing like the little birds of the catredanto?" The blade tickled at my exposed cock, prodded my eggs again. "Would you even miss your eggs, Davico? You hardly knew what to do with these when you had them. Would you even miss them?"

I stared at her in horror as the men laughed. I wanted words to form, to find some way to convince her not to do this awfulness. But all I managed was a strangled terrorized whine. I could feel myself somehow both inside my body and outside of it, watching as Celia played her gleeful role, first playing at my cock, then threatening to fuck my ass with the blade. She was playing to her audience, making all the men laugh. I lay beneath her, watching her do it, but somehow separate from it also. I was far above, even as I lay beneath.

Celia's eyes narrowed with new malice. "You know," she said to the Parl, "even without the cock and balls, he will still be dangerous."

She dragged the knife up my belly, leaving a red line. It scraped up my stomach, hissed up my chest. The stiletto's point came to a pause, pricking at the hollow of my throat.

"You're sure you have a use for him alive?" It was an idle question, a sort of bored curiosity.

"He has uses."

I swallowed. The knife pricked my throat. Celia was gazing down at me like a piece of meat. I wondered if she would push the blade in anyway, even against the Parl's desires. I was not even human to her anymore, let alone someone she had known, someone she had lain with. Someone she had loved. Her eyes held nothing for me at all now. Her eyes were as dead as Scuro's caves.

All the men were watching with bated breath, enthralled by the tableau of the girl exacting her long-awaited revenge. Celia's knife slid up to my cheek. I tried to draw away.

"Hold his head still."

Strong hands gripped my skull. She drew little scraping circles on my cheek, and then I saw a new idea flicker behind her eyes. She leaned against the blade. I felt the sting as it cut. She dragged the blade down my cheek. I cried out, but she did not pause. The blade cut my flesh.

"Sfaccito," she whispered.

"No."

"I own you," she said.

"Please," I whimpered.

"Please? Your family made me as your slave." She dragged the blade down my other cheek, another cut. "You made me sfaccita."

"We made you family," I whispered. "Please. I loved you." I felt blood trickling from the wounds.

"You owned me," she said. "And now I own you." And then with a sudden ferocity she cut, and cut again. "You are mine!" Two more slashes upon my cheeks.

My blood flowed hot. I cried out as she made the third cuts, wild with rage, slashing. "Slave," she hissed. "Slave!"

Even the men who were our captors seemed appalled at her ferocity, but she was not done with me. She straightened, turning to the Callarino and the Parl. "He will ever be your enemy if you let him live," she said. "Just as I was to him."

"Do not kill him," Dellamont admonished.

Celia shrugged. "Then I will make him harmless." She smirked down at me. "You should thank me, Davico. I've decided to spare your manhood."

And with that, she flipped the knife into the air.

I remember watching that stiletto rise. I remember the glint of steel in torchlight. How it spun. I remember thinking how skilled she was.

How skilled at faccioscuro. How skilled with a blade. True Navolese, if ever there was such a person. I remember thinking how extraordinary it was that I had never known this part of her.

I remember that long thin knife spinning, and I remember it falling, and I remember how expertly she caught it.

And then she hammered that stiletto blade into my eye.

My eye tore, ripping like egg yolk. I screamed and bucked but the soldiers held me down. Cold steel scraped the bone of my socket, probing, invading, ripping, finishing the job for all time.

"This is for my family," Celia said grimly. "This is for di Balcosi." And then she twisted the knife once more.

I screamed and screamed, but the torture continued. At last I fell mercifully into darkness.

And when I woke, I was still in darkness, for Celia had taken both my eyes.

Terzi Abacassi Senzi Gattimensi

There was once a numerari who found a magic abacus. He found that simply by flicking the beads, copper money would appear in his pockets. It appeared in his lockbox. It appeared under his bed. It even appeared in his cooking pots. He found another abacus, and discovered that by flicking the beads, he could make silver appear. He found a third abacus, and this one made gold.

Now, with the numerari, there lived three cats. And they found that if they played one abacus, they could make tasty crickets appear. And if they played another, they could make fat mice. And if they played the third, bright songbirds would be theirs.

During the day, the numerari made his copper, silver, and gold out of nothing. But at night, the cats played instead. And they made clouds of songbirds that ate all the wheat in the fields. And they made plagues of mice that ate the grain in the warehouses. And the crickets, well, the crickets filled the crevices and cracks of the city, and the armpits, buttocks, and assholes of every person who lived there.

So the people came to the numerari and they skinned him, and they skinned the cats. And they broke the abacuses, for nothing should be made from nothing.

Such is magic, and such is a numerari, and such are cats, so never trust them.

Chapter 46

I woke to the sound of crowds chanting. I did not know at first what I heard, for it was a rumble and then a roar. I felt around myself, trying to understand my place. My fingers discerned that I lay upon a hard platform with a thin mattress, very narrow, from the edges that I followed. I smelled straw, the mattress ticking.

The chanting continued, the roar of crowds.

Bruised and sore, I slowly drew myself up to sit at the edge of my bed. I was blind. It seemed impossible, and yet I was, and I felt myself begin to cry, a welling of self-pity that I fought back. I could almost hear Cazzetta sneering, asking me if I was weak. Was I a dog?

Yes. I feared to even cry from my ruined eyes.

I carefully felt my face, touching the bandages. I didn't want to know what ruin lay beneath. Celia. My mind shrank from the memory of her.

Are you a dog? Or are you di Regulai?

I forced myself to remember those final moments. And then I forced myself to remember all the others who had betrayed us. The Callarino. Sivizza. Dellamont. The Parl . . .

There was a story I had read once, of a priest of Virga, tortured, one of those barefoot mendicants who wandered begging, dependent upon the weave and the care of others. He had wandered into foreign lands, a mountain kingdom, where men rode short-legged ponies and carried spears and bolas and wore fur hats, and they tied him to a post and roasted him alive. It was said that he blessed them as he burned, and forgave them, singing out that he was one with them, and could never die while they lived, that they were all one.

I was not that priest.

If I somehow survived I would have revenge against them. All of them. They would feel my wrath. It was an impotent wish, but it filled me with a certain strength.

Are you a dog, or di Regulai?

The crowds continued to roar and chant. Music wafted up to me, horns baying.

Determined now to take action, I felt about myself. I didn't dare stand, blind as I was, and so I eased myself down to the chill marble of the floor and began to crawl about, leading with my hands, trying to discover the shape of my surroundings.

Beneath my bed, I found what I quickly discerned was a chamber pot. In another corner of the room, I found the shapes of a desk and a chair of splintery wood. The walls were stone. The room was small, perhaps four paces across, if I were to stand. I found a roughly finished wooden door, bound with thick cold iron bands. Also, by following the breezes on my skin and the shouts of the crowds, my hands encountered a slender slit of a window, not much wider than my fist, which allowed fresh air, and amplified the shouts and chants far below me.

I was confined in the Callendra's own prison tower, I realized. The Torre Justicia. How many times had I gazed across the city to the thrusting profile of this very construct, knowing that some ambassador, or spy, or famous duke or general was confined within, awaiting sentencing or perhaps ransom, depending upon the political winds of Navola. How many times had I gazed up at it from Quadrazzo Amo, seeing the thin slit windows and wondering at the lives of the sad confined occupants?

And now I sat in one such cell and listened to the crowds below, great masses of them, all of them cheering and roaring at some sight or pageant. Their roars nearly shook the tower they grew so, and slowly the cacophony began to form into words, a collective chant, all of them joining together.

"Mortis! Mortis! Mortis! Mortis!"

Death.

I could claim that the chant did nothing to discomfit me, but it would be a lie. Even in my pathetic and ruined state, still the chant chilled me. There were many ways we executed criminals, and none of them were pleasant.

The chant broke apart as the crowd lost the rhythm, became a garbled polyglot of voices, then, like some wriggling dismembered sea worm, its parts came back together and became unified once more.

"Mortis, mortis, mortis!"

The tumult was extraordinary. I could imagine the people, packed shoulder to shoulder, angulo a angula, as they say, all those people chanting.

I turned away from the window and carefully felt my way to my bed. I curled up beneath the thin blanket that had been provided as the chants continued. The day chilled to night. Fireworks crackled over Quadrazzo Amo, echoing around me. Drunken songs wafted up, songs whose words were muddy except occasional snippets. Regulai. Dogs. Shit. Those words featured often. We were dogs, we were evil. We were sorcerers. We were Scuro's canipedi. We were all the evil contained within men's souls.

Too, there were screams. Our allies being tortured and murdered, I assumed, but I could not see, and in truth I had lost any ability to be truly surprised or horrified. I had seen too much already, had felt too much.

I tried to sleep but the revelry and tortures went on all night, sporadic. Firecrackers and shouts. Glass and pottery shattering. Screams of pain and jeering laughter. Whenever I did manage to sleep, nightmare memories of Celia and her stiletto assaulted me so that I woke shouting and thrashing, fighting back, impotent as she leaned over me, her face a mask of hatred, and myself, unable to move, unable to stop her, and then I was awake, swinging wildly, my eyes full of fire, and then I was sobbing, clutching at my bandaged missing eyes.

It was not a good night.

I was awake already when I heard footsteps outside and the rattle of keys. My jailers said nothing, but I smelled a porridge and heard pottery being set upon the table. I listened, pretending sleep as my chamber pot was taken and replaced. And then the door was locked again and I was alone.

I told myself that I should eat. Aghan Khan had told me tales of being captive during his campaigns in Zurom, and how important it was to keep strength, to keep alert for escape, but after a bite of the thick porridge I found I could not swallow, and gave up.

Down in the quadrazzo, the sounds of filth dealers cleaning up from the revelry, picking apart those things that could be resold from those bits of food and garbage that could be turned to use in fields. The sound was distant and desultory in the otherwise silent city, slumbering at last after its debauch.

By and by, my door rattled again and I was given water and a meal of dry sausage and bitter Pardi cheese, and hard bread that was not stale, much to my surprise.

Below me, I heard the hammering of some sort of construction. I wondered if they were building a gallows or a stage. I heard music, the strings of lutes, the bleat of horns and thump of drums, sometimes together in song, sometimes competing with one another. More and more voices filled the quadrazzo. People arriving for some purpose. The quadrazzo buzzed with a growing anticipation and so I was not entirely surprised when my door rattled again, and this time it was not food that came but rough hands that dragged me up as irons clanked.

I did not fight as they clasped the irons about my ankles and my wrists. They took me by each arm, hauled me upright, and forced me out of my cell and down the stairs, down and down, round and round, until we reached the echoing marble halls of the central Callendra.

I heard people around me. Though I could not see, I knew where we were, and I knew, too, where I was being led. I did not need to see as I was led through the great doors carved with the story of Amo's protection of Navola from the invasion fleet of Vesuna. I heard them boom open, and the banging of the first secretary's staff upon the drum. Its echoes filled the great rotunda. The murmur of archinomi fell silent as I was led in.

Even though I could not see, I knew I was being led to the center of the forum, and I knew what I would encounter there. A trial box. I was instructed to sit inside of it. I felt my way inside, my hands encountering its smooth wood, worn by many hands and many trials. And then more iron clanked, cold upon my wrists, and muted upon the wood. I was chained to the box and would not be freed until after the trial.

Someone cleared their throat beside me.

"Yes? Who is there?" I asked.

"Giovanni."

"Giovanni?"

I could not understand. It was too strange. Giovanni . . .

"I represent your defense."

My friend. I felt a wash of relief. "Giovanni." I clutched toward him, trying to find him, trying to find his hand, but found nothing. "I did not realize that you had finished studies. You are now one of the litigi? You are not an apprentice? I did not know."

"We have grown apart," Giovanni said. "It's true." His words were cold, but I could not help but be happy that he was near. Giovanni, always with his books. Giovanni, always so decent.

"I am . . . I am . . ." I could not find words. "Giovanni." I felt for him again, this time accidentally touching his fingers. I captured his hand. "Thank you."

"Boviculo!" He shook me off as if my hand were covered in shit. "Let go of me!"

He took a breath. In a more measured tone he said, "Do not thank me. The Callarino's allies are fussy about observing the forms of Leggus, that is all. I am chosen because I am the lowest lawyer in the guild, and you are a known enemy to my family. My duty here is entirely clear. I am here to fail you."

"Because of your cousin," I realized, with a sinking heart.

"Just so."

I thought back to the moment in our gardens when I had refused to help Giovanni. Failed to speak for his cousin. Chosen not to rein in Cazzetta. I tried to recall the cousin's name and could not.

"Is he . . . dead?" I dreaded the answer.

"Vettino? Nai. He returns from exile in Gevazzoa."

"With the Speignissi," I realized.

"We are closely allied, now. And yes, they are coming home as well, now that your family is no more."

"I would not have thought to see it."

"Nor I, but times change."

I wondered if I had behaved differently, if this moment would have been different. Had my failure to save Giovanni's cousin somehow ensured this moment? If I had extended mercy to him, would some salvation have come to us in turn? Some whisper? Some warning of the Callarino's betrayal? Or would it all have happened just the same? Would Giovanni still be standing here, just as cold?

"And what coin will the Callarino pay you to fail in my defense?" I asked.

"I will be given a position as second secretary in the Callendra's Diplomatic Secretariat."

"But your family is nobilii anciens. You should not be eligible."

"The nobilii anciens are rising in Navola. We have taken many places in the government that were vianomae before."

"Well, I'm glad someone will benefit from all of this." I tried to make my voice light, but could not stifle the bitterness.

"It wouldn't matter," Giovanni said. "They will condemn you regardless. This is for show, to make the people hate you, that is all. You still have a few supporters."

I was surprised. "I assumed they must all be dead by now."

"Many, of a surety. But still, there are too many archinomi, and certainly vianomae who remember old favors. So. You will be humiliated publicly and proven to be a traitor to Navola."

"But it's not true! How will the Callarino prove something that is not true?"

"Ci, Davico, so pure of heart. We are not here to show truth or falsehood, we are here to play our parts. We are un spetaccolo. An entertainment. We all have our parts. We all have our lines. We all have our songs and our steps. It is all arranged."

Before I could reply, there was a rustling of bodies in the gallery, accompanied by a rising murmur.

"The Callarino," Giovanni whispered. "He arrives."

The first minister's staff hammered upon the marble, echoing. Once, twice, thrice, calling the chamber to order. A voice rang out, the Master of the Chamber, announcing the business of the Callendra. "Archinomo di Regulai stands accused of plotting against La Citta Republica da Navola. They stand accused of seeking Scuro's profit from our subjugation, and to yoke us to the Empire of Cheroux."

A few voices shouted for my head, but there was also a strong murmur of discontent, and I thrilled to it. We had many who owed their fortunes to us, to our loans, to our support, to our friendship, and with that murmur, I wondered if the Callarino had overplayed his hand.

"This one, this man, this servant under Amo's hand, Davico di Regulai da Navola, stands accused of treason," the Master of the Chamber concluded.

The murmur of resentment grew stronger. Spoken out loud, it sounded fanciful and absurd. The idea that our family, who was so deeply tied to Navola, would sell ourselves to Cheroux, whom our people had resisted for nearly a centenato?

A voice rang out: "These are strong words, Maestro!"

The archinomi stilled. Even I froze, surprised. The speaker was Lady Furia.

"How is it that the Regulai so plot," she demanded, "when they are so deeply tied to this city?" Her voice, which I had always found gratingly sly, wicked, and knowing, now was turned against the Callarino.

"Their roots dig deep here," she continued. "Archinomo di Regulai is as much a part of our city as the Great Piers, as the Convent of Tears, as the Callendra and this gallery. As much a part of us as Catredanto Amo, for which Deiamo di Regulai himself laid the foundation stone. Their very name is Navola. Does the first secretary support this action? Is this truly the will of the Callarino?"

A shout of agreement broke out. *"Aivero! Veritissimo!"* More voices rang out, and there was a stamping of feet as well. "*Veritas. Veritas! Aivero!*" Truth. Truth.

"You see?" I murmured to Giovanni. "I still have friends."

"Ci. It is a play, Davico. All the players have their roles, Siana Furia as well. Ai." He grunted satisfaction. "Here it comes."

"There are witnesses." It was the first secretary. "There is proof."

"What proof?" Furia mocked. "I was no friend of Devonaci di Regulai, but he was no traitor. What proof?" More shouts of agreement echoed. In a moment, I thought the entire Callendra might rise up and tear the first secretary apart, perhaps even the Callarino. But then there was another voice.

"I am witness!" The shout rang out. "I am witness!"

My heart froze. I recognized the voice.

It was Merio.

Chapter 47

The Callendra fell silent, as stunned as I. All the guild masters, all the representatives of the trades, the vianomae of the quartieri, all the archinomi of the city, stunned to silence.

In that silence, I heard Merio's steps echoing down the main aisle to the center of the Callendra.

"I am witness!" His voice rang out again. "I saw what transpired! You know me well! I am Merio Pevecho da Pardi! I knew all aspects of Banca Regulai. I was its most trusted numerari. Many of you know who I am, for we have sat parlobanco and negotiated. I have been privy to your plots and mistresses and bastard children and secret wives and clever business deals and more. I know all the secrets of the Regulai, and I say it is true!"

"How do we know?" the first secretary asked. "How do we know the truth you speak?"

"With my cheek upon Amo's foot, I am witness. I have seen many things, many plots, how Devonaci di Regulai and his son sought to control this Callendra, how he took favors and marked cheeks. I thought he took too much influence, and I was silent. But this, I cannot stand in silence before. I cannot." His voice choked.

"To see him plot with Cheroux, to see his secret letters! To hear his plans, was too much. He sought to make Cheroux the master of Navola, and he sought influence there, he thought to use his son, to bind a match . . . That one"—I knew he was pointing at me—"that one was the chariot of his ambition. We all know that the Regulai have business in many lands. They are no longer as a tree, well grounded in their city, but more a serpent vine, happy to tangle anywhere, to crawl and spread and root everywhere. They long ago lost their way, and their love for Navola, and conspired with Cheroux to take control and with their help to strike down all other banks, and make all the world their profit—"

"It is a lie!" I leapt to my feet and shouted into darkness. "It is a lie!" My words echoed against the cold galleries of the Callendra.

"—and there he is, the last of them," Merio went on, undeterred. "The dog of Cheroux, who would have sold us all into slavery—"

"It's not true!"

"It is!"

I whirled to face the new voice, coming from a different quarter. It was General Sivizza. "They directed me away to Merai, to take my Wolves away, leaving the city ill defended, and then to return—Merai, Cheroux, and I all together—to sack the city. I could not do it. It went against all my honor."

A roar of horror filled the chamber; my own voice was drowned.

"Mortis, mortis, mortis . . ."

The banging of the first secretary's staff fought against the tumult, finally bringing the galleries to order. I could imagine the Callarino, enjoying the spetaccolo he had written and perfected, watching as each of his players came before the audience. I imagined him guiding the actors, moving the audience, causing the music to swell . . .

It truly was a performance of brilliance, for in addition to Merio, there were others:

The young numerari from our bank who had spied for the Callarino. In a quavering voice he described the secretive comings and goings of my father and me, and the dark ways of our stilettotore, Cazzetta.

Garagazzo stood and spoke of how members of our household had come to him under secrecy, in terror for their souls, and confessed to him, so no, he could not say their names, but they were blessed ones who had seen what we were about, and could confirm that we had plotted truly.

And then, in the last, there was the Parl of Merai himself, standing to say that he, too, had been taken in by my father, by me, by our dangerous plots, and that only in the end had he discovered that we intended not just for Navola to fall to Cheroux, but also Merai.

Oh, the crowd howled for justice then.

Furia's voice rang out. "I am convinced! They were traitors! Their secret dealings, their banking, their secrets. They sought to profit more from misery even than the misery trade. Do what you will with this one. Skin him like a dog. Burn him like a nerisa religia."

The chants began for fire. *"Inferno! Inferno! Inferno!"*

"And now," Giovanni murmured in my ear, "the play is almost complete. It is only for me to perform my role."

I barely registered his words, for the chant filled the Callendra, so loud that it seemed the edifice would surely shake and collapse with the stamping of boots and the chanting for my death. The chamber fairly boiled with archinomi baying for my blood.

Giovanni's voice rang out.

"Archinomi da Navola! Great names! Hear me! Davico di Regulai is as much a victim as any!" he cried. "He is not the one whose blood you seek!"

A booing rose up, booing and catcalls. Something wet struck the rail beside me, making me flinch, but Giovanni's voice still rang out. "He has a right to defend himself! It is our way! I will speak!"

"There is no defense!" someone shouted, and more booing fell upon us, this from the upper galleries of the observing vianomae. The upper and lower chambers of the Callendra were all arrayed against us, and yet still Giovanni gave no ground.

"I will speak, and I will be heard!"

The boom of his voice was unexpected, for in my experience Giovanni had always been mild. The crowd seemed surprised as well, for they quieted to mutters of resentment.

Giovanni pressed on. "Those who know Davico—and there are many in this chamber who know him well, have seen him grow from a babe. Many of us have seen him with his dog Lazy, and his cute little pony"—there was a titter of knowing laughter—"we have seen him, and we know that unlike his father, who was as sharp as a fish knife, that Davico, he . . ." And here he paused, and I knew that Giovanni was giving one of our famous shrugs, the Navolese shrug, that speaks whole conversations in a single movement.

"Well, let us be honest, amici, vianomae, archinomi. Our Davico . . . he is not so sharp."

A titter of laughter went up.

Giovanni pressed his advantage. "Our little Davico has not the plotter's mind. I myself have played cartalegge across from him, and never once seen him play a sharp card."

Another laugh rippled around the Callendra.

"It is like playing with a child," Giovanni said. "Like playing cartalegge with one of the cow-minded."

Another laugh.

Encouraged, Giovanni's speech gathered momentum. "So, I say again, Davico di Regulai is as much a victim of his father's plots as we. His crime is not one of clever plots or plans, but simply being born into Archinomo di Regulai. Whatever twisting plots his father might have entertained, this boy before us, he is not one of the shrouded cards, he is merely prince of fools."

And that made everyone laugh yet again. I felt my face burn with embarrassment. The first secretary banged his staff for order.

"He may be innocent of planning, but he is not innocent," Garagazzo said when the crowd had quieted. "He did not speak out. He did not speak up. He did not warn. He was a part of the plot, nonetheless."

"A tool, perhaps," Giovanni protested, "but nothing more."

"An accomplice," General Sivizza said, "one who cannot be allowed to walk free."

The muttering of the crowd rose, but then settled abruptly. Soon I understood why, for at last the Callarino spoke. He affected a tone of neutrality. "These witnesses. Are there others, First Secretary?"

"I witness," the Parl said. "He came to me and did his father's bidding. He may have been a pawn, but he was most willing."

"I do not say he is innocent," Giovanni countered. "I say that he is not a danger. Surely there is some room in this great chamber for mercy. A measure of mercy for one who was caught up in plots he did not understand. I myself had a cousin who was once caught up in similar plots against the Regulai, and I say that to be caught up is not the same as to be a leader, and so, even though this one here never raised his voice to defend my cousin, I recognize that mercy demands we see the difference between one such as he, who follows because he is weak, rather than one who leads, because he is strong.

"I do not argue his innocence," he concluded. "But I beg for him, a measure of mercy."

The Callarino's voice rang out. "What say you all? Does this creature deserve vengeance? Or pity? Discuss amongst you."

Voices rose up as the Callendra argued my fate. I heard words advocating for my freedom and for my being torn apart by horses. I leaned over to Giovanni. "I must say, I'm not particularly in love with your defense of me."

Giovanni laughed. "I must defend you not just before the Callendra, but before Leggus. I have only spoken truth, and this I can swear. Leggus will have no complaint with my honest words. You always were terrible at cartalegge."

"It would be an irony if that were to be my saving grace."

Before Giovanni could reply, I heard the Callarino clearing his throat, signaling that the discussion was to end. The first secretary banged his staff. "Let us make our votes, then." There was a general clatter as the archinomi found their seats.

"How many call for death?" the Callarino asked.

I heard a general rustling, all around the Callendra. Giovanni sucked in his breath. "It's bad?" I asked.

"I'm sorry."

"And how many for mercy?" the Callarino asked.

Not a single rustle, not a cough. Only silence. Such an awful silence as I have ever heard.

Such was politics in Navola. It had now, suddenly, become too dangerous to give mercy, to identify in any way with our family. I wondered if this, too, was part of the Callarino's plan, to try to discover where we might still have support, a way of smoking out his prey from where they hid.

I suddenly felt exhausted. There was no hope here. I wondered that I had even hoped. In this, as in all things, I had been the fool. By the fatas, I had been a fool.

"So," the Callarino said, "it is the will of the Callendra that this one be put to death, for treason. By law, he shall be beheaded, and his head displayed before the Callendra for the time of one month, his limbs torn and scattered so that he may not be collected by Scuro's dogs."

And then there was a shout of protest. "You are all cows and laundry women!" It was Furia. "That one is nothing. He is a speck of nothing. And you are children jumping at shadows! He has no eyes! Look at him! He is nothing!"

"It is the law—" the Callarino said.

"*É letigi justia? Ci, siete fescatolo cane!* Is this Amo's light? Make him your dog, let him live eyeless as a warning for the rest of his days. Let him beg in the quadrazzo, for all it matters. What good does another head on a stick do anyone?"

Merio spoke up, his voice oily. "There is one thing, if I may."

"What is that?"

"The wealth of the Regulai. Much of it lies beyond the borders of Navola, in other branches, far away, subject to different laws and customs, but all of them subject to leggus mercanta. If the last heir is allowed to live, we can recover the wealth of Banca Regulai. It can be put to good use, to pay our guard, to make a statue of our independence, to feed the poor. If the last Regulai agrees to bring his wealth back to Navola, perhaps it would be sufficient payment for a sort of mercy. I can tell you as their numerari that vast wealth lies in the vaults and accounts of the bank branches which they have scattered up and down the hook, across the Cerulea, and over the Cielofrigo."

Suddenly the pantomime made sense to me. "This was their shrouded card," I muttered to Giovanni. "This is why we all perform. So that I will be a different sort of puppet for them."

"I think so," Giovanni murmured. "They want your wealth, and seek to use the authority of the unified Callendra to draw it to them."

"What say you, Davico di Regulai?" the Callarino asked. "Will you swear yourself to your city once more? Will you pay a ransom for your life? Will you swear to do as we demand?"

I didn't answer. I didn't know how to answer. It was everything that my family had been. The work of my father, my grandfather, my great-grandfather, all of them. Was this to be my legacy? Deiamo, the Kind; Destino, the Bull; Devonaci, the Brilliant; and Davico, the Weak—the one who marked his cheek upon the boot of the Callarino and surrendered like a dog.

Davico di Regulai, the last shriveled stump of a once proud name.

Giovanni nudged me. "I would rather die," I murmured. "Let it be done. Let them end me."

"Don't be a fool," Giovanni whispered. "Think how they will torture you if you refuse. Buy your life. They want your wealth, that is all. They care nothing about you. You are not a threat to them. You are not their object. Let them gorge upon gold and move on. Why should you die because your father made enemies? You are not a threat to them. They care nothing about you."

Such kind words, such brutal judgment. I was not a threat to them. "So I should mark my cheeks upon the boot of the man who destroyed my family?" The thought nauseated me.

"They have already won. At least this way you live." I laughed bitterly at that, but Giovanni pressed on, "Yes, live, Davico. Live. Time passes. There are still pleasures to be had in this life. Don't lose heart. You have lost much, but still you have Amo's light within you. Do this thing. Buy your life. It is gold that is already lost. So buy your survival with it at least. Live, Davico. At least live."

At least live.

I do not know the right or wrong of acquiescence, the good or bad of obedience to one's enemies. I know that surrender tastes like ash and emptiness. To mark your cheek upon the boots of those you hate is to fill your heart with worms. Is it honorable to submit to men who already dominate you, who have already won? To wag your tail and beg their mercy, to roll over and show the belly and placate their bloodlust? I do not know the good or bad, the right or wrong. I only know what I did.

Slowly, I bowed my head.

A shout of approval went up. The Callarino's voice rang out, exultant. "Then, as mercy is a virtue of Amo, so mercy shall be a virtue of this Callendra. Come before me, Davico di Regulai da Navola, and swear your fealty. Swear fealty before all."

Giovanni helped me down from my seat and guided me across the rotunda. I could feel the eyes of the Callendra watching and then I smelled the scent of cloves, the chewing leaf that the Callarino favored, and knew we were close. I had never associated the smell with the Callarino before, but now I knew that it had always been there. I had never noticed. So many things that I had never noticed.

"Kneel," Giovanni whispered.

I heard an uncomfortable rustling of silks as I knelt, as if the Callendra were discomfited by this humbling of the Regulai. As if they could not believe what they were seeing. As if our destruction was something that they could comprehend, but this humbling was something else, not of nature. I heard the boots of the Callarino scrape before me. I could sense him standing over me, looking down upon my wretchedness, savoring it.

"You wish to say something?" he asked from above me.

"I wish to swear fealty," I croaked. The words were like shit in my mouth.

"Louder. The Callendra must hear you."

I cleared my throat. "I wish to swear fealty!"

"Good. Now show me."

Obedient as a dog, I felt blindly for his boots, found their shape with my shaking hands. I crouched low and pressed my lips to leather. It stank of shit and I knew of a certainty that he had stirred his boots through dung deliberately before coming here.

"Go on." The Callarino's voice was amused. "Mark your cheeks, di Regulai."

The gathered watchers had gone utterly still. The whole great chamber was silent.

Giovanni told me later that seeing me prostrate before the Callarino felt like the shattering of an age, as if the vase of Navola had been thrown down, its shards scattering and skittering in every direction, never to be repaired, all order lost. What had been Navola before, in that instant, became memory. To slay me would have been one thing, but the humiliation of Archinomo di Regulai was far more powerful.

It was the end of us. It was the end of Navola. It was the end of all history.

I marked my cheeks on shit-smeared boots. They stank and I gagged, but I marked my cheeks and swore fealty to Callarino and Callendra, before Amo and the assembled audience. Archinomi and vianomae watched from the Callendra floor and from galleries on high. Dimly, I heard Garagazzo intoning prayers in Amonese Anciens, acknowledgment of oaths and binding. As formal a marking of the cheeks as had ever been.

At last it was done. The Callendra seemed to breathe again. A snickering wave washed over me, whispers accented with uncomfortable laughter.

"Did you see? Did you see?"

I felt as if I were a rag, wrung out. Within me there was emptiness only, a terrible exhaustion. My limbs felt as if they had turned to water. I wanted to collapse with relief that the Callarino's spetaccolo was over. My part was concluded. The Callarino had triumphed. I was done.

It had been masterfully executed. The Callarino had cowed those who might have supported my family still; he had made me his dog;

and he had guaranteed that our wealth would be given into his hands. To simply murder us all would have been a success for many a player of Navolese politics, but this was the play of a master.

I wondered if it had been on the advice of Merio. Or perhaps the Meravese, Dellamont. I doubted it had been the Callarino. He was too blunt. It hardly mattered, though. The play was done, and as Giovanni had foreseen, we had all played our parts. And yet here I remained. Or at least the husk of me. All my emotion was gone. All my grief. All my shame. Even my anger at all the betrayals was a smothered fire, nothing but char—

The Callarino's voice intruded on my thoughts, dark and oily. "This oath of yours," he said. "Should I value it?"

I fought to rouse my exhausted mind. "I do not understand, lord."

"Nai?"

To my consternation, I heard the Callarino begin to pace, to circle me, slow and lazy. "Your father was a man of his word," he mused. "He kept all his promises." His words dripped an arsenic pleasure. I struggled to follow the Callarino's movements, following his voice and footsteps. "He was a man who valued promises." The footsteps stopped, directly behind me. "He collected them, remember?"

My hackles prickled. "I do."

Suddenly he was close, his lips against my ear. "Why should I trust the shit on your cheeks?"

I flinched. "I . . ." I strained to hear what was happening around me, trying to understand what the Callarino's game was, but my ears were not enough. I felt as if I were swaddled in black Borraghese velvet, all the world muffled to me, indistinct, and yet real enough to bite. I could not locate the direction of the threat.

"I—"

"He has sworn," Giovanni interceded. "It is enough, Lord Callarino. He has sworn. All have witnessed."

"Nai!" The Callarino stamped his boot beside me, making me jerk with surprise. "It is not enough! Not enough at all! I smell the twisted plots of the Regulai, still!"

He was playing to the crowd, I realized. His voice was not turned to me, nor Giovanni, it was turned to his audience. I felt a terrible foreboding.

"How shall I ensure our city's freedom?" he cried. "I ask you all, how can we trust this dog that has attempted to bite us once already? I say we must still make certain!"

With a chill, I remembered the chanting crowd outside the Callendra. *Mortis, mortis, mortis . . .*

The Callarino went on, "Nai, my friends. I know what you are thinking. Not death. Death does not teach. A head upon a pike does not teach, as our beauteous Archinomo Furia reminds us. That behavior is for his sort." He kicked me. "The sort who would hang a body from a palazzo window. But that does not teach. And I say to you all, this traitor, he must teach. I see cuts upon his cheeks, but they will heal in time. I see mud upon his cheeks, but that washes off, with time. And in time, a man can forget his oaths. Can think them past, and worthless. That must not happen. This one must not forget. We must assure that no one ever forgets! No one in this Callendra! No one in Navola! No one in all the hook! All must see, for all time, that the Regulai are no more! No mud or scar is permanent, but his oath will be. This I swear to you all, as Callarino! This Regulai dog *will* obey Navola! *Today, we make him ours!*"

I heard Giovanni protesting and the Callarino's puppet names all cheering. Hands seized me, soldiers clanking in armor dragging me up to stand. Cold iron manacles clamped about my wrists.

"Strip him!" the Callarino ordered.

Of course I fought, but I was no match. They tore my clothes from my body, jerking me this way and that, ripping seams. My shirt tore, cold air gusted across my back. My breeches were slit from my thighs, something sharp scraping my skin, and suddenly I was naked, shivering and exposed to all. Instinctively, I crouched, covering my cock with my hands. A murmuring arose and suddenly I was almost glad I was blind, for I could not see their faces. I could not see who saw me so.

"See him?" the Callarino intoned. "See this traitor? Now see the correction of this twisted one, see this Scuro's child. Observe him, and let no Navolese say they do not know what shall befall them should they plot against our city. Scars will heal, mud washes off, but this one's cheeks will never be clean again. Brand him, I say! Mark him with the three-and-three!"

A gasp went up.

It is strange to think that the gathered archinomi would feel shock at the three-and-three when they would have quite comfortably watched me beheaded, or hung, or torn apart. But there are taboos in every land and every city, and to drag an archinomo down to slavery, well, that was something that not even the most diseased of my father's enemies would have considered.

"Mark him well, and mark him deep! All will tremble at the lesson of the Regulai!"

I tried to run, but blind and shackled I immediately tripped and crashed hard upon the marble. Hands seized me. Strong men cursed as I fought them. They bound me. And then I smelled it. Sulfur smoke. Charcoal burning. I heard the scrape of iron upon marble and felt the heat of a fire being brought before me, a brazier of some sort. The stink intensified, that Scuro stink of slave holdings the world over.

They dragged me to the source and forced my head into something that clamped me tight. A branding vise, I realized. Leather straps and metal tightened about my head, squeezing until I groaned. I smelled the sweat and fear of thousands of slaves who had been branded before. A leather bit prodded its way into my mouth, pushing my teeth apart, my mouth wide. My head was adjusted in the vise, turned so that my left cheek was up and exposed.

The heat of the approaching brand felt like sunlight at first, a gentle warmth. I tried to draw away, but my head was clamped. The heat increased—

Iron seared into my cheek. My skin sizzled, burning, smoking with the piggy stink of my own flesh cooking.

"Mark him well! Mark him deep!"

I was cooking. I was meat, cooking.

Again, the brand pressed hard into my skin. My flesh sizzled. Char choked my nostrils. I gagged. Again the brand descended, and again my flesh was seared.

The vise that gripped my head was cranked around. It clanked and clanged on its screws, twisting my head, turning it, turning it, turning it until my right cheek faced upward, well exposed.

Three times left, and three times right, they marked me.

I screamed and fought but I was bound, and in the end, I was their slave.

And they had uses for a slave.

Part 4

Chapter 48

For you to understand why I was not executed, you must understand a little of the customs of banca mercanta.

Our world is made up of petty kingdoms, greedy republics, mad principalities, rapacious dukedoms, and rotten empires. The lands between are rife with bandits and piracy. Under such circumstances, one would be forgiven for thinking that the might of the sword was the only law, and the sole necessity for collecting the spoils of a victory. An enemy is slain, his strongbox prized open. His women are raped. His wine is drunk from his silver goblets, served up by his children in chains, their cheeks marked with the blood of their patro, smeared there by the bloody boots of their vanquishers.

Sfaccire, truly.

Such has always been the way. In Navola, certainly. Witness how the Callarino now dominated Navola much as the Parl dominated Merai. And of a certainty, my family coffers in Palazzo Regulai had been prized open and well plundered. Merio knew all our secret hiding places and had all the keys to our vaults, and he was eager to make himself useful to his new masters, lest their swords fall upon him.

But as Merio had stated in the Callendra, the strongboxes of our bank and palazzo represented only a small portion of our wealth. Banca Regulai conducted trade in many foreign lands, and each one of those distant cities and kingdoms had its own bank branches, with their own partners and representatives, with their own coffers, locked with their own double keys, and stuffed full with their own gold.

A bank is not a kingdom with soldiers, not a city with walls, not a palazzo with locks, and the sword does not rule this demesne. A bank, despite appearances, is not beams or stone. It is not even gold.

A bank is promises.

A promise is not something an enemy can fill his pockets with, nor drag back to his own palazzo to hang as a trophy, like a boar's head hung upon the wall. My father used to say that we dealt in trade, but more in promises, and this was the crux of the Callarino's conundrum. All those promises we had made, words inscribed in vermillion ink—all those tricksy terms of art that I used to memorize in our scrittorium under Merio's tutelage: *lettera di credita, in caso di guerre, Sotto Gli Occhi di Leggus*—all those words, looping gracefully across our specially prepared paper and stamped with our private chop that lined the shelves of our scrittorium in ledgers, sheaves, stacks, piles, all locked behind iron lattice. This was the beating heart of our wealth.

These were our promises.

"I promise, I have done you a favor," Merio said.

I felt something slide under my hand, a whispering rasp.

Paper.

I patted my fingers across it, curled up its edge, recognized it. The paper we used for our most important bank correspondence. My fingers stroked the familiar surface. Its texture would be embedded with fine black and gold and red threads, saffron-thin, our colors, pressed for us specifically.

"There's no use being bitter," Merio said. "You should thank me, instead. I saved your life."

The paper's method of creation, the embedding of the threads, even its heft and cut were specific to our bank. The paper was one of three unique aspects of our correspondence, created to ensure that no one doubted the authenticity of our missives. I had not realized how deeply familiar it was until my fingertips caressed its face. I knew this paper as well as I knew the velvet softness of Lazy's ears. It echoed with memory.

I was surrounded by echoes of my former life. Indeed, if I closed my eyes—ai, if I had had eyes to close—I could have been a child again, surrounded by the heavy smell of ink, the rot of vellum, the click of abacuses on the floor below—

"Do not smear the ink," Merio admonished.

—and Merio pacing behind me, giving instruction.

Here I sat at his desk in our scrittorium, just as when I had been young, the chair itself an echo of that time when I had been too small even to sit in it, but had knelt upon it instead.

"It's already written on then?"

"You could hardly be expected to inscribe the terms."

I lifted the page to my nose and sniffed. The ink, too, was unique, and it, too, carried memories. Long afternoons spent writing filthy jokes to Filippo di Basca in Torre Amo. Days spent prying open wax and slitting open envelopes. The scent of this very ink, wafting out, promising to share intelligence and rumor that had been scribed to us months before.

"I thought we might draft the letters together," I said.

"It seemed simpler this way," he said.

Merio sounded brusque, perhaps even embarrassed at the farce we both participated in. Warm air wafted across my cheek, anise and the sweet scent of the tea he drank. He was leaning close, leaning over me, just as he had when I was a child. The paper was tugged from my hands. A moment later it rustled upon the desk. Squared before me, I assumed.

"There," Merio said. "That should do."

Carts were rattling over the cobbles on the street far below. I caught a whiff of dry and powdery manure, carried upon the warm whisper of a breeze that eased through the bank's slit windows. From the warmth, I knew it was a sunny day. How many youthful days had I spent in the shadows of the bank while the sun shone outside?

"Afterward, I would be grateful if we could take a walk," I said.

"I'm sure you would be grateful for a great many things. Right now, though, you should be grateful the Callarino has a use for you, and that I explained to him the Laws of Leggus. So let's not delay or frustrate him." Merio's warm dry hand closed around mine. He guided my hand—nai, my whole arm—and set it so that it rested where he had squared the paper.

"Are you worried about what the Callarino will do to you, if you fail?" I asked.

"Worry less about me, and more about yourself, Davico. What is past is past. Your bitterness will not change it."

There was a rattling sound beside me on the desk. A pause. Another rattle. From the noise, from its arena upon the desk, from my long history in the scrittorium, I knew what was coming. Merio's warm hand closed around mine once more. He turned my wrist. A thin brushy length slid between my fingers. The quill. From the sounds, I knew that it had already been dipped in the inkpot.

Merio's hand guided mine downward until the prick of the quill scraped paper.

"There," Merio breathed. "Just there. Sign your name."

From the tightness of his voice, I knew he felt the transgression of our act.

You know the story of the man who could speak and gold would spill from his mouth? And how his greedy captors tore him to pieces, cutting and slicing, desperate to loot the gold within?

Such is a bank.

Slit it open. Chop it into a thousand pieces. Still you will not find the source of its gold.

In some lands, our trade was treated with suspicion for this very reason, for gold to those people seemed to seethe and breed within our bank's vaults. Though it had no root or fig, still it multiplied. A numerari would inscribe words upon paper and gold would appear in a vault. Unnatural, this. Sorcerous, almost.

If you are not well versed in the methods, customs, and law of banca mercanta, it may seem amazing to you that the seizure of the bank does not result in ownership of all its promises. But banks are most strange beasts. Not here. Not there. Not rooted to the soil like a tree. Not planted upon the top of a hill like a castle. More like a mist: hard to seize, harder to pin, impossible to control. Or perhaps (less politely, but more to the point) think of a bank not as a single creature at all, but instead as that mad rogue priest Magare Malatesta enjoys calling us:

A nest of vipers.

Imagine Banca Regula as entangled serpents, all twined and coiled, knotted to one another by promises. Now imagine you seize the largest serpent from that tangle—fat and long and thick and vital. Call it Devonaci di Regulai da Navola. Cut off his head and drain his blood and declare victory.

And yet.

And yet all the promises that my father used to knot himself to all the rest of his serpent nest are not contained within his own serpent body. They are contained within the entanglements. So you might chop off the fattest head of the fattest serpent, but still there are many other heads—in many other lands—and all those little heads care not that the great head is gone. In fact, the death of the head inspires not many heads newly regrown (as in the hydra myth), but instead an unraveling of the entire knotty serpentine mass, each bank branch slithering quickly away to pursue its own profit interests, so that the killer of the bank is left holding nothing but a single limp and rotting serpent, while all the rest of the tangled snakes slip and slither away through his clutching fingers, carrying their gold with them.

This was the central problem the Callarino and his conspirators faced: They had slain the serpent head, they had taken the paper, but still they did not have the promises.

But they had hope, if I were left to live.

How could this be?

In a word: history. Banca mercanta and its peculiarities grew from the ancient practices of the Amonese and their worship of numerous gods—and one in particular: Leggus, the one-eyed god of weighing, and of measure.

According to legend, Leggus showed Desmetonos the tricks of triangles, circles, arcs, and domes, scratching them in the dirt with a stick, showing their divine relationships, and showing Desmetonos the path to build the dome that sheltered the Temple of Argo, that edifice in Torre Amo whose dome was said to be so large that it hid the very sky, and angered Urulo so much that he struck it with lightning, and left it as nothing but crumpled columns.

According to the Amonese, Leggus was much obsessed with counting, weighing, and measuring. He did it compulsively, counting anything he encountered upon his travels. He counted souls, sheep, urns of wine, Khusian lion spines, Cerulean eyes, children, acts of good and evil, and—eventually—gold.

Now, a cynic might suggest that it was not Leggus who loved to count gold, but in fact Leggus's priests, who saw an opportunity to profit from their knowledge of misura. But perhaps those ancient priests were wise and saw that order was necessary, whether in weighing flour, counting sheep pelts, trading pigs for wine, or coinage.

The question of how Leggus became so attached to gold is lost to history, but it became common for his acolytes to oversee trade and agreements between merchants, examining the health of horses, measuring the purity of gold in coins, and creating scales and certifying accuracy so that a cut of meat was true, the length of a bolt of silk was standard, and the strength of a sword reliable.

These acolytes were called numerari—devotees of numbers—and the place in their temple where they used their scales and abacuses was called the Judicio. Its symbol was a circle bisected by a horizontal line, with a triangle dangling from each side: an eternal promise of accuracy in the form of the geometry that Leggus loved so well.

Now, because these customs worked well, the priests' methods spread far beyond Amonese borders. People in other lands might speak different languages, they might despise this or that Amonese god, they might even war against the emperor who sat upon the white rock of Torre Amo—but Leggus and his practices, his principles, his rules, his measures, those were shared amongst many people, indifferent of language or station. Indeed, at Leggus's temple, any who came—tall or short, speaking Amonese or Khusa, wearing the silk robes of Xim or the bearskins of the north, man or woman, crippled or poxed, child or even dog—would be taught to write numbers, to use the zero, to create confirmed weights and lengths, and to play the abacus.

Though the Amonese Empire eventually fell to ruin, and though the hook of the Cerulean Peninsula became a shattered land of warring dukes and princes, Leggus's books of laws, and the scrolls detailing the duties and practices of numerari and the Judicii, persisted. Though Cheroux and Wustholt might war against each other, or Pardi against Navola, or Merai against Vesuna, or all of us against the hated Borraghese in Gevazzoa, Leggus's laws held strong.

Admittedly, sometimes, these laws were twisted, sometimes abused, but they largely held intact, even as empires crumbled, for no meal has flavor if spice merchants refuse to journey to your demesne, and no fief or kingdom flourishes if no one will buy your wool or wheat, your iron or pottery. Breaking too often with common trade practice meant isolation. Isolation led to hunger, to unrest, and oftentimes to a change in leadership.

And so, though we could not agree on a single other thing, we all agreed that life was better under the tutelage of Leggus. So it was that Leggus (no longer a god) and his followers (no longer religious acolytes) still presided over us. The sacred Judicii, where knowledge had been kept, became places of scholarship and repositories of knowledge—our first universities. Leggus's followers, who had been most associated with the documentation and preservation of his rules and tools, became instructors, and called themselves litigii, and took to drawing up contracts and promises according to standard practices. Those acolytes who had been most associated with numbers, the numerari, came to be masters of household accounts, merchant ledgers, and, of course, bankers' balance tables. And so we continued on, sensibly, with the methods of the ancients. The religion might be nonsense, but the practices were wise, and upon this sensible foundation Banca Regulai was built.

A merchant could arrive from Avillion with a piece of paper from the Banque Tourlis saying that he should be paid an amount of navisoli, and it would be honored by Banca Regulai, without contest or argument, within two days of presentation. We could send a man to travel the breadth of the passes of Khim and Kharat to arrive at last in Zurom and present our letter of credit there, and he would immediately be paid from existing accounts, to make his purchases of ivory. A contract for armor and swords could be drawn up, even in bloody Gevazzoa, and if there were dispute about quality on delivery, it could be brought to the guild, and a panel of litigii would weigh the dispute according to agreed-upon standards.

The Laws of Leggus bound us all, and now his practices were the crux of the problem for my enemies.

The Parl could kill my father. The Callarino could scar my cheeks. They could slay our servants and hang them from our walls. They could loot our coffers. But the laws of Leggus and banca mercanta retained their iron strength. And of all the laws of banca mercanta, in all the known world, none was more iron than that a man's gold in his bank was his gold and no other's. If a man died and no heir was legitimate, then his wealth was dissolved according to Leggus's custom: a portion to the bank, a portion to that city's clergy and gods, and a portion to the king or duke or prince or sultan or shangto of that place. Such was the custom, and such was the law, and such was the problem for the Callarino.

And so my life was required. My life, my signature, my inked chop, my secret words and phrases all to be compared at our various distant branches where they kept those same phrases in their secret books to assure their authenticity. Archinomo di Regulai could not be exterminated. I had to be kept alive so that the Callarino and his allies could repatriate the vast fortunes that were spread across the world. I had to be kept alive to exercise my family's ownership rights and to close those far-flung branches one by one, like a Cerulean sea flower pulling in its tendrils at the touch of a finger, bringing the profits and wealth of those places back to Navola.

"Go on . . ." Merio urged. "Write your name."

"How can I?" I lifted the quill from the page. "You took my eyes. How can I write?"

I heard breath sniffed inward. Suppressed irritation. "Your name is memory, nothing more. You do not need to see." I felt my hand taken up again. I felt the tightness of Merio's grip as he guided my hand back to the parchment. He was irritated, of a certainty. I felt a certain pleasure at this, even as I felt the point of my quill touch the parchment once more.

"There. No more games, Davico. This is how you survive."

"Nai." I struck the quill across the parchment, a fast scrape, dragging it hard, hoping to cleave paper, hoping I was spilling a great deal of ink. "This is how *you* survive."

Behind me, Merio sucked in his breath more sharply, and I knew that the page had been ruined. Three perfect copies, but now one was not. How long had it been since he had taught me that three perfect copies were necessary? It seemed a lifetime. "Davico . . ." I could feel his seething anger. It emanated from him like a bonfire, rage at me, impotence in his gritted-teeth voice. "You, Davico, are a child, still."

"I am no longer a child. And you are no longer my instructor. I will not sign."

"You will sign, or the Callarino will hurt you, and then you will sign. It is as simple as that."

"Did my father treat you so badly? Did he insult you, to make you such a traitor to him?"

"Davico . . ."

"Did you not flourish with him? Did you not drink fine enough wine? Eat fine enough cheese? Spend your navisoli with ease? Did you not have estates? Servants? Lovers? How much more gold could you have wanted? Were you not rich enough?"

"Is that what you think, Davico? That this is because of gold?" Merio laughed bitterly. "How like a child of the bank to think only of gold."

"Are you not about to be wildly rich? Rich beyond any measure you have ever known? This idea to retrieve our gold under the Laws of Leggus, that was you. Your plan to get rich."

"You are naïve."

"You are a traitor."

"I bargained with what I had!"

I flinched from Merio's shout. Below, on the floor with the abacuses, there was hiccup of pause in the clacking of beads. Merio lowered his voice, but still it quivered with rage. "I have done you a favor, Davico. You may not think it, you may despise me, but I had no choice. Your father gave me no choice."

"No choice but to show all our secrets to our enemies, for profit. We all thought you trustworthy, and instead we kept a master of faccioscuro within our midst. You must be proud that you fooled even Cazzetta."

Merio didn't reply.

Carts below rattled. A man was selling pears, I could hear his voice, passing beneath the windows as he walked up the street, calling out, passing, passing . . . Still Merio said nothing. I began to wonder if he had left. Had he stalked away, leaving me alone at the desk? I sniffed for him. For anise, for fennel, for sweet tea—

"I do not wield a sword," Merio said heavily, "but knowledge is a sharp enough weapon. I tried to teach you that once. To use your wits. But you did not listen. It gives me no satisfaction to have fooled you. I would have saved you better if I could. I would not have . . . ruined you so."

I could hear regret in his voice. Genuine pain that made little sense.

I groped clumsily toward his voice. My fingers found cloth, his robes. I fumbled and found his arm. Gripped it. "Then why? Without your help, without your help to open the gates, we—we would have—Why?"

"Ai, Davico. Still you do not understand the workings of the world." He shook off my grip, sounding exasperated. "Do you remember your name day?"

"How could I not?"

"The same could be said for me. I nearly died that day. Your father's power was clearly waning. He had offended too many of the old nobilii, forced too many to his boot. It was clear he rode a precarious steed. And even if he beat back one attack, what would happen next? What would happen when you were expected to do the same? How long would you survive in his role? How would you, kind Davico, soft Davico, do what was necessary? We all saw it. We all saw you. You . . ." He trailed off. "Well, perhaps you were equipped to oversee a branch of the bank. But your father dreamed of empire. Can you imagine? He was a fool with a father's love, and you were weak, and I could not pin my survival on someone so lacking." He sighed. "Ai. It is done. There is nothing for it. You were always right. You were not meant for this life. You are not Navolese. Not truly. Too soft. Too chiaro. I wonder sometimes if the blood of the Regulai even flows in your veins. I could not yoke my fate to yours, whatever your father might have hoped. He forgave you all your faults. I could not afford to do so."

I heard papers shuffling on the desk. Merio moving about me, tidying.

I could not pin my survival on someone so lacking.

I felt numb. We had been betrayed . . . because of me? I had been weak, and Merio had turned against me? They all had? Grief welled up within me.

"Come now, Davico. Stop the whimpering," Merio said. "Stop the self-pity. I have more letters for you to sign. Ones that you have not yet spoiled. Do not make this difficult. There is no purpose to it. If you wish to live, then you must be useful. If you are useful, you will not be treated badly." He guided my hand once more to the paper. "Here. Now sign your name."

And so I did.

With a heavy heart, I did as I was told. I did as I was meant to do. I did as the failure to my family that I was. And so the wealth of far-flung lands began to pour back to Navola.

My letters went out to Avillion, Bis, Wustholt, Nordur, Zurom, and Chat, and in turn a great river of fevigs, loden, kingheads, sefi, and khu poured back to us, and poured into the purses of the Callarino, the Parl, General Sivizza, Merio, and Garagazzo.

They fed upon the wealth of the Regulai as vultures feed, and they grew fat.

Chapter 49

And what of my life? What sort of existence did I purchase with my obedience?

I became a sort of ghost, haunting the halls of the home I had run through so freely in my youth. Of course, the palazzo was no longer mine, no longer Palazzo Regulai. It was now Palazzo Corso, for the Callarino's own patrinomo, and his green and gold colors were splashed garishly across the entrance gates—at least, that is what I was told. I had no eyes, so they could have been painted with the languorous curves of Erostheia for all I knew.

In any case, Borsini Amoforze Corso held the keys to the palazzo now, and I became . . . well, I was a strange sort of creature. Like the beauty and horror of the Princess Lis, depending upon which mirror she looked into, I, too, appeared different in different lights.

I was a slave, but my labor was light. I was dressed still in the finery of my rank, some of the clothes very fine indeed. I stood as a ghostly memory of the palazzo's past, and a shadelike warning for others' futures. I was not dead, as were all my family and retainers, but not alive, either. I became a sort of fata, a symbol of failure, gliding through the halls and across the quadrae, a warning to any who might think to raise themselves as the Regulai once had.

My abode was high in the palazzo's defensive tower, in a room much similar to the one I had briefly inhabited above the Callendra. Particularly, it locked from without. Within, it contained a small desk that gave splinters if I ran my fingers too quickly over its surface, and a three-legged stool that creaked. A rough straw pallet lay upon the floor with a chamber pot beside it. And of course, upon the desk there rested the all-important inks and quills and stamps that were required of me whenever Merio came knocking. Letters to sign. I had many of those.

Stacks, in fact. It had a chest for my clothes. Once a day I was taken to the baths and ordered to scrub and shave myself, for the Callarino liked me presentable, a better contrast to wear finery against the sight of ruined eyes, better for my skin to shine clean and clear, to show the brands upon my cheeks.

Each day I signed and stamped the documents that were required of me, and when I had done my tasks to Merio's satisfaction, I was allowed to roam within the bounds of the palazzo, a pet rewarded for obedience with a longer leash.

Of course, I could not roam at will. A servant named Aqba was assigned to watch me, a vicious creature, whom I imagined as a crabbed gaunt man with sunken resentful eyes and a ferret's face. Of course, he could have been handsome, but I do not think so. Those who chew kheem leaf are not known for their pretty teeth, and he stank of that plant. Too, he was small of mind, petty and cruel. The sort who would secretly move your three-legged stool to trip you, or who would sprinkle sand in your tea.

I think that those who take pleasure from hurting others are never pretty, even when their features are even and their skin is clear; their ratty piggy natures shine through. I have seen women with hair like spun gold and skin smooth as porcelain who showed themselves as Scuro's beetles, so much that you would expect not jaws but mandibles to open when they gaped their mouths to spew their minds. So I imagined Aqba as a skinny sneaking slinking ferret, and with that image fixed firmly in my mind, he never disappointed me.

With this inconstant companion I was allowed to walk the halls and galleries of the palazzo and to sit in the gardens in the sun sometimes, and I was tolerated.

This was the life I purchased with my many missives to our many branches and managers, with my sincere entreaties and explanations of how the ventures would be dissolved and the wealth carried back to Navola.

And Celia? The girl who saved herself and took my eyes? She disappeared like mist off the harbor in the sun.

I dreamed of her sometimes. In some of my dreams she was the Celia I had loved, and she turned her knife on the Callarino, and she defended me to the last. In others, she was the Celia of that fateful night, practical, cruel, and vengeful, and her knife fell upon me once more. In others, I was the one who held power over her.

I dreamed of stabbing her body a thousand times, her blood spraying the walls of her chambers, her body torn and ripped and shredded, and when I woke I was horrified and ashamed and giddy at my hatred of the girl I had once loved; and then depressed and despondent that I would never have my revenge upon her, then nauseated that I still missed her laugh and her capricious mind, and then once more enraged, knowing that even if I were to drive a knife into her heart, I had no way to see the life drain from her eyes, or collect her apology.

I heard rumors of her, of course. Conflicting stories of her exploits and whereabouts. I heard that the di Balcosi name had been restored in Navola and yet she was not seen amongst them. I heard that she lived as mistress to the Parl in Merai, kept in luxury and comfort. I heard that she had left Navola and traveled to far-off Cheroux, where she was now a queen. I heard she was dead, strangled by the Callarino, murdered in his bed after sharing a goblet of viscous sweet wine. I heard that she had been sold into slavery and sent to the Khur Empire, where she now decorated the harem of a brother of the sultan.

I suspected more likely that my enemies had simply killed her after using her to blind me, enjoying the cruelty of turning her against me, and then the further cruelty of teaching her that her debasement of herself was not sufficient to make her one of them.

But I did not know. I could never ascertain if any of these things were true. As in so many things, I was in the dark.

And so this was my lot. I wandered the halls of my family's palazzo, a deformed ghost, haunting. I did the bidding of the Callarino. I learned to keep quiet, to fade away, much as I had used to disappear into forests, so that people became so used to my pathetic form that they did not trouble themselves much with me.

You will judge me for my failure to hold myself with honor, I am sure. To see me so debased. Perhaps you are a better, stronger person than I.

In truth, I do not know the right or wrong of surrender. I know stories of men and women who refused to surrender their honor to their enemies. Men and women who killed themselves rather than be dishonored. The women of Archinomo Vazzini, who cut their own throats, one after another, rather than allow themselves to be raped by their enemies. The whole city of Zathyros that fought unto the last child, and any that were captured killed themselves soon after, so that none were sold as slaves. Even the children were so fierce in their honor that they stabbed their own bellies rather than be enslaved.

And yet, I allowed it.

One night, in despair, I attempted to hang myself. I managed to wrap a pair of breeches around my desk and fashion a noose, and sat myself down so that colors, despite my missing eyes, began to fill my vision and I gaped for breath, but I found I had not the bravery to go on when my breath became labored. I ended madly scrabbling to get my feet beneath me and unloop the noose I had fashioned. I fell coughing and gagging upon the floor, my heart pounding, my lungs burning, loathing myself for my weakness.

After this attempt at suicide, I found insufficient bravery for another. I do not know if this was weakness on my part. I do not know if the strong are the ones who end themselves, or if they are the cowards. I do not know if the cowards are the ones who mark their cheeks with the shit of their enemies' boots, or if they in fact are the bravest—those who continue living even as their souls are defiled with shame.

Many a night I lay abed, full of self-loathing and rage, but still I continued to live. I ate the food of my enemies. I obeyed the bidding of my enemies. I wore the garments of my enemies.

I lived in darkness.

I do not know how long this period lasted. More than a month, certainly. Two? Three? Time becomes a dim dream in such circumstances, one day melting into the next like butter melting into olive oil in the pan, all of it becoming mingled and liquid.

But even so, voices began to intrude upon my thoughts. As I stamped my chop upon the various letters that Merio set before me, these voices scurried through my mind, unwelcome as rodents. As I sat warming my face in the sun, Cazzetta would rise from a shadowed corner of memory, asking me if I knew what it was to be sharp.

When I heard the Callarino's guard clashing at sword practice, Aghan Khan would come to stand behind me, demanding to know if my blood was that of surrender. Late at night Ashia would come and sit beside my bed, and ask if I was yet a man or if I was—and always would be—a child. And then, most painful of all, as I stamped those seals and signed my name and convinced our fortunes home, my father would lean upon my desk beside me, his hawk's eyes unrelenting, inquiring in that piercing way of his, if I still thought myself di Regulai.

And so my mind began to churn. It began to stew upon pleasant fantasies of vengeance. At night I dreamed seductively of bloodshed and by day I imagined elaborate many-splendored triumphs over my enemies—all of which were quickly shattered when I stumbled over that three-legged stool of mine that Aqba had set once again in my path.

And Aqba snickered.

Bruised and shaken, I lay upon the flagstones, fuming at my keeper's cruelty, and suddenly Cazzetta's shade was beside me, crouching down, peering at the visage of my impotence, amused.

"Sfai. Davico," he mocked. "You cannot even walk across your own cell without falling on that ugly face of yours! Who are you to think of vengeance? You are a worm in the dirt, dreaming of standing proud atop a castello's ramparts." He smirked in that infuriating self-satisfied way of his. "You have not the legs for it, boy! Where are your legs, boy? Where are your legs?" He shook his head, as disappointed with me in death as he had been with me in life. "No worm storms a castello without legs. And here you lie, upon the floor, like a worm. Are you a worm, princeling? Is that your ambition? If so, you make an excellent one."

Ai. If I could have dragged him from death to murder him again, I would have.

Later in the cool of night, as I sat upon my pallet, with my arms around my knees, despairing of anything, feeling the cool night breezes wash over me and smelling the scent of the lusca flowers wafting through my slit window, he came again to sit beside me.

"So you've chosen self-pity then?"

I scowled at his shade. "Why can I see you when I see nothing else?"

"You're talking to yourself." He smirked. "Your mind is sharp, after all. So it tells itself stories." He paused. "Of course, I only compliment your wits because you want to believe you're somehow special. You pull my strings to compliment you. But in fact we both know you are a worm."

I glared at him.

"Oh? Does that sting, princeling?" He made a flick of three fingers, off his cheek, at me. "I have never seen a problem solved by denial. You are a worm. That is truth. So . . ." He gave me a piercing look. "What will you do about it?"

Ai. I hated him for that. Hated the truth he spoke. My mind twisted upon itself like a serpent, trying to escape his judgment, seeking an excuse for myself, but at every twist and turn and coil, it came back to the undeniable truth: I was weak, and I was alone, and I was powerless. No one cared for my fate. No one would ride to my rescue. And, too, my time of shelter under the Callarino's hand would inevitably come to an end.

"There's nothing left to do," I muttered. "They destroyed everything. Look at me. I'm useless."

"Ci. You choose to be weak," Cazzetta said.

"I am blinded!"

"Matrae fescatae! You are weak, and you choose to be weak! I once saw a man from Xim fight three others while blindfolded! He fought with only his hands, though his enemies had swords, and he left them all as corpses in the combat sands of Gharat. You are blind because you choose not to see."

"I didn't choose to have my eyes stabbed out."

"You certainly chose not to see that the Parl was your enemy, that Merio was afraid and cowardly, that . . ." He trailed off, considering. "I think you were always blind."

"You also were blind!"

Cazzetta shrugged. "And? Does it make you feel better to know that others are failures? Does that make you some success?"

"I am broken!"

"*Mi dicti fescato!* You are a child. You want someone to come and save you. You want someone to salve your wounds. You want someone to tell you they love you. You want to be told that you will be rescued." He laughed. "Those are the dreams and wants of a child. There is a time to look to allies, and there is a time to look to oneself, and if there was ever a time to look to oneself, it is now, princeling, for you are alone. If you keep on as you are, you will not just be a worm, you will be food for worms. If you wish to escape your tower of despair, then you must climb down."

"I am blind!"

"You do not see. That is different."

He stood and straightened his clothes, gazing down on me as I huddled miserable on my pallet. "Your fate is your own, Davico. Pray to Amo. Pray to Scuro. Pray to Soppros and all those philosophers you admire. Pray to the foreign gods of Wustholt, Zurom, and Xim, and they will all tell you the same. Your fate is your own. Sia Fortuna gives not a shit for you."

By the fatas I hated him. I hated his smugness. His conviction that my victimization was my own fault. That I was to blame for my powerlessness. They had done this to me. I had not asked for it. I had not allowed it. I was wounded. I was damaged. I was not whole—

Ai. Self-pity. It was all self-pity. I was broken. I was damaged. It was all true, and it was also all excuses. An escape not from my prison, but from my responsibility. I was blind. I was damaged. I was frightened. I was alone. Those things were true. So . . . would I quietly die?

Would I let my enemies triumph?

No one will save you, Davico.

So.

Did I have the will to save myself?

It was a painful thought. That despite my impairments, I must go on. It seemed a violation of all the doctrines of Leggus and Amo. It was not fair—

"A stag hunted by wolves does not complain of fairness," Aghan Khan observed. "The stag runs, it fights with all its might, it does not trouble itself with fate, or luck, or fairness. It troubles itself only with the necessity of flight."

It is a painful thing to abandon all excuse. To accept that all responsibility is yours alone. To know that to forge through, or fail, is simply what is.

Ashia smiled sadly at me. "Ai. Now you know what it is to be a man."

And so at last, I accepted that I was indeed the blind worm that Cazzetta suggested.

And so I set about growing legs.

Chapter 50

In the morning, I pushed impotent fantasies of revenge from my mind and turned my energies to the practical: acquiring mastery over my circumstances. The start of this was to live—nai, not live but *thrive*—without eyes.

Under the guise of exercise, I began to walk back and forth in the gardens, back and forth, back and forth, while Aqba sat in the shade like the lazy beetle that he was. In the hot summer sun I paced.

Back and forth, back and forth, back and forth.

Step, step, step, step, step, step . . .

This was not as it appeared, mindless movement, but in fact serious practice, my first foray into deception, my first attempt at something approaching the faccioscuro of my birthright.

Aqba thought that I was exercising like some pony in a field, but I was in fact working my mind, furiously.

Close your eyes. Close your eyes and walk everywhere that way. Tune your senses. Remember your steps, practice the length of a stride. Vary it. You will never approach the discipline that I focused upon my task. It was more focus than I had ever given to the examination of accounting books with Merio or the practice of the sword under Aghan Khan. I was more intent upon my learning than even when I had studied the flowers and salves and anatomy that I had loved under the hand of old Dellacavallo.

To and fro, across and back, this way and that, feeling my way around fountains and flower beds, pricking my fingers on thorny rose-bushes, running my hands around stony columns, inching across cool terra-cotta tile and smooth marble floors. Each step I counted, each wall I touched, each column I noted. Slowly, I began to scratch out a map in my mind, a cartography of my unseen world, like the sea charts that guide sailors through the deadly shoals in the Straits of Nerarocca. Inch by inch, flagstone by flagstone, portico column by portico column, I scratched down each new discovery in the map of my mind.

But even as I built that physical map by feel, I was surprised to find that the map was coming alive with other layers, as if onionskin were being laid over it, and other details were being inked in, not by feel, but by other senses. You who live with sight forget your other senses, and so had I. But now my senses slowly awakened, opening like lusca flowers that offer scent only at night, my own senses blossoming in response to the darkness of my eyes.

My skin felt every breeze and told me its direction and strength. My ears became attuned to the echo of servant voices and footsteps, and the rustle of wind through leaves and branches. My nose became acute to the scents of people and animal and flowers, even the differing scents of granite and marble. And each of these senses, in turn, told me more about my physical world. The echoes of voices gave me the shapes of halls. The winds told me if doors or windows were open, told me if I faced tight passages or open galleries. My nose told me of gardens and of people, and whether they were near or far.

Indeed, my senses became so attuned that the hairs upon my arms seemed to fairly quiver with an awareness of subtle motion around me, became so attuned, in fact, that I could feel Aqba's hand near mine as he sprinkled sand into my tea, his oh-so-close but not touching presence. So in this and many more ways, my sharpening senses aided me as I constructed a new understanding of the palazzo where I had lived all my life.

If, in my youth, I had discovered the ways of climbing out a balcony and stealing across the red-tiled roofs to peer down into the bathing chambers of our servant girls—that hidden path and hidden way others were ignorant of—the awakening of my senses now pried open nooks and crannies of the palazzo that I had never noticed.

I became a listener. A counter. A feeler. A sniffer. It is difficult to describe to one who has not lost their sight, but my mind seemed to grow capacious.

From the door of my cell, I circled down eighty stairs through the levels of the tower, down and down, until I eventually spilled out into the echoing arched gallery that I knew from memory had the painting of Urulo's storm being quelled by Urula. From there, it was thirty-three further stairs down to the garden quadra. From the north side of the quadra to the south, from the east to the west, I measured steps. To the fountain in the center, to each of the corners, where the roses and wild vivena grew. I knew those steps, and I built a shadow palazzo in my mind, a mirror of that place where I lived.

Ai, it is impossible to describe such a thing to you, with your sight. My words are a poor metaphor. Suffice to understand that despite my blindness, I became increasingly confident within the walls of the palazzo that I knew where I stood.

But of course, a palazzo is not just granite and marble and gardens and columns and doors and vaulted ceilings. There are things more changeable as well. If the structure of Palazzo Regulai was Firmos, strong, steady, true; then the people, the furniture, the animals, anything that could move, that was the realm of Cambios.

And Cambios was indeed treacherous.

I learned to be always alert. I learned to listen for footsteps, voices, echoes, whispers. I felt the breezes of a chamber when a door was open and smelled rose, and knew that the Callarino's daughter would soon be approaching. I learned to smell if candles or oil lamps burned, to distinguish between servants and masters at night. I learned to listen for the echo of conversation between servants and guards, to know if I approached the kind or the cruel. I distinguished people by soft slippered tread and heavy boot.

Particularly, I learned to track the Callarino's own family. His children Tiro and Aviana, Tiro always sweaty because he never bathed, Aviana with her rose perfumes. His wife Carizia with her sniffling as if her nose was always running. His wastrel brother Vulo, always loud, always announcing himself from one side of the palazzo to the other, only silent when he lay redolent with the fumes of grape spirits, sprawled across a passageway, immobile as a log. Vulo's wife Ana, who limped unevenly and avoided him. The Callarino's vulturous mother Marza, smelling of piss and fishy sourness whenever she moved her legs. These were the people who now inhabited my family's great halls and private chambers and ordered the servants to their own liking, and all of them I listened to.

And so it was that my nose, my ears, the hairs upon my skin—everything about me—became attuned to the palazzo. Indeed, over time, I learned to walk from one side of the palazzo to the other, up and down stairs, through gardens, around servants, down passages, and along galleries, all without bumping into a single obstruction.

I did well—until the Callarino's children rearranged the potted plants to present unexpected barriers.

The Callarino apologized profusely. "They forget that you have no way of knowing," he said after I tripped over a planter in the garden and lay sprawled amongst dirt and broken pots. "They are children. We must forgive them."

But I had heard the children giggling at the far side of the garden and understood that he had set them to the task. Even now, he could not resist mudding my cheeks. Power does not change a man's nature, but only makes it more so. Such was the Callarino.

But the lack of power, well, that is something else, for the lack of power was most certainly changing me.

Chapter 51

The days of summer fell to the cool of autumn. My mind worked furiously at the problem of my captivity, for the river of gold flowing into the hands of my betrayers would soon become a trickle.

I turned my discoveries of the palazzo toward those places that I had so far avoided, those places close to the main gates. This was where the stables lay, and a pearl of a plan was forming in my mind. If Stub still remained, I thought we might together manage an escape. We knew each other's minds well—had we not fooled the woodskill of Aghan Khan?—and I thought that perhaps aided by Stub's loyal friendship and his eyes, we might pick our way south to the wilds of the low Romiglia and the lands of the Sfona. It would be difficult, but Stub had made the journey before. I didn't know exactly how it might be accomplished, blind as I was, but I thought it might be possible. Too, Cazzetta had been lurking in my mind of late, urging me to plumb the defenses of my captors, to see what might result from testing limits.

By roundabout explorations, I made my way to the palazzo's quadra premia. Of course, Aqba was in tow, always irritated, bored, and feral, but he did not prevent me from arriving at the fountain of Urula in the center of the quadra. I ran my hands under the chill water, listening to it splash and gurgle as if fascinated, but in truth listening to the sounds of this new quadra, tracking its smells. The gates were open. I could hear the rattle of carts on cobbles and hear people calling out. The wind was coming from there, through the gates, carrying the scents of dust from the street and fish from the nearby market. As if lost, I wandered toward those sounds and smells, ears pricked, nose sniffing, curious, like the dog that I had become, a simple puppy exploring—

I was herded away by Aqba. "Nai, slave. Get away from there." He seized my ear and dragged me away. "That is not for you, slave."

I turned then, most compliant and obedient, bending and bowing, wincing at the pain, but also, as if by accident, turning myself toward my true destination. And Aqba, placated for having demonstrated his power over me, released me to follow my nose instead toward the thick feathery scents of straw and manure coming from the stables.

I was pleased that my shadow map of the quadra was accurate, and that I had placed myself correctly. I arrived almost perfectly at the stable doors, within the number of steps that I guessed would be required.

I paused at the entrance, sniffing at the nostalgic scents. Remembering long ago when I had mounted Stub and ridden out, thinking to flee—and been turned back by Cazzetta. How my life might have been different had I ridden over that man, had I fled the city on the day of my Assumption . . .

A wet nose pressed into my palm. I felt a shock of recognition. I knew that damp muzzle instantly, and knew, too, that if I showed any love for her, Aqba would use her against me, or else the Callarino would. They would wound her, to wound me.

I patted Lazy absently, ran my hand over her head, found her ears and stroked them. Feigned disinterest even as my heart sang. "What is this?" I wondered. "Some mongrel it seems."

Lazy whined and pushed her nose against me and rubbed about my legs. Aqba hissed at her, and she growled in response.

"Go away, dog." I pushed her sharply off, not wanting Aqba to focus his pettiness upon her. She returned to me, but I shoved her away again. "Off with you!" I said. "Go!"

My heart broke to send her away, for she was the only friend I had found since our family's fall, and perhaps the only one who remained, but I was relieved when she went away, whining. Still, I sensed her lingering, wounded by my disloyalty.

Stifling my guilt, I felt my way inside. Stable scents enveloped me. Horses. Their well-washed coats, their long manes, their snuffled exhalations, their grassy breath. Hay. Manure. Oiled leather. So many horses.

My hands touched a wooden gate, the first in the line of stalls. I again felt pleased. This part of the palazzo I only knew from memory, and yet still I navigated it. I was blind, but like a sailor with a map and compass, I was able to sail and find a port that lay hidden over the horizon. I went from stall to stall, calling softly to the horses. Many came forward, hoping for carrots and sweets, but Stub was not one of them. Indeed none of them were familiar to me.

"These horses are not yours," a man called out. "Those have all been sold."

I turned toward the unfamiliar voice. "You know me?"

"Everyone knows you, blind one." I could hear the amusement in his voice. "But your horses are gone. Sold as soon as Archinomo Corso arrived."

"The Deravashi, even?"

He grunted. "Especially the Deravashi."

"Oh." My chest tightened, and not entirely because of the crumbling of my plan to escape. Stub was gone. Another victim of my family's fall. My rejection of Lazy hurt now, even more. My last friend.

The man approached. He had a heavy tread, good stout leather boots undoubtedly, and what I thought must be a halter clinked in his hands. This was confirmed when the jangling sound was hung upon the wall with the rest of the tack.

"The Deravashi were not to the Callarino's taste," the man said gruffly. "Too short. Not a steed for an archinomo. Noble names must have noble steeds."

"Ah." The stable was no longer mine. The smells were the same, but none of the occupants were. It had been foolish to think that anything would be other than changed, but still, a sadness welled up within me. I reached into one of the stalls, feeling for the creature that now inhabited it. A moment later, I heard a snort and felt a damp muzzle pressing and snorting breath into my palm, warm lips seeking a carrot that I did not have.

"The patro is a fool," I said. "The Deravashi are more noble than any breed I have ever known."

The man grunted amusement. "The Deravashi are an acquired taste." He was a big man, I judged, wide and tall. His deep-voiced words seemed to spill down upon me from a height. I liked the sound of him. Stout. Direct. Huge. The sort of man who had grown up on a farm wrestling livestock into and out of paddocks, and raised himself in station through his knowledge of animals. I heard him coming closer. I took a step back, wary, but his huge hand took mine. He pressed something cool and thin into my hand. A carrot. "You've found Sia Aquia," he said.

"Sia Aquia." I offered the carrot to the horse and she nipped it from my palm, snorting contentedly.

"She's a Russo," the man said. "Five clean generations."

The Russo was a breed from the south, quick for racing, but lacking stamina.

"I like the Deravashi better."

"They are stout," he agreed.

"You're the horsemaster?"

"I am. Herges is my name."

The name was strange. "You come from Chat?"

"I do. You have an ear for names."

"It was once my family's business to know such things." I patted Sia Aquia. "What is that dog that licked my hand?"

"A hound," Herges said. "I found her lurking outside the palazzo. She's a good dog. Quite clever. Trained well, too. She doesn't like many people, though. Surprised she didn't bite you."

"I always liked animals better than people. They're more trustworthy."

He laughed. "I've found it so as well."

"You're not afraid to talk to me?" I asked. "Even though you know me?"

"I am very good with horses," Herges said. "Without me, the Callarino would still be begging Sia Aquia to let him straddle her."

"So you're not afraid."

"I fear many things. But not the Callarino."

Our conversation was interrupted by the arrival of a person running into the stables. Soft sandals but a heavy man's tread. No scent of perfumes, so, a servant . . . I strained to identify him. He whispered to Aqba, but I could not make out the words. Whatever they were, they stung Aqba for he was instantly upon me, yanking my ear.

"Time to go, slave."

"Hold there!" Herges commanded. "I have not dismissed this one, and you do not stand above me."

Aqba hissed, "It is the Callarino's will."

"And yet still I have not dismissed you, sfaccito."

"My cheeks are clean!" Aqba bristled.

"Some men are slaves in their souls."

Aqba hissed again. If Herges had not been so powerful and Aqba not such a ferret, they would have fought then. But all Aqba did was hiss.

"Ai. He's a slave and a coward," Herges said. "You have made a terrible choice of companion, blind one."

"The Callarino will have your head," Aqba said.

"And yet still, I have not dismissed you."

"It is better if I go," I said. "I am dependent upon Aqba's goodwill. Please, we should go."

Herges seemed to consider, his dislike of Aqba warring against the force of the Callarino's call. "All right," he said at last. "Off with you, then." But then his voice became dark with warning.

"Treat this one well, Aqba. It's not many animals that like a man by instinct. This blind one is a creature of Virga's weave, and she does not take kindly when her creatures are tortured. Remember how she dealt with King Nemaius."

Aqba hissed at this, but I could feel him draw back as well, made wary by superstition.

Chapter 52

Despite Herges's warning, Aqba returned to form as soon as we were out of the horsemaster's sight.

"Hurry, slave! Hurry!" He yanked me along by my ear, his grip a crab's claw as we made our way through quadrae and under arches. "Up the steps. Up! Lively! Up."

I tried to keep count of the steps but he was in a rush. I stumbled and fell, cracking my shins upon the stone. He dragged me upright. "Hurry, slave!"

I smelled catredanto wood ahead and knew suddenly where I was being taken. I felt a sudden dread and instinctively balked. My father's library. I had not been inside or even near it since my family's fall. It was a place too painful to approach. It was almost as if I had a superstitious belief that if I avoided that refuge of my father, the truth of our fall would not be realized. Much like the girl Meraillia and her dreams that became real, as long as she did not see something that contradicted them first.

I had not seen my father fall. I had not seen his final defeat. The Parl might have claimed it, but it remained only a story, rather than a fact. And so, against all logic, I had unconsciously clutched to fantasies of his continuation. I could pretend that he lived yet, just around the corner, just beyond in the next quadra, just behind the doors to his library—

The doors opened. Aqba shoved me through.

I stumbled into the library, caught myself, and froze, overwhelmed by the sense of trespass. It was almost exactly as it had been. It still smelled of the books. The carpets were still soft underfoot. It was all there, and yet everything about it felt defiled.

"Davico!"

The Callarino was sitting behind my father's desk. I could hear exactly where he sat. In my father's place. My skin crawled.

Aqba seized my arm and dragged me forward. "I have brought him, lord." He shoved me to my knees. "I have brought him. He is here."

"Good. Get out."

If Aqba had hoped for some reward for dragging me to his master, he must have been disappointed, but he scampered out obediently, closing the doors behind us.

"Get up, boy. Get off your knees." The Callarino sounded irritated. His chair scraped, my father's chair, and I knew he was now standing. His footsteps began pacing, back and forth, behind my father's desk. Despite all logic, I found myself stretching my senses for hints of my father, as if his spirit might still linger here where he had spent so much time poring over ledgers and correspondence—

"*Once a cat called to a bird,*" the Callarino recited, "'*Come down that I may eat you.*'" He paused. "Do you know this poem, Davico? Is it original?"

My heart fell. I knew now why the Callarino had summoned me.

"My lord, Callarino—"

"*Once a cat called to a bird,*" the Callarino began again.

> "'*Come down that I may eat you.*'
> *The bird looked down and laughed,*
> '*Stand still so that I may shit upon you.*'
> *The cat was angry,*
> *The bird cared not,*
> *And shat upon him freely.*"

Paper crumpled in the Callarino's hands. A second later it bounced off my chest, making me jump, and fell to the carpets at my feet.

"Filippo di Basca da Torre Amo has a sense of humor," the Callarino said.

"My lord—"

"Filippo di Basca controls the bank in Torre Amo, and he sends poems."

"My lord—"

"Silence! When I want my dog to speak I will tell it to speak!" The

Callarino continued in a more moderate voice. "That man controls nearly half your family's wealth. Torre Amo is the gateway to the Khur Empire, and Filippo di Basca is its gatekeeper, and he sends poems."

"That poem was not meant for you—"

"Nai? It had my name addressed. The messenger brought it to me directly."

"Filippo has always been difficult. My father indulged him."

"I am not your father. By law and right he cannot do this."

I did not say what I thought about his laws and rights, but it did not matter for he was still speaking. "This man di Basca thinks me weak. He thinks himself far. Aqba!"

The door opened. "Lord?"

"Bring me that fat asslicker."

"The banker?"

"Yes, Merio! Merio da Pardi! What other fat asslicker?"

The image of Garagazzo immediately sprang to my mind, but if it entered Aqba's he had the sense not to mention it, and instead scuttled out. A few minutes later, Merio was back with him, and the Callarino was still pacing. Merio read the letter, then it crumpled once again.

"Filippo has always been difficult. Devonaci indulged him greatly."

"I feel as if I'm in an echoing cave!" the Callarino said. "Filippo is *difficult,*" he parroted. "Devonaci *indulged* him." His pacing came to a halt. "Why? Why did the great di Regulai allow this fop and fool to represent the bank?"

Merio sighed. "Torre Amo is unique, because of its trade with the Khur. Tea and spices that cannot be procured elsewhere come through its port, and the Khur refuse to trade with any others than the princes of Torre Amo." I could almost see him shrug. "They think of Torre Amo as a Khur principate. The princes claim lineage."

"And this Filippo?"

"He has done favors for the princes. They like him. He is . . . debauched."

"He cannot be invulnerable."

"Nearly so. It is why Devonaci indulged him. Filippo is a power unto himself. The relationships with the Khur and the princes, the trade, the discretionary deposits, all of it flows through Filippo's hands. In this relationship, we are the weaker partner, not the greater."

"Devonaci was a fool!"

I fought to stifle a laugh. It was such a pleasure to hear the Callarino's impotence. To listen to him in a rage over that which he could not reach and could not control. And to see Filippo, of all people—that crass and clever man—caper and dance outside the villain's reach.

The bird cared not and shat freely upon his head.

Indeed.

Merio and the Callarino continued to debate impotently, as Filippo's shit rained down upon them.

Suddenly the room fell silent.

"What is this?" The Callarino breathed.

At first, I thought that I must have betrayed my feelings upon my face, like the faccioscuro incompetent that I was, but then Merio whispered, "They said that he had some attachment to it."

Suddenly I realized what they were talking about. The dragon eye. That ancient fossil still sat upon my father's desk, just where it had sat when my father lived. And now it was alive. I could feel it. I could feel it pulsing with warmth, and without even realizing it, I had turned my face to it, as a flower turns its petals to the sun, soaking in the radiance.

Warmth seemed to pour from it, bathing me. I had laughed at the Callarino, and the dragon had laughed with me. Laughed at the petty world of humans. Laughed at us, laughed with me. By the fatas, I could feel it there, could feel its life pulsing, could feel its dark pleasure at the Callarino's petty wraths. We were one, enjoying his suffering, and in the darkness of my mind, I could see it.

Of course, I was not truly seeing it, for I remained blind.

And yet.

And yet I felt as if I could. I could see it resting upon the ancient carven desk that my ancestors had constructed, with its engraved obeisances to Leggus and its depictions of fatas and fauns and gold and gems and merchants and abacuses and gold scales. The eye sat before me, that strange fossil with its long trailing ocular spines, sharp and glittering, the light within it alive, the cat's-eye slit seeming to wink at me from beneath the milky sheen of its surface—

The blow came without warning. My face blazed with pain from the Callarino's hand.

"Stop it!"

I fell back crying out, my cheek stinging. Another blow followed.

"Stop it, I say!"

I realized that I had been reaching for the eye, all unknowing, stretching my hand toward it.

Now I cowered back as the Callarino struck me again and again. I fell to the carpets, cowering under his blows. The Callarino continued to pummel me. The dragon eye disappeared from my mind. It was as if black Borraghese velvet had been dropped over it, muffling light, blocking heat, snuffing out life. I fought to find it again, to touch that great and powerful creature, but it was gone as if it had never existed.

I felt as if I were mad for even imagining it, it was gone so completely.

I lay upon the carpets, my face stinging, my body aching and trembling. A final boot slammed into my ribs. I flinched and whimpered. It is an awful thing to be beaten when you cannot even anticipate the blows.

The Callarino stood over me, panting heavily. "What was that?" he demanded. "What happened there?"

Merio sucked his teeth thoughtfully. "Cazzetta once said that the boy had an affinity for the thing. That its soul stirred for him somehow. He told me he saw the boy mesmerized by it. He wanted Devonaci to get rid of it, but Devonaci refused."

"Superstition?"

"Nai. Cazzetta was not one for such."

"I do not like it," the Callarino said. "Take him back to the tower. He is not to enter here again."

"You yourself brought him here," Merio pointed out.

"Get him out!" the Callarino shouted. He took a deep breath, fighting to regain control of his emotions. "Make him useful. Make him write to Torre Amo again. Bend Filippo di Basca to our will."

"It will not work," I whispered.

The Callarino crouched down beside me. "For your sake, Davico, it had better."

And so I was taken back to the tower and there confined, and there I dictated letter after letter to Torre Amo, begging Filippo to close our bank's partnership and repatriate the gold that was my family's back to me.

I ordered, begged, and entreated, just as I did with all the other branches, and all the other branches obeyed me. The gold of my family was pouring back to Navola, a mighty river, branch after branch obeying my bidding. Cheroux. Vaz. Chat. They all did my bidding.

But not Filippo.

Not Torre Amo.

Filippo refused my letters.

I dictated to Merio again and again, and at last, after many letters and entreaties, we received a new poem from Filippo:

The Callarino may bugger di Regulai,
And the Regulai may spread their assholes,
But I am not di Regulai!
I am the one who pours the olive oil,
Not the one who fills my ass with it!

What is mine is mine, and what is yours is mine,
And the men and women of Torre Amo love my cock!
Now bend over, esteemed Callarino
And oil that wrinkled bung!
Brace yourself for buggering!

For you, dearest Callarino, are fucked!

The Callarino was enraged, and made me correspond again, and this time, very quickly, we received a new poem.

There once was a young bull who sucked an old goat.
The old goat was dry, and his cock was shriveled.
I am glad I am not a young bull.

That letter caused the Callarino to beat me heavily.

"He defies me?" the Callarino raged. "I will have his head. I will . . ." He mastered himself. "I will send an assassin. A stiletto for his neck."

"It won't work," Merio said sourly.

"Why not?"

"Filippo seems a fool, but he is alert. He has survived the intrigues of Torre Amo for years. I myself know of two attempts to kill him, once by poison, once by the blade, and both stilettotore died." He paused significantly. "And later, their employers as well."

"But by all the Laws of Leggus he must give up that money! Is that not what you told me?"

"You speak truly," Merio said. "And yet he who holds the rope owns the goat."

"More goats. There must be some way to force him to the plank."

Merio sucked his teeth. "Filippo was always a law unto himself. I fear that without his loyalty to Devonaci, Filippo has taken this opportunity and made our gold his."

I did not point out that the gold in question was not theirs at all. It galled to hear how easily they had assumed ownership of something that they had taken by treachery. But still, they were incensed and angry, as dogs who have been denied a stag in a hunt, and so now they circled, baying and barking at one another in their frustration.

"Does di Basca not care for Devonaci's son?" the Callarino asked. "Does he not understand how precarious the young Regulai is?"

I did not like the silence that fell between them. It was predatory. Speculative. Their gazes crawled over my skin like spiders seeking a way under a man's collar.

I cleared my throat. "Filippo cares for nothing except bawdy jokes and other men's wives. He cares not for me."

And yet still the silence stretched.

"Convince him," the Callarino said at last. "Convince him that your life hangs in the balance."

The letter I dictated was as impassioned a treatise as I have ever written. I poured all my eloquence into that letter. I even included a joke about goats and nuns. But the Callarino was not satisfied with my efforts. He added a message of his own. A gift to accompany my impassioned begging: the bloody severed stub of my littlest finger—a token of seriousness for an unserious man.

Filippo returned my finger, withered and black, strung upon a golden chain.

Chapter 53

There is the darkness of blindness. And then there is the darkness of a dungeon.

Though you might think blindness worse, a dungeon—deep and dark, without a sense of passing time—well, as it turns out, that is a recipe for madness.

After my final failure to sway Filippo, the Callarino had no further use for me, and so he sent me to the catacombs.

Aqba and the Callarino's guards dragged me down into tunnels I had never known existed deep beneath the palazzo. Not the catacombs of the ancient city that I had journeyed through with Cazzetta and Celia, but some other deep hole. Scents of ancient death wafted through there, so perhaps my hole and those catacombs shared bones somewhere. Mostly I smelled torch smoke and felt the mist of cold dripping water on my skin as we descended. The gritty scent of damp stone. The must of mold.

And then, before me, the clang of iron gates, the scrape of rusting metal. Another crash behind me, and then, silence such as I had never known, a heavy cold weight of silence. It felt as if the palazzo were squatting upon me, all that stone piled up above me, all that weight. All that cold dripping silence.

The first night I spent in the deeps, the Callarino came to me, observing me as I was served my dinner, the scraps of his table, dumped wet and splashy into a trough outside the bars of my cell, so that I had to reach through and feel for anything I hoped to eat. I did not know he was there at first, thinking only guards to be present, so it was with my hands threaded through the bars, fingers deep in cold slop, that I discovered myself observed.

I was picking through crusts of bread, feeling and separating the textured rinds of cheeses and melons, and discovering the half-gnawed stub of a chicken bone along with the thigh of some creature that I supposed might have been a pig. A heavy pork bone, well stewed perhaps? There were other scraps as well, bits from the kitchen I assumed, the tops of carrots and turnips, wads of trimmed raw fat, cold and rubbery. Something wet that pulped when my fingers touched it, perhaps tomato—

"Does my pig fatten?"

I froze at the Callarino's crooning words. Then hurriedly yanked my hands back through the bars, in case he planned to seize or stab them. My attention had been upon the mess before me. I hated that he had managed to sneak up on me. Now I drew a little farther away, wiping my filthy fingers upon my shirt.

"Merio once said I could live as an abacassi if I did your bidding."

"Did he?"

"He said you had no interest in torturing me."

The Callarino snorted. "He lied."

I had suspected such but had still held out hope. When we are dependent on the charity of others we become as dogs, always hoping that the next time a stranger approaches on the street he will not kick us.

"Why do you not kill me then?"

"It pleases me to see the Regulai living in filth. Rooting like a pig."

"So you only treated me well while I was of use."

"Is that a surprise?"

"We never treated you so. My father did not humiliate you."

"You're more blind than I thought, Davico."

The Callarino's footsteps scuffed softly. I followed the noise of his movement, straining to locate his slippered feet. I didn't like that he had stopped talking. He was pacing before the bars of my cell, a soft velvet sound. Back and forth, back and forth. It raised my hackles.

"We never—"

"I ate shit from that man every day that he was alive!"

I flinched and scrambled back from his fury.

"I ate shit! I ate shit and I ate shit!"

His words crashed over me, echoing and re-echoing, surrounding me, reverberating from the stone walls of the cell. I crouched amidst the storm of his rage.

"I ate shit, and Devonaci di Regulai made me smile!"

A wet noise from the direction of the trough was my only warning. Something cracked against the wall beside me, light and hard. The chicken bone? I ducked away, crouching, covering my head. "We—"

"I ate shit!"

Something heavy slammed against my shoulder. I cried out, numbed, "That was not me!" I tried to cover myself better, not sure where the next attack would come from. Afraid of what else he might throw. "I didn't do that!"

"His blood. His get. His seed!"

Something wet and nasty spattered against my ear. "He made me smile and he fed me shit! And now you're my sfaccito fescato dog and you will pay!" At any moment, I was sure he would enter my cell and murder me.

It is terrifying to cower before such rage, but also—and I know that you will think this strange—in that moment, even as I cowered and crouched, blind and vulnerable, I saw—in a way that I could not have seen when I still had eyes—that the Callarino was trapped in a cell as dark and cold as mine.

Despite the man's triumphs, he lived not with pleasure in the present, but caged within the rages of his past. Borsini Amoforze Corso lived shackled and chained down by memories of how my father had once held power over him. The man was haunted by the ghosts of his past.

And seeing that, I saw, too, that he was small.

I had thought him powerful. I had thought him dangerous—and he surely was—but I also saw in that moment of insensate rage that he could control neither himself nor his hatred of my father, nor of me, and he could not set down the past that he had triumphed over. This man owned Palazzo Regulai. He had slaughtered all my father's family. He had taken all our lands, our warehouses, our vineyards, our wealth.

He ruled Navola.

And yet still he felt my father's grip upon his neck.

For a moment, I felt pity and even a sort of hollow triumph, knowing that these memories still ate at him and that even I—despite my loathsome and pathetic state—even I held a sort of grip upon him.

But in truth, it was a small comfort, and it was soon extinguished under the rigors of the dungeon.

We are all as dogs before pain. We all, in the end, are of a shared weaving—and we all howl when we die.

—VITTIUS, AS RECORDED BY THE HISTORIAN
LIIS OF KHUS, ON THE EVE OF HIS QUESTIONING

Chapter 54

My cell was five steps wide, and five deep. Exploring by feel, my fingers discovered rough flat stones stacked and mortared as a wall, with sharp edges and nooks protruding. Stones perhaps even older than those of the catacombs and foundations that had been made by the Amonese. Thick rusty iron bars made up one wall of my cell, with a simple door inset. If I stood with my back to those bars, the left wall made a trickling sound. It was covered with moss and algal slime. There, water dripped down its face and ran into a shallow trough, so shallow that my fingers at first could not discern how it stayed in its channel, that ran down the center of the room. The water flowed until it encountered the far wall, where it pooled along the edge. It must have somehow found its way between small cracks in the stones, for there it seemed to disappear. My new abode was clammy and damp. I had been given rough wool blankets; they were soon damp as well.

I saw no more of Merio, nor of the Callarino. I was forgotten, except by Aqba, my tormenter.

Aqba. How I hated him. I tried to keep track of my days by scraping marks into the rough walls with a shard of stone that I found, marking my feeding times, trying to keep track of my one meal of the day, but I soon became convinced that Aqba deliberately came to me at odd hours, that he fed me sometimes more and sometimes not at all, so that I would lose all sense of how time passed.

When at first you are thrown into prison, you imagine that you have some power over yourself. Some resilience. You know that your enemy's object is to drive you mad, and so you set your mind to calmness. For myself, I brought to mind the pages of Soppros's wisdom, concerning stillness and listening and the pleasures of it. I brought to mind the breathing and calmness exercises that Aghan Khan taught, ways to settle a mind and keep it focused before a battle. I cataloged my memories of our family gardens, each flower and herb and plant and tree, and their uses, their Navolese and their nomae Amonese Anciens. I bathed myself by hand with the water that dripped from the wall.

All this I did and more.

But eventually, inexorably, my willpower waned. I became despondent. I became enraged. I shouted at Aqba, I challenged him to kill me. Anything to end my filthy existence. For I was filthy. My cell had no chamber pot or bucket. I shat at the low side of the cell, and it came to reek. I lost interest in attempting to clean myself, for it was a choice between becoming cold or becoming an illusion of clean.

I lived in a filth that you cannot imagine, and then as my shit and crumbs of food accumulated, the rats and roaches and beetles came. After them, the spiders came to catch the beetles. Fleas found me, I think from the blankets that were given to me. Firmos had found me, even here, deep in the bowels of the earth.

I slept only in glimpses, for when I stilled to sleep, rats would visit and attempt to nibble at my ears and toes and I would wake, thrashing. When Aqba did not come for a long time, and my stomach became too hollow, I began to catch and eat cockroaches and beetles. I became as a beast. My skin became abraded and soft, suppurating with sores from the bites of the rats and fleas.

And yet still I lived.

Hours became days became years, became as one. I imagined sometimes that I was a creature of the caves and darkness myself. Scuro's acolyte. One of shadow. One of filth.

Davico receded, and another replaced him—one that slept and paced and snuffled as an animal. I became so adept at sleeping that when a rat came to bite upon my ear, I caught it and broke it against the wall in my sleep, never waking, and only realized later, when I woke and found the shattered creature in my hand.

I drank its filthy blood for sustenance.

I survived.

I do not know how long I lasted so, but suddenly there was the smoke of burning wood in the air, and footsteps echoing. My nose—sharpened and quivering—smelled the men as they descended, their scented oils, their sweat, the well-cooked meat that they had eaten that day. My ears—cocked and alert from listening for the footfalls of spiders and cockroaches—counted the heavy boots. I scuttled to the farthest corner of my cell as the boots halted before my bars.

Someone retched. There were four of them, and one was Aqba. I smelled his breath and his kheem leaf.

"He's filthy," a man said.

"He is vermin," Aqba said.

"Get him out."

"Lord?" Aqba's voice was laced with puzzlement.

"Get him out. The Callarino wants him." The man gagged. "But clean him first."

"He is filthy," Aqba said doubtfully.

"Ai. You're a fool. You, clean him!"

"Yes, Captain," another said. Footsteps retreated—the two guardsmen, I assumed. Two guardsmen, plus this captain, plus Aqba. I wondered if I could reach one of them, perhaps bite their throat, drink their blood—

Icy water deluged me. I leapt back. Another icy bucketful hit me in the face.

"Take off those clothes," the captain ordered.

Another bucket of water gushed over me.

"Hurry up about it."

Shivering, I did as I was ordered. The men went away and returned. More buckets of water gushed over me. Something thudded at my feet.

"Bathe yourself."

I felt for the object, and found a clod of something slick and heavy. Soap. It felt strange in my hands. Smooth.

"Be quick about it."

I soaped my body, feeling the sting of my sores, fascinated by the strange smoothness of soap. More buckets of water gushed over me.

"Again?" one of the guards asked.

"Nai, it'll do," the captain grunted. The gate squealed open. "Come on then. Come out. Let's get a look at you."

Cautiously I felt my way out through the gate. The captain sucked his teeth. "This is your doing, Aqba."

"I followed the Callarino's will."

"We keep our horses better than this man. Clean out his cell."

"Me?" Aqba protested. "It is not my—"

"Clean out his cell or by Amo I will have your head buried in that pile of shit!"

And then I was being guided out of the catacombs by the two guards, who still seemed reluctant to touch my filthy body. We climbed stairs. Round and round, up and up, and up. And up.

And up.

And up.

By the fatas, I had not understood how deeply I had been buried.

At last we emerged into warmth and sunshine. My skin felt as if it were being seared. I felt as one of those dung beetles that scurries away when hot sun strikes its carapace, scrambling for darkness and safety. But I had no choice. I was guided through the palazzo and eventually to chambers that I recognized by scent. I was being taken to the baths. There, I was handed off.

"Ready this one for tonight," the captain said.

"He is filthy!" a female voice protested.

"Do your best."

And so I was handed into the care of the bath girl and from there guided into a tiled room that I knew from memory. It was the one that the servant girls used to bathe themselves. The one I had used to spy down upon. The girl brought me a steaming bucket of water, and laid a hot wet cloth upon my skin. I flinched.

"I won't hurt you," she said. "Be still now."

"The water," I rasped. "It's hot."

"Ai." She sighed. "Wait."

A minute later she returned and I heard water splashing into the bucket. Again the cloth touched my skin. "Better?"

"Much."

Her name was Aya. She tried to wash me but I was too tender and so she gave me the cloth to scrub myself, with her to supervise. And so I stood and dipped the cloth and tried to rub the filth from my wretched skin. She clucked her tongue. "We will have to soak you. Perhaps that will help. But not yet."

She called to another girl, Ana, and they had me sit on a wooden stool while they took my hair in their hands and began to cut great fistfuls, discussing between them the knots and mats and filth that lay within, gasping at skeletons of beetles, at small rat bones. They cut my beard, first trimming it and then shaving it away entirely. They cut my nails, commenting on their gnarled lengths and how they protruded from my fingers and toes. At last they guided me to a deep soaking tub. I slowly managed to immerse myself in the heat, and the girls sat beside me.

"You looked dark when I first saw you," Aya said. "But now you are pale as a corpse."

"So much filth," Ana agreed.

The warmth of the water was making me dizzy. "Is there . . ." I hesitated, afraid to ask. Afraid that if I made a desire known, it would be snatched from me.

"Yes?" Aya prompted.

"Food?"

The girls burst into peals of laughter. "Of course!"

A few minutes later, Aya returned with grapes and cheese and bread, and fresh water and none of it filthy.

"Ai! You're like the wolf that ate the baby!" Aya exclaimed.

"You can't eat too much," Ana counseled. "You will be sick."

I knew that she was right, but I could not stop my convulsive gobbling, so Aya took it away. "A little now, a little later. Not so much. I have seen starving men kill themselves from eating too much."

I wanted to fight to get the food back, wanted to tear at her, but I was weak. They drew me once more from my soaking tub, and set about scrubbing me all over once again.

At another time, with my eyes, with my sight, I might have felt self-conscious at their hands upon my naked body, scrubbing me as intimately as a mother washes her babe, but I had been an animal too long, and could not in any case see their eyes upon me, and so I merely stood obediently and let them wash and rinse me. Then I was soaked again, with new water, and at last I was judged clean.

Ana and Aya cleaned my wounds and put salves upon my fleabites and all the time they talked and chattered.

"You are kind," I said, "to care for me."

"Ci. It is nothing," Aya said, and then, hesitatingly, "Your family was good to mine."

I was surprised. "I thought all our friends dead and gone."

"Not all. A few, here and there. Vianomae remember. I had a brother who was paid to join your father's militia. We were saved from starvation because of it."

"Does that still exist?"

"Nai. The Archinomi did not like vianomae with so much swordskill. He is a mercenary now, and sends us silver."

"Ah."

We were silent for a while as they clucked over my wounds.

"I used to spy upon this bathhouse," I said.

"Oh?"

"Up there." I pointed to where I knew the high windows must be. "When I was a boy. I hid upon the roof and watched all the girls as they bathed."

"Ai!" Aya cried. "You were a wicked boy."

"The boy at the keyhole!" Ana exclaimed. "How naughty of you!" But they did not sound angry, only amused.

"It was a different time. I was a different person. I remember . . ." Suddenly grief washed over me. "I had eyes."

I do not know why it was this memory that filled me with grief, but it was sharp and bright, where my losses had all been dull before. The memory of pretty girls bathing, covering themselves with soap. And me, peeking down, not knowing the gift I was stealing. Not knowing what lay before me in my life, not knowing that soon I would never see any such thing ever again.

"I wonder if my wounds are punishment," I said, drawing a ragged breath.

"Ci. You were only Caliba's acolyte. Everyone likes to peek if they can," Aya said. "I peeked at my brother. I wanted to see a root."

"I watched the Callarino's neighbor," Ana said. "Siana Trucco and her guardsman. I was sent to deliver a message to her cook, but it was Siana Trucco on the kitchen floor. I watched them grunt like pigs."

"Everyone peeks," Aya said.

"Everyone," Ana agreed.

"Why are you being kind to me?" I asked.

"It's the Callarino's birthday. We are here to make you presentable for the event."

"How long have—what birthday is this?"

"He turns forty-five."

A year. More than a year I had been in that hole. It seemed both impossible that it had been such a long time, and impossible that it had been so short. More than a year. I had been taken down into the bowels of the palazzo in the spring, after failing to convince Filippo, and now it was not one summer but the second. Not all that far off from my own name day, though I struggled to remember if the Callarino's came before mine, or after.

But I had no time to dwell on this for Ana and Aya still had tasks to complete. They rinsed me once again, then wrapped me in towels so soft that it felt as if I were being embraced by clouds. They groomed me one final time, shaving my face perfectly smooth and trimming my hair to a style that they approved of, then dressed me in clothes that were soft and light and told me how filthy I had been before.

They guided me from the baths and once again out into sunlight, still hot, still shocking, but not as painful as before. I smelled roses blooming and heard bluetips cooing in the garden's trees. Evening was approaching.

They took me to a bench and saw me seated, and bid me goodbye. I loved them greatly. I still do, in fact. But in that moment, I would have died for them.

A whipped dog takes what love it can.

Chapter 55

After such a long time under the earth, the gardens seemed to be bursting with life.

When I had first been blinded, I had thought the loss of my eyes had made more me fully aware of my childhood home, forcing me to experience it in new ways, forcing me to see it truly. But now I understood that I had been wrong in thinking I had noticed anything at all, for now my senses were drunk, as if they were all coming awake for the first time, like flowers bursting into blossom in the spring.

The marble bench I sat upon had its own scent. Different from granite, as in my cell. Different from sandstone. Different from another marble bench that sat baking nearby in the sun, even. I smelled the flowers, but I smelled, too, that the roses were dry, and that their petals were beginning to desiccate. The earth in the planters was dry, a feathery scent rather than a damp one, so I knew it had not rained recently. But too, the hot air felt moist and anticipatory, and I knew clouds were forming, building, not for today, nor for tomorrow, but soon there would be monsoons and the hot season would break. I heard the rumbling buzz of fat bees. The scents they knocked free as they scrambled through flowers told me that they were particularly attracted to the coneflowers—I tell you these things, but still I am unequal to the task of explaining. Suffice to say, my childhood palazzo seemed more vibrant, alive, and real than at any time in my entire life. The familiar made strange made familiar again.

Guests began arriving. I found this frightening. I had not been surrounded by people for such a long time that I had a sudden urge to scuttle away, to crouch in corners, to hide from their eyes, to protect myself from their loud voices, their laughter. They were so close that

I could touch them and so far away that they might as well have been Borraghese for all the humanity we shared.

Fortunately, I was saved from conversation, for each time a guest drew close thinking me someone of interest, they would gasp and turn away sharply. I was indeed of interest; too much of it. With my sightless eyes, slave-scarred cheeks, and gaunt appearance, they knew me instantly. They whispered amongst themselves. They thought themselves subtle and secretive, but I heard all their words.

"Di Regulai. The son."

"Sfaccito! A di Regulai sfaccito!"

"I would not have thought them so low as to accept such humiliation."

"I always heard the son was weak."

"Why, he is nearly a cadaver!"

"Look at his eyes."

"Ai! What's that creature doing here?"

"Is he a warning? I thought him dead."

"He looks a monster."

"How does he yet survive?"

"Those eyes! I had heard that he was blind, but what a ruin!"

"His eyes."

"His eyes, his eyes, his eyes . . ."

There was more like this, all of their reactions and feelings shared with me because their senses were blunt where mine were sharp, but their horror was nothing to me. To them I was a beast, but I did not mind. To myself, I was a beast.

Left alone by the celebrants, I eavesdropped on their conversations, the ebb and flow of the Navolese at ease. Warm tones of women flirting. The strut of men preening. The give-and-take of negozziere and mercanta, the world I had grown up with.

"Two navisoli a yard—!"

"—Have you seen *The Milk Maid*?"

"Arestophos's old comedy?"

"Yes, but Zuzzo has reimagined it . . ."

"Sia Devina, you are more lovely each day—"

"Really, Avo, you are too much. I have a servant girl from the Romiglia and she has never bitten a single soul—"

"—marble downriver to Venna for half the price that di Corto is quoting—"

I had never noticed when I had been sighted how conversation flowed. Who dominated and who attended, and what it indicated about the power of various players. But now I listened: no longer a participant, no longer trying to find the gap for my own voice, to show myself interested, or witty, or any dozens of other reasons to make noises with my mouth. Marooned at the margin of their conversations, I listened, perhaps for the first time. The words lost their meaning, concerning a world that did not concern me, but I found the voices fascinating. The tones and rhythms of conversation were nearly musical, the way they twined and rose and fell through the warm night air. Men booming with bombast, women twittering in deference. Men clashing as bulls. Women stabbing as stilettos.

The tenor of the conversation shifted abruptly. Someone important was forging through the crowd, cutting through the revelry as a ship's prow cuts the Cerulea. Waves of conversation were stopping. A spreading wake of rustling cloth followed. People were bowing, I realized.

"My lord Parl!" The Callarino, his voice booming with pleasure. "Welcome once again to Navola." Rustling clothing told me that the Callarino, too, now bowed deeply.

"Patro Corso!" came the reply. "The city is even more beautiful than when I last visited!" The voice was not the young Roulait's. "Felicitations on your name day."

"You're too kind," the Callarino preened. "It is an honor to host you once more."

It was absolutely not the young Parl that I had known. The voice was deeper, thrumming with confidence, familiar . . .

The Duke Dellamont.

I almost laughed. The first secretary was now, apparently, Parl. The man who had been Roulait's best support had revealed himself as the hungry wolf. Cazzetta had been right. Dellamont had been too much a force to remain content under the shadow of a brash young inheritor.

My thoughts were interrupted by the approaching steps and chatter of Dellamont and the Callarino.

"Ah. The young bull," Dellamont said. "I'm surprised you are still alive." A pause. "Though you do look worse for the wear."

"Do I?" I forced myself to smile up at him, sunny. "I haven't a mirror."

"I've seen losing dogs in a betting fight look better."

"I'm sure the Parl looks worse than I."

"I am the Parl."

"And yet I could have sworn there was some man you had sworn to protect."

"Ignore him," the Callarino said, but Dellamont only chuckled.

"That boy was not the man he thought he was. A problem you both shared, as it happens."

"Did you poison him?" I asked. "Did you send a stilettotore?"

"I did it myself," Dellamont said. "I put the dagger up under his ribs while he celebrated the death of his uncle Ciceque, and the successful clearing of his father's debts."

"And you then blamed his death on his uncle, I'm sure. Even though Ciceque was already dead, you found some way to blame him."

"Ai. I think you see more clearly now that you're blind, Davico. In fact, one of Roulait's closest men was torn apart by four horses for the perfidy. A man named Ceinot. You met him."

"I did."

"A man of no real account, but still, a relation of Ciceque's and therefore guilty of a terrible vengeful plot."

"Convenient."

"Efficient. Another was implicated as well. The capo of your bank's Merai branch. I think you knew him. Paritzio Ferro?"

I remembered Maestro Ferro. The man with the abacus-callused fingers, who had worried about the expense of chilling bitters with snow from the Ruia. I had written to him early in my enslavement. Indeed, he had been one of the first and most punctilious to send my family's money back to Navola.

"What did he ever do to you?"

"To me? Ai, Davico. As your partner in Merai, obviously, he was plotting revenge against us. Also, he was wealthy in his own right."

"You are a monster."

"I am Parl."

"This younger generation," the Callarino said, "has an overweening sense of their own importance. But come now, the first secretary of Vesuna is here. He has a proposal to curb the Schipians and their piracy."

They drifted away. The intermingling of people resumed. I wondered if I was glad or sorry that the young Parl had fallen to Dellamont's treachery, or if I cared at all. I decided to feel happy.

"Oh my. The last seed of the Regulai."

I startled, for I had not heard or smelled her approaching. Still, I recognized the purr of self-satisfaction. "Siana Furia."

A small laugh. "You're more observant without your eyes than you ever were with them, Davico."

"People keep saying that."

She had once greatly frightened me. She and her black stallions and her poisonous slaves and her foreign warriors. Now I could not muster the urge to spar with her. I only wished her to leave me alone so that I could feel the warm night air upon my skin. I resolved to focus my attention there.

Confoundingly, Furia settled upon the bench beside me. "I never expected that I would see a Regulai reduced to slavery."

"I still don't see one."

"Oh," she purred. "You've acquired a droll sense of humor."

I didn't reply.

"No one will sit near you," Furia said. "They are all afraid. You should see them. They can barely look upon you. They look, and then they look away, and then they look again."

I didn't answer. It took all my will with Furia beside me, but I focused my attention upon the garden. The warm night. The perfume of flowers. The moisture of the storm that would come—

Something touched my cheek. I flinched.

"Ci. Let me look at you." It was Furia's hand, turning me to face her.

"You want to see what you have wrought?"

Furia snorted. "Not I. I would have made prettier marks. The Callarino is ruled by his emotions. He runs down paths that he has not thought through, and then is angry when he arrives."

"I'll tell him you said so."

"I have told him myself." She turned my face this way and that. "You look like a creature that's crawled from Scuro's Unseen Realm." She dropped her hand. "I would not have seen you treated so, Davico. Whatever else, I would not have done this."

"And yet you went along."

"I am as wheat before a winter wind."

"Avinixiius. I think you profited more than wheat."

"Am I not Navolese?" Furia laughed. "If you had been half this wise when you had your eyes, things might have turned out differently for you."

"You would have been loyal?"

"Do not speak to me of loyalty. I was not even of your father's circle, and yet I warned him. He would not listen."

"I don't believe that."

"Nai? I warned you as well."

I thought back on all our interactions. "The finger bones. On my name day."

"Indeed. No one feared you, Davico. Devonaci refused to see that you were not the son he desired. You were a good boy, with a lovely hound and darling little pony, and no one feared you. You were not the sort who bent others to your will. Devonaci was a great man, but he was more blind than you are now, when it came to his son. He had so many plans, so many ideas of how his world could be shaped. But they all depended on men's willingness to follow you. He believed that because he called you his heir, others would believe it, too. Would obey it. He saw many things clearly, but he loved you too much. It was his downfall."

"And you have no such weakness."

"What we desire and what is real are not the same. Men forget that. I do not."

It was a strange conversation. From Furia's tone, I almost had the feeling of apology. It left me unsettled, trying to understand what she gained from speaking so to me.

"Do you like my pet?"

It was the Callarino, returned.

"He would have been worth more unscarred," she said, her words becoming once more the threatening purr that I was most familiar with. "I could have sold an unmarked Regulai for a thousand suns. If you had given me the brother and the sister, I could have trained them to do wonderfully unspeakable things."

I tried to hide my startlement at the mention of Celia. Was she a slave as well? Did Furia own her? Had she been sold as sfaccita? My mind roiled with questions that I dared not ask, and feelings that were too complex to untangle.

"But then someone else would have had the pleasure of his suffering," the Callarino was saying. "Some treasures are far too dear to sell."

Furia's hand grasped mine and lifted it. Her fingers ran over the stub of my missing pinkie. "But not too dear to mangle, it seems."

"He's more intact than he has any right to expect. He has nine fingers still, and his life. He even has his cock."

"You should kill him."

"One minute you complain I damage my toy, the next you say I should throw him away. Make up your mind, siana."

"A living Regulai is a dangerous Regulai. You do not know what you're playing with."

"Ci. It's my birthday, and you come with prophecies of doom. You're just jealous that I won't sell him to you."

"I am not."

"Would you have liked him in your bed? One of your pleasure toys? I've heard you like a firm lad."

"Sfaiculo. He is a wreck now, hardly worth a navisoli. If you will not sell him to me, slit his throat and end his line for good. He is dangerous to Navola."

She stood and departed with a swish of silks, leaving a perfume that smelled of citrus.

"Women," the Callarino observed, "do not like it when you keep them from their baubles."

"Why am I here?" I asked. "Why did you bring me out into the open air?"

"So that you can enjoy my birthday, Davico!" He clapped me on my shoulder. "To celebrate! On this anniversary of my birth, I show mercy to my enemies and give gifts to my friends." He squeezed my shoulder, proprietary. "Enjoy your wine, slave. Enjoy the night. Enjoy that you breathe warm air."

The Callarino departed. I sipped the wine and realized that I was light-headed, a dizzy relief and a surprise, for a mere half glass to cause me to feel so. I heard torches crackling and smelled their smoke. I supposed that the quadrae were well lit and festive. My face felt warm, tingling with the wine.

Soon there was a bell rung and I was guided toward where voices chattered and cutlery and dinnerware clattered, a great long table, I deduced, set in the heart of the courtyard. I was guided by a servant past all the people scraping their chairs, gossiping with one another and taking their seats, guided along the length of the table until I realized I was being led to one end of it.

I was distant, of course, from the center, a creature relegated to the edge of importance, but still, where I sat would be supremely visible. The Callarino's trophy. I could not have given him more satisfaction had my head been mounted upon a wall.

I ate. I drank. I listened to the birthday revelry. I listened to the voices of my enemies as they all joined in toasts to the Callarino's long life: Sivizza, Merio, Dellamont. Garagazzo. Furia. I heard the voices of others, people who had attached themselves to the Callarino's risen star. Some of whom I recognized. Some of whom had once been allies of my father. Some of whom had I never known. All of them dined with pleasure.

At the end of the night, I was dragged back to my cell deep beneath the earth and left to rot once again.

But in that world above, I had managed one thing:

I had stolen a spoon.

Chapter 56

A spoon.

Upon such fragile foundations are hopes built.

A spoon.

The first real tool I had held in my hands in more than a year.

I had regained my mind, I had a spoon, and as I descended into the bowels of the earth, new determination filled me.

I would dig my way out. I would escape.

To that purpose, I used all my senses to track my return to my cell, counting my steps, noting details as we descended: the smells of torches and of the rotting ancient dead that told me the crypts and catacombs were not entirely separate from my prison; the kiss of breezes on my skin, on the stairs, in the tunnels, those winds that felt and smelled dank and deep, and those of a fresher, warmer nature.

All the way back to my cell, I mapped the passages in my mind, memorizing turns and steps and doors and gates. Truly, it was a place that I never guessed existed. I wondered if any of my family's own enemies had languished down here, perhaps tortured by Cazzetta, suffering, hopeless, alone. I realized that I didn't particularly care. I think a different version of me, perhaps one with eyes, would have felt differently, but after my time in the dark at the Callarino's hands, I only wished that Cazzetta had gotten to him as well.

Once I was interred, I set to work.

If I had hoped for better treatment after the guard captain's intervention I was soon disappointed. Left to his own devices, Aqba once more let my filth accumulate. He threw the Callarino's scraps into my trough outside the bars or, when he was feeling particularly irritable, hurled them upon the floor of my cell. He also took a liking to spitting upon me when I sat too close to the bars.

But I was immune to his abuses, for my new determination fortified me. Scraping and prying mortar, first around the edges where the bars were set into the walls, and then between the stones that surrounded the bars, kept me busy and optimistic. Feeling each stone, I chipped slowly at the mortar. For long hours—and sometimes days, depending on whether Aqba was trying to starve me—I was left alone to scrape and burrow, and so I did. Like Scuro's blind white worm that he rode to consume the mythical city of Ach, I burrowed. I burrowed with purpose, thinking about how Scuro and his worm had opened a vast sinkhole and swallowed that city, to punish them for turning their worship from Amo. I imagined opening a hole beneath the Callarino, and swallowing him up entirely.

I scraped and chipped and pried enough to at last unseat a bar sufficiently that I could work on the next. I intended to pull the stones from beside the bars, to slowly open a gap that I might squeeze through, but the weight that sat upon those stones was great, and the mortar was as good as any used on the dome of Catredanto Amo. Still, I was not deterred. I was Scuro's worm. Each waking moment that Aqba was not present, I whittled and dug at those stones, loosening more of them. Weakened by imprisonment, it was not easy labor for me. But slowly, mortar gave way. And slowly the spoon was worn down. It became a sharp stake. It became shorter. And shorter.

And shorter.

At last, I accepted that I would need more than a single spoon to dig my way free. I would need dozens at the pace I progressed. I had little hope of escaping this prison by digging, but now my spoon was very sharp indeed, which made me think of other exits.

If I could bait Aqba to open my cell . . .

It took some taunting, but at last, driven by rage at my musings on how his mother had coupled with dogs to father him, he decided to open the gate and beat me like the slave I was.

He came with all the fury of a fata. I rammed my sharpened spoon into his belly.

Unfortunately, it was not a good weapon. It slipped in my hand as I stabbed through the cloth of his shirt. It took me three strikes to puncture him. And then the spoon became even more slippery with blood. It slithered from my grip, caught in his belly, and I was unable to finish the deed.

I scrabbled for the gates then, but I had overestimated my own speed and strength, and underestimated Aqba's. He seized my foot and dragged me back, and then clawed his own way out. The last thing I heard was iron slammed closed and the lock in the gate and then his footsteps stumbling down the tunnel, his breath ragged and bubbling.

After that, I was left alone for a very long time.

Eventually, another came to feed me, accompanied by a guard.

"Where is Aqba?" I asked.

They did not answer, only dumped my feed into my trough and walked away.

I wondered if perhaps Aqba had died. Perhaps his wound festered. Perhaps I had pricked his bowels and now his belly filled with shit. I liked that thought. I might have stabbed deep enough in my last attempt. It was possible. But without a spoon and without news, I was left much as I had been before, alone in the dark. I tried working the stones with my fingers, but my nails broke before I prized free even a small amount of mortar.

Time passed. It began to twist and untwist like the dark plaits of Celia's tresses. Aqba returned, hissing and vicious, and sadly alive, to spit in the slop of the kitchens that he served. To give and withhold food, as he pleased.

Entangled in darkness, my sense of time became confused, I became once more a crouched and scuttling beast. Nai. Not even a beast. Perhaps a cockroach. I was exomentissimo. I became one, not with Virga's weave, but with Scuro's legions. A creature of filth and pestilence. I was a beast of the dark, like one of those blind hairless rats that are found in sewers and deep mines. My ears became such that they pricked up when any new noise fell upon them. When the farthest chains and doors rattled, I froze. With the first scent of feed for my trough, my mouth salivated, long before it arrived.

In that ratty state, I listened often to my brothers and sisters, their squeaking and scuffling and skittering, their tiny claws upon stone, their nosing about my chamber. I woke more than once to find them chewing on my ears, but I caught them easily and ate them, so eventually they learned to respect me. After that, I imagined myself their friend. I learned to identify them by their scratching footfalls. I named some of them, even. Creatures that had once been indiscernible became as my companions. Dolce, the rat without the tail. Spera, the one with the torn ears. The fat slow one who came too close one day, and that I ate.

I called him Garagazzo.

I do not know how long I lived as an animal, except that I eventually emerged, as from a dream, to find myself shaking and shivering upon the floor, feverish and horrified at what I had been.

I was not sure if I had been sick and imagined myself as an animal or if it had truly happened. For a while I clung to my recovered sense of self, but then I slipped away again, exomentissimo.

My sanity went on like that for quite some time, emerging and disappearing, like the rocks and shoals of Navola's harbor. Exposed during low tide, drowned during high. Lost and then recovered.

It was a shock and a terror when I heard boots tramping in the tunnels. Many men, and lacking the smell of food. Only leather. And steel.

I smelled steel.

I scuttled back, shielding myself from the stinking smoking torches and their scalding heat on my wormy skin. The booted men came to a halt before my cell. In my animal way, I knew that this was my end. The Callarino no longer needed me. No longer enjoyed even my debasement. Chains rattled. The gate squealed open. A man entered, then retched and retreated. When he spoke, his voice was muffled, as though covered with some cloth.

"Clean him," the man gasped. "The Callarino wants him cleaned."

I perked up at this, remembering the baths of the palazzo. Remembering their warmth, the steam of the great baths, the tile, the scents of soaps. Two girls . . . their names . . . they had names . . . there was kindness there—

Icy water gushed over me. I scrabbled back, crying out, but more bucketfuls of ice water crashed down upon me. I huddled in my corner, shivering, unable to even form words as more water was heaved upon me.

"Strip."

I tried to understand the words, but they failed to make sense.

"Is he mindless?"

"Who can say?"

"Strip!" the first man repeated. "Take off your clothes!"

My skin. He wanted me to shed my skin. I plucked ineffectually at the sopping garments pasted to me, stiff with grime and shit. Slowly,

I began peeling myself free of those protective outer layers, wincing as my skin—nai, my clothes—tore away from my flesh.

"He's a mess."

"We can't hide those sores."

"It doesn't matter, take him up."

And so they dragged me out of my cell and up the stairs, the men nearly carrying me, for I was too weak now to climb, and then the air was warming, and then I was in the palazzo baths, submerged in water that was warm, and yet I shivered. Hands caressed my body—soft hands, and gentle.

"Hush," I heard a girl saying, "hush now, hush."

She kept saying this, over and over. "Hush now. Hush."

I realized that I was sobbing.

Ana and Aya worked harder this time to make me presentable. Clucking at my sores, at my slack skin, at my filthy hair and beard. At my bones pressing against my flesh like the ribs of a dead and desiccated cow.

"How long . . . ?" I rasped when my lips finally remembered how to form words. "How long has it been?"

"A year," Ana said, as she tended my sores. "It has been another year."

Chapter 57

It was as the previous birthday. I was given new clothes—very fine, my skin told me—and I listened once more to the guests and the pleasures of people who lived in the above world. I did as was expected. I sat on my bench. I drank my wine. I played the part of warning sigil to the Callarino's friends and enemies.

But I was a withered creature in comparison to my previous attendance. If I had thought myself a ghost before, I understood that I had been wrong. I was fading, right before these people's eyes. In another year or two I would be a memory. A true ghost at last.

The Callarino's steward announced the feast and I was led to the end of the long table once more. I heard the Callarino's voice purr behind me as I was guided into my seat.

"I've given you a fine companion tonight, Davico. A lovely girl. A pity you can't see how pretty she is."

I did not know if he was taunting me or not. I could smell jasmine perfume to my right, but the person could have been a crone, or leprotic, or a man perfumed and I would not have known. I was not sure what jest the Callarino played, so I said nothing.

Ritual toasts were given to Amo, and wines were sipped with ceremony. A servant stood behind me and guided my hand to the various cups and glasses for the toasts, the small bitter cup of history, the pewter one of the present, the glass one of the future, and then platters redolent of fowl and game were being set upon the table, making my mouth water.

It was with great restraint that I did not shame myself by lunging upon that meal, that I did not leap onto the table and scuttle down its length to where the meats were being carved before the Callarino. Though my mouth flooded with saliva, I restrained myself. I would not be the madman, ripping and tearing, the juice of duck and pork and beef running oily down my chin as I fed like a golgozza, tearing hearts from the warm bodies of the living. I would not play that part.

Still, my whole body quivered.

To distract myself, I forced my mind away from the scents of food. Beside me, the stiff silks of a woman's skirts rustled, accompanied by another wafting of jasmine flowers. The girl the Callarino had mocked me with. She had not said anything to me, and in fact I sensed that she shrank from being seated beside me.

I wondered what she had done to prick the Callarino that he would place her so. To my left, I smelled the sweat and labored breathing and the clinking ornamental buckles of a man. Someone else the Callarino didn't like, or wished to frighten, I supposed.

At last the first course was placed before me, a cold duck in a sauce of vinegars. Around me, conversation flowed, tableware clinked. The duck lay before me, wanton and beckoning.

The man to my left had begun a flirtation with a woman farther down the table, turning his body entirely away from me. He was apparently most pleased that he had successfully raised the rents on his tenants in Quartiere Pescane. His voice had a strut of confidence that sounded fragile as he preened to the woman. His target, too, sounded a false creature, twittering about a brooch of malachite that she said was expensive.

Farther still down the table, I picked out more voices. The Callarino, delighted with his party. Garagazzo, laughing and insatiable for the duck. Dellamont's molasses tones, thick with hidden intention as he discussed the problem of Cheroux. Sivizza's gruff rejoinders. Merio's appreciation of the wine. My enemies, all so close, and yet out of reach—

"Will you not eat?"

It was the girl to my right. Her accent was strange. From somewhere to the north. Venazza, perhaps, with that slight lisp, or even Merai. An educated voice, and surprisingly gentle.

"Forgive me," I said. "I was not sure if the Callarino played me for a fool, or I should have introduced myself sooner."

"There is no need to apologize," she said. "I remember you." Her fork clicked on her plate. "Will you not eat?"

"I am wary these days of things that the Callarino sets before me."

She was quiet for a moment, and then, in a low voice, leaning close, she said, "It is not poisoned or soiled. It was cut from a duck here at the table, the same as all of ours."

"You are kind for telling me."

"It is a small thing."

I felt for the food. "Forgive me, I must use my hands to know my plate." My fingers dipped into something wet. I sucked my fingers, tasting the vinegar sauce, sweet and tangy over the duck breast, the juice of the duck, the meat so tender, the skin so crisply seared. I fought the urge to seize everything in my fists and shove it into my mouth. "It is not polite, I know, but my hands are my only way of seeing."

"It does not offend me."

"You are very kind then." I finished my exploration of my plate and wiped my fingers on the tablecloth. "What, pray, is your name?"

She hesitated. "Your hand . . ."

"Oh, this?" I held up my hand with its missing finger. "Best not to speak too loudly."

She lowered her voice. "But . . ."

"Another token of my lord's displeasure." I changed the subject. "You were about to tell me your name."

"Allessana."

"And you say you know me?"

"It was a long time ago," she said. "Years, really. But I still remember it."

"Ah. You remember my eyes, then." I tore at the duck breast with my fingers, swabbed it in the sauce. "You do not remember me."

"No. I remember you." She paused. "You are changed, it's true, but I recognize you."

"You have the better of me, then." I took my first bite. Saliva flooded my mouth. A pleasure so intense that I should have been cavorting with Caliba and his fatas. I wanted it all. All in my mouth. To devour it, snuffling and grunting like a pig. I assumed that this was the Callarino's intention in placing me next to a woman he called beautiful. To make her disgusted by me. To disgust them all. I forced myself to chew slowly. Such pleasure . . .

"Are you all right? You're shaking."

"I—it has been a long time since I ate well." It was a surprise to me to discover that I still had vanity. Carefully, I tore another piece of the duck and ate it, savoring the juices on my fingers. Feeling my will crumbling—

"We dined together in Merai," the girl said.

"Ah." I fought to return my attention to the girl. "I thought I heard an accent."

"It was a long time ago. I was a silly girl then."

"I doubt you were as silly a girl as I was a silly boy."

"You didn't seem silly at the time. It was in the Parl's palazzo. You were visiting. It was a diplomatic visit. The Parl wanted to honor you. I was not important, but my friends and I drew cartae di scuro and I was permitted to sit beside you."

I tried to summon up those ghosts of memory. "I'm sorry. I do not remember you. Too much has happened."

"We discussed the wines of Navola and Merai. And the twisting intrigues of your city." She paused. "We were not kind to you. We teased you. We said all the things we say to one another about the Navolese. We said things like, *The Navolese are as twisted as the plaits of their women's hair.* That sort of thing. You took it well."

I remembered.

I had flirted with her. She had been pretty. Cazzetta had called her bait. One of those young women who decorated the Parl's court, hoping for well-placed husbands and lovers, hoping for advantage for their family. A girl of lower rank, and lucky to be included.

"You wore peacock feathers," I remembered.

"You said that the heart of a Navolese flies straight and true."

"I'm surprised that you remember whatever foolish words I spoke."

"Oh, you were very handsome. And you spoke with eloquence." Allessana hesitated. "I had heard that your family had fallen. I didn't guess . . ." She trailed off uncomfortably.

"Such are the intrigues of Navola." I tried to make my voice light. "You were right. We walk twisted paths here."

We were quiet for a time. I ate more duck. Each bite a pleasure and a torture.

"It's the same in Merai," she said. "We called you Navolese twisted, but now I think we threw insults upon you because we were ashamed of our own twisted ways." She sounded bitter.

"Your new ruler?" I hazarded. "How does dear Dellamont enjoy his power?"

"I cannot speak ill of my Parl," she said warily.

"Nai. We wouldn't dream of it. Though I confess that I don't see much difference between your new Parl and your old one. They worked together to ruin me and mine. Neither was ever going to be Virtus incarnated."

I must have spoken loudly, for down the table, Garagazzo spoke up, "No man is Virtus incarnated. We must strive to find Virtus within us. Charity, Kindness, Wisdom. And we must beat away the Envies and the Fatas of Lust and Rage."

"You lead us in all things," the Callarino said drily. Even people with ears less attuned than mine heard the mockery, and there was a titter of laughter.

"Yes, well, we all strive," Garagazzo said, sounding resentful.

"We do indeed strive for Virtus," Dellamont said, sounding more sincere. "We are humbled in our striving."

A murmur of agreement rippled down the table and I could imagine people kissing their amulets and touching them to their foreheads, bowing heads as they did so. Indeed, Allessana beside me echoed them.

"We must strive," she whispered. "We must strive," and I heard her make her own motion of obeisance. Heard her lips upon her amulet.

I felt a breath of movement as a servant placed a new course before me. The plate with my duck was being taken away. "No!" I flailed for his arm. "Please. No." I fought to control the begging that invaded my words. "Thank you. I still eat."

Aromas of sweet oranges and sharp onions over bitter greens wafted up to me from the new plate.

Around me, tableware clinked. Wine gurgled into cups. The festivities, the pleasurable braiding of good wine and good food and music and company continued. My senses, attuned after years squatting in darkness and listening to the creeping of spiders and the differing gait of skittering rats, feasted upon the activities around me.

I found I knew the number and places of the participants at the table. I counted thirty, seated down the length. I could separate voices, attach names, and set the people in their seats. There was Merio, down the length on the left, commiserating with a pair from the loom guild over the difficulties of Schipians and their inconstant ways. Sivizza, seated at the center on my right, directly across from the Callarino in a place of honor, alongside Dellamont. Sivizza was bragging about his villa's vineyards and the winemaker who oversaw everything from the pruning of the grapes to the barrels that the wines now aged in. "They are Wustholt oak. It took a pile of navisoli to bring them over the Cielofrigo."

"How far is your villa?"

"Just up the river, against the first hills, for good drainage."

This could have only pleased the Callarino, that the general was tying himself ever more tightly to the prosperity of the city.

There was Furia, just beyond Sivizza, complaining to the Callarino that Archinomo Boccatta was now allowed to keep their slave pens within the city, a privilege, I gathered, that she had enjoyed alone, before.

"You yourself do so, why should others not?" His oily voice implied that for a price they could be banished once more.

"Because I am Furia, and they are Boccatta, and if this is not resolved, then someone will find their Boccatta friends hanging by their necks in Quadrazzo Amo."

"That is . . . not subtle."

"It is not. Nor am I."

And then there was Dellamont, wryly engaged with a woman, a voice that purred, tantalizingly familiar—ai. Sia Allezzia, the famous courtesan who had once taught Celia. Even after all these years, I recognized her voice. He was urging her to visit him in Merai, and she was evading.

The table was full of archinomi, mercantae, and nobilii anciens. Many voices, many conversations. Mostly, I listened to my enemies. All my enemies, seated at one table. If I had had poison, I could have avenged myself against them all, could have listened as they gurgled and collapsed around me, as Avinixiius did to all his cousins before becoming emperor in Torre Amo and taking his place upon the White Rock.

"My dear, that gown is a lovely shade of blue."

The words drew me back to my near surroundings. It was a merchant speaking, seated on the far side of Allessana, and she was recoiling from him. From the way she did, I understood that he not only admired her, but also touched her.

"The sia was speaking to me," I said.

He started to retort, but I leaned forward. "The sia finds you unpleasant. Perhaps because you touch her too familiarly, perhaps because you smell of manure and olive oil, which makes me think you've been buggering your groomsman."

"You—" I heard him moving, knew what he was doing.

"Take your hand off your knife," I said.

He gasped, unnerved at being caught out by a blind man. I continued speaking, voice low, leaning toward him so that he could clearly see my ravaged eye sockets and disfigured face.

"The young sia is a ward of Siana Furia. Under her name and under her protection. Think hard on what you do next."

The man hissed at me, but he withdrew.

I was somewhat surprised at myself. I had known the man's intentions, had felt them, and been quick to act. My old self would have dithered, worrying about propriety, about telling lies, about making a noise. Instead, I had reacted as I would to a rat that had bitten my ear while I was sleeping, smashing it against the wall without hesitation. I wondered what I would have done if he had continued to challenge, and was interested to discover that I simply didn't care.

"Now," I said, turning to Allessana, and making my voice pleasant. "Tell me, how is it that you come to Navola? Have you found a higher rank, to travel so far in the company of Dellamont?"

"I . . ." She broke off, and a false brightness entered her voice. "Well," she said, "as you once said, the Navolese have hearts that fly straighter than any arrow. I wanted to see if it was true. I came looking to see if there might be a match in your fair city." The words were playful, but her tone was laced with something akin to panic.

"That hardly seems credible."

"I go where the Parl goes." There was another hitch in her voice. A hint of desperation. "I serve at his pleasure."

"Ah. Even the Red City with its sunny streets and warm flowers has twisted paths."

"My family . . . depends upon my good service."

"Forgive me, you seem distressed."

"Merai . . ." She lowered her voice even more. "It is a cautious place now. Even when the young Parl was our lord, even when Ciceque made him paranoid, there was still some . . ." She hesitated. "There was as least light."

"Light." I mused upon the word, thinking back to my own impressions of the young Parl, and of Merai. "Yes. I suppose there was light. And yet the darkness was always there as well. You didn't notice it, of course, but the darkness was already there. It was all around you in fact. It permeated everything. It's just that now it has made itself apparent to you."

"I don't think so. It was better, before."

"*Veridimmi?* Come now. It was the same for me. Darkness lurked at my elbow for years, but I did not see it. Darkness sat with me at my own table, rode horses beside me, laughed with me. Darkness was there, and I did not see it. And now I see nothing at all."

"I have heard the tale."

"What tale?" I said it more sharply than I intended, and immediately felt sorry. I was snapping at the one person who had treated me as a human being in more than a year. I touched my heart in apology. "Forgive me. I do not mean to lash at you. Tell me. What did you hear?"

"Oh, I don't know. It was just a story," she said. "About your family's fall." She hesitated. "You had a sister. There is a song about her."

A new plate arrived. The seared scent of a whole redfin. I set about peeling away its crackling skin, feeling for the innards, but my hands were clumsy with hunger.

"Let me," she said. "It is easier for me."

Her hands were soft, moving mine aside. I heard her opening the fish with her silver tongs, setting aside the innards. Her breath was sweet. Her scent. Her warmth. "There." She took my hand and guided it to the meat, to where I could now draw it from the skeleton of the fish, rib by rib, the flesh peeling easily now that it was undressed.

"A song?" I pressed. "About Celia di Balcosi?"

"At first I didn't know what it was about."

"Tell me the words."

"Oh." She cleared her throat. Her tongs clinked against her plate. "I cannot sing it."

"Tell me, then."

"It was a song of a young girl who lived with a powerful bull. The bull was kind to her and guarded her, but one night when she walked under the moon in the fields, a wolf came to her. And then every night thereafter he came to her. And eventually he seduced her. He convinced her that the bull was her enemy, and she should run away with him, and that he would dress her in diamonds. But in order to escape the bull, there was something she was required to do."

My chest tightened.

"In the darkest night while the bull slept, she tore out his eyes and made a dowry amulet of them to prove her love to the wolf. But when she asked for him to help her run away, the wolf instead brought more wolves and they fell upon the bull and all the herd that he had once protected. When the slaughter was complete, the girl was left standing amongst the dead. Surrounded by the growling wolves, sobbing for her betrayals, and sobbing for her fate.

"Now, whenever the moon is full, you can see the tears she shed upon the grasses, bright as the diamonds that she was promised. But she is gone. The night cannot even find her now."

I found I no longer had appetite.

"I'm sure she is not so badly off as that," I said, wiping my fingers.

"I do not know. I have heard many songs since. Some say she was sold as a slave to the Khur. Some say she has been given lands as reward. I know that the songs of serving the Parl as a consort are false, for I have never seen her in Merai."

It had been a long time since I had thought of Celia.

Perhaps she, like me, languished in some damp dungeon. More likely, I suspected that she had simply been thrown into the Livia to feed the fish in the bay. The very fish we ate at this table might well have fed upon her disintegrating corpse. I had thought my wounds concerning Celia healed, even if my eyes had not, and yet here Allessana brought her back in an instant.

Celia. I wondered if I would ever be free of her. The confusion of my attraction and love, tangled with my terror and rage as she had ripped out my eyes. I didn't want to cry, and in any case the damage Celia had done made tears impossible, but I didn't like the feeling in my chest.

Allessana's hand hesitantly touched my shoulder. "I am sorry for what has happened to you. You seemed kind when we met before. I would not have wished this on you."

"Ah. Kindness. Yes. I am kind. I think this is why I still survive. If my enemies thought me capable of the least violence, I would be long buried. My ineffectualness is what has saved my life, such as it is."

I did not hide my bitterness.

"It makes me grateful I am not part of the great intrigues," she said.

I felt a flare of irritation. "I also thought I was not part of the intrigues." I turned to face her, opening my eye sockets as much as their scarring allowed. "But then, clearly, I did not see clearly."

She jerked away. "Ai! You are—"

"A lesson," I said sharply. "Just because you are a weak card in some-one's else's hand, does not mean that they will not play you, and that you are not in jeopardy."

"What do you discuss, dear Davico?"

It was the Callarino, calling down the table to me, and with his words he attracted the attention of everyone seated. His voice was as oily as always, pleased with himself and condescending to me. A new dish was arriving. A soup with tomato and chilies, cold and spicy at the same time.

"Well?" he pressed.

A wiser man would have smoothed the moment. A more strategic man would have turned it to his advantage. I was neither. "I was telling my pretty companion that a swine may strut in robes of gold, but in the end, all he can do is snort."

Pity the man who struts to impress a woman. Despise the man who flares his plumage, like a peacock flashing the pathetic memory of feathers long ago burnt down to melted spines.

The Callarino's chair scraped abruptly. He was standing up. I immediately knew that I had gone too far. The humiliation was too much. I could hear his footsteps approaching. He would cut my throat for his honor—

Laughter broke out. Furia, gay and pleased. "Your little dog still yaps!"

"He won't yap anymore," the Callarino said. "I assure you."

Furia was still laughing. "And so you'll waste the value of the Regulai once again."

The Callarino's footsteps slowed. "What are you talking about?"

"I? Nothing. He's your slave. Do what you will. If it were me, I would not throw away a toy so easily, but you always let your anger rule you."

"You think I let my anger rule me?" The Callarino's voice was a dangerous warning. The table had fallen silent, shocked at her temerity.

Furia only seemed to enjoy the attention. "I think you will slit the

Regulai's throat tonight," she said, "and then you will regret it tomorrow. But you will pretend to all of us that you don't."

"Furia . . ."

"Either that, or you're a fool, and you won't even see that you wasted something valuable."

I wondered if she was harassing the Callarino because she was angry about the Boccatta and their slave pens in the city, or if she was simply seeking to mark the Callarino's cheek. Either way, she played a dangerous game. I half expected the Callarino to come after Furia instead of me. The silence stretched between them. I felt for my meat knife and slid it beneath the table, thinking that I might yet have the chance to give the Callarino a surprise.

"I take it you have some proposal," the Callarino said, his voice clenched with the effort of control.

"The sfaccito is your property. Do what you like. Waste him. Keep him. It's not my affair."

"And yet you keep speaking."

"If you hate your little dog so much, why not sell him? At least make a profit."

"Ai. There it is. You want to buy him still."

Furia laughed. "All right. Why not? I'll give you half a naviluna."

"A half-moon for the last di Regulai?" The Callarino snorted. "I'd rather slit his throat."

"You can hardly call that creature di Regulai anymore. You've ruined most of his value. A healthy chicken has more value than that scrawny creature."

"A moment ago, you said he had great value. And you still seem to want him. Why?"

I, too, wondered why Furia involved herself. Did she seek to somehow save me? It seemed unlikely. My bank was bled. My body spent. Furia would not act for mere pity. What use could she possibly have for me? Perhaps she was simply showing the others that no man ruled her. She had certainly been disruptive enough at our own dinner parties.

"I'll toss you a navisoli to cut his throat," Dellamont interjected. "He should have been hung already."

"You were not invited to this conversation, foreigner," Furia said acidly.

"And yet here I sit, comfortable at this table."

Garagazzo cleared his throat. "I think it would be wiser to make an example of the slave. Have him slowly pulled apart at Quadrazzo Amo for all to see and learn. Make an example of him, so others will remember the cost of treachery. Best to make a lesson of him."

"This reeks of dishonor," Sivizza rumbled. "He has paid his ransom. Kill him quickly and be done with it. We are all lowered by these tortures."

"Lowered?" The Callarino's voice turned dark. *"Lowered?"*

It was apparent to me, if not to him, that he was losing control. It filled me with a certain satisfaction to see my enemies bickering, even if it was bickering over what they would do to hurt me. They were not friends. They were barely allies. And it was a pleasure to see them fraying now that they had no common enemy. It was particularly pleasing to see the Callarino lose control.

"Ai, Borsini," Furia was saying, "you're like the cauri bird that has found the emerald. You have seized something that you think is valuable, and so you hold it tight—not because it's valuable to you, but simply so others cannot have it. You worry too much about this person's opinion or that person's desire. You don't even like this slave and yet you clutch to it. And when I offer you the favor of unburdening yourself, you refuse, because you worry that I might enjoy the toy more than you. I repeat, you don't even like this slave. If you gave him to me for no silver at all, I would still be doing you a favor. You would be doing yourself a favor. Unburden yourself, Borsini. Let the past die. Move forward."

There was silence.

I listened to that silence and I wondered if I should hope for Furia's petition to succeed, if I would fare better under her, or if I should hope for simple death at the Callarino's hand. My meat knife was clenched in my fist. If the Callarino came for me, I would fight. I might take him with me . . .

"Nai." The Callarino cleared his throat. "Nai. I do not think so. You are wrong, Siana Furia. I do still gain something from this one. He does have value to me. But you are also right, and I acknowledge that as well. It's true, I do not enjoy this creature anymore. He does not *amuse* me, anymore."

To my surprise, I heard the Callarino's footsteps receding back down the length of the table. His chair scraped. Tongs clinked. I realized he was eating. Eating as if nothing had happened. When his next words came, they were from around his meal. "This example business, Garagazzo, I like it. But I think my little sfaccito is too skinny to provide a proper lesson. I think I will fatten him first."

"He hardly needs fattening to pull him apart," Garagazzo said.

"But my dear friend, you are too simple." The Callarino's tongs clinked on his plate as he took another bite of food. His wineglass thumped on the table. "I have decided to make a lesson of him worthy of his offense. His tongue offends me. I intend to cut it out and feed it to him."

The merchant beside Allessana sucked in his breath. A woman down the table laughed uncomfortably. The Callarino was still eating. I could hear him chewing. No one spoke. He held their attention.

At last, Sivizza said, "Tongues don't get fatter with feeding."

"Ai. True." The Callarino set down his tongs with a clink. "Tongues do not fatten. But we do not fatten pigs for their tongues." A pause. A sip of wine, I heard him straining the wine through his teeth, savoring it. His glass thumped again on the table. "But I want a pig that is nice and fat, for after I cut out that intemperate tongue of his, I do not intend to stop. Every day, I intend to cut a bit more from his fat little body and set him grilling. I will let him smell himself cooking before himself, and then I will feed him nothing but himself, and I will teach him to salivate when we light the coals to cook him more."

His words were gathering momentum, flowing more and more easily. And as he spoke, a sort of power seemed to gather around him, like mists gathering upon the River Livia.

"And when I have trained him," the Callarino continued, "I will hang my slave in a cage in Quadrazzo Amo. And I will tell all the people that the allies of the Regulai plot against Navola still, and we must smoke them out. And I will order that all the great names of Navola, all who love our republic, prove their loyalty."

It was an awful sort of power. A feeling of inevitability. Irrefutable. Immutable. Fear, I realized. The power of fear. The power that I had never mastered, the Callarino wielded.

"I will cut a little, for all to see. And the Hundred Names will cut a little, for all to see. And the names around this table—if they are good and loyal Navolese—they, too, will cut a little, for all to see."

Around the table, the powers who had been bickering and splintering, raising their voices in challenge, making the Callarino a figure of fun, had gone silent. There was only one voice now, and one authority: Borsini Amoforze Corso, Callarino of Navola.

"Every archinomo will cut a little, and we will roast his fattened buttocks, and smoke his thighs, and pry out his ribs, and grill his cheeks, and pickle his fingers, and he will feed upon himself until he is nothing but a fat wriggling worm, eager to feed and unable to stop . . . and still we will not slay him, for you are right, Siana Furia, it would be waste. Instead, we will keep him dangling there, that all may be reminded what it is to betray Navola. And then I will let him starve. The Regulai worm will die slowly, legless and armless, wriggling and desperate to consume just one more bite of himself. And so the slave will be punished, and Navola will be united."

A pall had descended upon the table. The guests were shifting uncomfortably in their seats, taken aback at the barbarity of what the Callarino proposed. But there was no more splintering of powers.

"Does that meet with your approval, my dear?" the Callarino asked, as his tableware clinked and he returned to his meal. "Does that seem like less a rush, and more a plan?"

"It seems . . ." Furia seemed to be groping for words. "It seems . . . sufficient."

"I'm so glad. I wouldn't want anyone thinking that I don't make useful examples of my enemies."

Chapter 58

The Callarino threw me back into my pit, but now Aqba each day delivered me rich food, redolent of fine spices.

"The food of the Callarino's own table," Aqba crooned. "Eat well, my pig. Fatten, my pig."

Fatten, my pig.

By the fatas I hated that man. And I hated myself even more when I broke, and fed.

I was still a starving man, so of course I ate, even though I was filled with horror that I did so. And then I would avoid eating, fighting the blandishments of sweet baked pies, rich stews, haunches of lamb—and then the food would pile up and the rats would come, and I would find myself fighting them for my meals, the largest of the rats.

The Callarino of Rats. The Parl of Rodents. The Sultan of Vermin.

I swung between the twin poles of starvation and gorging excess, the asceticism of the barefoot priest and the debauchery of Caliba. I fought battles between the dignity of man and the raw instincts of the wolf.

At last, bloated after feeding and sick with myself, I determined to at least deny the Callarino the satisfaction of his final tortures. I would muster my will. I would deny his blandishments. I would starve myself to death.

And starve I did.

The food arrived. The rats fed well. But my will held strong, and I went elsewhere.

I turned my attention inward, delving deep into my soul and memory.

My hunger grew.

My concentration sharpened. I delved deeper into myself.

Aqba poured food between the bars. "Fatten, my pig, fatten," he crooned, but I did not reply, for I was far away.

I was standing on the Great Piers of Navola, feeling the kiss of fresh wind rushing off the waters, redolent of salt and fish. I was walking the hills in spring, amongst fields of purple and yellow flowers. I was kicking through Romiglian forests amongst fallen autumn leaves, smelling the damp chill and rich humus of the ending season. I was hunting mushrooms, and spying foxes, and I was far away.

Deep underground, turned inward to memory, I escaped to the world above.

And there was so much to explore.

I practiced swordcraft in the gardens with Aghan Khan, working again and again to perfect my movements. I wrote filthy and debauched poems to Filippo di Basca da Torre Amo. I chased Lazy through the palazzo as the servants shouted after us to be more careful.

I reconstructed the palazzo in my mind, walking it as I had when I was first blinded, imagining every step, building and painting in more and more detail, bringing that dead map within my mind into full and living life. The palazzo rose and bloomed around me. I could place myself in the sunny herb garden, or in the quadra beside the splashing fountain of Urula, or in the solitude of my chambers. I could wander down into the kitchens and steal apples. Each of these places I painted with exquisite and increasing detail in my mind. I added the color of memory to all my other sensation memories of the palazzo, sharpening them, using the tools of concentration and obsession that I had discovered down in my deep pit.

I returned to the baths of the servant girls, and watched them soap themselves once more, reveling in their beauty and diversity of figure, lusting and reminiscing. I sat in the gardens beside Dellacavallo, naming plants and medicines and discussing the philosophies of Soppros.

I even walked with Celia, that girl I hated now, and had loved so deeply then. Ai. Such a madness of confusion with her memories. An entanglement of lust and fear and love and care and rage. A knot without end or beginning. But she was there—as much a part of the palazzo as my father or Ashia or Lazy or Cazzetta—and so I let myself touch the pain of her memory, and even return to that moment when we had stood before the library doors, when our hope was lost.

And there, I forgave her.

I forgave her for what she had done to me, and I hoped that her decision had saved her at least. That one of us had escaped Palazzo Regulai alive. And if she had not survived, I hoped that her shade would one day find its way from Scuro's caverns and she might make her way into Amo's light.

Even as she stabbed my eyes, I forgave her, and I felt a terrible weight lift.

I felt relief, but more than that, I found that I could now turn away from the pain of her betrayal and touch what she had blocked.

My father's library.

As if dreaming, I placed my hands upon those handles of bronze, fashioned into the shape of the bull, and pulled. The doors swung wide. The orange light of evening filtered through the shutters. Within, everything was as it had been when I was young and still stealing glimpses of girls at their baths.

I walked along the shelves of books. I touched the scrolls. The histories of Avinixiius and Venxian. The revered teachings of Libri Luminari Amo. The treatises by the acolytes of Leggus on shapes and volumes and divine ratios. I crouched down and found the art of Adivo and Milas, those sketches and eroticisms. I found the women who had once fired my young imagination, leaving me trembling and shaking with needs that I could not yet fully understand. Those images of great monstrous creatures ravishing women, of fatas beguiling men, of the harems of Zurom. The women, so lush, the men rippling and virile, the looming beasts, the sinuous octopi, the beckoning fatas, and the debaucheries of Caliba.

I turned the pages in my mind, my memories so sharp, my mind so well tuned that I was able to recall every page as I turned it, to feel every shock of discovery, to see the images just as they had been, in the light of the sun where it squeezed in through the wooden lattice shutters, orange with evening, that dying light.

And I remembered something else. Something so powerful that it could even distract a boy from sketches of lust.

The dragon eye.

It glinted in the light upon my father's desk. Bestial and strange. Swirling and alive. A terrible artifact, that fossil object, with nerves like spikes trailing behind it, gleaming like the comet seen in skies from Losiccia to Pagnanopol. I remembered how it had drawn me to it. How it had cut me when I touched it, all unwary.

Even now it drew me.

Even in my imagination, it seemed alive, seemed to stare back at me, seemed to call. I remembered how it had seethed with life, its hungers and malevolence, and how it had drawn me.

I leaned close, peering into the milky crystal, meeting the gaze of that slit reptilian eye and the fires that raged within. I reached out to caress the thing. And as my fingers touched it, I felt a surge of life, and realization crashed in upon me.

I was not in my cell at all, but in the library.

I was beside the dragon eye, and I saw it truly.

And it saw me.

Chapter 59

For a heartbeat, we regarded one another. A fateful frozen moment that we shared, the dragon and I.

And then it attacked.

I tried to withdraw my hand from the orb, but the dragon flooded into my mind, scrabbling and clawing, heaving its serpentine body forward, and as it did, it took my body. It flexed my fingers as claws. It bared my teeth as fangs, and still it surged and burrowed into me. The dragon occupied me the way it had once occupied the fossil eye. And still it came on, ramming itself into the tiniest corners of my skull so that I howled and clawed at my empty eye sockets trying to tear it out.

The dragon roared. I covered my ears and howled with pain. Aqba came and shouted for me to be quiet. He banged upon the bars of my cell with his poker but he was as the wings of mosquitoes, far away and minuscule in comparison to the awesome creature that filled my mind. The only thing I can compare it to is the great wave that swallowed Navola in ancient times, leaving nothing upon its shores. The whole city simply gone—so was I engulfed by the dragon.

I tumbled in the froth of its memories, a bit of flotsam drowning under the crash of millennia. I remembered what it was to cut across an open sky, my wings beating hard, rising. I knew what it was to search the land and then fall like a falcon. I felt my wings furl and I plummeted, eager for my prey. Bones shattered between my jaws. Hot blood spurted across my tongue. I curled to sleep amongst the high steep crags that stood sentinel over the passes of Zurom. I hunted sheep in fields and burned men in towns. I perched upon red sand cliffs and watched empires rise and fall. I hoisted camels with my claws and bore them away to feed, leaving caravaners to desiccate in deserts that they would never escape on foot. I flew and fed. I flew and mated.

I flew.

And still the dragon came on. Its scales scraped the interior of my skull, its claws gouged crevices. It coiled, twisting and slithering about inside my mind, finding home, and then it flexed its body and my skull cracked for I was too small. I shattered. I screamed as blood poured from my ears, from my nose, from my ruined eyes. I screamed and screamed until my throat was raw and still that creature grew. I was overwhelmed at every turn. I was hunted, swallowed, crushed, and burned. I fled and retreated and still that monster came on. I was dying. Nai. More than that, I was being annihilated.

And yet . . .

And yet, I did not perish.

I clutched for the shattered fragments of my self. Memories of Lazy, memories of Stub, memories of my father, of Cazzetta, of drunken nights with friends at the Bear, the play of light amongst whitebark pines, anything . . .

Celia.

Ai. By the fatas, I hated her. But now, as I fought to hang on to the fragments of my soul, I clutched for her, too, and she bore me up, and in that moment I understood her, and forgave her all the more because of it.

We are all flotsam in the maelstrom. To swim at all is triumph.

It was Celia who guided me to sanctuary. A will so strong that she would pay any price in order to survive. A will that never faltered. I clutched to her example, the way a drowning sailor seizes upon a shard of timber wreckage.

I would not surrender.

I do not know how long I lay in a stupor. Days, I think, overwhelmed by the immensity of what had been the dragon. The terror and glory of the dragon's memories tore and tumbled me, and each time there was less and less of me that remained. But I clung to Celia and her iron will. The girl who had destroyed me now buoyed me through exhaustion, pain, and terror. And at last, when I thought I could not survive more, she dragged me to a shore of stillness, a place within myself that did not die.

The vast mind of the dragon rumbled all around me, inhabiting me, but I was not finished.

Slowly, painfully, stealthily, I began to gather back the shattered parts of my self.

Much as glass from a shattered window may be gathered together and remelted and made whole once more, so too I gathered the shards of my self and labored to fashion something new. Bit by bit, shard by shard, memory by memory, I made myself whole. With the discipline of a mind honed by isolation, and senses honed by darkness, and with the iron example of Celia guiding me like a fata's flame, I regathered myself, not as the soft creature that had been manipulated by my family's enemies, nor the trusting boy who had fallen beneath enemy knives. Not the last di Regulai, a victim tried and tortured by the Callarino. And not the child who had collapsed beneath the onslaught of the dracchus.

My soul—if such can be said to still exist—was too broken to simply repair. Instead, I took parts and pieces of my self and refashioned them into something new. The process was almost as awful as the destruction that had been wrought upon me by my enemies, for it meant becoming something that was not my nature.

There are stories of creatures built from many other creatures, the head of a bull, the body of a man, the hands of a crab, the hooves of a goat. This was how I refashioned myself. Each action I took to make myself into a new creature felt anathema. I stole cruelty from the Callarino, and faccioscuro from Merio. From Furia, I took pleasure from disquiet. I took relentless darkness from Cazzetta. I took fearlessness from Aghan Khan. I stole a lack of shame from Filippo. From my father, I took strategy. From Ashia, I took strength. And from Celia, I took her iron will.

Anything and everything, I took and used. All the pleasures, all the humiliations, all the love, all the pain, all the tortures . . . I used it all to forge a different self. It was a blasphemy, for those parts of me that the dragon had not annihilated, I now immolated myself. I melted, twisted, beat, and reforged whatever was left of me, and whatever I could steal, and made myself into a new creature—sharper, harder, more determined, and more vicious.

And then I turned on the dragon, and I struck.

Ai. We fought. Ai. It is terrible thing to feel such a scaled creature within your own corpus, controlling muscle, tendon, bone. It breathed with my lungs, it thrummed from my heartbeat. I cannot describe such violation, the sense of your enemy within you, invading you . . . it is worse than steel sliding into your guts, worse than a poker rammed up your ass, to feel a dracchus breathing beneath your skin.

I fought, though. I fought, using every weapon I had.

I used my honed senses to anchor myself first to the cold stone floor of my cell, then to the drip of water, then to the echoes of Aqba beating the bars outside my cell, then to the skitter of rats, then to the smells of shit and rotting food, and from these sensory threads, I rebuilt the stairs up out of the ground and strode up them. I filled my mind with the palazzo, and all its architecture rose up about me as I marched through it. Stone by stone and column by column, I forged my way back to the library, and there I flung open the doors and faced the dragon, and there, I vanquished it.

I made myself separate.

With all my will, I placed myself not within the dragon orb but without, and the dragon not within me, but without, and with a roaring shifting grinding howl, I hurled the dragon out.

I was whole.

I opened my eyes. I lay in my chill dark dungeon once more.

My throat was raw. My body ached. I was covered in sweat.

I rolled over and hauled myself to where the wall dripped water. I collapsed, my face on the floor, trying to lap cool clear liquid. My tongue touched lichen and moss and damp. I drank and rested.

I lay there for a long time, exhausted, bruised, shivering, and weak. A sadness tried to come and sit upon me, along with a self-pity and a fear, but they sought a different weaker Davico, and they went away.

I drank more water. I felt for food with my hands and ate it. I gathered my strength. And then I reached for the dragon eye once more.

Of course, it reared up and attacked, but I was ready, and this time we fought not inside the territory of my body, but inside the territory of its eye. I rammed all my force and all my will into it, smashing and invading and growing, and though the dragon beat at me, and roared and slithered and coiled and clawed and spit acid and flame, I did not stop, for I was not the same Davico that it had crushed before.

Eventually, when both of us were torn and exhausted, I invited the dracchus to sit and bargain.

Had I served sweet tea and bitter cheese and we two sat across the plank, our negotiation could not have been more formal. Who can say, amongst all the great figures of banca mercanta, that they have bargained, parlobanco, with a dragon?

We did not like each other, but we did not have to. My father once told me that we don't make truces with allies, but only with enemies. And so it was with us. We were not friends, but we were beneficial to one another. As much as I desired its powers, it had hungers of its own, and upon that basis we reached agreement.

And so it was that beside the Callarino, I opened my great eye.

Chapter 60

To say that I *watched* is too small a word.

To say that I *saw* is too trivial.

I devoured. I gorged. I fed upon the world around me. The library was alive. Grains of wood, the texture of stone, the weave of carpets, dances of color. Motes of swirling dust. And even sounds. It took all my effort to watch the Callarino, for he was no more fascinating than the strokes of paint by the master artists who had brought forth the ceiling murals, and which, I noted with annoyance, the Callarino had painted his visage upon.

Did a fly buzz in an upper clerestory window? Did a mote of dust spill from the Callarino's sigil? Did Sivizza have a sheen of mucus upon his finger? Did a raven flap before the window? Did the carpet threads crackle like wildfire with every step that Merio took? Everywhere was light and noise and smells, and I devoured it all. I caressed rippling conversations, I licked thrumming colors. I watched scents as they drifted like dust through the sunlight. I captured motes of rose and sweat, puffs of age from books . . .

My father had cast nets of influence and spun webs of intrigue, but he had been only a man, fallen from Virga's weave. The dragon was still a part of that ancient design, woven fully into Virga's artistry, just as Soppros had described. Man had fallen from the weave and sat crying in the dirt, but now for this moment, I was part of it once again.

I was in ecstasy.

I smelled bread baking in the kitchens. I eavesdropped on the conversations of the Callarino's servants. I could hear the rustle of bedclothes as the Callarino's children snuck from their beds and the grumbling of his ancient mother as she complained about her joints. I could hear the guards talking at the gate, and knew almost as soon as I started to listen that one did not like the other, and that the one contemplated a betrayal of some sort, but the other was ignorant of this. It was lust, I realized. One lusted for the other's wife. Their voices told me so, a truth revealed as if they were shouting.

These were the patterns of men, I realized.

This was not something I knew, it was something the dragon knew. The dragon had watched empires rise and fall. It had listened to thousands of conversations of men as they made caravans and marches through its demesnes. It had seen a thousand betrayals and a thousand loyalties.

This was not the knowing of the mystical, it was the knowing of patterns. Simple humanitas, observed for millenati. Wisdom. This was wisdom. Wisdom such as the philosopher kings of ancient Ebezzu could never hope to achieve, for they lived a single short lifetime, where the dracchus had seen all of humanity, for all of time. It had seen our petty human dramas and comedies too many times for anything to surprise it. It knew the intentions of a man perhaps before the man himself knew them.

And now, while we were bonded, I knew these things, too.

I could see the Callarino, how he sat with the archinomi of Navola. I could see how he recoiled slightly from Garagazzo. I could see how he hung attentive to the words of Serena Romizzini, whose family had become influential with the fall of my own. I watched how he hungered for her, and also how he feared to press an interest for her. I watched his disdains and his regard. It was painful to watch, for it brought with me another awareness as well.

I had always thought my judgment suspect. I had lived so long amongst men who considered themselves expert in the knowing of the hearts of men and their motives that I had doubted my own instincts. I remembered long ago when the Callarino had come before my father and I had watched with awe at how my father had guided that man he had called Borsini, playing him, using him, accomplishing the business of Navola. But I had felt the boiling rage and hatred of the Callarino. I had seen the true danger he presented.

And my father had not.

Cazzetta had not.

Merio had not.

All my life I had doubted my own mind, had thought it dull and skittish in comparison with the men of substance who surrounded me. And yet I had been right in my assessment of the Callarino. My father had caused Archinomo di Regulai to ring out across the oceans because he understood the dangers that surrounded him, the risks, the opportunities . . . and yet he had not seen everything.

Now I lay in the filth of my cell and sought my opportunity. I watched the Callarino preen in front of those who were weak. I watched him storm and bluster and command. I watched him gloat about my coming tortures—the spectacle he planned and how he would use it to draw out any last remaining di Regulai allies.

"We'll put them all in the front row," he said to Garagazzo. "Watch their faces when they hold the knife."

Ai. I could have lashed out then. The dragon desired to. With its power I knew that we could draw the Callarino to us, and then we could destroy him. We could feed upon his soul, and wasn't that what I had promised the dragon? Prey? Blood? Death? Vengeance? Howls of pain and souls leaking out to be devoured?

I wrestled with the dragon then, for its nature was to prey upon anything that was weak before it, not to plot or plan or manipulate. Ai. We fought then, the dragon calling to the Callarino, and I muffling its call.

Prey. Prey. Prey.

The Callarino stared into our swirling colors, mesmerized. He reached for us. With all my will, I shoved the dragon down, and held it there as it slashed its tail at me and its teeth snapped. But when the Callarino touched our surface, we held quiescent. He lifted his hand unscathed.

Ai. What an effort. To forsake the satisfaction of easy blood.

I felt sullied after, doing something so much against our nature. We could have sucked away his soul and destroyed his mind with our onslaught. But he was but one man, and I was in the dungeons. His death would not release me. His fall would not provide salvation. And so I forced the dragon to wait.

We watched and waited for my opportunity, seeking a person from my past whom I might reach and turn to my needs. But no one presented themselves, and my tortures were fast approaching. I began to contemplate Merio. My mentor, my betrayer, the only one of the plotters who might still carry sympathy for me.

Twice in the library, while he discussed the discretionary accounts of the Callarino and his family, I thought to reach out to him, and twice I hesitated. Even with all the wisdom of a dragon at my disposal, Merio was a cipher. I held back, reserving him for desperation.

Unexpectedly, I was rewarded for my patience. Not by the arrival of some old Navolese friend, but by my new Meravese acquaintance.

Allessana.

The girl who had twice been my dinner companion. She stood before the Callarino, and his eyes traveled over her, hungry. I could smell his lust. She came as supplicant. The girl who had given me the uncertain gift of my own pride now stood before the Callarino and begged his aid. Her family in Merai was bankrupt. Her father had invested badly on a merchant's caravan to Deravash, a horse-trading venture that had ended with sickened animals that were put to the sword at the border of Merai. He had gambled at cartalegge then, and lost more, and then killed himself. Now her mother and a young sister had lost their home and were adrift and vulnerable. She begged his shelter.

It was an old drama; they both knew their roles.

I watched as the Callarino sent away his guards, and watched as he stripped her while she stood trembling. With eager fingers he unbuttoned her bodice, and then yanked her dress off her shoulders. Seams ripped, exposing her breasts to his old hungry eyes. Nothing he did surprised me. I knew the sort of man he was. He forced her to her knees and made her unlace his breeches. And I watched.

I watched with the empathy of one who had suffered at his hands, and the indifference of a dragon. Nothing the Callarino did to her was new. When he forced her mouth to his manhood, he behaved as powerful men have always behaved.

Eventually, he left her sullied with his seed, collapsed upon the floor, and surrounded by blue puddled silks. His last words to her were dismissive. "You'll do. There is a priest I want you to entertain tonight. Make yourself obedient to his tastes. And listen well to his words when he has finished. I want to know what he thinks of me. Then I will see to your family." And then he was gone.

I watched as Allessana numbly gathered her torn gown and hitched it back about her shoulders. I watched her unsteady movements as she sought to repair her dress. She did not sparkle as she had the first time I had met her in Merai. She was a shadow of the girl who had been kind to me at the Callarino's table a mere month previous. We are all cards in a vast game of cartalegge, I had told her. None of us are immune. I felt terrible pity for her, a girl caught in a web she could not escape, a girl thrown upon the rocks of desperation.

She would do.

Was I different than the Callarino? Or was I just the same? In truth, I do not know. In truth, the creature I had become did not care. I was as the dracchus. We had fed upon whole villages without hesitation or regret. What was one more girl in the face of that?

I reached out to her. Using the power of the dragon eye, I forestalled her departure from the library. Just as the dragon eye had once called to me, I now called to Allessana.

Allessana.

Come to me. Look upon me. Come. Come closer.

Closer . . .

It was a keening seduction. A trick the dragon had used all its life to lure its prey out of dense sheltering forests and deep stony caves to be attacked from above. It was a hypnotic song and I used it now, without hesitation or shame. I called to her. I commanded. I beckoned.

At the doors to library, on the verge of departure, Allessana paused. She looked back, searching the library, sensing that she was not alone. She gathered her torn clothes more tightly around her, protecting her modesty against a presence that she could not see but sensed most clearly.

Allessana . . .

Her gaze fell upon the dragon eye.

Come closer.

She could not resist my call. She came warily, but she came all the same. Closer to the desk. Closer to the eye. Closer to me . . .

She bent and peered into my eye. I whispered longingly for her touch. She raised a tentative hand, on the verge of caressing the crystalline fossil.

And stopped.

Frustratingly, impossibly, she stopped. Her hand hovered mere inches from contact, and came no closer. And then, like a rabbit sensing that she explored a wolf's den, she drew back.

By the fatas, I could have raged. If I had had the power, I would have seized her and dragged her to me, but I could only woo. I was as the fatas who lured men to leap from cliffs. I could woo, I could lure, I could entice, but I could not force Allessana to cross my threshold.

And truly, she was right to stop, for I was a danger to her. I cared only for myself. I was a monster. And I would not stop.

Allessana. I would be your friend.

I would help you . . .

Her touch was a shock.

It happened so quickly that I almost lost my concentration. One moment she was drawing away, on the verge of flight, the next her face screwed with determination and she stepped forward and laid her hand firmly upon the dragon eye, and when she did, it was as if her soft palm rested upon the skin of my bare breast.

That shock of human flesh, of human contact, was overwhelming.

The feeling of a woman touching me so intimately—ai. It dragged forth feelings that I had buried ever since my fateful night with Celia, that I had thought thoroughly annihilated. My sense of intimacy had been so horrified by Celia's betrayal that I had closed myself entirely from any feeling of desire, attraction, or trusting intimacy. But now, against my will, touched by Allessana, I opened to her.

I was like the lockbox that springs open at a skilled thief's touch. I had been trying to seduce and manipulate Allessana, but now, like the hunter who has caught a lion by the toe, I realized my mistake. I had brought her too close.

The two of us were suddenly one, so intimately intertwined that we might as well have lain in bed. Nai. More so. Allessana was within me. She *knew* me. All my desires were exposed. She could see clear into my ravaged, rageful, desperate soul. She could feel my sudden lusts for her tangled with my rages for Celia, my tumbling fantasies of revenge against my enemies, my plans to manipulate and use her—

She jerked away as if scalded.

I cried out, ashamed and enraged and horrified that she had seen so much of me. I was as Scuro revealed to Erostheia. Twisted and vile. She had seen all of me. Every failure, every lust, every betrayal, every hunger, every fear, every shame, every cruel desire . . .

She was rightly horrified. She fled from me as if pursued by wolves.

With one last frightened backward glance, she yanked open the library's door and escaped my reach.

Chapter 61

"Davico?"

The whispered voice woke me. I was surprised that I had been asleep. I reached out to the dragon eye and saw that it was deepest night. It was strange, after so long in a dungeon without day or night that I would bother to check, but as soon as I had made alliance with the dragon, I had become attached once more to the rise and fall of the sun.

"Davico?"

Again the whisper. I recognized it, but I was disoriented, for the voice was not within the library.

"Davico?"

Allessana. Just outside my cell door. She was here, in my prison, so close that I could reach through the bars and touch her. I suddenly became aware of my filth, my fetid state. That was followed by the horror that she had seen into my soul. I scuttled to the farthest corner of my cell and crouched there, trembling, hiding in the darkness.

"It is you!" she exclaimed.

I realized she held a candle. I could smell its smoke. Of course there was no hiding. What a fool I was.

"Welcome to my abode," I said, mustering what little dignity I had left. "I'm sorry I cannot offer you wine."

"I . . ." She gagged. "I had no idea . . ."

"We are all dirtied in our dealings with the Callarino."

I heard her lift her candle, and heard my ratty friends skittering away from the light. "By the fatas," she murmured.

"Is it so bad as that?"

She only gagged again in reply.

"Why did you come?" I asked. "How did you find me?"

"I—" She hesitated. "I just knew. I saw the path to you. I saw the door in the servants' passage. I saw it, and I knew every stair down, and then I knew the way through the passages. It was like a dream, murky and not quite right, but the path was true—You told me, didn't you? It was you in the library, wasn't it?"

"Yes."

"I felt it so. I felt . . . You wanted to do terrible things to me."

"I have become a monster. You should not have come."

"You aren't the same person I knew."

"Free me and find out."

"You are as bad as the Callarino. As that priest Garagazzo." She shuddered. "Why did you call me?"

"You know why. I want to escape."

"And you will do anything to achieve it."

I couldn't help a bitter smile. "Better than feeling myself cooked and then forced to dine upon my own flesh," I said.

"I cannot help you."

"You can," I said. "If you seduce the creature called Aqba who feeds me. He has the key to my cell. Seduce him. Bring me the key."

She was quiet for a long time.

"You are a monster."

"I can help you," I said.

She laughed darkly.

"I can help you where the Callarino will not," I said. "He is not trustworthy."

"And you are?"

I crawled to the bars and pressed my face between them, my filthy features staring blindly out to her. "You have seen into my soul. I am a monster, but I am true. I will use you as my shrouded card. I will use your body and your honor for my own benefit. And I will not apologize for it. But I will keep my bargain, and this makes me a better ally than you will find in all of this palazzo."

"And you offer?"

"I know a man in Merai, who will aid and shelter you. A stilettotore. Dangerous. Useful."

"You have an ally still? I thought they were all dead."

"He may be dead," I admitted. "But he is the sort who survives, so I think not."

"You think not? That is the aid you offer me? A man who may or may not still live?"

"I also know where some money is buried."

"And now a dragon's hoard?" She scoffed. "Like that awful eye in the Callarino's library? How did you speak to me through it?"

"I have always had an affinity for Virga's weave, I think, from the time when I was young. A long time ago the dragon called to me, and I heard it where others did not. It stole my blood. I found it again in my madness."

"Along with its hoard?"

"Not a dragon's hoard, a banker's. A cache for our agents in Merai. Kept for the unexpected. It will not be easy to reach, but I think it still remains."

"A man who may or may not be dead, a hoard that may or may not exist." She laughed bitterly. "You need some practice at wooing women."

"Allessana." I reached blindly through the bars and captured her hand. She gasped and tried to pull away but I gripped tight and drew her toward me, inexorable, until we were face-to-face. I could smell her beauty and I knew she could smell my filth. "I am Scuro's now, that is true. I am darkness, hunger, filth, and rage. That is also true."

I released her, pushing her away, and turned from her.

As manipulative as my father. As coy as Celia.

"Help me, or not," I said over my shoulder. "Go back and suck the prick of Garagazzo if you can find it under that belly. Lift your skirts and give yourself to all the Callarino's friends. Pray to Amo that his word is true and he will help you. Make your choice."

"My choice?" she asked. "My choice would be to rid myself of all of you."

"And my choice would be to have my eyes back. But none of us can pretend we are not a part of this game. You may play cartalegge down here in the dark with me, or up there in the light with the Callarino. Make your choice, Allessana. Choose your allies."

I held there, waiting for the answer that would determine my fate. Another bargain. Another gamble. A last card laid upon the table. I heard her breathing. I felt her thinking. My last hope, my prey, balanced on the edge of decision—

"I am yours," she said. "What must I do?"

Chapter 62

Allessana did not appear again for several days. I waited with growing concern. I had begun to feed myself once more, trying to gather strength, but now I wondered if I gathered strength to escape or fattened myself for the Callarino's tortures. And those tortures rapidly approached. Servants all over the palazzo were speaking of a festival that the Callarino would throw. A great spectacle, within mere days.

And still Allessana did not bring the key.

Finally, late one night I heard voices and footsteps and smelled torch smoke. A man and a woman . . . Allessana, but not alone with the key. Alongside Aqba.

"Ai . . ." she gasped as they drew close under the crackle of the torches. "He stinks!"

"He is an animal. Of course he stinks."

"Somehow I imagined him to have more presence. He is but a weakling wretch now."

"Sfaiculo," Aqba said. "Do not be fooled by his state. He is dangerous. He stuck me once."

"Stuck you?"

"With a stolen spoon that he had sharpened." He spat upon me. "He is clever and vicious. Now I am not allowed to touch him."

"Not allowed?" Her question prodded his ego.

"The pissioletto Callarino wishes him to live. But I am patient, and on the morrow I shall be rewarded. When the sun sets I will feed this Regulai his own tongue. I will slice it from his mouth, and grill it before his nose with the finest sweetest vinegar of Venzi, and then I will feed it to him, piece by piece."

"The Callarino must value you, then. To give you such an opportunity for your own revenge. Ai." She sighed. "I wish I, too, could have such satisfaction."

"Tomorrow I will let you watch."

My skin crawled. *Tomorrow?* Allessana's role took on a new urgency. If she failed tonight, I would have no second chance.

"Let us go," Aqba said. "You have seen the Regulai, as you asked. And"—his voice lowered and became lascivious—"you promised further favors."

"Bide a moment. You feed him, yet what is all this mounded food in his cell?"

"Sometimes he eats like a pig. Sometimes he starves. Right now, he starves himself. He is stubborn." A moment later, something struck my face, making me flinch. A stale crust of bread. "You see, he is nothing but an animal. I don't know why you wanted to see him."

"He insulted me once, long ago."

"Oh?"

"He found me as a simple girl and took advantage in Merai."

"Ai." Aqba sucked his teeth. "All the Regulai are such. Rogues and rapists. It will be good to be rid of the last of them."

Another chunk of bread bounced off my head. "There!" Allessana cried, clapping her hands delightedly. "I have struck him!"

"Well thrown." Aqba laughed. "You have skill, sia."

"It is a poor revenge," she said sadly. "I wish that I could roast that tongue of his."

"Fear not. You will see him suffer. I will make sure of it."

"Still, it's not the same. I wish to hurt him as he hurt me."

"Would you beat him?" Aqba asked.

"I would ram this poker up his nerasfica . . ."

I heard a scraping and realized that she had taken down the poker that Aqba used to shove food in at me, and to hook back bones so that I could not throw them at him. She clanged it against the bars. "I would push it up him until it came out his throat . . ." She trailed off. "Ai. Forgive me. He fills me with hatred."

Aqba sucked his teeth. Animosity and sybaritic lust fairly radiated from him. He liked the thought of me raped by a poker very much. "You cannot kill him," he said. "But perhaps we can play with him."

"Aivero?" She clapped her hands again. "You would do this for me?"

"Perhaps. What would you offer me for this opportunity?"

"Ci! You are as much a beast as he!"

"Nai, do not say so. But you must understand, what you ask for, it is not the Callarino's will. It is a risk for me to give this gift to you. A great and terrible risk."

"I will make it worth your risk," she said. "Please, let me make him suffer."

"He is dangerous.

"He is shit. I will feed him shit!"

I began to wonder at Allessana's true intentions. She sounded too eager. She sounded like a young Furia.

"He must be alive when the Callarino comes for him tomorrow," Aqba warned.

"I'll only hurt him. Let me pay that monster back. He is Scuro's spremi. Please. I will please you . . ." Her voice became low. "My lips, my mouth, my fig, my . . ." She trailed off seductively, and I heard Aqba draw a sharp breath and I knew she must be touching him. "I will serve you as if you were Caliba himself. You will be my master . . ." Aqba drew in another sharp breath. "I will be your slave . . ." she cooed.

"Yesss . . ."

Keys jingled and then rattled clumsily against locks as Allessana continued to tease and urge Aqba on. I heard more chains clanking. "We will restrain him with these, and then he will be ours," Aqba panted.

"Yes," Allessana whispered eagerly. "We will pay him back."

I did not have to pretend horror as they entered. I scrambled back, fearing I was betrayed.

"Chain him," Allessana said.

"Take the poker," Aqba said. The chains jangled as he circled toward me. He was too smart and too wary. I tried to track his movement as he closed the distance between us. The manacles clinked in his hands. "Time for fun," Aqba said. "I owe you for that spoon."

"Please . . ." I whispered. "Please do not."

"It begs." Allessana laughed. "Did you hear it beg?"

"He'll beg now!" Aqba shouted and he seized my leg. I tried to kick him away, but a manacle snapped around my ankle and then he yanked me so that I fell backward. He leapt upon me and caught a wrist. I swung a fist at him, but my blow was weak, too weak for that vicious ferret. Another manacle closed about my wrist. I struggled, grunting, trying to throw him off—

There was a thud. Aqba cried out. Another followed. He fell upon me, scrabbling, trying to get off. *"Aiutame! Aiutame!"* I heard Allessana grunt above him, and then a wet crunch. Aqba sagged heavy upon me, limp and silent.

I struggled to roll him off me, but he was like a stone, and I was fettered. I heard Allessana breathing heavily.

"A filthy ending for a filthy man," she muttered as she hauled him off me.

I tried to free myself from my fetters, but they were locked tight. "Help me get these off."

Silence.

"Allessana?"

"I'm sorry, Davico. You must tell me first. Tell me what I need to know."

"You don't trust me?"

She laughed bitterly. "Isn't that how this game is played?"

I slowly sat up. I could hear that she was staying out of my reach now, cautious. Treating me like a dangerous animal. I wanted to be angry at the distrust, but I could not find it within me. A part of me even admired her.

"You have seen too much of me," I said, and I felt a terrible sadness in my chest, for I knew I deserved her suspicion.

"I've seen too much of all men," she said.

"I think you must be an excellent cartalegge player."

She laughed at that. "Were you telling me the truth, or not?"

"I am di Regulai," I said. "I always keep my promises. The man's name is Lugo. He is vastly ugly. Slave-scarred as I am, and more, as if his face has been chewed on by a great bear. He was my family's shadow man in Merai. He is deadly, and he is loyal. Find him, and tell him that you aided me. Tell him . . ." I thought for a moment. "Tell him Cazzetta was right. We make our own luck."

"We make our own luck?"

"Exactly like that, and remember to say that Cazzetta is the one who said it. Lugo often drank in an ugly small taverna called the Shoe Dog. Do not go to our bank in Merai. It is long ruined. Go to the taverna. Go there and tell him I owe you my life, and that he is to take you to where I first met him, and to reward you with all that is guarded there."

"And if I cannot find this Lugo? Most of your family's allies have been exterminated."

"If anyone has survived, it will be Lugo. He once bargained with a stone bear for his life." I laughed, thinking of his ruined visage. "He is a tough one. But if he is dead, you must seek the treasure yourself. It is five days or more into the wilderness, in the deep forests south of and west of Merai, at the base of the Ruia. There are no trails that lead there, and you must avoid the ranger patrols. I pray that you do not have to do this alone, for it is not an easy path, and I do not know anyone else who can be trusted to help you seek such wealth. You will know you are close when you see a mountain, cut asunder at its top, so that it forms two peaks, like the ears of a rabbit. Water spills from there, down into a high valley, and at the mouth of that hanging valley, it spills again, down to the forest floor, and there it makes a stream. That stream is what you must seek. Follow it out until you find a wood cottage and a few cleared fields. There is a man who farms there. You must go to the hearth, and pry up the stones. Below it you will find a chest. It is not a vast treasure, but managed carefully it will be enough to protect yourself and your family for many years. The man does not know about the gold and I think he will be surprised." I paused, considering. "I think you should kill him first."

"This is what you give me?" She laughed bitterly.

"It is all I have," I said tiredly. "If I could offer more, I would. I'm sorry I cannot." I felt wrung out. I had done everything within my power. I had used every weapon at my disposal. "Do as you will," I said. "But if you will not release me, at least strike me as you have Aqba. Save me from being cooked."

"You would have me kill you?" she asked incredulously.

I sagged back, exhausted. "I would have you save me."

"I will not kill you."

"Do as you will, then."

My life was out of my hands. There was nothing more for me to do. I was entirely in Allessana's power. To save. To leave. To kill.

There was a long silence. Allessana did not move.

"Go," I said quietly. "Save yourself and go. My shade will not haunt you. Go."

Suddenly she was beside me, taking hold of my wrist and unlocking its manacle. I stifled a sob of relief as it clicked free. She turned to my ankle fetter, working the key. It clacked open and fell away.

"I was afraid to trust you," she said. Her hand touched my cheek, making me flinch. It returned, gentle, and lay soft upon me. "This place is ugly. It makes us ugly. I was afraid."

I turned my face away, fighting to control the wash of my emotions. I tried to make light of it. "Well, I am a Navolese, after all."

"With a mind as twisted as the plaits of your women's hair." I could hear the smile in her voice.

"Just so."

I tried to get up, but found my legs were weak. I crawled to Aqba's body and began stripping off his clothes. "What time is it?"

"The second call of Amo."

"Is there a guard?" I asked. I began stripping off my filthy clothes.

"Nai." I heard a rustle of movement. When she spoke again, her voice was turned away from me, and I knew she was trying to give me privacy in my nakedness. "Aqba told me they don't bother with guards when the dungeon is barred and locked."

I managed to stand, and tugged Aqba's breeches up around my waist. They were loose. All his clothes were loose on me. He had not been a big man in my estimation, but he had eaten better than I, and I felt it in how his clothes hung off my body.

I pushed his corpse into where I knew the darkest corner lay. "Help me cover him. I don't want them to know it is he who lies here."

She crouched beside me, rearranging his body and clothes. I could hear her breathing through her mouth, trying not to smell the stinks around her. "There," she said. "It will have to do." She took my arm and helped me up, and guided me out of the cell, then locked it behind us. "Here," she said. "Take the key."

"Did you . . ." I hesitated, afraid to hope. "Did you manage the other thing . . . ?"

I felt another key pressed into my hand. "It was not easy."

"I'm sorry," I said. "I owe you more than I can repay, but I swear someday I will aid you better."

"Do not make promises," she said. "Promises are for people more powerful than you or me." She pulled me toward the stairs. "Now come. It's this way."

"Nai." I pushed her away. "You've done all I asked and more. Go on ahead. I will make my own way."

"But how will you find your way out of the palazzo?"

"That is not your burden. You have done your part."

"But—"

"Listen!" I reached for her, found her arm and gripped it. Pulled her to me. "Listen. Dawn will soon be upon us and you must not let waking eyes fall upon you. A single whisper from a guard or servant will destroy you. Go back to your chambers and forget that you ever knew me. Go!" I gave her a shove in the direction of the stairs. "Go! Live to seek out Lugo and your fortune. Go, and live!"

She hesitated for a moment longer, and then to my surprise, pulled me into close embrace.

She pressed her cheek to mine, her clean skin against my filthy ruined flesh, and whispered in my ear, "You are not a monster. No matter what you may pretend, you are not a monster to me." And then she kissed the scars of both my cheeks, her lips as gentle as butterflies, and then she was gone, her footsteps echoing up the stairwell, leaving me to my darkness.

Chapter 63

Silently, stealthily, I followed Allessana's receding footsteps up the stairs. Up and up, I climbed, counting steps, measuring my progress out of the bowels of the earth, stopping often to quiet my breathing. The climb was demanding, and I was weak. I had grown terribly weak and had not guessed how much until this unaided climb.

For a moment I regretted sending Allessana away, then berated myself for the thought. In the few moments I had known her, she had shown me more kindness and sacrificed more for me than all my family's former allies. I only hoped that she would not pay a price for it. I dreaded that she would.

I reached the top of the stairs and squeezed out the door. Using the keys we had stolen from Aqba's corpse, I locked it by feel. With luck, they might not discover his body until well into morning.

I was standing in a servants' passage. One of the many narrow halls that Celia and I had often snuck through, frightening servants, pretending to be fatas. I had seen this door many times and never paid attention to it. It had been the domain of servants, and therefore unimportant. And so I never discovered the secret prison below. How strange that such an awful place had lurked so close to me. It had not even been hidden. I had had my eyes, and yet not seen it. A lesson, there.

All around me, the palazzo slumbered. Nothing stirred. I heard no footsteps. I heard no talk. I heard no breathing. I smelled no smoke of candle or torch. I slipped down the passage, guided by the palazzo in my mind.

As I neared the kitchens, I heard early-waking servants. I avoided them, knowing they went to gather wood to warm the baths and kitchen hearths, and so knew their paths. Soon more would wake, then more and more. I hurried my steps. I reached the kitchens and heard rustling in the storeroom. I stole through the kitchen as they rummaged. I was as a rat in the shadows. I knew my steps, I knew the way.

In the garden quadra, I smelled a guard before I heard him. Kheem leaf on his breath, wafting to me. From the breeze, I knew his general location, and knew he blocked my path. I listened closely and finally heard him shift his body. He was leaning against a column at the garden periphery. I was suddenly struck by the fear that he would smell me, despite the direction of the breeze. I knew I stank. I hunted though my mind and memories for a solution—discovered a cherry tree. I eased over to it, keeping portico columns between him and me. My fingers slid through the leaves, hunting, hunting, my breath held, hoping—*There.* The cherries were hard and small, but made good noise when they bounced through the gardens.

He moved. His footsteps marked him as he made his way into the gardens, searching for my cherry noises.

Quickly quickly, past the guard's post, silent silent, up the stairs like a ghost, up the very stairs where Ashia had died. Up more stairs to the long gallery where my family's portraits had once hung, and then to that fateful door.

With the key that Allessana had procured, I clicked open the lock. I could feel the dragon's power beckoning. It bathed me as the door swung open, a pulsing warmth and hunger. When I approached and laid my hand upon it, the library flared to life, the two of us seeing it as one. Outside, it was still dark, but I could discern a slight brightening to the east. Time was passing.

With my hand upon the dragon eye, darkness was no hindrance. It is a disorienting thing to watch oneself from outside. It gave me a headache, but with the sight of the dragon to guide me, I took up the dagger of the Sag man that my father had kept, and tightened its scabbard straps around my forearm. I was on the verge of taking up the eye and fleeing, but a new thought made me pause.

Instead of running, I began searching the Callarino's desk. My father's desk. I could fairly hear Cazzetta calling me an arrogant fool. If I had been my old self, I would have agreed. My new self had a different perspective. After a few moments, I found what I wanted: paper, ink, and quill.

I wrote quickly, fighting my growing headache, then held the words before the dragon eye, reading over what I had written. It would do. I stabbed my hand with the quill and smeared my blood upon the paper, then snapped the quill and tossed it down as well. Cazzetta muttered curses in my mind, but the deed was done.

I gathered the dragon eye into my arms, gazed about the library one last time—so much the same, so much changed, so much a part of me—and then I was out the door and down the stairs.

Everything was easier, using the powers of the dragon. With it to guide, my senses were sharper. I heard guards breathing far away. I heard their footsteps and knew their paths long before I was close. I heard the servants stoking the fires back in the kitchens. I even smelled the smoke.

Thus aided, I ghosted to the stables. I gathered a bridle and managed to haul over a saddle despite my weakened state. It was a clumsy process, for seeing clearly required me to hold the dragon eye, and saddling a horse required both hands. I chose the closest horse, one of the Callarino's racing steeds, Avalonia by the name upon the stall. I hoped it was his favorite. I rested, panting, then began the task of securing the saddle by feel, and after that lashing the dragon eye awkwardly ahead of the saddle. I felt the increasing pressure of time and regretted my lingering in the library. More and more servants would be waking.

Behind me, a familiar snuffling broke my thoughts.

"Lazy?"

She was older. She was white about her muzzle, but still she knew me. She came, panting and grinning and wagging her tail. I crouched and hugged her to me, running my hands through her fur and scratching behind her ears. "Ai, I've missed you, my friend."

"She's a good dog," a voice said.

"Herges." I straightened to face him, and my hand fell to my dagger. "Do not try to stop me." I eased back to touch the dragon eye, and suddenly I could see the horsemaster clearly, a looming presence in the shadows.

I had guessed rightly about him. He was a big man, broad in the chest. Bald, with a heavy brow and a jutting jaw, as those in Chat often have. He held an axe in one huge hand, and I knew that should he strike, I would be hard-pressed to defend myself, even were I not weak. I waited, straining all my senses, watching with the eye, tracking the barest movements of his body and breath, trying to discern his intentions—

"Nai," Herges said, shaking his head. "I will not stop you. I saw before you were part of Virga's weave. Not many are tied so closely. I will not slight Virga."

I was surprised. "You people in Chat, you follow the old Amonese gods?"

"They are not Amonese to us. Nor old. Nor broken, as some of your people think. They have always been the gods, and Amo is but one, and not the greatest in the weave." He nodded at Lazy. "Too, Regna likes you, and I have never seen her judge falsely."

"You call her Queen?"

"Of course. What other name fits?"

"I called her Lazy."

He snorted. "You did her a disservice."

"I've been told." I let go of the eye and crouched again. Rubbed Lazy behind the ears. "You'll take care of her, won't you?"

"I will."

Lazy rubbed her nose against my face, wagging her tail. I hugged her close. My last true friend. "You are too old to journey where I must go," I said. "Stay here. Keep the palazzo for our name."

With a final hug, I gave her up.

As I was leading Avalonia from her stall, Herges said, "The thing you carry. The eye. It is full of malice. It is dangerous."

I laughed and turned my eyeless scarred face to him. "More dangerous than I?"

He shrugged. "Virga protect you, then."

I did not hear from him again, and Lazy did not follow. Avalonia's hooves echoed on the cobbles. Ahead, at the gates, a guard stirred himself and straightened. "Who's there?"

"Aqba," I whined, leading Avalonia closer, keeping my hand upon the eye. "I am to bear a message from the Callarino to Merai."

"At this hour?" the guard asked doubtfully. "You?"

"Ai." I nodded, knowing my face was covered with shadow. "That matra fescata gives me no rest. Why me, I ask? Why poor Aqba?" I shuffled closer. "But I follow his will, no matter the time—"

The guard gasped. He had seen my face, but by then I was close, and I was ready, and he was not. I drove the Sag dagger into his belly, and shoved it upward, seeking and then finding his heart. He was heavy as he collapsed, and he fell clumsily for I was not strong enough to support him, but he did not cry out, and when I checked, he was already dead. Blood came from his mouth as I wrestled him back to his station. I propped him there, seemingly sleeping. I did not feel regret that I had killed him. I felt nothing at all. But the dragon was different. I could sense it rising and circling about me, wild and eager, hunting and snapping for the man's soul. It was hungry, and I had fed it, as I had promised.

I opened the palazzo's small door, embedded in the larger gate, and guided Avalonia through. The city was beginning to wake. I heard the calls of milk and bread sellers. I heard carts rattling. The city, yawning.

I hauled myself into Avalonia's saddle and turned her west. She felt to me like a good horse. Not Deravashi, but not everyone can be perfect. I urged her into a canter, guiding us through the city's twisted streets and alleys. Fish sellers were carting in their catch. Farmers from the fields were arriving with their carts and baskets to sell their vegetables. Behind me, the first rays of sun came pouring across the city. The tall defensive towers of the archinomi gleamed orange.

I was in awe of the color. I was in awe of the dawn. It had been a long time since I had seen it.

A short while later, we reached the Andretta Gate, with wide green fields and rising hills beyond. In the farthest distance, the sun was striking the high peaks of the deep Romiglia, sharp and snowy and wild.

Soppros once said that only that which was not man could be trusted. He called it Firmos. Firmos was reliable. The hearts of wolves and stone bears and shadow cats and rabbits and deer could be trusted. The kiss of the wind upon whitebark and catredanto pine was always true, and never false.

Firmos.

I craved it.

Soon, the Callarino would begin searching for me. He would be enraged and frantic, but by then I would be in the embrace of Firmos, in that place I understood best and belonged to most. Herges said I was close to Virga's weave, and that felt true. The Romiglia was a place I understood—perhaps the one place I had ever understood—and there I would seek refuge. I would rest and heal beside clear laughing streams and walk under the green canopies of rustling whitebark. I would dig my fingers through the dirt for portola, bellabracchia, and carnecapo mushrooms and I would forage for sweet blackberries in warm sunny meadows. And with the dragon eye to aid me, I would hunt as the creatures of Virga hunt, and I would dine as the creatures of Virga dine, and I would become one with the weave. And if the Callarino sought to find me, he would have to brave me in those shadows and whispers of the wilds where I was Firmos, and he was but a man.

I passed through the city gates, and out into open verdant fields.

Navola's twisted streets fell behind me.

In Merai, they say that the Navolese are as twisted as the plaits of their women's hair, and I cannot disagree. But, too, as Aghan Khan said, when we find that which we desire, our hearts fly swift and true. I would also add that our promises are as hard as the ice of the Cielofrigo, and just as cold.

I spurred Avalonia onward, and she showed me her speed. Ahead, the Romiglia beckoned, and behind me, upon my father's desk, a message for the Callarino waited.

Something to think on.

Borsini,

I'm sorry I couldn't say this to you in person, but my time is, as you can imagine, limited. Still, I'm sitting here at my father's desk—which you have warmed for these last few years—and it strikes me that you should have slit my throat when you were able. But then, as they say, greed makes a man blind. How strange it is that I, who have no eyes, can see this clearly. And you, who have both of yours, could not. I'm sure there's a joke somewhere in that. Perhaps Filippo will make one up for you. In the meantime, keep this seat warm for me. I like knowing where to find you.

—Davico di Regulai da Navola

Acknowledgments

Navola would not exist without the kindness and support of many. Above all, I would like to thank (and also apologize to) Jonathan Strahan, who long ago asked for me to write a short story about dragons. I never delivered the story to him because the short story became a long story, became a novel, became . . . well, here we are. But without his instigation, I would not have discovered this rich world, or fallen into it so deeply. I would also especially like to thank Blake Nicholoff for encouraging me to tag along with him on his journeys abroad. Without his invitation to come out of my shell and once again explore the wider world, *Navola*'s tapestry could never have been woven. I could not ask for a better friend or companion in the hunt for orange wines or squacquerone.

I like to think I'm an amiable writer, but suspect that I am not, and so I want to thank my editor, Edward Kastenmeier, for his patience as he read draft after draft, and guided me to a better version than I thought possible. Holly Black and Charlie Finlay helped me more than once, and talked me off the ledge more times than that. Their insights and encouragement were critical. Rob Ziegler read early drafts, and just when I would have given up, fortuitously intervened. My agents, Russ Galen and Danny Baror, were incredibly patient as I worked for years on this secret project, and I'm so grateful they were still enthusiastic when it was finally ready to be seen by others. I'd also like to thank my writing crew, Carrie Vaughn, Tobias Buckell, Daniel Abraham, Kameron Hurley, Ramez Naam, Maureen McHugh, and Ty Franck. I feel lucky to be surrounded by such kind, supportive, and wise friends. Closer to home, I would like to thank Morgan MacInnes, for his brilliant coffee, his excellent company, and his many wise insights as I struggled with revising this book.

Finally, I would like to thank my wife, Anjula, and my son, Arjun. I feel so lucky to have you both in my life.

A NOTE ABOUT THE AUTHOR

PAOLO BACIGALUPI is the author of *The Windup Girl* and *The Water Knife,* as well as the young adult novels *Ship Breaker* and *The Drowned Cities.* A National Book Award finalist, and winner of the Hugo, Nebula, Theodore Sturgeon Memorial, and John W. Campbell Awards, as well as a three-time winner of the Locus Award, he lives in Colorado with his wife and son.

A NOTE ON THE TYPE

This book was set in Adobe Garamond. Designed for the Adobe Corporation by Robert Slimbach, the fonts are based on types first cut by Claude Garamond (ca. 1480–1561). It is to Garamond that we owe the letter we now know as "old style." He gave to his letters an elegance and feeling of movement that won him an immediate reputation and the patronage of Francis I of France.

Composed by North Market Street Graphics,
Lancaster, Pennsylvania

Printed and bound by LSC/Harrisonburg,
North Harrisonburg, Virginia

Designed by Betty Lew